Ashes of Paradise

Ashes of Paradise

❧ ROGER ELWOOD ❧

WORD PUBLISHING
Nashville·London·Vancouver·Melbourne

ASHES OF PARADISE

This novel is a work of fiction.
Names, characters, places, and incidents are either the product
of the author's imagination or are used fictitiously. Any resemblance to
actual events, locales, organizations, or persons, living or dead, is entirely
coincidental and beyond the intent of either the author or the publisher.

Library of Congress Cataloging-in-Publication Data
Elwood, Roger.
Ashes of paradise / Roger Elwood.
p.   cm.
ISBN 0-8499-3390-0
1. South Carolina—History—Civil War, 1861–1865—Fiction.
I. Title.
PS3555.L85A56   1997
813'.54—dc21
97-26525
CIP

Printed in the United States of America

7 8 0 1 2 3 4 9 QKP 9 8 7 6 5 4 3 2 1

To
Joey Paul,
my editor, my friend,
my brother in Christ,
and to
Laura Kendall,
in Christian love
and appreciation.

There is no fear in love; but perfect love casteth out fear.
1 John 4:18

Prologue 1

❦

The Plantation Letters Society . . .

LITTLE KNOWN OUTSIDE the Deep South, it would lead, many years later, to scores of books featuring letters written from various Civil War battlefields, as well as the publication of private diaries by husbands, wives, sons, and daughters caught up in the cataclysm of that tragic era, a cottage industry spawned, as it turned out, by what outsiders seemed to view as the pointless efforts of a few forlorn, elderly women unable to cope with what had become of their lives.

The Plantation Letters Society was well funded by the discretionary wealth of its half dozen members, though occasionally there were as many as eight or ten women who got involved, which simply meant that, due to their advanced ages, some ebb and flow of the total was unavoidable. A greater number of members would not have been in keeping with the intimate nature of the Society as it had been originally envisioned.

A tiny organization, if it could be called that, the Society had been founded for a unique purpose during the final years of the nineteenth century. It served only widowed women who had no family left; they gathered the first time not long before the turn of the century . . .

THE ORIGINAL MISSION of the Plantation Letters Society was to enable its members to collect large stacks of letters written before, during, and after the Civil War, letters invariably revealing an avalanche of thoughts and emotions that, they anticipated, would seem remarkably akin to their own.

In the intimate writings of wives and mothers such as themselves as well as the battlefield writings of beloved husbands, sons, and brothers, the members of the Society hoped to find relief for the continuing and debilitating emotional anguish they had been experiencing . . .

These women, who had no financial worries thanks to the large estates that had been left by their husbands and the worthwhile investments encouraged by their financial advisers, originally went so far as to hire a long list of detectives to help them find the letters. They also established contacts with collectors like themselves, sent telegram after telegram to virtually every state in the union following every possible lead, and enlisted the aid of dozens of political figures to gain access to invaluable government archives. They pressured a wide range of institutional presidents and civic group chairmen—from museums to historical societies to veterans organizations—asking them to part with letters or hand-copied facsimiles of letters that had little or no importance except to the Plantation Letters Society itself.

At first the widows were viewed as just a bunch of eccentric old pests, but they were grudgingly tolerated, and some onlookers even betrayed a flicker of admiration from time to time. Then President Teddy Roosevelt, not always the tough-as-nails leader he pretended to be, became aware of what the women were doing and was more than a little sympathetic to them, opening many more doors than they ever could have done on their own. He showed to them a genteel and touching side of his personality that the general public never saw because of the image of bulldog toughness he cultivated.

Twice a year, the Plantation Letters Society members came from entirely separate places to converge on one location: Winchester, Georgia, a town that had been taken and lost and retaken by opposing forces dozens of times during the Civil War.

For more than a decade, the Society's members had been meeting in the same house, which was every bit large enough to accommodate twice their limited number. The women were drawn to the meeting place like devout Muslims to Mecca, though they all professed a long-held redemptive faith in Jesus the Christ.

Not coincidentally, tranquil little Winchester—an archetypal embodiment of true southern gentility, having shed the tragic state of existence that the war had brought upon it daily, making life continually unsettled and violent for its residents—happened to be the hometown of the Society's very determined founder. Loreta Ashby, now nearly eighty years old, was, to the astonishment of everyone who knew her or knew about her, still completely in control of herself in an era when living to such an age was far less common than it would become during successive decades. Anyone who did aspire to such longevity could never be assured of the continuing ability to speak or think as coherently as Loreta managed to do, with a clear head and heart, crediting her mission as her life preserver.

Yet Loreta was of utterly joyless demeanor, her very manner closing off any attempt even at half-hearted frivolity in which a hapless visitor might have been tempted to indulge. There was a somberness about Loreta, not cold or mean or angry, but a weariness, actually—sad, concerned more with death than life, living in the present only insofar as it could gain her the access she craved to the past.

Loreta was uncommonly tall, straight-backed and thin-boned, and her eyes were a striking aquamarine that made avoiding her gaze when she was determined to impose it a nearly impossible task. In her earlier years she could have dominated any audience if she had ever decided to engage in public speaking.

Advanced age had brought much gray among her once bright crimson strands, and her face had become more deeply lined than even her many decades should have made it. Every moment of sorrow Loreta Ashby had experienced was written across her countenance as deeply as though chiseled in stone on the side of a mountain.

Especially in her latter years, Loreta did not often venture far from the environs of her splendid mansion. A throwback to the antebellum era, little of its well-appointed interior had changed from the rugged days of the Civil War when it had served as headquarters for the Confederacy when the South's forces had control or for the Yankees when they had wrested Winchester away from Johnny Reb.

The Society's members had been astonished at how well kept the house proved to be. When they first stepped inside, they were witness to a home of expensive furnishings, many of which were imported.

"Look at the walls!" visitors and members alike would exclaim the first time they entered the century-old structure.

Much of the wall space was given over to a vast collection of photographs and daguerreotypes showing Civil War generals from both sides who had communicated with her. Scattered among the pictures were framed letters from presidents, senators, doctors, and others, including a particularly treasured one from the great black leader Frederick Douglass, who had written to Loreta Ashby with great affection, indicating his conviction that if every Southerner were like her, there would never have been a War between the States.

"You are remarkable," the man expressed with apparent warmth. "I wish those in the Deep South who control the halls of power would spend one day with you, dear lady. You have had, as your guests, black and white, soldier and statesman, cotton-picker and noted physician. I myself enjoyed your company.

"After having gained my freedom way back in 1847—so long ago it seems!—by the good offices of some dear English benefactors, I started publishing the *North Star*, a newspaper in Rochester, New York. I have had the enriching experience of meeting many different kinds of people, but few have seemed as intriguing as Loreta Ashby.

"As I learned more about you, I knew that I had to get in touch with you. You seemed so young, but I found you wiser than your age would indicate. Thank you again for a stimulating time. Perhaps I shall be allowed to stand at the gates to heaven one day and welcome you to the eternity we shall be spending together."

It was a letter she especially treasured, one that would be kept in her collection of important correspondence for decades after it was sent.

"There has always been something about my house here," Loreta had told Society members early on, "something that was truly special. It was never less than a place of love, faith, and reconciliation. None of the soldiers sent by General Sherman in the closing months of the war disturbed so much as a picture on any wall. They seemed to hush their loud talk as soon as they entered.

"This house was like a church to those men. When Sherman first found out, he was enraged, yes, but only until he personally came here to visit my dwelling. He told me later that day, 'Not a single flame shall touch your home, ma'am. It offers no military advantage. Rest easy. You have my word!'"

She looked out over the members as she added, "General Sherman then said something that, I think, voiced the longings of his heart."

"What was it?" someone asked.

"This house reminded him of the one in which he had been raised as a young child, a place he hoped to return to someday before he died. 'There is some peace here,' this brutal, weary soldier said in a tone that struck me as sounding not anything at all like a general but instead like a lonely man, a very lonely man."

None of the members interrupted her with other questions, because they were becoming transfixed by her story.

"Then, in a complete departure from his reputation as a godless man, General Sherman asked me if I would join him in prayer," Loreta continued, "and so I knelt beside him. I said that, yes, sir, I would be happy to do that.

We prayed together a few minutes later. He spoke to God about the blood on his hands. My prayer, as his own, was that he would be forgiven and come to be at peace."

"It came out of your heart, your soul," someone interjected. "Even Sherman must have sensed that, Loreta."

It was difficult for any of the women to think of the man in any way that was remotely sympathetic. Members from Georgia and the Carolinas had either experienced Sherman's "scorched earth" ravages directly or had friends and relatives who had been caught up in it. The massive destruction and the pillaging behavior of many of his troops had earned Sherman the most venomous hatred, hatred so strong that even the most forgiving of Christians were known to feel it.

"I think he did," Loreta replied. "He returned more than once after the war ended. We talked for many hours about life, death, living beyond the grave. I cannot say if he truly became a Christian. I sensed something about him that was holding back.

"I suspect that he had seen so much blood being shed, so much pain on the faces of the men from both sides of the war, that, though he survived physically, part of his spirit was wounded and never healed. He had been obliged to send out too many death notices to too many bereaved loved ones. He was not some cold stone of a beast but a feeling man with a heart that had broken an uncountable number of times."

Her own husband and her sons—there were no daughters—did not return to her when the war ended.

All died in battle.

At first she herself wanted to die, and if she had been completely alone, she might have been driven to take her own life. But there was always someone else in the house with her or perhaps a dozen others, sitting in the living room, sleeping upstairs, wandering the grounds.

"I was not allowed the curse or the blessing of solitude," she recalled. "I see now that the Lord knew what he was doing."

So many memories to sift through, so much to share with the other women, as they would do likewise with her . . .

"One of the Confederate soldiers came up to me the day we all heard the news about Appomattox," Loreta recalled, "and, you know, he broke down crying. I put my arms around him, and he told me that he had just learned that everyone in his family had been wiped out by General Sherman's plundering forces. That poor young man . . . his face was so pale. I could see the greatest sorrow rapidly spreading across it."

Loreta cleared her throat, that poignant scene as fresh thirty years later as it had been days after it occurred.

Then she continued, "'Stay here,' I suggested to him. 'My family is gone, too, it seems. I am all alone.'"

"Did he?" several of the women asked in unison.

The others waited for Loreta's answer, drawn by her bittersweet story and eager to know the answer to something they had not heard before.

Loreta's eyes grew watery, tears slipping from them and sliding down her cheeks.

"Yes, that young man was here for nearly two years."

"What happened?" a member asked.

"He just wandered off one day, and I never saw him again."

Loreta had learned over the years to keep her emotions as tightly bottled up as possible. And that determination seemed to be shared by everyone in the Society. Emotions meant pain, and they had had too much pain.

He just wandered off one day, and I never saw him again.

That soldier would never be mentioned again.

Prologue 2

It seemed that only death—by heart attack or cancer or other natural cause—could stop any of the members from attending a meeting of the Society. One elderly woman named Estelle collapsed shortly after she had started climbing the front steps to Loreta's house. She gasped for breath as massive pain gripped her chest. The others hurriedly called for the yardman to carry her inside.

Just before her death, Estelle reached out for Loreta's hand.

"It has been so long," she whispered, smiling, "and now the search for peace is over. It is finally over for me, dear friend."

"You are the fortunate one," Loreta replied. "Should we mourn for you? Or should we rejoice instead?"

"You must thank God . . . for your salvation," Estelle pleaded, her weak voice fading rapidly. "Death . . . is not an enemy to any of us . . . who know and love the dear Savior . . . It only brings us to . . . our precious Father. How can death be less . . . than a welcome friend?"

Estelle was taken back to her hometown a dozen miles away and buried in a plot next to her husband and two boys, all dead because of serving the South during the Civil War. A large part of the cemetery was filled with those whose lives had been claimed in one way or another by that war's monstrous carnage.

The other members of the Plantation Letters Society attended the funeral, even Loreta, one of the few times she ventured from Winchester. They gathered again afterward, more than one processing some regret that they were still alive and searching while Estelle had found the peace she had coveted for decades.

Should we mourn for you? Or should we rejoice?

To the surviving members, the answer was obvious.

Not even weather conditions, no matter how threatening, had ever been successful in keeping the Society's members from attending the biannual meetings. The fact was, none of the women had found it necessary to journey to Winchester during freezing weather or hurricanes or floods, a fact that they agreed was one way God seemed to continue blessing them in the common purpose that had been drawing the group to one another since the beginning, a purpose that was treated with increasing seriousness as time passed.

As each meeting neared, the members would pack a few personal items, making sure they had the stacks of usually very old letters with which they had been so careful, and then, like aging human swallows returning to Capistrano as though guided by instinct alone, they came from their individual locales, always completing their journey successfully as though guarded by some sort of mysterious protection.

A mysterious protection . . .

They discussed this periodically by letter or in person, wondering about being utterly shielded from harm as they journeyed. No robbers had ever accosted them over the decade-plus of the Society's existence; no horses had gone lame on the way, stranding them. Nor did any drivers get drunk and fail to take them to their destination.

And now began the latest gathering of six by-and-large age-riddled women, unhappy souls all, women from whom any cheerful person would have fled because they wore their tragedies like gaudy banners that proclaimed unmistakably that they were miserable and did not expect to be otherwise until the day they died . . .

The year: 1912. Historic trouble was stirring in Europe.

At one time the United States of America had seemed immune from whatever went on "over there."

But politicians were now whispering what had been a once unthinkable possibility, that America could be drawn into whatever conflict was undoubtedly going to erupt on the European Continent, though isolationists were not giving up their fight to stop any such intervention on the part of the United States.

For no people did the specter of potentially thousands of Americans being killed on foreign battlefields seem more disturbing than those who had formed the Plantation Letters Society, women whose relatives had been killed during the American Civil War or, in some instances, gone off to battle and perhaps been so destroyed in mind and body that, though alive, they did not return, ashamed of what they had become and unwilling to inflict themselves upon their loved ones.

My beloved . . . where are you? Alive and a wanderer . . . or in some unmarked grave? You are gone from my arms but still in my heart.

That was the typical thought-cry of several of the Plantation Letters Society members past and present, plaintive in its hopelessness, for there was now no rational chance, after so long, that any of their beloved ones could be expected to show up miraculously as in some dime-novel melodrama.

"We have known sorrow," one of the women, Angelina, a faintly Mexican-looking, rather majestic woman with pronounced cheek bones and thick lips, remarked knowingly at the start of the latest biannual meeting. "But at least, with a new war coming any moment now, we can sigh with a little relief, because today, dear friends, none of us has any more men to lose nor any more loved ones to be sacrificed for our country," Angelina continued "We have been bled dry, the lot of us, and there is nothing left."

That was a statement with which the members could agree, all nodding as they acknowledged their assent.

"But there has been some joy as well," another member, Charlotte, spoke up. "We must not lose sight of the joy."

She was actually smiling as she spoke, scattered, blissful memories momentarily supplanting those that were far sadder; but then her lined, pale face hardened again into its more customary look of perpetual melancholy, making her seem much like a blind person who abruptly sees the flickering of a beam of light, reaches expectantly for it, and finds that it has slipped through her fingers and she is once again in darkness.

At that, the rest of those half-dozen women murmured approval, though it was a somewhat mechanical gesture on their part since all of them had come to focus so obsessively on the personal losses they had experienced, which were at the very center of the reason for the Society's existence in the first place.

"Just like the Bible says," several said in ready unison, "there is truly a season for everything in life."

Yet no one in the group truly believed that, because for them, there was nothing but one season, a prolonged season of grief from which they never strayed, a wintertime of their souls that was full of dark skies and mournful, chill winds, a bleakness that cast itself around them, forbidding the joy of spring.

The Bible was mentioned more than once during their meetings.

While the Society was not a Christian group as such, it was nevertheless comprised entirely of elderly Christian women, which made their often melancholy nature all the more contradictory.

"On top of everything else," one or another of them would admit out loud, "I have this guilt over not being able to hand everything over to the Lord and allow Him to take my yoke from me."

The speaker sighed in resignation and let that moment pass without delving into it further. Whatever the Society offered to its members on a certain level, it was not a group therapy session every six months, for that sort of thing was quite unknown in those days and there was no certainty that the women would have participated anyway.

Christian as far as their spiritual beliefs were concerned, yes, but none seemed able to grab hold of and apply the providential wisdom of verses that dealt particularly with "the peace that passes all understanding" or those suggesting that all things worked together for the good of those who knew and loved the Lord.

Any such promises were continually being buried under a suffocating avalanche of self-pity, perhaps understandable in view of their losses but only compounding their grief because they refused to let go of it, clinging to it now for half a century. It had been with them over such a long period of time that they assumed nothing would change until the day each died "and went to be with the Lord."

"I look forward to that moment," a member named Henrietta had said wistfully sometime earlier. "I look forward to the peace it will bring, the joy. That is all I have that sustains me, you know. What else is there? We have no one but ourselves."

Once every six months, during the first week in January each year and again toward the middle of July, they would gather together and pore yet again over their respective findings, some old and much discussed, others bits and pieces newly uncovered. But this rather basic objective quickly expanded beyond whatever any of them had had in mind at the beginning.

"We share once again the thoughts of those who chose to write so long ago," the founder, Loreta, always seemed to announce in some form during her opening remarks, "because we all here have a real need of knowing what it was like for those other wives, mothers, sisters, and their loved ones who endured what we endured. By the act of sharing, we hope to find release from our own anguish."

Her expression was one of wistfulness bordering on self-mockery, revealing that the hope she had spoken of seemed nothing more than a foolish old woman's fantasy long held but never experienced in reality.

"How was it that these other women were able to survive their grief? Could it be from some unquenchable embrace of their Christian faith? Or was it their natural gumption? Perhaps luck? Might that have been it?"

She cocked her head as though listening to some voice within her, a voice that only she was able to hear. As she started to speak again, her own voice trembled, and she stopped for a moment before going on. "Some are no better off than we all are, old women wallowing in our sorrows, but others, only a few perhaps, have gone beyond this ghastly stage in their lives, leaving it behind them in the mercifully scattered dust of the past.

"They have been able to pass from their own valleys of the shadow of death to something quite different, something that is no longer elusive for them.

"Yet not one, I repeat, not one of us present today has really *triumphed* in any similar manner. It is one thing for us to survive. Oh, yes, we all have done that, and to those who do not know us well, we seem quite content with our lot in life. Yet we know it is altogether another matter to find real serenity, a state of being that has proven its utter elusiveness for everybody here."

None of the members of the Plantation Letters Society had experienced more than fleeting glimpses of that serenity, and then only to find it cruelly vanish by their own fault, for the insistent memories of their wartime experiences continued to haunt them all to the point of needing medical care, and all clung with abiding stubbornness to the very elements in their lives that were destroying them.

One had lost a husband and three sons, going from a state of shock to perpetually dreading any new relationships out of fear of having anyone else she grew to love ripped from her grasp. Another had faced the wrenching truth that her father and five brothers had been wiped out by the ravages of the battlefields upon which they had fought. As a result, she had had to be institutionalized for quite a period of time, committed by her mother, who was the only other surviving member of that family, though anyone who survived confinement in a sanitarium in those days and eventually gained release from it must have been of naturally stronger stock than originally suspected. The others had dramatic stories also, experiences to share that were not at all dissimilar to what the other women had undergone.

All were searching through the dusty letters of other women and their loved ones, admitting their own failure to cope while hoping that one day something penned on the by now tattered, yellowing paper would somehow speak to them decades later, becoming one of the emotional keys they needed, keys that would succeed in unlocking a life free from sorrow, free from the lingering ghosts of what once was, ghosts to which they somehow were clinging and of which they did not seem able to let go.

Until the member named Sarah began to read from a pile of letters written by a woman named Charity more than half a century earlier, letters that none of them would ever forget . . .

Prologue 3

AFTER THE FIRST few letters, Sarah paused, gauging the reaction of the members. No one was talking; all sat back in their chairs, looking stunned.

"What I have read to you are some of the later letters," she told them. "Are you ready to hear more?"

A pause.

They were trying to get control of their emotions after hearing what Sarah read of the content of some of the most remarkable letters ever to be read to them as members of the Plantation Letters Society, letters whose sentiments left none of them untouched.

Finally, all the women, including Loreta, nodded solemnly, some dabbing their eyes with tiny handkerchiefs.

"I think I shall have someone else take over the reading," Sarah told them. She was answered by protests.

"No!" Loreta herself spoke. "You have done so well. Please continue. You have us in the palm of your hand."

"But I am really tired," Sarah told her. "You will be very pleased, I am sure, by the one who takes over for me."

"But who among us could do so well?"

"My replacement is not from the membership."

"*What?*" Loreta reacted.

More protests could be heard.

"You have not spoken of this to me," the founder told her sharply. "What you are suggesting is not agreed-upon procedure. I am disappointed that you—"

Knocking . . .

At the front door.

Loreta's maid scurried to answer it.

"A driver has brought your guest," she said somewhat nervously a moment later as she approached Sarah.

"Let her in," Sarah said.

"But you cannot—!" Loreta protested, as tradition bound as ever.

The maid, though, hurried to the front door and opened it, and they all saw someone framed in the doorway.

Someone whose apparent age made the rest of them seem young in comparison.

"She has to be over a hundred years old . . . ," someone whispered.

Sarah overheard this.

"Charity is only eighty-one," she said softly. "But she's lived the equivalent to two lifetimes in her eight decades; I'm afraid she's just about worn out her beautiful old body, haven't you, dear?"

Several of the members gasped.

The woman named Charity walked slowly toward them, using two canes. She could not look directly at them because her back was bent just enough that she was unable to hold her head up straight.

"Where am I to sit?" she asked in a soft, raspy voice.

No one moved, struck first by her appearance and then by her voice, surprisingly strong and sweet-toned.

Loreta got to her feet and helped the visitor to her own chair, which, of course, was at the front of the group.

"Is this sufficient?" she asked.

The old woman told her it was. After catching her breath, Charity spoke again.

"You must be wondering why I am here," she said slowly. "I am here to tell you the stories behind my letters, as many stories, at least, as do not bore you."

"We are so glad you could come," Loreta answered. "But you need not have tired yourself," Loreta pointed out. "Sarah was doing very well reading the letters. And any one of us could have taken over when she became tired."

"I came because Sarah invited me; that was one of my reasons," Charity replied. "And I came because I wanted to share with you the many facets of the people whose lives the letters describe; I wanted you to know us as we were. I wanted you to understand why things happened as they did. And there is one other reason why I came. But it is something of which I want to speak only later."

No one objected.

She seemed so extraordinary that they were willing to accede to whatever she desired, a woman who seemed incredibly old but who, now that they looked more closely at her, was still incredibly beautiful, with exquisite white hair and finely etched features that gave her dignity despite the wrinkles and pale skin and liver splotches and the inevitable marks of aging shared by the other women there.

This one was special.

Sarah handed her the pile of letters, and Charity took it carefully, grimacing as she moved arms severely touched by arthritis.

"I was very young when I started writing these," she told the members, holding up one that illustrated her point, for it showed the scrawl of a child. "Something made me do it."

"The Holy Spirit?" a member asked.

"I think so," Charity replied. "Few of us will live on in history books."

"But why should we?" the same one spoke again. "None of us has had any influence upon its events. We have done no great works."

Charity looked right at the member who had just spoken.

"We have lived, we have loved, we have contributed children, and we have stayed firm in our faith," she said. "Is that not enough for us to be remembered?"

And before anyone else could speak, Charity picked up one of the letters and began to read from it. After only a few sentences she paused, drew in a breath, and let her hands, still holding the letter, drop to her lap. "Let me tell you about my life when I wrote this letter," she said, a far-away gleam coming into her eyes . . .

AND SO IT *began that midafternoon for the Plantation Letters Society, that which was to prove to be an extraordinary departure from its usual routine.*

And it was an experience that even the controlling, dominant, and autocratic Loreta herself found remarkable as she swept aside all the normal rules and notions and sat captivated by the story of Charity Littlepage. Under normal circumstances, sharing the spotlight so dramatically would have been an irritant to the Society's founder. She was accustomed to being in charge, and along with this, relished the control that her position gave her.

Because of Loreta's controlling demeanor, not everyone who joined had stayed in the Society. More than a few women were eventually rankled enough by Loreta's demanding and unyielding style of leadership that they left. Loreta then, predictably, would profess her relief at their departure, shift the blame to them for their disloyalty, and launch whatever it was that she could manage to throw at them.

It was different now. Charity seemed, in a strange way perhaps, very much in charge, with Loreta relegated to the sidelines.

Part 1

❧ ❦

Faith is a living and unshakable confidence,
a belief in the grace of God so assured that a man
would die a thousand deaths for its sake.
Martin Luther

I REMEMBER MY *father so well," Charity said as she paused for a moment from*
the letter she had been reading. "I remember . . ."

And then she stopped, a hint of tears in her eyes.

The members of the Plantation Letters Society knew what must have been
tumbling around in her mind just then, for they all had experienced moments
when an image from the past would spring up and tease them, recalled
glimpses of happiness once enjoyed then dead and gone.

As though anticipating how the other women were reacting, Charity
smiled and pushed her glasses back up her nose.

"There was so much joy!" she exclaimed with a vibrancy that belied her
years. "I try to think of that instead of wallowing in the misery of no longer
having my father in my life in the flesh-and-blood body the Lord gave him."

Several of the members became uncomfortable as Charity continued to
speak in that vein, but Loreta especially tried not to show any reaction—
while secretly wondering if the old woman had been put up to this by
Sarah, who seemed to be manifesting some sort of agenda that was increas-
ingly discomforting.

"My father was a Christian man of intelligence and decency and so
much else."

She had put the pile of letters down, and her gaze roamed over them.

"Let me tell you a few things . . . ," she said.

Charity need not have wondered if they were paying attention.

1

"MASSA'S BACK!" Whenever red-haired, thin-faced Charity Elizabeth Littlepage heard those words shouted with special gusto by Little Isaiah, a six-foot-one, very broad colored man just over fifty years of age whose name surely must have been a clumsy but well-meaning attempt at sardonic humor by his parents since he did not spurt up late in life, surprising everyone, but came out of the womb bigger and heavier, it seemed, than a set of full-term twins, she would look up instantly, her tiny brown eyes widening.

And then Charity would unceremoniously drop whatever she happened to be holding at that time—perhaps an heirloom doll from before the American Revolution or a plate of food or one of her always-forgiving cats—and run as fast as she could on her spindly little legs, tripping sometimes, frustrated by her ever-evident clumsiness but ignoring any pain as she got up right away and hurried on, this time from the second floor of her large plantation home, down the elegant, curving staircase, the railing made of imported mahogany and always polished to a glass-like shine, and head straight for the front door, which her black mammy, already alerted, was holding open wide for this exuberant child.

As Charity burst outside, arms flailing, she finally saw her tall, sandy-haired, dimple-chinned, decidedly handsome father, whose eyes had always seemed slightly Oriental in their shape though there was no part of his family tree that would suggest why.

This charismatic gentleman was now walking toward her in that familiar, slightly bow-legged gait of his up the long, straight dirt pathway to the whitewashed, three-story plantation house, its porch fronted by four large Grecian columns. It was one of the more splendid mansions in an era that boasted of its share, a structure that had been built on a foundation of so-called tabby, a hardy material made of a blend of oyster shells, lime, sand, and water, sitting like a serene and benevolent monarch on a small hill surrounded by more than a hundred prime acres of land.

The dominant feature of the front lawn, unlike any of the other front lawns in that entire region, was a triangular-shaped garden plot in the center comprised of perennial tulips in a variety of colors—which bloomed each spring and lasted many seasons unless afflicted with some kind of blight. They were surrounded by a hedge not more than eight inches in height so as to avoid hiding the vibrant blossoms.

The subtle smell of precious jasmine was being carried through the air by a humid summer breeze, and the instant chorus of unseen birds, jays and others, became audible as though they, too, were caught up in the sudden joy of that moment and had elected to join with a young child in her exuberant greeting.

Little Isaiah, lumbering though he was, always managed to get to Alfred Monroe Littlepage first, the two men hugging one another as though they were not simply master and slave but dear friends who had been separated for some time and now could express their affection openly and unmistakably.

Not everyone found this sort of public display endearing. Other slave-owners of that region in the middle part of South Carolina were openly repulsed when it happened that they were riding by at such a moment and saw what was going on, at first disbelievingly then with growing resentment, resentment aimed directly at Charity's seemingly unconcerned and, they would say, arrogant father.

While in theory Alfred could do with his blacks whatever he wanted, his critics would frequently ruminate among themselves, the man surely must know that he was under obligation to take into consideration the established standards of the rest of the community and avoid whatever would do injury. Better to treat savages for what they were than offend the sensibilities of one's fellow *white* citizens.

None of this was written down. Nor was any matter of actual civil law involved.

But Alfred felt the presence of those invisible "standards" as surely as though he had seen them chiseled into permanent tablets of stone placed before him several times each day. By his conduct, he was setting an example, and no one in that region wanted to have to emulate his behavior with their own slaves.

"My genteel prison," Alfred would say jokingly from time to time as he sat with his wife and their one child at dinner in the large, high-ceiling dining room where several generations of Littlepages had gathered. Charity would stick her nose up, trying to discern what had been prepared as aromas came in from the kitchen, which was a separate structure unattached to the main house, as was the case with most plantation homes in those days since there was great concern about possible fires. Charity generally did not know what her father meant by the words "genteel prison," but her mother,

Elizabeth Carswell Littlepage, was well aware of her husband's inference since she felt as he did toward their half-dozen slaves and often incurred the scorn of other women who would try vainly to bring her to her senses and get the Littlepages to accept slaves as slaves and not as adopted members of the family.

"He treats them like children," Alfred once heard someone sneeringly hold forth, "because he was able to have only one of his own."

Though normally not at all given to violence, Alfred knew he could not let that remark stand without some forceful rebuke. Much of his Christian restraint fell by the wayside as he hit the man so hard and did so much damage, breaking the jaw in several places, that the offender could not speak for many weeks.

This encounter occurred at a community picnic in which everyone from many miles around participated annually. The purpose of such events was to maintain a bond between the aristocratic families of middle South Carolina, enabling them to continue their cocoon-like existence free of any dreaded abolitionist and Yankee pollution.

"Yankees are uncouth hypocrites!" a man from one of the more prominent families had been saying. "They call us the crudest of names, and yet their free blacks have conditions that I wouldn't allow for my pigs, let alone my slaves."

There was some truth in that.

In New York City, not a single free black of any age could claim to live in anything better than the worst slum quarters, presided over by uncaring masters of a different sort, with rats and cockroaches and an escalating incidence of disease that would be appalling to anyone who took the time to gather the available facts. Sometimes the conditions were bad enough to prompt riots, but to no avail.

None of the black men and women living in New York had anything better for themselves than cast-off, thread-bare clothes to wear along with shoes showing more holes than leather. It was not at all uncommon for whole groups of black people to be overheard voicing a wistful desire to forsake the so-called virtues of freedom and return to the South as slaves, particularly when they felt the gnawing ache of real hunger. Whereas most slaves were at least adequately fed, and sometimes even well fed due to their masters' realization that they had to be kept strong and healthy in order to perform profitably in the fields where they harvested cotton or any of the other crops so important to the southern regional economy, freed blacks in New York had to fend for themselves in a hostile environment.

He treats them like children . . . because he was able to have only one of his own.

The veneer of civility and politeness that dominated South Carolinian society was especially maintained at public gatherings such as parties and various other celebrations, but it was frequently cast aside at other times. And the comment that had enraged Alfred Littlepage was probably being thought by most of the well-bred men with whom he came in contact, even though only an occasional foolhardy one of them would voice anything of the sort.

Large families were the norm in those days, with five children the average number of offspring, but many families swelled by twice that number. One's children were the pronounced outward evidences of real southern manhood, and children meant grandchildren and great-grandchildren. It was commonplace for a family to number in the dozens of members if all the surviving generations were counted, which made reunions and other kinds of familial get-togethers eagerly anticipated because these proved to be the highlights of many social calendars and were seldom less than boisterous affairs with a great deal to eat, drink, and be merry about.

"Massa's back!" Little Isaiah shouted again, his deep, clear voice alerting everyone who happened to be on that part of the estate.

Those words, spoken with the most visible eagerness born not of duty but of genuine warmth, also stirred reactions within a quite different group, those with abolitionist sympathies, their kind convinced that, given other circumstances, no colored man would ever claim to feel that way toward his master. It was just a common, learned response, they said, not unlike the training of a mongrel dog, and it had nothing to do with what was really in anyone's heart, for no heart could possibly be content under the enforced domination of another human being, whatever his color.

Little Isaiah would have none of what he called the "gimjack nonsense" spouted by what he considered to be such poor white trash.

"They's jus' wantin' to stir up trouble," he reassured Alfred again and again. "There's somethin' unhappy in their own lives, and they want to make ever'one else feel and act miserable like they is."

Alfred nodded sadly, realizing the wisdom of his friend's words.

"I will give you freedom anytime you want," he promised more than once. "I can have the papers ready whenever you say the word. Please believe me when I say that I mean this truly."

He kept hoping that Little Isaiah would say yes; at least one part of him did, but the other part wondered what would happen if that were the case.

I think I want him here as a slave, Alfred thought, *because I would hate to see him go and lose him as a friend.*

Little Isaiah usually wore, on very hot South Carolinian days, a white, floppy-brimmed straw hat, now very old and more than a little tattered, which he would take off momentarily whenever something especially serious was being discussed.

"There's three reasons why I couldn't do that, Massa," he replied, resting his hat on one hand, his forehead cut deep with several rows of frown marks. "One of them is that I ain't sure that freedom means anything these days if I is just a slave to being poor somewhere else. You see, my cousins up north is hungry all the time. They's begging for food every day and for places to sleep, and them Yankee hypocrites don't care what happens to 'em. That's what they calls freedom up there, Massa!"

Alfred recoiled from the awful images that the other man's words produced in his mind, images that made him want to travel up to Washington, D.C., and demand that the lawmakers do something about the plight of the blacks in northern cities. But he knew what he would run in to if he were to do so, a hypocritical barrage of insults thrown in his face about his way of life, especially his slaves, demands that he let them go free and then come back to talk, to which he would have to respond in a manner similar to how Little Isaiah had addressed the situation. Reminding Yankees of their hypocrisy was not a way to get Yankee lawmakers to do anything he was asking of them!

Dear friend, Alfred thought, *you know so much truth, and yet so few will ever listen to you in all of your lifetime.*

On the day that particular conversation occurred, Little Isaiah happened to have a letter stuffed in a side pocket. He took it out finally and handed it to Alfred. Though he had learned to read, he obviously found the contents of that letter too emotional to recite.

A cousin . . . it had been written by a cousin named Old Jim.

"He seemed old even when he was a child," Little Isaiah reminisced wistfully, "always so serious, you know, dreamin' what it was going to be like when he grew up and became a man. Jim never changed his ways. And now—"

Old Jim's son had been killed by a rat or, more accurately, a group of rats. The remains of the little body had been found hours later.

"Jim went huntin' for work that day, like on lots of other days," Little Isaiah said sadly. "His missus had took to beggin' for food. Their older son had went out alone, tryin' to get pennies from strangers. That's when the rats came. Nobody helped the boy even when they heard him screamin' and screamin'. Somethin's been done to their spirit, those folks up north. They's no longer carin' for nobody but themselves. Isn't that an awful thing, Massa?"

Little Isaiah's eyes were quickly filling with tears as he added, "What's the good of being free for them?"

A moment later, he took the letter Alfred handed back to him and said, "Ain't no reason to leave if that's what I go to."

After scratching the top of his nearly bald head, he said, "The second reason is that girl of yours. Miss Charity is like my very own, Massa."

Alfred interrupted him and said, his voice showing his distress, "Please, Isaiah, no more massa. You can call me anything else but not that."

Little Isaiah seemed to sputter, not knowing what to say. He was far from being an ignorant man, yet in that single moment he seemed very much like a bewildered child unable to cope with the current situation.

"I don't know what else to say," he said humbly after a short while. "My mammy called your father massa. And so did my grandpappy. I—I—"

Little Isaiah was becoming more and more flustered.

Smiling, Alfred reached out and placed his right hand on the other man's broad left shoulder.

"It is long overdue that you begin to call me by my name," he said gently. "Please, friend, call me Alfred."

Little Isaiah shook his head in an exaggerated manner.

"Oh no, Massa! I—I couldn't! It's not respectful. Generations of my family owe you and your family our very lives . . . the clothes on our backs, the food in our bellies, the good health we's been enjoyin' for so long."

Alfred smiled as he said, "Then call me what you want, my friend."

Little Isaiah bowed his head briefly, and it seemed that he was praying. Then he looked straight up, a grin crossing his pitch-black face from big ear to big ear.

"I call you massa then. It's what I say to my Lawd Jesus when I's on my knees and prayin' to Him."

Alfred had seen Little Isaiah in prayer often as the years passed, particularly when Charity would injure herself or have a fever perhaps or when he or Elizabeth were not feeling well, but never more than that tragic day when she miscarried.

"But that's not the same," Alfred continued. "He is our Master, no doubt about that, but I am not like that, and I don't want to be, Isaiah."

"Jesus is massa of our souls, but you is massa of my body."

Alfred Littlepage grimaced, seeing the sincerity on Little Isaiah's face, an expression he knew all too well, one that, from past experience, left little doubt that the emotion his friend was feeling then was not born from anything shallow by its very nature, easily shown and then gone just as quickly, but from something that ran much deeper and would be harder to change, if that ever was to be the case.

"Jesus is Master of your soul, Little Isaiah, because you allow Him to be so," Alfred said, trying to help the other man clarify what he assumed was some degree of mental confusion. "I must tell you that this is what Scripture teaches and—"

He stopped himself, his face reddening as he realized the trap into which he just had fallen, for he knew that he was guilty of assuming that Little Isaiah had been incapable of any kind of truly clear-headed thought.

I call you my friend, Alfred thought with candor that was wrenching, *but still I regard you so unequally.*

He recalled word for word what one of the other local slave-owners had told him some time earlier.

"You seem to be trying to atone for the sins you imagine the rest of us somehow to be guilty of, Alfred," the man, Jeremiah Huger, opined reasonably, not with any bitter sarcasm but as one earnest friend trying to enlighten another. "And yet I wager that underneath it all, you still consider those six niggers of yours to be as inferior to you and your family as the rest of us plantationers view our slaves.

"Of course none of them should be abused. Frankly, Alfred, I treat my own darkies truly well, but not to the same extent that you have been doing for so long. It is as though you are trying to convince yourself that you are not like the rest of us, who have no illusions about what the slaves are. Yet your true feelings sometimes must confront you. How could it be otherwise if you have eyes to see that they are a mere step removed from acting like the apes they so closely resemble?"

He thought Alfred would interrupt, but that was not the case.

"What is your response when this happens, my friend?" the man prompted. "Buy them all more food? Is that it, Alfred? Go and put a fresh coat of paint on their living quarters? Does that help somehow, I ask you now? Or furnish each one with better clothes, thinking this in itself will work? That happens to be a pretty liberal outlook for someone as conservative as you have been all these years."

Alfred started to object, to tell the other man that he was dead wrong. "I love them, Jeremiah," he said. "I—"

"Oh, I do believe you," Huger replied sympathetically. "But so does my son love the bird whose broken wings he fixes. The difference is that when the bird is well again, that boy has the good sense to let the little creature fly away."

"Jeremiah, I have tried again and again to do just that. Each time they tell me no, that they prefer to be with me and my wife and our little Charity."

"You have offered them what you say, Alfred, yes, I shall give you that, but what do those actual words cost you when that offer has been turned down? You always end up seeming so kind, so caring, so very Christian, shall we say, but there is no danger involved. You know in advance what their answer is going to be."

Huger smiled broadly.

"I am glad your views as a Christian forbid you from joining a group of us in our weekly poker game," he said, laughing. "You would make a wonderful player. Poker is ninety percent bluff, you know."

I call you my friend . . . but still I regard you unequally, Alfred now thought to himself, watching Little Isaiah's anxious face.

The two men had been sitting on soft grass under a large, centuries-old weeping willow tree, both of them trying to escape the heat of an August afternoon, the humidity so thick there seemed to be a perpetual mist in the air.

Minutes later, Little Isaiah jumped to his feet, waving his hands excitedly through the air, his thick lips parted in a smile.

"It is the same," he said quickly, with passion. "You are massa of my body 'cause that's what I wants you to be. When I's come to you with my pain, you always takes it upon yourself, as da Scriptures says. And you's never failed me, Massa, not me or any of the other coloreds here!"

Alfred was uncomfortable with this testimony as a Christian and as a man, but he could see that these convictions were deep-seated as well as tremendously affecting in ways the old colored man could not have known, and he decided not to contradict Little Isaiah, at least for the time being and perhaps never, since destroying a man's illusions carried with it the possibility of destroying the man himself.

"Then massa it is," Alfred agreed, trying to keep his reluctance from registering into his voice.

Little Isaiah sat down again, and the two of them stayed in the shelter of that familiar old willow, saying little more for another half an hour or so as breezes that were cool and soothing stroked their sweaty faces.

"Let's go inside and have some fresh-squeezed juice," Alfred suggested finally, getting to his feet and starting toward the plantation house.

Then he snapped his fingers and stopped walking.

"Wait!" Alfred said. "Didn't you tell me that there were three reasons why you felt you couldn't leave. What was the third?"

Little Isaiah seemed suddenly embarrassed and turned away.

"You don't have to tell me now," Alfred assured him.

"I do, Massa, oh, I do."

Little Isaiah turned around, tears on his cheeks.

"I love you, and I love Charity and Mrs. Littlepage," he said, his voice breaking. "I ain't like no slave, not like those down the way, them who're beaten day in and day out. Life's awful for coloreds like that. I gots no chil'en of my own 'cause I never married. The other mens I know all has wives and little 'uns. You's my family, Massa. I don't need anyone else. Why in the world would I want to leave my loved ones behind?"

I got's no chil'en of my own . . .

Alfred caught his breath when Little Isaiah said that, knowing all too well why this remarkable man whom he had known for so long had never become a father.

At a younger age, this gentle soul was castrated by a previous slave-holder because he said Isaiah was "a randy sort" and he didn't like the idea of the slave siring a great "whole passel of pickaninnies running around all over the place," though a critic or two ultimately did confront Little Isaiah's massa, not on moral grounds but because the black children he might have fathered could have been put to use as sturdy workers, making the barbaric owner guilty of economic madness.

"My sons, my daughters . . . ," Little Isaiah whispered wistfully, his mind filled with the ghosts of those who might have run up to him over the years and lovingly hugged him as their father.

"I hope Charity has been able, in some way, to take their place," Alfred said, knowing that anything he said might seem presumptuous but wanting to do whatever he could to comfort the other man.

"Yes, Massa," Little Isaiah assured him, "yes, she has. That sweet, sweet child surely has done that."

The big black man never felt that sweetness more deeply than when little Charity would be swept up in her father's arms after he returned home from a business trip. Those sometimes bloodshot eyes of Little Isaiah's could see clearly enough the joy on the faces of daughter and father alike, a joy he shared as a member of that family, while, in the South Carolinian community surrounding them, the hatred against him and his massa seemed to be growing year after year.

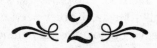

*C*HARITY WIPED HER *eyes for a moment before continuing. "I remember him so well . . . ," she told the Plantation Letters Society members. "Alfred Littlepage was the most handsome man around."*

She chuckled as her cheeks became a bit red.

"But then every girl child thinks that of her father, I am sure," she said as the members were drawn to childhood recollections of their own families so many years before.

And Charity resumed the reading . . .

ALFRED LITTLEPAGE REPEATEDLY, and with some relish, violated the Deep South norms of that period in various other ways, one of which happened daily when he provided his half-dozen blacks, or "his coddled niggers," as neighbors called them, with the very same food as he, his wife, and his daughter enjoyed eating. But he insisted upon going even further by letting the household slaves have their meals in the same room as his wife, his daughter, and himself, and at the same time, though he did keep them at a different table. The justification for this curious act of separation was unclear, like a barnacle clinging to an otherwise immaculate vessel, and seemed utterly anachronistic in light of Alfred's liberal ways in nearly every other aspect of his relationship with the slaves he owned. There would be moments when he and Elizabeth were alone and would briefly discuss it, deciding that the practice was nothing more than an odd holdover from the more rigid customs of their ancestors. Both ended up making a vague promise that they would deal with it someday.

It was not that slaves on various other plantations were habitually being cruelly mistreated by the most hard-hearted of villains; some owners in that region and elsewhere certainly *did* fit squarely that description, but most did not, however much the biased northern press tried to stereotype everyone with the same cruel image. Rather, it was that their diets, though healthy, tended to seem rather more monotonous than harmful and were often concentrated in a bland, daily repetition of what they called "hogs and hominy."

But then that may have been true of many less than wealthy non-slave-owning white families as well. What this diet translated into was between two and three pounds of bacon each week plus some chunks of fat pork along with fresh-baked cornbread and especially large amounts of grits. On occasion, slaves ate dried beef, and occasionally some poultry was added to their diets by compassionate owners. Whatever else came to be part of their "menu" was grown by the slaves themselves, with the women in each group raising vegetables of their own in garden plots, which usually included sweet potatoes, cowpeas, watermelons, and turnips.

After securing special permission, the men often learned to expertly bag game on regular hunting and fishing expeditions, usually under the attention of a hovering white overseer appointed by the slave-owner, though sometimes the master himself would accompany his slaves, never openly admitting that he actually enjoyed going out with the lot of them on a hunt that always started his blood rushing. As a result, slaves who were industrious enough could supplement what their owners gave to them with additional provisions of venison, turkey, rabbit, squirrel, and opossum, but they had to find the time and the energy to do so after being worked hard all during the day. It was only on weekends, when some of them were given lighter schedules, that they could go out hunting and trapping, and they made the most of it.

Alfred Littlepage's approach was altogether different. No one in the Littlepage family, going back over several generations, had ever developed the taste to be a hunter except in a more primitive time early on in the settlement of that region, and then only as a matter of survival. Alfred was no exception, though he recognized that imposing any prohibition on his slaves would deprive them of an activity that they enjoyed very much, and so he put aside everything he felt about the subject and let them hit the forest nearby several times a year.

It must have something to do with how they all survived in the wilds of Africa, Alfred thought, *something primal in them, a need that other owners foolishly have ignored, a return to the roots of the way they once lived.*

"Do it if you gain pleasure from hunting," he would say to his blacks. "But I want there to be no hunting by any of you from this plantation simply for the goal of satisfying any hunger that you might be experiencing. It is my obligation to take care of you, an obligation that is a matter of honor as far as I am concerned. Is that understood?"

None of the other owners who were neighbors of the Littlepages ever talked to their slaves in that manner, for they had another consideration that took precedence.

Profits . . .

These were always at the heart of the various slave-owners' purchase of food. Every dollar spent feeding slaves was that much less profit in the bank for them and their families. Even when slaves caught or grew their own food, most owners took a percentage and either ate it themselves or sold it for additional revenue.

This system seemed to work well, especially since the slaves had all the work and the owners none of the expenses. So, it was understandable that when Alfred Littlepage seemed to be continually upgrading his slaves' diet without an equal amount of effort on their part, he was met with animosity and a certain puzzlement over his motives.

"If we spent money on those slaves of ours the way you do yours," Alfred would hear again and again in angry tones, "why, we'd be going bankrupt in no time at all, can you not see that? Word gets around, Alfred. If we run into any trouble, well, our trouble's suddenly going to be yours as well. *Remember that, neighbor!*"

Whatever the case, Alfred did not change the way he treated his slaves

If anything, he pampered them more than ever, with food only a part of it. He gave them better clothes, fresher blankets and sheets, and whatever else they needed.

"I enjoy seeing them happy," he told friends and detractors alike. "They have a way of expressing their feelings that you and I either have never known or have lost somewhere along the way as we have become more 'civilized.'"

Yet the quality and quantity of food were hardly the only differences that existed between the lifestyle of those fortunate slaves living and working on the Littlepage plantation and those who were elsewhere in that region of the state.

For many, living conditions were cramped at best, with the typical wood cabins averaging about fifteen feet square, each usually housing more than one black family. The structures were usually rickety and unpainted, cold in the winter and stifling in the summer, and frequently swarming with insects

Alfred took more pride in the way he treated his slaves without any sense of economics ever being involved.

"I could not sleep at night," he once told Elizabeth, "if I followed the examples of those who so despise me. When I go to be with our Lord, I will not have to admit to Him the sins of those other owners."

"Remember Brawley?" she whispered.

"Oh, I do, Elizabeth," he replied. "I do."

Years before, he had overheard a slave from another plantation singing to himself while taking a break from picking cotton.

"Massa sleeps in the fine bed," the man sang. "Nigger sleeps on the floor. When we all get to heaven, we'll be slaves no more."

Alfred surprised the man by abruptly stepping up to him and commenting about what he had just heard.

"Don't tell my massa," the slave begged.

"He would hurt you, wouldn't he?" Alfred asked, knowing all too well the expressions of slaves who feared for their lives.

"Hurt me bad, sir. Whip me. He'd whip me 'til my poor back's raw. You won't tell him, will you?"

Alfred saw before him a tall, broad man in his mid-thirties—but a man who was reacting like a scared child.

We treat them like children, helpless little children, he thought, *and that's exactly what they continue to be.*

He smiled as he said, "If I could buy you from this creature and set you free, would you like that?"

The man nodded excitedly.

"I would free every last one of my people any time they wanted," Alfred told him, "but they refuse me."

"I knows your slave Simuel. He done told me about you, sir."

"What did he say?"

"That he would never go, that as far as he is concerned, there ain't no life 'cept what he has with you."

"Where will you go if my offer is accepted?" Alfred inquired.

The slave scratched his head, a slight smile crossing his face.

"Out west, sir," he said. "Yes, sir, that sure would be it. As far as Wyomin' if I could make it there."

"But things aren't so good there in a whole lot of ways, I hear. Coloreds have as hard a time of it in the West as they do everywhere else."

The slave's smile became broader, more spirited.

"My cousin's out there; he's a blacksmith. I could help him. He's wrote to me and told me he's got more work than he can handle."

Alfred was genuinely glad to hear this.

"I pray that your master will listen to me," he said, "and not turn me down. What is your name, by the way?"

"Brawley, sir."

"Are you married?" Alfred asked.

Without venturing an answer, the man lowered his head, obviously ashamed and finding it difficult to respond.

"What is it, Brawley?"

"I know Little Isaiah, too, sir. Simuel went and got us together one day some few years ago; he sure did."

"You mean he introduced the two of you?"

"Yessir, that's sure 'nough what I meant."

"What about Little Isaiah then? Help me now, Brawley, please. I just don't understand your meaning."

"I's like him, sir," Brawley told him. "I can't get married, and I can't father no chil'en of my own."

"You were—?" Alfred gasped, astounded that castration seemed as widespread a punishment as it was.

Brawley nodded, a look of sorrow replacing the smile.

"Did your present owner do that to you?"

Brawley hesitated, looking nervous and fidgeting as though he expected his master somehow to be eavesdropping and dreading the possibility of provoking anger from a man who was apparently merciless.

"I asked you a question, boy, and I want an answer," Alfred demanded in a harsh tone, hoping to startle the man into telling the truth.

Brawley looked at him, knowing he could be in a dangerous situation, big eyes as wide as they could be.

"He did. Oh, he did! He took a knife and . . . and—"

Though Brawley was a large man, comparable in size to Little Isaiah, it was impossible for Alfred not to pity him.

"So much pain, sir," he went on. "I thought I was goin' to die; I did . . . I did. I thought I would see my blessed Lawd Jesus any minute, yessir! But that's not the only kind of pain—at least that pain went away after 'while.

"But I feel somethin' else achin' inside me ever' time I see any little boy run up to his daddy and they's huggin' and huggin' each other. That's the worse part of my pain, you know? It jus' hang on. It not go away, now or ever!"

Though Brawley was sweating from working in the field, Alfred put his arms around the man and whispered, "I cannot give you children, of course; but I can get you out of this place and send you elsewhere with some money and a continuing prayer from the center of my soul that you will have the Lord's protection."

Poor Brawley was almost comically flustered, unable to speak coherently and managing only to nod in appreciation.

"Go on working for now," Alfred told him hurriedly. "I shall be back with good news as soon as I can."

He smiled as he added, "Let us shake on it, friend."

Alfred extended his hand, expecting the other man to reach out in a similar manner and grasp his own.

But Brawley, unaccustomed to any display of kindness like this from a white man, did not quite know what to do. So Alfred took that big, rough-skinned hand into his own, and shook it with great energy.

"Praise God above," Brawley whispered, still acting like someone who had finally gotten what had only been a wistful dream for the greater part of his life but wondering how long it would be before all this evaporated.

"I do," Alfred replied, "every day."

He could not explain, then nor later, why he seemed so drawn to this one black man. Even with his resources, he resigned himself to the fact that he could not afford to buy and set free every slave; yet Brawley seemed so special.

I would be bankrupt in a fortnight, he had to acknowledge, *but if I had endless sums of money I might at least try!*

He glanced at Brawley.

How many thousands are there like you through this country I love? Alfred thought to himself as he stood a moment more, watching Brawley. *How many men have been robbed of their—?*

He felt his throat tightening at the thought and clinched his hands into fists as anger started to take hold.

Someday, all of this barbarism must stop, Alfred thought. *People cannot be allowed to go on this way.*

Alfred was climbing back on his one-horse carriage, which he had taken out by himself without the help of a driver, when he felt a chill that raced up and down his spine. So severe was this premonition that it caused him to shiver for several seconds before it passed, leaving him to wonder if he was becoming ill.

"Or is it something else, Lord?" he whispered as he looked up toward the sky, which was completely devoid of clouds that day.

Then Alfred waved a temporary good-bye to the slave named Brawley and began guiding the horse down the dirt road to the main house. As he passed a number of other slaves in the vast cotton fields of that particular plantation, he saw that their condition was similar; scores of tired men and women much like Brawley working alongside more than a few so old that they should never have been allowed to continue performing such hard labor out in the heat of a blazing overhead sun.

A<small>LFRED DID WHAT</small> he had promised, waiting while Brawley's owner pretended to be mulling over his offer.

You are not a very good actor, he thought impatiently about the little man, *especially after admitting to me that you happen to be strapped for cash just now. That was stupid, but then your kind usually are never very smart.*

Moments later, his offer was accepted, though that did not preclude some momentary face-saving haggling, which was a usual part of the process of any such business, and both men were accustomed to it.

I could even allow myself to feel a bit sorry for you, Alfred thought as the other slave-owner went through his patently amateurish routine, *but then it may be that your need for cash comes because your slaves are working at less than their greatest efficiency because you have treated them all so poorly, and you just are not smart enough to realize that you are the one at fault, not these poor people.*

And then it was over, the two men shaking hands to seal the deal but with no friendliness in the gesture.

"What in the world is so special about this buck?" the weasley little man asked, frowning after the agreed amount of cash had changed hands. "I have others I would stack up against him any day of the week."

"I'm getting Brawley away from your kind, nothing more, nothing less," Alfred replied brusquely as he carefully folded the precious single sheet of paper that gave him legal ownership and virtually the full power of life and death over Brawley. "That happens to be the whole story, neighbor, though I regret more than you could ever understand that I have been forced into the position of referring to you as a neighbor of mine."

The other man seemed to find such indignation amusing. "I guess you can throw away your money, if you want, on something as stupid as principle or whatever. Your loss is my gain; yeah, that's the way I figure it."

Cackling smugly to himself, the man walked slowly back to his plantation house, and then inside.

Now that the deal was concluded, Alfred had permission to go back to the slave quarters and bring Brawley out to the carriage where Little Isaiah was sitting, holding the reins in his hands and looking with some disgust at the comparatively run-down condition of that plantation, including the owner's house, which needed some paint and other repairs, not to mention dead or dying plants and shrubs.

Alfred stopped as he came upon a series of dilapidated log cabins, each about ten feet square, with sorry-looking darkies crowded into each one.

Brawley was standing in the splintering doorway of the one in which he and half a dozen other slaves had been living.

There were no windows . . . and not all of the chinks between the logs had been filled in, which made living conditions even more ghastly during the cold winters that roared down on South Carolina seemingly on a direct path from frigid Canada.

"Some's gets to doin' the coughin'," Brawley said later when Alfred asked about the health of the cabin's occupants. "They can't stop, and the blood comes, and they die."

He's talking about consumption, Alfred thought. *They are probably allowed to just cough their poor lives away!*

"What happens to their bodies?" Alfred asked. "Are these people given any kind of proper burial?"

Brawley shook his head.

"Some hole somewhere," he replied. "When the grass grows over and flowers sprout up, it's real nice where they are."

Brawley had managed to sneak away sometimes, with the other slaves covering for his absence, and spend a moment at that place, standing there with a quiet solemnity born of helplessness, realizing that people who had been living, breathing, talking men and women were now just the deplorable fertilizer for a beautiful meadow of yellow and red and orange flowers casting the sweetest of scents to heady breezes. Every so often, Brawley would bend down and gingerly touch one of the delicate-looking blooms, then pull back. He might whisper a prayer or else just stand and consider where he was and on what ground he stood.

. . . It's real nice where they are.

Alfred could tell that the other man had lost some very dear friends during his time of slavery, his sorrow causing a thin trickle of tears to slip down his right cheek as those memories abruptly took him back over the years.

"You and I have to get away from here as soon as possible," he told Brawley, "before your owner changes his mind, which is always possible, you know. Is there anyone you want to say good-bye to among the other slaves, Brawley?"

"Any of them's I got is out workin' in da fields now, sir," Brawley told him, pointing wearily in that direction.

"We can go by there on the way to my plantation, if you like. You could stop and offer your good-byes. That would be fine with me."

"I's better not," Brawley said, with some reluctance.

"Are you certain?"

"Yessir, I is. The bunch of them sees me goin' free, and it's gonna make them all feel real bad, sir."

Alfred understood, nodding in response.

"Get your things," he said.

"Don't have much," Brawley told him.

"Then get what you have!" Alfred added impatiently.

Brawley went inside the cabin.

Hoping he was not being seen or heard, Alfred started gasping quite violently after walking just a little distance away from that deplorable, ramshackle cabin, unable any longer to continue restraining himself or to endure the overpowering stench.

Even so, after he had recovered from that seizure, he knew that his experience of encountering those ghastly odors from inside the cabin would never be forgotten.

Right out of the rancid reaches of fervid hell itself! Alfred thought then as well as during later moments—in fact, whenever he recalled that wretched moment. *Waste products infrequently cleaned away, and sweat, and other—*

He was glad that he saw Brawley finally emerge from the cabin.

"Have you lived here long?" Alfred asked.

"Don't hardly know nothin' else," Brawley replied, scratching his head and trying to think back over the years.

"And you have no mother and father left?"

"We was once together as a family a long, long time ago, sir. All of a sudden they was gone, and I's left alone."

"Died? They died?"

"Can't say. We was split apart. My daddy went with one massa and my mother with another. I was turned over to someone else."

"How many years has it been?"

"Maybe twenty years, sir . . . yessir, maybe that long."

"I would like to help you find them," Alfred spoke immediately without thinking of the consequences of his offer.

"But I's bein' set free. I don't need nothin' more than that."

"What I think you need is to be with your loved ones, Brawley. No man ever deserves less than that."

"Am I a man, sir?" Brawley asked. "Am I really a man?"

As Brawley spoke, Alfred wondered if he would be able to reply, so moved was he by that question.

"God created you as a human being," he managed to say. "And that has not changed for thousands of years. Of course you are a man!"

Brawley seemed puzzled.

"Then why's nobody ever treated me like one before now?"

If only you knew the whole truth, Alfred thought.

The two of them walked to the carriage.

"A fine horse," Brawley observed, admiring it. "I used to think I wanted to be with horses; ya know, there's somethin' about them. I guess that's why bein' with my brother in his business is appealin' to me."

"Get in," Alfred said kindly. "It's getting late."

A bit awkwardly, Brawley climbed up into the carriage and sank down into the comfortable seat.

"Feels so good," he said.

"The leather?" Alfred asked.

"And the smell of it, sir. The feelin' of the air 'gainst my face, the first air for me to breath as a free man."

"You know, Brawley," remarked Alfred as he started the horse on its way, "I feel ashamed when I hear you talk like that."

Brawley was alarmed.

"Does I speak out of turn, sir?" he asked, barely able to say anything.

"Not a bit. What I mean is that I breathe every day as a free man and think nothing of the privilege."

Alfred sighed as he enjoyed savoring the sensation of a gentle breeze that rippled across his fine-boned cheeks. "My family and I take so much for granted," he went on. "We have had clean clothes all our lives. We certainly wouldn't have a clue as to what hunger is like. We have a roof over our heads that does not leak."

"Now that is somethin'," Brawley chimed in. "Yessir, that surely is some-thin' to praise the Lawd for."

"A roof without leaks? More than clean clothes? Or a full stomach?" Alfred asked, taken by surprise.

"Oh, yessir, a lot of gifts from sweet Jesus. Ain't that somethin, though, the way things turn out? No good havin' clothes and food if the rain's pourin' in on you and you gets to coughin' your lungs out and you die in them nice clothes, with food on the table just waitin' to be eaten but you can't eat it 'cause the sickness done took your appetite away."

"You shall sleep this night under such a roof!" Alfred declared, very glad that he could do this for the man.

"Sir . . . ," Brawley asked tentatively. "There's somethin' I's been meanin' to ask you."

"Go ahead."

"Your man Simuel . . . he told me 'bout your Charity."

"My daughter?"

"Yessir. That Simuel done told me there's sure somethin' right special 'bout that little girl of yours."

Alfred was pleased while realizing from personal experience that slaves were hardly immune to currying favor with a new master—or anyone else, for that matter. It was one of their few tricks, little survival tactics their servitude made necessary again and again.

"She's a wonderful child," Alfred agreed with Brawley. "Her mother and I love our Charity dearly."

"Simuel's got a real gift," Brawley replied, nodding. "He's no good tellin' the future or anythin' like that. But he gets to feelin' a certain way 'bout people sometimes, and he's seldom been wrong that I's heard."

"And he's felt like that about Charity?"

Alfred knew his daughter was a sweet child, free of any meanness, devoted to Jesus in her youthful, trusting way, and, of course, there was her special relationship with Little Isaiah.

"I will plan on talking to Simuel about her one day soon."

Alfred smiled warmly.

"Thank you for telling me this, Brawley. Thank you very much."

"Sir?"

"What is it?"

"Could I . . . I meet Charity?"

"Of course. First, I want you to have a good night's rest. I'll make sure you get to see my daughter in the morning."

"That would be fine, sir, just fine."

The two men glanced at one another.

"I am very glad that I met you today, my friend," Alfred admitted, hoping his words and the tone of his voice would make it clear that this was how he truly felt. "I think it was God's will that this happened."

Brawley turned away for a moment.

"What is it?" Alfred asked.

"I gets ev'rythin' you gives me this day, and yet here I is with nothin' to give you in return. Ain't right."

The carriage was nearing the western edge of Alfred's property. He stopped it for a moment and faced Brawley.

"The greatest act you could ever give to me in return is to go on and build a happy, fulfilling life for yourself, Brawley," he said. "I could not ask for anything more, my dear man. Believe me, it is true. I could expect nothing greater than that from you.

"When I appear someday before our dear Lord in His kingdom, I want very much to know that I have done something right in this life of mine before it ended and that I have as few regrets as humanly possible."

Suddenly Brawley reached out, wrapped his thick, strong arms around the much slighter Alfred, and squeezed him hard enough to cause some pain.

"Bless you . . . ," he whispered. "Someday maybe the good Lawd Jesus will provide for me somethin' else that I can do. I's gonna be prayin' to Him regular that He opens the door He wants me to step through one of these days. Gotta tell you, sir, that He ain't gonna have to show this darkie what to do more than once!"

"Someday, I suspect, Brawley," Alfred assured him, pulling away, aware that the man needed a bath as soon as the water could be poured into a tub. "Remember to take His blessings one day at a time."

"I sure will do that. Yessir, I sure will."

As they were getting out of the carriage, Alfred happened to glance up at Charity's second-floor bedroom window.

My dearest, Alfred sighed, glad to see that she had pushed the curtain aside and was standing there. She appeared to be looking with her usual unrestrained curiosity at the new visitor.

What a beacon you are, child, her father thought, his heart beating faster at the sight of her perfectly formed little head with its curly hair and rosy cheeks, a familiar frilled dress showing through the windowpane. *I hope the Lord, in His boundless mercy, allows me to live to be old enough to see you unleashed on the world around you. How much you will affect everybody you meet!*

Just then Charity waved to both men.

Brawley was transfixed as he, too, noticed her.

"There she is! She—" he started to say something then interrupted himself. "By jiminy, whew! I sure needs to get some clean water on this body of mine. I needs to be just right, I sure does, to meet that little girl. I needs to—"

Suddenly fidgety and becoming quite flustered, Brawley, his manner suggesting a bit of desperation, turned to Alfred.

"Where do I go?" he asked, disoriented after so many years of living on another plantation. "I's not knowin' where to go."

"Simuel is coming now. He will show you."

"Can I use some . . . soap?"

Alfred laughed despite himself.

"Plenty of soap," he assured the other man.

Simuel had come around from the rear of the plantation house, ready to greet the newcomer.

"Simuel!" Brawley exclaimed happily. "You old coot! I never thought I'd see you again, least of all the way it's happening now."

The two of them faced one another for a second or two, then each let out an ecstatic holler; they seemed to be almost dancing as they hurried on toward the separate building where all six slaves regularly bathed.

"You mean, everyday if you want?" Brawley was muttering in amazement at what Simuel had just told him.

Alfred sighed with satisfaction as he watched the two men disappear inside.

"Daddy!" Charity shouted as she ran outside, eyes wide, looking toward where they had gone. "I wanted to meet him!"

"Our new friend needs to clean up," Alfred told her.

"Why's he dirty?" she asked logically.

"It's because his previous master never wanted to take care of Brawley the way we do our slaves here."

Charity got a glum look on her face.

"Is it because they thought he's an animal?" she asked, showing a stark clarity that surprised her father.

"Something like that, dear," Alfred replied, knowing that, after eight years, he should never be surprised by the directness of this child's questions; still, he was always taken aback anyway.

Charity wrinkled up her nose in frustration.

"They don't know Little Isaiah!" she declared confidently. "Nobody could ever call him an animal."

Alfred sat down on the front porch and motioned for Charity to join him.

"I want to hug you real good," he said.

That was the only invitation Charity needed.

Alfred reached out, carefully picked his daughter up, and set her on his left knee, grunting as he decided that he would not be able to do this simple act much longer since the child was growing far more rapidly than he and her mother could ever have guessed, her little body seemingly becoming heavier by the week.

"When you get older," he tried to explain, "you won't be able to avoid people who think that Little Isaiah and our new friend Brawley are just like dumb mules, good for working real hard but nothing else."

"That's mean," Charity answered contemptuously, saying a great deal with just those two little words.

"It's more than mean," Alfred said solemnly. "In time you will understand, dear child, even better than you do now."

At the moment, all that little Charity was able to grasp, reasonably so for someone her age, was perhaps a vague notion that not every slave on the other plantations bordering her family's was being treated like those fortunate ones who had been owned by her father or grandfather all their lives and whose lineage traced back through her great-grandfather and great-great-grandfather as well.

But as Charity grew older, wiser, and more knowing, she was destined to learn the full extent of the inhumane treatment that did exist.

Oh, child, child, when your ignorance goes, which happens in this cold, sinful world, what an awful time that will be, Alfred thought mournfully. *God has kept you pure so far, but one day your eyes will see what has always been there.*

Though the worst aspects of slavery in Dixie were never as universally widespread and as accepted by most southerners as Yankee reporters and their sympathetic politicians would have unsuspecting readers and constituents believe, still the lies continued to be pushed—and pushed relentlessly. An endless parade of not-so-subtle attempts at painting a bleak and devastating portrait of the South.

The anti-slavery movement's campaign of cruelty charges did seem, in its intensity, a maniacal portrait concocted chiefly by grudge-tendering political enemies that was riddled with documentable and deliberate inaccuracies, which were obvious to any fair-minded person who took some time and delved into the truth. Nevertheless, high-level and powerful factions in the North seemed to conspire to destroy the South, leaving it ashambles and remaking that region into one that was more acceptable to Yankee sensibilities.

How are you going to react when you come to know later what your innocence now is denying you, child? Alfred thought lovingly and with the greatest concern over her future welfare. *I pray that the Lord will give you the discernment you shall surely need and the courage to act as you must, whatever the costs might be.*

"Daddy?" said Charity.

"Yes, dear."

"What's his name? When will I meet him?"

The eagerness Charity showed was nothing new, but Alfred hoped that he would never take it for granted.

"Brawley . . . our new friend is named Brawley. Count on being introduced to him tomorrow morning, just before we sit down for breakfast. I want him to get clean and grab plenty of rest. Savilla is going to make something special within the next hour or so, and she will make sure Little Isaiah takes it out to him right after that."

"Give him my cupcakes," Charity offered cheerfully. "I don't have to have them for dinner tonight."

"We have plenty of those. Anyway, Savilla can always make more. You don't have to deprive yourself."

Charity frowned cutely for a moment then shrugged her shoulders.

"Okay," she told him cheerily then impulsively dashed back into the plantation house, where she scooted up the curving stairs to her room and an irresistible bed full of dolls that were waiting for her attention.

Alfred bowed his head and folded his hands together.

"Lord, keep Charity from harm throughout the whole of her precious life," he prayed out loud. "Precious, precious Savior, send, I beg of You, whatever number of Your angels You see fit to protect that child."

Hearing a familiar voice behind him joyously declare "Amen!" Alfred glanced back at the front door.

Old but still healthy, white-haired, pitch-black Savilla stood in the opening.

Wearing a bright red dress with white polka dots on it, she was pausing in the doorway, smiling, a heavy rolling pin held between both hands, a butter- and custard-splattered yellow apron tied around her waist.

Standing there for another second or two, Savilla, so important during the course of Alfred's life, winked at him just once, then, humming to herself, disappeared back into the house.

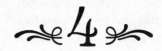

THE BIGGEST SHOCK for Brawley was actually being confronted by the place where he would spend the night.

So big! he told himself. *These slaves ain't cramped at all! I know some white folk who live a lot worse than this.*

Just in front of him were quarters nearly 70 percent bigger than what he had left behind at the other plantation, with oversized windows that allowed sufficient ventilation during the summer but could be easily shut tight in the cold months of November through March. Modest drapes hung over them, and there was a large wood-burning stove that served as both a heater and a cookstove; the stovepipe extended through the roof.

A table that had been imported from England where it was fashioned by craftsmen stood in the middle of the room on a bare wood floor that was kept polished.

Brawley could hardly believe what he was seeing.

As he was entering the building, he noticed a large supply of wood stacked near the outside wall—enough so that they could use as much as they needed and not have to worry about running out, which was hardly the case on many other plantations, not the ones where he had been a slave, anyway.

"If the Lawd sends us a real bad winter," Little Isaiah told him, following his gaze, "we's always sure that we can git more wood to take care of our needs. All any of us has to do is ask. Massa Alfred will say ever'time, 'Get it from the stack that has been laid up for the plantation house. Take as much as you need.' Yessir, that's what he'd say."

Everyone inside murmured agreement at that.

Brawley noticed something else inside that he could not recognize.

"What is that?" he asked. He was pointing toward an object that looked like a large, white wood box measuring roughly four feet by three and a half feet. Inside it was another box four inches smaller on all sides, the space between it and the outer box packed tight with powdered charcoal. The smaller box held five pecks of ice, which lasted for twenty four hours, keeping butter, meats, and other foods from spoiling.

"I never seen nothin' like that," Brawley admitted, examining it as though he were a quite young child suddenly introduced to something extraordinary from a world of adults and thoroughly beguiled by it.

"The massa got a bigger one in the plantation house," Little Isaiah told him. "We gets a whole lot of ice all the time."

Brawley also marveled at the building itself, which had been repainted just a few weeks before and thoroughly cleaned inside as well.

"We had to handle the work ourselves," Simuel remarked casually, "but that's jus' fine because Massa Alfred did give us whatever we needed, all the supplies, and 'nough time off to be able to do ever'thin' right."

"We even made the paint ourselves." Now a man named Hester spoke up. "The massa said that he never minded buying ready-made paint, but we got it in our heads that this would be somethin' we could do and be proud of, and he thought that was fine."

What they ended up with was a substance called milk paint.

"We took six ounces of slaked lime," Hester continued matter-of-factly, "then mixed in some good ol' skim milk that wasn't even a little sour and added six ounces of boiled linseed oil, then poured on three more pints of milk. After stirrin' it well, we crumbled across it 'bout five pounds of Spanish white, let that sit for awhile, and, finally, worked up the stuff with a wooden spatula."

Brawley started crying.

"What's wrong, brother?" Little Isaiah asked.

"I thought the devil had taken over the whole world," Brawley acknowledged. "I thought it would never be no different. I thought I's lookin' at nothin' but pain and sorrow for the rest of this life of mine."

He looked from Simuel to Little Isaiah to the others who were gathered together to welcome him warmly.

"I was tellin' myself that I wanted nothin' more than to die," he went on sadly. "I was plannin' on puttin' a big old rope around this scrawny neck of mine and . . . and just . . . just, you know, just hangin' from . . . from—"

He collapsed to his knees without finishing the sentence.

"And then your massa came up to me," he sobbed, "and we talked and talked, and he bought me from the devil who made life so bad. Massa Alfred took back my soul; he told the devil to leave, and the devil left!"

"You have your freedom now, don't you?" Simuel asked.

Brawley nodded, a smile replacing his sorrowful look.

"We could have been free years ago," Little Isaiah added. "Massa Alfred's offered it to us a lot of times."

"And yet you stay?" Brawley managed to ask.

Little Isaiah was smiling broadly as he said, "You will see why . . . Surely, my brother, you will see that."

IN ADDITION TO Little Isaiah, Alfred Littlepage's slaves included: Kindly
Willis, a man in his early sixties, quite thin but also very strong, with a
long, narrow face and a dimpled chin.

Rugged, sometimes ill-tempered Simuel, who actually dwarfed Little
Isaiah in terms of his girth but was a couple of inches shorter.

Hester, a man in his twenties, the youngest of the men by many years
and the shortest, but very nearly as powerful as any of the others and sometimes embarrassingly shy, considering his physical condition.

Savilla, an elderly woman who seemed almost to have angelic powers
with food, concocting some of the finest dishes anybody on that plantation,
including visitors, had ever had.

The remarkable Violet, even older than Savilla and anybody else around,
and hardly bigger than a circus midget, who was not much good at anything
but the most exquisite examples of careful knitting, taking intricate and
beautiful images that she had stored endlessly, it seemed, in her wondrous
old mind and turning them into sweaters, shawls, gloves, and other items.

Tiny Violet had one other gift . . . a gift that was directly connected to
her very soul.

Singing.

She could turn even a mediocre hymn by a run-of-the mill composer into
the music of heaven itself.

And she did this often.

Long into the night, when she was feeling well, which at her age was
hardly a regular occurrence, she would sit outside the whitewashed slave
quarters on a rocking-chair that Willis had made for her, Violet inspiring that
kind of love from everyone she met.

While puffing periodically on a corncob pipe that had belonged to her
father—curiously, none of the men had ever adopted this particular habit—
Violet would hum a certain tune or, holding the warm pipe in one hand, let
out with tender lyrics in a sweet voice that seemed far younger and stronger
than the ancient, frail body from which it sprang forth, and wave the other
hand through the air as though conducting a choir that only she could see
but with which she was in the most blissful harmony.

"Jesus, Jesus, my Savior, my Savior . . . ," she sang just a few hours after Alfred Littlepage had returned home, bringing Brawley with him.

Elizabeth was standing at the single-pane window in the master bedroom, listening to the old woman.

"How could it be that the angels above sing any more sweetly, Alfred?" she asked, her voice husky.

"If they do better than Violet, I scarce can wait until we get there," he said as he walked up behind her.

Elizabeth spun around, her eyes widening.

"You must never say such a fool thing again!" she admonished him, her voice unusually stern.

"What do you mean?" Alfred asked dumbly.

"I . . . I do not enjoy the thought of losing you. I do not enjoy the possibility of Charity having no father. I—"

Alfred put two fingers to her lips.

"You truly never have to worry yourself about such things, and yet you are always worrying, it seems, my dearest. Why is that, love? We have everything around us that is necessary for the truest peace of mind here and now, and we have had it like that all our lives. I mean, this grand home in which we live . . . all the clothes we shall ever desire . . . all the fine food we could conceivably eat . . . and there is the unstinting help of Little Isaiah and the others, help with every possible task for which they are needed. And you mustn't forget that we have our health, Elizabeth. What more could there be for you, for me, for our daughter?"

He was trying to be sympathetic and bolster her spirits without letting any sarcasm creep into his voice.

"There is no hatred in this blessed home of ours," he told Elizabeth admonishingly, "and there has been only love through the dozen years of our marriage. We maintain the deepest respect for one another, respect of a kind that most other families around here surely do envy whether they admit it or not, for it is essential to the happiness of any husband and wife.

"And we do know that the Holy Ghost Himself is standing with us. So please then, dearest Elizabeth, please tell me: What is there really for you to concern yourself with so grievously, my love?"

A slight smile edged up the sides of her lips. *You have always known how to reach through to my soul, dear husband,* Elizabeth admitted to herself. *If I could but do the same with you as you so deftly are able to do with me, I would be a much better wife than I am.*

She looked sheepishly at him.

"How long will what we have in our lives last, though?" she asked, not comfortable, even after a dozen years of marriage, with having to admit any such feelings to him. "Those dreams that I dream, Alfred, such terrible dreams, as you know. There was a new one, new but old and mean and awful at the same time, just last night."

Alfred had been concerned about these but had no idea of what their cause might be. Even so, he tried to be as comforting as he could. Right after she awakened each time, covered with perspiration and shivering frightfully, he would hold her in his arms and stroke the back of her head and kiss her again and again.

"What can I do? The dreams have never been anything less than abidingly harsh . . . so cold. They go away for a while and then return."

"Do you want to talk about the latest one?" Alfred asked. "Would that help rather than keeping their content to yourself?"

Elizabeth nodded nervously.

"I see our dearest, dearest Charity crying—how much she cries this time, this fine child," Elizabeth said, her lower lip trembling. "Alfred . . . Charity . . . she seems all alone in this dream, alone and sad. I want to reach out to her, to touch her, to tell her that she should not be acting like that, but I cannot . . . I cannot.

"It is hard to think of that perfect little princess becoming as distressed in life as she seems in this dream. Charity has been such a joy to us, to Little Isaiah, and to the others."

She was shaking, the color draining quickly from her face, giving it an eerie, almost ghostly look.

"You are especially upset today," Alfred observed, more concerned than ever. "I wish we had a minister who could provide true spiritual help. But not that Marmaduke, hardly him! I think I should ask around, try and find someone with considerably more depth than I have ever seen from him. Would you travel?"

Elizabeth nodded without hesitation, seeming so vulnerable that he could do nothing other than put his arms around her.

Jesus, Jesus, my Savior, my Savior . . .

"Let's just stand here and listen for the moment," Alfred said, his voice low and filled with tenderness. "Listen to what dear Violet is singing right now. Let her faithful words speak to us, Elizabeth. Let them come into our souls as though from the good Lord Himself.

"It is all we can hope for until we find someone to help. Lord willing, that old woman will be His instrument today when we need her the most."

Elizabeth did what he had asked. And her manner gave the impression that it was what she herself needed equally as much just then, to soothe her soul.

But, still, her worries did linger, refusing to allow Elizabeth any significant degree of peace, though she chose to keep this fact to herself, hiding with great success the pile of worries that made her wonder when that insular world of hers would come apart and fall to pieces at her feet.

~❧6❧~

Brawley had bathed twice by the time breakfast was nearly ready, that first night before going to bed and then in the morning not long after sunrise, both times using real soap, which he had seldom so much as touched or smelled in the past, lathering up very much like a delighted child, his glee evident, using an entire bar in the process.

The other slaves snickered as they listened to Brawley singing joyfully from the bath shack.

"Will the massa be upset?" Brawley asked of Hester, the youngest slave, when he realized that he had gotten carried away and there was no soap left.

"If it makes you smell better than you did last night, he's gonna sing hallelujah, hallelujah!"

Brawley beamed from ear to ear.

"This massa ain't perfect," Hester told him. "But he ain't cruel, either. And he listens if any of us have problems."

Then Brawley was given some fresh clothes and told by Little Isaiah to report to the plantation house at 7:00 A.M. sharp.

"Why are we going there?" he asked the other man, self-consciously unaccustomed to the routine.

"For a hearty breakfast," Little Isaiah said rather casually, not elaborating beyond those few words.

"We pick up our food there and then bring it back with us?" Brawley persisted while gesturing with his hands and assuming he surely was misunderstanding what the situation seemed all about.

Little Isaiah began laughing with gusto now, and the other slaves joined in with him, all except Savilla, who had gone on much earlier to the plantation house where she was busy preparing the morning food for everyone.

"No, Brawley, my friend," Little Isaiah finally managed to say at last, "we have breakfast inside the main house."

Brawley shook his head disbelievingly, realizing that he really had gotten it very wrong after all.

"Is the kitchen large enough for *all* of us?" he asked tentatively, not wanting to appear to be critical or argumentative.

Again the rest broke out heartily, not able to control themselves at the expense of their new friend.

It was Hester's turn to speak up.

"We eats in the room with the massa and his family!" he declared zestily, enjoying the other's dumbfounded reaction.

Brawley thought that the group of them must be playing some friendly kind of joke on him as the newcomer.

"Okay, okay . . . ," he said, deciding to humor them, hoping he was convincing enough so they would not realize that he was in on their little joke.

I can't spoil their fun, Lord, he thought. *They's so nice to me, all of them. I's got to go along with this.*

So Brawley told Hester, "I's ready whenever you all are."

They formed a line and walked the short distance from their quarters up the pathway to the plantation house.

Savilla.

She was standing in the doorway, waiting for them.

"Hope you all are hungry," she told them. "The massa wanted to serve something special today. I done cooked enough to feed an army!"

The old woman talked expansively, delighted by any special occasion that justified going all out for a meal.

"Eggs, bacon, fresh-brewed coffee . . . ," Savilla went on. "Normally, I'm too old to work this hard, but I'm doin' it 'cause you're a fine young man, and besides, the massa wants you to consider this your new home!"

Brawley took in what she was saying, wondering if anything was behind it. Might the tall, kindly white man have an evil purpose of some kind that would only come out later when nothing could be done to stop it?

It's not normal, he told himself. *Nothing like this is done for dirt-poor darkies like me. He wants to get on the good side of me, and then, like everybody else, somehow he's gonna try to work me into the ground. Under that pure white skin—*

Brawley turned and started to walk back down the path, but not in the direction of the slave quarters. Instead he was going in the direction of the country road that bordered the front side of the Littlepage property.

"Where's you headin'?" Little Isaiah demanded. "What's wrong with you, all of a sudden, acting like that?"

At first Brawley did not answer, confused over his own actions; then he called back over his shoulder, "I don't deserve this."

"What you talkin' about?" Little Isaiah excoriated him. "You don't deserve the good Lawd Jesus either. Are you gonna cast Him out, too?"

"I'm just a piece of black trash," Brawley persisted as he continued walking. "I can't 'spect to sit next to—"

A thin little voice yelled out to him.

Charity.

"Don't go!" she was begging. "Stay with us, mister."

Brawley stood still, looked with longing at the open road directly ahead of him. Just a few yards more and he would be on it, finding its appeal strong after so many years of being captive to other men and now unsure of what was ahead for him. But somehow that very uncertainty seemed appealing.

"I can't, child," Brawley said as he turned around. "This ain't my place. I gotta go where I belong."

Charity started racing toward him, tripped, skinned her left knee, then stood again, brushed herself off, and continued in his direction.

Not her, Lord, he whimpered to himself. *I can stand up to everybody but that sweet Charity! With her, I have no will power, none whatever!*

He wanted to continue on, leaving everyone who was white and rich behind him, and find his own way in the world, a world he knew would be harsh especially to a colored man but still, he would find out on his own.

Except for Charity.

Her thin, child's arms closed around Brawley's thick muscular arm, her immature but sincere words pleading with him in a cute voice that could scarcely be ignored by anyone, and Brawley knew finally that he could resist this little one no longer. He knew that he had to give this family a chance and that the road to the outside world would have to wait, a road he might travel someday but not now . . . not now.

Brawley decided to stay on at the Littlepage plantation for a few months. He proved a worthwhile addition to the laborers already there. Apart from doing his chores well, he revealed a talent that seemed to surprise even him.

Storytelling.

What Violet accomplished so triumphantly with her singing, Brawley was able to do with his stories.

"How did you come by these tales?" Alfred asked him when they were sitting together on the back lawn.

"It's not hard," Brawley told him. "I hears so much that's still with me from all them old, bad days."

"In Africa?" Alfred asked cautiously.

"Yessir."

"I would be happy to hear about them."

"After a day of huntin' food, everybody would sit 'round a fire at night and talk and talk 'bout whatever they could from days gone by, tales passed to them by their daddies and their grandpapas."

"Jesus was a teller of stories, too, you know," Alfred said. "He used parables so that certain truths would become clear for those who were listening to Him."

"I heared a Bible story about the man with a house built on shifting sand, and the other man whose house was built on solid rock. Is that one of Jesus' stories?"

Alfred was very pleased.

"Yes, Brawley, that is one of the parables."

"I knows others."

"Why don't you teach them to Little Isaiah and the rest?"

"Maybe they know 'em already."

"Even if that is so, the way you express yourself is so wonderful, so beautiful and fine, it is almost as though the Lord is speaking through you."

Brawley had been examining every inch of Alfred's face as his benefactor was talking. It was his own way of discerning whether someone meant what was being said, for he had the ability, it seemed, to peer into the center of any human soul and learn quickly whether truth or hypocrisy were behind the words being spoken.

. . . It is almost as though the Lord is speaking through you.

That whole idea was foreign to Brawley.

"I'm nothing more than a misbegotten creature," he said slowly. "I just can't see, Massa, the Lawd Jesus wasting His good time with a no-account buck like this one here now. He'll never stoop that low, no way."

"What kind of men *does* Jesus use then?" Alfred inquired, careful to keep any tone of sarcasm out of his voice.

"Good people, people like you, people others respect. I ain't had no respect in my life . . . until I came here."

"Of course," agreed Alfred. "There was the apostle Matthew, a hated tax-gatherer. And Thomas, a very tiny man who used his mind but seldom paid attention to what was on his heart and who was often scorned by people around him. John was quite young, naive, impetuous, not regarded seriously at all by very many members of the older generation. I could go on and on. You have no reason to feel as though you cannot qualify for discipleship."

Brawley fell silent then, leaning forward, elbows on his knees, hands pressed hard against his cheeks.

"And Jesus, remember Him above all . . . ," Alfred continued. "Jesus was despised and forsaken even by His apostles at one point. His death was demanded by a crowd that contained some of those same people who witnessed more than one of the miracles He performed, who had listened to His wisdom in the Sermon on the Mount."

Brawley remained in that position, saying nothing for several minutes as he reflected on what Alfred had told him.

Then Alfred spoke slowly. "And Jesus Christ was spat upon by many, mocked, abused by soldiers of Rome. They made Him carry His own cross on His bloodied back. They nailed Him to it and watched Him die—"

Brawley suddenly straightened himself.

"—'fore their very eyes. They left Him there, rejecting the precious Son of God, and damnin' their souls."

Alfred was deeply affected.

"Where did you learn that?" he asked.

"I had nothin' but tattered scraps of pages from a New Testament," Brawley replied. "I'd found some pieces of it here and there, and I collected them all together. Some of the other slaves knew a little readin'. I asked them for help."

"But that could hardly have been enough to teach you to read."

"A storekeeper in town took some time to help me when I was pickin'
up some things for my massa."

"He taught you more?"

"He did. He was a kindly little man, that one. He's gone now. I 'spect to
find him waitin' for me at the gates of heaven."

"But kind acts in themselves are not enough," Alfred pointed out. "You
do know that, Brawley, I hope."

The other man nodded.

"I do, but the Bible also say that if you love the Lord with all your mind,
heart, and soul, us will want to do things to His honor and glory. What you
do don't get you to heaven. Your love for the Savior done that."

Brawley was struggling, and Alfred wanted to help him win whatever
battle it was, but he needed to know more.

"I can see that you are in some real pain, friend," he spoke. "Will you tell
me what I can do for you?"

Brawley's frustration poured out.

"I don't know, sir," he said. "That's what's got me bad, you know. I think
of one thing, and nothin' happens. I think of somethin' else, and it's just
silence from above."

He cleared his throat nervously.

"If I was white, I could do a lot, I guess, but since I ain't, since I's as pitch
dark as though I'd been dipped in the blackest tar, what is there left for me?
No white man will ever listen to Bible talk from a black man."

Alfred had to admit that Brawley was right.

In the South of those days, black preachers always kept within the confines of their own race's groups, and there was absolutely no overlapping
of evangelization. Any free black who would dare to approach a white man
or woman in an attempt to witness for Christ invited being ridiculed if not
beaten!

"How can the Lawd use me then, sir?" Brawley asked plaintively. "How
can He do that? I need to know, Massa. I need to have Him guide my steps.
My mind tells me nothin' while my soul keeps on searchin'."

After being in control of his life for all of his adulthood, Alfred had experienced hardly any situations where he himself felt 100 percent powerless.
And as far as the slaves were concerned, he could order them to do whatever his will was at any given moment, and they would have to obey. The
fact that, in his case, fear of punishment played no part whatsoever did not
change the outcome; Alfred got what he wanted from his slaves while other
slave-owners used physical abuse to achieve the same result: obedience.

"Then we get down on our knees," Alfred spoke, "bow our heads, close
our eyes, and ask Him the same question directly."

"I's ready," Brawley replied. "I's ready."

Both men started to kneel, but the former slave did not stop at that.

Without pretense or hesitation, he fell forward onto his well-muscled chest, groaning with the need to be in deeper prayer.

Alfred saw what Brawley was doing out of the corner of his eye and immediately followed suit, though not with the same sort of innocent spontaneity that had abruptly gripped the other man and left him no choice but what he had done.

There was a time when, despite Alfred's sympathetic attitude toward blacks, he would never have gone this far in communion with any of them, but that time had passed, and with it, during the remainder of his life, other conventions also would be swept away, yet these would go awkwardly, clinging to him until the last minute.

The men remained prostrate for a very long time, moving scarcely at all as they began their separate prayers, first Alfred, followed by Brawley, around four o'clock in the afternoon of that mild September day.

And they did not cease until colder breezes touched them and odors from the kitchen alerted them to the fact that evening was on the way and it was time to go inside. But even then they were reluctant to end what had seemed the most sublime moments of communion with Almighty God that either had ever known.

Alfred opened his eyes first and saw that Brawley was still praying in that same prostrate position, little groaning sounds issuing from him.

To those given much, much is expected of them, he repeated to himself. *I have everything this man does not, and yet he gives back so much more than I ever have done. Oh, Lord, it seems that every black man I meet has taught me something new, something that You must pass on to them so that they can go and tell the world.*

His body tensed.

But how many get the opportunity? How many die with Your message frozen in their throats, never spoken to bless those around them?

Alfred was hardly a mindless captive to some absurdly romanticized view of black people in general.

I've become aware of too much of the truth ever to fall for that, he thought.

He knew from personal experience that only a handful of Negroes were like Brawley and the others under his care. The rest were often a varied lot, hardly people of one personality any more than white folks were.

But it was true that many of the free blacks had shown themselves to be thieving, raping, no-good savages, retaining the grossest barbarities of their native lands, surreptitiously living off the underbelly of decent society, and proving worthy of nothing but harsh punishment when they were apprehended, just as was the case with any law-breaking white men.

He glanced at the darkening sky, shivering as the temperature started to drop even more. Yet Brawley, a man reviling in being free for the first time in his life, was going on as before, seemingly unperturbed, his entire body covered with perspiration.

Another fifteen or twenty minutes passed.

Savilla had come to the doorway and was leaning against one side as she waited, holding a towel in her right hand. She raised the other hand and waved to Alfred, indicating that dinner was waiting; but he realized that, since he had begun with Brawley, he should leave only after the man had finished his two and a half hours of soul-wrenching prayer. Then and only then, the two of them would walk into the house together.

Finally stirring, Brawley said, "Amen."

And he struggled to his feet as though he were a hundred years old.

"It has been good here this day," Alfred told him.

"Yessir, it has been real good, praise God," Brawley replied with an earnestness that came from his very soul.

But then he started to shuffle his feet uncertainly.

"Anything wrong?" Alfred asked.

"I'm all sweaty, sir. I's not able to have the evening meal with you 'cause I gotta dry myself first and put on some decent clothes likes those you done left for me.

"Then go take a bath. It really is as simple as that. My family and I will wait a reasonable period of time for you to join us."

Brawley appreciated that kindness, but he felt fidgety about accepting it, not wanting to inconvenience his benefactors.

"Everybody must be real hungry by now," he replied. "I can't have you doin' anythin' like that, sir. I just can't."

Alfred struck a determined pose but not a stern one, hands on hips, frown on his well-tanned forehead.

"You are *not* my slave and never will be," Alfred pointed out, "but you are my guest this day and, I trust, for many more days after this one. I do expect, though, that you will accommodate yourself to my wishes as your host."

That insistence touched Brawley deeply, causing him to nod sheepishly and head back to the slave quarters, whistling an ancient spiritual as he walked with a greater sense of joy than he had known through his whole life until then.

Glancing toward the plantation house behind him, Alfred Littlepage saw his wife and daughter looking out from a second-floor window just before they were to go down for dinner. Both were smiling with the kind of pride in him that had become almost commonplace for such a man.

❧ 8 ❧

IT WAS ALMOST two years before Brawley started down that road that seemed always to be beckoning him away from the Littlepage plantation. He clearly was reluctant to leave, but to him being free was something more than it was to Little Isaiah and the others.

"I knowed only fear and pain and hunger until Master Littlepage freed me," he told the others as he paused at the front gate. "All y'all have had the best massa in the world to take care of you, so freedom would mean nothin' more to you. You have it here on all these acres of ground. That's where your freedom begins, and that's where it ends."

Charity came up to the group just then and motioned for him to bend down, which he did. She kissed him on the cheek.

"If I could keep this voice inside me quiet," Brawley went on, "I surely would; the Lawd Himself knows that to be true. But it's there; it stays where it is, calling me away, telling me about the world outside."

"It's a cruel world," Little Isaiah said, shaking his hand for the last time. "And we have so much here. The Lawd's blessin' us ever'day. Please stay, friend. The devil's out there, ready to pounce. Don't give him a chance."

The two men embraced.

"The devil is anywhere we are," Brawley said. "Our natures give him entrance or keep him out. I'm gonna fight him hard wherever I am."

Then he proceeded to ask one favor of Alfred.

"Massa?" he started to say, clearly nervous about doing so.

"What is it that you want?" Alfred replied, trying to make him feel less ill-at-ease.

"The plantation house, Massa. Before coming here, I ain't never been allowed to see the inside of one, let alone been welcomed inside as you've done. I'm gonna miss it. Could I go in this . . . this one last time? Or is that too much of a bother?"

Alfred assured him it was fine to do so.

They walked through together, master and slave, and Brawley looked around, still in awe. Every hallway had columns at each end supporting the twelve-foot-high ceilings. Perhaps the most unusual part of the house was a divided, so-called "good morning" staircase, a layout that was comprised of four separate flights of stairs leading from a common landing that was situated between the first and the second floors. Two flights ascended east and west, each to the upstairs bedrooms. A third descended east to the center hall, while the remaining one led north to the kitchen. This architectural design allowed privacy to any family members who might want to go directly to the kitchen without having to confront guests who happened to be downstairs in the two parlors. Men in those days had a parlor to themselves, and so did the women. These were not particularly an outgrowth of any notion of the men's superiority but because it was thought that women had interests wholly distinct from those of men, and the arrangement of a ladies' and a gentlemen's parlor seemed more a courtesy than anything else, allowing each group to talk among themselves quite freely.

As they stepped outside again, Brawley noticed the "warming kitchen," a lean-to structure adjacent to the cookhouse. Here, food was kept hot before being served to dinner guests. Originally the warmer had been built into the back wall of the kitchen fireplace, but ultimately that system was replaced by a cast iron stove Alfred had had shipped in from Boston.

"You's so blessed," Brawley said as he stood outside the cookhouse.

"I have never known anything else. Although I hope that my happiness is not based on all this," Alfred replied, "but rather on what is inside here." He tapped the center of his chest.

"Praise Jesus for you!" exclaimed Brawley, knowing that if he did not leave immediately he never would.

Now he ran his hand over one of the smooth, white columns at the front of the wide, welcoming porch of the main house.

"So beautiful," he said softly.

As he walked slowly away he turned a number of times to wave at the Littlepages and their small group of slaves before, finally, rounding a bend in the road and disappearing from sight.

Little Isaiah approached Alfred Littlepage.

"You don't never need to worry," he spoke earnestly. "We's here on this plantation until the day we all die."

Alfred thanked him and remained outside while the slaves returned to their quarters and Charity dashed inside the plantation house to play with her dolls, though, now nearly ten years of age, she was not spending as much time with them as before.

Only Elizabeth remained with Alfred.

"What are you thinking about?" she asked as she stood with him at the gate, a gentle breeze touching her long hair and stirring it a bit.

"How Brawley could ever leave what we have here," he speculated. "I know what he told us, but I still am unable to understand choosing certain danger above real security. If Brawley were white it would be different, but that pitch-black skin of his is going to be a beacon for all the secret political parties in the region. If any of the Dark Lantern societies get hold of him, there is no hope for Brawley, none whatever."

These groups, named because they usually did their violent work in the middle of the night, carrying lanterns to light their way, were forerunners of the KKK and other such secret societies that would be organized after the Civil War.

"For him, it was still captivity . . . ," she mused.

"And it isn't for Hester and the rest?"

"Because they *choose* to live their lives that way. Is a man still a prisoner who refuses his own release? Ponder that, my love. Or has he secured the greatest freedom of all?"

Elizabeth was making some sense, as usual.

They had decided many years before to be Christians through mutual acts of free choice. Certain atheists in the community around them continually found Christianity to be enslaving, stultifying, readily mocking any Christians they met as simply "white niggers with a heavenly massa." These individuals were few and far between, but they were loud and they were mean, and they decried any form of faith in God and Christian worship.

"Slaves for Christ," Elizabeth added. "That is what we are, you and I. We have chosen this for ourselves, just as Brawley did a moment ago with the direction of the rest of his life. We are no more prisoners than he is. For our people, it is the same. They are here because they trust us, they love us, and they see some measure of the Holy Spirit reflected in and through us, Alfred."

"We call them slaves," he protested.

"And they call you massa. But they could leave tomorrow because you would let them. Nevertheless they stay in willing bondage of a sort. Their world is strictly what we have here, nothing more," she said gently. "Where Brawley is heading has no appeal for them. Let it go at that. There need be no serpent in our little Eden unless we invite it in by our misgivings. Satan feeds on doubt. Have no doubt but only faith, and he shall flee."

"You seem to be comparing me to Jesus," he pointed out, greatly uncomfortable with that notion.

"Is it so wrong to do that?" Elizabeth persisted. "Are we not to be Christlike? Are we not to imitate the Savior?"

She took his hand in her own.

"It means one very important thing that has seemed so obvious to you and me for so long but now, I think, has become even more important," she said, her forehead lined with deep frowns that seemed quite incongruous considering the porcelain beauty of her face.

"What is that, my love?" Alfred asked.

"We must protect those dear people in every way we can. We have discussed this often before now. But having Brawley here and then watching him leave us as he has just done makes it seem of even greater consequence because of what he has given up. We can do nothing beyond the boundaries of the land that we own. But here . . . by all that is holy, yes, that is another story!

"I think they should know what we intend to do to protect them—if not now, then someday, a day we must pick with wisdom only God Himself can give us. And so we should tell Charity when she has reached an appropriate age."

Elizabeth had started to wring her hands.

"We wanted Brawley to stay here, and he did not listen for very long to us because he had the freedom of choice, and he made it, God bless him. Right now Charity has no choice, and she is content; but when our daughter becomes a bright young woman, will she decide as he did? Children are like that, wanting to fly free. She might feel eager to break out from this cocoon that you and I have created around her and . . . and—"

She turned away from the gate.

"—and try to live out there. That frightens me. There are forces gathering that may make a nightmare of the future. You know what they are, and you can be no less disturbed."

Alfred sighed as he put his arms around her.

"I see what you see," he agreed, and not for the first time in their marriage. "I see the Yankees with an unquenchable thirst for power. I see them conniving in every way imaginable to take over the South and turn it into a mirror image of the North or else drain us dry of our crops and our various manufactured goods in order to keep their own manufacturing base going.

"That is their great weakness, of course, a heavy reliance on industry very much at the expense of any substantial kind of farming. Perhaps they could overrun us, but only if they do not starve to death first."

He nodded back toward the slave quarters.

"And they are increasingly going to use the issue of slavery as an excuse for all manner of clandestine actions once enough fools start to believe them!"

CHARITY WAS SILENT *as she placed another letter gently on top of the others.*

"I never heard that conversation, of course, but my parents did tell me about it later," she told the members.

"Clouds on the horizon," Loreta offered. "Was that it? How well we all know what you are telling us."

"Oh, yes, storm clouds of the most ominous sort."

"How ominous, truly ominous they were, and yet we engaged in a grand game of pretense," Sarah added. "We just could never admit to ourselves that generations of living a single way of life could be wiped out in a very short while."

"Life as we knew it would disappear, and with it would go so many of our loved ones," Charity remarked.

"That is why we have formed this Society," Loreta told the newcomer, "to keep at least the memories alive."

Charity looked at her strangely but said nothing just then.

It was only later that Loreta would find out what she had on her mind.

Part 2

~❧ ❧~

God washes the eyes by tears until they can behold
the invisible land where tears shall come no more.
Henry Ward Beecher

Even as I became a teenager, I was not aware of anything but the happy sur-
face of the life I was living," she said while reaching for another letter. "I had
my friends from the surrounding plantations, and I was happy in every way
a child could expect. My nearly always cheerful personality won over all but
the grumpiest of other children, as well as their parents.

"I had my moods, especially during adolescence, times when I sulked in
my room alone, leaving my parents to wonder what was peeving me. It could
have been anything: the evening meal unacceptably later than usual or a
friend down the road not being able to play with me. In a perfect world,
imperfections in the form of trivial things not going my way were hard to tol-
erate, and I did not learn quickly to do so.

"I was most content when I was home, alongside my mother and father,
and also when I was with my family's slaves. Years later, I would wonder why
that was so, why I enjoyed myself more with common black folk than with
white youngsters my own age and of my own social station, but it was
enough, when I was so young, for me simply to live in this manner and not
question in any way the foundation of it all."

The old woman's wistfulness was apparent and mirrored the similar feel-
ings the members of the Society would have when thinking of their own
younger, happier years.

"For a very long while, I was accepted just as any other bright little girl
would be into the community," Charity mused . . .

IN FACT, CHARITY was accepted by the community more than her father
was. It seemed probable that other parents in the community exercised a

measure of fairness in assuming that she was simply too young to know or understand or approve of what was going on in her father's head and in her mother's, too, since Elizabeth chose to be fully supportive of Alfred. As a result, Charity did not come under the kind of animosity others aimed at her parents. Instead, her innocence was separated from the "sins" of her parents.

Charity experienced no retribution against her because of her parents' conduct, no sudden mushrooming of resentment spilling over and entrapping her as well. Anything that arose later came about moment by moment, offense by offense, bruised feelings along with trespassed cultural taboos waiting like dormant volcanoes, ready to erupt their destructive content.

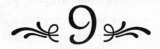

WHY DO OTHER folks around here hate you so much?" Charity asked Violet one Sunday morning.

The teenager was supposed to be getting dressed for church, but she could no longer hold the question to herself since, while she was in town, she had overheard some talk about Violet's "uppity" ways.

The old woman turned toward her attentive little friend and wondered briefly what she should say in response, wanting to be honest but hoping not to say anything that would truly upset Charity.

"I don't think they do, young lady," Violet finally replied then grimaced, unconvinced of her answer's truthfulness.

"What's wrong?" asked a concerned Charity.

"Age," she said simply. "You sixty before it grabs you and then it never lets you go."

A sharp jolt of pain had hit her as she moved to a new position in the old rocking chair where she had taken to spending so much time in recent years, her manner suggesting a certain ageless wisdom that went largely unappreciated by one so young. "They's doin' what their parents did, and their gran'parents 'fore that."

The old woman paused, catching her breath as the pain finally passed, and slowing her rocking to a more normal beat.

"They just ain't stoppin' and thinkin' rightly," she went on. "That's not meanin' any of them's evil; don't ever believe that. They's just plain dumb, child, 'member that. You mustn't upset the Lawd by turnin' 'round and hatin' 'em in return."

Charity shook her head energetically.

"But they look at you," she protested with real energy, "and Little Isaiah and all the others, and they say such mean things when they think you're not able to hear them. I listen sometimes. I try not to, but I surely do. And it's hard, Violet, so hard not to say anything when they . . . they are being just plain nasty!"

Probably the people she spoke of made the assumption that Charity, as young as she was, could not be aware of what was going on so they felt free to speak their minds when she was around. But she was proving to be more intelligent than many other youngsters her age, inquisitive but not to an extreme, and she immeasurably benefited from the rearing of a father who encouraged her in every way to reach out, to study, to decide for herself about the world around her, making himself always available to answer whatever questions she might raise.

Since Charity had lived from birth in a family environment that included slaves who were never treated less than well, she did not know any other way of life, and when she learned of the cruelties often inflicted upon other black people by men with none of the unvarying decency of her father, she did not have to wonder if this was proper treatment, since she already understood clearly that it was not.

"I do know, child," Violet replied lovingly. "But the Lawd don't want us to return evil for evil."

The old woman fell silent for a moment, her mind forcing her back to that harsh time when she had not been nearly so restrained, the pain of some harsh and cruel words stinging her like the literal lash of a cruel master's bullwhip, or the first occasion when she learned that a great many white people thought of her kind only as animals, like gorillas or monkeys and "only slightly smarter," as someone said a long time ago.

"They's thinkin' we ain't human.'

Violet spoke with conviction, but still, Charity could scarcely believe what the woman just said. Then, realizing this was someone who was not given to untruths, she jumped to her feet, her face flushing a bright red.

"Not human?" she repeated, not quite grasping what she had been told but, also, not liking the very sound of it. "How can they say that about you, Violet?"

"'Cause they be the ones who're ignorant!"

Violet and Charity broke out laughing at that.

"I want you to go to church with us," Charity declared resolutely after she had calmed down just a bit.

Violet turned toward her and smiled.

"I would love to do that, dear child," she said, her old voice cracking, "but I couldn't if I had to leave behind the rest of the slaves here. It wouldn't be right, you see. I couldn't just cut 'em out like that."

One of Charity's most noticeable shortcomings, her temper, flared up, perhaps inevitable in a wealthy family where she was denied little. She snorted, much like an impatient young bull ready to charge.

"My father will do it!" she exclaimed. "He'll take you with us. I'll make *sure* he does!"

Charity did not often play the "Daddy" card in any of her youthful relationships, somehow sensing that this would not have been proper and eventually would backfire. But she sensed something in this instance that made doing so necessary.

After winking at Violet, she scurried on back to the plantation house but was almost sidetracked by the very tempting aromas drifting in from the cooking kitchen, where Savilla was busy preparing the latest meal for everyone.

"Daddy!" Charity screamed as she dashed up the curving staircase that led to her parents' bedroom.

She started banging on the thick, solid oak door.

Elizabeth opened it with considerable alarm, concerned about what was obviously upsetting her daughter.

"Charity!" she said. "What in the world is wrong?"

"Violet and Little Isaiah and Savilla and . . . and—" Charity told her, sputtering as the words rushed out, making her suddenly seem more like an overwrought child than a rapidly maturing young woman.

"Calm down," her mother urged. "What about Violet and the others?"

"Church!" Charity declared.

"Yes, I know, your father and I are nearly ready to leave."

"They're all going with us."

Elizabeth had a blank expression on her face, momentarily not comprehending what her daughter was saying.

"Mama!" Charity stamped her foot again, frustration building up. "They're going to church with you and Daddy and me."

Alfred had come up behind her mother and heard what Charity had just declared.

Elizabeth glanced up at him hesitantly, looking rather helpless in the face of her daughter's sudden demand.

Breathing deeply, Alfred said, "Well, tell them to get ready. We need to leave in just a little over fifteen minutes."

Charity let out a holler and rushed back downstairs to inform her black friends of what their master had told her, while her parents stood, looking at one another, aghast at what they had just agreed to allow.

"Can we do this?" Elizabeth asked.

"How can we not do what seems so right to Charity in her admittedly youthful naiveté?" Alfred replied. "If we tell her what it is to be a Christian and yet we serve mere social custom instead, shaming dear Little Isaiah and the others, what does that say about us, Elizabeth?"

"You sound uncertain. That isn't like you."

"And what we are about to do isn't like us either, despite our attempts to be Christian in deed as well as word."

Both of them had tried so hard over the years of their marriage to be faithful to their beliefs in every aspect of their lives together. And yet they knew there were weaknesses in their Christian witness just as there were with other men and women like themselves.

"We must never stop asking the Lord to help us always to be open to His leading when He tries to show us whatever our failings might be," Elizabeth said as though to remind herself of that commitment.

Some Yankee Christians gloated over this by pointing out that slavery was a demonstrable example of seething hypocrisy with virtually every southerner who dared to defend such an institution, particularly by resorting to any so-called biblical justification for the generations-long practice of one human being owning another.

"I wonder if the Lord is enlightening us through our sweet Charity," Alfred posed. "Are we being told to—?"

He waved his hand through the air.

"What is it?" she asked.

"Nothing at all, my dear," Alfred assured her, "nothing that matters very much now anyway."

Elizabeth doubted that her husband was telling her everything, but she decided not to pursue the matter with him just then because she felt certain that the next few hours would bring quite enough pressures for the entire family to handle.

❧ 10 ❧

Everyone was waiting for Alfred Littlepage to join them, not apprehensively but with an air of joy.

More minutes passed.

Only Elizabeth felt uncertain as she waited with Charity and the others on the front lawn, for Little Isaiah, Violet, Savilla, Willis, Simuel, and Hester had trained themselves simply to trust Alfred, with no room for questioning anything he did.

Fifteen minutes.

Elizabeth was beginning to feel embarrassed, wondering whether her husband had changed his mind, but she decided to leave them all to come to that conclusion by themselves without any announcement from his lips.

Dear Lord Jesus, Elizabeth prayed silently. *Please bring him through that door, not with a changed mind at all but with the same purpose as before, so that these good people are not disappointed*

She glanced from one to the other, saw the expectation on their faces as they awaited such a simple joy.

To be able to go to church, to sit and hear the Word of God, Elizabeth thought. *Alfred and I have taken that privilege for granted, I suspect, throughout our married lives, and all of that time, we have left behind dear Savilla and . . .*

She found herself staring at Violet while the old woman's lips moved silently, her eyes sparkling.

She sings so much of the time, either to herself or out loud . . . so happy with so little compared to the people who call us names behind our backs.

Elizabeth remembered Christmas the year before. She and Alfred had given the slaves gifts, as always, but it was Violet's reaction that would never be forgotten. Her present was a leather-bound songbook.

You sat for hours holding it as you rocked back and forth in your chair. It was as though that little book seemed somehow holy to you.

Elizabeth had asked her about this some days later when she found Violet sitting in her rocker on the porch of her quarters.

"It ain't holy, ma'am," Violet replied. "I's holdin' it like this 'cause you gave it to me out of your love, and I's enjoyin' holdin' your love as close to this stooped-over, wrinkled little body of mine as I can."

Elizabeth sat down on the thick, somewhat damp grass in front of the porch.

"Let's sing something together," she said.

Violet, who could read as well as Little Isaiah and the others, leafed through the book and found a hymn that appealed to her.

"I knows this one a real long time ago," she declared. "Some of the others ain't so familiar to me."

"I thought we could learn them together," Elizabeth told her, honestly looking forward to such a time.

"I'd like that, ma'am; I'd like that very much."

Violet smiled.

"Thank you," she added simply, but with an earnestness that could not be mistaken.

Elizabeth had acknowledged that sincerity by nodding and returning Violet's smile with her own of equal warmth.

Now the sound of a door opening nearby brought her back to the present, directing her attention toward the big house again.

Praise God! she thought. *Oh, Lord, I should never have doubted my husband or Your plan for our lives.*

Alfred had finally emerged from the house and was striding toward the little group a short distance away.

"I have something to say." He started in, clearing his throat, a gesture that Elizabeth had come to know well.

She swallowed hard, waiting for her husband to say whatever he had on his mind while not sure she would like it very much.

"I feel that you should not go to church with us today . . . ," Alfred started to announce to the slaves.

It was what Elizabeth had not allowed herself even to momentarily dread, and yet her husband was saying those very words.

No choice.

She felt there was no alternative left except to contest her husband's judgment, while very much aware that social convention dictated that this not be done in front of anyone.

As Elizabeth was about to ask that he step back into the house with her, Alfred continued speaking after a pause that lasted no more than a few seconds.

"You must realize that I approve of what we all were going to do," Alfred said slowly, "but it is an opportunity to witness for Christ that cannot be thrown away out of haste—understandable haste, but haste just the same."

His expression was not stern or critical but unmistakably kind.

"We should proceed carefully," he continued, "and make the most of what our God may be about to provide."

Little Isaiah and the rest seemed to be hardly breathing as they waited for their master to tell them the rest. Violet's lips began to move, and her eyes closed, asking the Lord to give Alfred wisdom and boldness at the same time.

Watching them and her husband at the same time, Elizabeth hesitated, for the moment saying nothing.

"Here is what I have in mind," he went on, his emotions gaining momentum. "Tell me if it sounds as though you can do this."

Alfred could have ordered the whole group of his slaves to do whatever he wanted at any given moment, but that had never been his way, nor had it been his father's or his grandfather's before that.

As a third-generation Littlepage in that region, he was acting, in some measure, out of family tradition, yes, but it was also a course of action that he would have undertaken entirely on his own in any event.

"I do not think it is best that any of you join my family in church this day," he told them solemnly, "because I am now going to ask you to spend much of your time over the next weeks rehearsing—"

Elizabeth suddenly realized what Alfred had in mind but did not interrupt.

"—several hymns," Alfred continued. "White people's hymns, yes, but that is where you will make a true difference, all of you. You will sing these hymns as though they come from the very center of your souls. And you shall surely make them your own. I do not see how any of the congregation can be less than deeply affected. I think our own Violet, if she is feeling up to the task and is inclined to do so, should be your instructor."

They all turned in her direction. She tried to pretend that she was unaffected by this attention but failed.

"I can do it, Massa, only if it brings glory to the name of precious Jesus," she told them, her voice unwavering. "He's gotta be the source of my strength. If I do anythin' in my own, I's goin' to fail."

"And that is the way it shall be, for our only purpose is to bring praise, honor, and glory to the King of kings and Lord of lords!" Alfred declared exuberantly. "Am I to gather that you will help us then?"

Her answer was to break out in a lively rendering of a black spiritual that neither Elizabeth nor Alfred had ever heard before then. By the time she had finished, everyone was weeping, including Violet herself.

"I have changed my mind," Alfred said abruptly. "You will sing one white people's hymn, and then you will join with Violet in gracing the lives of everybody in that church with such beautiful words, such beautiful emotions."

He walked up to the old woman, put his arms around her, and hugged that frail body as tightly as he dared.

"I love you," he whispered.

"God and I sure enough loves you, too, Massa," Violet told him. "I's goin' to my grave thanking you for bein' so kind to all of us."

Alfred knew how she and the others felt by their actions, but hearing her speak as she did meant a great deal to him.

. . . I's going to my grave thanking you for bein' so kind to all of us.

There was no phoniness whatsoever in aged Violet's words, no transparent attempt to curry favor with the man who was legally able to control every aspect of her mortal life until the day she died. She had been with the Littlepage family over the course of two generations, had seen tiny Alfred as a baby in his crib, had held the boy in her arms when his mother contracted influenza and died far too young.

Even Alfred's father had come to Violet during the days that followed and cried himself almost to the point of being physically sick, telling her that he did not know how he could manage to hang on, that his wife had been the center of his entire life, and with that center vanished, he felt terribly, terribly empty.

Violet reminded him that if he did not live, his son Alfred likely would have to be raised by strangers over whom he would have no control, a prospect that could destroy the boy's decency in short order.

"Does you want that, Massa?" this wise old one had asked pointedly. "He's all you's got left. Give that son of yours twice as much love. Keep young Alfred out of the hands of those who's maybe gonna wreck his life."

Moments later, after he had exhausted himself and could not sob any longer, Alfred's father saw that Violet had been crying right along with him; he touched her gently on the cheek, just under her eyes.

"Let me wipe away your tears," he whispered. "I think I can deal with the reason for my own now."

She and the family were part of one another, and it was little different for the other slaves, though only Savilla equaled her in the time that had been spent working and living on that single plantation.

If the truth was known, Lawd Jesus, Violet told herself, *we would die for our massa. And he would die for us.*

"I cannot call it kindness, as you say," he said now. "It is my duty, for I made it an important part of a pact with our Lord. You are human beings. The Bible nowhere tells me that human beings should be treated any other way. It is a part of me, the way I think you all should be treated. I could no more stop doing it than cut off my hand and pretend that everything continued to be normal."

He stepped back for a moment.

"Y'all can leave today," Alfred added with unflinching earnestness. "That is no secret around here. I mentioned it yet again to Little Isaiah not too long ago, and he told me that he preferred to stay on since he had come to believe that freedom meant nothing if he simply exchanged one master for another."

Elizabeth could tell by their grimaces that they knew precisely what Alfred was talking about.

"There are plenty of other kinds of masters up north," Alfred spoke knowingly. "You know them as well as I do, perhaps better: poverty, hunger, the hatred toward niggers that the Yankees only barely manage to conceal some of the time while pointing those familiar accusing fingers at us down here."

He waited to see if any of the slaves wanted to respond.

Savilla was the sole one to speak up.

"And when we's got home from church that next Lawd's day after our singin' is done, if you all leave this here old gal alone, I's goin' to get the best meal these bony hands of mine can manage," she said, effectively ignoring everything that Alfred had just said and with it, his invitation to be made a free black.

Savilla was smiling as she added, "And I knows what it'll be. The Lawd's gonna take care of your souls, and He went and told me right now, 'Savilla, their bodies is up to you!' Just you wait and see. I ain't got too many more meals left in me, you know, and this one's sure enough goin' to be the best I did in my whole life!"

Without hesitating, the ancient little woman, her hair long ago turned a brilliant white in striking contrast to the darkness of her skin, fell to the ground, wincing a bit as her bony knees made contact with some stones embedded in the dirt.

"Take these hands, Lawd Jesus," Savilla prayed aloud, "and make this meal a blessin' to ever'one who eats of it and that bounty from which it came, for it is a real witness to You, Lawd, of what Christian love's like, if people just let it flow!"

✎11✎

"FOR A FULL WEEK," *Charity said, "all the slaves practiced their singing while my father allowed as much free time as they needed. He often either sat back and listened or joined in before realizing that their talent was not his own."*

Finally, it was Sunday again, and they got ready for the church service . . .

The church that had been attended by every member of the aristocratic Littlepage family for several generations was located just a bit less than three miles down the road from their plantation house; in fact it was the only place of worship in that entire region that could be deemed "suitable" for the gathering together of the families who enjoyed a standing similar to their own in the aristocratic community of that day.

Despite the extensive profession of Christianity throughout the Deep South, the region, surprisingly, was not overloaded with churches for the wealthy or the middle class, though an abundance of these centers of worship did exist for the poor folks, especially the poor black. Usually these were just ramshackle structures, some barely standing. It was a commonly held truth in those days that the wealthy were disposed to housing their family dogs in a clearly superior manner. The condition of these buildings reflected the extreme poverty endured by the worshipers, but in no way did it indicate a poverty of their spirit, for their beliefs gave them considerable strength and a greater sense of bonding as they participated in the emotional atmosphere that dominated the black church groups, making the services elsewhere for their masters seem rather embalmed and even spiritless in comparison.

Yankee critics would say that blacks had more churches because religion was one device the upper class used to keep them in line. If slaves, or bondsmen, as they also were called, could be made to feel fulfilled in a spiritual sense, then there would be less likelihood of open rebellion being fostered among them.

"Keep their souls content," sneered the cynics, "and then you can mistreat their bodies any way you want."

There were also several so-called "suitable" churches near the county line for plantation families such as the Littlepages, but that would have meant a burdensome amount of travel time each and every Sunday and on most Wednesdays when prayer meetings were held, not to mention additional services at Christmas and Easter.

And so it was that this one building, so conveniently located, was packed every Sunday morning except when the weather closed down everything in that area, as people gathered to hear stirring sermons by the current minister, John Covington Marmaduke, a fire-and-brimstone sort, fierce in his own way but self-admittedly no relation to the army major general who would later direct brutal governmental military campaigns against the Indians and the Mormons throughout the frontier lands west of the Mississippi River.

A physically impressive man with thick-boned face and neck and an almost bearish quality to his appearance, whose big voice fully matched his physical frame, Marmaduke adhered to a distinctly southern theology that accepted the Bible as God's literal Word from cover to cover. But, like so many other preachers of that era, he was routinely capable of applying certain verses out of context in order to justify upholding the cherished southern position verifying the morality of slavery.

So successful was he at this mixing together of Holy Scripture as a justification for slavery in the form that was being practiced and so well known did he become throughout the South, that John Covington Marmaduke would eventually join the staff of Confederate President Jefferson Davis and prove adept at rallying the troops with a call to "God, country, and the slave in bondage to his white master."

Many Yankees and not a few southerners with abolitionist sympathies were prone to describing the Reverend Marmaduke as a clever but transparent hypocrite through and through. And yet that label did not stick to him very well by-and-large as any such description could be used in a normal fashion, because this man did not sermonize one way and go about acting altogether differently in another.

This unusual consistency to his walk as well as his talk actually earned Marmaduke some grudging admiration even from those in the North who disagreed vehemently with just about all of what the man happened to stand for and loathed that which he continually defended Sunday after Sunday, either directly from the pulpit of that church or during regular after-church social gatherings.

What a sight the reverend was on such occasions, his already bulging eyes widening, his nostrils flaring whenever he saw an opportunity to engage someone in an on-the-spot debate, winning these confrontations more frequently than losing any. In the latter instances, Marmaduke would wave the victor aside, utter a curt, "The wisdom of God is as foolishness to man," and strut with calculated pomposity from the scene.

The church, on the outside, looked very much like a considerably smaller version of one of the many plantation houses throughout South Carolina, featuring two tall-ridged columns in front but with red brick as the facade instead of the more traditional whitewashed wood siding. An extraordinary hand-polished, gold-toned bell hung inside the steeple that was adorned with a large cross atop the peak.

Replacing individual rooms inside was a single large hall with a high ceiling supported by large pine cross-beams, the hall large enough to produce a slight echo effect for those voices occasionally raised loud enough.

The worshipers sat on customary hard pews, designed not so much as a concession to frugality but to guarantee that they keep awake. There were no adornments such as stained-glass windows or statuary as seen in the classical cathedrals throughout Europe, a reflection of the church-goers' deliberate attempt to shift attention toward the scriptural truth that the church was a gathering of people of like spiritual conviction rather than simply a means of displaying architectural magnificence.

"We worship the God of heaven and earth, not the mere physical buildings in which we gather," Marmaduke would thunder with great emotion from the pulpit in one of those pronouncements of his that had earned him his reputation as a theological conservative, a pronouncement that was quickly mixed with the seeds of secessionary sentiment. "Far more than slavery, far more than the gentle use of God's savage creatures who have been rescued from the jungles of their homeland and domesticated to have many of the advantages of civilization graciously bestowed upon them. Yea, my fellow Christians, it is my conviction that far more dangerous than any such benevolent institution to this still young and fragile nation of ours, this much-blessed United States of America, is the devilish infestation of unholy Romanism from Italian shores whose man-concocted ceremonies and rituals are infinitely more loathsome than humanity and God Himself should have to endure. Martin Luther and others saw the truth, and it is that truth we worship, and no other."

Listeners would then express their agreement with him by shouting "Hallelujah!" several times. And, always, after each service, his hand would be shaken until it was sore to the bone, shaken by members of the congregations who were absolutely in agreement with his various stands, whatever the subject might be.

Alfred Littlepage had no difficulty supporting Marmaduke in terms of his stand on Catholicism and a number of other issues that stemmed from their similar interpretations of Scripture. This meant that their directly opposite views on slavery in general and blacks in particular did not scuttle their relationship.

For a long time, Alfred hoped he would be successful in softening Marmaduke's outlook a bit in that one area, clinging to the notion that if such a man were so properly grounded in biblical truth in other respects, his darkness on a single subject surely could be altered as time passed. Nevertheless, many years of trying produced no fruit, and Alfred had come close to giving up.

"How can that so-called clergyman preach as though he is so close to the dear Lord above and yet be so filled with loathing for the poor coloreds?" Elizabeth asked as she stood before a mirror and made sure that her powder had been correctly applied and that her dress, a new light-blue frock imported from England, was as it should be. "How can he sacrifice true Christian love for the way he feels toward people with skin color that does not happen to match his own?"

"That is the man's blind side," Alfred replied. "He is so solid in every other way. I feel as perplexed about him as you do."

He was standing just behind Elizabeth, seeing if his own clothes, also new, were fitting properly.

"We are among the very few around here who see any contradiction at all," she observed with a wisdom tinged by sadness. "The other families do not bother to question anything because the foundation upon which they have built their lives is involved, particularly what their minister preaches to them every Sunday morning."

Alfred nodded as he recognized the truth of what Elizabeth was saying.

"Because everyone else takes what he says as the gospel truth," he agreed, "especially when Marmaduke seems to be finding justification in Scripture for how slaves should be treated."

A Bible was on the dressing table. Elizabeth reached out and picked it up, holding it against her chest.

"If they only looked inside, studied it by themselves, and understood its message on their own," she said.

She thought of the biblical passages about sheep following their shepherd. *How tragic it is when the one they trust blindly is guided by instincts other than those his Creator had given him,* she told herself.

"Marmaduke is so commanding an orator that they would not think of questioning him. They accept the message because of the messenger."

She turned and faced him.

"Why don't you challenge him?" she asked.

"We have debated in private many times."

"But why not do it in front of the congregation? Think of how many of them you could sway, Alfred. I know of no man more intelligent nor more articulate than you are. You could do very well against Marmaduke."

Elizabeth really had been hoping, for some time, that her husband would do this but was not surprised by his response.

"Marmaduke is likely to win even with his falsehoods," he said. "I would be far less convincing even though I would speak the absolute truth. He has been trained as a public speaker while I have not."

"How sad," she said, genuinely upset.

"But we must face reality, my love, and reality is that deception is easier to accept than God's truth."

She nodded in agreement.

"If the other members started to agree with us, they would have to treat their slaves differently or release them."

Elizabeth thought of those women she knew so well in the community who would be quite horrified at one or both prospects, either having common slaves eat in the same room as the plantation's white family or watching them go free, leaving no one behind to do the housework.

"I could name three wives now," she said, chuckling, "who would think their world had abruptly ended—"

The image made her laugh so hard she had to wait until she stopped to continue speaking.

"They would think that their world surely had ended if they were forced to wash any clothes or cook any meals or do anything, I suspect, but sit back and enjoy watching everybody else's hard work."

"Or worse yet," Alfred added, "clean up after the meal."

After both of them had finished laughing heartily, Elizabeth touched her husband's hand for a moment.

"I love you so much," she said, her expression leaving no doubt as to the sincerity of her words.

Alfred put his arms around her.

"And I love you equally," he whispered, his lips touching her ear.

As Elizabeth and Alfred were ready to leave, she glanced briefly through their bedroom window.

Not unexpectedly, their six slaves were gathered quietly outside, waiting to board the two wagons that would follow behind the carriage carrying the three Littlepages; one wagon would be driven by Little Isaiah, the other by Hester.

Charity was standing with protective Little Isaiah, who could always be counted on to look out for her even if it would have meant giving up his own life in the process, not entirely because of any orders to do so but arising primarily from his feelings for this young girl, feelings which made him nearly as protective toward Charity as her own father would be in any moment of danger.

Elizabeth squinted as though not quite believing what she was seeing; she backed away from the window an inch or two while pointing outside.

"Look at that!" Elizabeth said excitedly. "They're . . . they're . . . oh, Alfred, look at the precious lot of them!"

All six slaves were waving up at her, beaming most proudly, as was Charity, though it seemed, in that moment, that they all were child-like.

We treat them like children, Alfred thought. *We provide everything for them so that they shall never want, and all we ask in return is obedience. When will we ever allow them to become what they are?*

Alfred came up behind Elizabeth and saw what had surprised her, but strangely, it seemed, he himself was taking the sight completely in stride.

Mouth open slightly, Elizabeth glanced at Alfred and then quickly turned her gaze back outside, blinking her eyes several times.

It was not because they had been obedient as always that Elizabeth would have registered such surprise, for this was expected of them. There was something other than that, something that Alfred thought would have thoroughly pleased his wife.

Their clothes.

The sight of them proved to be what had made Elizabeth react as she was doing.

It was true that not one of the Littlepage coloreds had ever had to resort to wearing tattered rags in the absence of anything better available for them, since Alfred never subjected any of the six of them to the indignity of sub-standard apparel that should have been thrown away instead of reused.

"They are not stray dogs," he once remarked to a visitor, "and none shall be treated as though they are."

As usual, none of the other family patriarchs in that region felt the same.

Typical owners could never be bothered getting nice new garb for their slaves other than when new clothes proved absolutely necessary, which usually meant at the point that their existing clothes were impossible to salvage by any more sewing or patching or just plain ignoring the poor condition of shirts and pants and dresses.

Again, the reason behind this frugality was largely economic, but that did not tell quite the full story.

"If we start dressing their kind anywhere nearly as finely as the standard to which we ourselves have been long accustomed," one slave-owner named Samuel Fulkerson had opined emphatically a number of years before when they had bumped into one another at a local farm market, "if we start feeding them much the same meals that we ourselves are eating, if we boost these niggers to a higher level than they deserve, these savages, and none of them are one load of dirt better than that, these filthy savages will start thinking that they are as good as the rest of us, that they actually deserve certain things. If we aren't about to provide whatever it is that they have learned to covet, then, I tell you what, Alfred Littlepage, they might leave us, maybe in the middle of the night, giving you and me and the other owners around here no choice but to go about hunting them down and punishing each one real good.

"Alfred, I tell you this: We must never allow that to happen, never! They have their place in our world, but that is all. That is where they must be kept, through whatever means are necessary to make certain of this. We have to guarantee that these creatures are not allowed to be contaminated by any fancy ideas."

"That gives you license to—" Alfred started to interrupt.

"Yes, I did say *whatever means are necessary,*" Fulkerson went on without paying attention. "And I meant every single letter, every single syllable of that. Hang the rebels. Skin them alive. Beat them to death. Nothing should be held back, for if we stop short for a single moment, if we show compassion, if they sense any weakness in us, they will be like animals sniffing out their kills."

Fulkerson leaned forward, his nose just inches from Alfred's.

"Fear smells different to animals, you know," he said, his voice hardly more than a growl. "It has a real odor of its own. Hey, you know, that may be why the darkies stink. I mean, they really stink!"

Alfred Littlepage never thought anything of the kind.

And along with feeding his slaves well and housing them properly as well as tending after their health, he saw to it that their clothing was simple but clean and never older than it should be.

Yet this time, preparing to go to church and surprise the congregation, Alfred had decided to add something else to the basics. Little Isaiah, Simuel, Willis, and Hester were now dressed in fine black suits with silk shirts underneath, all fashioned of quality, imported materials; Violet and Savilla had donned finely designed, medium-blue dresses embossed with a gentle, cream-shaded floral pattern and lace trim, white silk hats on their heads, and each holding a blue parasol. All seemed anxious to present themselves in the public showcase of the church.

"Where did they get all those beautiful clothes?" Elizabeth mused absent-mindedly for a moment, not really grasping what the answer must have been until it abruptly seemed to grab hold of her.

Alfred, why are you saying nothing? Surely this must—She couldn't imagine how it had happened. *Surely you must be as startled as I am!*

Then, suspicious of her husband's silence, she swung around and confronted him. "Did you enable these dear people to dress up like that, Alfred?"

Alfred felt embarrassed by the way his wife seemed to be accusing rather than complimenting him.

"I could hardly let them go to church—" he started to say defensively but then stopped himself.

"Dressed like slaves?" Elizabeth interrupted. "But that is what they are! Should we pretend otherwise? Should we dress them up like cute little organ-grinder monkeys and trot them out for everyone to see? You think, I suppose, that fine clothes will be a defense against generations of condemnation or worse?"

Elizabeth narrowed her eyes.

"Are we *really* doing all this out of a desire to show kindness to those precious souls outside?" she asked pointedly, her voice unsteady, showing the strain she was feeling. "Or does it have more to do with making you and me feel good about ourselves, Alfred, with little real concern for them after all? Here we are, giving these good people a taste of refinement, a few minutes of respectability of a sort, and then what do we do? We send them back to their shack to live—a rather nice shack admittedly, as far as shacks go, but still a shack, no matter how we try to dress it up."

Alfred responded with a display of anger that was not customary for him.

"That just is not fair," he told Elizabeth. "You *know* that I have offered Little Isaiah, Simuel, and the others their freedom again and again and again. Why, it was just two weeks ago that I spoke the latest time to—"

"Yes, I realize what you are saying, husband," she interrupted once again. "I surely am aware of all that you are trying to tell me."

Elizabeth paused, that intent gaze of hers capable of reaching into her husband's very soul.

"But why is it, then, that they have not left us?" she asked without relenting. "Can you answer me that, Alfred?"

"You know the answer," Alfred retorted, his irritation apparent. "Those people have repeated it every bit as often as I have told them that they can leave, that I am willing to give them legal freedom, with whatever papers are necessary. Why does all this need to be stated yet again in order to please you, my dear Elizabeth?"

His wife's large brown eyes seemed to widen even more as her emotions continued to heat up.

"Are you being entirely honest when you give these six human beings everything they could possibly need, providing them, as our slaves, with such a vastly better life than they could ever obtain as free blacks anywhere else in this country, and then you go and tell these dear people: 'By the way, my friends, you can leave anytime, and you can do so with my full blessing.'"

Alfred was beginning to see his wife's point, but he would not admit this to her right away.

"What would you do in such a case, Alfred," she said, "if you were black and someone had said that to you?"

She paused, letting that sink in, and then went on, "Think of what I am saying; I beg you, my beloved. I agree that Little Isaiah, Violet, Savilla, and the others clearly have never been slaves to Alfred Littlepage's iron rule as we speak of it at this very moment, for you have never been that kind of man."

Elizabeth smiled slightly, an expression of affection that came from the very center of her soul.

"It is not in you to mistreat any slaves," Elizabeth declared. "And you may not be keeping them here on this plantation with whips and chains and whatever else some other owners use to intimidate them into submission. But, dearest, they still are *bound* to you just as strongly—Open your eyes!— just as tightly as though they were locked away in the foulest of prisons from which there is no escape."

She glanced out the window again and looked at the six slaves waiting patiently and with such great trust for a man with whom they had spent the greater part of their lives, a man who never struck them in anger.

"Look at them, dearest," she said, sadness in her voice, as she pointed toward them. "What if something happens to us?"

Elizabeth's manner softened as she said that, her voice lowering.

"Some other slave-owner will undoubtedly buy all six, like heads of prime beef from some cattle range. The only difference is that it won't be to slaughter them but to work those people, those fine, good people until they drop. How will they endure that after the way you have spoiled them?"

Alfred seemed to have caught some of the same mental images that Elizabeth was now apparently seeing, tumultuous scenes of great and continuous cruelty, human beings being forced into the lowest level of living, working as glorified beasts of burden carrying whatever was being piled upon them by those cold-hearted men who would not care if one or more of their blacks were to die on the spot from the strain. Instead they concerned themselves far more with the considerable cost of replacement labor, what with the incidence of rising inflation in recent years and the necessity to spend precious hours training every new colored man, woman, and child.

I wish I could say that all this was wrong, he thought, *that it was concocted by the Yankees and nothing more, but I cannot.*

Alfred remembered hearing about just such an incident, related to him one morning by another slave-owner who, though not as generous as himself, nevertheless abhorred the sort of treatment it portrayed.

Two years earlier . . .

This occasion involved a middle-aged black man who had been abruptly downed by a massive heart attack after an especially heavy day of work in mid-August of that year, always the hottest of months.

As he fell, gasping desperately, into a roadside ditch, his master had yelled at him, "Don't you go dying on me, you stinking piece of trash!"

The man's owner strode over to the trembling, twitching body and kicked it with the tip of one of his heavy boots.

"I would never be happy, not happy at all, about finding another wretched nigra just now to replace you, boy," the white man growled. "You surely don't want to make me mad, real mad, do you?"

The black man actually tried to stand when he should not have been moving at all. His eyes were filled not with anger but with choking panic along with the convulsive pain that raced through his entire body.

"I's okay," he lied desperately, though barely able to speak. "I's gettin' up . . . Don't be upset with me, Massa . . . I'll be along now . . . Ain't no need to whip me this time. Jus' give me a minute, Massa, just a minute to—"

The poor man stumbled forward, collapsed in the owner's arms, and died after gasping just once more. Without delay, his body was thrown to one side and never picked up. That night wild animals took care of the scrawny, discarded body.

Remembering that story, the Littlepages now asked themselves . . . *what if something happens to us?*

That "something," of course, was nothing but a certainty.

Whether it occurred ten years hence or thirty or whatever time in the future when both went on to be with the Lord, left behind would be whatever slave holdings they had been able to maintain until then.

They will be cast adrift after we are gone, cast adrift and ill-equipped to cope with a world that scorns them, Alfred thought with a regret that seemed to grab hold of every inch of his body and squeeze him tightly. These feelings aligned him solidly with the more principled families living in the South, people with whom he had been having a number of discussions over the past several years. *Little Isaiah, Simuel, and the others—especially the women—are so helpless, vulnerable to the ever-present perversity of life beyond this life. It is only here that they are able to enjoy the safety that all of them deserve.*

Children.

Simple, unsophisticated, totally dependent children, children who would remain the way they were for the rest of their lives.

Their blacks were but children to them or, perhaps, retarded adults who deserved to be shielded from the brutal realities of the world that was just beyond the boundaries of the family's plantation acreage.

Thinking of grown men and women accordingly would seem unspeakably condescending to succeeding generations of white and black people, but not in the South Carolina of the late 1840s or anywhere else throughout the South.

A matter of affection. For some, it was not more complicated than that, and the slaves themselves seldom took it any other way.

Kindness . . .

That was what it genuinely proved to be at the time, a true motivation for kindness, however misguided, and it drew a line of demarcation between those who sought only to exploit their hapless slaves as mere beasts of burden, or worse, and those who harbored genuinely paternalistic feelings toward their property.

What if something happens to us?

Elizabeth's words, repeated in Alfred Littlepage's mind as she said them again, brought him sharply back to the present. He had no doubt as to what he would do.

"I would arrange for their freedom, you know that," he protested, though not altogether confidently, "making that an irrevocable part of my will, if necessary, in order to be certain that everything was going to be safe for them after I was gone. Every last one would be protected. I give you my word before the Lord!"

Elizabeth persisted, trying not to sound snappish.

"But where are they to go?" she asked. "We all know what it is like for those poor blacks who are up in Yankeeland. Or out West, perhaps, to be slaughtered by heathen Indians? Who can say? More likely some soulless trader will grab them all and resell them in no time."

"But, Elizabeth, that . . . that would be quite illegal!" Alfred protested stupidly, his cheeks reddening.

She could not believe her husband's strangely naive reaction.

I cannot let this pass, she decided with not a little reluctance, *only to have it flare up some time later.*

Elizabeth's challenge was a rare one in the South of the mid-1800s, and she was very much a southern woman of the times, deferring to her husband in all other matters, although he let her feel the natural freedom to be a separate individual, able to raise her voice when this became necessary.

"In a world where free *blacks,"* she struck back at him, her eyes wide, glaring at him with amazement as well as anger, *"free* blacks feel no guilt whatsoever over committing what we both surely believe must be the greatest of all hypocrisies by paying top dollar for a whole cattle car load of prime young bucks, healthy slaves gathered from among their own people. Think of that, my love!"

She lowered her voice, reaching out and touching his cheek so gently that it might instead have been a feather on his skin.

"In such a world as we have today," she added, this time less stridently, her anger at him dissipating as quickly as it had flared up, "how could either of us expect any illegal act to be stopped with that ugly horde of traders at every dock, every depot, some of whom are themselves black? They are dealing in an awful trade as grossly as any of the white traders I have seen.

"Their kind are human monsters, Alfred, tearing entire loving, close-knit families apart and counting only their filthy gain from these abominable acts, for nothing matters more to their kind than financial and material gain. Laws of man and God mean little to them; surely you comprehend that better than most people."

Alfred hesitated, caught off guard by Elizabeth's erupting ire and unable to speak for a moment.

She was right, he realized, since he had heard many of the stories that seemed to be perpetually circulating about those arrogant blacks who had deserted any standard of decency when, sometimes after earning their own freedom, they would go on to set up and maintain a large stable of their own black slaves.

Not a few tried to salvage some scraps of credibility by claiming that they were doing this only for the altruistic goal of keeping various family members together. But these protestations usually carried with them the attendant suspicion by their critics that this was no more than a flimsy facade, that the real motive was getting, as always, cheaper labor so that their profits could be enhanced no matter how much of a crime was being committed against the very people among whom their own roots could be found!

Though surface appearances were treacherous to use as measuring sticks to judge anything by, it nevertheless seemed to Alfred that the very principle of a black man enjoying all the privileges of his own freedom and yet then turning around and engaging in the unrestrained buying and selling of other black men, women, and children should have posed a problem of extraordinary proportions for those in the South as well as the North. But even those northerners who had become committed to the abolitionist "doctrine" perpetrated destructive myths about blacks that suited their purposes, making those slaves whose interests supposedly motivated the entire movement instead only helpless pawns in a power game between federal interests and the rights of individual states.

And yet . .
Silence.

Odd as that was, little was being said by the other camp about the hypocrisy of black owner-ship of blacks.

It would burst the balloon created around the lingering myth that their kind enjoy perpetuating, Alfred told himself. *They insist that the morality of black people was clearly better than that of any white slave-owners, painting them as poor, noble savages suffering dire exploitation at the hands of their oppressors.*

Losing the viability of that potent and insinuating image was a looming prospect hated by the various militant Yankee factions. They needed it to wave around in their heated speeches and their newspaper columns; losing it would only help to undermine their campaign to gain ever greater public support, on both sides of the Mason-Dixon Line, for either legislative action at the federal level or for fomenting violent rebellion by masses of slaves through clandestine contacts.

They are no better or no worse than the rest of us, Alfred grumbled to himself. *But listen for a little while to any of those loud-mouthed Yankee idiots and their lackeys, and it would be easy for most folks to be duped into thinking that those of white skin were actually the inferior of the two races because we would dare to buy and sell coloreds, supposedly showing by that alone a so-called streak of moral defectiveness!*

He sank down on the large bed, his hands shaking, his face pale, as though sickness was coming upon him.

"Forgive me . . . ," Elizabeth said, concerned, as she sat down next to him, putting her arm around his waist and her head on his shoulder. "I didn't mean to make you feel in any way as though you were being——"

"I do love them, you know," he interrupted, voice trembling. "It may have been as you say at the beginning, that any kindness I showed had strings attached to it. But that ceased being so a very long time ago."

Alfred grimaced as soon as he realized that he was admitting this to himself as well as to Elizabeth.

Oh, Lord, he thought. *Lord, how we follow the deceiver of our souls while thinking ourselves righteous.*

Alfred glanced toward the high, white ceiling, not able to meet her gaze since Elizabeth was demanding complete honesty; that was not usually a problem for him, but this time the circumstances were different.

"After all, if I could give Little Isaiah, Simuel, and the others the gift of some simple Christian kindness and get back, in return, unbroken obedience from each and everyone of them," he finally acknowledged, "I would have what every slave owner truly does crave. Yet, in truth, any who have succeeded in attaining it have done so only with the greatest effort as well as far more unpleasantness than has seemed necessary."

. . . *and get back, in return, unbroken obedience.*

"Then what does that say of my heart?" he added, agonizing over the image of himself and his actions that loomed in his mind. "I get the very same result that Samuel Fulkerson has been achieving all these years, just in a contrary manner. We both arrived at the same destination, however. How can that make me really all so different from him?"

No answer came to him, none at all, just a growing sense of guilt that seemed like a loose bull in one of the finer china shops that Elizabeth and he visited from time to time in Charleston and elsewhere.

Alfred looked at his wife as though he were a helpless child confronted by a problem that had no apparent solution.

"It may have been pure business early on, with a little sugar-coating, I suppose, but then they started to show me real appreciation," he told her. "And out of that grew love, Elizabeth, theirs . . . and mine."

For a few minutes, the two of them shed tears together, then, wiping their faces and straightening their clothes, they headed outside to join their slaves.

~❧ 12 ❧~

G IVING SLAVES AT *least part of each Sunday off was hardly uncommon,"* *Charity recalled to the gathering Plantation Letters Society members.*

For some owners, it was merely a bit of good business, adopting the same principle they used with common work mules: If you worked them too hard without rest, you had to expect the poor things to drop eventually; obviously, this was a very short-sighted approach. For men who cared about the well-being of their flesh-and-blood property, especially the Christians among them, dollars and cents had little to do with it, with earnest consideration given to the blacks' spiritual as well as their physical health for moral and ethical reasons.

Usually this rare leisure time was spent in church, where entire families of slaves from various plantations gathered together to worship in pure faith, faith as well as trust that was daily tested by the circumstances of slavery for those trapped into ownership by the more uncaring owners.

These families were, by and large, not the *original* families of each black man, woman, or child but a new family, fostered by years of living together. A man who was married in Africa probably also would be married in the South of the nineteenth century but seldom to the same woman as before, since previous relationships were seldom maintained in an auction environment where the husband might end up being sold to one owner from Virginia, the wife to another in Tennessee, and their children to others.

Church represented a welcome coming together for black people, a community in itself, even if it was not being shared with loved ones they had known in their villages back in the various regions of Africa that were being continually plundered.

So, when the Littlepages' carriage and two wagonloads of their slaves pulled up in front of that South Carolina church, a number of the members assumed that Alfred, Elizabeth, and Charity would stop there and their slaves, in the two wagons, would continue on to their worship service elsewhere, perhaps in the familiar building three miles down the road.

But when the wagons as well as the carriage were tied up across the way from the sanctuary and the six black passengers all got off, and started to walk toward their master, several people gasped.

A broad, burly-looking man named Ambrose Pegram, whom Alfred just barely knew, stepped in their path.

"Not allowed," he declared simply.

The slaves stopped immediately, conditioned to obey without dispute what any white man told them.

Pegram folded his arms smugly and waited for them to turn around and promptly head back to the carriages.

"Wait, Little Isaiah!" Alfred called out. "You will not be leaving!"

Little Isaiah spun around, recognizing that authoritative voice but saying nothing in response. He stepped aside as Alfred strode toward him, gently grabbed his shoulders, then pushed him ahead, waving at the others to follow behind.

"What you are doing will not be tolerated," Pegram insisted. "Be careful that you are not digging your grave with black hands on the shovel."

"I wonder, sir, if you could be threatening me?" Alfred said as he clinched his hands into ready fists.

"I wonder, sir, if you have not lost your mind," the other man replied, mocking the haughty manner that long had been a Littlepage trademark. "This church is for white folk only."

"Do you think coloreds have a god of their own? Or do they worship the same God we do? May I have your response, sir?"

Pegram resorted to biting his lower lip, sensing that he was being set up and not happy about the prospect since most of the members of the congregation were still outside and eagerly standing by, witnessing the confrontation.

"I have no idea what those darkies do when they go into *their* churches," Pegram growled. "For all I know, they could be cutting off the heads of chickens and covering themselves with the blood—some kind of Santeria ceremony, like they do in the jungles of Haiti."

Many of the other members were nodding, and a few murmured in agreement.

"I mean, Littlepage, I myself have never been in any nigger church ever," added Pegram, playing to the crowd. "But I suppose that you surely have. In fact, I would be willing to *wager* that you have."

Alfred saw an opening and seized it.

"On a Sunday in front of His people?" he shot back, broadly feigning disbelief. "You can propose before everyone here a bit of gambling, and that seems fine and dandy to your way of thinking. Yet these simple, Christ-centered black folk, you are saying, cannot be allowed the immeasurable benefit of teaching from the notable Reverend Marmaduke because they are black. You would not mind, I assume, if they waited outside, near the carriages perhaps and played a game of craps on the Lord's day?"

Pegram was sweating, conscious that he was losing the battle.

"But I will let that one pass," Alfred told him, "in order to get back to the question I raised a moment ago, the one about Almighty God. Do you remember it, or are such matters like sand between your fingers?"

Pegram started to say something, but Alfred cut him off.

"If this church is for white folks only," Alfred went on, "then God must be for white folks only. But that cannot be so, sir. You see, you guessed correctly. I *have* been in a colored church. And I have witnessed their love of the Lord. I have heard songs of adulation and joy coming from deep within them.

"They do not sing as you and I, but then they are on fire for Him in a way I have never seen in any of our staid services. We sing the words, oh, yes, we do that, but they *feel* those words from the very center of their souls."

He lowered his voice.

"How often have you gone only through the motions, sir, the bland, dull, ritualistic motions?" he asked ruefully. "How often have you knelt in the heavenly Father's presence with a deadened conscience and a rancorous heart?"

Pegram reached out to slap him, but Alfred grabbed his wrist in midair.

"How often, sir, have you reacted with blinding anger because someone has simply confronted you with the truth about yourself?"

He held Pegram's wrist for a moment longer then dropped it.

"I know what anger is justified!" Alfred exclaimed. "It is the anger felt by Almighty God when He hears such as you daring to claim the name of His only begotten Son. That, sir, surely must be the rankest of blasphemies!"

With a motion speaking of the utter contempt he felt for the man, Alfred turned his back on the other man and walked the rest of the way with his family and his slaves up to the church, entering it as those lingering in the doorway stepped aside.

Pegram, ridiculed as he had been, stalked off without attending the morning's service, and a number of the other members followed suit while the majority of the congregation, their murmuring quieted for the time being, fell in line behind the Littlepages, none of them wanting any more of a scene such as that one to develop on the Lord's Day.

But there was still John Covington Marmaduke to contend with . . .

❧13❧

THE REVEREND MARMADUKE stood behind his freshly polished cherry-wood pulpit, one of his few concessions to any kind of material improvement within the church, palms pressed hard against the top, his gaze fixed on those who were coming into the sanctuary. The church was one of the many areas where his control was complete, down to the placement of the pews, the exact schedule for each service, and every other facet of church life. The kind of commotion occurring that day was guaranteed to raise his ire and loosen the veneer of godliness that he pulled around himself whenever it was convenient.

At first he said nothing.

"Why is he not protesting?" whispered Elizabeth, surprised.

"Simple reason, my love," Alfred replied knowingly. "Our reverend needs an audience. Having lost part of it a little while ago, he wants to make certain that the rest are seated before he says anything."

After everyone had been seated in the pews, Marmaduke's attention drifted to the empty seats, about a third of the total.

"What a pity!" he exclaimed. "Hungry souls left out in the desert."

"It was their own choice," someone spoke up.

"I see . . ." Marmaduke pondered the statement like a cow chewing its cud. "You are blaming those loyal members and not the *conditions* that made their attendance in this house of worship intolerable to them and, perchance, to any decent white man."

"They had a choice," the same member added nervously, unaccustomed to taking a stance that defied Marmaduke.

"If that is true, then it was, I daresay, a choice *forced* upon them," Marmaduke countered. "If a man had to kill another in pure self-defense, we would say that it was a bad choice but he was forced to do it. And there would be no condemnation. Furthermore, under certain circumstances, he might be called a hero."

The member was silent now, intimidated by this man.

"No response, I see," Marmaduke said, acting as though he was not at all surprised. "Darkness has fled before the purging light of truth. That is what I seek in all of this life, the truth that only God Himself can give to any of us."

Surprisingly, he continued with the rest of the service, glancing occasionally at the Littlepage slaves.

"He may be hoping that they will just disappear," Alfred confided to Elizabeth, who was tempted to chuckle but restrained herself.

Alfred had made one concession to the times by asking his slaves to sit in a rear pew. Even Elizabeth voiced no objection over this, considering prudence a virtue they should not completely cast aside.

After Marmaduke finished his sermon, he was about to ask the congregation to sing a certain hymn. Alfred turned back and nodded at his slaves, and they were on their feet before anyone else could stand. Now everybody turned and stared at them, some with obvious relief because they assumed the six blacks were simply getting ready to leave.

Instead, the four men and two women started to sing, Violet first, her voice clearly stunning the church's members, and then the other slaves joining her.

"They *are* wonderful!" a woman declared in her husband's ear. "Listen to the passion that resonates in their voices. I never thought I would hear such singing this side of heaven."

It was not that they or any of the other members were ignorant of the musical ability of slaves but, rather, an admission that *these* six were quite extraordinary, going far beyond what could have been expected.

"I feel as though they have taken hold of my very soul," one man whispered to his wife, "taken hold and will not let go as long as they are singing like that."

The couple next to them overheard and essentially repeated the observation.

Marmaduke detected what was happening. Though not pleased, he had the good sense to wait until it seemed that the slaves were finished.

What demons are troubling that man? Alfred thought with surprising sympathy, studying the other's face and seeing, undisguised, the distaste that showed on it. *What awful visions pummel him, oozing out of every pore of his body with hatred for them, masquerading as a single angel of light but with a heart of the rankest darkness? Why does he show such distaste for the sublime beauty of these wonderful voices?*

All but one of the slaves sat down again. Only Violet was still standing.

Finally, at the end of whatever fragile bit of patience he possessed, Marmaduke jumped to his feet and started to bolt down the center aisle.

"That is quite enough!" he bellowed. "This house of God shall not be turned into a haven for common niggers! Get out of here, woman, you and the rest of—"

That was when Violet started to sing again.

The impact of her voice seemed like a physical blow to Marmaduke. He stopped about halfway down the aisle, saying nothing further as her singing filled the sanctuary with a voice laced with the pain of her people but somehow possessing an overriding joy as well.

"Praise His holy name," she sang, "sound the trumpets, open the gates of heaven above. The Lawd is near; the Lawd is dear, His arms outstretched in glory."

Violet sang with an urgency that Alfred had not noticed before. He could see perspiration on her forehead, her eyes half-closing as though she were mere seconds from a fainting spell.

He was halfway to his feet as he said, "Violet, are you—?

She turned to him, smiling, and then began to walk toward Marmaduke, who seemed unable to move, frozen where he stood.

Violet was just inches from the man when she abruptly stopped and looked up into his face as she narrowed her eyes. "I love you, sir, 'cause the Lawd Jesus loves you, and that's why He died on the cross, out of love, not hate," she said simply. Then, clutching the frilled collar of her new dress, she fell against him, her mouth opening and closing rapidly as she gasped for air.

Marmaduke found himself holding Violet, slumped across his arms. Looking around at the people who were staring at him, he seemed less like a towering figure ranting against Negroes than a confused child, caught in a situation that made him feel quite desperate.

Violet was only a moment from death as her gaze met his own.

"The Lawd's told me jus' now that He loves you, too," she muttered. "He's gonna wait for love to replace all that hate in your heart."

She smiled sweetly and died, her eyes yet open, glistening.

Marmaduke seemed numb, confused; then, noticing Alfred, he walked over to him and whispered, "Please take this poor soul's empty shell. Take her now, as Jesus has claimed her risen soul."

While handing over Violet's limp body, he added in a voice so low that Alfred had to strain to hear it, "Be careful now; be very gentle with her, my brother."

After glancing around him at the congregation he had shepherded for decades, John Covington Marmaduke extended his arm, gently closed ancient Violet's lids, then left the sanctuary, his shoulders slumped, his walk uncertain, tears flowing as never before in his life.

He left that community where he had been involved for so long, and it seemed that no one would ever hear from him . . .

⚜14⚜

DESPITE THEIR UNWILLINGNESS to admit the truth about their hypocrisies, Alfred's neighbors were beginning to let their resentment against him die.

One indication of this was that almost immediately after Violet's death there was an increase in invitations to dinners, various arts affairs and other festivals, and whatever else was being hosted at the time. Along with this went the absence of stares at Elizabeth or Alfred as they rode or walked past.

Bringing the Littlepage slaves to church that providential Sunday morning achieved more than Alfred could have hoped. And yet it always would seem so sad because of Violet's sudden death in front of the congregation. That any thawing in relationships between plantation patriarchs had not happened sooner was the underlying tragedy beneath what her death had succeeded in bringing about.

What the other aristocratic South Carolinian families realized after so many years of jealousy and antagonism directed squarely at the Littlepage clan was that, while most of them did profess to hold to basic conservative Christian beliefs, they were unquestionably inconsistent in their daily witness for Christ compared with Alfred and his loved ones—and the Littlepage slaves as well. Honest Carolinians admitted this between themselves in much needed candor, and once they did, the walls between the families began to crumble.

This alone succeeded in earning the Littlepages more and more respect, though it was but a step-by-step, gesture-by-gesture situation, a cesspool of old grievances disappearing slowly but disappearing just the same.

Even more than used to be the case with his father and his grandfather, Alfred had become determined to let his Christian testimony witness to a greater extent than all the pamphlets he could have printed and all the passionate speeches delivered on street corners and in front of country stores and in the midst of city parks and elsewhere.

Being Christian was synonymous with being southern in those days. And Alfred Littlepage, while proving the sincerity of his Christian witness, also attested to how genuinely southern he proudly would always be in attitude as well as ancestry.

He was perplexing to his many southern critics until, in many cases, they got to know him and became his friends, and then their antagonism changed to an unabashed admiration, even to putting him on some kind of pedestal as the ideal southerner who could be presented to the world as an example of what the region was all about.

Yankees frequently snickered to themselves when slave-owning Christians from the South dared to speak of such matters as spiritual values and biblical principles and related subjects, countering that their unwavering stand on slavery largely nullified the sort of Christianity that was being manifested by a majority of southerners.

Yet few of those below the Mason-Dixon Line would ever plead guilty to hypocrisy on this issue, since they were always quick to point out that they did not talk of anything that had to do with faith and redemption one moment and then go on to mistreat their slaves the very next.

Yes, it was true that some were harsh and abusive owners, the majority freely admitted. But it was truly rare that those abusers pretended also to be committed Christians. For the most part, the more devoutly Christian a typical Deep South plantation family happened to be, the more humanely its various members treated the slaves listed among the family's many possessions—while, in most instances, resolutely and expertly sidestepping that most central issue: whether Christians should be "owning" other human beings in the first place.

Reality for these folks was that, yes, they had slaves and, yes, these slaves were treated decently. And that was the end of it!

For their part, many of the more vocal Yankees were not necessarily as well-prepared to debate the opposite viewpoint. A principle, they would say, they were "merely" defending a principle, one that only recently had been gaining exposure on any widespread basis. On the other hand, southerners had had plenty of time to justify the way of life that had been theirs since soon after the first settlers entered that region so long ago, a way of life about which few, if any, of them felt guilty.

"If I didn't own them, somebody else would," one plantation patriarch replied in absolute seriousness when a visiting Yankee businessman brought up this matter. "I cannot speak for whoever that might be, sir, but as for me and my family, I can say, with all authority, that we shall continue as we have by considering them human beings created by the blessed heavenly Father. And we will deal with these slaves of ours accordingly."

"But, still, enslaved human beings, isn't that wrong, if I may be so bold, sir?" the brash, cigar-chomping, rotund Yankee in this instance pressed on with rankling condescension. "Are you not robbing these unfortunate people of an essential part of their very humanity, something the God of whom you speak would never have intended?"

"When I am fully convinced that you, too, are redemptively in intimate communication with our blessed Lord and that you speak with His voice and come here as His divinely appointed and anointed messenger," burst forth the emotional reply, "then I will seriously consider what it is you have to say."

The patriarch's voice deepened tellingly as he added, "But until then, you may be assured that such dismal spoutings as you have flung forth in my presence are regarded by all true southerners such as myself as hardly more acceptable than a large pile of fresh horse dung swarming with flies. We do not care to surround ourselves with either!"

Not surprisingly, that particular business trip would be cut short, and the meddling stranger from the North returned empty-handed, no cotton or corn or any other goods to show for his trouble.

~15~

"IT WAS SUPPOSED *to have been only a little walk, pleasant and relaxing, in large measure to get some fresh air after spending most of the day indoors, embarked upon sufficiently before dusk so that my father and I could manage to have a quiet, happy time together, and yet still be able to get back home early enough to avoid the possible dangers of the night,"* Charity told the members.

"What dangers?" someone asked.

"The ones that occasionally intruded on that region in the middle part of South Carolina, dangers that were not epidemic but still needed to be taken into consideration despite the genuine lawfulness of most of the people."

As Charity knew all too well, there existed an implicit acknowledgment of the truism that stated, *"Though I honor the laws of God and man, I cannot vouch for the next fellow and, especially, the one after him."*

That one memorable, awful night . . .

Elizabeth had remained back at the plantation house, supervising the evening meal's preparation.

A special night, that night.

Early in September in that year of our Lord 1848 . . .

THEY HAD JUST passed, on both sides of the country road, a densely wooded area with considerably tangled undergrowth competing with exposed tree roots for ground space. Above them was the frequent chatter of birds seeking refuge from predators.

Nearly a quarter of a mile in width, this section of land was situated between the boundaries of the Littlepage and Fulkerson plantations and extended far behind both properties, literally into the next county.

Alfred kept glancing with great wariness at this site, seemingly displaced from some gothic drama but as real as the setting sun, until it was well behind Charity and himself. As he studied the sinister darkness of the tangled briars and bushes, he succumbed to random, resurrected memories from his own childhood and the continuing myths or folk tales about that forested region, an admittedly rather eerie place. For decades there had been unsettling stories of strange goings-on amidst the lush undergrowth and tall, thick-leaved trees. The tales involved everything from gruesome goblins and fancy leprechauns to another creature similar to the legendary "New Jersey Devil" that supposedly had been roaming the pine barrens of that state for more than a century. The far greater probability was that the creatures were the operators of well-hidden moonshine stills put in place by poor blacks and whites alike, and the trembling occupants of underground tunnels where various fugitives had been able to avoid capture over the years, the woods becoming for them a kind of haven of safety or city of refuge.

Alfred had heard most of the often laughable tales; some were used more than anything else simply to scare impressionable little children into obedience. Yet the rest assumed a certain credibility by their proven durability.

It is as though some evil things really do dwell there undisturbed, ready to break out and pounce suddenly, he thought.

He felt foolish, of course, a grown-up Christian man succumbing to infantile skittishness about a place that children feared, perhaps, but should not bother any adult to the same extent, especially since fantasy and reality had become so completely intertwined that it was impossible to tell the boundary lines of either.

Dusk . . .

Alfred felt the first tell-tale cool breezes of that time of the day and looked up at the sky, which had not as yet begun to show the beginning of darkness. Instinctively, he sensed that the two of them should turn around soon, though Charity would be disappointed since she enjoyed looking at the quietly grazing cows that were on other plantations in that area and, in a typical happening, making friends with one or more of the sheep owned by a family next door to the cattle.

One of the bigger, fluffier sheep was conveniently pressed right up against the fence at the edge of the road, sitting down on what was left of the grass, its legs folded comfortably beneath it, making it look like an overgrown, cotton-topped white cat of some peculiar and uncommon breed.

Charity reached her left hand through the split-rail fence and soothingly stroked the animal's back.

It did not move or seem startled since she was so gentle, as she was with all animals; the sheep seemed to settle down even more as she stroked its curly wool.

Everything that has been created by Almighty God seems to trust that child of mine, Alfred remarked to himself. *I wonder how she is going to use or need that gift when she becomes a mature woman.*

"We have to return home now," Alfred finally told his daughter.

Charity went on rubbing the sheep for another few seconds and then stopped obediently, jumping to her feet.

"Okay," she said without protest, which was almost always the way she responded to whatever her parents asked of her.

They had been enjoying the cooling air after an especially humid afternoon that seemed nothing less than the final dying gasp of a suffocating summer.

Alfred, as it turned out, saw another reason to head back.

Just ahead was Samuel Fulkerson's plantation.

"Charity," Alfred said, "do you know why we have to leave?"

"Bad people at night?" she asked simply.

"Sometimes," he replied. "It is better not to take chances, dearest. Is it all right with you if we go now?"

Charity nodded, happy to abide by her father's wisdom.

As they were turning around to go, someone called out to them.

"Alfred!" the familiar, strong voice bellowed. "May I perhaps speak with you very briefly?"

Samuel Fulkerson.

Satan's emissary, Alfred thought with barely disguised contempt and without feeling the least bit uncharitable or judgmental, for the man's unrelenting and thoroughly abysmal record of atrocious behavior toward his pathetically scared slaves gave ample justification for that description. *This little encounter will be ended in no time!*

Fulkerson had just walked through the front gate at the western end of a long walkway up to his plantation house and was now in the middle of that dirt road, waving to the two of them.

"Come on here," he said, half-joking. "You needn't expect me to turn into some mean old cougar and devour the two of you."

Fulkerson waved again and pointed in the direction of his house.

"Please, do come," he repeated at a shout.

"All right, Samuel, we will be right there," Alfred yelled back wearily, not certain what tirade it was this time that he would be expected to endure while his daughter was forced to stand by and watch. "But make it quick. You have not earned an infinite amount of patience from very many decent people, certainly not me."

A bit nervously, he glanced back over his shoulders at the wooded area on both sides of that country road and at the coming darkness which was just beginning to spread across the sky.

"And the hour is getting late," Alfred shouted with even more volume.

Fulkerson was a genuinely robust man who lived and breathed with vigor.

That was part of the foundation for his success at intimidation over the years, the role of a bully an easy one for him to assume. While not more than five-feet-eight in height, he was exceptionally well muscled, with a full head of flowing, pearl-white hair that appeared quite striking when properly groomed. Tiny veins appeared in a network across the surface of both his cheeks, readily attesting to years of more than occasional drinking. He had a forceful manner and a deep voice that gave him a magnetism that belied his height, and he used these attributes to full advantage.

Samuel Fulkerson had been one of Alfred's most obnoxious detractors. Their previous confrontations had brought out his dictatorial instincts, but now, as they stood facing one another that night in early fall, there was something about his manner that seemed rather self-consciously vulnerable.

"Good evening," Alfred said as pleasantly as possible given the circumstances surrounding the man's conduct and having to grit his teeth in the process. He hoped he could hide any natural inclination toward cynicism as he saw the other man smile expansively, something unusual in itself, his more typical expression one that was closer to something that might be seen in a Gustave Doré woodcut about Satan.

How silly! Alfred exclaimed to himself. *I make him seem more evil and therefore more dangerous than I should. He is a man, a sinner like the rest of us, not some incarnation released from the very pit of hell!*

"Good evening to you, neighbor," Fulkerson replied with equal apparent cheerfulness as he also nodded at Charity then winked at her, causing her to blush, for he was obviously appreciating how much of a young woman she had become.

"What can I do for you, Samuel?"

"I think you have done it already."

Alfred had no idea what Fulkerson was talking about.

What absurd ploy is this? he thought. *And for what purpose? Perhaps the man has finally gone over the deep end.*

"I must say, Samuel, in all candor, that you really are not making any sense," Alfred remarked, hardly surprised.

"All these years . . . ," Fulkerson said, his voice cracking.

His eyes were half-closed, and he seemed weak.

"Are you feeling ill?" Alfred asked, concerned to a degree that was surprising since on other occasions he would have wished the man anything but good health. "How can I help, Samuel?"

Fulkerson shook his head slowly as he leaned against the recently painted white-rail fence stretching around the edge of that part of his extensive land holdings—more extensive, in fact, than the land that had been owned by the Littlepages for generations. The main plantation house set back from the property line nearly half a mile and was partially obscured from view by a large number of trees.

The fruits of treating your slaves so severely, Alfred thought cynically. *You could cut back just a little in this lavish lifestyle of yours and make life a whole lot easier for those poor folk under your control.*

"No, I am not ill," Fulkerson began muttering. "I was just recalling that a great deal has gone on between us."

"That is so, Samuel," Alfred agreed without emotion. "But I wonder if you realize that I had no choice those times we have tangled. What choice might there have been? I could not sacrifice my principles or anything else that I hold dear just to achieve some kind of peace with you."

Steeling himself, he expected the other man to react angrily, but that was not the case this time.

"Would you come with me?" Fulkerson asked as though not paying attention to what Alfred had just said. "There's something I want to talk to you about."

"But what about Charity?" Alfred asked, nodding down at her. "You have never had children, although she can no longer be thought of as a child. It is not a responsibility you can understand. You treat your slaves like animals, so none of them can substitute as children."

Fulkerson winced at that but kept calm.

"She will not be upset by what I am going to tell you, Alfred," he said, his voice oddly calm. "It might be said that your daughter Charity is going to be as pleased as her angry father will be."

His manner had not proven to be forbidding in any way but, still, Alfred hesitated, out of habit perhaps, knowing how much of a transformation this represented from the past few years.

Samuel Fulkerson glanced over at Charity, who was standing just a foot or two to her father's right.

He reached out and touched her thin shoulder with obvious tenderness, displaying a degree of affection that surprised Alfred, considering what had been the man's previous behavior.

"At my worst, I would never endanger that dear, dear child," Fulkerson remarked plaintively. "You must never think me anywhere near that kind of monster, though you undoubtedly continue to think me a villain."

Alfred was becoming more and more impatient and finally could not hold his peace any longer.

"It is late now," he said, his feelings transparent. "Charity does need to be returning home, to get her sleep tonight."

He turned to go when Fulkerson spoke again, "You should know that what I want to say has to do with my darkies."

Alfred flashed a look of disdain at him.

"There isn't much to discuss," he said. "You cannot stand there and tell me that you have no idea how I feel."

Recollections of those encounters when the two of them had gotten in verbal sparring matches remained fresh for Alfred.

"We have collided many times over the years, Samuel," he pointed out. "You seem patently unable to tell me what could be so compellingly different now. I cannot remember one whit of change on your part for all the time that our paths have been crossing. The last time we tangled, you were as objectionable as ever."

Fulkerson chuckled knowingly, letting the insults pass as though they had never been spoken.

"You may be right. And, yes, I am aware of probably every precept involved in those staunch convictions of yours, my dear Alfred. Realize I speak now the absolute truth, neighbor: What you believe so fervently is precisely why you should understand, more than many other men around here, what has happened to me and my reason for calling you over here this evening."

As he said that, Fulkerson was beginning to show some impatience of his own.

"Alfred, Alfred, you can surely perceive how awkward it is for me," he went on, "yes, me, of all people, to approach you as I am doing this evening. Is it not out of character? Can you at least admit the truth of this?"

That remark struck a little closer to home for Alfred.

"But please realize that I have an honorable and decent purpose for doing so," Fulkerson told him, almost a pleading tone to his voice.

. . . an honorable and decent purpose for doing so.

Alfred frowned at that thought, hardly convinced by words alone coming from someone who was no stranger to spouting the most inhumane comments imaginable without regard for their impact.

And yet Alfred was somehow hooked by a curious edge to Fulkerson's manner that he had started to detect.

Honorable and decent behavior has seemed as far from you as the moon is right now, he thought sarcastically, *and yet there is something else, something that stops me just short of throwing up my hands, snarling at you with some well-chosen invective, and walking away with my sweet daughter.*

Alfred lingered while Charity started to shift her feet restlessly, anxious either to return home or to see what all this commotion was about.

"I must ask that you let this be enough to satisfy you for the moment," the other man spoke again. "Give this Lord of yours some credit for a miracle even with a rascal such as myself."

Alfred had not seen Fulkerson conduct himself like this before, betraying a curious mixture of attitudes.

Something is going on with this man, he told himself. *I have seen Samuel Fulkerson hypocritically attend church, yes, and sing any number of hymns wholeheartedly, listen intently to various sermons, then pray fervently, but never have I heard him use the Lord's name in such a manner.*

Alfred decided he would take whatever minimal risk there was and agreed to stay for a short while.

"Come inside," Fulkerson asked, waving his arm toward the plantation house behind him. "It is getting chilly."

Alfred was uncomfortable about the hour and about Samuel Fulkerson, and hardly forgetting the dangers of the forest area nearby.

Oh, Lord, get us out of this, he prayed silently. *Extricate my daughter and me from the spell of this awful man!*

"Is this all right, Charity?" her father asked, his tone nearly a whisper, genuinely wanting not to displease the child by going against her wishes but hoping she would simply shake her head so that he could use this as a ready excuse for returning home at last. "Are you up to staying out just a bit longer? Or should we stop this right now and hurry back to some of Savilla's good cooking? We shouldn't be walking that road when there is only the moon's glow to light our way."

The little girl smiled broadly, her eyes widening, tempted by the image of the meal that awaited them, since Savilla, in her zestful opinion, was quite possibly the greatest cook that the good Lord had ever put in the world.

Yet though she was young and not able to fully comprehend everything that was going on, there seemed to Charity something fascinating about this Samuel Fulkerson, a coarse, cruel man, according to what she had overheard through the past couple of years, and she wanted to find out what it was, even if this meant delaying supper.

"Okay," she told him, fascinated by whatever the next few minutes might hold in store. "I'm not tired yet, Daddy. Jesus will protect us after we leave."

But what about now? Alfred thought. *We may need that protection inside this house as much as outside.*

Alfred smiled at the beautiful girl, who seemed so perfect that he knew he surely would die if he ever lost her.

When you climb up on my lap and rest your head against my chest, he recalled, *and I feel your warmth, oh, Charity, Charity, how I do praise God for the blessing that you are, child.*

"You love Charity so much," Fulkerson said, observing this little moment between the two of them.

"I surely do, Samuel."

And that love drives me to think about her safety right now more than anything else, he thought, *particularly chatting with the likes of you!*

Alfred imagined an hour-glass with the sand rapidly running out, that instrument representing any hope they had of getting back home before there was total darkness.

"Samuel, we really should be concerned about the hour," he suggested nervously, looking at his daughter.

"I agree," Fulkerson responded. "But remember that there are solutions even to problems such as what the night holds."

He was not being sarcastic, nor did Alfred take him as such, but Alfred still grew increasingly apprehensive.

"Yes, but we have no carriage with us just now, Samuel. We must go back home by foot and that is—"

Fulkerson shook his hand. "Stop it!" he fairly shouted. "Look at that child who holds onto your hand so lovingly. You may love dear Charity even more—I can just about guarantee that, Alfred—when you realize that she is the sweet angel very much behind what I feel compelled to share with you in a few minutes."

Alfred's irritation was rapidly growing as he became convinced that Fulkerson was up to nothing but constructing a quite elaborate charade of some sort with only the purpose of trying to make a fool of him so he could brag about this to others, a goal he undoubtedly coveted, this despite the polite, kind, conciliatory words he had been spouting endlessly, which were now seeming as insubstantial as the early evening mist that had begun to appear.

You are a splendid actor, he thought. *It is a shame that you are not part of some traveling theatrical troupe.*

Alfred regretted any polite concession to attentiveness he had chosen to accord someone who deserved nothing of the kind, nothing, in fact, but permanent isolation from the company of decent men everywhere.

"You continue to go on and on in the most absurd of riddles," he replied. "I shouldn't be wasting my time and my daughter's in this manner, as you have asked us to do. We will leave you now, Samuel. And I trust that you and I will bump into one another as infrequently as possible."

Alfred reached out to take Charity's soft, slender hand and started to turn back down the road toward home, fully intending to call an end to what seemed merely the mindless palaver of a despised neighbor, a man with whom he usually would try to avoid all contact.

I will tell Elizabeth all about what has happened, he thought, *and then I shall dismiss all this from my mind.*

"Be calm, dear man, please!" Fulkerson urged, perhaps a bit more franti-cally than he would have preferred, but then he was hardly accustomed to betraying such feelings as openly as he was doing, let alone in front of someone such as Alfred Littlepage, and it was not surprising that he had overreached himself. "It will all be clear in just a few minutes; I can promise you that."

As he frowned, all the wrinkles on his face were exaggerated, making him seem a good deal older than his nearly fifty actual years.

"You ask for calm, but you know the stories about the woods as much as I do," Alfred protested. "How can you be so callous?"

Fulkerson spat on the ground, his contempt unmasked.

"Stories reeking of pure fable!" he retorted, his own temper rising. "Where is your faith in that protective Savior about whom you have never been loathe to speak in my presence or anyone else's, for that matter?"

Fighting hard to control himself, Fulkerson reached out and not too gently grabbed Alfred's shoulder.

"I petition only for a little time," he added, abruptly lowering his voice, "and a greater amount of your patience."

He gave an exaggerated sigh.

"Try not to insult either of us tonight by hiding under the flimsy excuse of a bunch of musty, antiquated rumors about a patch of woods," he said. "That is hardly worthy of an intelligent and forthright man such as yourself. I had thought you would be the sort to venture into those woods and slay all the dragons hiding there!"

Alfred bristled at the notion that he was a coward or a hypocrite or both, his blood pressure shooting up.

"It is not what you say, not at all!" Alfred responded. "Why is it that you scoff at being prudent? Is this not far better than throwing all those tales to the wind and then regretting it? What if there is somehow a measure of truth, a tiny fragment of it perhaps in at least one of them?"

Samuel Fulkerson smiled.

"I have slaves, Alfred," he declared, some sarcasm coloring his voice. "I have carriages. And I have more than ample ammunition to deal with any army of robbers that could assault us. That kind cannot prevail this night.

"What I find more alarming is your reluctance to listen, my good man. Is it possible that you are but one of those Christians who feel that once a man's character has been set during the early years of his earthly life, even God Himself is simply powerless to work any miracle of transformation?"

He paused, letting a few seconds pass.

"Will you not allow me this one concession?" Fulkerson asked, cupping his hands together as he spoke. "Please forget the lateness of the hour. That can be dealt with so that no one is harmed because of it. Or is it, Alfred, that—"

Fulkerson cut himself off momentarily and just stared, first at Charity and then, for just shy of a minute, at her father, undoubtedly trying to make him feel awkward or embarrassed.

If that is your goal, Alfred admitted, *I hope I never have to confess out loud that you are succeeding very well.*

And then Samuel Fulkerson went on to tell him, "Or is it simply that the two of us, grown men that we are supposed to be but terribly, terribly head-strong, both of us, with more than a touch of arrogance in our blood, is it that we have become entrenched in our personal battle positions for so long now that, in reality, any kind of quiet talk, man to man, seems sadly beyond our furthest reach? We view one another strictly as foes to be vanquished. But I wonder how much of that is unnecessary now."

. . . Be calm, dear man!

Alfred repeated those four words to himself, still unable to believe that they and others of the past few minutes had come from the man standing before him, looking up into his face, a man who seemed so eager to tell him about whatever mysterious circumstance it was that had presumably barged unannounced into his well-fortified life and which somehow held beloved little Charity at its very center.

What in the world is going on inside Samuel Fulkerson's head? Alfred wondered but found no obvious response. By now he was far too weary of questions to worry about any more answers that he might perhaps gain.

Fulkerson swung open the large metal gate, its creaking hinges needing attention, and stepped aside.

"Please," he said, betraying a vulnerable expression, "go right in. If it turns out that you aren't interested after about fifteen minutes, you can get up and leave without saying so much as a polite good-bye."

Lord, I suppose since You parted the Red Sea for Your servant Moses, Alfred decided, *You can open a path through the differences between Samuel and me. If that is Your will, praise You, Lord; praise You for doing this!*

Shrugging his shoulders, he winked at little Charity, who did the same in return, and they both reluctantly followed Samuel Fulkerson down the long pathway, bordered on both sides by tall, thick hedges with ruby-red blossoms that had not yet given in to the early fall that year. Finally they all entered a massive plantation house that had been maintained by the sweat and the blood of far too many hapless black people over the years.

⊱16⊱

ANY VISITOR COULD see that the exterior of Samuel Fulkerson's home was anything but customary, with eight grand columns supporting the roof over a porch that ran the entire width of the house, a total of nearly a hundred feet. The front door was enough to leave the average newcomer speechless, fashioned of solid oak and lacquered to a dark, almost-mahogany color, every inch of it taken up with a hand-carved and very imaginative montage of clusters of coconuts, papayas, bananas, and other fruits. Something similar could be seen on the hulls of certain boats of that era, the more elaborate ones owned by wealthy shipping magnates who were headquartered in Europe but conducted business in the United States.

"The closest I shall ever get to the Sandwich Islands," Fulkerson wistfully told Charity and Alfred as they stood and looked at it. Alfred's mouth was hanging open in amazement as much as his daughter's was, but there was no way he would admit this to someone like Fulkerson.

The entrance hall was uncluttered and painted a basic white, with a high arched ceiling and a single hanging Napoleonic lantern hanging from it.

Directly ahead, in the large living room, the remains of animal kills by Samuel Fulkerson hung from two walls—deer, buffalo, antelope, cougar, a hawk, a grizzly—dead creatures whose heads put up for display bothered Alfred immensely.

Fulkerson saw that his attention was shifting from one preserved head to another, then back again.

"A hobby of mine," he explained, with no apparent pride in his deep voice. "I go out west every so often and bag as much game as I can. I am a very good shot, you know. I can kill any animal the first time I pull the trigger."

"But then you are killing only for pleasure," Alfred pointed out, "since you surely do not need the meat to keep you from starving. Does that ever bother you, that you are bringing down these magnificent creatures just so their heads can be hung as trophies on your wall?"

"It never has. If I stopped it for the rest of my life, there would be other hunters to take my place."

Alfred noticed that Fulkerson did not speak with much conviction, detecting the slightest hint of uncertainty. "You speak with no bravado," he said. "I wonder if you are feeling some stabs of conscience about this."

Fulkerson's left cheek started twitching.

"Not only about this," he spat out the words.

Fulkerson was leaning against an impressive floor-to-ceiling fireplace that he had had built years before using flat blocks of fieldstone taken from a large nearby quarry that had been opened during the previous century. Just below the five-foot-long mantle was a carefully sculpted single slab of marble portraying a scene with hounds bounding after a fox followed by their masters on horseback.

Trying to be civil, Alfred commented on how much he admired the design of the fireplace.

"Few residences show the kind of attention to detail that I see in this house," he acknowledged. "Those beautiful brownstone steps, that hand-carved, well-polished oak door . . . We have used only cypress or perhaps heart oak in our home; it seems quite plain in comparison. You have decorated yours as well, and with some real flair. My congratulations, Samuel."

"There was a problem at the beginning," Fulkerson replied as he stood before the fireplace, running his fingers over the long piece of marble. "Getting the right air flow—yes, sir, that was the killer! This room filled with black smoke more than I care to admit. But once that was okay, well, I have enjoyed it very well, especially on those freezing nights we have in January and February each year."

"Other personal touches abound, from what little I have glimpsed tonight. Can I assume these details were your ideas as well, Samuel?"

Fulkerson nodded, though quite gravely, with no real life; there was no energy in that simple movement, making him seem like a worn-out marionette whose strings were being pulled in a listless way by an aging puppeteer.

"Since I have no one telling me what to do, no wife hovering around," he said, "no horde of children making demands on my attention, I have been able to get done what I wanted all these years."

Alfred had never made it a point to find out very much about the man, but he realized then that he had not seen Fulkerson in the company of women; his companions, which were few, were always men.

"Why have you not married?" he asked, now curious about the reason behind this but aware that it was none of his business and prepared for a rebuff. "You must have some very lonely moments."

Fulkerson seemed almost to ignore that comment for a few seconds, closing his eyes and tilting his head to one side.

"I have proposed three times, Alfred, and they all, with the ugliest coincidence, have left me, each of them dying tragically," he replied finally. "After a while I simply gave up and built another kind of existence around myself, one that you likely have been calling most cruel. I suppose I have done this because I could not control the lives of those I loved, so I would control others instead."

"But why, Samuel?" Alfred demanded. "Why the awful decision to inflict your pain upon others, men and women who cannot fight back because of the greater fear of losing their lives in retribution?"

Fulkerson wiped his eyes with the back of his right hand.

"To see your daughter, to think of what it would be like to father a beautiful little girl as you have done so successfully . . ."

Charity and her father were sitting on plain wooden chairs, each with a leather pad stuffed with goose down.

Suddenly, Fulkerson turned in their direction.

"I could not sleep well after seeing that colored woman die," he admitted just as abruptly.

"That shouldn't be a strange sight for you, Samuel," countered Alfred. "Your work habits imposed on those people have driven more than one to an early grave. What was so special to you about Violet's passing?"

"The expression on her face," Fulkerson replied. "She seemed to be holding no hatred, only love; I mean, how could anyone love the Reverend Marmaduke? But that old woman certainly looked as though she did. I could detect no phoniness, no attempt to ingratiate herself. She was what she was."

"And what she was . . ." Alfred started to respond, but talking about Violet brought out emotions he tried to keep buried, not wanting to risk that the sorrowing process might start all over again.

He bowed his head briefly.

"I can imagine well enough," Fulkerson spoke. "I can understand why it is difficult for you to talk about her."

Alfred looked up at him.

"I would not have thought that you could even begin to do so, Samuel," he said. "You hated her kind. You periodically work colored women like that dear soul into the ground, and then you refuse even to mark their graves. You would have exploited Violet to death if she had been your slave."

Fulkerson strode forward, facing Alfred without blinking.

"It seems that you are not adverse to indulging more hatred against me than that poor old woman did," he pointed out sternly. "Can you call yourself a Christian now with such feelings as you have?"

Alfred's face flushed angrily.

"Violet probably did not know who you are, Samuel!" he protested. "If that dear soul had, I suspect that her attitude would have been quite different. How could she have felt otherwise, considering your treatment of her kind?"

Fulkerson laughed as he replied, "Is that what you say?"

He slapped the palms of his hands against his thighs.

"So now, it seems—correct me if I am wrong, Alfred—that you believe you have kept those slaves of yours isolated from everything! And you undoubtedly congratulate yourself for having made them little more than hot-house plants.

"But why do you do this, I ask? Is it out of kindness alone? Or are you afraid that someone will enter your narrowly defined little world and perhaps fill their primitive minds with the worst abolitionist heresies? At least my behavior is honest. I despise their black skins. All I can see when I look at them are some naked creatures swinging from trees in Africa like stupid gorillas."

Alfred kept his silence, as difficult as this was to do.

"Surely that old woman had heard of me," Fulkerson went on. "How could she not? Surely she knew the kind of man I was. I have to believe that some of the others must have spoken to her about the so-called cruel and disgusting Samuel Fulkerson and how fortunate she was not to be under my barbaric rule!"

Alfred pretty much knew where his slaves were at all times, but he acknowledged the possibility that some contact could have occurred during one of the hunting trips he allowed for sport and extra food purposes.

"She may have heard a few stories, I suppose," he conceded, "but those were secondhand at best. I am in a much better position to comprehend what kind of man you are, Samuel, simply because I know you. I need not depend upon a mere handful of unreliable rumors that have been bruited about."

Alfred paused, adrenaline flowing rapidly as he tried to get his thoughts together, not wanting the other man to best him in any kind of unofficial debate such as the one in which they seemed to be engaging.

"There is no doubt in my mind that Violet was convinced as a Christian that she—" he started to add.

"—should do what you could not," Fulkerson finished the sentence for him, obviously assuming that he had anticipated the rest of what Alfred was going to say. "Were you about to offer that as a choice bit of insight, neighbor?"

Fulkerson cleared his throat then continued, "Think carefully about this: Are you suggesting that some common, off-the-boat nigger, the smell of darkest Africa still clinging to her, somehow went on to achieve a higher level of spirituality than either of us adult white folk tonight?"

Alfred hesitated. Fulkerson saw this and did not allow the other man to catch his breath and offer a convenient retort.

"Why are you not coming back at me right away, neighbor?" he demanded, though not in anything like a shout and without any vicious edge. "Look at what I have given you, the rope to hang the hated Samuel Fulkerson, rhetorically speaking."

He smiled crookedly.

"With all this talk about treating your slaves properly, yea, about the Christian requirement to treat all slaves like human beings, you still cannot bring yourself to think of Violet or any other slave owned by you as your equal and certainly not your superior in any area of life, let alone personal spiritual testimony."

Filling with rage at what Fulkerson had said, Alfred was preparing to jump to his feet and tangle with the man when Charity quickly slid off her chair and dashed between the two of them.

"Violet loved everybody!" she exclaimed, folding her arms defiantly in front of her and looking first at one man then the other. "She didn't care who they were. She . . . she saw what they could be . . . because of Jesus!"

Both men were transfixed by the girl's words.

Alfred's manner softened instantly.

"I was not heading where you obviously thought I was with what I just said," Fulkerson told him a bit smugly. "What you do not know, what you could not know, what I have not had a chance to tell you is that I feel Violet was . . . was . . ."

The words seemed to be caught in his throat. He turned away, struggling to control his own vocal chords.

"She was superior to both of us in at least one way, and not just to you, Alfred," Fulkerson finally said, "because of her willingness to accept God's love into her life and send it forth even to a wretch such as Marmaduke."

. . . a wretch such as Marmaduke.

Alfred started to say something about the kettle calling the pot black, but Fulkerson raised his hand and quickly interjected, "Keep that impetuous spirit to yourself for once! You see, I add myself to that list of scoundrels such as the dear Reverend Marmaduke, his poison filling your mind and mine Sunday after Sunday. If I had gotten to know Violet, I suspect that she would have poured out her love over even me."

He brought his hands to his face and started sobbing.

"Even me!" he repeated.

Samuel Fulkerson dropped to the floor, and Charity knelt beside his trembling body, while her father grappled with a sudden, suffocating onrush of shame unlike any he had ever known before then.

ᵔ17ᵔ

I T WAS GETTING very late now, time having passed without the hour being paid attention to by anyone.

The sounds of several animals howling in the darkness could be heard inside the plantation house. A stiff breeze had started to kick up, rattling shutters pulled across the many windows on both floors.

Noticing Alfred's anxious looks toward Charity but not wanting to end their conversation, Samuel Fulkerson offered to have one of the most dependable of his long-time slaves take Charity back home in his carriage with a second slave, armed just in case, to sit beside the girl.

"Bring Rufus and Johnny," he ordered his housekeeper. "Tell those two I need them right away."

The heavyset black woman smiled.

"You is doing the right thing, Massa," she declared happily, "protecting that dear, dear child."

"Thank you," he told her. "Now see to it."

She nodded and scurried out of the room.

"Alfred, do your slaves still call you massa?" Fulkerson inquired a short while after she was gone.

"Yes, they all do," Alfred replied. "Believe me, I tried to stop that sort of thing more often than I can remember, but I am just not able to get past their conditioning. I sometimes think that the word and the control it has over their lives seems to have been born into those people. It has become an actual *need,* and they are not even aware of this. I am their massa in their eyes, and there is nothing more to be said."

"What need is that?" Fulkerson asked, seemingly fascinated. "You are saying something quite intriguing."

"I suppose I could describe it as the need to be subservient to their owners. Consider how dogs or horses respond after just a relatively short period of training. What they learned in the short term becomes their life-long conduct. They know nothing else. It seems well-nigh instinctive from that point on."

With the love that he had for his slaves, Alfred felt ill at ease advancing such an argument, but he did see kernels of truth in it.

"Dogs are taken from their mothers without having any control over what happens and thrown into a strange environment," he said. "They depend upon others for everything whereas, left to themselves in a wild, natural environment, they would tend to become more self-sufficient—either that or die."

Alfred's personal distress at linking insights about common house dogs with those about human beings could not be kept hidden; beads of perspiration trickled down his forehead and his cheeks.

"Imagine what it must be like for people who have been treated like dogs or worse for many, many decades," he suggested, "taken from truly naked freedom in their native Africa and abruptly deprived of everything they once had taken for granted."

He seemed about ready to leave the matter there without elaboration, but Fulkerson wanted to hear more.

"Go on," he urged Alfred.

"I know of a true story wherein the master of a particular plantation wanted to test the loyalty and devotion of his slaves, so he asked one to cut off a finger of another. The order was obeyed instantly. The injured one stood before the master and asked simply, 'Do you want me to cut off another one myself?'"

Fulkerson was presumably pleased by Alfred's response.

"I have thought about that, too," he spoke. "What if that really is all that Almighty God has ever intended for all the black folk in this land of ours, and ironically in that case, it would be the thoroughly blind abolitionists who are the ones acting in wanton disregard to His divine will? I mean, when they rant and rave as they do, do they think that the louder they become the more they will be able to get a greater number of people to listen, to support repeal of the slave laws that provide for ownership?"

Fulkerson's quavering voice was betraying the man's deeply rooted irritation over the whole issue, showing that he was someone who was convinced that he had seen truth and was frustrated that others seemed blind to it.

"The Bible talks about Christians being slaves to the Lord Jesus. Was that just some sort of cultural admonition, or was it supposed to remain in effect for all succeeding generations until the end of time?"

"I have not thought about that, Samuel. I just know that I love them and treat them with respect."

"Always with respect, Alfred?"

"For as long as I can remember."

"You never asserted your superiority?"

"Not with arrogance, I trust."

Just then, Fulkerson's housekeeper came back with the two slaves. Both were young and strong looking.

"Boy, you ever shoot a gun?" Alfred asked of the one named Rufus, trying to be as intimidating as he could manage.

"Yes sir, I done shot a rifle lots of times. Brought down many a buck deer. None ever got away that I can remember."

Alfred turned to Fulkerson.

"How accurate is that, Samuel?" he inquired, depending upon the other's judgment in a way he could not have predicted a short while before.

Fulkerson obviously seemed confident.

"Very!" he replied enthusiastically. "You need not worry, Alfred. Rufus here can hit anything that moves and do so more often than I have seen before in my entire life. I have to tell you that his skill makes you and me look half-blind on our best days; that is how good this boy is, believe me."

He walked over to Rufus, who flinched noticeably as he approached, apparently remembering what it was once like to live under the rule of this master. The slave's muscular body bore the scars of whip lashes that would never disappear.

Noticing this, Fulkerson reached out and rested his left hand gently on the other's shoulder.

"Rufus, Rufus . . . ," he repeated, nearly whispering, a softness to his voice that Alfred had not detected before that night.

Their faces were but inches apart.

"You must learn not to flinch anymore as I come near," Fulkerson stressed as though it were a matter of life and death. "As time passes, you will see that I am not the pitiable wretch of a man who used to treat you so hellishly. Yes, you are my slave, I own you, but I am not your tormentor any longer. Can you grasp that, Rufus?"

The black man smiled and relaxed a bit, nodding. Johnny, standing behind him, shuffled his feet nervously.

"I would stake my own life on their ability to do what they say," Fulkerson now told Alfred. "Charity will be safe in their care."

Alfred still needed to be convinced of a remaining point and continued addressing Rufus directly.

"Ever wounded or killed a man?" he asked sternly, though trying not to sound like some dreaded interrogator from the slave's cruel past while also convinced that the right precautions could play a huge part in his daughter's safety on the way home. It was a short distance that was not at all significant during the day, but nighttime transformed it into another story altogether, with wooded areas along the road on both sides, precisely the ideal sort of hiding places that robbers and other criminals would be seeking.

"No sir."

"How do you know you can do it?"

He could tell that the black man resented the question and quickly added, "I am sorry, but I have to ask that. My daughter's safety is all-important to me. Downing a buck deer is child's play compared to aiming at another human being and wounding or killing him. As her father, I would not hesitate. But what about you, Rufus?"

Rufus looked at Fulkerson, who nodded approval.

"If someone tries to harm Miss Charity, I's ready to kill 'em with ma bare hands if I have to," he declared without hesitation. "Johnny here feels the same way, sir."

The expression on his face left no doubt that he was not saying simply what Alfred wanted to hear but instead speaking very much from the center of his soul.

"Miss Charity is special," Rufus added earnestly. "Nobody's gonna dare to touch a hair on that sweet head whiles we is around!"

Before that night, Alfred would not have believed that those slaves could ever have felt as they did; indeed, he would have greeted their comments with the greatest suspicion, what with the history of mistreatment that had been heaped upon them, but after what Fulkerson related to him, he could not anticipate any questions.

In so short a period of time, Alfred thought, *in barely an instant, it seems, the Lord can change any man's soul.*

"Both are fine, Samuel," he agreed graciously. "If you have such strong confidence as that in Rufus here and Johnny just behind him, so shall I also, especially now that I see what fine, fine boys they are."

Can this be happening? Alfred asked himself. *Lord, what are You bringing into being here this night?*

Charity kissed him before leaving then walked gracefully over to Fulkerson and planted another kiss on his cheek.

When they were alone, Alfred admitted, "I had no idea you felt this way, Samuel. What you have told me is remarkable."

Gone was the savage antagonism, whatever the valid reasons that once existed for it, gone in the wake of revelations so astonishing that his earlier attitude toward Samuel Fulkerson could never have survived.

"I once heard that the Lord works in strange and mysterious ways," Fulkerson replied, sighing, as he glanced at his guest out of the corner of his eye. "Well, praise God, He has proven the truth of that to me beyond any doubt."

That such words were coming from Samuel Fulkerson made what had happened all the more striking.

Will I ever be able to forget what he had been doing to his slaves before change overtook him, Alfred asked himself, *the lives he wrecked, the families he tore apart, the deaths that he caused? Lord, Lord, let this not be a false alarm, some well-intentioned new beginning but one that fails, like seed that falls on stony ground.*

"And to me as well," he agreed after a few seconds. "You can count on having a new friend now and for the rest of our lives."

Fulkerson closed his eyes for a moment.

"Is there any doubt that God has brought this about?" he asked. "You and me sitting here, talking like this?"

Neither thought the situation would have turned out at all as it did through any other course except that of divine intervention. The details giving texture to Fulkerson's story were so unexpected, so startling in themselves, that nothing short of the miraculous could account for any of it, let alone all.

Both men pulled their chairs across the bare wood floor to face a quite large crackling fire, the odor of burning wood pleasant. Alfred Monroe Littlepage savored the details once again while Samuel Fulkerson was lost in them as well.

～18～

I T BEGAN ON *a day and in a way that seemed quite routine," Charity continued, "without any hint of what would soon occur with wrenching force within the soul of Samuel Fulkerson . . ."*

Little Isaiah often was sent into Columbia on errands for the Littlepages, usually to pick up orders of new linens, clothes, and such items, and to replenish stocks of food, including confections for Charity. He generally took with him one of the other slaves. This time it was Hester, as strong a buck as Little Isaiah had ever seen.

As soon as the carriage pulled away from the stable area, the two of them got to talking about how Alfred Littlepage had found Hester at a small slave market near Macon, Georgia. The market was noted for its better quality stock and its somewhat more humane treatment of black people.

Hester was a fortunate member of a very small group of blacks, those who did not have to spend much time in the market environment but were snapped up immediately.

"It's been good here," he admitted. "I was just twelve years old when the massa found me. I'd never been mistreated, you know, praise the good Lord for that. My mama and my papa worked for an old lady down Savannah way. They was like a family. She was all alone and allowed us to sleep in the plantation house."

It was a familiar story, told in idle moments like that, but Little Isaiah enjoyed hearing it again since there was little else to talk about on the way into the city, which was one aspect of slave life that even Alfred had never confronted: Theirs was a way of life that was so predictable, so confined to the same set of circumstances day after day, year after year that slaves fell into the sort of routine that made boredom a persistent problem.

Alfred had made many trips to the other southern states and on over to Europe as well as out west so he had plenty of variety in his life. Any restrictions faced by Elizabeth and Charity in his absence were self-imposed, for they simply enjoyed their estate.

The Littlepages also enjoyed going to county fairs and other events that took the family away for a day or two but never longer than that. Of course, they had parties at the plantation house and other activities to vary the makeup of each season.

Not so their slaves. They ate, they slept, they did their chores, they hunted, they warmed themselves by the stove, sang together at night, and shared more such activities, but still, that was it. They had become familiar with every detail of every corner of the estate, but that was all they knew, except for brief trips into the city as Little Isaiah and Hester were on that particular day.

While most of the Littlepage slaves had been born on southern soil and had no memories of the past in Africa, Hester was an exception. As a child Hester had listened to his mother and father telling him about hunting gazelle and other animals for food, and about the tribal wars that flared up every few years, making peace between the tribes transitory at best.

Hester had slipped into silence as he thought about the old woman, his former owner. Now he spoke again. "When she died, her kin got hold of the property and divided it up, and my folks and I were split apart. Somebody bought them the same week the old woman died. I never saw them again. The old lady's kinfolk sent me to the Macon market."

Though the slave auction to which Hester was sent was better than most, cleaner by a considerable degree and feeding the slaves adequate food while the poor black men and women awaited sale to another owner, it was still a terrifying and depressing place for Hester to endure, especially so soon after that separation from his loved ones. Men were sent to one location, women to another, and children to a third spot altogether.

Near twilight a few days after he had been taken to the Littlepage plantation by his new master, Hester was steadily working alone, planting a plot with new flower seeds that Elizabeth had just purchased in Columbia. He was startled when Alfred quietly approached him and asked for some information about his parents.

"You are so young," he said. "I have never inquired about your parents. What happened to them?"

Hester told him all the details.

"Just a few weeks ago then?" Alfred asked.

"Yessir, that's all the time it's been."

"What would you think about me trying to find out something about them—where they are, that sort of thing?"

"You sure don't have to, Massa," Hester replied, trying to conceal the anticipation he was feeling then.

"I know that, but I have never liked the practice of splitting up families. It is cruel and very antiChristian."

"It surely would be fine if I knew somethin' 'bout them, maybe send 'em a letter or two sometime."

"You can write?" Alfred asked, surprised, since he was well aware of how rare it was for young slave children to be able to read or write.

"The old lady who owned us taught Mama, Papa, and me."

"Why not write a letter tonight? I will take it with me into the city tomorrow morning, right after breakfast, and check around a bit. Finding out who bought your folks shouldn't be difficult, I expect. Your papers tell me a little bit, and I know some well-placed politicians. They can return a favor or two at long last."

"Would you tell 'em I love 'em if you find out where they are?" Hester asked.

"Say that in your letter. It would mean more if you did it, Hester." He paused, rubbing his chin, then added, "Forget the letter."

"Yes sir," Hester replied quickly, though his disappointment showed in his eyes.

"If I find them, I will buy them and bring them here," Alfred went on to tell him matter of factly, with no intention of any grand, empty gesture.

Hester did not comprehend at all what had just been said; he looked completely blank.

"I mean, if you really want to be back with them," Alfred continued, then said more sternly, "Hester? Are you hearing me now, boy?"

The slave shook his head.

"Sorry, Massa. I miss them so much, and I guess I was daydreamin' a little. I even thought I heerd you sayin' that you'd go and find 'em and bring 'em back with you."

"I did say that!" Alfred exclaimed, chuckling heartily. "You were in no way imagining anything."

"You—"

"Yes, I did!"

The boy's natural impulse was to reach out and hug anybody who supplied good news of that magnitude, but he knew this would not be considered proper, so he restrained himself, smiling instead and thanking Alfred over and over.

"Calm down," Alfred told him. "I have to tell you that there is no certainty whatever that I ever can find your mother and father. But I happen to think that there is enough of a chance that I should spend the time on it."

"But you is gonna try, and that's what's meanin' a lot to somebody like me now!"

Alfred saw the joy on his face.

"You can be sure of that," he responded. "God knows you can be very sure that I will do nothing but my best, Hester."

Beginning the next day, Alfred spent the better part of his time in

Columbia, tending to certain business interests but also making inquiries. And what he uncovered was the worst that he could have expected. Hester's parents had been killed in one of the rare slave revolts of that era, even though they had not been a party to the incident. Caught in the crossfire, they died immediately, or that was what was first thought to be the case.

When peace was restored, the black casualties were piled on two large pyres of firewood, which were then set ablaze.

Somebody heard a series of screams coming from one of the bonfires, the smoke from it reaching up into the sky to be seen for miles in every direction, a warning to other slaves not to attempt a similar insurrection.

"One of them is alive!" exclaimed a slender, thirtyish black man peering into the flames. "I think it's that pretty one, already a mother, but looking young enough to be her own daughter. We've got to do something."

His companion, who had helped him light the fire, was greatly distressed but saw the reality of the situation.

"It's too late, Jonathan," he said, tears starting down his cheeks. "Honest to God, it's just too late!"

They saw movement within the spewing flames.

"That's her, I think," the one named Jonathan cried out. "She's kneeling, her hands pressed together. Oh, Lawd! She's praying!"

And then she had tumbled to one side, no further sounds coming from her.

Jonathan's boss decided that the best way to dispose of the ashes was to ship them "to any slave owners suspecting that their slaves are becoming restive," to be used as an example of what happened when black people tried to assert their so-called rights.

That was what Alfred had been told by someone who had witnessed the brutal events, a man in his sixties with long white hair and bushy eyebrows who had been a life-long believer in the institution of slavery.

"It is a disgrace!" he protested vigorously. "I tried to stop it, but no one would listen. Slaves are human beings, no more, no less. To take their remains and . . . and . . . just . . ."

"I cannot tell their son," acknowledged Alfred.

"Tell him anything but the truth. It would sadden and enrage him, and you might have to face an uprising of your own someday as a result."

So Alfred returned home with the most devastating news, deciding to lie to Hester about the final "details."

Elizabeth urged him, "Hold nothing back. We both know who the father of lies is, don't we? Do not serve him, dearest husband, in any way. Serve only the God of truth instead. And He will do the rest."

Alfred decided that his beloved had spoken with wisdom, and so he walked back to the slave quarters.

Hester was sitting on a tree stump, playing a sad tune on his harmonica, and doing it well.

He waited until the twelve-year-old had finished.

Hester glanced up.

"It ain't good, is it?" he spoke.

"Do I look as bad as that?" Alfred replied.

The boy was silent.

"Your mother and your father are with the Lord."

Hester nodded.

"I 'spected that, Massa. Since you went, I's been prayin' a whole lot. I said to the Lawd, 'I sure don't want them to be sufferin' none. If they is with You, Lawd, they's happy. That's the way I'm prayin' it'll be when the massa gets back.'"

"There's more, Hester."

"You don't need to tell me the rest."

"But you have to hear the truth."

"Jesus has them now, and they not got to face the pain of this life no more."

Hester buried his head in his hands. Alfred knelt beside him.

"Lean against me now," he said.

"I can't do that. It's wrong. I could be hurt real bad for it."

"I am your master now, Hester. You need never worry about being hurt like that while I am alive."

The boy was fighting back more tears.

"Let it out," Alfred urged. "I have no whip for moments such as this. I have no whip at all. Cry as you will, for however long your soul must shed its sorrow."

Hester seemed bewildered, wanting to express his pain more completely but not quite able to do so in the presence of even this kind master.

"I will go then," Alfred told him. "You know where I am. Whatever you might need, just ask for it."

He stood and started to walk away then heard Hester speak behind him.

"Massa?" the boy asked.

"Yes?" Alfred replied without turning around.

"A Bible, Massa . . . Does you have a Bible I could read? I's thinkin' that's 'bout the only thing can help me now."

"I will bring one right away."

"Massa?"

"Yes, Hester?"

"The other darkies says they love you. I's beginnin' to see why."

Alfred went back into the plantation house and walked down the hallway to his den, where he retrieved one of the three beautifully bound copies of the King James Bible that had belonged to the Littlepage family for many years and headed outside again, though slowly, gripping it in his left hand as he prayed silently with every deliberate step. He quickened his pace as he approached Hester.

"Here it is, Hester," he remarked. "Keep it for as long as you may want. I have another."

"Never knowed nobody with more than one copy," admitted Hester as he eyed the precious volume.

"My family and I have had them, this one or others, for generations. I have always needed to know what it says rather than depend upon the interpretation of others."

"That's my feelin', Massa. I want to learn more."

"And I would be happy to help."

"You would? Oh, Massa, that would be mighty nice of you."

Alfred was tired from the trip to Columbia, unusually so.

Oh, for the vigor of my youth, he thought.

But the opportunity to sit down with Hester and direct him to certain passages stirred his soul.

"I would be happy to," he told the boy.

And so Hester sat down on that stump again, and Alfred sat next to him, and the two of them shared God's Word by lantern light until long past dark.

~19~

NEITHER OF THEM realized that Little Isaiah had stopped the horses. Now the carriage, with its two horses resting motionless, stood squarely in the middle of the country road.

"We's been chattin' and rememberin' and goin' nowhere!" exclaimed Hester. "You'd better start 'em up quick, or we's gonna be late gettin' back home!"

Little Isaiah nodded, but before he could do anything, they both gasped as they heard a piercing sound nearby.

Screaming . . .

The sounds of someone screaming.

"What—?" Hester started to say.

Samuel Fulkerson's plantation house was just behind them.

Little Isaiah and Hester immediately jumped out of the carriage and started running toward the front gate and beyond it to the massive structure itself. Both thought that perhaps Fulkerson was in some difficulty.

Though the man had a reputation that everyone was aware of, regional convention dictated that the slaves of one master be taught to respond at whatever cost if the slaves of another were experiencing some form of danger or if the master himself needed help. Failure to respond would be considered an insult to their own master.

Little Isaiah and Hester realized immediately that if they went right on by without trying to investigate the agonizing sounds, they would be letting down the man who had been so kind to them for much of their adult lives, and they knew that they also invited some kind of punishment from him, punishment that would hurt him nearly as much as it did them, knowing Alfred's kind heart as they did.

Generally, Alfred Littlepage tried to avoid administering anything of the sort, certainly no action that was even remotely brutal, but the admonition that his slaves should never shirk their duty to come to the aid of another white man or the slaves owned by that individual was an indispensable and unalterable fact of life for them.

It stemmed from a streak of decency in Alfred, yes, but something else as well.

Survival . . .

A key factor for the survival of the southern culture at that time was the instincts of those plantation owners like Alfred, instincts that were quite rational, actually, and honed by years of experience.

At the center of this was a man's unquestioned right to defend his life and property, and to expect that any and all neighbors would help if need be.

Little Isaiah and Hester got to within a hundred feet of the plantation house when the front door was swung open.

Fulkerson himself stepped out, carrying a black teenage boy's body.

He looked helplessly at them and asked, "Can you two help me? He hit his head on a rock, and I . . . I think he's dying."

Little Isaiah hurried to Fulkerson's side and looked at the body.

"He . . . he is dead, Massa," he said. "This child ain't breathin', and I can't find any beating' of his heart."

Fulkerson staggered, nearly falling. Hester took the body from him, and Little Isaiah helped him sit down awkwardly on the dew-covered grass.

"I was shouting at his father," Fulkerson said, "and I guess I was gettin' a little loud and nasty. The boy ran toward me with tears in his eyes and begged me not to beat his daddy. 'Don't do that, please, Massa! Beat me instead,' he told me. 'I'm younger. Daddy's not been feelin' well lately. I don't think he could take another whippin'.' I—"

Fulkerson was having trouble swallowing and seemed on the verge of choking but forced himself to continue speaking.

"There was Zack, running so fast across the yard and so worried. He wasn't looking where he was going and tripped on the grass and fell, hitting his head on that big rock yonder."

Fulkerson glanced at the blood on his hands.

"I was about to tell Zack that it was nothing serious, that I would not beat his father for any reason, but I never got the chance. I guess the boy was dead instantly. Jacob's in the back, doing nothing but sobbing.

"When you two came along, I was hurrying to get a wagon because the others are out in the fields, only Jacob and me around. I thought a doctor could do something for poor Zack, that he might be only unconscious."

Little Isaiah and Hester were astounded that a man like Fulkerson would go to so much trouble explaining his feelings to another man's slaves.

"I liked Zack," Fulkerson continued. "If I was a black, he'd be one young buck I would be proud to call my son."

Fulkerson seemed on the edge of a breakdown.

"Nothing like this has ever happened before," he told them, his voice rising to a thin, nasal pitch. "I could yell at them and kick them and, yes, even use the whip on one or the other of them now and then, but I was never directly responsible for one of them dyin'. Plenty of my slaves have died naturally over the years with whooping cough and chest pains and the rest, that sort of thing, you know, but this is different. I have so scared those people that they think of me as—"

And then Sam Fulkerson simply passed out, dropping at their feet.

20

"HOSE POOR BOYS must have been beside themselves," Samuel Fulkerson recalled later. "There I was, collapsed at their feet, completely motionless. They must have thought I had died right before the two of them."

Scared. And confused.

Nothing like this had ever happened to Little Isaiah and Hester.

Until now . . .

A white man on the ground, unconscious or worse.

And a dead slave near him.

"We gotta get help," Little Isaiah said apprehensively as perspiration started to soak his body. "We gotta tell Massa Littlepage what happened. He's gonna believe us, you know that. He'll do his level best to protect us."

Hester agreed that his friend was right but added, "What about the father out back? What do we do with him?"

"We can't be everywhere," Little Isaiah protested. "He won't stray far; that's for certain. We gotta hurry. The massa and his missus were 'posed to be leavin' for a few hours—some church meetin' or whatever it was."

"I hopes we catch 'em."

"We doesn't have no chance if we jus' stand here yappin'."

Samuel moaned slightly as the two slaves lifted him into the carriage; then they took young Zack's lifeless body inside the plantation house, looking with great apprehension from side to side as they wondered if anyone was witnessing their actions.

Seconds later, they were headed back home.

The Littlepage plantation was only a mile or two down the road, but for Little Isaiah and Hester, it might as well have been in the next county.

Fulkerson was groaning again. A couple of times he took to thrashing about in the rear seat of the carriage.

Hester had to reach back from the front seat, grab his arms as gently as the circumstances permitted, and stop him from moving like that, letting go only when Fulkerson seemed to have calmed down.

"I wonder what's gotten into him," Hester whispered.

"You's claimin' you don't know?" replied Little Isaiah. "I thought you wasn't no dumb nigger, that's what I thought."

"I isn't dumb. I just asked a simple question. Look, I'm jus' as worried and 'fraid as you is. You don't have to snap at me like that."

Little Isaiah felt immediate regret over his sharp words and said so.

Hester accepted his friend's apology, realizing that they were in the midst of a crisis, especially if Fulkerson died while he was with them.

Given his reputation, nobody would believe that his death was accidental, with enough Carolinians reasonably assuming that Alfred Littlepage's two Negroes must have had something to do with it.

"It's plain old guilt," Little Isaiah said. "That man there's got a whole heap of guilt pressin' down on him now, and guilt's what he's been wrestlin' with, Hester; it's as plain and simple as that."

The other slave nodded.

"I think you's right," he replied. "And it's over more than jus' that one slave. He's startin' to think 'bout all the others he's had, beatin' 'em and all."

"Maybe we should try and help him. Maybe there's a chance to reach his soul somehow. What do you think?"

Hester scratched the top of his head and wrinkled up his nose.

"The Lawd sure wouldn't be pleased with us if we just turned our backs on this man and didn't try."

The truth of that stayed with Little Isaiah and Hester, though it made life suddenly very difficult for them.

The Littlepages had already left for church.

And now the two slaves were left with the motionless body of Samuel Fulkerson and no one around to help them.

"They's not here!" Little Isaiah exclaimed, panicking. "They's gone and took another carriage . . . and . . . and—"

The other slaves were in their quarters or at the far end of the property, staying late in the fields to finish their work.

"I's glad they ain't here. The less they know," Hester ventured realistically, "the easier it will be for them if something goes wrong."

"Good thinkin'," Little Isaiah admitted.

They started to take Fulkerson out of the carriage with the intention of bringing him into the plantation house and administering whatever treatment they could manage, either simple cold rags across his forehead or some of the headache powder they knew Mistress Littlepage kept in a pantry closet.

"Pray that nobody around here sees us," Little Isaiah said so low that Hester could hardly hear him.

But somebody did, a witness both of them hoped would be upstairs in her room, sound asleep.

But she wasn't.

Standing in the doorway, eyes widening.

Charity.

Not a child to wander about if her parents told her to stay in the house, she had been looking through a window and saw them.

"Miss Charity . . . ," Little Isaiah said, trembling. "We need to get inside. This man's fainted. He may be in a bad way."

"I'll go and get a wet cloth," she said before disappearing back into the house.

"I SHO' HOPE Miss Charity can keep a secret," Hester fretted.

"We ain't done nothin' wrong; you know that. The Lawd's gonna be with us. We just gotta be careful is all."

Little Isaiah wanted to believe it was as simple as that, but he was concerned.

"That's a lot to hope for, Hester. But we ain't got no other choice open to us, friend, no other choice at all."

Anxious and nervous, both men drenched in sweat, they entered the plantation house and waited anxiously for Charity to return.

Finally, she called to them.

Little Isaiah and Hester moved anxiously, not sure of what they expected of their young mistress but also knowing that Charity was not ordinary in any respect. She directed them to lay Fulkerson on one of the settees in the parlor, carefully spread a cool, wet cloth on his forehead, then disappeared down the hallway, returning quickly with a quilt.

"You work fast," Hester told her admiringly.

"Mama taught me," she replied matter-of-factly.

The two slaves tried to help, but Charity refused to let them do anything and handled it herself, lifting the damp cloth, dipping it in the basin of water she had set on the bedside table, squeezing it expertly, then carefully laying it across Fulkerson's forehead again. Then she held his hand as she began to hum a tune that neither of them recognized.

"What's that you's hummin', Missy?" Little Isaiah asked.

"I don't know what it's called. It's something Mama sang to me when I was little and something had upset me."

"But he might not even be hearin' you, honey-chil'."

"If the Lord wants him to, he will."

Little Isaiah and Hester said nothing further but sat down on the floor and waited with Charity for Samuel Fulkerson to regain consciousness—if he ever did. Suddenly both slaves began feeling calmer though having no idea why.

Rocking slowly back and forth, Charity continued humming . . .

~❧ 21 ❧~

FULKERSON STIRRED ONE finger at a time. Then he moved his head but with even greater difficulty, for it was throbbing.

And finally he opened his eyes.

Charity was standing over him, smiling cheerily. The two slaves sat to one side.

And then Fulkerson remembered what had happened.

"Oh God!" he started to say. "First, that old woman in church, and now Zack right in front of me."

Bending down, Charity held one finger to his lips and said, "Shush, Mr. Fulkerson. You can't use God's name like that."

Fulkerson blushed as he struggled to get to his feet.

Little Isaiah and Hester hurried over to him.

"Be calm, Massa," the younger slave cautioned. "You's had a shock, a big one. You gotta be quiet for jus' awhile."

"But that boy!" exclaimed Fulkerson, seeing in his mind Zack's motionless body. "What about that boy?"

"He's gone," Little Isaiah told him. "Nothin' to be done about it. No sense in throwing yourself away too."

"But what will I tell everyone?"

"Tell 'em what happened."

That prospect unnerved Fulkerson.

"What . . . what will everyone think of me? How will they look at me from then on?"

"Around here, some folk might raise their eyebrows, yes sir, and my massa would be real upset," Little Isaiah went on. "He might want to come over and talk to you real good. But that's all. Zack was nothin' but a colored boy. Nobody's gonna be up in arms or anythin' like that."

"But I would know," Fulkerson commented.

"That wouldn't change whether you told anybody else or not. You'd still be havin' to do with your guilt, Massa."

Charity touched his hand again with her own.

"The truth . . . ," she muttered. "The Bible says the truth's going to set you free, Mr. Fulkerson. You don't have to worry about anything."

Fulkerson shook his head, wishing he could have agreed with her but deciding that he could not.

"The truth is that Zack thought of me as such a monster that he misunderstood what I was saying to his father, and he tried to stop me, thinking I was going to punish his daddy in some way. How am I ever to be free, knowing that?"

Abruptly, Fulkerson pulled away from Charity, struggled to his feet, and rushed through the warming kitchen and down the hall.

Charity and the slaves waited to hear the front door slam shut behind him.

There was no sound at first. Then they heard something, but it wasn't the sound they expected.

A grown man sobbing like a child would have cried when faced with an experience so awful that it shattered his stability and forced him to stand face to face with a mirror of sorts, the kind that reflected not his physical form but his very soul.

They raced out of the warming kitchen and into the hallway, following the sound, until they found Samuel Fulkerson huddled on the floor.

He looked up at them.

"How many more are dead inside because of the way I have been treating them?" he muttered. "That old woman in church . . . she was happy because she was treated like a human being. I could see it in those eyes of hers."

Charity did not answer Fulkerson directly but walked up to him, pulling a delicate pink hanky from a pocket in her dress as she knelt by him.

She used it to wipe away the tears that had started to trickle down his cheeks, then she stepped back a few inches, hands on her hips.

"We'll help you!" she declared.

"You are only a girl," Fulkerson said though not with any unkindness in his voice. "How could you do anything to—?"

He studied her eyes for a moment.

"If only I could be even a little bit as sure, as confident, as you are this very moment, wide-eyed and at peace and full of faith," Fulkerson remarked. "Please hug me, Charity. Please hug this rotten old devil, and may it be that some of your own goodness passes to me."

"I won't!" she declared, her nostrils suddenly flaring.

Eyes half-closing, Fulkerson bowed his head, taking her refusal as though it were a very real dagger she had plunged into him.

"You aren't a devil!" Charity went on to rebuke the man. "Daddy says it's just that you've been mean so long that you don't know how to act any other way. He says it'll take something awful to change you."

Bewildered, he looked from Charity to Little Isaiah to Hester.

"But what can I do?" Fulkerson asked helplessly. "Where do I turn? I may not be kicked out of the community for this sort of thing, but my slaves . . . how will this affect them? Oh, the hatred they will feel toward me!"

"That boy of yours done had an accident and died on you," Little Isaiah said slowly. Then he stopped, not wanting to risk being an affront to someone who, while not his own master, was a white man nevertheless.

"But what about his father?" Fulkerson persisted. "I should not have treated that poor man as I did. If I hadn't, then Zack would never have had what he thought was ample cause to act the way he did."

Charity seemed to be studying Fulkerson with great intentness for a moment, her pale forehead frowning in puzzlement.

Then, looking quite determined, she spoke. "Forgiveness, Mr. Fulkerson. Isn't that why Jesus died, so that God could forgive us? You . . . you must forgive yourself, that's what you have to do, 'cause that's why you're acting like this."

"You think God listens to a wretch like me?" Fulkerson replied. "I have done much more than you know, the nastiest, cruelest actions against those slaves of mine year after year. I could hardly list everything because there is so much of it!"

"Charity spoke wisely, Massa," Little Isaiah told him. "Hester and I be glad to go back with you, and if we can say somethin' to help, we will!"

"You and the young buck there by your side know who I am. And you know what I am. Why would you make such an offer?"

Little Isaiah pointed to Charity.

"If that child sees somethin' decent left in you, then we gotta go along with what she's feelin'. Charity's pure and good. She would never waste two seconds on you if you was nothin' but a hopeless wreck."

Little Isaiah gulped, then added quickly, much like an impudent child himself, "That's how I feel, Massa."

Hester asked if he could add something to what the other slave said, and Fulkerson told him that he could.

"Maybe the Lawd's in this," he said, shuffling his feet uncertainly.

"You aren't saying that He's somehow involved in the accidental death of that healthy young—?" Fulkerson answered the slave incredulously.

"Maybe it came 'bout the way it did so that, seein' it happen, you might change those ways of yours, Massa. Maybe poor Zack would have died early anyway, never reachin' old age, an accident or somethin', you know.

"Then, too, there's been an awful lot of lightning lately, you know. And cottonmouths have been comin' back after bein' away for a long time. Maybe he was gonna be bit by one, with nobody around to help.

"I think God just up and said that was too much of a waste, with nothin' good comin' from it, and so He made Zack's death mean somethin' instead of him bein' found by the side of some road somewhere after a bunch of mean ol' scavengers had their way with his body. That would have been worse, Massa, with nothin' to show for it."

Nervous, he had expected Fulkerson to wave him to silence, or possibly worse. But this did not happen.

"I ain't got nothin' more to say," Hester said. "Guess I shouldn't have said what I did. But I gave you what's on my heart, Massa, and that's all I have."

Fulkerson sighed as he replied, "We should go back. I would be grateful if you would stand with me."

Charity thought he meant her, and she started to walk toward the front door.

"No, my dear," Fulkerson said as he got rather unsteadily to his feet. "Your father would think me quite crazy in the head if I allowed you to go. Please, you have done more than you might know. Remain here, please, and keep all this to yourself for the time being. Will you do that for me, Charity?"

"Okay . . . ," the teenager told him without protest. "But I'll be praying to the Lord Jesus to help you."

Fulkerson hugged her.

"Your parents adore you," he said, his voice breaking. "I can see why."

Then he left with Little Isaiah and Hester, regretting the course of a life that denied him an opportunity to call any such child his own.

~❧22❧~

SAMUEL FULKERSON WALKED up the pathway to the front door of his own home as though he were instead approaching a dreary funeral parlor. He dreaded gaining entrance, for he had no idea how he was once again going to face the sight of that dead body inside.

Voices . . .

"Listen!" he exclaimed to Little Isaiah and Hester, who were directly behind him.

A mournful, dirge-like chorus of voices singing.

"It's comin' from 'round back, Massa!" Hester said, as surprised as he was.

"How could they be singing?" Fulkerson asked. "Tell me: How could their kind ever be doing that now?"

Neither Little Isaiah nor Hester could answer that.

Instead of entering the plantation house, they walked around its western side and back to where the slave quarters stood.

Little Isaiah recoiled at the sight.

Shacks . . .

A series of half a dozen shacks . . . none of them looking much different than ramshackle outhouses.

The odor was similar.

Fulkerson saw the expressions on Hester and Little Isaiah's faces and started to speak, but then he noticed the assemblage of slaves behind those miserable quarters.

They walked slowly between two of the buildings, the stench coming from both sides assailing them.

A circle.

Three dozen slaves were gathered in a circle, holding hands, as one of them prayed with great heaviness of heart, "May the massa let us get poor Zack's body. May the massa let us bury the boy as he should be instead of throwing him away like a side of beef, for the creatures to feed on him. May the massa let us weep as we say good-bye."

Fulkerson did not interrupt them.

"May the massa have mercy, Lawd," the prayerful voice continued. "May the massa show us just this little kindness."

They sang and prayed on for fifteen more minutes.

. . . May the massa let us weep as we say good-bye.

It was difficult for Fulkerson to get past those words.

They fear my wrath so much that they must pray with such fervor for my willingness to let them mourn properly, he thought.

He became weak, and Little Isaiah and Hester had to hold him up.

"Could it be so awful for these people?" he whispered hoarsely. "Could it be so great a nightmare?"

"We knows only what we hear," acknowledged Little Isaiah.

"You called them people just now," Hester put in. "But from what we's told, you sure don't treat them like they is, Massa."

Little Isaiah shot a warning glance at his fellow slave. But Fulkerson let that comment pass without showing any anger.

"I shall tell them now that I am here," he said.

Fulkerson pulled away from the two slaves and walked toward his own.

Someone spotted him and quickly shushed the prayer.

Several of the women started whimpering, convinced that they had done something that would cause Fulkerson to punish them.

"Go on," he said. "Please, I have never been against any of you praying."

And then Fulkerson remembered that there were moments when this had not been so, moments when one or more of them would stop their work for a few seconds or perhaps a minute or two, and he happened to notice.

Oh, God, he thought half-prayerfully, *what have I done to them?*

Abruptly, as though seeing them for the first time, he noticed the multitude of scars . . . on the cheeks of some slaves and the foreheads of others, on the arms of several; and he saw a few slaves whose legs were scarred, including one that was so grotesque he had to avert his eyes from it.

"How did that happen?" he demanded.

"Don't you 'member, Massa?" the youngest of the slaves, a lad named Nate, replied.

Fulkerson started to shake his head but stopped because he suddenly knew the answer.

"I nearly bled to death, Massa," Nate told him. "You gave permission for me to be taken to a colored doctor in the next town, and he sewed me up real good. I's thankful, Massa."

"How can you claim that you are thankful?" Fulkerson asked in disbelief. "You say so only because of being afraid that I will punish you again if you say anything that accuses me."

"I could never accuse you, Massa. It was me. I was wrong."

"But I remember what happened. How could you ever think that you were at fault?"

"I knows I was bad, Massa. Because I didn't please you, Massa. You always punish us when we don't please you. That's why I deserved this bum leg."

Fulkerson had thought Nate was not working as hard as he should be while digging a new irrigation ditch. He demanded that the boy's pace be stepped up. But Nate, though young and healthy looking, had proven to be more frail than any of the other slaves.

Half an hour later, Fulkerson had returned to that section of his estate to find Nate more tired and less productive than before; he had grabbed the shovel the young slave had been using.

"I slammed the sharp edge against the middle of your leg!" blurted out Fulkerson, "not once or just twice but three times, and then again for good measure. I tore nearly all the flesh off. I   . I could see white bone underneath!'

"But ı's fixed up real good now, Massa," Nate told him again.

He walked forward but with distinct effort.

"You limp!" Fulkerson noticed.

"Don't matter."

"And your face . . . I can see your pain on your face."

"This is a world of pain, Massa. You get used to it when you's one of eight chil'ens. My mammy and my pappy were never without pain."

"Did they ever work for me, Nate?"

"Yes sir."

"What happened to them?"

"You had Pappy hanged because you thought he done stole somethin' from you. Mammy went on for as long as she could until her heart just gave out."

"Was that Ria?" Fulkerson gasped as he recalled the woman.

"Yes sir, my dear mammy was called Ria."

Fulkerson clamped his hand over his mouth, thinking he would be sick to his stomach any second.

Ria was one of the most beautiful black women he had ever seen, and she had possessed a will that made her seem as though she would never be broken by anything.

Except her husband's so-called execution.

"She was strong, my mammy was," added Nate. "But the sight of Pappy hangin' from that rope and kickin' and screamin' . . . she couldn't take it. The memory of it attached itself to Mammy like some awful leech and sucked her dry."

Fulkerson wished he had not heard those last words.

"The other members of your family, are they still here?" he asked.

"I ain't sure where they is, Massa," Nate replied honestly. "We's been divided up so often over the years! You bought my pappy, my mammy, and me but not my brother or my sister. The rest is gone away to God knows where."

He bowed his head.

"I guess I might be the only one left," he added. "Sometimes I miss them so much I ask the Lawd to make it so that I not wake up in the mornin'. There isn't much in this world to look forward to no more."

Because of the shame he was feeling, Fulkerson had not been facing Nate or the others. But now he turned around and looked from one to the other.

"I have a body in my house," he said. "I think it is time that young Zack be given a proper burial."

"Where should we put him?" the father, Jacob, spoke up. "The nearest cemetery for black folks is down near—"

"Too far," Fulkerson interrupted. "You can put him right in the spot I will show you . . . follow me."

Little Isaiah and Hester fell in line behind him, with Fulkerson's slaves next. None of them dared to speak, fearing that they had said too much already.

Finally they all had gathered in front of the plantation house

In the middle of the front lawn was Fulkerson's most prized growth, a giant loblolly pine tree. He had had it transplanted here many years before, determined to make it grow even though the normal regions for it were the coastal areas of South and North Carolina.

"Right there," he said.

"Next to the loblolly?" one of the slaves asked.

"No . . . where it stands now."

"You want to cut it down?" Nate spoke.

"It shall be cut down."

"You's loved that tree since you become massa here," one of the others pointed out. "I can still remember seein' you help cart it in right from somewhere near the ocean. Even then, it was big. Can't you bury Zack in place of one of the rose bushes yonder?"

"I want him here!" Fulkerson declared. "I want to give up something that I treasure. I must do this!"

None of the slaves had ever seen him acting in such a vulnerable manner.

"Get me an ax," he demanded.

"It's real late, Massa," Nate reminded him. "You could wait until mornin'."

"Get me an ax immediately," Fulkerson said, his voice louder.

"Yes sir!" another male slave replied, hurrying toward the tool shed at the rear of the plantation house. After about a minute, he returned with a large ax.

"Here, now!" Fulkerson ordered him. "Give it to me."

He grabbed it and swung it once directly into the trunk of the loblolly, then a second time, a third, a fourth. He was not a man who had spent much time keeping himself in shape, and the effect was showing right from the start.

"Massa," Nate told him, "let us help, let us—"

"No!" Fulkerson declared. "I shall do this alone if it kills me, and then you can take over afterward. That is the only way I shall step aside this night!"

On and on he went, his face red, his lungs heaving from the unaccustomed exertion.

After ten minutes, he had not managed to cut very deeply into the loblolly.

Dropping the ax, Fulkerson seemed ready to pass out but steadied himself a bit and continued on.

Then his strength was come, and dizziness took hold of him; he fell at the base of the tree, dizzy, exhausted, and heaving up the food he had eaten earlier that night.

He tried to stand but was too weak.

"So sorry . . . ," he muttered, "so very sorry."

No one else moved for a moment.

Then Fulkerson felt a hand on his shoulder.

"My turn . . . ," a voice said.

He glanced up, trying to see with vision that had become blurry.

"Who dares to—?" Fulkerson asked.

The slave bent down, smiling kindly.

"I's taking over," he said. "It's my son. I have the right."

Jacob . . . young Zack's father.

"You rest now, Massa," he said. "We'll have this done in no time."

"We?" Fulkerson repeated, not comprehending. "What are you babbling about? I've got to get on with—"

"It's my son's body that will rest where the tree stands, Massa," Jacob told him. "What's goin' on now is my 'sponsibility, the last act I's ever gonna do for him in this world. Rest easy, Massa, and God bless you."

He spoke firmly but without insolence.

"And they will help me," he pointed to several of the slaves who had retrieved additional axes. "Look, Massa, see them behind you? I ain't alone in this."

"But I . . . I wanted to do it, to be able to say . . ." Fulkerson stuttered, which was unusual for him. "That . . . that—"

"By allowin' it, you say 'nough," Jacob remarked with great dignity. "We don't have to be here watchin' you die 'fore our eyes to believe you."

Fulkerson stood, his legs wobbly. Jacob reached out to steady him.

"How can you be like you are with me this moment?" he asked, genuinely wanting to know. "How can you let go of all the hate that must have been inside you?"

"The Almighty done forgiven those who caused the death of His dear Son. Can I do less in return, Massa?"

"No . . . ," Fulkerson whispered, shaking his head sadly. "No, you can't."

He started walking toward the plantation house then stopped and faced them all again.

"Give me an ax," he asked firmly. "I cannot retreat to my fifteen-room cocoon and not help with this. I see that the job of uprooting that tree was too much for me alone. Why don't we all do it together?"

The slaves glanced at one another then murmured a collective "Yes sir."

"Can we go inside to get my boy's body?" asked Jacob.

"I will bring him to you," Fulkerson said. "While we are doing what we must with the loblolly, the women can be cleaning him up."

"That's fine, Massa, real fine."

Fulkerson continued on toward the house. When he was inside, he hurried to the hallway where Zack's body remained.

Darkish fluids had formed a large circle around it.

The women cannot do this, he thought. *And I need help.*

He stood in the back doorway and called out to Jacob, who came quickly.

"You and I should do this," Fulkerson said

"The body, Massa?"

"Yes. We need to take care of him ourselves. Your women folk shouldn't have to clean him up. Are you up to it?"

"I ain't got no choice. Zack is my only child, Massa. He would do the same for me. I help you, Massa."

"How will you get along without him?"

"Only with the Holy Ghost inside me helpin'. Ain't no other way."

Fulkerson had never discussed with his slaves matters of faith or anything else that was personal, so he had no idea what they thought about any aspect of life.

"You honestly believe that?" he asked.

"You and me here now doin' what we's 'bout to do is proof, Massa."

They carried Zack's body into the bedroom.

"You get the boy's clothes off," Fulkerson told him. "I'll go and fetch some water from the well so we can clean him up."

Jacob nodded and proceeded to pull off the boy's tattered overalls.

Fulkerson grabbed a bucket from the pantry and hurried outside. The rest of the slaves were waiting near the loblolly as he had ordered.

He stopped, looked at them, seeing how obedient they were, dependent upon whatever he ordered them to do.

. . . like sheep.

Dumb, blind sheep.

Yet what I have done to them over the years, he thought, *I would not have inflicted upon any creature.*

He waved to one of them.

"Parker!" he called. "Tell the boys not to wait for us but to get started now. This is going to take awhile."

A simple nodding of the head in response, together with what had become an instinctive "Yes sir!" with no hesitation whatever . . . obediently following all orders . . . every last one of the slaves trained brutally well.

They seem to have no will of their own, Fulkerson observed with great shame. *How have they continued to be as happy as they are?*

Another thought, this one more disturbing, erased the first.

All this time I have been doing it to them . . . all this time I have been squeezing from them so much of their humanity.

Fulkerson wiped a single tear that welled up in his left eye.

And yet the irony is that they have stayed human while I have become less so.

When he reached the pump, he filled the bucket as quickly as he could and hurried back to the house. As soon as he entered, he heard the sound of Jacob's hysterical sobbing and rushed to the bathroom, spilling some of the water on the floor as he went.

Jacob had carried his son onto the bathing porch and had gently laid the thin body into the old tub. Now he was hugging the boy's now stiff shoulders, rocking back and forth with it and moaning.

"I wanted to see you grow up and 'come a man," Jacob was saying. "Now I's 'bout to put your body in a grave and throw dirt over it."

He looked up toward the ceiling.

"Lawd, it should have been me!" he cried. "I've had more than enough of this world. But my boy here never had a chance to make it better for himself. Oh, Lawd, take care of this poor child real good. Let him know that his mammy and I will be thinkin' 'bout him for the rest of whatever lives You see fit to give us, Lawd."

Fulkerson left the bucket in the hallway and sat down beside Jacob. The man leaned against him.

"The last time I did this," Jacob said, "Zack was not much more than a baby, just beginnin' his life, you know. He had falled into some little puddle of mud, and I was washin' him off down at the creek yonder."

He closed his eyes and sighed.

"We was laughing and cutting up and having a high old time. I jus' didn't know what was gonna happen these fourteen years later. That's not some mud on him now . . . It's my baby's life, flowed out of his body!"

He shook with the sorrow that had overtaken him. After he had quieted down, the two of them remained like that, master and slave leaning against one another for some while before they began the task of cleaning that cold, lifeless body and then dressing it again, wrapping it in a sheet, and taking it to where the loblolly once sank its roots deep into the ground.

THE FIRE HAD dwindled to nothing but coals by the time Samuel Fulkerson finished telling Alfred his bittersweet story of his conversion from .harsh skeptic to humble believer.

Alfred gazed into the glowing embers, lost in the depth of his new friend's experience, when another thought suddenly pierced his peaceful reflection.

Charity.

"I hope she made it home safely," he said, breaking the quiet mood. "It was foolish of me to hand her over to others; I . . . I was so caught up in the thrill of what you were telling me, I wasn't thinking clearly. And now I have this sudden, urgent sense of . . . of . . ."

Without another word, Alfred fell into silence for a moment, praying that the Lord would keep his daughter safe.

～23～

RIFLE ON THE floor at his feet, Rufus was sitting next to Charity while Johnny drove the horses back toward the neighboring Littlepage plantation, moving along at a faster than customary pace because of the hour.

They were nearly past the dreaded woods, prepared to sigh with relief when they no longer had to be concerned with this sinister stretch of the road.

The two slaves felt a gut-deep fear that Charity sensed but did not understand. The two men had come from a huge continent where the practices of native black magic and voodoo held vast numbers of men, women, and children in terrifying sway. In their ignorance, natives worshiped strange gods given form through grotesque masks and statues. Ceremonies involved bloodletting and, in some cases, cannibalism, the latter with the belief that eating the body of another human being meant also ingesting the other's soul.

From Africa, such occultic domination had spread to the Caribbean where it took up residence principally on the island of Haiti before moving on to the United States by gaining a foothold in New Orleans, the most morally and spiritually evil and politically corrupt city in the country through the 1840s and much later, mired in a pervading cycle of occultism that would weaken then return strong as before.

New Orleans, a miserable, fetid hell on earth . . .

The city and its environs had a surfeit of apostles of darkness, most of them black, more than a few leaving that city and spreading their satanic worship elsewhere, especially among the slave populace throughout the South. Voodoo in Africa and Haiti became what was called hoodoo in the southern states.

Charity did not know any of this; nor would she learn it for many years, but she did sense the cold fear that Rufus and Johnny were feeling just then, the nervousness they betrayed in their mannerisms.

"It's silly to be afraid!" declared Charity, pointing in the direction of the forest. "It's just a bunch of old trees and stuff like that."

Rufus looked at the teenager with considerable affection, not wanting to destroy her illusions because that would have meant she would share the panic that was working its way through the two of them.

"No, Miss Charity . . . not silly," he assured her solemnly while reaching down and tightening his grip on the rifle.

Charity shook her head in exasperation, tired of all the nonsense that was surrounding her. She had the faith and the trust of someone still young and no patience with anyone less confident.

"Daddy's afraid, too," she added. "He's not like that at other times, just now, tonight. But I don't understand why he's afraid."

"He jus' wantin' to make sure that nothin' happens to you," replied Rufus, his voice a kindly tone.

"But Jesus'll protect us," Charity announced, her eyes wide, her expression supremely confident.

"Sometimes that's true," he agreed. "The Lord saves us from harm."

His expression was more serious.

"But child, sometimes He not do that," Rufus added. "Christians sometimes got to die real early."

Charity was beginning to hug herself, a touch of fear entering that normally carefree head of hers.

"Sorry . . . ," apologized Rufus.

She shook her head.

"It's okay," she said.

Just as the carriage was approaching the far edge of trees and growth so densely packed together that even in the daytime the interior was, at best, semi-dark, the two horses started to act nervous, slowing their gait and glancing frantically from side to side, their odor-sensitive noses picking up disturbing scents that were unfamiliar, their ears hearing sounds they liked even less.

Incense.

"Somebody's burnin' somethin'," Johnny said uncertainly as he sniffed the air. "Do you smell it?"

"I do," Rufus told him, his muscles tensing.

Johnny looked back over his shoulder at Rufus.

"No need to worry, I guess," he remarked. "Animals sometimes pick up things from us. If we is afraid, they is afraid. If we is happy, they seem happy . . . just the way it is. Pay no mind, Miss Charity. We're acting strange, so it's catchin' on with these horses, that's all. No need to be concerned 'bout anythin'."

She reached out, patted Johnny on the knee, then settled back again, not entirely convinced that she had nothing to worry about.

Nor were the horses placated either.

Neither of them calmed down but remained tense, ears straight up, noses testing the breezes that passed by.

And their behavior became more and more erratic.

Twice the horses tried to bolt on ahead, but Johnny grabbed the reins tightly, slowing them down.

The woods were now just behind them.

All three cast one last glance at the trees, now with the evening mist making them seem unreal, a mirage of sorts.

Suddenly both horses reared up on their back legs, kicking their front hooves into the air, their eyes wild with terror.

"Look!" Rufus said, trembling.

He was pointing a shaking finger straight ahead.

A single figure.

Standing in the middle of the road.

He was a black man wearing a stovepipe hat, a pitch-black, long-tailed jacket over a high-neck silk shirt, and wide trousers with shredded edges. His eyes seemed to glow in the darkness.

Johnny had to steer the horses to his left or, it seemed, they would have trampled him underfoot.

"Look at his hand!" Rufus shouted.

A tattered doll not more than six inches long.

"Hoodoo Jack!" Johnny screamed. "That's him. I thought he was gone. I thought he had been kicked out and—"

The horses became so frenzied and uncontrollable that Johnny had to cut them loose, realizing that they would head back to the plantation for sanctuary and that this would serve to alert their master. He jumped down from the carriage then turned to help Charity to the ground.

"So you know about me!" the man exclaimed. "You must be a little smarter than you look, boy."

"I's known 'bout you for a long time," Rufus said with a confidence that he in no way actually felt. "My cousins up north send me letters, telling me tales. Thought you was run clear out of the country."

"Stayed in Haiti for a while. Getting back was easy. I come and go as I please. No man stops me. I'm driven by a more powerful master than you are!"

Rufus was sweating despite the nighttime chill.

"Sweet Jesus!" he muttered in sudden shock as he glanced behind him, words spoken not profanely but as an instinctive prayer.

More figures, not like the one in front, three of them for the moment, though he half-expected yet others to appear out of thin air, these three just standing there for the moment, waiting for instructions.

Their eyes, Lawd! he thought. *Starin' but not seein'!*

Charity clung tightly to Rufus's middle while he raised the rifle.

"I shoot you, mister," he called out while hoping that he did so with enough ferocity to wipe the arrogance off the intruder's face, "and they's all gonna scatter. Now git the devil out of here right now!"

The figure in front of them spoke with a lilting accent.

"I have been sent by the devil of whom you speak," he declared grandiloquently, "to liberate the black man from his oppressive bondage. And you there can be one of the very first to embrace what you have never had."

"We's not wanting the kind of freedom you sellin'," Rufus yelled. "Besides, who's you to talk? You don't sound like no black man I ever knowed. Fancy words and fancy clothes—you's not one of us. Not your kind!"

What he was saying seemed to be affecting the stranger, who shook himself in a single, wrenching motion.

"And what is my kind?" he asked. "What primitive thoughts come from that monkey brain of yours?"

Johnny broke in then, proving that he was becoming every bit as angry as his fellow slave.

"From the devil himself!" he screamed. "No darkie would say anything like you just did, that his own people come from monkeys."

Hoodoo Jack held out a bony finger, with its long fingernail, and wiggled it at Johnny.

"Hah!" he spat the word out.

Both slaves could feel their skin almost crawling on their backs, their bodies as tight as boards.

"I'm only repeating what it is that your white massas are saying behind your back," Hoodoo Jack snarled. "If you can't take it from me, another colored man, why do you bow and scrape before them?"

The man spat some disgusting dark-brown chewing tobacco on the ground only a few inches away from Charity's feet.

"You've been God-fearing all this time, bowing and scrapin' for that massa of yours," he added with sarcasm thick enough that it could easily have become physical. "What has that gotten you? You should murder the bastard."

Grimacing, Charity straightened herself up and walked forward as much as Rufus would let her.

"You shouldn't talk like that, mister," she firmly rebuked Hoodoo Jack, a tiny frown on her narrow forehead. "You'll be punished for it. You surely will!"

Then she stepped back, still glowering at him.

For a moment, Hoodoo Jack was speechless, never expecting a mere teenager to be as brave as Charity had shown herself to be.

"A soul that's headin' for heaven, that's what we got." Johnny spoke again, answering his question. "What's the use of us gainin' our freedom by your hand if we lose our souls? It's better to work for our massa."

Still unable to shift his gaze from beautiful young Charity, Hoodoo Jack blurted out, "You're both fools! And that little child is going to suffer because she happens to be in your company."

Attached to his waist by a leather tether was a long wood reed, hollowed out inside.

An instrument of death . . .

Hoodoo Jack's hand flashed down and grabbed it. Then with his other hand he took a six-inch needle-like splinter of wood from a side pocket, the tip glistening a bit as moonlight caught a small splotch of poison that had been smeared onto it, and slipped this dart into one end of the reed before raising it to his mouth.

"Watch out, Miss Charity!" Rufus shouted, pushing her slim form to one side hard enough that she tripped and fell, wrenching her side and letting out a cry as she hit the ground, staying there without moving.

Stepping in front of Charity, Rufus raised the rifle and took careful aim straight at Hoodoo Jack's chest, which was difficult because his hands were trembling. But his concentration was broken when Johnny screamed, "Behind you!"

Rufus spun around and saw what had made Johnny react.

One of the three black men behind them had taken a similar reed and was starting to aim it toward them.

Rufus was drenched with perspiration, and the rifle slipped a bit as he tried to hold it steady and aim it accurately.

Don't let this fail me now, he prayed. *I gotta protect that little girl. I's not carin' for myself; you know that, Lawd.*

Finally Rufus pulled the trigger and caught the strange-eyed black man in the chest, though he seemed only to be staggered by the shot. Then Rufus recocked the rifle and fired a second time, hitting him in the right leg just above the knee.

Snarling like a beast with rabies, the stranger toppled to the ground but did not remain still. Instead he managed to raise himself to his knees and shake his fist wildly, his face contorted with rage that made the veins on his forehead bulge.

His two companions rushed to his side, lifting him up between them, all three stumbling forward.

Their eyes!

Charity let out a cry of fear and turned away, unable to look into those large, bloodshot eyes for more than an instant.

"Miss Charity!" Rufus yelled as Johnny rushed over to her. "Go, Johnny! Take that precious child to the massa. Take her now!"

Hoodoo Jack had paused, waiting for an opening.

Now he blew hard into the reed, and Rufus cried out as the splinter entered his shoulder near the neck, penetrating to an astonishing depth.

Still able to lift the rifle, Rufus spun around, tottering in the process, and let go another shot, this time at the bizarre Hoodoo Jack, who seemed surprised when the bullet actually hit his left arm, jerking it backward like a puppet's.

Johnny swept up Charity in his arms, grunting in surprise as he found her to be heavier than he expected.

Hoodoo Jack seemed to be faltering, blood dripping down his arm and off his fingers, forming a small pool on the dirt road.

He's done for, Johnny thought gratefully. *Good shot, Rufus! Thank the good Lawd for that aim of yours!*

For an instant, squinting in pain, Hoodoo Jack leveled his gaze directly at Charity like a hawk drawing a bead on his prey. Slowly, his body trembling, he raised one hand and seemed to aim his long, pointed fingernail directly at her heart.

"May the gates of hell swallow you up along with your loved ones forever!" Hoodoo Jack screamed.

"No!" she cried out in terror but also bravely, shivering as though a large wave of freezing water had suddenly submerged her beneath it. "Jesus is here. Leave us alone!"

Then Hoodoo Jack, weakening, fell on his back with a thump and was unable to stand, his eyes glazing over.

Jesus, Jesus, Jesus, Charity repeated silently, little differently from what she would have prayed as a young child. *Stop that terrible man from hurting us. Protect Johnny and me, please!*

Never before had she seen such darkness in another human being.

The man's eyes! They revealed the evil of his soul!

Her relative isolation from the extreme harshness of life beyond the plantation prevented Charity from understanding completely what she saw, only that it made her desperately afraid.

Instinctively taking advantage of Hoodoo Jack's momentary woundedness and his obvious disorientation, Johnny darted to the right of the tall, prostrate figure and raced on past him.

"I'll have you back with your daddy in no time," he spoke soothingly into her soft ear as he ran. "Don't be afraid, sweet child; don't be afraid. You're right. Jesus will protect you. And I's gonna be the one He uses!"

Behind them, they both heard the sound of poor Rufus, screaming horribly for only an instant before his voice was snuffed out.

~❧ 24 ❧~

"I HEAR HORSES," Samuel Fulkerson, turning his head slightly, spoke up. "They must be back already."

He set down the cup of tea he was sipping.

"That seems awfully strange," he mused out loud. "The horses are running—and I didn't expect them back so soon. Something must be wrong!" Both men rushed to the door. The carriage wasn't there. The sound of the horses' hooves had stopped.

"Rufus? Johnny?" Fulkerson shouted into the darkness.

Nothing.

Standing on the quiet porch, the two men were becoming increasingly restless.

Now there was another sound. The wheezing, huffing voice of a man, out of breath, somewhere out there in the darkness, coming nearer, calling out for help.

"Massa!"

"It's Johnny!" Fulkerson cried out, stepping off the porch in one long step. "Johnny? Johnny? What's wrong? Is Charity all right?"

Johnny finally emerged from the darkness, limping up to the yard, his shoulders heaving with every breath. And in his arms . . .

"Charity! Oh, dear Lord! Is she all right?" Now it was Alfred's turn to leap from the porch and run toward the edge of the yard.

"I'm fine, Daddy. I'm okay, really, but Rufus . . ."

Johnny had gently set Charity onto her feet and now was babbling disjointed half-sentences, with Charity standing next to him, trying to fill in the blanks in Johnny's panted explanation. Her face flushed, her eyes bloodshot, the look of fear gripped her face as well as Johnny's.

Dear girl! Alfred exclaimed to himself, his heart nearly stopping as he looked at her. *What has happened to you?*

He reached out and gently took his daughter into his arms, momentarily stopping the jumbled cacophony of words. Abruptly, feeling her father's arms around her, Charity started to cry, unable to speak any words, her thin body shaking fitfully.

"Get the truth from that boy! Get it now!" Alfred demanded. "If you cannot, Samuel, then believe me, I will!"

Fulkerson grabbed Johnny by the shoulders.

"What the devil happened, boy?" he yelled with a mixture of rising anxiety along with his anger.

Johnny was scared of the bizarre stranger and the others he had left behind on the dark road, but he was also terrified of Samuel Fulkerson, who could order Johnny's death, if he chose to do so, and never be brought to trial for the act.

"Yessir, that's who it was, Massa," Johnny told him, eyes wide, bloodshot, lids red-rimmed. "Sent by the devil Satan himself! Yessir! We's met him face to face out there near them dark woods down the way, and we—I—I mean, me and Charity—done hightailed it back here. But I knows that one's gonna follow us. I knows he's right behind us."

"Where's Rufus?" Fulkerson said, his eyes squinting to peer steadily into the young man's face.

"He's . . . he's . . . oh, Massa, I fear he's dead! He . . . the man shot him with somethin'—blew it through a reed, and Rufus went down. He yelled to me, 'Go on, Johnny! Go take Charity to the massa. Take her now!' And I . . . I . . ."

"He carried me all the way," Charity interrupted. "He ran and ran until I thought his heart would burst, Daddy. We were so scared!"

"Do you know who this . . . this man was?" Fulkerson asked.

The slave nodded as he said, "Hoodoo Jack, that's who it was. He's called Hoodoo Jack, a mean, cruel creature. No decent man wants any part of him."

Johnny had begun to move toward the house when, abruptly, his mouth opened wide and he fell forward against Fulkerson's chest.

"He got me, Massa! He's coming for us. We gotta get away, get in the house! Hurry! Lock the door!" the black man begged, his features contorted with pain. "Please, Massa, please!"

Just then, something seemed to fly directly past Fulkerson's right ear.

He could only sense whatever it was, feeling nothing more than the hint of a tiny breeze caused by the object.

"What the—?" he started to say.

"Poison!" Johnny sobbed. "He's blowing his poison darts at us. He got me, Massa! Now I's got hoodoo poison in my veins like po' old Rufus! Oh, Massa, it's hurtin'; it's hurting' so bad."

Alfred scooped Charity into his arms and ran for the door. Fulkerson wrapped one arm around his slave, half dragging him up the steps, across the porch, and through the door, slamming it shut behind them with his free hand.

"I's so weak, so trembly," Johnny said as Fulkerson gently helped him onto one of the parlor chairs. "I don't mean to be a bother to you, Massa. Please, help me get back to—"

"Quiet," Fulkerson insisted. "Sit down here."

As he helped Johnny into the chair he noticed a splinter-like piece of wood lodged in the back of the black man's neck.

"Look at this," he said, motioning Alfred over to take a look. "I wonder what that could be."

"I've seen something like that before," Alfred told him.

"Where?" Fulkerson asked, surprised that he knew anything at all about it.

"Later . . ."

There was no time to talk just then, because in an instant, Johnny was having convulsions.

"What is causing this? Can you tell me anything?" Fulkerson asked frantically. "What can I do, Johnny? Tell me, please, what can I do?"

"Nothin', Massa," the slave whispered hoarsely, barely able to swallow as the poison spread through every blood vessel in his body. "I's goin' to be with my Jesus, my blessed Savior now. He'll make sure I ain't got no more pain. And I's lookin' forward to that. There's been too much pain for too long, and I's ready for a rest."

Though he wished it could have been otherwise, cursing the timing, Fulkerson was not able to stop himself from crying while hating the fact that he was doing this in front of both Alfred and, worst of all, young Johnny.

"Isn't there any way to stop this?" he pleaded. "Some kind of remedy I can give you to counteract that—?"

The black man shook his head weakly.

"Too late, Massa, too late," he said. "I thanks you for caring. I thanks you for crying over this worthless piece of black flesh. Ain't never been no good to nobody, I ain't. Pick some cotton. Lift some bales of hay. Clean some outhouses. That's my life, Massa. That's all it's ever been. I don't give up much by dyin'."

"No, Johnny, please!" Fulkerson blurted out, the veins bulging on his forehead and neck. "That was how I made you feel. And that's what I did to Zack and his father and so many others like them and you. That is not how it's gonna be from now on, not at all. I can learn so much from Charity's father. You shouldn't—"

Johnny's expression had not the slightest trace of rancor in it, but instead gentleness, a peace that seemed wholly unfathomable coming as it did from a man who was dying of some unknown Caribbean poison.

"Not just you, Massa," he told Fulkerson. "Everybody done that . . . my kind's jus' their mules; we's sure good enough to carry their burden, oh, surely that. But when we don't do right, they kick us, they beat us, they force us to eat slop. No more of that for this black boy. No, sir! Jesus ain't got no whips in heaven."

Johnny's eyes rolled upward in their sockets, and he coughed up some dark green fluid, some of it splattering on Fulkerson's arm.

"Hoodoo Jack's gonna go after the others," Johnny gasped, surfacing again, and whispering in a rapidly failing voice. "He's gonna goad that whole bunch into leaving, Massa, by telling them to throw off their bondage and be free, be free, be free . . . and then he's gonna start takin' their eternal souls right on to damnation in hell forever and ever."

Johnny shuddered.

Fulkerson immediately wrapped his substantial arms around Johnny's muscular, once strong body, now drenched in sweat, and hugged him tightly.

"I am so sorry that I have done what I have to you and the others before now," he sobbed just short of hysterically, either forgetting that Alfred was still there or simply no longer caring. "I . . . I . . . made life nothing but the bleakest kind of hell for you, Rufus, and for dozens of other slaves over the years of my life on this plantation."

"Not hell, Massa," Johnny said less than a minute before death would sweep over him. "Hell's right outside with Hoodoo Jack . . . the Lawd done changed you . . . The Lawd's gonna give you strength . . . all that you need . . . I wish—"

He let out one desperate cry of pain.

"I wish I could be there . . . to see it," he managed to say. "He needs to be sent packin', that devil does."

Johnny smiled then, a deep-down smile that transformed his wrinkled, thick-boned, scarred face with its broad, chafed lips and those eyes of his, oddly ancient-looking in one so young of flesh and bone.

"Love every last one of 'em, Massa," he begged. "Show all them slaves out back that you really love 'em, not just sweet words to make 'em feel good . . . do this, Massa . . . and they will follow you anywhere . . . do whatever you want of 'em. Prove to every last one of 'em that you know Jesus, and they will stay without bellyachin' by your side for the rest of their lives."

~❧25❧~

"Badly wounded, *Hoodoo Jack and at least one of his followers never-theless seemed possessed of an astonishing ability to regenerate them-selves physically,*" Charity recalled, her gaze going from one member to another. "*Though very wobbly, the fact that they could walk at all was remarkable.*"

"Look at him!" Hoodoo Jack growled, pointing at poor Rufus's body sprawled on the dirt, his arms and legs stretched out almost in the position of someone who had been crucified, frozen in death, his eyes open.

Yet there was no hint of terror or pain on his face, rather a certain peace, which was curious under the circumstances.

That he should be this way had enraged the four intruders.

Encouraged by Hoodoo Jack, the two who had not been shot committed unmentionably grotesque and bloody acts against that lifeless body, but they could not change the peaceful expression on Rufus's face.

"He is hopeless!" Hoodoo Jack proclaimed. "We leave him now. Maybe predators will do our job for us."

The four villains headed in one direction, toward a single destination: Samuel Fulkerson's plantation. It would not take long at all for them to reach the boundaries of his property. Upon their arrival, they had been ordered by Hoodoo Jack to avoid the main residence and head straight for the slave quarters.

Not something new for him.

Hoodoo Jack had been practicing his occult road show for so long and with such success that there was very little variation from place to place.

He had one intent that evening: to take over more slaves, stealing them from Samuel Fulkerson and adding them to his private demonic army.

That purpose and one other: *To destroy those who had dared to oppose him* . . .

Inside the plantation house, Fulkerson and Alfred had wrapped a rug around Johnny's body and put it in one corner of the large living room, just below a moose head hanging from the wall.

Fulkerson glanced up at it and winced.

"He mustn't be left here after all," he spoke. "This spot makes poor Johnny look like just another trophy!"

"Only this time he isn't yours," Alfred said sarcastically, regretting his words and apologizing immediately.

Alfred could see that Fulkerson was on the verge of becoming ill, his face pale, his throat muscles constricting rapidly.

"Charity!" her father demanded. "Turn away!"

"I've seen somebody throw up before," she protested. "You must think I'm still a little child. I can endure a lot more than you think."

Startled by her outspokenness, a trait that she was to be increasingly noted for as the years passed, he and Fulkerson glanced at one another and, despite what had happened to Johnny and Rufus, they could not help but burst out laughing, in no way trivializing those tragic deaths but both desperately needing even a fleeting moment's relief, which Charity's brash outspokenness provided.

"Anytime you want to send this girl out for adoption," Fulkerson joked, "I would pay good money for her."

Realizing that he was kidding, Charity squealed in mock protest and pretended to cling tightly to her father's leg.

Those few moments were an oasis for the three of them, but the merry mood was gone soon enough as they heard a ghastly cry of pain outside.

"Where is your help?" Alfred asked.

"In their quarters," Fulkerson replied. "Where else would they be at this hour?"

"Can Charity hide somewhere . . . upstairs perhaps?" Alfred asked.

"In the attic. The entrance is concealed. Nobody could possibly find it. They would never know where to look."

"Would you take my daughter there?"

"Of course," Fulkerson said, beckoning Charity to follow him up the stairs. Another cry.

Fulkerson seemed to recognize even such a distorted voice.

"My slaves!" he spoke. "That Hoodoo Jack character and his zombies can only be after my slaves."

Fulkerson touched Charity's shoulder with such gentleness that Alfred could only watch in wonderment, given the brutal reputation of the man.

"But they shall never touch you, my dear," he spoke reassuringly, smiling at her. "They would have to go through your father and me first, and only then would they try and find out where I've gone and hidden you. You and your daddy and I are much too smart for any old bunch of crazy goblins!"

Nodding energetically, Charity kissed him on the cheek and waved goodbye to her father as Fulkerson hurried her up the curving flight of stairs.

Alfred heard the sound of a trap door being thrown open.

Make it quick, he prayed to himself, *but, Samuel, be careful with her.*

Two minutes later, Fulkerson came back down.

"Weapons . . ." Alfred said. "Where is your gun rack?"

"And knives! I have plenty of them, including some vicious-looking hunting knives. Jim Bowie himself gave them to me a number of years ago."

"Any bows and arrows?"

"Yes! I have three sets. What do you have in mind? Using all of them? The two of us could never handle that many weapons."

"When I was in Canada last year, working with some fur traders who wanted to set up a few outlets here in South Carolina, I was able to spend the better part of a day with one of the French-Canadian Indian tribes in the Quebec province. It turns out they have many interesting potions of their own."

He narrowed his eyes, remembering some details.

"Most of what I heard about or was actually shown were special mixtures concocted basically for the simplest medicinal purposes, such as purportedly curing colds or other lung ailments as well as a variety of tropical infections and a heart problem or two," Alfred continued, his heart beating faster as an idea took shape. "There were others that could be used as effective antidotes to save the lives of braves bitten by poisonous snakes or spiders while hunting game or after being surprised by a seven-foot-tall grizzly bear, which would hardly go down with a few untreated arrows in its hide."

"Are you piecing something together?" Fulkerson asked. "I have seen that expression on dogs about to give birth."

Alfred, scowling a bit, silenced the other man by waving his hand authoritatively through the air.

"Some of what those Indians had been storing away had yet another purpose, a totally opposite purpose, not curative at all but intended for use in killing or incapacitating any of their various enemies. They kept this supply in a special secret location for use in the event of hostilities with another tribe."

Alfred was grimacing.

"They produced horrible results, Samuel, most horrible! I learned of total paralysis, heart attacks or strokes, or often the most awful fits, with people foaming a brownish fluid from the mouth and losing control of their bodily functions."

"Get to the point, Alfred."

"Their weapons were poisons made of common ingredients that could be found, in some cases, in homes like this one."

Fulkerson's eyes widened in disbelief, and his mouth dropped open.

"You all but dismissed the fact that I have a good collection of rifles.

Quite amazingly, I find you more interested in my archery sets, hardly a modern weapon. What am I supposed to think? And now homemade poisons? Are you serious?" he asked, dumbfounded. "Besides, I honestly doubt that I have all the necessary ingredients. Anything that mind of yours could concoct surely would require a very odd mixture of different—"

Abruptly, Samuel Fulkerson stopped such chattering and closed his throbbing eyes for a moment.

"And yet . . . ," he mused as he rubbed his chin and recalled items in various locations in that house. Then he opened his eyes.

"Yet I just may," he announced triumphantly. "I just may have every last drop of whatever it is that you need, here or in either of the kitchens. We have pests just as you do, moles, rats, snakes, others. Because of that fact of life in this soggy region of our state, I have made it a point to keep on hand a supply of—"

Fulkerson clapped his hands together once and let out what was for him an out-of-character whoop.

"Praise God!" he exclaimed then added, with some embarrassment over that display showing in his expression, "The first time you and I truly get together, for a friendly meeting, and look at what is happening between us!"

Alfred nodded in agreement then told Fulkerson urgently, "Samuel, this is what I want you to do."

He outlined the plan that had taken shape in his mind with speed so remarkable he knew he could never claim credit for it.

"What do you think, Samuel?" Alfred asked after he was finished, not certain how the other man would respond but also aware that he was unable to do what he had in mind without some assistance.

Fulkerson, still nervous despite his outward bravado, admitted that the plan did make a fair bit of sense.

"A year ago, I most likely would have thrown my whole bunch of slaves to any pack of wolves that happened along and run straight for the nearest exit, seeking whatever safety I could find," he said, grimacing. "Now those wolves are right at my door, and I find myself about to risk my life for their ignorant black skins."

He bit his lower lip.

"I should not be saying that anymore," Fulkerson acknowledged ruefully. "These people are ignorant. Neither of us can, with any integrity, dispute that truth, but it is a situation that has happened entirely because numerous men like Samuel Fulkerson and Alfred Littlepage and others of our ilk scattered throughout our beloved South have kept millions of them entrapped by their own stupidity."

The man seemed in some anguish as he continued speaking.

"How can we continue depriving them of so much that should be theirs," he went on, "and then abruptly declare our dependence upon them for our lives in one situation or another, as though any of them would ever want to help their masters after the way we have treated them since we started kidnapping them? Have we become so hypocritical, even those who are the so-called Christians among us?"

"I have not kept my slaves ignorant, as you say," Alfred protested defensively. "I have made every effort to make sure that—"

"Neighbor, neighbor," Fulkerson interrupted, "if you asked any off-the-road stranger you happen to meet to determine, out of a single assembled group of ten slaves which are yours and which are mine by the way they speak, I would wager that this stranger's task would be but an impossible one."

Alfred wanted to say more, to refute what the other man had said, but he knew there was little time for any kind of debate, so he kept silent. The implications, however, were not to be easily discarded.

"Oh, yes, you can give any darkie some books containing a few simple stories for him to labor over, and you can teach his kind some semblance of rudimentary arithmetic and other skills perhaps," Fulkerson added. "But what results from all this is hardly what any of us would call an educated human being."

More cries outside . . .

He sucked in his breath.

"Poor Rufus," he whispered, "poor Johnny."

"Show me what you have," Alfred said urgently.

Fulkerson led him through the house to the back exit and across a short walkway to the main kitchen.

Just outside the entrance, he pointed to a small storage shed.

"Some of the ingredients you need are in there," he said as he handed Alfred the lantern. "Each is labeled clearly."

Alfred got what he needed from a dusty collection of old bottles, some of which contained yellowish liquid and others seemed as clear as water; he also gathered some small leather sachets of herbs and some jars of salve. Then he closed the heavy door of the shed.

The two of them hurried on into the kitchen, Fulkerson stopping in the doorway as he heard an eerie chanting sound nearby.

I have heard that before, he thought, his nerve ends vibrating. *I have heard it in the darkness of a Caribbean jungle as a night of evil began, and I ran to safety before they got me and buried me alive for their pleasure.*

Alfred's voice snapped him back to the present.

"Are you all right?" he asked. "We need to hurry."

"The battle has begun," Fulkerson announced, his voice sounding cryptic. "I know that sound . . . that chilling sound . . ."

The only thing missing from the horrifying scene was the drums; in the jungle their sound had filled the air relentlessly, nearly freezing his heart because he knew what they meant, a battle cry of sorts, Satan on the move amidst the tropical beauty of that isle . . .

"I was in Haiti last year," he recalled. "I heard it more than once, coming from the countryside, especially at just past midnight, when voodoo men usually came out in the open and terrorized anyone who opposed them."

"In Haiti? Why?" Alfred asked, startled.

"The slave market had temporarily dried up," Fulkerson told him, shrugging. "I had need of several new bucks at that particular time. I went to that pathetic country to tap what I believed was a reliable alternate source."

"But the normal avenues for slaves . . . what happened to those, Samuel?"

"Too many Atlantic storms during the earlier months had been interfering with the regular shipments that had been coming from Africa. In retrospect I am glad things turned out that way, frankly.

"What I did see there in that misbegotten country was so deplorable, so unhuman, that I suppose such sights formed the beginning of a soul-deep change in my outlook.

"Any man who was not under some kind of dark delusion himself would be appalled that other human beings, whatever their color was, could be treated the way those poor people were."

His face had turned pale.

"Someday, Alfred," Fulkerson told him, "I shall be obliged to fill you in on all those terrible details."

He lowered his voice, more than a touch of affection in it.

"Then that dear, dear woman, Violet, and your very special daughter came along, and I had a different tune in my life, a symphony replacing the clanging, ugly series of the most discordant sounds that had been nothing more than noise."

. . . a different tune in my life.

Alfred thought of how beautiful a description that was and how accurately Fulkerson had described the "noise" in his own life before this night.

Once inside the kitchen, Fulkerson pointed to two lacquered-wood cabinets, both attached to the wall on their left.

"The rest of what you probably require is stored in there," he indicated.

Hoping that despite his haste he had been able to recall all the ingredients mentioned to him by the chief of that Indian tribe, Alfred managed to take less than five minutes blending everything together, following the remembered steps as best as he could. Then, using a teaspoon, he dripped the thick, salve-like, milky-white substance with a slightly bitter odor into a tiny leather pouch he had retrieved from a corner of the shed.

In the meantime, Fulkerson had returned to the plantation house and had hurriedly gathered together a couple of freshly cleaned shotguns, a large Indian-made hunting bow, and half a dozen long, copper-tipped arrows.

"I understand what you have told me about this plan of yours," he insisted once Alfred had rejoined him in the front parlor. "And, yes, I acknowledge that it is a very good one, a bit of genius actually, I suspect, but, still, you have to be prepared for the possibility that it could fail, my friend, and in doing so, place us in the greatest danger. You must be aware of this, surely you must."

He held up the shotgun.

"In that case, nothing can replace this old-fashioned hardware, not even those poisoned arrows you have just concocted. Take one, my friend, and stick some rounds of ammunition in your pocket."

His manner was as demanding as his words.

"I trust that we are in agreement here?" Fulkerson added sternly. "Or, as the Italians say, *capeice?*"

Alfred agreed with that.

"Correct, Samuel. We have gone beyond the argument stage, you and I," he said. "Now, give me to the count of thirty . . . and then come outside, ready for whatever might be happening." Adrenaline started to flow as he quickly visualized what could happen during the next several minutes.

Fulkerson patted him on the back and remarked, "May God be with your every step—and with mine, too, neighbor."

And so it was that an armed Alfred Littlepage headed outside just before midnight, ironically just a few nights before Halloween, praying that Charity would still have a father to take her away from that hideaway long before morning light.

❧ 26 ❧

Hoodoo Jack and his three men were standing before Samuel Fulkerson's gathered group of slaves.

Despite being almost comically disheveled, that commanding quartet was still able to project the coldest, darkest sort of menace.

Though outnumbering the intruders by more than five times their number, these men, women, and children standing tightly against one another in front of their simple living quarters nevertheless showed that stark fear was still an effective weapon that could be used to force them into submission, whether the one wielding it was black or white, especially after so many years of learned behavior under the rule of their master.

They were on the edge of outright, uncontrolled panic as the tall, thin, strangely dressed and grim-looking devil glowered demonically at them, waving his long-nailed hands around in a manner that bordered on the hypnotic.

He had learned well what the occult masters in Haiti had taught him, learned well the secret of voodoo and its so-called powers, the power to entrance and control. More than any physical attack, he knew that gaining access to the mind of an adversary could convert that individual into a follower who would be chained to his every instruction.

"I am a master," Hoodoo Jack shouted at the cringing slaves, enjoying their fear as a kind of elixir that he let wash over himself, "a master of hodun, hoodoo. You are not wrong to cower before me."

His power over them made him very much like a sinister puppeteer, pulling mystical strings that controlled human beings instead of toy figures.

"None of you can possibly stand against me," he went on. "Bon Dieu gave his loa to me. You cannot know how important that is. Do you not understand that I am a houngan? Your very souls are in these hands of mine."

Hoodoo Jack held out his hands, palms up, the skin covered with scars. He threw his head back and let out a screech as his mind filled with the numbingly repetitive sounds of music from old Haiti, drums pounding and bodies swaying, voices chanting amid the odor of fire and incense.

"I command the gods of the abyss to—" he started to say.

That was the moment Samuel Fulkerson picked to show himself after frustrating moments of waiting, watching Hoodoo Jack begin to work his magic.

Their master's sudden appearance greatly startled the slaves as well as the four strangers.

"No!" Fulkerson demanded in a scream. "This evil will stop immediately! I will not allow it to continue!"

Carrying his heavy shotgun, Fulkerson strode quickly in front of his slaves and stood between them and the four strangers.

"You are not going to invoke any demons on my property!" he declared. "Nor will I let you remain here as the trespassers that you are. Surely you know that you have set foot on this private plantation illegally."

Pointedly tapping the shotgun with a couple of fingers, he added, "And now you must leave, stranger."

Hoodoo Jack's eyes were bulging grotesquely. "I find that amusing," he laughed. "I find that more amusing than you could ever imagine."

He snapped his head up then stared directly at Fulkerson.

"By property, are you referring to this land?" he asked, a slithering hiss in his voice. "Or that house perhaps?"

Hoodoo Jack pointed at the slaves.

"Or do you mean these poor souls who have been treated like brute beasts for so long according to your every whim?"

Fulkerson was taken aback but got his nerves together again quickly enough. Without saying anything in response, he slowly raised his shotgun and aimed it at the stranger, who simply laughed and pointed a bony, pale-brown finger at him.

"No answer, I see," Hoodoo Jack snarled. "You have no answer, despite all that aristocratic book-learning."

He sniffed the air.

"I smell the certainty of victory this night," he said, "real victory, and that's because I speak only the truth, and that is why you have no answer. All of you slave-owners act the same way, think the same way.

"Niggers are just mindless cattle to you, no better, no worse. When they cannot be of use to wait on you any longer, you toss them aside like so much garbage!"

Sweating over every inch of his body, Fulkerson lowered the shotgun, his muscles tensing even more. He gulped a couple of times, overwhelmed.

Niggers are mindless cattle to you . . . when they cannot be of use any longer, you toss them aside like so much garbage!

Fulkerson wanted to offer a strong denunciation of that statement as he saw his slaves looking at one another and then at him, but he could not.

Beads of perspiration were slipping down his forehead and stinging his eyes even at that time of night. He knew he had to say something, that any continued silence on his part would condemn him in the eyes of his slaves and hand Hoodoo Jack a victory he must never be given.

Help me to sound convincing, Fulkerson prayed. *Let me know that what once was true, for me at least, has been buried forever.*

His new feelings for the slaves made losing any of them seem tragic now—and for other than just the old financial reasons.

"It used to be that way," he said. "Six months ago, you would have been describing the situation here; yes, I know that. But no longer!"

"Oh, you have changed, have you?" Hoodoo Jack persisted. "You are now kindness and generosity brought to life? Is that what you want me and my friends and those captives to believe?"

"I am trying," Fulkerson admitted. "I have confessed my sins to God and to these folk, and I have been forgiven by Him and by them."

Hoodoo Jack's blood-red lips were pulled back into a loathsome snarl that revealed his uneven teeth, the middle two so black with decay that it was a wonder they had not dropped out, leaving only the diseased gums.

"And what has brought about this transformation?" he demanded. "It must have been a giant tongue of flame from heaven or a whirlwind that grabbed you and spun you around, surely?"

"A child—no, that is wrong, a young woman in nearly every respect," Fulkerson interrupted. "A dear young woman led me. She opened my eyes, her simple sweetness as yet unspoiled, like a child's."

For a moment, Hoodoo Jack said nothing.

Fulkerson's attention shifted to one of the three men standing behind their leader.

The tallest had streams and splotches of dried blood over most of his muscular chest, and there was what appeared to be a small hole just below his right shoulder, a ragged edge of inflamed flesh around it. Then he noticed the bloodstains on the sleeve of Hoodoo Jack's tattered coat.

Rufus . . . Didn't he shoot two of them? he asked himself, recalling what details Johnny had been able to provide. *But how could they be here now, standing straight and strong-looking . . . ?*

He was too transparent in his amazement.

"We four here have amazing powers of recuperation," Hoodoo Jack said, noticing what had caught Fulkerson's attention. "Nothing can keep any of us down for very long. We rise and walk."

The biblical analogy was not lost on Fulkerson. As Hoodoo Jack stepped forward, Fulkerson retreated a foot or two.

The intruder stopped then, his expression changing.

"I mean no harm now," Hoodoo Jack said, his voice softer, a seeming kindness supplanting his anger. "I want only to help and to beg your forgiveness for being too harsh in my judgment."

He was a bare few inches away now and slowly reached out to touch Fulkerson's cheek.

"You are white only on the surface," he declared in a monotone, his malevolence even more chilling as the play-acting of a moment ago ended. "Underneath you look just like us, with the same red blood that flows just as freely."

Without warning, Hoodoo Jack ripped a long nail across Samuel Fulkerson's smooth skin.

The slaves gasped collectively as they watched this happening.

"Lies that are spun in the service of the master cannot be called venal," Hoodoo Jack pronounced, grinning broadly. Then he glanced contemptuously around at the frightened adults and children only a foot or two away.

"This tyrant, this master of your lives, is but mortal flesh!" he bellowed. "I drew blood from him just as easily as with any of you. It is red like yours, it flows just as freely. There is no difference between master and slave."

Hoodoo Jack strode over to one of the women and slashed another sharp nail across her neck, which she gripped in pain as she fell to the ground. This proved too much for several of the younger men, who advanced angrily toward him.

"Touch me now, any of you, and I take you all to the pit of hell this night!" Hoodoo Jack shouted, waving his hands in front of him as though he were in the process of casting a spell over them.

The young men stopped, seemingly transfixed. Then a woman started to pray, then another, some children joining them and several of the men, one after the other.

"You shall not do that!" Hoodoo Jack commanded them, seeming unnerved. "I shall kill you right now if you persist. The use of that name will not be tolerated this night! Stop immediately!"

Despite the dizziness that had grabbed him and had not yet let go, Fulkerson never dropped the heavy, cumbersome shotgun but was able to bring it up swiftly and whip the barrel across the stranger's head.

Caught off guard, Hoodoo Jack staggered sideways, stunned by the blow, suddenly yelling in pain.

The huddled slaves were still terrified, and yet, despite themselves, they let out a murmur that sounded more like a cheer.

Fulkerson glanced at them and smiled, nearly forgetting the condition of his cheek and the blood trickling down his neck. On the ground, Hoodoo

Jack rubbed his head, shaking it from side to side, then he stood up in pseudo-military fashion and spoke sarcastically: "Is that the best you can do, brave Mr. Slaveman? Does it not surprise you that a nigger has not started begging you to stop about now, that a nigger has taken your best blow and yet not dropped to his feet before you, proclaiming you as his massa?"

He raised his arm and pointed directly at Fulkerson.

"Now I have a go at *you!*" he announced before getting ready to spring forward like a cougar after its prey.

A sound.

One that did not seem unfamiliar to Hoodoo Jack. He turned in the direction of it, his eyes widening.

An arrow!

In a split-second, it caught him in the right shoulder, the arrow tip poking through his back.

"No!" Hoodoo Jack screamed, not so much as a word but rather as a cry of rage and burning agony, an agony that started where the tip entered and quickly spread down his side and into the rest of his body.

Alfred Littlepage came out from behind a nearby tree, leaving behind the shadows cast by moonlight.

"I believe it is stronger than what you have been using," he announced confidently. "I found some poisons that are home-grown here and available nowhere else in the world, and I mixed them in for good measure. You should be dead in less than a minute—a minute more of life than you deserve."

Mouth opening, closing, opening, closing, but no sounds coming from him, Hoodoo Jack had fallen to his knees.

With a single motion, he pulled the arrow out—and part of his shoulder with it—holding the weapon before him and shaking it arrogantly at Alfred as spittle began to drip over his lips and down his chin.

"Even this will not stop me!" he declared as he struggled to stand but fell forward instead and was still.

Alfred stepped up to his body and nudged it cautiously.

Motionless. There was no response.

"This madness is over," Alfred, celebrating, told everyone. "And it will never disturb any of you—"

He was interrupted by someone gasping, one of the women, then someone else, another, and another.

No one moved, not the slaves, not Hoodoo Jack's followers, nor Alfred Littlepage or Samuel Fulkerson.

They watched as Hoodoo Jack's body, which had remained immobile for only a second or two, moved again, slowly, agonizingly, hands grabbing for Alfred's leg but missing as he stepped back in shock. Then Hoodoo Jack's long arms pushed against the ground, lifting him one inch, then another.

Alfred reached for another arrow, raised the bow, and aimed it at the stranger. And Fulkerson, with renewed strength, pointed the shotgun.

Hoodoo Jack glanced from one to the other.

"Can you not realize from what your eyes have shown you that nothing can stop me? Nothing can stop me tonight or tomorrow, not anytime!" he boasted. "Do you not know that I have been to other plantations this year and the year before and the year before that, in Tennessee and North Carolina and Georgia, and have caused other slaves to rebel against their masters.

"My mission! That is my mission right now, as it has always been, to break the backbone of the South by robbing your kind of the cheap labor that is so central to the way of life you have been living for generations."

There was no emotion showing as Hoodoo Jack spoke, his mouth with its thin, red lips barely moving, his gaze fixed.

. . . by robbing it of the cheap labor that is so central to the way of life you have been living for generations.

Something odd happened in Alfred's brain when he heard those words, so carefully spoken, so well-crafted, so—

Rehearsed . . . well-rehearsed.

It cannot be, Alfred told himself, an explanation surfacing that he could not allow himself to accept, nor even contemplate seriously. *Surely what I am thinking cannot be! No mere man could be so evil!*

What Hoodoo Jack had said just then sounded inexplicably familiar. And the way he said those words, seemingly by rote, as though they had been taught to him, repeated countless times until they could not be forgotten.

"Daddy!" His daughter's voice called out to Alfred.

Alfred spun, saw Charity running toward him.

"Go back!" he shouted at her. "You mustn't see this. You—"

She stopped, cocking her head, looking at Hoodoo Jack curiously.

"Jesus loves you," she said in as loud a voice as she could. "Don't look so mean. Talk to Jesus, mister. He'll help you. Isn't that right, Daddy?"

Hoodoo Jack moved with such unexpected speed that no one had time to react. He knocked Alfred nearly off his feet in the process. Grabbing Charity, he took her lithe young woman's form upward, his fingers pressed tightly around her neck so that she could say nothing else or even swallow.

She looked instinctively toward her father as she struggled, but Hoodoo Jack would not release her.

"I am dying," he told them. "You did your work well. But I will not die right away. I have partial immunity from poisons deliberately shot into my body to give me that immunity. I can be completely protected only against that which I know about. Where did you get your knowledge, white man?"

"From Indians near Quebec . . . ," Alfred muttered, waiting for an opportunity to rush him but desperately concerned about Charity being injured or worse.

"Too bad for you that it is not quick enough to save your white hide," Hoodoo Jack was saying. "I hold your future in my hands. The child you love could die in an instant, and you would be destroyed along with her."

No one noticed the figure walking quickly toward them, a tall man with exceptionally broad shoulders and the stance of someone accustomed to taking command of everyone around him.

John Covington Marmaduke.

"Your power this midnight is ended!" he declared with greater solemnity than anyone had ever before seen from the man.

Hoodoo Jack, still holding Charity, turned away from Alfred and Fulkerson and confronted Marmaduke.

"I know you," he said. "I know your kind."

"And how is that?"

"You take the so-called Holy Bible and twist it to justify keeping my people in chains, controlling their lives."

"Yes, I have done that."

Marmaduke's face showed the shame he felt. His arrogance was gone, only the truth about himself apparent.

"I am naked before you all now," the minister told not only the bizarre stranger but everyone else there.

Hoodoo Jack blinked, prepared for a rebuttal not an admission. "Black children have been perishing at the hands of white men," he continued, his voice not as certain as his words. "Should not a white child die in a black man's fatal embrace? Can I not use that precious Bible of yours to justify this, as you have done against my kind? An eye for an eye? A child's life for a child's life?"

Hoodoo Jack seemed to be tightening his hold on Charity's neck. She squirmed and whimpered in pain.

Alfred was preparing to lunge, whatever the consequences. Marmaduke saw this and shouted, "No, Alfred, no! You must not! This devil would snap her sweet, sweet neck in an instant! There is another way!"

"But what?" Alfred shot back. "I must—"

"Dear man, you must not! Please, please, listen to me, my brother; listen to me for the first time in your life . . . because for the first time in my life, I may have something that is worthwhile to say!"

Alfred hesitated, hearing Marmaduke but also the painful sounds his daughter was making.

Marmaduke walked closer to Hoodoo Jack. As he passed by the three other men, one of them reached out and grabbed him, but he broke loose.

"You have no power over me, demon!" Marmaduke shouted as he faced the three of them who were now backing away from him. "I claim the blood of Jesus Christ and the protection it offers this night!"

Now he approached Hoodoo Jack.

"Release that innocent one you hold," Marmaduke demanded. "You have no claim whatever on Charity."

"I learned a hard lesson when I was a child myself, that no one with white skin is truly innocent, preacher man."

"You are evil?"

"Yes, I am evil. Good failed me a long time ago."

"Are all black people evil?"

"No, but they need to be. For being good, being obedient, being what they have been has gotten them nothing but grief!"

"Are these dear people evil?"

"They are not yet evil."

Marmaduke turned to the two dozen slaves.

"On your knees!" he ordered.

All of them obeyed without hesitation.

"Even now, you make demands of us!" Hoodoo Jack rebuked him. "Even now, what you are breaks through all that meaningless pretense, rips that preacher's facade right off your cold-blood hide and—"

Marmaduke was clearly being stirred out of a long slump after those weeks that he could not be found, his old fire renewed.

"God Almighty Himself makes demands of all of us, white and black alike!" he interrupted. "You have forgotten that, or ignored it for much of your life, I suspect. But this night—mark it well, you devil from hell—for this night, I and they remember the most precious eternal truth. We remember it well, accept it totally, and cast our very souls at His blessed feet because of it."

Hoodoo Jack's cheeks started twitching. Abruptly he grabbed Charity's neck and swung her out in front of him.

"Father!" she cried. "Daddy—!"

"I shall gladly cast this horrid soul of mine into hell's fiery corridors, lined with living walls of doomed niggers like myself!" Hoodoo Jack suddenly blurted out. "And I take this child with me to the very gates!"

Hoodoo Jack turned toward Marmaduke and with something of a plaintive tone in his voice said, "The burden of her death is laid at your feet. Can you not see this, preacher man? I would have taken her with me as a hostage. She could have survived. She . . . she could have been introduced to a whole new way of life."

"Life or damnation?" Marmaduke shot back. "Do you not see the difference, whoever you are? Is life amidst the red-hot rubble of hell the kind of life you crave for dear innocents like Charity? Have you no corner of compassion left in you?"

Hoodoo Jack hesitated, listening to some distinct siren call in his mind, perhaps something from the past, a portion of memory long discarded but now returning to his consciousness.

"I once—" he started to speak, his voice not much above a whisper. "I once—"

But he could not continue. The evil within him was too strong for whatever that fragment was, and he started to shake Charity. An instant later, he abruptly flinched and let go of her.

Hoodoo Jack stumbled forward, first in the direction of his men, but they backed away, and then toward the slaves.

"I just want you to be free . . . ," he said, his words slurred as he stretched out both hands toward them. "Why is that so wrong in your eyes? Why have you greeted me with such hostility?"

One of the women, Fulkerson's cook, spat in his face.

Her enormous bosom shook like chocolate pudding as she told him, "Being damned is not being free. Why can't you understand that, whoever and whatever you are? We's got no chains now. They's gone! Our massa is different today from what he was. That little girl you tried to kill was used by the Lawd to change him.

"But even if them chains was a-hangin' from us right now, they wouldn't be on anyone here forever. You forget that, Mr. Jack. As soon as the Lawd calls us home, we is goin' right to be with Him. We'll walk those golden streets by His side. But where is you goin'? Where there is no more pain or where there is only pain?"

His eyes widened as she pulled a long carving knife from behind the apron she was wearing.

"I hid this months ago in my shack yonder," this very large woman spoke sadly. "I was going to kill myself, cut my own throat maybe or my wrists or somethin' like that while hopin' that I wasn't sinnin' beyond redemption. But that was before Jesus entered this plantation through that child yonder."

She glanced briefly at Charity.

"She's gonna live," the woman proclaimed, "and she's goin' to mean somethin' in this world, more than you and me and the rest of us here. She has white skin, but that don't matter 'cause the Lawd's inside that girl."

Closing her eyes, she asked Charity's father, "Massa, don't let those darlin' eyes see this. Don't let those pure eyes see what I's 'bout to do."

As a prominent landowner, someone who, though unable to control the outcome of any legal action in that county or anywhere else throughout the state, could nevertheless greatly influence what happened, Alfred Littlepage realized that he had every right—even an obligation—to object to what was going on, to try and stop it by demanding that Hoodoo Jack be held for trial, along with his three lackeys.

That would be better, he reasoned to himself. *We would be using the law, not violating it by an act of murder.*

But the slave woman would not allow him to convince her that the legal alternative was the right one.

"This creature will never make it to a jury," she spoke wisely, seemingly reading his thoughts. "Or maybe some smart-ass Yankee lawyer'll get him off somehow and he'd go free to cause some devilment in other places."

She saw Charity look away, burying her head in her father's chest as he held her trembling body in his arms.

"No more," Alfred said resignedly. "Let me take this child back into the house before you do anything."

The woman nodded, waiting until the two of them were heading toward the house, with Fulkerson behind him. Marmaduke did not move at first, trying to decide whether to try and stop the woman or let her do what she surely intended. Finally, grunting, he turned and followed the others.

"Now . . . ," she said, seeming to gloat a bit as she examined the long, shiny blade of her deadly knife.

"You fool!" Hoodoo Jack gasped in terror as he painfully reached above his head and tried to peel her strong fingers from the handle, but she would not let him get away with this.

"Shake hands with the devil!" she yelled at the man as she plunged the blade into his chest just once.

Hoodoo Jack fell backward. He should have been dead that instant, as tortured as his body had been, but he managed to hang on a little longer, kicking and snarling as some new pain grabbed his nerve ends.

Finally, too impatient to wait for his death, one of the men walked to within a couple of feet of his convulsing body and said, "You have only hate in your dark soul while we know love now, love from the folks you want to destroy."

"I was born in Haiti," he said. "My name's Crispus. I know about you. Everybody there does. Why's you here, railing against whites?"

"I know not what you talk about," Hoodoo Jack replied so weakly that only the other man could hear him.

"You must have changed a lot then," Crispus accused him. "Word was that you were a spy for the richest slavers, goin' from place to place and lookin' for strong bucks like me to buy. I hear that you once turned in some members of your own family because you needed the money."

Hoodoo Jack was silent, death nearly taking him.

"You's here, doin' what you doin' for some reason," Crispus spoke, "but I's not knowin' what it could be just now. I jus' thinkin' that you is a liar, Hoodoo Jack, and a phony, and your soul's goin' right to hell this night."

The prostrate intruder coughed up some blood then grabbed his stomach as pain raced through it.

"You destroyed yourself, Jack," Crispus said, standing over him now. "You let that evil of yours eat you up, and that's why you dyin'. That woman provide the means for somethin' that's been long overdue."

Abruptly, Hoodoo Jack's jaw started moving slowly, then his lips opened just a little, the words coming out in an uneven and anguished flow that was almost unintelligible.

"You . . . have become the same . . . as the white trash are . . . but too . . . ignorant . . . to . . . realize it," he gasped, so close to death yet still not dead. "You sound like . . . one of . . . their turncoat puppets. Where is that love of yours now toward one who is black like yourself? Isn't love . . . supposed to bring with it . . . forgiveness?"

Not much time was remaining for Hoodoo Jack, but he used it to speak out with special contempt.

"You forgive those . . . who have always beaten you . . . and denied you even the proper, nourishing food you need. They send you to bed hungry sometimes . . . and those clothes you wear, just cheap stuff, not much better than rags . . . yet you stand over me . . . rejoicing as you watch me dying and seem happy in it. Your massa here gets all that love . . . and you deny . . . even a tiny crumb . . . to a poor, misbegotten coon who is just standing up . . . just standing up . . . for the rights of our people?"

Crispus snorted as he replied, "It's got nothin' to do with any of that. We's rejectin' *you*. We's turnin' our backs on what you stand for 'cause you's hating those we all now love, and you's tryin' to destroy them."

Hoodoo Jack started to object with whatever strength he had left, but Crispus interrupted him. "Hold on there! It's more than just hate, I's thinkin'. I mean, the way you act and all, the awful things you think, the hell-fire blazin' in those eyes of yours. You got a worse problem than any of us; that much is clear."

Even the other slaves were amazed at what Crispus was saying. "But I can't figure it all out," he went on without catching his breath. "I ain't able to put any of the pieces I see and hear together 'cause I don't got the kind of learnin' you must have, or the mind, I guess. I's sure smart enough to know that you is crazy but too dumb to find out what caused that burr you got under your saddle."

He frowned, aware that he had stumbled suddenly upon some special nugget of truth, but knowing that there was probably much more left.

"How you managed that fancy kind of talk and those educated ways of yours is somethin' you ain't told nobody here," Crispus added. "But none of that's important no more, Jack . . . or whoever you really is."

He pointed toward the plantation house behind him, a large dark shape outlined by moonlight, dominating that spot in more ways than one.

"You want to destroy them, even that sweet child!" he exclaimed, his anger making the veins stand out on his forehead and his neck.

Bending down over Hoodoo Jack, Crispus added, spitting the words out, "That makes you our enemy, not those white people! Them's tryin' to be good folk. Them's done their real best these past months. I'm telling you, Jack.

"We don't need the likes of you filling our minds with garbage that's not fit for pigs. We's freer than you 'cause we ain't chained to hate that's so strong it might as well be a jail cell with bars keepin' you in. You understand me, Jack? You understand what I's sayin'?"

But by then he was speaking to a dead man.

~❧27❧~

MARMADUKE INSISTED UPON taking Alfred and Charity back home, though Fulkerson urged him to spend the night at his plantation house. "You should rest, John," he said. "Stay here overnight, will you, good sir? I see no reason why we cannot talk about matters of faith in the morning when you are refreshed."

The minister was quite unprepared for that.

"I had heard that you were changing," he acknowledged. "I never did know until now how completely."

"You and I both are evidence of the redemptive power of faith."

Charity dozed peacefully on one of the couches in Fulkerson's parlor, unperturbed by any of their talking, her head resting on her father's lap.

"I suppose you could say that God used that child in a wonderful way," Fulkerson explained, pointing to her quiet form. "It had been going on for some time, her growing influence on me. Nobody but that little girl and a couple of my slaves knew.

"That was the way I wanted it at the beginning. Now, sometimes I feel as though I want to tell about what happened to me to everyone on earth. Is that not a truly strange thing for a man such as myself? And now I have learned that I am not alone, that your dear one has worked her magic on someone else."

Marmaduke spoke up about Violet. "You mustn't forget that dear old woman. She and that child both changed our lives forever, Samuel. No one could have predicted any of this. I would have said anyone who did was ready for confinement to some asylum up north."

"Will you be my guest then?" Fulkerson asked, wanting very much for the minister to accept his offer.

"I would like to take you up on that another day for certain," Marmaduke replied, "and quite soon, my friend. But this night I have need to spend a bit more time with Alfred. Will that be all right with you? You are not offended, I trust."

Fulkerson's manner changed altogether.

"Fine, but I really do think that I am a better host," he said with a telltale air of his old trademark arrogance.

He had spoken with such a convincing deadpan look that both Alfred and Marmaduke took him seriously, their disappointment with the "new" Samuel Fulkerson showing unmistakably on their own faces.

And then, suddenly, Fulkerson burst out laughing, riotously so.

"Forgive such humor, please," he told them when he had calmed down. "After what has just happened, I am hoping that you both will allow me this one harmless little moment of levity, however inappropriate."

His face was showing the strain. "It is my own peculiar way of somehow dealing with the tension of this night. Even so, shortly, when I go to bed upstairs, I know that I shall be unbearably restless despite my best efforts to calm down."

Alfred was sympathetic.

"By the time I have been able to explain everything to my dear Elizabeth," he said without sarcasm, "and by the time she in turn has finished expressing, shall we say, her profound relief over my survival, I shall be far too exhausted, I daresay, to get much rest myself, though I just may collapse into unconsciousness rather than sleep."

He gently eased his legs from beneath Charity's head then stood and lifted her into his arms. She stirred but did not awaken as Fulkerson walked them out the front door.

"Could anything that Hoodoo Jack said cause trouble, I wonder," he mused, "when my slaves think over some portion of it and realize that that creature was actually telling them at least some few truths?"

He looked intently at Alfred and Marmaduke, ashamed that he was bothering with such concerns and yet aware that they were not altogether invalid.

"I do worry now about that, you know," Fulkerson admitted. "It is a good thing none of your own slaves were around, Alfred. I would hate to see any ravings from that man affect the way they behave toward you."

"Or it may bring your people closer to you," Alfred countered. "That just may happen, you know, when they compare you with that mad man. Crispus was already at the beginning of that process; that's what I think."

"That would be wonderful, friend," Fulkerson replied. "I could not ask for a better outcome."

He bade them good night as they settled themselves into Marmaduke's carriage. Marmaduke sat on the front seat beside his driver, a trusted slave named Henry, and Alfred gently lay Charity on the backseat then eased in beside her. When they arrived at the Littlepage plantation, they were greeted by a large group of people, with Elizabeth in the center of the crowd.

Alfred recognized everyone there, principally the families of landowners from miles around, together with groups of their slaves. Virtually everyone was armed. Word of their confrontation with Hoodoo Jack had quickly and mysteriously spread throughout the countryside.

Elizabeth ran up to her husband as he stepped down from the carriage.

He handed the still-sleeping Charity to Little Isaiah, who immediately headed toward the plantation house.

"What happened?" Elizabeth asked as she kissed him with a passion that was surprising in view of the onlookers and southern propriety about such matters. "Is Charity all right? Are you?"

He nodded and said, "It is a very long story."

"I shall tell it all if you like but not this very moment," Marmaduke spoke up, enjoying the attention of that gathering. "You two should go inside without delay and comfort one another. I must go on home to bed and rest since I am older than any of you."

"But you did want to talk with me about something," Alfred reminded him, though very tired and anxious to be inside his home with his wife.

"That can surely be taken up later. Like Samuel, you see, I have no one who has waited up anxiously for me to return. Go with her, my friend. We will get together in the morning; you can be quite sure of that."

Alfred thanked him for his help. "That encounter at Samuel's place could have turned out very differently if you had not arrived when you did," he said. "I might not be here now. And Charity could have died, John, or . . . or . . . I mean . . ."

Momentarily forgetting about words, Alfred hugged the big man. Marmaduke, nonplused, tried to minimize Alfred's expressions of gratitude.

"It had nothing to do with me, friend," the minister remarked modestly after Alfred had stepped back. "I was driven purely by a very distinct leading of the precious Holy Spirit. Without Him, I would have no idea, none at all, where any courage might ever have come from. I certainly had little or none of my own."

To make matters worse, as far as Marmaduke was concerned, Elizabeth now approached him, and took her turn at putting her unusually short, thin arms as much around him as his substantial girth would allow.

He desperately hoped no one would notice that he had started to blush.

"I have no idea what happened," she admitted, "but if my husband hints that you helped to save his life as well as Charity's, then that is all I need to know right now."

There was some sustained grumbling from the crowd about filling them in on what had occurred earlier.

"Go back to your own homes, people!" Marmaduke insisted but with appreciation, not impatience, in his voice. "I love you all, but I am terribly tired. You will learn everything during the next worship service. I promise to leave nothing out."

As he got back into his carriage, he told Alfred, "Henry here has been patiently waiting for me; it's time for both of us to get on home."

A MOMENT LATER, Marmaduke and Henry disappeared down the road, while most of those in the crowd drifted on back to their own homes.

After Alfred had said good-bye to Marmaduke, he and Elizabeth went inside. Little Isaiah was just coming down from Charity's room.

"She woke up and seemed so startled," he told them. "I did the best I could to calm her by humming a little tune to her, one I remember from my own younger years. Mama sang it to me whenever I was afraid. Miss Charity is nearly a grown woman now, but still, it worked, and she's real peaceful now."

"Bless you," Elizabeth told him. "Bless you, friend."

The black man started to go out the back door and go back to the slave quarters but turned and said, "She was mumblin' somethin' about Hoodoo Jack. I's been hearing stories about him for a long time. Bad soul, that one! Is he really dead now?"

Alfred assured him that he was.

"Praise God!" Little Isaiah exclaimed. "He's been behind a whole lot of bad stuff, hurtin' some good people."

"I had never heard the name before," Alfred said, frowning a bit. "How could that be? I am hardly ill-informed about most important matters."

"There are secrets sometimes, Massa." Little Isaiah sounded unusually cryptic.

If Alfred had not been so tired, he would have pressed the matter more vigorously. Instead, he shrugged, thanked the other man, and said good night.

But as he and Elizabeth started up the stairs, Little Isaiah called to him, "Massa?"

Obviously he felt the need to say something more about the intruder and sensed that his strange manner was perplexing.

"Yes?" Alfred replied.

"None of us here wanted to worry you about anything like that. We even thought, once, that maybe Hoodoo Jack wasn't real after all . . . too many stories comin' from too many places. We couldn't believe 'em all!"

"Any idea who was behind what he did?" Alfred asked. "He had to have money from somewhere. The Yankees . . . was it the Yankees?"

Little Isaiah nodded.

"That's just what I hear, Massa. And someone else, too."

"Who could that be?" Alfred asked curiously, unable even to guess who it might be.

"Satan himself, Massa. Satan himself."

Alfred had no trouble believing that.

"It's a good thing Hoodoo Jack ain't 'round no more," Little Isaiah added with apparent relief. "Now I's best be goin'. You and Mistress 'Lizabeth need to rest this night."

"You sleep well also, dear friend," Alfred said.

Little Isaiah waved to him and went outside.

Elizabeth and Alfred looked in on their daughter, saw that she was sleeping, and then prepared for bed.

A short while later, they fell asleep in one another's arms, too tired for anything else.

~ 28 ~

ALFRED COULD NOT stay in bed any later than usual, nor could Elizabeth. All that had transpired during the past twenty-four hours continued to saturate their emotions, making them more than typically restless.

After getting up, washing, and dressing, they decided to take a long walk on the grounds before breakfast.

"The morning air almost always helps," Alfred remarked.

A white, cotton-like mist was clinging to the scene, making the gray strands of Spanish moss hanging from the trees seem a bit ethereal, shifting slightly as breezes sighed through each strand.

Elizabeth observed, "This is a very special world, yours and mine and our daughter's. We have known little else. Out there is yet another. Despite being separated from it, as we are here, we hear things, you and I; we somehow hear imagined rumblings from somewhere in the distance, barely perceptible, the sound of rifle fire, the smell of burning wood and hay. How about you?"

"I know what you mean," he assured her, "and it has nothing to do with dreams. We are well-educated. We read whatever we can get our hands on. We listen to intelligent conversation. And I travel a great deal. I pick up various insights on the road.

"You and I are the kind of people who will try and put this or that piece of information or supposition together, whatever we have learned, rather than let seemingly random bits and pieces of information float aimlessly around like so much flotsam, unconnected, in our minds."

He shook his head.

"We analyze, we sift, we engage in responsible conjecture; that's the kind of people we have always been, Elizabeth. We understand the value of discernment, and at the end of it all, neither of us likes what we are seeing."

"If only the people who want to destroy our way of life would stay up north where they belong," she said. "We never bother them. They should leave us alone."

"Human rights, dearest. They will ride this issue until there is nothing left but war. And they will not hesitate to devastate this land of ours."

. . they will not hesitate to devastate this land of ours.

Such gloomy thoughts were interrupted when Elizabeth said suddenly, "Look at that! Will you look at that?"

She was pointing to a carriage and horses.

"It looks like Marmaduke's, doesn't it?" Alfred told her as he also noticed it, anticipating her own observation.

"Still here!" she exclaimed. "He never left when we thought he did. Where could he have spent those hours?"

Just then, Hester was coming out of the slave quarters holding in his left hand some clothes that looked familiar.

"What do you have there?" Alfred asked pleasantly.

"The good reverend's things," Hester replied matter-of-factly. "He asked to borrow some of the clothes you gave us."

"Where is he now?"

"Out back last I saw, sittin' by the stream, readin' his Bible. I was just 'bout to hang these up to dry."

"What happened? Can you tell me?"

"Sure 'nough, Massa. After you went back in and ever'body was left, he unhitched his horses and left his carriage here."

"He's been with you all since then?"

"Yessir, he has."

"Asleep in one of your beds?"

"Right after we's done finished talkin' a blue streak, yessir!"

"Talking? About what?"

"Different kinds of things, like how much he needed to learn 'bout all God's folk, not just the white kind."

Elizabeth and Alfred could hardly believe what Hester was telling them.

"Why don't you go 'round and talk to him?" he added casually. "He won't mind at all, I'm supposin'."

"We might embarrass him. He could want all this to be a secret."

"Not likely, Massa. He's writin' some kind of sermon right now . . . plans to preach it this Sunday and says he wants all of us there."

"Alfred, you go," Elizabeth said. "I'll tell Savilla we have a guest for breakfast."

He thanked Hester then walked around the side of the slave quarters to where a tiny, clear stream cut diagonally across the property, the sound of water trickling over pebbles audible in the morning quiet.

John Covington Marmaduke was sitting on a flat rock, his head bowed, a Bible opened across his lap.

Alfred stood a short distance away, waiting until the man seemed to pause, then he walked up and tapped him on the shoulder.

"Good morning, Alfred," Marmaduke said, acknowledging his presence without glancing up at him.

"You spent the night with my slaves! You could have been in my house instead. I would have gladly put you up for as long as you wanted."

There was a serene smile on Marmaduke's face, one that seemed wholly in contrast to the self-satisfied expression of the weeks before.

"The Lord guided me along a different path," he announced.

"But I just do not see—"

Abruptly Marmaduke stood, facing him.

"You seem so surprised," he said. "Yet you are the one who has been preaching better treatment of those slaves. Are your words just sugary glaze, Alfred?"

"Feeding them well, clothing them properly, making sure they have clean, comforting quarters to live in," Alfred protested, "that is what I have been preaching, as you call it. But I surely have resisted any notion to spend the night with them."

"Which of us is suddenly the more enlightened?" Marmaduke posed. "Where is all that liberalism of yours when it comes to what I have done?"

Marmaduke's words hurt Alfred, an arrow hitting its target.

"I just think you would have been more comfortable with us," he offered lamely, trying to camouflage what he was feeling.

"Comfort was hardly what I sought," Marmaduke told him. "I have come to believe that comfort is the Achilles heel of wealthy Christians."

He turned away and sat down again. "Alfred, Alfred, if you only knew all that I have experienced since leaving the church so short a time ago," he said, "you would understand why I am the way I am now, and probably will remain until the day I die."

"I will listen, John, if you care to tell me what's been going on," Alfred promised him.

Marmaduke sighed as he spoke. "Sit down then on that rock there, please, and I shall relate everything."

Alfred did just that. "I will repeat what you say to no one," he reassured the other man.

"Wrong!" Marmaduke corrected him brusquely. "Everybody will learn it all, every bit, I daresay, when I speak from the pulpit in a few days. As for you, go out and tell the world, Alfred. Do that, yes!

"This man of God no longer wants people to look at me in the same way as they did just months ago. They must know that I have been transformed, and they must be told how this came about."

"Anyway you want it," Alfred said. "Go ahead, then. I promise I will listen without further distraction."

Marmaduke started speaking slowly, each detail coming with obvious pain.

"I could not sleep after what happened in church that morning," he said. "Everything about that woman stayed with me—the genuine love she showed, the forgiveness, none of it forced, none of it adopted for show or effect. I knew she was incapable of the ability to contrive or to be devious that the better educated among us find so natural."

Alfred had to acknowledge that Marmaduke was correct. He had known the little woman for the better part of his life, and she was like every last one of the other slaves in their singular and unmistakable lack of pretense.

"You have described her well," he said. "She was what you say."

Marmaduke nodded as he went on, "I started to look at the whole of my life, at the lack of love in it, at the way I had slipped, over the years, into a dismal legalism that was not even a shadow of what I should be manifesting not just as a Christian but as a teacher, as a man of God who was supposed to be leading the flock."

He was shivering.

"That I was doing, Alfred, leading the flock, surely I was, but not on to the throne of Almighty God; rather, I was leading everyone who listened, who paid any attention at all, to a kind of moral and spiritual precipice, filling their minds with what their own tradition wanted them to hear, heaping error upon error!

"How many lives had I distorted during all that time? How many black men, women, and children was I responsible for giving the most miserable of lives? How many were dead because of me and my thunderings?"

He reached out his right arm before him.

"I saw that face of hers in the darkness, evening after evening, that midnight-black face, so pure in spirit it was, so forgiving. She was always smiling at me, Alfred."

Marmaduke's expression showed his shame.

"Even then I would shout the most awful of names at her, obscene words spewing from my sanctified lips, words that I would counsel others never to utter, yet there they were in abundance, coming up from the very center of my being, and, still, she would not change her own attitude, that woman, she would send back to me only that sweet Christian spirit, flying in the face of my abuse."

He was shaking so badly that Alfred became concerned that he might be in the midst of convulsions certain to injure his heart.

"I must get through this somehow with you!" Marmaduke declared. "It is but my final hurdle. I must clear it in your presence or I fear that I will never mount that pulpit nor any other again in my lifetime."

Alfred respected his wish, and did nothing but listen.

Arms folded, rocking back-and-forth, Marmaduke continued as best he could, "As you know, I waited until the next Sunday to disappear, not because of any plan, not because of any terrible desire to shock the people who had come that day to hear me yet again.

"I intended to preach, Alfred, oh, that I did. I got so far as dressing, and headed outside. I was getting into my carriage, and, suddenly, it happened, suddenly, I sensed everything collapsing out from under this large frame of mine, and I fell to the ground. Henry, my driver of many years, jumped out, and rushed to my side.

"I would not let him touch me, a man who had served me so well since I was a child, Alfred, all that time! I told him, 'Get away from me! Get those dirty black hands off me! You must never touch me again. I will not allow you to do so!'

"I got up and backed away from Henry as though he were more like Hoodoo Jack than what he was, a dignified man, soft-spoken, a bit more literate than other slaves I had known. I mean, I could actually talk to him about matters of theology, and more, much more.

"Though I had never admitted it to anyone, especially myself, I felt very close to that dear Henry. It was almost as though that man wasn't black at all, just another human being, his color meaning nothing.

"He was just standing there without moving at all, Alfred, standing there so very quietly, no anger on that face, that fine old face, nothing to show that my cruel words were cutting deeply, which they surely must have been doing.

"I couldn't stand that, you know. I wanted Henry to cuss me out, to show blinding rage. I wanted that old boy to turn away from me in naked disgust, go back to his own quarters and not speak to me again for a very long time."

Marmaduke was sweating.

"But he did just the opposite. He finally said, 'You will get through this, John. You will get through this, and I will be there with you in it.'"

Alfred nearly fell off his stone in reaction to that revelation.

"You allowed him to call you by your first name?" he spoke, thinking that he had not heard correctly.

Marmaduke ignored that and continued, "That was not what I wanted to hear, given the terrible state I was in. And so I backed away from him, turned, and ran, ran so fast that I thought I was having a heart attack from the strain and nearly passed out.

"Then I heard the familiar sound of a carriage behind me. I looked behind me and saw Henry coming right along, ready to go almost as though without interruption. I kept on running, and running, and running, until I had lost him."

He became silent for a number of minutes. Alfred did not prompt him to continue but gave him the respect of waiting.

"I ended up you will never guess where," Marmaduke continued. "Not in this state or anywhere nearby."

A bemused look crossed his face.

"I had gone on to Florida somewhere, near the swamps. Everything in between here and there is a blank to me. I just cannot remember.

"The next thing that does come to my mind is being picked up by the side of some road, and carried off. I half-expected that I would be fed to the gators, I suppose.

"Then I lost consciousness altogether. I hoped that, when I opened my eyes, I would be standing at the throne of grace, looking at the countenance of Jesus Himself."

He was facing Alfred now.

"A black face, that was what I saw when I came to!" he exclaimed, smiling slightly. "'Lord,' I begged, 'please, don't let this be heaven, and don't let me see that you are black.' Well, Jesus answered that for me!

"I found myself not in heaven, of course, nor in hell either. But I was in a shack on the edge of the Okefenokee, just after it leaves Georgia and extends into Florida. And I was surrounded by darkies! But it was hardly heaven. And for that I was very glad!"

Despite how somber Marmaduke seemed until then, he could not resist chuckling, and Alfred was caught up in this with him.

"I think the Lord sometimes sends humor," the minister spoke, "in whatever form He chooses, as a special gift."

Alfred could agree with that, enjoying the irony.

"You of all people . . . going to heaven where a black Jesus comes to greet you!"

This time, though, Marmaduke did not laugh.

"That no longer would bother me," he confessed. "What those good people did for me changed my mind . . . and my soul."

"Tell me the rest," Alfred asked, eager to hear the details. "I am anxious to hear whatever you want to recall for me."

"And undoubtedly very curious about how anybody like me could be turned inside out as I have been."

"Yes, that is true. Forgive me for this. I did not mean to be prying. I want to hear but only if you are comfortable telling me."

"I counted on that, my friend. Your reaction will guide me greatly when I get up before the congregation."

"Let me have some beverages, at least, brought out to us."

"Good idea. My mouth is very dry now."

Alfred went back into the plantation house, as Marmaduke remained by the stream, pouring all of his being into a prayer as he waited at that quiet and peaceful place.

A moment or two later, Alfred stopped by the family room and heard a familiar voice, no longer like a child's, abruptly addressing him.

Charity . . . he saw her standing to his left.

"Is everything all right?" he asked.

She nodded convincingly.

"Do you think I should spend a little time with the pastor?" she asked, a certain maturing wisdom in her manner.

"Sure you should. But why?"

"Something the Lord laid on my heart," Charity replied.

"I am sure he would enjoy your company just now."

She smiled prettily at him and walked outside, heading toward that little stream.

MARMADUKE WAS DELIGHTED and flattered that, as beautiful as she was, Charity would want to spend her time with an old man.

"Jesus told me something last night," Charity proclaimed cheerfully. "It was in a dream that I had."

"Dreams can be dangerous," he cautioned her. "People can depend upon them too much for truths that they should be getting from the inspired Scriptures."

"Yes, I know," she replied a bit defensively. "But sometimes they can tell us certain things. Was not Daniel an interpreter of dreams?"

Marmaduke had admired Charity for a long time, observing her passage from cute little baby to precocious little girl to an older, astonishingly alert and knowing child and, now, a young woman in her late teen years, and he was not surprised that she showed the spunk and the intelligence that was obvious to anyone spending more than a few minutes with her.

"You have me there," Marmaduke confessed. "Tell me about yours."

"I cannot remember the details so much as the message, but it was a powerful message, Reverend Marmaduke."

"And what was that message?" he asked, smiling a bit as he remembered a time when she had great difficulty pronouncing his name.

"The Lord seemed to be saying that you are going to be here for a long time, and you'll be doing some really good things."

His expression brightened even more.

"How delighted I am to hear this!" Marmaduke exclaimed. "And I believe it because you have said so, Charity."

She smiled, then told him, "When I was a child, I was scared of you."

"I have heard that I had that effect on little ones," he told her, not at all surprised. "Perhaps I still do."

Just then, Alfred returned, carrying a tray with a large clay container of cherry-flavored anisette, minus the whiskey often blended with it.

"I suspect I should leave now, father," Charity announced without prompting, then kissed Marmaduke on the cheek, winked at him, and returned to the house.

"She told you?" Alfred asked as he put the tray on the ground between them, sensing what had happened.

"She did. I gather she let you know as well."

"Just a short while before I came out here."

"Remarkable young woman, my dear Alfred, most remarkable, I have to say that, I surely do. I can only imagine an extraordinary future for her. You must do everything you can to foster her well-being. I think she is destined to have considerable impact upon everyone who is fortunate enough to get to know her."

"Perhaps you will play a part in it, John."

"It was only a few weeks ago that I would have considered myself unworthy of anything of the sort."

"No longer?"

"I cannot imagine what the Lord has in store, but I know there is something. I know that I am grateful to Him for guiding me to those darkies who were so kind to me."

"Why not tell me the rest now?" Alfred suggested.

"That I shall do!" agreed Marmaduke. "That I shall do."

~❦ 29 ❧~

During the night in that little shack, Marmaduke had dreamed. "It was unquestionably the most vivid vision of my life," he told Alfred. "I was in a graveyard, and yet that should not have concerned me. As a minister, I have performed more services in these places than I can possibly ever recall. However, this graveyard was far from being an ordinary one. There were headstones, of course, but they were in the form of statues, large ones, statues only of angels.

"A hundred markers like that . . . angels with beautiful wings outspread, angels with trumpets, others sitting in contemplative positions, some as though ready to embark on a battle, wearing helmets on their heads and swords in their hands.

"Everywhere I looked, Alfred! I said that there were hundreds, but there must have been more. I could never see the end of them. I turned left and right, I walked straight ahead, I went here and there, but always I found row after row of these extraordinary statues. If it were not a cemetery, then it could have been a forest without trees, a forest of angels.

"I touched many of them, thinking within the dream, which I assumed was reality, that I was dreaming. I know how strange that sounds, but the dream appeared so vivid to me, so palpable that it seemed real unto itself and yet so odd that it could only have been a dream.

"Nevertheless, those statues were quite solid to the touch, Alfred. I felt them, some with smooth surfaces, others more uneven, porous, a few of such roughness to the touch that I had to pull away immediately or cut my fingers.

"Then I heard a voice. I knew it was the Lord's from the start. He was using that dream to speak to my very soul, Alfred, cutting through everything else, all the years of hatred, the domineering ways, the—"

Marmaduke was shivering though the temperature was several degrees above seventy that morning.

"Oh, friend, friend," he spoke, "to know that my Creator was communicating in that way! To hear Him!"

"What did the stone angels signify?" Alfred asked.

"My life until that point! I had angels all around me, guardian angels every minute of my day, ready to help me, ready to empower my ministry as never before."

"But they might as well have been made of stone . . . ," Alfred said gently, realizing what was coming.

Marmaduke had been bowing his head but jerked himself straight at that.

"That was it!" he exclaimed. "How could you have known?"

"I think God sometimes communicates with us through our dreams. He has been doing that, I believe, with Elizabeth and myself. To depend upon dreams can be dangerous because at night Satan can get through our defenses but, then, so can the Almighty."

"I woke up and found those free blacks still hovering around me. One of the women was swabbing a simple wet cloth across my throbbing and burning forehead. Another was standing nearby with a bowl of what turned out to be some kind of gumbo soup, very rich, very strong, but it was what my body needed at that moment."

Marmaduke's demeanor was changing as he spoke.

"I never wanted to leave those people," he confessed. "I wanted to stay with them in that basic world of theirs, living off the land as they were doing . . . growing the vegetables they needed, trapping gators and smoking that meat for suppers for weeks to come. Other times, I suppose, it was rabbit or fowl instead.

"I had the greatest difficulty coming to grips with their acts of sheer kindness. I was but a stranger, and a white stranger at that, yet they shared everything they had with me and asked no questions.

"'How can you do this so unselfishly?' I asked disbelievingly. I shall never forget the response I was given: 'You's sent here for a reason. God's gone and done that. We ain't askin' no questions where's He's concerned.'

"Such simple trust, Alfred, and then the shame I felt afterwards! It was the worst part of that period for me. I went to sleep with it, and I arose with it. It threatened to destroy the spiritual blessings I had started to receive.

"Then I was baptized by an eighty-year-old black preacher. He said I needed to be cleaned in the sight of God and man. They took me to the edge of the swamp, and I was held under the water for a few seconds then lifted out as a dozen black people sang, "Swing Low, Sweet Chariot," which I was hearing as though for the very first time."

"I would have stayed with them, I think, for the rest of my life, but I knew I had to return. I knew I had to come back and demonstrate what had been done in my life. That is why I am here, and that is why I need to stand before that congregation again and tell them all that the Lord has revealed to me."

"And look at the moment the Lord chose," Alfred pointed out, shivering as an image of Hoodoo Jack came to his mind.

Marmaduke snapped his fingers.

"That is it!" he said.

"What?"

"I was telling the truth when I said that I thought I was being directed to return to my pulpit here. But I have not told you until now that I kept feeling there was something more that I should be doing."

"What else could there be, John?" asked Alfred. "You have scores of people whom you will be shepherding, with the responsibility of changing the way they treat their slaves. Is that not enough, good sir?"

"It isn't," declared Marmaduke. "I want to reach the Negroes directly. But I have not been certain how."

"Are you any more sure now?"

"When you directed my attention to the moment of my return, facing Hoodoo Jack as I did, the Lord let the other pieces fall into place within this puzzle of mine. There are others like that scoundrel. Perhaps I should spend some time alerting slaves and free blacks so that they will never fall under the spell of creatures like him.

"If I do that, Alfred, owners certainly will be happy and more inclined to grant me greater access to their slaves and perhaps be much more open to treating those poor souls like the human beings they are."

Alfred had to admit that Marmaduke was making sense.

"It is good that you have come back, John," he said.

Both men stood.

"Not everyone in the congregation will agree," Marmaduke suggested. "We may lose some members."

"But those who are left will be the ones worth having!" Alfred remarked.

"My friend?"

"Yes . . . ?"

"May I sleep here again tonight?"

"Only if you will stay in my house. You proved your point earlier. You shouldn't have to do so again."

"Then I shall find another place." A hint of disappointment made his voice suddenly sag.

Alfred was irritated by that, for it sounded like the old John Covington Marmaduke trying to get his way.

"You surely need not become any kind of martyr," he said, his tone of voice leaving no doubt about how he felt.

"You are bothered by this, are you not?" observed Marmaduke.

"I must say that I am."

"Why?"

"Because—" Alfred began.

"Spare both of us any excuses," interrupted Marmaduke. "Be honest with me, my brother: You are afraid that my conduct will set an example, that perhaps you might have to go in there and share a night with those slaves of yours."

Alfred's irritation should have become outright anger, but it did not, because that was in fact what concerned him.

"I do a great deal to offend the sensitivities of the other families around here," he said. "Dare I go one step further? I could try it secretly, but there is little that remains secret for long, I have discovered over the years."

Alfred's manner softened.

"It is not because I care little about their feelings," he added. "I think you make more of a statement by doing it than I would."

"Particularly since you have already been showing where you stand?"

"I would say so, John. Can you not accept this?"

"For you, of course, but not for me, Alfred, not for me. I am reminded that the dear Lord Jesus, the transcendent Man of all men, was born in a misbegotten stable." Marmaduke continued without waiting for a response. "Can I do less than that for just one more night, a few hours in humble surroundings?

"You have given them a better home than our Lord knew in His incarnate infancy. Tomorrow, after everyone realizes I am back, I shall find myself returning, I suppose, to my much grander parsonage."

"But what if people find out what you have done? Your risks are the same as mine, are they not?"

"You said it yourself, I admit. You have already run a gamut of risks in matters regarding your slaves. This one is my first. There may be many more that the Lord directs me to take, and I had better get accustomed to them."

"Go ahead then," Alfred relented. "How could I object under the circumstances? You are as effective as ever, my friend, surely you are."

"Is that why you never debated me in public?"

"You realized that?"

"I was once deluded, good Alfred, but not necessarily blind!"

The aroma of cooking came to them on a gentle breeze.

"And now breakfast," Alfred reminded him.

"You mean eat with all them niggers?" Marmaduke said, adopting an expression of mock distaste.

"Absolutely!"

"Then it will be my privilege to accept your invitation."

Just then, four slaves emerged from their quarters.

John Covington Marmaduke broke away to go and greet them, hugging each one, acting as though he had been gone from them for a long time instead of only a short while.

Alfred watched, and as he did, words immortal came to mind, like a benediction from heaven itself: *Well done, thou good and faithful servant, well done.*

❧ 30 ❧

FIVE DAYS LATER . . . John Covington Marmaduke proceeded to give his first sermon since returning after his disappearance.

The sanctuary had only standing room left, and not much of that.

"I am sorry that I had to leave you as I did," he told everyone. "I spent most of my time living in the shack of a wonderful black family, sleeping with them, eating with them, working side by side with the men. I worshiped our risen Lord with them as well."

He enjoyed the moment, still capable of controlling any crowd, and his powers were no less evident that Sunday morning.

Alfred anticipated that fully as many as two-thirds of the church's members would get up and leave.

He was wrong.

Everyone stayed, and all seemed to be giving full attention to what their pastor was now telling them.

"I think we sin greatly when we abuse our slaves," he went on. "I would hope that someday slavery could be abolished, but in a way and according to a time table different from what the abolitionists favor. But in the meanwhile, any man who uses the Bible to justify brutality toward these men and women is skirting heresy and, I would add, blasphemy as well if he attributes his actions to the Almighty's commands.

"I believe quite firmly in slavery because I do not think that these folks are able to survive on their own—at least, survive very well. The family that took me in was kind and generous and loving, yes, they were that. But they were poorer than the slaves owned by any of you in front of me now. They possessed few clothes. They had to work three times harder than your slaves to be able to eat half as much. They had no one to protect them.

"Gators and snakes and other creatures attack them. Disease is common. They are free, yes, and they seem happy; but I can point to the Littlepage slaves to show you that being a slave does not have to be a sentence to hell.

"But for some, that is what their slaves do experience, I am afraid, a hell on earth, my brothers, my sisters in Christ. God gives us the care of these poor souls for a reason, and we must never bring shame to Him by beating any slave, by denying any man, woman, or child the proper food in the proper amounts, by not keeping their black hides warm in the cruel cold of winter and as cool as possible in the oppressive heat of summer.

"If slavery could exist only as a notably inhumane institution, supported by repeated acts of cruelty else it would cave in on itself, then I would transfer my allegiance to the abolitionists in an instant!"

He looked out over every man, every woman, every boy and girl in that sanctuary.

"We are told to feed the hungry," he emphasized, "clothe the naked, and all the rest. If we do not take care of even the lowliest among us, we might be turning aside an angel in disguise. If that is the case with those who come to us along city streets and beg for mercy, how can it be less so for our own property?

"Remember, friends: We have the obligations of ownership. Would we abuse a fine piece of furniture? Would we deliberately crack a rare old mirror? Or a piece of cut crystal? Of course not! Only a madman would mishandle that sort of possession."

He slammed his fist down so hard on the podium that Alfred wondered if Marmaduke had broken any bones.

"Only a madman would do such a thing—or so we say as we hide behind our personal delusions. Yet I ask you, how many do that and worse to living, breathing human beings entrusted to us?"

Marmaduke was genuinely enraged—this was no performance heightened for dramatic effect—and the members of that congregation could only sit back, astonished, unable to move, his words pinning them to the pews.

He took the chair he had sat on for twenty-odd years of church services, lifted it up, and threw it partway down the center aisle where it came to rest in a pile of half a dozen pieces.

"You would never do that to furniture, would you? Yet some among us treat their slaves with even greater contempt. Those who do are out there at this very moment, sitting in those pews in God's house of worship, listening to my words and either feeling morally superior or racked by a conscience that will not let them rest."

He leaned forward, his elbows on the flat, upper surface of the podium.

"Abusive slave masters are sowing the seeds of ruinous rebellion and giving the abolitionists the very excuse their kind needs to wage war on our precious land someday."

At the mention of the word war, several in the congregation moved nervously in their pews, for that was something they dreaded even as they saw its warnings on the horizon.

Marmaduke's nostrils flared in vintage fashion.

"It must stop," he demanded, his voice louder. "I serve you notice: I shall personally confront, on his front porch, if necessary, any man from any family who does not cease and desist the cruel treatment of his property. He can expect to be barred from this church and shamed throughout the county. Something must be done to take the enemy's knife from our throat."

He paused, mulling over what he had just said.

"Did I say take the enemy's knife?" he continued. "Instead, I should have said, '*take back the very knife that we handed to him in the first place.*'"

Someone dared to speak up at that point.

"You talk as though you want us to free our people," a short, balding, pale-faced man said as he stood.

"That is not what I am saying," retorted Marmaduke. "Slavery is hardly wrong, and no one can convince me that it is. Every Christian should be a slave to Christ, the Master of all who accept Him as Savior and Lord.

"So, then, if that form of slavery is not wrong, then surely being a kind owner of a well-treated colored is also not wrong. There are many free blacks who are trapped in conditions far worse than slavery imposes upon them.

"Hear me good, and if you want me to repeat it a hundred times over, I shall: Slavery is not the moral evil our adversaries make it out to be. But when men like yourself and Ambrose Pegram label talk of simple Christian kindness—acts mandated by Holy Writ—as somehow seditious and unseemly, a bouquet the fragrance of which the Yankee abolitionists and the southern turncoats love, I say you are quite stupid—in plain language, stupid like the dumbest mule ever to see the light of day."

The man began to object, but Marmaduke shouted him down.

"This may be the Lord's house spiritually, and so shall it remain, but it is I who takes charge while the flesh and blood steer it through the shoals."

He raised his right arm and pointed toward the rear of the sanctuary.

"Go, thou slave of Satan," he roared. "Stop polluting the purity of this place by your foulest of stenches!"

The man and his wife stepped over to the center aisle, then left.

"If anyone else cares to follow in the dubious footsteps of such human vermin as that man," Marmaduke added, "they may go now . . . go and never return!"

Even the intimidating veteran of church battles waiting expectantly at the podium found his heart almost stopping in dread as every individual, man, woman, and child stood at virtually the same time.

Not to leave him behind, forsaking his leadership, but to give Marmaduke sustained, loud applause.

Finally they all sat down again.

Marmaduke seemed momentarily weak and had to grab hold of the pulpit to steady himself. Then, visibly weeping, he told them, his voice resonating more than ever, "A chorus of angels could not have been any sweeter."

He asked that they bow their heads so that he could deliver a closing prayer. It was probably the humblest he had offered for a long time, certainly shorter than most others.

"Lord," he spoke, "take this broken vessel and make me your instrument of edification for these thirsty souls . . . Amen."

After that, the congregation continued to stand as he left the pulpit and strode down the center aisle to wait outside as they exited.

One by one, he shook the hand of every man, woman, and child, not with the haughty air that he projected as recently as a month before, but with a newfound kindness.

Finally, Little Isaiah and the other Littlepage slaves approached him. He reached out and hugged each one.

Then Elizabeth, Charity, and Alfred were standing in front of him.

"You are tempting fate by all this," Alfred said softly with a mixture of concern but, more than that, with admiration.

"There is no such thing as fate," Marmaduke corrected him. "Only the destiny determined by our Holy Creator matters at all, you know. Fate is nothing but a deception hatched by the enemy of our souls."

He turned to Charity, who was smiling at him.

"You must never lose the ability to smile like that," he told her. "When you are eighty years of age, I hope you can still smile like you are now."

Charity was delighted by that.

Finally, they left him and started toward their awaiting carriage.

"Mama, Daddy, look!" Charity screamed. "It's that awful man!"

Her parents swung around and saw Ambrose Pegram racing across the road toward the church and Marmaduke, who was starting to go inside.

"Alfred, he has a knife!" Elizabeth shouted. "Warn John!"

Alfred did, raising his voice so high that Marmaduke turned around with a jolt, startled by the sound of it.

Thinking quickly, Little Isaiah tossed Alfred a rifle that, ever since the Hoodoo Jack episode, they had carried with them as a precaution. By the time he had raised and aimed it, Pegram was only a foot or two away from Marmaduke, who was now standing with his arms outstretched toward them.

"If the debased mind that you have can be shown even more clearly for what it is by my death in this evil manner," Marmaduke said, "then take my life, for I sacrifice it gladly toward that end."

Pegram was gripping the knife handle tightly as he started up the steps.

"Shoot, Alfred!" Elizabeth urged. "Shoot him now!"

But Alfred knew he had to aim with great care since Pegram was not entirely blocking Marmaduke. It would not be hard to miss and wound or kill the minister instead.

"Are you sure you want me dead?" Marmaduke asked Pegram with great kindness.

"I am not going to kill you, not now," replied Pegram calmly. "Yes, I confess that, only a bare half an hour ago, I was waiting around the corner, hoping to catch you for that very reason. But, you see, the window was open. I heard those words of yours, truly good words. And the Lord soon sent me right to my knees.

"After I had remained like that for some while, I felt very ashamed of myself and started to leave. I had made it across the road before I heard a voice in my head whispering, 'Go back, Ambrose. Tell the man how you feel.'"

Suddenly, Marmaduke glanced over the other man's shoulder, immediately noticing Alfred and the rifle.

"No!" he shouted frantically, pushing Pegram to one side as he stepped forward. "Put it down. Everything is going to be—"

Alfred had started to lower the rifle an instant before he noticed Pegram scoot behind Marmaduke, using the minister's much larger body as a shield while he raised the knife and plunged it downward.

Marmaduke stumbled down the steps, his hand darting behind him, then he turned, facing his assassin. Pegram followed Marmaduke like some ghoulish predatory creature, lifting the knife again and swinging it down toward the minister's chest.

Alfred fired, catching Pegram in the chest and dropping him to the ground.

Marmaduke could barely stand but managed somehow to stagger over to Pegram.

"You spoke of the Lord sending you to your knees!" he exclaimed. "How could you say such a thing? You are guilty of using His precious name in vain!"

"I have lived by the hatred you taught every Sunday . . ." Pegram gasped as blood spurted out of his mouth and from his chest. "I am your offspring, preacher man . . . for you have fathered the grotesque thing that my soul has become.

"And I now leave this world. I leave it by the same road you mapped out for me and others a long time ago. Nor am I alone . . . Your children walk this land by the score, preacher man . . . each one carrying your message . . . as a beacon on their way to hell . . . which is their destination and surely mine as well."

"But you said *Lord* a moment ago," Marmaduke reminded him. "You cannot lose your salvation; even you cannot."

Pegram chuckled the last few seconds of his life away as he said, "It depends upon which lord sits upon the throne of my life . . . does it not?"

In a fraction of a second, Pegram slashed the knife across his own throat but not before he mumbled something about the terrible heat of an approaching wall of eternal fire and, among the flames, demonic faces crying out in gleeful welcome.

∼ 31 ∼

A<small>FTER HE HAD</small> been examined by the nearest country doctor, John Covington Marmaduke was taken to a doctor in Columbia who determined that the wounded pastor needed immediate rest and continual care in a facility there if he was to survive his wounds.

Alfred wanted to go with him to Columbia, but Marmaduke, barely conscious, pleaded, "Your family has seen all this. Be with your wife, your daughter. That is more needful for now."

But there were numerous other volunteers.

Their minister's pulpit statements and the violent aftermath had seared through even the most entrenched viewpoints about the kind of slavery he condemned.

While waiting for word about Marmaduke's condition, the people of that county did much talking within their families and friends.

As they talked, the attention of most was returned to the earlier evening's confrontation with Hoodoo Jack, the scene in which Marmaduke had played such an important part.

This time, the location was the comfortably furnished and decorated living room of Alfred Littlepage's plantation house.

Dinner had not as yet been served. Elizabeth sat down next to her husband on a French Provincial sofa while Samuel Fulkerson was across from them in a high-back wing chair. They were discussing what had happened the week before.

Crispus stood before them, repeating for them the statement he had made while standing up to the demonic stranger.

I said, "'Word was that you were nothing more than a spy for the slavers, goin' from place to place and lookin' for bucks like me to buy.'"

That burst of insight by Crispus had seemed stunning at the time, and, now days later, it was no less so.

"And then I told him, 'I hear that you once turned in some members of your own family because you needed the money,'" he finished, proud of himself for having said that in the first place and especially that he remembered every word.

"Thank you for telling us," Alfred remarked.

Crispus hesitated, acting as though he wanted to say something.

"What is it?" Fulkerson asked. "Is there something else?"

The slave was biting his lower lip.

"Please, go ahead," Fulkerson assured him. "Things are different now; I thought you understood that."

Crispus smiled as he said, "That be the very first time any white man thanked me for anything, Massa."

Fulkerson was not angry. If anything, he seemed regretful.

"It will never happen again," he remarked. "You will be treated as you should be."

The slave flinched at those words.

Fulkerson noticed this and promptly added, a bit amused, "The part about not thanking you, I mean!"

Crispus was immediately more cheerful.

"Thank you, Jesus," he said. "Thank you, Massa!"

He seemed to want to say something else. Fulkerson gave him leave to speak again.

"The preacher man, we is prayin' and prayin' that he pulls through," Crispus said.

Then he excused himself and walked quietly outside where he would spend some free time with the Littlepage slaves, several of whom he had known for years.

"Amazing what happens when we are the least prepared for the Lord's intervention," noted Alfred. "We could not have anticipated anyone like Hoodoo Jack's entering our lives or that the man Marmaduke had become was returning at just that moment, to stand up to the devil like that in more ways than one."

Fulkerson sucked in his breath, then let it out slowly.

"Hoodoo Jack's whole manner of speech did seem different," he mused. "The man, if you could call him that, was well-educated, clearly so. I wonder whether we will ever know the real story about him. What connections did he have? If the words he spouted were intended as a facade, hiding the truth, what was his purpose?"

"This matter isn't over, my friend," Alfred told him, "I suspect Hoodoo Jack represents only the start of something much, much wider in scope. There are others out there—in different sizes and shapes, perhaps, but spreading similar poison."

Fulkerson was puzzled.

"I don't follow you," he said.

"I think . . . ," Alfred said slowly, "that certain interests were behind Hoodoo Jack, pulling his strings."

Fulkerson burst out in self-conscious laughing.

"Thank God you said that," he remarked with relief. "I suspected that I was losing my mind in the midst of this conspiracy business that seems to have been gaining momentum in recent years. I think we are onto something here."

"You feel the same way then?" Alfred asked, surprised, but pleased that he was not alone with his suspicions.

"Precisely! I have been able to consider little else." Suddenly he recalled Hoodoo Jack's ominous words.

. . . That is my mission right now, as it has always been, to break the back-bone of the South by robbing your kind of the cheap labor that is so central to the way of life you have been living for generations.

"When he said that," Alfred went on, "I thought I was listening to a well-rehearsed speech by the head of one of the abolitionist groups."

"The way Hoodoo Jack spoke, you could hardly escape that conclusion," Fulkerson agreed. Abruptly, he jumped to his feet and started pacing rather frantically.

"What in the world happened?" Alfred asked, not expecting that sudden movement.

"I fear for the future of our way of life," Fulkerson acknowledged. "Until recently, I was unabashed evidence of how far astray that way of life can go.

"But then you, Alfred, provide the best proof of how right it can be. But the Yankees see us as a prize, orchard after orchard of fruit trees to be plucked as they pass by, ravaging us."

"Are you convinced that it will come to that?"

"Not tomorrow, Alfred, not for some years perhaps, but it has to come, and it will roar in like Satan himself. Their interests and ours are in competition. They need what we grow, and we need what they manufacture."

"But we can get along without them, if we had to," Alfred pointed out, "whereas they cannot do without what we in the South provide for the entire country. Food is a commodity more indispensable than anything the Yankees possess. They know this, and it gives them pause."

"Correct. Furthermore, they can purchase a fair amount of their needs from overseas sources but not nearly enough. And if war ever comes, maintaining those sources would be questionable. We could cut most of those off!"

"War, Samuel? Is that what you are saying . . . *war?* Surely not so, man! This nation would be torn asunder, split in half. Even the politicians would not be stupid enough to let a war between the states occur."

"The fact that anything like that is unthinkable is not, I fear, a barrier necessarily to its inevitability."

Alfred reacted with surprise at the other man's hard-nosed reaction to his statement, and this registered in his expression.

"You seem taken aback," Fulkerson pointed out.

"I am getting to know you, Samuel," Alfred told him.

"And you are surprised that there is some depth to me."

"If I answer that, you will be offended."

"I once would have been offended, but no longer. The fact that I was the way I was is now the offense, as I look back."

Elizabeth Littlepage had been sitting quietly beside her husband, listening but not speaking, for that was the custom of that era, women seldom interrupting any kind of earnest conversation between men.

Alfred turned to his wife then, and asked, "Why don't you tell us what you think about all of this, my dear?"

Some husbands did treat their wives rather like simple-minded children at times, and an invitation of that sort from another man to another woman might have been tinged with sarcasm.

But with Alfred, that was never the case. For him, marriage was not merely a sexual union but an intellectual one as well.

Elizabeth replied without delay, "I have been hoping that those dreams of mine are not prophetic."

"May I give Samuel here some idea of what you mean?"

She nodded her consent, and Alfred told their guest what one of the dreams was like.

"What you have described is not so different from the dreams that have plagued my nights," Fulkerson acknowledged.

"You, too, Samuel?" Alfred spoke.

"Afraid so. And if you talk to others throughout the South, I suspect you would get much the same response."

Alfred had not even suspected that anything like this could be true.

"Just a collective kind of fear?" he asked.

"More than that, my friend. I think we are being prepared for something, sometimes gently, sometimes not so, a cataclysm that will change our lives forever."

"A cataclysm by God, is that what you are saying?" Elizabeth inquired, alarmed. "Could it be that the Lord has been trying to warn us, sir?"

"Frankly, I see no other possibility, Ma'am. How many are likely to heed Him in time remains to be seen."

Alfred was alarmed, unsettled.

"But what can we do," he said, "set all our slaves free?"

"You have offered to do that very thing, have you not?"

"Yes, but—"

"Calm down, Alfred. I happen to think that that would never stop the worst of the abolitionists. Once any such particular pretext for interference is removed, they would simply substitute another and another after that, if necessary. And another after that, if required to do so. They are quite fanatical, you know."

"We would be outnumbered, for certain," Alfred mused.

"Their armament stores are growing rapidly; we know that for a fact, with no official reason being given for this phenomenon. It is almost as though they are planning for some future confrontation. I cannot believe that even a political hack like Zachary Taylor—if he wins the next election—would be stupid enough, as president, to allow the situation to get out of hand. But then those money interests up north are powerful; they want the prize of war, and Taylor, as good a soldier as he was, may be too weak, too vacillating, to stand up to them."

"And too much tilted toward the South, anyway."

"You believe that?"

"I do, Samuel. He's a Virginian after all. I think Taylor would be on our side in the event that war ever does come to our land. He appears weak because he is loathe to do anything to hurt our interests."

Alfred smiled at Elizabeth.

"My dear, we have been chattering along with the excuse that your dreams have given us. Forgive us, please."

She shook her head as she said, "I am not a prophet."

"Nor am I," Fulkerson spoke up. "Yet we have dreamed alike."

"Of death and destruction, of fire and smoke," Elizabeth ventured musingly. "I wonder what it all means."

"The end of everything?" Alfred said somberly.

They looked at him, then at one another, because the very possibility seemed so terrifying that they could do nothing else, frozen where they sat, silent.

Just then, Savilla came across the walkway to the main plantation house and announced that dinner was being served.

It was the break they needed, a time to take their minds off the apocalyptic turn in their conversation.

Exhausted by mealtime, Savilla had clearly gone overboard, and intentionally so, but with Elizabeth's hearty approval, for the old woman was wise enough to understand that this was a fine opportunity for her to be able to take everyone's mind off what had happened so recently when Hoodoo Jack had entered their lives.

The meal Savilla prepared, which had to be started early in the morning, and which Nester and Little Isaiah helped serve, was an extraordinary one, bringing together a number of culinary origins. There were two appetizers: shrimp and okra gumbo as well as smoked sausage. The side dishes she prepared were sweet squash with nutmeg and vanilla, buttery baked maca-roni and eggs with caramelized onions, black-eyed peas with bits of bacon, and finally, warm beet salad. The main course was stuffed pork chops with onion gravy. The meal ended with a dessert that included cream cheese and roasted pecan cookies, fig sweet-dough pie, and Indian black strap molasses pudding. The beverage was mint-flavored iced tea.

The slaves decided to eat in their own quarters, sensing Elizabeth's and Alfred's need to eat alone with their new friend.

"Unbelievable!" Fulkerson exclaimed after he had finished. "Is your Savilla available to teach my people how to cook? I have never had a meal as good as this one in my life. Even my mother couldn't touch this!"

Elizabeth did not take this as well as he had intended.

"Good cooking is an activity that has to be learned over a long period of time," she replied, her indignation not disguised. "Like the meal itself, Samuel, it is not something you can just pop into an oven and expect or hope that something good will come out after just a day or two spent try-ing to learn how to do it all."

"I meant no offense."

"Nor did I," Elizabeth assured him, not altogether truthfully.

❧ 32 ❧

LATER, SAMUEL FULKERSON stretched his legs and excused himself. "I must go," he told his hosts. "This dinner was wonderful! I see now that I have no such cooks of your Savilla's caliber working for me. They keep me healthy, of course, but not, I must say, particularly satisfied."

After Elizabeth and Alfred had shown their guest to the door, the three of them stood outside for a moment, Fulkerson luxuriantly breathing in the cherished night air, finding it clean and pure as always, devoid of the sootiness apparent in certain regions of the North.

"Nothing burning as yet, I see," he observed sardonically, "and, hallelujah, not even the hint of gun powder."

He shook hands with Alfred and kissed Elizabeth on the cheek.

"The French would take your hand," he said, "and kiss the back of it. But you have such a charming cheek."

"You are civil in more ways than one these days," Alfred noted appreciatively. "Congratulations, Samuel."

Fulkerson thanked him and added, "You may be right. I beat my slaves only twice a day now instead of half a dozen times."

He had spoken so seriously that Elizabeth's and Alfred's faces went pale.

"Only jesting," Fulkerson, grinning, told them. "It is a streak of mine that remains unconquered."

His manner became somber.

"You are a better man this day because of this precious lady," he told the two of them, "and a luckier one, I might add. Never be ungrateful, my friend, for Elizabeth is a true gift, one that should be treasured."

He turned toward the house.

"And in there, sleeping so well by now, I am sure, is the greatest blessing you both could ever have," he told them. "Someday, somebody will have much to write about her, I think, for she will live a remarkable life and have a remarkable story to tell."

Beckoning to Crispus to bring the carriage, Fulkerson prepared to return to his own plantation house.

"Bless you," he whispered warmly. "I am glad we can be friends; I do not need another enemy."

The carriage pulled up, with Crispus at the reins.

"We must not drift apart, you and I," he said, with Alfred nodding in agreement. "I think when we spend time ruminating about the threats beyond our precious region, as well we should, we are prone to ignore those lurking within our boundaries, waiting to pounce.

"The attack against Marmaduke may be a hint of what to expect, a tiny peek that we are being allowed, as the Lord's warning. There are many traitors, Alfred, truly many in our midst whom we will have to defend ourselves against, if not a year from now or this decade, then the next or the one after that, coming to us under various guises, men and perhaps women whose souls have been sold out to the Yankees, prowling our roads and sitting in our churches and eating from our tables as our guests, innocently invited by us into our very homes.

"They will look like us, Alfred; they will talk like us, but their hearts will belong in New York and New Jersey and Washington, D.C., not Richmond and Charleston and Natchez."

Shrugging forlornly, Samuel Fulkerson climbed into the carriage and waved good-bye to them, slowly disappearing into the darkness, his shoulders slumping, an aura of regret and loneliness surrounding him as completely as night itself.

Elizabeth and Alfred decided to remain outside for a short while longer, soaking in the quiet of that moment.

Then, as they were going back into the plantation house, Elizabeth ran her hand over the door frame, examining it in a way she had not done before that moment.

"How much longer?" she asked wistfully.

"This house, the land, the way we live?" Alfred asked, instantly understanding what his wife meant.

"Yes . . . the holocaust, dear husband . . . when will it come?"

"It may not come, Elizabeth, it may not come at all. Nothing of the sort is necessarily ordained, not as far as I can tell, anyway. Remember, certain political forces are in our favor, as well as those forces against us."

"Oh, it shall come, my love," she insisted as she shook her head. "Make no mistake about that. Our dreams have opened the door, and as we peer beyond it during these nights of wary sleep, we catch but a glimpse, and it is enough, a vision unassailable."

Elizabeth laughed at herself.

"I sound like a second-rate Shakespearean imitator," she said, chuckling at her own morose words. "Whatever happened to the admonition 'Take no thought for tomorrow, for sufficient unto this day are the evils thereof.'"

Alfred hugged her.

"We will not be squashed like bugs under a hundred thousand Yankee boots!" he proclaimed. "For one thing, Jefferson Davis from Mississippi has been a very able senator. I understand that he is being mentioned for a Cabinet post, perhaps as Secretary of War.

"Davis already has amassed some considerable influence, and he is learning to wield it well. Any such appointment will only heighten his power. The man is impressive. I met him during one of my trips a few months ago. And I am encouraged."

"Yes, but for every Davis you can mention, I am afraid, there are ten or more others to oppose him."

Alfred shrugged his shoulders and suggested, "Whatever the case, we should forget this gloomy stuff, at least for tonight. What we should do is hurry upstairs this very minute and proceed to make the wildest, most passionate love imaginable in our four-poster bed and forget the rest of the world until we have to awaken to it in the morning."

His forehead touched hers.

"I wonder if you would be willing to do that?" Alfred Littlepage added.

Elizabeth's expression told him everything he needed to know.

❧ 33 ❧

MARMADUKE'S LIFE WAS not lost at the hand of an assassin. No vital organs had been touched by the blade that had pierced his body. He lost a considerable amount of blood, but transfusions were started immediately after he entered the hospital.

The pastor recovered after a week of the best care available during those days and was taken back to his parsonage, where a hundred people waited for him. It was a large home, befitting his stature in those days, sprawling over several acres of ground. Land holdings were generous for men such as Marmaduke who were leaders of one sort or another, as well as for families and anybody who was upper middle class or higher.

Land . . .

It would be one reason, pivotal at that, why southerners would later fight with the ferocity they did. If their numbers had been equal, the armies of Johnny Reb would have overwhelmed the Yankees.

As the Richmond Daily Dispatch would publish on May 12, 1862, "Then call us Rebels, if you will, we glory in the name, for bending under unjust laws, and swearing faith to an unjust cause, we count as greater shame."

Passion.

That was a part of what separated the South from the North in the coming hostilities. The Yankees were to be marching according to the political dictates of their superiors. But for the South, it was survival, fighting to preserve their homes, their land, their government, everything that was anchored in the heritage they had carried for many decades.

Now Marmaduke saw the group of them gathered on the front lawn of his parsonage and grunted, not happy with the fuss.

Even my critics, he observed, *even they have come. How extraordinary!*

Quite a few should not have been waiting since their views seemed no longer the same as his own, but it did appear that their Christian consciences had won out over mere political or social tradition.

How can I get them to understand? he thought. *We are not so far apart as they may assume. There is but one difference: kindness. I think slavery is defensible, but only if the slaves are treated humanely. For them, kindness is not superfluous, especially if it costs too much in the form of better and more food, clothes, or whatever else.*

Something mouthed by Ambrose Pegram had refused to let go of Marmaduke's mind, the accusation that Pegram and others like him were but their pastor's children, raised spiritually under his pastorship for long years of maturation—as men and women and as Christians.

I think, Ambrose, as far as you were concerned, Christianity probably amounted to just a social club comprised of fellow tyrants, a club that opened to you if you announced yourself a Christian and would have been closed if you had not.

It also isolated you from any possibility of your conscience accusing you because if the way you treated your slaves was, according to your twisted outlook, ordained by Almighty God and there were around you other so-called believers reinforcing that outlook, then—

Marmaduke felt a chill as he imagined a line of people headed toward a distant lake of fire, and there he stood, behind them, urging them onward.

Lord, Lord, if their souls are at my feet and I have been sending them to damnation, how can I survive without losing my mind?

Seeing the group of them waiting on his front lawn was the fastest answer to a prayerful question that he could remember, as though God sensed his urgency and refused to let him be burdened any longer.

They continue to look to me, Marmaduke told himself. *They seem to have put aside any and all obstacles and returned to my fold, which is, in turn, the good Lord's . . . in love or respect or pity or whatever. But that hardly matters right now, because they are here, in any event, and surely, it is that nothing else has any bearing but only the opportunities ahead for undoing some of the harm for which I have been responsible.*

He saw Charity beside her mother and father, once the most charming of children and now becoming a young woman, tall and beautiful and exceptionally intelligent, someone who stood way above the common crowd.

Even someone such as Charity, Marmaduke thought, *even that sweet, sweet child now becoming a maturing and impressive woman . . . She hardly knows me, but she cares, and she cares in large measure because that is how she has been raised. Praise God that she has never been corrupted by the "doctrine" I have been handing down.*

One by one, people stepped up to greet him after he had been helped from the carriage. One among them was a considerable surprise.

The widow of Ambrose Pegram.

"Julia, I have no words," Marmaduke told her honestly. "That you would be among those greeting me . . . . I don't know what to say!"

"I loved Ambrose passionately," she remarked without hesitation, "but love accepts the whole person as it tries to overlook the blemishes. For my husband, there were a vast number of these blemishes, yes, but also, to make matters worse, an unholy sickness that managed to corrupt him, a sickness worse than anything physical. For Ambrose, no healing came to him. And I think we are parted forever, this man and I.

"That is the problem, Pastor. My husband was a reprehensible fake, Christian only on the surface, and only barely that. It was something he flaunted to gain him relationships through the church, people who might become his customers. He went to the worship services and the social functions for no other reason."

She was just tenuously in control of herself, a tall woman, thin-faced, wearing a dark purple dress with a high frilled collar and large, mother-of-pearl buttons down the front, someone who could be disdainful and domineering within seconds but who now seemed frightened and sad, grasping for something to keep her going.

"As horrible as he could be, as artificial and manipulative and barbaric in his conduct outside our home," she went on, "I never stopped loving that man, I think because when he was with me and our children, he was not the same.

"We were the very center of my husband's world. Ambrose never touched me violently or in anger. He was generous to the point that I would sometimes become worried about our family's financial health."

Julia seemed about to faint, but Marmaduke, though still rather weak himself, was able to catch her.

"Thank you," she said. "Having to bury my husband, having to explain what had happened to our children, having to reach out to his side of the bed nightly only to find nothing there but the cold, cold sheets . . . this is when it seems that my stability is not what it once was. I am a strong woman of noble birth, but I now . . . thinking about the man Ambrose became and the murderous crime he tried to commit—"

She cut herself off then quickly added, "Please forgive me for that, pastor. But I do miss my husband so. I miss welcoming my dearest at the front door and having him sweep me up into his strong arms. I find it so very hard to consider that I might have to spend eternity without him by my side."

Marmaduke cupped his palms on the sides of her face.

"Look up at me, Julia," he said. "I believe God gives each of us a final chance, before it is too late, not a second chance, mind you, but that one final moment in time when He demands redemption, confession, and repentance.

"It is then that our eternal destiny is determined, Julia, if not before. I think this could be what happened with Ambrose. I think there was a chance that he cast off his shackles and bowed in adoration before his Lord."

Julia fell to his feet, wrapping her arms around his legs, unmindful of his lessened strength. Alfred rushed to Marmaduke's side and steadied him.

"If only that is true!" she cried out. "If only I could approach my final days without this dread, this awful incertitude about whether my beloved is in heaven or is now being punished forever in the ghastly reaches of hell."

She quieted down a moment or two later and managed to stand, refusing the pastor's hand. Then, glancing at the people staring at her, she primly straightened her dress, aware that they must have been startled and embarrassed by her behavior.

"It is from love that I act like this, driven by the tragic mischance of my loss," Julia, both cheeks twitching just a bit, told them all, trying to shed the pedantic manner that was her trademark but not succeeding very well.

"Do not ever be ashamed of the indignities to which love someday may reduce you," she continued. "Worry instead that you might never love so deeply that you are willing to risk the ridicule of your countrymen."

Despite that kind of verbiage, she managed to connect with everyone there, especially the Reverend John Covington Marmaduke, who felt some semblance of the pain that was intimately hers.

❧ 34 ❧

*I*F ONLY I *could approach my final days without this dread, this awful incertitude about whether my beloved is in heaven or is now being punished forever in the ghastly reaches of hell . . .*

After speaking with the Reverend Marmaduke as he returned home, Julia Pegram did not venture out of her house for the next several days, preferring its familiarity to anything on the outside. She would walk from room to room, remembering places where Ambrose had stood, moments between the two of them, especially early on in their marriage before his behavior had deteriorated, as though by focusing on the one set of memories she could pretend that the other either did not exist or was unimportant.

If only I could stay here for whatever time I have left, she thought, looking wistfully at surroundings she had known for many years. *Outside, it is all mean and cruel, but here I have a chance to shield myself from all that.*

In the past, Julia had been able to control everything that happened within the walls of that house. Once she left them, she was at the mercy of others, many of whom deeply resented her husband. And so she had found a security, a comforting predictability, inside her home that she was reluctant to give up even for a short time.

Even our children were only doing their duty by attending the funeral. They all left as soon as they could. We have driven away from us everyone who has mattered, she told herself. *There were so few at the service.*

Most of those in attendance were business clients of her husband's, there only because it was "proper." She knew no one had come out of affection or a sense of loss, not even, she suspected, their son and two daughters.

"No one but me cried!" Julia suddenly blurted out as she stood in the middle of the den where Ambrose had planned most of his business strategies.

He had won some achievement awards, and there were a few letters from some of his customers, each one framed and hanging from part of one wall, now mocking his absence.

"You displayed each one as though receipt of it gave you some worth," she said out loud, her slaves elsewhere in the house or in their quarters. "'Here I am,' you seemed to be saying. 'This shows that people do care. This

shows that I have substance as a human being, that I will be missed when
I die someday.'"

Julia had to sit down, a spell of dizziness hitting her. She picked the hard
wood chair at his desk, hesitating as she took up its emptiness.

. . . *that I will be missed when I die someday.*

"Not even by your own children," she countered. "You were their father,
but you drove them all away, Ambrose. I remember your kind, wonderful
moments, but they were swallowed up by the others in time. Even at the
beginning, they seemed to be reserved for me, not the slaves, not those over
whom you held so much power.

"You couldn't dominate me because I would never let you, and I suppose
I earned your respect as a result, but from the time when the children were
toddlers, you tried to break their spirits. Later, as young adults, the moment
they could leave, they did."

No tears.

That struck her hard again.

"You bowed your heads at the grave but that was all," she said of those
grown children. "You took me in your arms and spoke soothing words, but
you meant little by them, for I used to push you away when you came crying to me about your father's austere ways. I left so much up to him while
I was busying myself with civic affairs and . . . and—"

She held up her hands in front of her eyes.

"Like shifting sand through my fingers," she moaned. "I have nothing left
except the presence of those whom Ambrose bought as personal property,
like any piece of furniture, people who may hate me, for all I know, even
as they surely hated my husband."

She spun around and nearly fell, apparently making enough noise to
bring the cook to the door.

"Anythin' wrong, Missus?" asked the middle-aged woman named Hannah.

"No . . . ," Julia told her. "I am just fine, thank you."

But she knew she could not have been convincing, her voice quavering,
the very tone filled with unmistakable pain. She hoped Hannah would say
nothing further, that she would simply amble off in that telltale way of hers,
a game leg making her limp.

Oh, Hannah, Julia thought. *I wish I could just send you off into the world
and—*

But that was not possible, for she had grown up with slaves and she
would not be surprised if she died with them around her.

How could I function without them? she asked herself. *I would have to sell
this plantation and get a smaller house in Greenville or Columbia.*

But Julia could not dismiss the sight of Hannah hobbling around with that bum leg; she could not because she had always suspected that her husband had been responsible, that a beating had done it or improper heating during the winter had caused gout, which, though most common in men, had attacked Hannah alone among the slaves.

Or diet, Julia added. *Some deficiency could have crippled her.*

When cold weather came, Hannah was worse, but she kept on working just the same. Ambrose Pegram threw dinner parties for his clients, parties that were elaborate because he had the money to make them so.

Shrimp was usually brought in from the Atlantic coast, expertly pickled with allspice, ground pepper, mace, and Spice Islands vinegar, and served as an appetizer. This became a standard dish in that household because it was one that Ambrose enjoyed more than any other. The main course was often country ham with brandied peaches, though roast duckling with sweet potato pie in orange shells was periodically served instead. Dessert proved to be either custard meringue, rice pudding, or pears poached in wine.

"Always there, doing whatever you had to . . . ," Julia whispered as she opened the door to the parlor and walked out into the adjacent hallway.

The back door was ajar, and she could see the slave woman in the kitchen across the walkway, puttering over something on the large oval table in the middle.

Julia walked out of the plantation house to the kitchen's entrance and stood there in the doorway, watching a lifelong slave seemingly enjoying what she was doing.

Whistling!

Julia wondered how that could be.

How can Hannah be so happy? she marveled.

But that was exactly what the woman seemed to be, her whistling as cheerful a sound as Julia had ever heard.

Julia walked into the kitchen, and Hannah jumped, startled.

"I didn't know you was there," she said. "What's you needin', Ma'am? Anythin' I can git for you now?"

Julia smiled and told her, "I was just watching you."

Hannah glanced up at her, puzzled.

"Me, Ma'am? I ain't doin' nothin' special, nothin' I know of, anyway. Jus' fixin' tomorrah's vittles."

"You were whistling."

"Did that upset you, Ma'am?" Hannah asked, swallowing hard, concerned. "I's sorry . . ."

"No . . . it was beautiful . . . and happy-sounding."

"Don't know anythin' else to do."

"Have you always been like that?"

Hannah became silent, pretending to concentrate on the fresh dough she had been kneading.

Julia touched her shoulder.

"Look at me." Julia spoke gently, not in the manner of her husband.

Hannah obeyed instantly as every slave learned to do early on, whatever the command might be.

"Have you always been so cheerful?"

"Sometimes . . . ," came the tremulous answer, a certain fear remaining though the cause of it was gone.

"Now is one of those times?"

"Yes, Ma'am."

"But why? Why are you so happy?"

"I's alive."

"You are feeling the way you do now, that whistling and all, simply because you are alive, Hannah?"

Julia had been born into wealth and the slave woman into poverty. Julia could buy anything she wanted, but Hannah and the other slaves had had to depend on fleeting moments of generosity from Ambrose Pegram.

"Simply because I is alive, yes, Ma'am, that's it," Hannah replied, but Julia sensed that there was something else.

"What are you holding back?" she asked.

Hannah tried to seem puzzled but failed to be convincing.

"I will not punish you for telling me the truth," Julia promised her.

"The massa would have!" Hannah blurted out.

"But my husband is gone. And I am not the same . . . as he."

At that, Hannah turned away, directing her attention back to the dough.

"Is that why you are happy?" Julia asked.

Reluctantly Hannah nodded.

"How often did my husband punish you?"

Hannah muttered, "Scars all over me."

"But what would make him do that?"

"If I slow answerin' him sometimes, you know . . . or if maybe I had a tone of my voice that he got into his head was not respectin' him . . . or if he no like my cookin' some days."

"But why did you never tell me? I could have stopped him."

"The massa coulda killed me quicker than that."

Hannah seemed to be pleading with her as she went on to say, "Ma'am, are you going to punish me now?"

As she spoke, she changed the way she held her body, for she not only cringed but seemed to be resigned to the pain of a whip or being punched or slapped or worse.

"You did that without thinking," Julia commented, "like a reflex, like you have learned to do it, a child hurt by flame flinching when he sees a fire close by."

"The massa enjoyed it."

"Enjoyed seeing you like this? Looking like some poor dog that has been kicked again and again?"

"Yes, Ma'am, but not as much as what he would do later, Ma'am."

So much of Julia's world had crumbled with her husband's death. The rest was now close to shattering.

"But he never raised a hand to me."

"You ain't a nigger, Ma'am."

Julia left the kitchen but stopped in the middle of the walkway between it and the plantation house as she heard Hannah calling to her, "Ma'am, can I say somethin'?"

"What is it? I am very tired. I want to go back into the house and up to my bedroom, and sleep the rest of the day and perhaps as many days afterwards as I can manage. If I am fortunate enough, sometime it might be that I shall never wake up."

Hannah walked to her side.

"You visited the preacher man," she said, "because you was forgivin' him, and you wanted him to know that."

"That's right. I could not blame Reverend Marmaduke for my husband acting according to that awful nature of his. I couldn't!"

"Can I speak freely, Ma'am?"

Julia told her she could.

"When is you gonna forgive yourself?" Hannah asked.

If Ambrose had been nearby, she would have suffered woefully for that sort of question, and probably the other slaves along with her, as the man's habit was to apply an ownership approach he called "group discipline."

"You know my heart . . . ," she conceded in a near-whisper.

"And the pain it feels," Hannah replied.

"Hold me," Julia begged. "Hold me, please, I am about to fall."

She leaned against the black woman, who felt like a strong tree that had been firmly rooted a long time before.

"You should be hating me!" Julia yelled. "But you do not. How can you be like this? How can you?"

"I have never felt hate," Hannah told her, "not toward you."

"Then what do you feel? Surely not love. I am hardly a lovable woman. I am vain, impatient. Some have called me hoity-toity, and they are right. I see that now. Surely you must have some strong emotions about me."

"You would punish me if you knew."

"I give my word that this will never be so from now on."

"Pity, Ma'am . . . I feel pity for you."

Julia started to push away from her, but the dizziness remained, and she had to hold on to the black woman again.

"How could you have only pity for me?"

"The massa was the way he was. The children is the way they is, Ma'am. You got this big old house all to yourself now and a lot of land and crops around it. You're not happy here no more, maybe never was.

"But it's not a prison, it shouldn't be no how, but you've made it that, Ma'am. You've gone outside only twice since the massa died—to his buryin' and to see that preacher man. You feel alone. And you's wantin' only to die. That, Ma'am, is why I feel pity."

Julia could not bring herself to protest because Hannah had spoken only the reality of what life had become.

"Do you want to go inside now?" asked Hannah.

"Yes . . . inside, please," Julia said. "I am not feeling well. Will you help me up the stairs? I need to rest."

Without replying, Hannah tightened her grip on the other woman.

The two of them walked slowly inside and headed toward the curving staircase that seemed a given in the design of many of the large homes of that era.

They were able to make it nearly to the top step before Julia's legs gave out from under her, and she collapsed, though Hannah was able to prevent her from tumbling down the stairs and seriously injuring herself.

Embarrassed by showing such weakness in front of someone she had always considered to be inferior, she suddenly barked at the other woman, "I can make it by myself! I don't need some nigger looking down on me."

Hannah stayed where she was, having learned to ignore insults after being the object of them all her life.

"I am not a child, however I may appear now," Julia added nastily. "Do get away from me . . . now!"

At that, nodding humbly, Hannah left her there and, betraying no emotion, walked back down the steps.

No . . . please! Julia said silently. *I mustn't let her leave me like that. I mustn't.*

She was about to ask for Hannah to return, but old social conventions refused to roll over and die, reasserting their control, and so she said nothing.

I will not grovel, her mind shouted with typical stubbornness, not before that nigger nor anyone else!

Julia had to pull herself along the hallway, her legs still perilously wobbly.

By the time she finally got to the other end, her arms were reacting painfully to the exertion.

I feel so old, she thought, *so old and useless and—*

If only she could reach the doorknob!

Finally, she was right below it, and she reached up, grabbed the knob, and turned it, using her shoulder to push the heavy door open, then crawled inside.

Out of breath, she had to rest for several minutes on the bare, tongue-and-groove floor before making it the rest of the way to the bed.

A short distance that seemed impossibly long.

After she lifted herself onto the bed, her head throbbing, her joints aching, Julia passed out, the rushing darkness a blessing that she embraced with desperate fervor because it brought with it a temporary oblivion to which she surrendered herself gratefully.

≈ 35 ≈

A NEW DAY PASSED, from the early dusk of the one to the full night of the next.

Hunger had started to awaken her, but it was the flickering of lights outside her window that completed the process as she opened her eyes with some regret, since she had been hoping the nothingness from which she was being pulled could have proven to be eternal, perhaps even a prelude to glory divine.

Lights.

Flickering.

Scores of them.

Dancing lights through the window and on the ceiling.

So many! she exclaimed. *Have stars come down from heaven at God's command to wait at my window and mock me by their cheerful glow?*

Julia wanted to close her eyes and return to a now familiar blackness, but that was when the voices commenced, singing a hymn she did not immediately recognize, and a moment later, they faded away until she heard just one, a young woman's voice, surprisingly in tune and unwavering, stronger than might be expected.

Julia struggled to a sitting position.

"Go away!" she shouted toward the window.

But the lights remained, and the girl's voice continued.

Finally Julia could endure it no longer. After managing to get off the bed, she pulled on a robe and stumbled down the stairs, onto the spacious front porch.

I will send them away immediately, she grumbled to herself. *They'll never do anything like this again.*

Julia was prepared to be quite profane in a society where this sort of language was heard only from saloon girls out west or streetwalkers up north along the Boston waterfront and elsewhere in that vulgar region.

What she saw as she stepped through the front door took the words away and left her gasping, mouth open, eyes wide, tears flowing like tiny streams.

More than twenty people! Each holding a single candle.

Among them all were the Pegram slaves, with Hannah at the front, and beside her Charity Littlepage, her parents standing close by, candles in their hands as well, and some neighbors, people she had assumed were not at all interested in her over the years.

Everyone else had started to hum as a backdrop to the girl's singing, which was surprisingly accomplished.

Her face . . .

It was a loving face.

A face with no trace of resentment or bitterness, but then that was as it should be since Ambrose Pegram had never harmed her or her family. And yet Charity was not alone, for others had the same expression, black faces primarily, including Hannah's, faces that seemed to be speaking a wordless but still powerful message.

Stepping onto the porch, dwarfed by the tall, thick columns on either side of her, Julia listened for only a moment then tried to turn away but seemed to have lost the strength to do so.

"I cannot accept what you are doing," she yelled to them, focusing on Hannah and the other slaves. "I gave no love to you, at no time did I do that. I turned away from you, hiding in the security of this family's wealth, pretending that it gave me all that I needed in my life. When you were in pain because of cuts and bruises inflicted by my husband, I pretended not to notice."

The singing had stopped. Only her voice was being heard.

"When you were hungry because you were not being fed properly, so that my husband's profits could increase, I spent money on dresses and perfume and fine linens and furnishings for this house. That should have been for food in your stomachs instead."

Julia again started to turn away, intending again to retreat back into that vast, womb-like house behind her.

"We is Christians!" shouted Hannah. "Folks like us ain't never had nothin' but our faith. But sick or well, hungry or full, achin' from the work piled on our backs or sufferin' from the lashes that broke our skin and spilled our blood but couldn't touch our souls, whatever was happenin', we knew the Lawd would take care of us. We knows we don't have to worry no how. We knows He would never leave nor forsake us.

"He never did, He never will, and He's brought us to this night. He has us standin' here now, with a whole lot of white folk all 'round, and that's the miracle of it, all of us comin' to you and sayin' real clear so's you understand that we hold nothin' at all against you, Ma'am. As the dear Lawd above forgives us, so we gotta do the same."

Charity stepped up to stand in front of Julia, who was still standing on the front porch. Charity's arms were outstretched.

"This young lady wants to hug you," Hannah said. "Walk down those big old steps, Ma'am, and let her do that."

Julia relented and, with sudden strength of step, approached Charity. More than twenty pairs of eyes wept cleansing tears as they embraced.

At the rear of the small group stood a certain preacher man who was behind it all.

CHARITY HAD BEEN *reading and talking, telling the stories for hours, a period broken only by her short breaks for water or other necessities. There was also a quick lunch of sandwiches and hot tea that Loreta's staff had prepared for everyone.*

It would soon be time for dinner. And the members, normally looking forward to whatever banquet Loreta had waiting for them, were uncustomarily anxious to eat and then hear more from the surprise guest . . .

Part 3

❧ ❧

Valor is a gift.
Those having it never know for sure whether they have it
till the test comes. And those having it in one test never know
for sure if they will have it when the new test comes.
Carl Sandburg

CHARITY'S TEEN YEARS *passed by, and her parents saw that she was as beau-. tiful a young woman as she had been an adorably cute child. She was well aware of her perfectly developed body and invariably chose dresses that showed off her tiny waist and eye-catching figure. Her parents worried that, on occasion, she could look too appealing and invite the wrong kind of attention from the wrong kind of people. At times they had to step in and take a particular dress away from her.*

To Charity's credit, even during the turbulent teenage years she never threw a tantrum, though she tended to sulk a bit for a day or two afterward.

As the years passed, the level of lawlessness in the area around the Littlepage plantation seemed to increase, and young women like Charity seemed to be the predominant victims, either of robbery, assault, rape, or other terrifying scenarios.

When yet another young woman was kidnapped from a community some few miles away, possibly by a stranger with red hair and expensive-looking attire, including a wide-brimmed gray western hat, Elizabeth and Alfred were compelled to caution their daughter about being too friendly with anyone she did not know.

Charity's immediate reaction proved startling, even to the two human beings who knew her best, for it turned out that she had already overheard the news when Samuel Fulkerson had dropped by to tell them, and she had figured out what they were going to say.

"Was it a white man?" she asked.

Alfred told her that that was what he had heard from Fulkerson during the early part of the conversation that she had missed.

"Praise God!" Charity said.

"Just because it was a white man?" he asked.

"I'm glad it was nobody black!" she replied.

Though already knowing the answer, Alfred wanted to hear how well his daughter was able to express herself.

"Explain what you mean," he asked.

"If a colored man did it," Charity went on, frowning, "there would be lynchings all over the place, innocent people strung up and killed."

"You are absolutely right, Charity," Alfred assured her with great paternal pride. "That was good reasoning, dear."

She seemed dispirited then.

"Anything wrong?" he asked.

"What if a white man kidnapped a black girl?"

"That would never happen. No one who was white and proud would want to do anything to any black girl."

"Are you sure, Daddy?"

"Of course!"

She stood on her toes and kissed him.

"Thank you for being honest," she said.

"You make it very easy for me," he told her. "You are not perfect, but then may the rest of us have only your imperfections."

SAVILLA HAD DIED a few years earlier, after a massive stroke had kept her paralyzed for the few remaining weeks of her life. The Littlepages moved her from the slave quarters into a room in the big house, hoping she would be more comfortable. But despite their loving attention, periodically Savilla could be seen crying, the tears streaking her cheeks, but this was not often.

"She's been used to so much activity," Charity lamented as she and her mother left Savilla's room one afternoon. "It must be awful for her to just lie there, doing nothing at all. That's why she weeps every so often, I think, remembering the times when she was up and about, with more energy than the rest of us."

Elizabeth agreed.

"We can only make Savilla comfortable," she replied. "I wish there were more we could do, but there isn't. The rest is in the Lord's hands."

They were downstairs now, standing near the dining room, both remembering the many meals Savilla had served in there.

"She will probably die in that bed," Elizabeth said. "If only there is no more suffering for that dear woman."

Savilla could move nothing but those marvelous, twinkling eyes of hers, not even the fingers that once had done so much cooking, sewing, and a great deal more. Charity developed a kind of "sight language" with Savilla, who was apparently aware of everything and everyone around her. "Yes" was indicated by a single blink of her eyelids, "no" by two blinks.

Alfred was grateful Charity could share a rapport with the old woman that seemed quite similar to what he enjoyed with Little Isaiah. As soon as he found out that Savilla could communicate, after a fashion, he went into her room at the plantation house and sat beside her fragile-looking form on the bed.

I am glad I moved you in here, he thought, *knowing what everybody else did, that you have only a limited time left and you needed more privacy than your normal quarters allowed, as improved as these were over what other slaves endure through South Carolina and elsewhere in the South. You probably have lived nearly eighty years without ever having something as basic as a room to yourself.*

He asked her that very question. "Have you ever had a bedroom all to yourself, Savilla?"

She blinked twice.

"I thought so!" Alfred exclaimed. "You really have no idea what true privacy is all about."

Two more blinks.

"How sad," he reacted, "how very, very sad, dear lady. I should have done it differently all these years with you, with the others, instead of loading everybody into a simple building that has no separate rooms and just a plain—"

Alfred was starting to weep as he spoke.

"I could have bought another home like this for you all, and more besides," he freely acknowledged to Savilla. "How limited my so-called kindness is, how concerned I am, after all, with what the community would think about anything like that! I, who have prided myself on ignoring its suffocating dictates; but then some fragment of that community's demands apparently does cling to me like a bloody leech, sucking from my body—"

Savilla interrupted Alfred by blinking in rapid succession, her sudden surge of anxiety apparent.

Puzzled, he turned to Charity, who was sitting next to him.

"What does that mean?" he asked. "What could be upsetting her?"

Charity answered without delay.

"Savilla wants to tell you something, but you need to ask the right questions to find out what it is," she replied wisely. "If you do that, she can tell you in her own way."

"But how am I supposed just to guess?" Alfred asked, more than a little frustrated by the prospect.

"You try. You try your best. I'll help you if I can, Daddy."

So Alfred looked intently at Savilla and said thoughtfully, "I wonder what it is you are trying to tell me now."

He thought quickly before suggesting, "Does it have something to do with privacy, Savilla?"

One blink.

"You have had little or none all these years. I can imagine how distressing that has been for a long, long time."

Alfred tried to envision what it would have been like if he had been stripped of the very privacy that had been so precious to him over the years, privacy that every other white family he knew would fight to maintain.

Two blinks.

She was saying no!

"Perhaps you misunderstood, Savilla," he said, bending lower because he assumed she had not heard him properly.

Once again she blinked twice.

"It hasn't!" he exclaimed in skepticism this time, then awe. "But why? Never to have something as basic, as—"

She was moving her lips now.

"Daddy!" yelled Charity, pointing at the frail old form in that strong, old, four-poster bed, a thick goose-down comforter covering a body that had deteriorated to less than ninety pounds. "Savilla's trying to speak. Look at that!"

He sat on the edge of the bed and leaned over Savilla, his ear next to her mouth, as she seemed to be trying to form words that could not be heard.

Alfred started to pull away, not able to grasp the meaning of what seemed essentially like guttural noises.

Several blinks in a row, seemingly frantic.

"She wants you to try again," Charity told him.

Alfred bent down one more time, praying to God that Savilla somehow could make herself understood.

Then, as he listened, Charity could see a smile slowly cross her father's square-jawed, still handsome face.

Finally Alfred Littlepage straightened up and then spoke. "Dear Savilla, I think this is what you said."

She seemed to be waiting expectantly, staring straight at him.

"You said that having no privacy was never as disturbing as it could have been," he said slowly.

One blink.

"Because—" Alfred started to say.

He brought the back of his hand to his lips.

"Daddy, is anything wrong?" Charity asked.

He shook his head.

"Nothing bad," Alfred assured his daughter, his voice breaking. "Savilla told me nothing bad . . . my blessed Charity."

And then he returned his attention to the barely breathing, shriveled little form on that oversized bed.

"Because . . . ," he continued with considerable sorrow, "if you love those you are with, it is never as bad as it could be, and sometimes it's not bad at all. Is that what you wanted me to understand, dear friend?"

Ancient Savilla blinked once and slowly closed those eyes that had seen so much, never opening them again.

❧ 37 ❧

EVERYONE ON THE Littlepage plantation had mourned Savilla greatly and felt the loss in the weeks that followed her death.

Charity had been in her late teenage years at the time, and having the old colored woman taken from her hit hard because Savilla was something of a substitute for Violet, a wise old woman who had become nothing less than a second mother.

Alfred knew he would have to replace Savilla, but this promised to take some time. Finding the right woman would not be a task he could complete in a day or two, for he would have to travel perhaps substantial distances until he found her.

Slave markets.

It meant having to go to more than one slave market throughout the state; if not successful within South Carolina, he would have to go to Nashville, a hub of slave-trading. Other trips might be necessary until he found the right woman.

"Whoever she is must fit in," he told Elizabeth. "She must fit in with you, with me, with the other slaves. After Violet and Savilla, the burden on a new slave will be unfortunate but hardly avoidable."

"And Charity . . . ," Elizabeth added quickly. "Charity as well must be comfortable with anyone new."

They viewed their daughter as God's supreme gift to them, second only to salvation. Every so often, something would happen that made the two of them realize how central their daughter was to their lives and how remarkable she was.

Charity's intelligence set her apart, which was gratifying to her parents since they both had done everything they could over the years to feed that smart, inquisitive nature of hers, not only through the best education available by private tutors, but also through the acquisition of as many books as they could gather so that she would have them at her fingertips.

And, then, there was also a regular stream of visitors who were statesmen, professors, authors, businessmen, the children and grandchildren of such renowned figures as James Madison, Benjamin Franklin, and others.

Charity had never been shut out of discussions before or after dinner or during any other occasion, unless, due to her age, these might prove disturbing to her.

Something else fascinated the people who met Charity.

Her astonishing sweetness.

The impact she had had on Samuel Fulkerson years earlier gave profound insight into this, for it came from a combination of everything that made up what Charity Dawn Littlepage was as a human being.

"We must be very careful with our daughter," Elizabeth said one day as she sat beside Alfred, watching Charity talking and laughing with young people from other plantations in the area. "Some folks of the wrong influences, and they are increasing here day by day, might see Charity's potential and enlist her in a cause that would bring her only grief."

For a moment, Elizabeth's attention wandered from the conversation she was having with her husband to Charity's way of relating to the other people around her, a cleverness that could never be called routine or ordinary. Telling her friends a clever story, Charity had quickly dawned a disguise for the role, brushing her hair back and stuffing the dangling curls under an old hat. Then she saluted sharply as though she were in charge of an army regiment. It was obvious that she was the center of everyone's attention.

"I agree," Alfred replied, breaking into her thoughts. "She must be kept healthy, she must be kept happy, she must be protected as much as we are able to do so."

He moved closer to Elizabeth, leaning his shoulder against hers.

"If only we could have had others like Charity," she interjected. "That is what you were thinking, isn't it?"

"As usual, you have guessed correctly," he admitted to her. "I think of the future, and I think of this world of hers, and I rejoice at what our daughter will contribute to it. But if there had been others, a boy perhaps, then—"

Elizabeth and Alfred had felt regretful about not having a larger family, at least one more child, but they also accepted that it was physically impossible since Charity's birth had caused so much damage to her mother, and they had long ago decided that they were fortunate and blessed to have even one child and to be alive to enjoy her.

Especially one like Charity.

"It is as though the Lord put into that dear, dear body all the joy and love of life that three children would have had," Elizabeth whispered, feeling a little foolish saying that but half-believing it to be true. "She is so much more . . . more . . . more gifted than the rest."

"I think most parents tend to feel that way," Alfred said. "But then you may be right. I wonder if we will be around when Charity begins her own family. I would like to hold a precious little grandchild in my arms—and so would you."

He was holding Elizabeth's hand, and his fingers tightened around it slightly.

"When that time comes, I would like to know that the way we have raised Charity is what the Lord truly did want. I do feel good about her so far, more so than I deserve, but it would be really wonderful someday actually to see what we now can only suspect. I guess it is what the Bible says, you know, like seeing through a glass darkly."

They were sitting comfortably beside one another on a pair of old rocking chairs that had been in the Littlepage family since their ancestors had come over from the shores of England more than a century and a half ago.

"How ready do you think we really are for these?" Elizabeth asked, playfully tapping one of the chair arms. "Have you thought about it whenever we sit like this on a quiet afternoon? Shouldn't we be up and about today, acting our age, which is hardly all that advanced, instead of engaging in some kind of dress rehearsal for being elderly?"

. . . some kind of dress rehearsal for being elderly.

Being old, if someone were a member of southern aristocracy, was not a dismal proposition by any means. The elderly were guaranteed to be waited on twenty-four hours a day, every need satisfied, medical care especially, handicapped only by the less precise standards of that day but provided lavishly just the same.

The greatest difficulty was preventing them from contracting one or more of the many diseases that went unchecked due to the lack of any cure, none of the later vaccines developed as yet: Respiratory ailments . . . an old man or woman was prone to any number of these, whooping cough, typhoid, and scarlet fever as well as dropsy, diphtheria, diarrheal diseases, nervous system difficulties, tuberculosis, and even ringworm could prove disastrous, even fatal, for older citizens—as well as the young.

One of the more deadly diseases, *vivas malaria,* was brought into the South by unclean slaves but also by European settlers. The most virulent strain was called *plasmodium falciparum,* a germ requiring warmer temperatures, which helped to explain why it was confined primarily to the Carolinas and states bordering on them. Simple mosquitoes were the main carriers. Not many slaves fell victim to this form of malaria, for they seemed to have a genetic immunity to it, though sickle cell anemia proved a ready replacement.

Yet none of the elderly white men and women afflicted by any of the prevalent diseases would ever be shunted aside by their children and, as a result, one strain or another often spread throughout entire, close-knit families, going from the first one taken ill to others charged with that individual's care. No one groaned over this; no one tried to figure out a way around it. They just accepted the consequences as part of the scheme of life.

Elizabeth and Alfred were fortunate.

They had escaped the ravages of the deadlier diseases and had occasionally discussed why this was so, why it was that some Christian families were devastated while others proved to be as they were, with no illness other than simple colds and the like.

"Perhaps it is because the Lord wants us here to see that Charity is able to grow up safe and strong, so that she can have the kind of impact on this world for which she seems destined," Alfred said zestily.

Elizabeth looked at him and said, "You shouldn't seem so facetious. I think that really may be the answer!"

"And when we are old and feeble, we know that she will be there with us, guarding you and me from harm."

In that, Charity would not be so unusual.

To the contrary, paying one or both aging parents any kind of disrespect or neglecting their care was a far more grievous offense in the South of the 1850s than would be so in subsequent generations to follow.

NEITHER ELIZABETH NOR Alfred talked for the next several minutes, the cool air of that autumn's late afternoon refreshing an image of the two of them, gray-haired.

"Elizabeth . . ." Alfred finally broke the silence.

"Yes?" she asked.

"There is something I would very much like to do, but I shall avoid it if you have any strong reservations."

That was the way the two of them had approached matters of this sort since the beginning of their marriage, each concerned about the wishes of the other, especially when the subject was their daughter.

"Go ahead. What do you have in mind?"

"I would like to take Charity with me when I go to that slave market on the outskirts of Nashville."

Steeling himself momentarily, he expected Elizabeth to be outraged at the very notion, surely so much so that she would put up the most violent protest. But, to the contrary, she replied with an altogether different response.

"I think that would be wise," she replied, the hint of an odd grin edging up the sides of her mouth.

He blinked at her several times.

"Are you surprised?" she asked, amused by his reaction.

"Well, yes, I am."

"I love you enough and trust you enough to know that you would hardly attempt anything that would hurt Charity physically or emotionally."

"I would like to go tomorrow," he said somewhat tentatively, still not quite believing what she had told him.

"Fine," Elizabeth assured him. "I think Charity will be thrilled, though I wonder if she will have any idea what is in store for her."

The first hint of uncertainty crept into Elizabeth's voice, a slight quaver that he had come to identify over the years.

"Are you perhaps not as convinced as you first sounded?" Alfred asked. "This is not life or death, of course. I could certainly wait a few months or not take her at all if you happen to have some misgivings."

"Her life has been so free of unpleasantries," she remarked. "All of a sudden, she will be surrounded by . . . by—"

"But she will have me," Alfred uncustomarily interrupted. "I plan on remaining her anchor, Elizabeth."

"And as Charity grows older, we will not be around every minute to shield her," she added, relenting. "It would be good for her eyes to be opened, for our daughter to see what these poor people have to go through.

"Right now, all she knows is how slaves are treated on our plantation and what others like them used to endure before Samuel Fulkerson changed so drastically and ceased treating his slaves with such cruelty."

Alfred sympathized with how she felt and tried to be reassuring.

"Believe this: If I find that Charity is being too terribly affected, and I will know even if she should try to hide this from me, that visit to the market will be ended immediately," he spoke, his voice unwavering. "Which means forgetting any new cook for the moment, Elizabeth, and going back there by myself as soon as possible."

He softened his tone as he said, "But better a delay, I would agree, at least under those circumstances, than causing our dear Charity too much discomfort of a sort that can only become harmful now or later."

But consider how you and I will feel, Beloved, if Charity somehow takes this in stride, he thought, *if the experience tomorrow firms up her views about slaves, views that she will hold for the rest of her life. She knows nothing but the kindness she has seen here. Except for Samuel Fulkerson, she has never encountered anything else.*

Elizabeth tried, in turn, to reassure her husband.

"I wish there were another way, but you really are right," she told Alfred rather mischievously. "The only problem I see now, however, is that until you can find somebody who is suitable to replace Savilla, then it does seem that everyone here will have to endure my attempts at cooking that much longer."

She paused, struggling to keep a straight face, but failed, and burst out laughing heartily as she told him, "Lose no time, good Alfred, my only love. Get that new cook here as soon as you possibly can, please!"

Enjoying the humor as much as she was, Alfred hugged her and then hurried back into the plantation house. Elizabeth lingered for a short while, chuckling to herself.

Anything that gets me out of that kitchen, she thought. *I never realized before now how accustomed I am to being waited on.*

Elizabeth called to Charity, who stopped what she was doing with her friends and hurried over to her mother.

"Is anything wrong?" she asked.

"Your father has something different planned for tomorrow," Elizabeth told her. "Here is what he wants to do. Tell me what you think. You can go if you want, but it is nothing you will be forced to do in order to please either of us."

Charity had heard a few scattered fragments of depressing stories for some time about the woeful slave markets that seemed to be prevalent throughout the South, but she invariably ignored these since they had all seemed so unpleasant and there was no need for her to be concerned with such matters.

Now, older and more aware, she finally had approached Little Isaiah about this subject just the year before, but for once, the man seemed reluctant to respond, a deep frown on his forehead, his eyes closed to the narrowest slits whereas they were usually wide open and sparkling when the two of them were talking.

Little Isaiah, hardy as ever, had been chopping some wood and seemed glad at first to take a break just then, but when Charity had told him what was on her mind, he started wielding the large ax again.

"It's somethin' that no one should have to visit or revisit, child," he said in a not unkindly yet still distant manner, a haunted expression settling on his weathered face. "It's part of what folks like me want to forget, yet we never seem able to—too much pain in that past, too much for each and everyone of us, Charity, too much pain and a heap too much sufferin'. We have seen what no one like you should ever have to see."

It did not take long for Charity to discern fully that this sweet, wonderful man she had known for so long, so gentle in his ways, reacted as he had done because of the veritable Pandora's box of dreadful memories that were periodically surfacing for him, chilling and unsettling memories of the abysmal shame and suffering his people had experienced for many years, memories and images shared by virtually every other slave on every plantation and probably on others for hundreds of miles around.

. . . We have seen what no one like you should ever have to see.

Recalling that inexplicable moment with Little Isaiah was all that Charity needed to react with anticipation as well as with a conviction that going with her father was at last an answer to a prayer she had raised to God regularly since seeing in her friend a dark pit of such sadness, sadness that was being communicated so powerfully to her.

In his eyes, she thought, *I can almost see wavering figures, people he's known and who are gone now, treated so cruelly that their bodies could not endure it any longer and their hearts stopped beating as they said good-bye.*

Charity took her mother's hand in her own.

"I want to go," she emphatically told her mother, hands on her hips. This was not particularly a sign of any sort of defiance on her part, for that was not Charity's way, but rather, was one of relentless determination. "I love Little Isaiah and the rest. But I don't always understand them, Mama. They seem to know me more completely than anyone except you and Daddy, yet I can't honestly say the same about any of them."

She was digging deep for those feelings that she wanted to express to a mother who had never resisted anything she had wanted to say, who was genuinely interested in every thought she wanted to express.

"I get so close, then they pull back. They would give up their lives for me, I know that, but they live in a world so different from what we here have ever known, and they don't much talk about it.

"I want to know everything I can about the black people's lives before they came here, before they ended up on places like the Littlepage plantation. I want to be a better friend than I have been. But I can't be if they seal off part of themselves."

Though young, Charity had an outlook and a vocabulary that seemed years ahead of what other young women possessed, and her mother could hardly contain the pride she felt when Charity was expounding on one subject or another.

"None of it will be pleasant," Elizabeth warned sternly while lamenting in silence the ill-considered willingness she had shown about sending their child to such a place. "You are certain, I fear, to be very upset by what you see."

"Mama, you and Papa raised me to cherish truth, truth from the Bible, truth from the world around me. You never have said anything about avoiding any of it just because it happened to be unpleasant sometimes."

When Charity was younger, she had used her cuddly cuteness to nearly always win whatever arguments or "discussions" ensued among the three of them, rare as these were in the harmony that bound the three of them together.

Now older, she was growing accustomed to using her mind, her reasoning powers, just as effectively as she once had used her cuteness.

"I still want to go," Charity declared. "Daddy will be there with me. I need fear nothing. I do want to see what it's like, Mama."

"Fine, dearest Charity," Elizabeth said. "I *have* let your father know I will not stand in the way."

Charity sensed that something was being held back.

"Are you sure this is all?" she probed suspiciously. "You can tell me whatever it is that's on your heart, Mama. You and Daddy have done that before. Don't stop now and leave me wondering, please."

Elizabeth shook herself in mock exasperation.

"Go!" she yelled as sternly as she could manage.

Charity kissed her mother on the cheek and dashed toward the house, pausing halfway to call back fervently, "I love you so much!" before hurrying on into the house.

Despite her daughter's exhilaration, Elizabeth's misgivings were growing like sudden fire in a clump of dry old straw. One stern question kept seizing hold of her, along with whatever its unperceived answer might portend.

What have I done, Lord? she asked. *Give me some peace about this or help me persuade my loved ones to call it off!*

❦ 38 ❧

I HAD NOT OFTEN *ventured far beyond that community where my only home was located,"* Charity admitted. *"When I was very young, there was no reason for me to do so. As the years passed, it seemed that I had no interest."*

"I don't care about other places!" Charity once declared, stamping her foot in exasperation. "I know what I have here, and I love it. I can't worry about anything else."

Even when young, she had spoken well, with near-adult language and precision, another benefit of the expensive tutors her parents provided for their daughter.

But, later, with maturity there grew an awareness that what happened elsewhere could directly affect that private world of hers. Charity opened up her mind to learning a great deal. She read more complicated books at a younger age than had other women or men. And she became curious about her father's business.

"Can I go with you sometime?" fifteen-year-old Charity had once begged with such a pleading manner that Alfred was amazed he could resist her at all.

"Dearest, the men I meet are annoyed by distractions," he replied, trying not to be curt with his daughter.

"Am I . . . a distraction?" she asked, a vulnerable expression showing unmistakably, making him regret that he had not chosen his words more carefully.

"Not for me, dearest, but for the others, I am afraid, that would be the case. None of them know you as I do."

Shrugging her shoulders, Charity smiled and skipped off to be with some friends. And that seemed to be the end of it.

Alfred had been relieved that she did not press the matter, uncomfortable as he was partitioning off any aspect of his life and running the risk of hurting her feelings in the process. In a household that knew few restrictions between family members, this sort of situation was rare, and he wanted to keep it that way.

She had walked away, seemingly resigned to accepting what her father had told her, hopefully without lingering emotional hurt.

But he had also misjudged the outcome, for Charity had something else in mind.

Ordinarily, when there were visitors for dinner, she seemed to enjoy being with them for a while then got bored or sleepy and either went outside or up to her room.

Two evenings later, however, she stayed until a prominent businessman from Natchez was ready to leave. Never interrupting her parents or the visitor, Charity managed to be captivating. She would smile and laugh at a comment or outright jokes, none of which were off-color since the man knew that Elizabeth and Alfred would not tolerate that kind of humor.

Whatever the topic under discussion, Charity would appear interested.

And when it was something that really did catch her youthful attention, she would scrupulously whisper into her mother's ear, and Elizabeth would wait for the proper timing so that this remarkable child could be allowed to speak.

"Where are you from?" she asked at one point.

"Mississippi," the visitor replied.

"Where in Mississippi?" Charity finally spoke determinedly, her expression one of satisfaction.

"Natchez," the man told her.

"That's a seaport, isn't it?" she replied.

"That it is."

"What do you do there?"

"I own a shipping company."

"What do you ship?"

"Food to places all along the Atlantic coast."

"What food?"

Alfred intruded at this point.

"Mr. Cruikshank is here to relax, child . . . ," he began somewhat sharply then turned to the visitor and added, "My friend, I am very sorry that—"

Charity burst out laughing.

"What in the—?" Alfred said, his face becoming red because he knew what had made her react as she did.

Cruikshank chuckled as he held up his hand.

"Nonsense, Alfred," he said, his substantial girth moving like a bowl of pudding. "Your daughter is just remarkable in every way! Besides, if I were her, I, too, would have laughed at the sound of Cruikshank!"

He rolled his eyes, showing a despair that was hardly of recent vintage.

"It is a perfectly awful burden to have to carry around all these years. But she does not know my first name. Shall we tell her?"

Alfred nodded, his face now a more normal color.

"Go ahead . . . ," he said.

"Charity, dear," Cruikshank spoke, "my full name is Archibald Cruikshank. Now you can have a good laugh!"

She did.

Nor was she alone this time.

That visitor ended up staying far longer than he had intended, which meant that, in addition to charming him thoroughly, Charity was able to delay going to bed, cleverly accomplishing two purposes at the same time.

Alfred expected her to corner him before going to bed and pursue the matter of going on a trip with him someday, now that she had shown how delightful she could be around a businessman such as Archibald Cruikshank.

But, again, he was wrong.

After he had bent down to hug her, Charity simply kissed him on the cheek and then hurried upstairs without saying anything.

He looked at Elizabeth in mild disbelief.

"I think she's forgotten," he said in an attack of wishful thinking. "All of this must be just more of her personality coming out. Is that not amazing?"

Elizabeth simply smiled.

"You think there's more to it than that?" he asked.

"Let's get to bed, Alfred," she told him, evading an answer. "Somehow I suspect that you can look forward to a very busy morning. As for tonight, I do have something special in mind! Now stop this guessing game of yours about our daughter's intentions."

Alfred Monroe Littlepage gulped a couple of times and went with his wife.

❧ 39 ❧

A T BREAKFAST AFTER Mr. Cruikshank's visit, Charity had been even more animated than usual, talking cheerily about a party being held soon at a nearby plantation. Before that, though, she had offered to say grace.

"Jesus . . . ," she began. "Thank You for this day and this food and for my parents and for Little Isaiah—"

And the fifteen-year-old went on to name each of the slaves sitting at the second table in the dining room.

This is unusual, even for Charity, Alfred thought. *She believes strongly in Jesus as her personal Lord and Savior but has always seemed loathe to get bogged down in anything that seemed at all ritualistic in nature.*

After that, she proceeded to eat her portion of the food that had been put on the table that morning and left nothing on her plate.

Finally it was time for Alfred to leave on the day's business trip.

His destination: a particularly poor white section of the center part of South Carolina where the local authorities were hoping to entice him to invest, whatever the business venture might be.

"It will be rough for me," he told Elizabeth as they stood on the front steps.

"Seeing all those people, hungry and sick?" she guessed.

He nodded, never surprised that his wife seemed always to know what was concerning him at a given moment.

"They will either gather around me and ask for help, or they will remain in their shacks, peeping through narrow windows at this well-dressed stranger. You and I live so well in comparison to most people, Elizabeth, and I don't feel bad about this because at least others around us have food to eat, clothes to wear, and pleasant homes in which to live. But those I will see in a few hours have next to nothing, and it turns my conscience inside-out."

"The worst part of it is that most of them are white, I understand."

"That they are. Some free blacks live better than they do, as blacksmiths, carpenters, stable men, that sort of thing."

"What can you really do?"

"Not all that they need, of course. I know it's a cliché, but I shall be only a tree-planter. Someone else will have to do the cultivation from then on."

"Should you take Charity, I wonder?" Elizabeth speculated.

"She's so young."

"We have shielded her a great deal, Alfred. Shouldn't we be thinking of the future, preparing our daughter for facing certain realities? Poverty is one of those. Help Charity to feel for people the way you do."

"I think you may be right. Perhaps next time."

Elizabeth nodded as she said, "You know best."

"Do not ever say that," he admonished her. "It speaks of the way other women view their husbands—I mean, as their master. I am not your master. I never have been, and I surely never want to be. We are partners, period, in every application of that word."

They kissed, and then he walked down the steps to the carriage that Simuel had pulled up in front of the house. Usually, Little Isaiah would be the one to go with him, but this time Simuel had made a special request which Alfred had honored. His reason was one that could hardly be refused.

"I want to find out if'n I can give them any part of what they's needin'," he said earnestly. "Thought maybe we all could get together, the other coloreds and I, and make some clothes for them, and raise some extra crops, if'n that be all right with you, Massa. We could make some preserves, too, enough to last some of them families a little while."

"But there are poor colored families," Alfred reminded the thin-faced black man. "Wouldn't you rather concentrate on them?"

"Hunger is hunger, rags is rags; don't matter no how what the color of their skin is. They's cryin' out for help. And Jesus wants us to listen and do somethin'. I can't go and pretend I ain't heard what He's been tellin' us."

After Alfred had climbed into the carriage's backseat, Simuel turned around and handed him a small square sheet of paper.

"What is this?" Alfred asked, holding the sheet rather dumbly, without opening it.

"A note from Miss Charity."

Alfred mulled over her behavior from the night before to just a few minutes ago, sure that he would not be surprised by what she could have written.

"Aren't you gonna read it, Massa?" Simuel asked.

"I almost know what it says."

But he unfolded it anyway, staring at the beautiful script his daughter had written: "Daddy . . . now may I go with you someday?"

"Simuel?" Alfred addressed the other man.

"Yes, sir?"

"Is it time for my daughter to see the side of life that those poor people near Columbia will show her?"

Simuel seemed pleased that he had been asked about this.

"I knows Miss Charity pretty good. She's stronger inside than a lot of men. I's thinkin' this might be a real good time for her to go along with you."

Alfred recognized the wisdom of that.

"Would you let her know then?" he replied. "Would you tell her for me? That she can go with me now if she wants?"

Simuel seemed nearly as happy as Charity would be when she was told about her father's decision.

"Yes, Massa!" he said, beaming at the news. "I'll do that right away. Will you be waitin' out here?"

"I will not move from this spot."

While he waited, Alfred thought of how completely he had been isolating Charity from white poverty without ever intending to do so. His daughter had witnessed more than her share of blacks living in sometimes subhuman circumstances, and this gave her more appreciation for how well the Littlepage slaves were being treated.

One such occasion involved a shantytown some fifty miles away from their estate. Its population was comprised of free blacks, a large number of whom had been given the so-called "gift" of freedom by their masters.

That place embodied everything I have been trying to say to anyone willing to listen for more than a minute or two, Alfred recalled. *Freedom is worthless if it means that slavery is being replaced by an even less desirable way of life. Yet so few people up north get past that one word . . . slavery. It is no more evil than those who impose it.*

Charity had been startled, startled by the smells, by the dirt, startled by the expressions on the faces of men, women, and children who seemed destined to walk about listlessly, getting whatever scraps of work they could but never finding enough available that would enable them to buy sufficient food and clothing for their loved ones.

"How many of them would accept the gift of slavery this very moment in return for what they are going to be facing out here every day of their lives?" he had posed to Charity as they rode in the carriage down the rutted dirt streets, their driver someone from the shantytown itself who was glad to get the money Alfred offered.

She frowned briefly, puzzling over what her father had asked.

"Why don't they just go back to being slaves?" she asked logically.

"Because their masters probably replaced them not long after they left or cut back on the number of slaves for economic reasons. Most would only discover that there is no longer any room for them in paradise.

"And then I do know of a few Christian families living at various places throughout the South who are under conviction about having any slaves, so they wouldn't be interested at all."

"You said paradise," she told him. "How did you mean that? You're not talking about heaven, are you?"

"No, I'm not. It's just my attempt at describing something. The way they used to live must seem like heaven compared with what they endure presently."

"It was paradise for them because they didn't have anything to worry about?"

"That's right. They got whatever they needed without having to beg, without having to behave like homeless animals. Some owners are terrible, cruel, vulgar people, and I can surely see why slaves would want to get away from them and never go back. But those are not the ones who would willingly release any slave from bondage."

One regret that Charity had was that they were just driving through the shantytown, observing the ghastly conditions without doing anything.

"Can't we help now?" she asked.

"We have no food, no clothes for them," her father explained.

"Well, why don't we drive somewhere," Charity persisted, "and get some stuff and bring it back?"

"Something like that has to be planned, dear."

"We could plan it right here, couldn't we? I saw a general store back aways. Why not go there, Daddy?"

As Alfred recalled that moment, he had to face again something that had not become easier since that day.

I looked at those poor people and would have passed them by, clucking self-righteously, he told himself, *and that would have been it.*

Except for Charity. She took the need for doing something as a given. It never occurred to her that they could not help.

Black people were looking at them as they approached, a flicker of expectation in their eyes that disappeared the moment the carriage passed by.

"Hurry up!" ordered Alfred.

In a few more minutes they were out of the shantytown and heading toward the general store some miles away.

"How much can we get?" Charity asked excitedly.

"Whatever we can pile into the carriage," replied Alfred.

"I'll hold some things on my lap," she announced.

"And I shall, too," her father agreed.

"Me, too, sir," the driver offered.

"We will do just fine," Alfred assured them. "Just fine indeed!"

~ 40 ~

THE GENERAL STORE was just ahead of them. As the carriage was approaching it, Alfred noticed that the apparent owner was hurriedly closing for the day.

Alfred jumped out and hurried up to the short, broad-nosed, fortyish man, a wide scar on his right cheek.

"I was hoping to buy from you whatever that grand old carriage behind me could be made to hold," he said.

"That's a whole lot of food, mister," the owner replied, eying the size of it. "But I'm leaving now. Got an appointment. Come back tomorrow."

"I will not be here tomorrow. I live inland. I would be happy to make it worthwhile if you were able to accommodate me."

The man looked at him curiously.

"There are a whole lot of mouths to feed," Alfred told him impatiently. "Will you not do this, mister?"

"You got a large family?"

"No, the food will not be for any of my family members. I shall take it all back to that colony of black folks down the road a bit."

The store's owner stiffened.

"Them shantytown niggers, you mean?" he asked.

"I suppose so," Alfred replied.

"I'm closed now," the man said.

"But you seemed ready to sell me whatever I wanted a minute or two ago."

"That's before I knew you were going to waste it on a bunch of lousy niggers. Jake Funsten ain't that kind of man!"

Alfred controlled himself from responding in kind.

"Many of them seem close to starvation," he said instead.

"I can do what I want, stranger. It's my store and my food stocks, and I don't have to sell you a grain of wheat if I reckon not to do that, understand me?"

"Yes, I understand what you are saying. But it doesn't bother you if babies die in their mothers' arms, if—"

"Don't matter much if it's black babies. Who cares? They'll just go ahead and have more, like rabbits."

"But I can pay—"

"I don't feed no darkies. Now go ahead and get out of my way."

"Because it's your store, right, mister?"

"You got it right at last, stranger!"

"Then allow me to buy the store."

The owner's mouth dropped open.

"I put years into this place!" he exclaimed, his eyes bulging. "You could never afford what it would cost."

"Give me a price."

The other man snorted and started to walk away.

"How about triple what your profits would be over a five-year period?" Alfred persisted, knowing well the enticements to which such a man would respond.

Funsten froze.

"Why, that adds up to something like—!" he replied, startled, gulping as he went on to name the figure.

"I have with me a blank draft from First Columbia National. It's guaranteed money. I would be happy to write down that exact figure plus a five percent bonus if we conclude the deal within the next hour."

Funsten spun around on one heel.

"What's the catch?" he asked, narrowing his eyes and looking with great suspicion at this seemingly calm, assured newcomer.

"No catch, just one condition."

"Go ahead. What is it?"

"That you continue to operate the store for a reasonable wage until I can find someone to take over from you."

Funsten seemed unable to speak for a moment.

"How do you know I won't cheat you blind?" he asked.

"Just because you hate niggers hardly means that you are going to go ahead and cheat a white man."

Jake Funsten chuckled and shot out his hand.

"You got a deal, mister. Let's go inside and put it all down on paper."

Alfred was amused by this man, having met his type often over the years. *You all are the same,* he thought, *whether you are located in the United States or Canada or England or anywhere else I have been. You have a price tag, and you can be bought.*

Once he was inside, he saw how so much of what Funsten had been stocking was critical to the survival of the blacks in the shantytown.

Beef jerky. Shelf after shelf of preserves of one sort or another. Salt pork.

Tins of hash. Meal. Flour, salt, and various kinds of bread, cakes, and biscuits including cornbread, gingerbread, beaten biscuits, and other treats
baked each day by the merchant's wife.

"What do you do with the baked goods that are left unsold?" Alfred
asked.

"Throw a lot of it out," Funsten told him. "Can't be kept too long. They
grow stale. Nobody wants stale or moldy cakes or any of the rest."

"But the niggers up in shantytown could live on what is left, even if it's
a bit stale. They surely cannot care if their biscuits are a little hard. Food in
their stomachs is what they need, however fresh it may or may not be."

"Sometimes I give the cakes and all to the birds, the meat goes to my
dogs and my neighbor's. You seem to think I waste all of it."

"You chose animals above human beings?"

Funsten, hands on his ample hips, looked at him in disbelief.

"You, a southerner, are calling darkies human?"

"I, as a southerner, have had relationships with black people all my life.
They are not animals. They seem much more like hapless children, torn
from their natural homes against their will, plopped down in the midst of
our world, and condemned because they look different, smell different, talk
different."

"I ain't selling no store of mine to nobody like you, mister!" Funsten
declared. "Now get the devil—"

"I will increase the bonus to ten percent and adjust your salary upward
by a similar amount," interrupted Alfred.

The other man smiled.

"On the other hand, since you are a fellow southerner, I don't see why
the two of us can't work this out."

~≈41≈~

So it was that Alfred Monroe Littlepage had unexpectedly become the owner of that general store located just a few miles from the only shantytown in all of South Carolina. Everyone else had seemed content just to let that ghastly place remain as it was, a rotting, reeking mess that some slave-owners felt the blacks had brought upon themselves, a problem that respectable white people could ignore for that reason.

But it was hardly the only location where groups of free coloreds congregated. Others tended to live in isolated, mountainous areas, keeping almost entirely to themselves and were generally a bit less desperate about food since they shot their own game, raised some few crops, welled their own water, and tried to patch together whatever else it was that they needed to eke out an existence better than the shantytown blacks.

As soon as the deal with Funsten was completed, Alfred felt the urge to head into one or more of those other sections of the countryside and see what he could do to help. He felt what he told Charity was "a real leading of the Holy Ghost."

"Those poor coloreds tend to be forgotten by everyone, even those of us with kinder instincts," he said. "They have a measure of sustenance, but it must be borderline. What about housing? What about clothes? And medical supplies?"

He saw that Charity was intrigued by what he was telling her, and that was when he dropped the subject, he hoped, in a way that did not raise her suspicions.

I shall have to go there without Charity, he thought. *Here, we are out in the open, but those other coloreds are so remote that they can get away with a great deal more than the ones in the shantytown, or anywhere else for that matter. That is why I have to be careful. How many of them hate people like me for making their lives so miserable?*

As soon as he left Jake Funsten and climbed back into the carriage, Alfred addressed the driver.

"What is your name, boy?" he asked the muscular-looking, round-faced teenager who was missing most of his right ear.

"Thomas . . . ," came the reply.

"I need help, Thomas."

"What can I do, sir?"

"That shantytown back aways . . . you live there?"

"Yes sir, I does."

"You know what just happened here?"

"You done bought da store, sir."

"You know why, boy?"

"I think you's wantin' to do somethin' about feedin' the other coloreds where I's makin' my home."

"Will they take this from a white man?"

"When you's starvin', you take food from the devil himself if'n you have to!"

Alfred winced at that.

Thomas noticed this and quickly added, "I wasn't tryin' to say dat you's a devil, sir; please forgive me."

The teenager was changing from someone who seemed calm and easy-going, however artificial that facade, to what he really was: a young man clearly very much on edge.

"It was awful, what I said," he went on, what was left of his right ear twitching a bit. "Is you angry, sir?"

"How could I be angry? I know what you meant to say, Thomas. I reacted the way I did because I am a Christian. That anybody would be desperate enough to turn to Satan seems a pretty terrible idea to me."

"When someone's handin' you a loaf of bread, you's not gonna worry about nothin' but eatin' it and making sure your wife and chil'en's got what they need."

Alfred leaned back, surprised that a teenager would be both husband and father, especially under the harsh conditions in the shantytown.

"How many children do you have?" he asked.

"Three, sir."

"How old are you?"

"Nearly seventeen."

"Nearly!"

Alfred had to pause and look away.

Thomas helped create three precious human lives, he thought, *and yet he cannot care adequately for any of them nor for his wife.*

Alfred knew his voice was trembling as he spoke. "Thomas, would you and your family like to come and live with my slaves? They are owned by me, yes, but I have told them that they could leave anytime they wanted. I would not require any ownership papers, just the pledge that you not tell them about any arrangement between us."

Thomas looked at him for a moment then jumped off the carriage and walked off perhaps a hundred yards or so.

"Daddy?" Charity asked.

"Yes, dear . . . ," he replied, though barely able to talk.

"Would you let me go after him?"

"We don't know anything about him, Charity. It would not be safe."

She touched her chest.

"What are you trying to say?" he asked.

"His heart, Daddy, we can feel what his heart is if we just try."

Charity was sitting next to him in the backseat, and he saw that she was staring at him, pleading with her eyes as only she could.

If I am really so uncertain about Thomas, he told himself, *why did I invite him to come with his entire family and join with my other coloreds?*

"You can go, dear," Alfred relented, "but I will go along after you if too much time seems to be passing. And you holler good and loud if anything's wrong."

"Thank you, Daddy," Charity replied with a typical burst of enthusiasm; she jumped down from the carriage and ran off into the patch of woods next to the general store.

But Alfred could not wait very long, misgivings about letting his daughter be alone with a stranger making him feel very uncomfortable. After just a few minutes, he left the carriage and headed toward the woods.

Voices.

He heard them right away.

Calm voices.

Alfred quickened his step and came to a little clearing in the woods.

Charity and Thomas were kneeling on the twig-littered ground, holding hands, first one praying, then the other.

Alfred stood quietly, not wanting to interrupt.

But Thomas sensed he was there and glanced up at him, questioning with his expression if what he was doing was all right with the massa.

Alfred nodded as he walked up to the two of them, went to his knees, and joined hands with his daughter and the young black named Thomas.

≈ 42 ≈

"ALFRED VISITED THE *shantytown and his general store any number of times over the next few weeks,"* Charity continued, still having the full attention of every member.

Before leaving the area that first day, he had hired a shipping company to bring in more food when the stocks ran low. He also organized a system that avoided chaos when word got back to the scores of hungry blacks, and he announced it to them in language that was tough but essential to everything functioning smoothly.

"You will pick certain men who will bring back just enough food to feed you and your families three times each day," he said to the gathered crowd. "There will be two trips daily, one just after sunrise, to bring back provisions for breakfast and lunch, the second around noon to get what is needed for dinner."

Alfred became even more stern when he added, "Allotments will be precise, and except for special circumstances, unchangeable. No departures from what I have prescribed will be tolerated. Repeated violations will result in all this good deed being canceled."

He had no intention of ever denying them food but had to make them think that this was a very real possibility hanging over their heads since they needed to be disciplined, as he felt was the case with all blacks. He had found out by hard, tough experience that many of them tended to be as shiftless as the stereotypes suggested.

At first he wondered why this was, the men most guilty of this. And then Little Isaiah gave him a glimpse of the explanation.

"In Africa the men does the huntin' and the womenfolk stay at home, preparin' meals, raisin' the children, cleanin', all the rest. But they ain't got no other chores. Once they come back with the game, the men's job is over, and they take to sittin' 'round and talkin' and talkin' and talkin' while the women do the work."

Little Isaiah hated to admit this was the case.

"It's the way my people lived for a long time. It's hard to change after so long."

Alfred had taken in such information early on and determined that he would not allow his own male slaves to fall into the same trap. So he made sure they worked at some task from morning until evening, whether planting and picking, painting, or making sure the flowers, in particular Elizabeth's roses, were being cared for adequately.

"If I fail to teach those coloreds of mine the value of discipline imposed by regular work," he had told Charity when she once asked him why he kept the slaves busy for most of the day, "should they ever go free, they would find it almost impossible to adjust to a world outside this estate that demands hard labor from their kind, and their survival would be very much in doubt.

"They have been called lazy, and, to a degree, judging by their ingrained natures, this is true enough. Leave a slave by himself without guiding him, and he would end up acting like a native in some jungle village.

"I am not being cruel or insensitive by saying this, Charity, just as realistic as I can be. They will never survive on their own unless they are taught the differences between the life they once had on this plantation and the one beyond its boundaries."

He sighed as he added, "White people have to realize that they cannot kidnap untamed savages on a wholesale basis without giving back something. Any other approach would be immoral."

Charity seemed to understand why he said this and nodded appreciatively, but he knew it was a lesson he would have to repeat before she fully grasped its significance.

The shantytown blacks adored Charity.

And she seemed to enjoy being with them.

It was almost as though their dirty bodies and the suffocating odors of that place escaped her attention. She would help them load the lighter items of food onto the carriage they were using to transport everything back to their homes. And whenever she heard any talking about their being thirsty, she would run into the general store and bring out glasses filled with lemonade. They would thank their politely, drink the juice gratefully, and continue with their work.

Thomas was one of the regulars who helped to transport the food.

One day he walked up to Alfred, who was standing outside while Charity was carrying some bottles of preserves from the store.

"She's wonderful, sir," he said.

"I agree with you, Thomas," her father replied. "I have been all over the world and met many children but have not seen any the likes of her."

"My wife is in a family way again," Thomas admitted to him, looking more than a little embarrassed.

"How can you manage?" Alfred asked, deeply concerned. "Surely you now have no choice whatsoever but to take me up on my offer to bring your family with you and stay on my plantation. You now have enough food to eat, but there is so much more to life than eating and sleeping. There are clothes, there are—"

They both sensed someone staring at them.

Charity.

She was standing a few feet away, a jar of preserves in each hand. After winking at them, she headed toward the wagon.

"Why are you resisting me on this?" Alfred probed.

Thomas shuffled his feet, nervous about answering.

"My people . . . ," the teenager told him. "It's my people."

"Your family, you mean? I thought I made my own wishes clear."

"The others. I have uncles and aunts and cousins."

Alfred could see a Pandora's box being opened right in front of him, but still, he wanted to believe that the teenager was not conniving something.

"I have room. If necessary, you all can cooperate, and we will build another structure for you to live in."

Thomas's expression brightened at that while Alfred started imagining that he ultimately would have the entire population of that shantytown making a not-so-grand exodus from where they were huddled together at present and traveling to his plantation, a spark being lit as far as his neighbors were concerned when they found out what was happening, a spark that could lead in only one direction: toward disaster.

"How many are there?" he asked, trying not to betray the anxiety that was growing with each heartbeat.

"Maybe fifteen of us, sir," Thomas replied.

Alfred did not know whether to rejoice over that relatively small number or wait for the other shoe to fall.

"Sir?"

"Yes, Thomas?"

"I mentioned my people, but, to me, that's not just my kin; it means our neighbors, their friends, all of us, sir."

Alfred was becoming more and more alarmed.

"Sir?"

"Yes . . . Thomas?"

"Them's all why I can't go to your plantation and live."

Alfred's whole perspective changed in an instant.

"You are turning me down because of fifty other coloreds? I just don't understand, Thomas. Can you tell me why?"

"It's because they would be left behind. I know in my heart that you càn't take 'em all or you's riskin' runnin' into trouble with the other owners."

Alfred was quiet briefly.

"Why be so concerned about the rest of those poor blacks back in the shantytown?" he finally asked.

"Because I can't be blessed like that while they's still livin' so miserable as they's doin'. I couldn't treat them like that, couldn't take all the good that'd be happenin' to me and my loved ones and see the rest of 'em goin' on with so little. They would end up hatin' me, and I'd be hatin' myself at the same time."

Alfred did not know what to say immediately, which was unusual for him, but he was confronted with a rather hapless black teenager who was the father of several children, with another on the way, no regular work, no other source of income except what he managed to beg from strangers who passed by or when he would go into Columbia, someone who had never had any kind of legitimate foundation in what resembled a normal life, yet who was willing to sacrifice a better existence for himself because of the impact upon his neighbors and friends.

Struggling with his own emotions, Alfred cleared his throat before replying, "I cannot tell you how much I respect what you have told me. I would like to be able to respond by waving aside those concerns about how other members of my community would react, but I cannot. As you have expressed your devotion to family and friends, so must I.

"Already some consider me strange, an outcast of sorts, even a Yankee in disguise, perhaps. I have to consider losing everything that has been built up over the years."

Thomas was nodding as he listened.

"But there is something I can do," Alfred added. "I can spend considerable sums of money tearing down the shantytown . . . and rebuilding it so that you have adequate surroundings. I cannot promise anything glorious. But I will not let you wallow in a cesspool any longer."

Surprisingly, the teenager did not seem elated.

"They won't let you, sir," he said flatly.

"Who are 'they'?"

"Certain people."

"Who are they? Where are they?"

"Everywhere."

"You haven't identified them, Thomas."

"A secret society, sir."

"What kind of society?" asked Alfred, though he already suspected the answer.

"They're fightin' against freedom for slaves."

"Does this society have a name?"

"I don't know it all. I think it's called Knights or somethin'. I's just not 'ware of what the rest of it is, sir."

"I thought that was what you were going to say."

"They're why we live the way we do. We ain't gettin' no jobs because of them. We ain't able to get no credit 'cause of them, to buy food, to buy things to help us raise crops. They's just wantin' us to stay here and starve to death."

"Because you happen to be free?"

"Not 'nough slaves 'round these days, sir. Prices is goin' up. That makes it cost more for them to do business. They want to force us to go back to being slaves. At least then we would have food, clothes. We wouldn't die of starvation. We wouldn't freeze to death in the winter."

"There might be some sense to that if you were doing it of your free will and if you could be guaranteed fine treatment by your new owners."

"But that'd never be, sir. Not everyone is like you."

Alfred thanked him for that and added, "I could even help by getting certain owners who need slaves to come down here, and you could deal with them directly. But there are so many of you. I might not run out of decent people who would treat you well, but I might run out of those who actually needed more slaves. Shortage or not, around here, anyway, the families I am in touch with are well stocked, by and large."

He reached out and gently placed his hands on Thomas's shoulders.

"I intend to build up that shantytown step by step, and no group like this Knights or whatever it is will dissuade me," Alfred said. "First, the food, which is now flowing; next, clothes. I know some kindhearted manufacturers who will help out with free goods.

"Can your womenfolk make clothes by hand? Is that a problem? If there is still any kind of shortage, I shall buy whatever else is needed. As for the buildings, that will be the next step, and it *will* happen. I do promise you that."

Thomas stepped back a few paces and shook his head.

"I just can't let it happen," he protested. "She is too precious, too fine."

"Who is that, Thomas?"

"Your little girl, sir . . . Charity."

"Charity? What does she have to do with this?"

"They's sure to strike you where it's gonna be grievin' you the most. And they's everywhere, sir, everywhere! In every town. In every village. They's of pure white stock, and they's living right with the rest of you, maybe next door, maybe down the road, but somewhere close by and far 'way. But they's not like you and the other good people you knows, sir.

"Their kind has been filled a long time with nothin' but hate, hate that eats 'way at their guts, sir. And all of 'em is blind to the meanin' of true righteousness. Their consciences is seared. And they will never change until every last one of them is gone. But that may never be, 'cause they's teachin' their own boys and girls to feel the same way they do."

"So Charity would be a target?"

"Their first target, sir. After that, they're probably gonna figure that you'd need no more convincin'."

Terror chilled Alfred, the terror of imagining her beautiful, perfectly shaped form lifeless at his feet, that sweet, ever-so-fragile body covered with spilled blood, her eyes open, staring up at him, as though to plead, "Daddy, Daddy, why didn't you stop them from doing this to me?"

"Give us some food and maybe some dress goods and wool for our women to use but nothin' more than that," Thomas's voice penetrated his distracted mind. "That'll be a help to us, sir. Don't sacrifice your family for our sakes."

All his life, Alfred Littlepage had been surrounded by the reality of power, the kind of power that substantial sums of money were able to command, first being protected by it through his parents then wielding it himself after he became an adult, and then even more with the resources that Elizabeth brought to their marriage.

He was hardly unaccustomed to using his influence to accomplish whatever he wanted, even to exerting control over certain politicians in the local and state governments as well as in Washington, D.C., but only by following careful thinking and exhaustive prayer about whether each of his goals was righteous.

"I think I need to leave now," he told the teenager.

"Go in peace, sir," Thomas told him calmly. "The Lord will look at your heart and know what kind of man you are. Don't you go home bein' ashamed no how. Us kind of folk thanks you for your kindness."

But on that matter, Alfred Monroe Littlepage would have little peace over the years to follow, the images of desperate black people coming back to him as he recalled that shantytown and the teenager named Thomas. And always when the thoughts came he would ask himself, *Should I have done more, Lord? Should I have risked everything?*

❧ 43 ❧

MY FATHER'S DESTINATION *on the day he sent Simuel to fetch me was a particularly poor white section of the center part of South Carolina,"* Charity continued. *"Authorities there were hoping Daddy would invest Littlepage funds there, allowing them to fulfill election-year promises with private money rather than drain the public treasury. Their plan would also make them look like financial wizards."*

ALFRED SNAPPED OUT of his extended reverie at the sound of a familiar voice and the creak of the carriage springs as Charity climbed in beside him.

"Thank you, Daddy!" she said excitedly.

"I decided to let you go along with me today," he explained, "because some people live quite differently from the way you and your mother and I and our coloreds are blessed to do. They are not evil or to be avoided for any reason just because they have no slaves and they are dressed in rags and have little to eat. The possession of slaves and all the rest has nothing to do with someone's worth in God's sight."

"Like Thomas and his people?" she asked.

Alfred nodded as he said, "That's correct, dear, but—"

"Most black people are poor," she told him. "I know that!"

"The people I am visiting today are not black, Charity."

That she was puzzled by this showed on her face, her nose wrinkled up, her forehead frowning.

"May I explain, Charity?" her father asked.

"Yes . . . ," she said hesitantly.

"God does not bring the burden of poverty to all people. The family they have had, the life they lead, these are some of the reasons behind how they are forced to live, but God is not to be blamed for this.

"There are more poor free coloreds around because so many white people will not hire them or else pay only very low wages when they do. This is wrong, I know, but nothing will change overnight, or perhaps ever."

"But today," she spoke, "where are we going today?"

"To see some poor white people," he replied.

For a moment, Charity did not react; then she looked at her father and said, "Why are they poor, Daddy, and we're not?"

Her father hesitated, uncertain how he should respond. It was a question, in one form or another, that had never been far from his own mind, along with a degree of guilt whenever he saw poor whites.

"Because God has blessed us real good," Alfred tried to explain but felt inadequate to the task.

"Why did God bless us and not them?" she asked.

He could not answer the same question when he asked it of himself, let alone face it from Charity.

"We just have no real answers," he tried nevertheless. "Maybe some are awful people, blasphemous, utterly controlled by the rampaging extent of sin in their lives. In their case, poverty truly must be the means God uses to get their attention, and then if they still do not listen to Him, He keeps every last one of them right where they are, their misery a just and prevailing part of their temporal punishment."

"But, Daddy, Mr. Fulkerson was once like that. And yet he was never punished."

"Our friend Samuel changed, Charity; he changed entirely."

"So God knew that he was going to change and never hurt him."

"Something like that."

"Then it's all right, Daddy, when people start out being evil if they change sometime. God forgives their old sins."

"Evil and sin and corruption are never all right."

"So why didn't He punish Mr. Fulkerson?" Charity asked, coming back to where she had started.

"Because—"

Alfred was not unaware that she had backed him into a corner.

"Nothing God does can be called unjust," he added. "There must be reasons for something that might seem that way in a finite sense but which we just do not know, reasons why there may be some good people among those who are so poor, and they must suffer along with the rest."

Charity closed her eyes for a moment, and Alfred recognized this as a sign that she was trying to think the situation through.

When she opened them again, he asked, "Do you still want to go?"

"Yes, Daddy," she told him most solemnly.

Later that day, poverty showed its white face to a child who had thought that only black people were poor . . .

CHARITY WAS SILENT on the way home. She had encountered an array of people and scenes that were beyond whatever she could have expected. But she reacted as her father had hoped she would.

When Charity saw a young boy, barefooted, wearing tattered clothes, face dirty, sitting in a ditch, crying, she asked her father to stop the carriage. Then she took out a little handkerchief from her own riding outfit, opened a jug of water next to her on the seat, dipped the cloth into it, and then declared, "He looks so hot and dirty. I'm going to wash off his face."

Alfred helped her down from the carriage and watched as she approached the boy and talked to him. Then she sat down beside him on the ground and ran the wet handkerchief over his forehead, cheeks, chin, and neck. The little boy smiled as she ministered to him.

Finally Charity returned to the carriage.

"His name's Timothy, Daddy," she said, "and he's very hungry."

"The only place to eat near here doesn't serve poor whites or blacks," Alfred was forced to tell his daughter.

Charity's response was immediate and typical of her.

"Then buy it like you did the general store!" she declared, having become familiar with how wealthy her father really was.

"This restaurant is owned by a man I happen to know. He is wealthier than I am. He would not want to sell it."

Charity paused, thinking over the situation.

"Let me see him."

"It would not do any good."

"Let me see him, Daddy," she insisted, knowing that she usually got her way whenever she was firm enough.

He had no resistance when she spoke like that.

"I know where he works and where he lives," Alfred told her. "I imagine he is at his office now."

She indicated that she wanted to be helped back into the carriage.

The drive into the nearest community lasted just under half an hour. Charity sat quietly, her hands pressed together as she prayed to herself.

"Where do we go?" Simuel asked.

Alfred gave him the directions.

A short while later, after finding the restaurant closed, they arrived in front of Matthew Randolph's house, the frontage derived from a style called Greek Revival, distinguished by an unusually narrow porch with a roof that was nevertheless twice as high as any other in the entire South, with only two tall columns supporting it, these dwarfing anyone who walked between them. Plantings of dogwoods, camellias, and azaleas distinguished the front lawn, which was fully a city block in width.

Simuel stayed with the carriage while Charity and her father approached the front gate, which was unlocked. They walked up to the front door, and Alfred knocked.

One of Randolph's several dozen slaves, who could not have been more than twenty-one years old, opened it.

"Would you tell Matthew Randolph that Alfred Littlepage and his daughter Charity are here to see him?" asked Alfred.

The slave nodded and stepped aside, indicating two plain wood chairs in the foyer. Then he turned and left them.

Less than a minute passed before Randolph appeared.

A man in his early sixties, about five feet eight inches tall, Randolph had an astonishingly thick, pure white head of hair that was obviously well-groomed. Large, bulging eyes were set in a face that showed ruddy, healthy skin and sported a silky white beard.

Charity's mouth dropped open.

"No, young woman, I am not the one you think I am," he said, "though I am often approached in December by youngsters who think I'm old Mister Claus, especially when there is snow on the ground and a full moon in the sky."

Randolph invited them into his parlor and offered them some tea, for which Alfred expressed his appreciation.

"It has been a long time," he said. "I think you were holding this beautiful little girl in your arms and rocking her back and forth when we last met."

"You have a fine memory," Alfred acknowledged.

"Why are you here?"

Randolph paused, his lips edging in a slight smile, then added, "Is it because of that starving little boy?"

It was Alfred's turn to look startled.

"How could you possibly know that?" he asked.

"One of my business associates was within sighting distance and recognized you, yes, but especially your daughter."

"Charity? How was it that he did?"

Randolph gasped loudly.

"You honestly do not know, do you?"

"Know what, Matthew?" asked Alfred, genuinely having no clue.

"She apparently is well-liked and admired by virtually everyone in your community and has been talked about more than you may know, both by those jealous couples who would love to be as blessed as you and Elizabeth have been and those who simply admire you for being the kind of decent and understanding father responsible for such a charming young lady. Some have tried hard with their own children and not proved so capable or so fortunate."

Randolph stretched his legs.

"You have whatever you need," he said. "Just tell me now."

Alfred swallowed hard, knowing that a little man to sell his modest general store had been easy. But Matthew Randolph could never be persuaded similarly.

"I want to buy your restaurant," Alfred told him, having decided to put everything on the table.

"It is not for sale," the other man replied simply. "Now, is there anything else? Or are we through?"

Alfred remembered that Randolph had never been less than a man with an amiable manner that hid a granite-hard heart.

"I had a special purpose in mind for it," he confessed. "I wish you would let me explain further."

"Though I respect you greatly, whatever you could possibly say now or later would not make me change my mind," Randolph reiterated in a monotone. "I am sorry to disappoint you."

Alfred nodded at Charity, and they both stood, getting ready to leave.

"I am sorry to have taken up—" he started to say, extending his hand.

Randolph waved his own hand impatiently.

"Timothy is being fed as we speak . . . ," he said, looking like a man who was enjoying a good joke.

"What—?"

Randolph repeated himself.

"I see . . . ," Alfred mumbled as, flustered, he sat down again.

"My staff is in the midst of preparing the food as we speak," Randolph told him smugly.

Alfred knew that Randolph believed in large payrolls and in servicing his customers in a quality manner.

"All this to feed one boy?"

"Nay, my friend, you are wrong. All this to feed his family and a great many others in that district."

Alfred had not anticipated that.

"But why are you doing this?" he asked, not completely convinced that Randolph was telling the whole story.

"A better question, Alfred, would be: 'Why have I not done so before now?'"

"Well, yes . . ."

Randolph pointed to Charity, his arm wavering as he did.

"She is the reason," he said with unabashed admiration, "that beautiful, sweet, loving child beside you."

Charity seemed as surprised as her father.

"I cannot fathom what you are saying," Alfred admitted as he scratched the back of his head. "You barely know my daughter, Matthew. How could she possibly influence a man like yourself in any way?"

"My associate saw clearly the expression on that lovely face as she was walking away from the boy. It was one of such utter sorrow and despair that it profoundly affected even him, and he is hardly someone who is given to brimming over with sensitivity for his fellow human beings. The man was in tears as he was telling me the details. Mind you, I had never seen this particular individual cry before!"

Alfred slipped his arm around Charity.

"All because of my daughter?"

Randolph extended his arms to Charity. She glanced at her father, who nodded slightly.

With a warm smile, Randolph enveloped her in his arms.

"You have been told before by others, I am sure, that you are very special," he said in a kindly manner as he held her back from him, looking her in the eye. "I agree, Charity. There is a spirit about you that sets you apart. When you are sad, I think the world would be sad with you if everyone on it could know how you feel.

"There is also a purity about you, young lady. And I think God is going to give you a life that someday, perhaps long after you are gone from this world, will inspire someone to chronicle your experiences."

At that, Charity became unusually serious, frowning, and did not say anything in response.

Randolph shook his small, round frame as though throwing off a layer of snow that had fallen on him minutes before.

"Forgive me for sounding so gloomy," he said, smiling broadly.

Alfred was grappling with an altogether opposite impression of Matthew Randolph than he had expected. They had never been more than acquaintances, yet this provided enough contact with the man to build an image of someone who was interested in profit for his various businesses, the restaurant being just one of them, far more than the men and women who worked for him, slave or free, black or white.

Alfred questioned him about this after he, Charity, and Randolph had gone on to the restaurant where they were soon eating a specially prepared meal of sautéed cobia steaks prepared with mustard, butter, and cider, along with several side dishes.

While Charity was finishing the plateful of food, Randolph and her father stepped outside, breathing in the fresh air.

"I surprise you, do I not?" Randolph asked, very sure of himself.

"You do, Matthew," admitted Alfred.

"Because I forbid poor whites and all coloreds from entering the premises and yet do not hesitate to help a poor, starving white boy? The former seems so callous, the other profoundly giving and kind."

"That is what came to mind, yes."

"May I explain?"

"I would be very interested in hearing, Matthew."

Randolph stuck his hands in his hip pockets.

"I have thought about this a great deal," he spoke. "Can I exclude these folk from my places of business on the one hand but not from my heart on the other? Is that not blatant hypocrisy, hypocrisy that would turn my stomach if I were to detect it in another man?"

Alfred was silent, sensing there was a great deal that Randolph needed to get off his chest and not wanting to derail his train of thought.

"I have come to the conclusion, Alfred, that I am doing nothing wrong by that facet of the way I conduct my businesses. Frankly, our society encourages such behavior on the part of those in authority.

"True, in Roman times, gladiator contests to the death and throwing Christians to the lions were activities encouraged by Domitian and others, but I am hardly suggesting that all kinds of social convention and political dictates should be obeyed if they go contrary to our consciences as human beings."

He pointed to the whitewashed colonial-style restaurant behind him.

"Forty years!" he exclaimed. "My father had it before me. And I am getting ready to pass it on to my own children and not wait until I die. It should be an enterprise that we enjoy together while we can.

"You have no idea how many people I have helped. I have a man in my kitchen who creates the most wonderful potato dishes. He approaches each day with enthusiasm and derives much satisfaction from his creations. He is, shall we say, not in his right mind, very slow at everything else, and can just barely take care of himself.

"Another is a former criminal, once a violent sort, a man with a terrible record, but I sensed something good and decent in him. And what a talent for main courses! He assists my regular chef, whom I brought over from Austria, of all places. There is absolutely no jealousy between them. They work very well together.

"Not everyone I hire is like either of these men, but a few are: I have someone in charge of my wine cellar who is missing an arm. Without me, each probably would be having a most miserable time of it."

Alfred started to speak, but Randolph silenced him.

"Let me finish," he continued. "Alfred, what I am telling you now, what you have seen . . . that is my way of earning a living, a most honorable one, of course. I have a cotton business and others as well. I do not mistreat any of my workers, though I may work them hard. If I learn of any injustice, I quickly reprimand, and often I punish the instigator. And I can tell you, whoever it is dare not repeat the offense!"

Randolph chuckled as he said, "I look so much like Saint Nick that I suppose my people are surprised to find that I can act like the hardest metal and just as unyielding."

Nodding toward a park across the street, he asked, "Could we go there and sit down? You are slimmer and younger than I, Alfred. And my legs are not now as sturdy as yours."

The two of them found a single bench that had ample space for them.

"I do not work as other men work," Randolph went on, puffing a bit. "Nor do you, for that matter. We have been much blessed with the absence of the heavy labor that weighs down other men. I look at those fathers who work so hard with their hands to provide for their families. They are often agonizingly tired at the end of each day, yet they seem happy, Alfred, even fulfilled at a soul-deep level. What they sweat over, what they earn, I have been given all my life. By rights, I should be feeling the way they do, but that is not the case.

"Not that I have any emptiness in my life, because I do not. I remain content largely because I avoid the pain that has been accorded so many other men, including most of those who are working for me. But I do not stoop to gloating when I say that, for I am simply doing everything I can to make their lives a little better."

"What does this have to do with excluding poor whites and blacks from your businesses?" Alfred asked.

"The fact that I have not had to work myself or my loved ones in a sweat daily for what we have does not mean that the people and the possessions in my life are any less precious to me," Randolph told him. "That hardly makes me less inclined to hold on to whatever I have and fight for every bit of it, whatever the costs might be."

"You will have to be less cryptic than that."

"Listen to me, Alfred! My restaurant business is supported by a certain kind of clientele. They are the ones who have money. They come here dressed in the finest clothes, and they order very expensive dishes. They also reward my employees with large gratuities.

"If I were to cheapen the atmosphere inside by allowing common folk to sit next to my high-society customers, I would be out of business in less than a fortnight!

"None of my waiters are like the men I mentioned who labor behind the scenes, Alfred. They all are refined, well-groomed, intelligent. They make my diners feel at ease."

He looked exasperated.

"If I served darkies, for example, I would be the only white man doing so. What would be the good of that, Alfred? The community would desert me. What help am I going to be, then, to my employees? I might lose it all! If that happened, so many would suffer. And how could I do for people what I shall be doing tonight and tomorrow and the day after that?"

His frustration was growing.

"I mistreat no one," he said. "I subscribe to the conventions of my time and my place. All I do is prevent—"

"But the Bible talks about not being a respecter of person," Alfred interrupted. "You know that as well as I do."

"Is there no such thing as the greater good, though? And are we not talking about a moot point? How many folks could afford to eat here in the first place?"

"A few, Matthew. You and I both know a handful who have small plantations of their own and large families."

"You missed my point. It just is not done! If only five niggers wanted to eat at my restaurant every few months but I turn them away, how does that compare to the livelihoods of a staff of underprivileged white folks that numbers twice as many as that?"

Alfred was answerless at first.

"You do the same thing with your slaves," Randolph continued. "You have become their great white father. But how often do you take any of them out to dinner with Elizabeth, Charity, and yourself?"

He lowered his voice.

"What is the difference between my refusal to serve any niggers off the streets who might happen to wander by—and your own unwillingness to take them out in the first place?

"I know your slaves eat their meals along with you and your family, but you make it a point to keep them at a separate table. What about that, I ask?"

Alfred could not defend himself against the truth.

"So, it appears that you and I may not be all that far apart . . . ," he said.

Randolph had been looking away but now turned his head sharply toward Alfred.

"Never say that!" he demanded. "There is no comparison between us. I do not have even a measure of your compassion."

"From what you tell me about—"

"Those are white people. Is it so wonderful if I help my own kind, Alfred? That young boy is white."

He bowed his head.

"But I have never lifted a finger to help a single nigger in my life."

"Yet you do not abuse your slaves. Compared with how some owners treat them, you are a saint."

Randolph shook his head.

"I just make sure they are clothed and that they eat properly and are never cold in the winter. But that sort of thing is handled through my orders performed by a man I hired for the purpose of managing my slaves. I have nothing whatever to do with them in the same way as you are doing every day."

Randolph was shivering.

"My sin, Alfred, is that I still cannot bring myself to think of them as anything but subhuman, jungle creatures at best."

He hesitated, perplexed, and then said, "But where is my humanity as a result?"

Alfred looked over his shoulder.

Several carriages were pulling up in front of the restaurant, and men, women, and children were getting out.

"Look, Matthew," he said, indicating the crowd with a nod. "That may be your answer over there. I doubt that you can be expected to change overnight after generations of the same kind of conduct in your family. Not everyone has a Damascus Road experience."

Randolph turned and saw the group of people.

"My lily-white beneficiaries," he whispered sadly.

"Look at how many individuals in this world do nothing at all," Alfred pointed out. "They sit back with self-satisfied complacency and reap the blessings and reinvest little or nothing back into society."

He knew of another train of thought, one gaining momentum among those white landowners who were sympathetic people, their concern over the underprivileged not at issue. What often ended up in debate was which group of the poor got their help.

"Why should I worry myself about those colored people when there are white people who need whatever I can give them?" Alfred had been told again and again after contacting businessmen for their assistance. "A baby with white skin should get my attention first, and only then, if I have anything left over, should I bother with the darkies!"

Matthew Randolph was different.

For the others, there was no crisis of conscience.

And Alfred quietly reminded him of this.

"You are not like this at all. Why do you not take that impulse of yours to do good and let the Holy Ghost apply it as He sees fit? What more can you do? I know one thing: Right now you should not be beating yourself bloody as you have been!"

"You were hardly thinking along these lines when we started this little conference," Randolph reminded him.

"I see your heart, Matthew, and I respect you all the more."

As they reached the entrance, Randolph stopped.

"What is it?" asked Alfred.

"I wonder what future generations will think of men such as you and me," the other man mused. "We live, we die, we do the best we can while we are here. Will we be considered villains, Alfred, or will we be heroes?"

"They may not think of us at all, you know," Alfred reminded him.

Randolph seemed to accept that rather mournful remark without rebuke and patted Alfred on the back. As they reentered the restaurant, both saw that Charity was already charming the newcomers.

❦ 44 ❧

A TRIP TO A *black shantytown . . . another to the depth of white poverty during the antebellum period . . . and now the possibility of a slave auction center.*

It had been three years since that last experience involving the poor white families.

Part of Charity's eye-opening maturation . . .

This was what Alfred and Elizabeth hoped would be the case, a process bringing her face to face with reality as it existed beyond the environs of the family plantation.

"It is so very risky . . . ," Elizabeth acknowledged as they sat on the plantation house's front porch, sipping some lemonade, with the swaying of weeping willows providing their distinctive calming sounds in the background.

"But a necessary one," Alfred replied, feeling increasingly powerless to anticipate all that might confront their daughter over the coming years but not willing to give up. "Charity's greatest blessing, her life here, could become her most severe curse."

The world outside was changing rapidly.

Stephen Douglas's "popular sovereignty" notion had achieved absolutely nothing except angering the abolitionists needlessly and giving them further impetus for their cause. As could be expected, they dismissed it out of hand by calling it 'squatter sovereignty,' insisting that it left slavery up to popular vote rather than law.

"How hypocritical are you and I being?" Elizabeth asked, obviously pondering a question that was not a new one for her. "At night, sometimes while you are asleep beside me, I have begun to wonder if it is right that we have slaves."

"It is very right," he said, more stridently than he would have wished. "Black people gain more from being slaves than they lose."

Elizabeth sighed, having heard that defense all of her life.

"That is true for the ones here," she remarked. "But we are not like everyone else."

"Nor are we alone. Even Samuel Fulkerson changed. And we both know what Julia Pegram has done to make amends since Ambrose died. The way it once was on those two plantations is no longer the way it is."

"I am sorry to be in such a mood. But life is far from simple anymore. When we both were children, having slaves seemed as natural as breathing the air God gives us."

Alfred did recall that simpler period, a time when there were no threats from the North, slave riots were rare, and it seemed as though the South's way of life would go on indefinitely without interruption.

. . . *Having slaves seemed as natural as the breathing the air God gives us.*

They hugged one another.

"All that is gone forever," Elizabeth whispered.

"And our daughter is beginning to understand this," Alfred said. "She leads a wonderful life, but it is also cloistered, in its way. She could be crushed if she is not prepared as best as we can manage. Charity is a sweet, sweet lamb, this daughter of ours, but lambs can be led to slaughter far too easily."

His eyes narrowed as he considered the future and all that a grown-up woman would have to face in an increasingly unstable world.

"She has to be toughened, made more aware of what is going on around her. Her life, a blessing until now, could become a curse as time passes."

"I still feel uneasy," she admitted. "The market is the cruelest of places. And you do have enemies. Neither of you will have any protection."

"Whatever enemies I have are not stupid. Hurting Charity and me while we are so visible would be suicide for them, especially in view of how everyone seems to feel about her."

Alfred smiled as he ran his fingers through Elizabeth's long, beautiful red hair.

"There is something else I must tell you," he said. "You may be upset, but I cannot keep it from you any longer."

He had debated whether to tell her but decided that their marriage had been one of unrestricted openness.

"Good or bad?" she asked with some apprehension.

"Good, I am sure. We will have protection, Elizabeth."

She pushed back from him.

"What are you saying?" her alarm showing in her voice.

"Certain people have already been sent on ahead. They will be all around us wherever Charity and I are."

"What people?"

"A rather rough crowd, Elizabeth. It really is better that you not know any more details than necessary."

For one of the few times during their marriage, Alfred seemed a bit condescending, and that was something she would not tolerate from any man since it was directed at her because she was a woman.

"That superior air of yours does not become you in the slightest!" she told him angrily. "I have to know! What is going on?"

He breathed in deeply and said, "I befriended someone on the docks years ago. He was being beaten by another two men, and I stepped in and, frankly, gave the attackers such a trouncing that they quickly limped away as fast as they could."

"You used martial arts?"

"I did."

Elizabeth remembered well how it came about that Alfred had learned to use his body in that way.

"I can still see the Oriental gentleman who saw some of Savilla's pottery that you were offering for sale," she recalled, "not to make money off her but to give that woman some self-respect, an outlet for her feelings

"He was charmed by what she had crafted and said that he could give you something that was better than any amount of money for that pottery she had made so carefully for so long. He had the cash in one hand, but you decided to take him up on his offer of teaching you fundamentals of the martial arts."

That was exactly how Alfred recalled the situation.

"At first I wondered why. It seemed so foolish. Martial arts for someone like me!" he admitted. "But the man seemed to have a certain wisdom, not from some pagan deity, of course, but a wisdom that the Lord surely must have granted him. I was able to lead this fellow to Christ the very next time we met.

"The man I helped seemed every bit as crude, profane, and yes, battle-scarred as those of his type come. He had no refinement whatever. He spoke far more crudely than any of our slaves, though his range of language seemed much greater. But what he lacked in all these areas, he made up in gratitude. He swore that he would be ready anytime I needed him.

"So, as soon as I finalized the trip with Charity to the auction, I posted a message that, fortunately, he received rather quickly, and when I was in Columbia not long ago, he was waiting for me at the hotel."

Alfred chuckled as he remembered the sight of them.

"This character had brought with him five very broad men who seemed to be even more tough-looking than he seemed. His first question after bear-hugging me was, 'Are they okay for what you have in mind?' Naturally I had no objection. Those men seemed able to defend Charity and me against a small army!"

"But what about weapons other than their fists?" Elizabeth pointed out. "The toughest of men are no match for any rifles."

"Knives, brass knuckles, rifles, they had it all," he assured her.

She turned away.

"Are you troubled?" he asked.

"Yes . . ."

"About what? I thought you wanted to know everything."

"I do. But how do you expect me to react when I learned that such precautions are actually necessary?"

He was prepared to say something astute and contradictory in response, but those few words from Elizabeth could not be rebutted.

"That is very true, dear," he said simply.

"All of this so that Charity can learn about the barbaric conditions at a particular slave market? Is any such experience worth the danger to our daughter? It could be so bad for the two of you that you have to solicit the aid of men with whom you would have no contact otherwise, because they are brawlers. I have never been eager about this trip, but now it seems even more foolhardy. Do you not see that, Alfred?"

Elizabeth knew enough not to dig in too hard but to give him some breathing room instead, for Alfred would only consider anything else an attack against his masculinity, coming from a woman as it did.

"How can we expect our daughter to be able to face the worst of life and the best of it," he finally asked, "to have the courage to deal with everything forthrightly, if her parents happen to fail the same test?"

"Or is it a matter of recognizing the cruelty that exists but not wallowing in the gutter along with such atrocities as those taking place at the kind of slave auction you want our daughter to visit?" said Elizabeth. "If you and Charity go, and if those men meet you there, and if something happens, my love, is there not the possibility that you could be responsible for the deaths of innocent people?"

"Including some slaves . . ." he muttered.

"Yes!" she exclaimed. "Praise God, Alfred! The very act intended to 'educate' Charity could cause an explosion that would be awful."

She frowned as she remembered his description of the men supposedly to be at the auction as protectors.

"And those men!" she declared. "While they sound like pretty brutal types, that does not mean their lives should be considered expendable. And it might turn out that, despite their presence, you or Charity or both of you could be injured or worse. When a crowd becomes a mob and goes berserk out of fear or anger, there are no guarantees of safety for anyone."

. . . When a crowd becomes a mob and goes berserk out of fear or anger, there are no guarantees of safety for anyone.

Alfred wanted to protest, to tell Elizabeth that backing out now would not send their daughter the right signal, yet their daughter's safety and his own were far more crucial, not to mention the safety of the strangers who would become involved and possibly die as a result.

"I think you may be right," he told her. "You are not a woman who sounds alarms needlessly. I have to feel that the Lord is telling you something."

Dusk was starting.

And they were not dressed warmly, so they decided to go inside.

Old Simuel greeted them at the front door.

Alfred had never found a temporary replacement for Savilla, which was in part because he had become so busy in his business and did not devote much time to the so-called search but also because the few women he managed to see never seemed suitable. His subjective reaction to them was somewhat bothersome to him and Elizabeth since it smacked of a subtle elitism lurking in his outlook, something that seemed to have been resurrected from past generations in the Littlepage family before it had been shed by his father, who had instilled in him an abhorrence of it by a very strict upbringing that mixed large doses of discipline with the love shown by his parents.

That was where Simuel came in quite remarkably. The old black man showed a culinary ability that blossomed quickly, many of his recipes owning a great deal to the dishes served at The Court of Two Sisters in New Orleans, because, as Simuel explained, one of his cousins was a secondary chef there and posted personal letters that contained some choice recipes.

That night proved no exception. Elizabeth and Alfred could smell the pungent odors of seafood gumbo coming from the cooking kitchen, this appetizer a mixture of bell pepper, white onion, okra, garlic, shrimp, scallions, crabs, oysters, cayenne pepper, and other ingredients. The main course was redfish baked with jalapeno peppers, mushrooms, red wine sauce, diced pimento, and whatever else Simuel secretively added.

The old man had brightened remarkably with his new duties.

Disconsolate after Savilla's death, he found that cooking was as much a Godsend for him as it was for the Littlepage family, sparing them the ordeal of breaking in a stranger, which was always awful, hard work.

Elizabeth breathed in deeply.

"Smells just wonderful," she told him as they entered the house.

"I's gone and sampled a little plate of it," Simuel replied, "and it seems pretty good to me, if I do say so."

"Is Charity inside?" Alfred asked.

"No, Massa, she's out back with Little Isaiah and Hester."

Alfred thanked Simuel, and he and Elizabeth walked through the house to the backyard, where they saw Charity sitting on the grass with those two slaves, the three voices carrying some distance.

"It's a place like hell," Hester was saying. "You shouldn't go there, Miss Charity. It's too dangerous."

Alfred and Elizabeth exchanged glances.

"He's right," Little Isaiah added. "I couldn't talk 'fore because the pain's still with me. It never leaves. Sometimes I think about it, sometimes I don't, but it never stays very far 'way."

"That was why I asked my father to take me," Charity said. "I wanted to know, but I didn't want to have you go back over the nightmare again because of me."

"I's willin' to relive those days, if you's willin' to cancel the trip," Little Isaiah told her.

"But you didn't seem to want to the last time. I decided I could never put that burden on you."

"I's puttin' it on myself."

She hugged Little Isaiah and then Hester.

Elizabeth and Alfred walked back into the house, deciding it would be improper to eavesdrop any longer.

A few minutes later, Charity left the two slaves and went inside where she found her parents sitting at the dining room table, holding hands.

"Mama and Daddy," she said, "I've got something to tell you."

When she let them know that she had changed her mind about the slave auction, Elizabeth asked, "Why, dear? You seemed determined to go."

"It's more important that Hester and Little Isaiah talk it out," Charity replied, "get it off their chests . . . and I don't think it's right that Daddy and I put ourselves in danger. You'd be left alone, Mama, if anything happened to us."

They embraced one another, staying like that for some while, and would have remained so even a bit longer if a loud, repeated knocking at the front door had not intruded.

~⧣45⧤~

THE MAN WAS every inch the way Alfred had described him: tough-looking, with thick cheekbones and a jutting chin, so scarred on his face, neck, and hands that, at some earlier point, he must have seemed like a freshly slaughtered piece of raw beef.

But his words were different, kinder, more concerned, the voice of a guardian.

"Elizabeth . . . ," Alfred started to say after he had regained his composure that had been momentarily upset by seeing the other man at his front door. "Let me introduce you to Max Cutshaw."

After the formalities, which included introducing Charity as well as the five men standing directly behind Cutshaw, Elizabeth, gritting her teeth, invited them all inside and asked if they had eaten dinner as yet.

"We haven't, Ma'am," Cutshaw told her. "But we are not intending to disrupt your evening more than necessary."

"It is not a disruption but a pleasure," Elizabeth responded while hoping that the Lord would forgive this exaggeration. "We always have food on hand to feed any number of surprise guests. I just need a few minutes for new places to be set at the table."

Cutshaw and the others were wearing sailor's hats, and they abruptly and self-consciously took them off, bowing slightly as Elizabeth smiled at them then turned and headed toward the rear of the house and the adjacent cooking kitchen to alert Simuel.

"I can see why you're a satisfied man," he told Alfred.

In the South of that era, such a comment between gentlemen would have stirred up a fistfight or worse for its salacious inference. But then Max Cutshaw was what he was, and Alfred let it pass.

Yet he could not altogether control his facial expression. And the other man picked up on it.

"I am sorry," he said. "Years of rough living, you know."

Alfred nodded understandingly.

"Quite all right," he replied. "Why don't you and your friends follow me?"

The six men did, pointing to the furnishings and the wall coverings and the rest of the details that bespoke elegance.

As they entered the dining room, Cutshaw, grunting, stopped short as he noticed Little Isaiah, Hester, and Willis taking their seats at the second table less than six inches from where the Littlepages themselves would be eating, and leaned over toward Alfred as he whispered with indignation, "Niggers in here?"

"It has always been that way in this household," Alfred explained.

"They're staying while we're eating?"

"Yes. Is that a problem, Max?"

Cutshaw was fuming as he turned around and walked out into the hallway.

"I've never shared dinner with darkies!" he declared.

Alfred could have asked him to leave but decided to resist that temptation.

"Max," he said, "you seem to feel that I saved your life."

"You did!" Cutshaw exclaimed. "No doubt about that."

"And that is why you are willing to risk your own life to safeguard my daughter and me at the auction."

"There's no other reason for us blokes to be here," he said. "We could be sipping some brew at a dockfront cafe about now."

"I have something to tell you," Alfred spoke. "I hope you will be pleased. But I need to ask you a favor while you are here."

Cutshaw and his men waited patiently for him to continue, though not without an air of defiance.

Alfred told him about the family's decision to cancel the trip to the slave market.

"Okay, fine," Cutshaw said. "I still owe you a debt, and even going to that ghastly place would not have satisfied it. What do you want instead for now?"

Cutshaw was not stupid, and he seemed to be bracing himself for what he suspected would be the answer.

"For you and your men to eat with my family at our table while my slaves are at the one next to it."

Cutshaw and the others glanced at one another, not pleased by the prospect.

"They smell so bad," he grumbled. "How can you stand it?"

"How badly did you smell when I saved your life, Max? As I remember, you were a sorry package, covered with sweat and blood and, I think, urine."

"But I cleaned up afterward!" Cutshaw protested.

"So have those four coloreds of mine after a day of work on my plantation!" proclaimed Alfred proudly.

The other man's eyes were bulging, for he knew that he was trapped, that he was obligated to grant such a simple request, and he loathed having to do what would surely sicken him, or at least that was what he had convinced himself would happen.

Finally Cutshaw mumbled, "I owe you, Alfred Littlepage. Otherwise there's no way I would be doing this!"

"One other thing," Alfred cautioned him.

"Yeah, I know. Pay attention to my language, right? Sorry. I owe you that, too!"

Finally everyone was seated.

Cutshaw and the five other men, catching aromas from the warming kitchen, were eager to dig in though awkward about being in such a home at such a table, dressed as they were in typical seafaring garb.

Alfred and his family were waiting while their six guests chatted among themselves.

Cutshaw looked up, and asked, "Anything wrong?"

"Grace," Charity told him.

Cutshaw shed his hard-bitten manner as he blushed, looking strangely like an overaged, embarrassed child, and said, "Sorry. We don't usually do that where I have been living. We're too interested in shoving liquor down our throats."

He shot a warning glance at the five men next to him.

"Bow your heads," he muttered to them.

"My daughter will be thanking God for His blessings," Alfred told them.

As Charity spoke, the six visitors did not move in their chairs or speak among themselves while she praised Almighty God for His gracious protection of the family and for His mercies in other respects.

"O Father in heaven, we also are so grateful to Thee for these six men who have come this considerable distance, at first to be our protectors," she continued, "now to honor us with their presence at this dinner table. May You guide them and be their haven of safety all the days of their lives. And, Lord, let this food be nourishing to our bodies and never let us forget whose hand has made all this possible."

Cutshaw and the others ate mostly in silence with just an occasional comment about the meal. Alfred had assumed they would be rather gregarious. That they were not puzzled him.

Afterward, as Charity and Elizabeth were helping Simuel clean up, another area of conduct that surprised the visitors, Alfred joined the men outside as they smoked cigars.

"They're Cuban," Cutshaw remarked. "Would you like one?"

Alfred declined.

"Because you're a Christian; is that it?"

"Not really, Max. Some Christians drink wine, but my conviction is not to do so. Others smoke cigars, and I am not foolish or judgmental enough to question their salvation.

"I happen to think that it is wrong in both instances. Alcohol brings little good while it is capable of fostering much misery. The same is true of smoking."

"But wine can be like medicine. And a strong shot of whiskey dulls a man's pain when he's to be cut open for a bullet wound or some side-winder that's gotten its poison into him."

"I can agree, Max. But just because ether, for example, dulls pain, is that to mean that we should be 'taking' it any other time, at dinner perhaps? Or soon after we get out of bed in the morning? And how many other times during the day?"

Cutshaw slapped his leg.

"Good for you!" he exclaimed, chuckling. Then he grew more serious.

"I once thought I might become a Christian," he remarked without warning.

"What stopped you?"

"Just what you've been saying now! I'd have to give up drinking and smoking and whoring as well."

"Definitely that last one," agreed Alfred.

"And not the others?"

"That would be up to you. I would like to think that your interest in such things would change as a result of accepting Christ in your life. But what can I say?"

"I am a crude man, a dirty bloke, as you know. I wish I wasn't. God don't want folks like me walking those golden streets."

"He especially wants people like you."

Cutshaw's cigar fell out of his mouth.

"What are you saying?" he asked as he reached down for it. "Aren't you belittling the Creator by saying that?"

"Before I invited Jesus into my heart and my soul, I was every bit as dirty in God's eyes as you say you are."

Cutshaw could not easily accept that, given his host's fine clothes and beautiful home and all the expensive furnishings and other items that were visible in every room.

"You don't know how much sin I've committed."

Cutshaw seemed genuinely ashamed.

"But then, do you have any idea at all how much sin has been typical of *my* life?" Alfred replied.

"But you are a wealthy man, a fine one, well-educated, your talk refined. You've never had to lie and cheat and a lot else to survive."

"But I used to lie and cheat and, yes, entertain lustful, carnal thoughts. If anything, it was worse for me to do all that because I had no excuse, given my family and church background.

"The difference between then and now is that I try today not to lie at all. I am no longer driven to cheat any of my friends, other businessmen, or anybody else.

"And while I still do battle with fleshly temptation, I do so far more successfully than I once could claim. What once was true in our lives no longer need be. Just as a good man can become bad, someone who is bad can be redeemed."

"I wish I could believe that," Cutshaw mused. "But I can't. I have committed adultery, rape, murder. I have been guilty of such filth in my life that you would not want me in your home again if you knew it all."

Alfred's face showed such a kindly expression that Cutshaw did not quite know what to make of it.

"I know more than you think."

Cutshaw almost dropped the cigar again.

"How could you? Before tonight, I wasn't about to tell you anything, no matter what you'd done for me."

"Each crime of which you have been accused is on record, Max. I am a man with well-placed friends, and I can find out whatever is on file about anyone. And I figure for every secret I found, there must be many, many more for which you were never caught."

"Then why have me and my mates as your guests? Letting us guard you at the slave market is one thing. Your life and your daughter's would be at stake, and we could be of real benefit. But here, well, you had nothing to gain."

Alfred paused, searching for exactly the right words.

"Because you were willing to sacrifice your life for ours, Max."

. . . *Because you were willing to sacrifice your life for ours.*

Cutshaw turned away and his friends looked elsewhere, because it was obvious that the man was on the verge of weeping, something he had never done in their presence.

"You chanced doing the same for me when I was a stranger, one whose appearance could scarcely have inspired someone of your standing to do anything at all except turn your back and walk the other way while I bled my life away. How could I do less for a man who, after all, is no longer a stranger but my benefactor instead?"

"Max, what really holds you back?"

"Holds me back?"

"From accepting Christ into your life."

"I've never thought about it."

"Do that now, please, as a favor for me."

Nervous, Cutshaw rubbed his chin, hesitated, then scratched the back of his head.

"Everywhere I look around me," he replied, "I see nothing but filth of one kind or another, enough to make any man with any feeling puke his insides out. And I *know* that I'm part of that. I wallow in the gutter along with so many others. *I am so unclean!*"

"But if you can wallow in the gutter, as you say, you can also stand up again and jump out of it, right?"

"No church would want me."

"It's true that some would frown on you. But look at how many people cast out the Lord Himself when He was incarnated as a Man."

"Incarnated? That's a new word for me. What does it mean?"

Alfred explained it to him.

"I see . . . ," he said.

"And as far as your imperfections, since your sins would be forgiven by God, forgiven *as well as forgotten*—"

Abruptly, he snapped his fingers.

"Thank you, Lord!" he said as he bowed his head in prayer for a moment.

"What were you thanking Him for?" Cutshaw asked after Alfred had opened his eyes and was looking at him again.

"For the thought I believe He placed in my mind."

"That can happen?"

"Oh, yes, Max, it can and it does—not every day perhaps, but when you really need guidance, God usually communicates with you somehow."

"What did He tell you just now?"

"My daughter, Max, how do you see her?"

"Young, smart, obviously a vir—"

His face seemed to freeze.

"Are you saying that that is the way—?" he started to speak.

Alfred nodded as he replied, "Washed as white as snow. You will be a virgin all over again."

One of the men, obviously listening, chuckled, and Cutshaw turned and shot him what must have been a look of icy anger.

"Isn't what you're telling me too much to expect of the Man Upstairs?" he asked.

"Or is it that you are expecting too little, Max?"

"This chap wants me to become a Christian," Cutshaw shouted to the other men.

Surprisingly, one of them replied, though sounding awkward as he did, "I will, Max . . . I will if you will."

The others murmured agreement.

"We're such a bad bunch," Cutshaw said, shrugging. "I'm afraid we'd pollute heaven."

He stood as though that part of the discussion was suddenly over, and the others instantly followed suit.

Alfred's heart sank.

I have failed, Lord, he thought. *Please forgive me.*

He was now on his feet as well.

"Sorry . . . ," he mumbled. "I wish you were willing to—"

"Where do we go?" Cutshaw asked, his eyes betraying more than a little mischievousness.

"For what?" Alfred responded.

"The baptism? Isn't that part of it?"

Alfred struggled to keep his surprise from showing.

"That *is* part of it, Max," he acknowledged.

"Then let's go."

"But only part, my friend. It *isn't* some sort of magical ceremony that, once completed, makes you set for time and eternity."

Cutshaw seemed genuinely disappointed.

"There's more?"

"Nothing is going to be easy about what lies ahead if you are serious about this. The act itself is simple enough, but *maintaining* the right direction in your Christian life is exhaustingly hard. You will be constantly tempted to go back to the way you once were living.

"After all these years, simply turning your back on certain habits and acts and never again indulging yourself will be a monumental task. But I can help you, Max. Do you have the time now? I can go through it all with you and the others."

Cutshaw glanced around at his men. All five nodded slightly.

"Whatever you say, governor!" he replied with great cheer, while exaggerating his very slight English accent.

Max Cutshaw and his men stayed on at the Littlepage plantation house for nearly a week.

On the second day, Reverend Marmaduke baptized all six in the little stream on the property while Charity, Elizabeth, and Alfred, as well as their slaves, watched.

Cutshaw, in particular, seemed desperate for more information about the Christian experience. Marmaduke was happy to invite the man to stop at the parsonage where a painstakingly accumulated library, large by the standards of that time, was one of the few material possessions over which he allowed himself any real pride.

"Every known book of any merit on theological and related matters is here," Marmaduke pointed out. "This collection is the fruit of many years' work."

"I can see that, pastor," Cutshaw replied admiringly. "Is it all right if I read through some of them?"

"You may use all that is here!" announced Marmaduke. "Nothing is off-limits. And I shall make myself available to you night and day for whatever questions you might have."

"When I get going, I might have too many questions," Cutshaw warned him.

"What is a night's sleep when we are talking about eternity?"

"I won't wear you out."

"I am but the Lord's instrument. And you cannot wear *Him* out!"

That these two men should get along well would have seemed unlikely just days earlier: one, a tall, courtly, well-bred individual with a soaring intellect; the other large and rough-edged, an ignorant man in some respects, an uncouth and vulgar one in others.

But friends they became.

"You know what Littlepage told me a couple of days ago?" Cutshaw said as the two of them were sitting in the den that also served as a library to hold the various books.

"About what, Max?" Marmaduke asked.

"That if it weren't for Jesus' death, burial, and resurrection, He would be viewed in God's sight as morally and spiritually like me."

"And *me!* That is very true."

"And *you?*" repeated a startled Max Cutshaw. "What are you saying, pastor?"

"I am saying that God knows my heart. Your heart is no cleaner or *dirtier* right now than mine. But once it was so much worse, in a way."

"How could that be?"

"Because I had a form of godliness, but the power of God was being restrained by my sin. Light cannot have fellowship with darkness."

"Now everything is forgiven?"

"Yes, Max, and—"

"—forgotten?" Cutshaw interjected.

"Exactly, my friend."

"Littlepage told me that. And so you agree with him?"

"Better to say that we—you and I and Alfred Littlepage—agree with God's Word, which is what the Bible presents from cover to cover."

"No mistakes in it?"

"None. The Bible is infallible and inerrant."

Marmaduke explained to him what such terms meant.

"And the God responsible for that kind of wisdom accepts this wretched self of mine?" Cutshaw asked, not entirely convinced.

Marmaduke nodded as a genuinely joyful smile crossed his face.

"Could I be alone here for a little while?" Cutshaw asked.

"Just call me if you need something."

As Marmaduke was standing, Cutshaw grabbed his sleeve.

"No, please, stay with me," he said, "kneel with me."

Marmaduke then listened to Max Cutshaw confessing to every sin he could remember. Even as a minister to whom people had admitted the worst of skeletons in their closets, he had to acknowledge to himself that he had never heard such a rank catalog of continuing filth from a single individual.

Oh, Lord, Lord, how much this man strains Your determination to wash him clean! he thought, wincing at each successive revelation.

Finally, though, Max Cutshaw was finished with his exposition but by then very weak due to the long, traumatic drain on his emotions.

"Until today no one but God Himself knew all this about me!" he exclaimed as he fell forward against Marmaduke, his body shaking from the sobs that continued to rack it.

"I think, pastor, that I am going to be very sick," he murmured.

Mouthful after mouthful erupted, soaking both men, continuing until Cutshaw's insides were so sore that he screamed in pain with each new spasm.

"I think I may be dying!" he groaned.

"No, Max, just being cleansed in every way," Marmaduke managed to say while understandably having to fight some nausea of his own.

They did not keep track of the time.

All that mattered, ultimately, was that Cutshaw's siege did end but not before exhaustion set in, neither of the two men moving for some while afterward.

Max Cutshaw and his men left three days after that.

It was a strange sight, these tough individuals, these hardened products of sordid life along the docks weeping like children as they mounted their horses.

They had hugged each member of the Littlepage family and Reverend Marmaduke as well and seemed ready to change their minds and stay in that vicinity.

"Ships are coming in," Cutshaw told them, "with cargo to unload. We have to be making a living!"

"I could find something for you all in this area," Alfred suggested.

"We aren't so happy being very far from the sea, you see. That salt in the air, the smell of fish, the sound of gulls. We've known little else all our lives.

"We couldn't give it up, not us. But we can live differently while we're there in the midst of it, like cutting out the wild parties. And the loose women. The—"

He blushed, glancing at Charity and Elizabeth.

"Everything that displeases the Lord!" he added.

The five other men cheered at that.

"I pray that you are strong enough," Alfred asked. "I think you will be, Max."

"I need to have you pray that I am," whispered Cutshaw, "for *their* sake as well."

"Remember what the Word of God says, my friend: 'Greater is He who is in you than the evil one who is in the world.'"

Cutshaw's hand was trembling slightly as he shook Alfred's.

"Bless you," he added, "bless you for casting out the raging savage in me."

"I did nothing from my own strength or wisdom or anything of the sort, Max. What happened *within* you was singularly the work of the Holy Spirit, dear man."

Charity, standing next to her father, leaned over to kiss Cutshaw on the cheek.

"If you *ever* need me . . . ," Cutshaw said, glancing from Elizabeth to Alfred to their daughter, "anywhere, anytime!"

And then the six men rode down the road and were soon out of sight, only a quickly dissipating cloud of dry earth marking their passage.

❧ 47 ❧

CHARITY, NOW A beautiful young woman, was always eager to learn, to hear new ideas, to explore the world beyond her home. She was delighted when at dinner one night her parents announced they were going to make a trip to Cincinnati, a journey that required several days' ride in each direction. Alfred had business there, and Elizabeth hoped she and Charity could accompany him. Her ulterior plan was that the three of them would be able to hear a celebrated speaker who was scheduled to speak in Cincinnati while they were there.

It took awhile for Elizabeth to make up her mind that she and Charity should go since traveling any such distance involved a great deal of planning and preparation—not to mention concern over possible hazards along the way. In those days, extended travel was not a simple matter.

"You really should take them, Alfred," Samuel Fulkerson commented as he sat in his least elaborate carriage while stopping one afternoon to say hello. "You are away on trips far too often; this way you can accomplish your business dealings and spend time with the lovely women in your family as well. It will do you all good."

Over the years since that encounter with Hoodoo Jack, the role he was playing in their lives had changed drastically from an antagonist to a friend and counselor, someone whose advice was nearly always on the mark.

"Though I have never had a family of my own," Fulkerson admitted, "I have rehearsed many times, in my mind, what it must be like, in part since your family is such a good example. You are fortunate, Alfred, my friend. A family gives any man's life the balance that it truly needs."

There was no mistaking his melancholy.

"Without this, a man tends to wander through his remaining years far, far more empty than he should be, an anchorless and pitiable vagrant of sorts, touching the lives of others and then going on, in a sense, unsatisfied; and then, ultimately, he dies, quite alone and forgotten."

Fulkerson's downbeat manner was unusual for him, the isolation and loneliness he felt playing across his face, his usual gregariousness evaporated.

He leaned over the edge of the carriage as he added, "But a home is more

than that physical building behind you. I have one the equal of yours, perhaps even grander, I suspect, and yet it has never been truly a home of any
meaningful sort to me. It is a place to stay, a spoiled child's dollhouse pretending to be a home."

He saw Little Isaiah carrying an armful of firewood behind the plantation
house.

"Your slaves have more of a home than I do," Fulkerson noted. "Sometimes
imagining myself living in a shack with my arm around my wife and my children at my feet and a simple meal waiting to be eaten seems more desirable
than all the material plenty I have had since the day I was born."

It was something that the man obviously had mulled over in his mind for
much of his adult life, because his response seemed well-worn, rather like
some of Hoodoo Jack's long-ago statements but for a different reason.

"It is so burdensome to possess all that this world can reasonably offer
and yet have no one to share it with," he observed. "I think that I sometimes
took out my fate on the helpless darkies whom I bought over the years. I
vented on them my anger, enjoyed giving somebody else pain. Why should
I corner the market on it?"

Fulkerson smiled, though rather weakly, which emphasized a one-inch
long scar on his right cheek that was otherwise nearly invisible.

"I think I may shock you, Alfred, with what I shall say now about my
slaves. But it's the only explanation that I have, frankly."

Fulkerson was uncomfortable, moving around awkwardly.

"Go ahead," Alfred assured him, "whatever you say will stay with me. No
one else is around. You came here by yourself, remember. My slaves are all
in their quarters. My family is inside. Speak freely, Samuel."

Grateful for the liberty to do so, Fulkerson went on to say, "I begin to
wonder that they may be not much more than animals, my friend, big, strap-
ping animals."

Alfred's face reddened, and Fulkerson noticed.

"It seems a terribly mean-spirited speculation, I know, though hardly a
new one. All the bigots have been using it as justification and will continue
to do so, that loathsome sort who get great pleasure out of skinning a black
woman alive after they have raped her.

"You may be thinking that I am slipping back into some sort of membership in that unholy group. But you would be wrong, Alfred. I am groping,
that is all, groping for an explanation to characteristics that seem so unusual
in any human being."

"What traits do you have in mind?"

"Have you had any pets?" Fulkerson asked, giving the impression that he
was sidestepping a direct answer.

"Not just now, but earlier, many of them; in fact, as a child and an adult I've had any number of dogs and cats, a raccoon, a squirrel, others."

"Except for the 'coon, I am sure, is it not true that, when you accidentally stepped on their tail or lashed out at them in irritation when they were trying to get your attention but you were too busy and found them to be a botheration, think of this, Alfred, and you will get my point: You discovered that, whatever the extent of your meanness, they came back to you. There was no lasting anger in them. You could smack a dog one minute, and the next, it would be wagging its tail at you and looking for affection.

"That is almost the way it has been with all of my slaves. I treated them so abominably before, Alfred, and yet they are being so kind, so forgiving toward me. How can that be? Is it just because they are true Christians? Or is it because of their animal natures that they simply do not know any better? If it's the latter, then their instincts leave them no choice."

"It has to be their Christianity," responded Alfred. "They must accept the leading of God more completely, more deeply than the rest of us."

"Like sheep heeding their shepherd . . . ," Fulkerson mused. "How often have we been the black sheep and not they?"

Suddenly that window into Fulkerson's soul closed, and he went back to the original topic of their conversation as though nothing else had intruded.

"Of course you shouldn't allow Little Isaiah or any other slave the sort of responsibility for overseeing your place while you're away," he pointed out, deliberately keeping his voice close to a monotone, "not by himself anyway and without any kind of supervision. If it would help you and your loved ones to get away for a change, I would be glad to pitch in by spending part of my time at your place, making sure your slaves are handling themselves properly."

Touched and pleased, Alfred thanked him, and then his neighbor was off on a trip of his own, this one to nearby Columbia.

Elizabeth had come outside to get some fresh air and to oversee a reworking of their front lawn area, with hedges being planted along both sides of the walkway to the front porch, a rose garden in another section, and various other changes.

Alfred approached her and recounted what Fulkerson had suggested. When she heard what he had said, she looked away for a moment.

"Is anything wrong?" he asked.

Elizabeth replied, "I was thinking that the reason Samuel offered and you accepted was that you seem to think Little Isaiah would not be able to handle the responsibilities. Or have I missed something, Alfred?"

"Correct, Elizabeth, as usual. Frankly, if I have any doubts at all about this, would it be sensible of me to experiment?"

He knew what she was getting at and tried to explain himself better.

"As much as I love Charity, I would never give her the full reigns of this plantation, not yet, anyway. She is unbelievably smart and resourceful, and she does know a great deal, but I think it would be too much for her just now. That does not mean I love her less or respect her less. I am simply recognizing her limitations."

"But Little Isaiah is old enough to be her father, or even her grandfather," Elizabeth protested. "He was here before our daughter was born, before you and I even knew each other."

"I treat him as though he is my dearest friend, my most beloved brother, regardless of the color of his skin, you know that," Alfred reminded her. "But, realistically, I can see some situations where putting him totally in charge of all that we have here would hardly be prudent. Am I less loyal, less loving because of that? Hardly, Elizabeth! Preserving our way of life is just as important for our slaves as it is for the members of this family."

Elizabeth had learned to love her husband's sincerity even whenever she might happen to disagree with what he was saying.

"But we will be away well less than two weeks, at the most," she said. "If you show this dear man that you have that much faith in his abilities, you will only strengthen the relationship between the two of you. The bond we all have with each one of those slaves is strong, yes, I know that. But are you saying, Alfred, that it cannot be made stronger still?"

Alfred disliked debating with his wife. Her record of winning was high, and he had to work far too hard to best her, so he often gave in, and this time was no exception.

"Any damage we suffer will be taken out of your budget!" he exclaimed, not altogether kidding about it.

"Will you go right now and tell him?" Elizabeth asked.

"I will, my dear; I will."

"Without the need for Samuel Fulkerson hovering around."

"Yes, Elizabeth, yes. Little Isaiah will have free reign."

"Wonderful!" she exclaimed, hugging him so passionately he was sorry he had not caved in sooner.

❧ 48 ❧

Half an hour later, Alfred came upon Little Isaiah and asked for a few minutes of his time then gave him the news.

The two of them walked to a large, round gazebo at the very front of the property, not far from the main gate. Climbing rose vines with scarlet, white, and amber blossoms circled it, adding much-needed hues to the lawn a few weeks after the beautiful cherry trees had stopped blooming, leaving behind only the pale willows.

"But I's not been in charge of anythin' in my whole life!" Little Isaiah exclaimed, looking a bit dazed. "I might do somethin' wrong, you know, that's possible, Massa, out of ignorance, since I am just an ignorant nigger."

Alfred did what he could to reassure him.

"No bills have to be paid during this period," he pointed out. "You will need to get in some fresh food supplies, depending upon what runs low. And keep the animals groomed and fed. But there isn't much else. I think you can handle every bit of it."

Little Isaiah was dazed, unable to say anything else for a little while, not having expected any such privileges, even with a Littlepage as his master.

Alfred gave him the courtesy of waiting, and not impatiently either.

The rugged slave, so strong and yet capable of the greatest tenderness, particularly where Charity was concerned, had bowed his head and seemed to be praying.

Finally he looked up, and said, "I's not able to do this in my own power, Massa. But I can, I's hopin', with the Holy Ghost's help."

"I would never want you to try without Him," Alfred answered happily and with respect that he hoped would be apparent to Little Isaiah.

"Massa, even with Jesus nearby, forgive me, Lawd, for this, I's still nervous 'bout doin' what you want, Massa. I sure 'nough hope I don't go and ruin ev'rythin' for you, Massa."

Alfred had come to know Little Isaiah's "ways" so well that the unusually frequent use of massa was a clue as to how nervous he was.

"I would not have asked if I had any—"

Alfred could not finish.

"You not sure, is you, Massa?" Little Isaiah asked perceptively.

"I think you will do fine, that you have the capacity for taking care of everything around here while I am away with my family. Forgive me for being nervous."

"It's natural, Massa. I's just a dumb nigger. You've never made me feel that way, but I still is what I is. You know that, and I know that."

Little Isaiah did something then that, in another household among the many in that region, was certain grounds for punishment.

He put his hands on Alfred's shoulders. No such motion, simple as it was, would ever have been tolerated under normal circumstances, for it was likely to have been construed as threatening or overly familiar and offensive as a result.

"I want you to be proud of me," he said. "I want you to say that I am a good nigger, that I am worth what you have put into me all these years."

Alfred did not pull back but leaned forward, his forehead nearly touching Little Isaiah's broader one.

"I know that you are a good nigger," he said honestly. "I have never doubted that, my friend, not once."

"But you need to feel that you and your missus and Charity can depend on the likes of me. I don't want you to think that I's just takin' and takin' and takin' from you and givin' back little. I ain't like that."

Little Isaiah was becoming agitated, and Alfred hated to see that happen since it was out of character for the man.

"I do depend on you. You are even now in charge of the other boys. You get your duties done just right. I have never been less than satisfied. You give back to me and my loved ones more than you realize, friend."

"But I don't want to stop there," Little Isaiah declared, "when I look at how other slaves are treated!"

"You would die for me if you had to," Alfred reminded him. "I know that. What more could you do? What more could I expect?"

The longing that Little Isaiah felt was written on his face.

"Tell me what you are feeling," Alfred asked. "I want to know. I want to understand your heart."

"What I do for you is easy, Massa," the slave replied. "Some of it is, I'm supposin', women's work, like helpin' with washin' the clothes since Savilla is gone. Even when she was here, you know, the cookin' kept her real busy after Violet died, and I had to do the wash then, with Hester and Simuel pitchin' in ev'ry so often.

"I also cut wood and dig holes for fence posts. I make sure the flowers are kept up. I do some paintin' though Simuel's better at that. You make me—you make all of us—feel special, but we ain't doin' nothin' different from other boys on other plantations."

"I had no idea you felt this way."

"If you tell me now to forget it, to go back and be what I have been all along, that's sure 'nough what I do, and I do it quick. But I love you, Massa, and I want to do more. I want to be more for you, Massa."

"Then you will have the opportunity, my friend!" Alfred replied, hoping that Little Isaiah was unable to detect any lack of certainty that had been working its way into his voice and producing tiny beads of sweat on his forehead.

Little Isaiah thanked him and headed back toward his quarters.

And so it seemed to be set, that "first" for Alfred Littlepage, giving over to one of his slaves temporary control of the plantation, which had been in his family for generations, a trusting act that, even as liberal as his father and his grandfather and other Littlepages before them had been in regard to their slaves, would have seemed far too extreme when they were running the family holdings. And yet there he was, agreeing to it, perhaps too impulsively, not sure what would be left of the place when he returned with his family.

This is foolish, he thought. *I have been far too hasty. If Little Isaiah does anything improper or ill-advised, I may not be ruined in so short a period of time, but still, who knows what could happen in my absence and how devastated he would be at disappointing me? I could never pretend that he hadn't; the man knows me too well.*

Instead of going inside, Alfred detoured around to the rear of the plantation house to the stable, which housed a dozen horses and was unattended at that hour.

The palomino horse with a flowing silver mane.

It had been a favorite of his for a long time. Alfred chose it above any of the others because he had spent more time with this one, and though it was hardly a pet, he still felt that when he was riding on it, it seemed to be a horse that could perceive his moods better than the others. That's the horse he needed at that hour, since he found his thoughts in turmoil as he set off toward Samuel Fulkerson's residence, where he intended to tell his neighbor he had decided to accept that offer of help after all, while not letting Elizabeth or Little Isaiah know, for the moment, that he was doing this.

Just two miles away . . .

A short distance, but traveling it gave Alfred some time by himself to think, the air bracing against his face as he passed that dreaded forest area again, which brought to mind what slaves like Rufus and Johnny had sacrificed all those years ago for his daughter. True, they both had operated under orders from a man they once must have had every reason to despise and who continued to rule them, however benevolently, but still, the circumstances were such that they could have run for their lives, leaving Charity as a convenient sacrifice and lied persuasively later about what had happened, with no disputing witnesses ever to show up.

Even so, the two slaves had refused to do this.

So you died as a result, Alfred thought, *died for a defenseless little girl you hardly knew while obeying a man who used to beat you for the slightest reasons and who regularly skimped on your food to increase his profits and kept you clothed in shamefully tattered old garb as you shivered through cold winters in a poorly heated shack.*

He mulled over Fulkerson's possible explanation about black people being little more than animals, showing the blind loyalty of common household pets, anything along these lines tantalizing while at the same time making another part of him recoil at the notion.

"I never thought of Little Isaiah, Violet, Savilla, or any of the others as mere beasts to be trained," Alfred said out loud. "They are human beings, period. Anything else would be an insult to their Creator."

He recalled the many conversations he had had with one or more of those slaves, the minds suddenly showing forth, sharp minds hobbled only by their lack of education.

"I think that is the one area where I caved in to social convention," he mused out loud. "I tried very hard to get a tutor for my slaves; again and again I tried, but no one was willing to let me engage them in anything of the sort.

"I could have kept up the search, but rumblings from other owners made me realize there was going to be trouble of one sort or another if I persisted. They put up with all the other taboos being broken on my plantation, but this would have been the final straw. I had to think of my family; I had to think of my heritage."

Educated blacks, it was assumed, were potentially a greater threat than the wholly illiterate ones on every plantation, according to so-called community wisdom at the time. After all, the handful of few blacks who managed to get an education up north were the uppity types with delusions that harbored rebellion.

"Look at Hoodoo Jack as one convenient example, and no one could misunderstand the pitfalls of giving their kind more learning!" another slaveowner had opined in Alfred's presence one day. "They've got some big ideas sometimes, but they're stuck with tiny little retarded brains lodged in those big old skulls of theirs.

"Think of this, Alfred: Take some loaded rifle, any gun will do, and hand it over to a chimpanzee from one of the circuses that pass through here once a year or so. Harmless, right? The thing is too backward to be a threat? But is it? No sir!

"True, nothing might happen, and it's little more than a silly experiment. Or . . . the chimp might be looking down the barrel at the same time it pulls the trigger and blows its own head off or kills one of us—by accident, of course, but that isn't any consolation when you're holding a dead child or your wife in your arms.

"It's worse with the darkies, as you can imagine. I have to say that they are far smarter than any monkeys, even if they smell a lot like 'em! That Darwin fella's only got it half right: Man as a whole never came from apes; only the darkies do. Suppose, though, that apes could learn to shoot or set fires or wield knives!"

The man seemed smug in his insinuations.

"The more you educate coloreds, the more they are able to plan schemes against us, armed with the knowledge they have gained. Rifles or shotguns are only the first step. Coloreds are starting to rise up in different places these days, brandishing rifles already, and those are the dumb ones, the typical kind, never far from their old primitive state!

"What happens if education gives them other ideas, Alfred? Corrosive ideas about how to plan the most elaborate calamities to assault us? We cannot allow that; we must stop the very possibility dead in its tracks!"

Alfred and Stapleton Telford Culp, standing just five foot five inches tall, had bumped into one another at a general store on the outskirts of Columbia, where many of the families in that region bought supplies ranging from gunpowder to soap to feed for their animals to a host of other items.

Culp had been reading an editorial in the local newspaper, grunting so often that Alfred had approached him to see if he needed any help.

"It's not my physical health that's troubling me," Culp grunted as he looked up . . . and thus, the conversation began.

Half an hour later it was finally winding down.

"Sorry to bore you with such palaver," Culp apologized. "I am hardly the tyrant I sound. But I think it is one thing to treat blacks humanely, which I have been doing all along, and quite another to give to them the weapons with which they can vent all those years of, I think, legitimate resentment that has been building.

"My slaves are fine; I am sure of this. I have precious few worries about them. And so it is with yours, from what I can surmise. But what about the ones we both happen to know are being abused perhaps daily? What if

some of them escape, get their education like future military officers training for battle, and come back to the South as Hoodoo Jacks all over again,
finally taking out their revenge on all of us, kind and cruel alike?

"Think of that scene, Alfred, think of it being repeated throughout this fair
land that is all we have known for more than a century, your family and
mine, our fields of lovely cotton drenched in blood."

A proud but nervous smile appeared on Culp's small, round face.

"My son is six feet two inches in height," he said. "My wife is two inches
taller than I am. I don't want to hold their bodies in my puny little arms after
some darkies have clubbed them or stabbed them or shot them to death."

"We inherit what previous generations have left behind," Alfred noted,
"their sins visited upon the rest of us."

"And it will take generations to come before men like you and me have
a chance to do what we in our hearts sense should be done."

"Are you talking about abolishing slavery—not overnight as the Yankees
profess but, somehow, gradually? Or have I misunderstood where you are
heading with this, Stapleton?"

Culp nodded, more than a touch of weariness about him.

"I fear as much for the survival of the poor, unprepared slaves as I do
for myself and my loved ones," he said. "A bunch of Yankee zealots fill
their hungry minds with enticing dreams of emancipation glory, and it all
sounds good."

Culp narrowed his eyes, adding, "But remember this singular truth about
most wild animals that are dragged kicking and screaming from their natural
habitats, Alfred. You surely can make good pets of quite a few, perhaps, with
some scratches along the way and a scar or two, but those that are domesticated cannot then be returned to the wild years later and be expected to live
on to an old age.

"Most do not; bet on that. They find themselves in a jungle with which
they cannot now cope, and they are swallowed up by it. Why? Their
instincts have been dulled by captivity to the point of being practically
nonexistent."

Alfred knew that a special meal was in store for him at home, but he
found Culp's ideas fascinating; breaking away was not easy.

"But we have caused their plight in the first place," he offered. "Naturally,
sending them back to Africa is hardly a rational prospect. But do we not have
an obligation, having created their nightmare, to do everything possible to
ease it?"

Culp found that a reasonable thought, and said so.

"Could this be an unsolvable dilemma, then?" he offered, clearing his
throat. Then he continued: "Is there no answer, even for intelligent men

such as you and me for whom answers are usually easier than for common folk not graced with minds like ours?

"Should the slaves we own be kept entirely from the outside world, as we try to protect them by all means at our disposal? Or should we instead thrust these ill-prepared folk out into that very world and let it eat them up?"

Culp could think of nothing good or noble coming from the latter course.

"The only appeal that has," he added, "is removing from the abolitionists undoubtedly their principal raison d'àtre."

His voice dropped nearly to a whisper.

"We created not what they were, Alfred, but what they have become, you and I. We and our ancestors did that as partners in this lunacy."

Culp had never spoken in that manner before, and Alfred was taken aback.

"Now they look to us as the helpless creatures they are," Culp continued. "How can we ever thrust upon them the alternatives to what they have now? Answer me that. We are like God Himself to them."

He looked away, not wanting Alfred to see the tears forming in his eyes.

"I think I love these black-skinned savages," he confessed, close to weeping. "You know, I think I do."

Alfred was not paying much attention but was gazing out toward the horizon, hearing over and over in his mind only that one question and not the rest.

How can we ever thrust upon them the alternatives to what they have now?

Alfred Monroe Littlepage could faintly hear the illusive sound of a lone bugle sending forth its mournful reveille through the white mists of a future dawn, of rifles being shot, of cannons thundering and men screaming as death swooped upon them across glistening fields of dew-touched clover.

"Someday," he finally said, a dark edge to his voice, "the choice may not be ours to make."

❦ 49 ❧

Samuel Fulkerson's plantation was just ahead. Alfred shook himself, trying to remove the accumulated cobwebs of those assorted memories that had spun themselves so quickly around him since he had left his own property not many moments before.

I seem to have nearly forgotten why I ventured outside tonight in the first place, he admitted to himself. *I hope Samuel is home. I—*

Abruptly, Alfred stopped the horse in the middle of the road. A thought bolted into his mind as though seared there by a hot branding iron.

The slaves who guarantee the profits of the plantations sprinkled throughout the South were taken away from their African homes, stripped of any power to control their own lives, and punished, even executed, if they protested. Something has to be done, a kind of penance paid.

And Alfred suspected that he was the one who had been chosen to start the process, however reluctantly he was working himself into it.

"I have to let Little Isaiah try, Lord, without someone hovering nearby, ready to pounce on him if he makes any kind of mistaken," he prayed out loud. "It was my idea, and I must show the man the respect he deserves by giving him a chance. I cannot allow my own uncertainty to add fuel to what he is feeling now."

The alternative was to withdraw from Little Isaiah the very privilege that had been dangled before him.

How could he trust me then? Alfred thought. *Perhaps You are trying to tell me that this whole trip is a bad idea. Is that it, Lord?*

Alfred was about to turn around and head back home when a voice called out to him in recognition.

"Is that you, Mr. Littlepage, sir?" shouted Samuel Fulkerson, good-naturedly feigning Southern formality.

"That it is!" Alfred replied loud enough to be heard a mile away.

"What brings you out here?" the other man asked as he approached the horse. "Did I not leave you just an hour ago?"

"You surely did," Alfred told him. "But why are you out here as well?"

"Thinking, neighbor, just thinking."

"I wonder if it possibly could be about the very circumstance that has been ensnaring my own thoughts."

"No doubt it is. In the short while since I came from your house, I have been engaged in prayer and the most profound thought. Afterward I spoke to Crispus about an idea that occurred to me."

"Crispus? What does this have to do with him?"

"I have been wanting to give him more say in the conduct of my business. He has a head for it, a surprisingly good one."

Still holding the reins, Alfred got off the horse and listened more closely.

"But, Samuel, you are the one who just cautioned me about my own Little Isaiah in the first place!" he reminded the other man, some irritation surfacing as he seemed to have caught Fulkerson in a contradiction.

"I cannot deny that, Alfred. Remember, though, that my concern was about him handling matters by himself."

"Because he had never done it before."

"That's right. Anybody who is a wet-behind-the-ears beginner needs supervision. I would think the same about a white man, let alone a colored."

"I spoke to Little Isaiah. The prospect was pleasing to him, but he also seems to feel very nervous."

"As he should, being given something so suddenly that had been denied him for so long! May I tell you what I have in mind?"

"Go ahead."

"Crispus could help."

"But why do you think so?"

"I gradually have been giving that boy a greater number of chores that are considerably more than the usual mere menial ones. He is learning to make decisions. And I must say that he seems to be doing well."

Alfred had begun to see the genius of what Fulkerson was offering.

"When a man has lost some natural ability, perhaps one of his senses, we try to rehabilitate him," he pointed out. "Someone without legs is given a set of crutches and taught to use them. A blind individual somehow develops other senses to a greater potency, and we reach out helping hands to make life a little easier for him. Those who are deaf use signs, which must be learned from teachers dedicated to the task."

Fulkerson was pleased that Alfred seemed to be catching on.

"The key is survival, Alfred," he said, "but, usually, that is possible only by adapting to a changed environment. Coloreds over here no longer are living in mud and straw huts that they built themselves. We have taken them away from all that and plunked them down in the midst of so-called civilization, with wonders to behold!

"Have their lives improved due to this? For hundreds of thousands of them, the answer is an ugly and pathetic no. I hear that some periodically moan that they would rather fight for their survival against wild beasts in a jungle than live as many are forced to do here. At least they could die with some personal honor intact in the jungle."

Both men stopped talking for a little while, visualizing how the calamity of being captured and taken into slavery must have been for the unfortunate blacks.

"We face shocks in our lives," Alfred ventured, before becoming silent again, "but eventually these shocks are put behind us, and we go on."

It could never be that way for hapless blacks being snatched from any of the African nations being plundered for their human resources.

"I'VE NOT TOLD you this before," Fulkerson said minutes later, "but there was another ingredient in my regeneration. One of my slaves died while that process of change was being completed in my life, and I was there at his side.

"I called him Nathan when I bought him. He was such a dignified man, even more so when he grew old, with that bushy hair of his looking like it had been covered with snow that never melted.

"Nathan could still talk clearly, with a strong tone, even on his death bed, the rest of his body weak and failing by the minute. I still find that to be amazing these many years later. He had a source of strength that carried him through a long life.

"He had been a chieftain in his tribe, and he always wore the most magnificent costumes—Nathan would describe these to me—including pieces of ivory, ostrich feathers, leather straps made from the hide of rhinos, and other bits and pieces to which they had ready access—all of this indication of his preeminence in the community.

"He told me of the power he wielded as a result, his voice so deep and rich, carrying with it the ring of great authority. He came to be well-nigh worshiped, the other natives believing him actually to be sent as a declaration of the gods that were a part of their daily lives, deities of the sun, the moon, the very earth itself.

"He'd tell me, 'I could stand on a hill, Massa, and look over them plains stretchin' on so far, and I could see giraffes eatin' the tree leaves. Lions sipped water from a stream. Birds suddenly took to the air when they sensed danger, beautiful birds, Massa, all colors, red and gold and white and, oh, how fine they looked!

"'We had campfires every night for cooking food and for heat when the temperatures had dropped during the night. I could see others like ourselves through the darkness in every direction. It was so pleasant, Massa, the cool air, the stars above, my family below, the warmth in front of us . . . the life we had known for generations.

"'Until the traders came. They had no interest in keepin' us together. We were split up. I never saw my wife, my sons, my daughters again. I was the father of a dozen chil'en, and in one day, Massa, they was gone!

"'I had lost ev'rythin' by the time I was brought here. But eventually, I met a new woman, and we got hitched, and I fathered other chil'en, a whole new family. Yet, Massa, I could never git them others out of my mind. I could never stop wonderin' whether my wife was still alive and those boys and the girls, what had happened to 'em.

"'A few times I hoped I could return someday to my old land and stand again lookin' at the plains, smellin' that air, watchin' those birds, but, of course, it'd do no good, no good no how. My family was my life then, and they was gone, gone forever, I knew.'"

Fulkerson was sniffling as he added, "Nathan died less than five minutes after he spoke those last few words. I buried him myself. The rest of my slaves stood nearby, singing some spiritual I had never heard before. I shall never forget that moment, never!"

He wiped his eyes quickly with the back of his hand.

"Heathen, they were, Alfred, and heathen they would have remained if not wrenched from that continent of supernatural darkness. So, I suppose, as far as their eternal destiny is concerned, the slave-traders did them a favor, bringing them to slavery in this life but redemption in the next. I guess that was something of a fair trade, when you think of it."

He was breathing deliberately, as though trying to deal with a pain in his chest. Alfred asked him if he was all right.

"I am, friend, I am," Fulkerson said. "It is not my heart that is in pain. My soul, yes! I was reasoning out what I just said. There is another side to it. While many coloreds became fine, fine Christians, many others drifted into the kind of 'religion' that Hoodoo Jack and his sort practiced, a religion of the demonic, losing their souls forever.

"Can God be pleased when all manner of human misery precedes the salvation of any of His creations? Is heaven as an end worth the means of hunger, fear, physical injury, the whole litany of what slaves endure?

"You and I, as Christians, would have to say yes, a hearty yes. And yet what a dilemma this presents us. Are their tormentors not then bringing about God's will? If so, how can they be condemned? They have wrought a good work from evil acts!"

Both men were sharing a sense of oppressing joylessness at that moment.

"Think of this: How many dream of the old times?" Alfred added. "How many think of what once was, and the images they see fill their hearts with sorrow? How many would get on a boat and return, given the chance to do just that?

"But, I know they cannot revert back to what they once were, swinging through the trees or whatever else it was that they used to do before the stinking Arabs started bringing them across the Atlantic Ocean, losing as many as a third or more of their 'cargo' to dreary afflictions of disease and shipwreck.

"Ordinary African savages did not have to deal with the same set of problems that newer generations must face today in this, for them, adopted nation that we mockingly call the land of the free. And yet, ironically, even so, some aspects of their lives have remained unchanged. In Africa, they could be hunted down by the predatory big cats. Here, in the United States, the predators are human and have white skin."

After Alfred had finished, Fulkerson put his hands side by side, palms up, and raised them several inches in front of him.

"We have to help our slaves pull themselves up," he emphasized. "You cannot break a man's legs and then berate him for not being able to run an errand for you."

Alfred wrinkled up his nose in reaction to that.

"And all this so that, one day, they can go free and be swallowed up by a world in which they will be treated like innocent lambs being led to their own slaughter?" he said, his pessimism unmasked. "What will we be elevating every darkie to, Samuel? Are we going to be giving them such an incredible blessing after all or a ghastly curse?

"If they should continue in their ignorance, is that not much safer than when they will be in a more educated state? Knowledge is not always a blessing because using it can bring the most serious repercussions.

"All my life, I have been waited on by dark-skinned men younger and older than myself. The thought of living without that level of comfort is distressing. It attacks my precious social sensibilities.

"Truly I have been spoiled, Alfred; and so have you, neighbor, though I suspect that you might try to deny this. We all are products of this society, and yet some have managed to be less corrupted by it than others. Nor are we alone. The Yankees have been corrupted by their society as well."

Alfred was tempted to deny that, expressing his offense at the same time, but decided to keep quiet.

"May I loan Crispus to you?" Fulkerson asked. "He is a fine young man, possessed of more than just muscle. Will you give this a chance to work?"

"I think you are on the right track. Will you drop by casually once or twice just to check on matters?"

"That is *all* I will do. If I happen to see Crispus or Little Isaiah or another, I might not even get out of my carriage but instead call whoever it was over to me and simply ask how things are working out."

He smiled reassuringly.

"They must feel that they are being allowed to stand or fall on their own. However, neither should be offended if I simply said hello."

Alfred agreed and accepted his offer. The two men shook hands, and Alfred was getting back into his carriage when Fulkerson tapped him on the back.

"It's new territory we are beginning to travel," he said. "We may be doing the right thing, or we may not, you know."

"My grandfather might have been appalled," Alfred replied as he sat down. "I think my father would have been skeptical. As for me, I hope and pray that this is the start of something that will be so successful that it may ward off what seems unthinkable now—but we have been thinking about it anyway, haven't we?"

"Every night, as I go to bed," Fulkerson spoke, "I glance by habit out the window that overlooks the slave quarters, and I think, 'You were my mules. Now you are nearer to being like my very children, but there are those who shout the call of liberation who want to make you nothing more than their pawns, to be sacrificed at their slightest whim.'"

He was ashamed but felt the need to admit his thoughts to someone else.

"'When will you truly be free to go your own way?' I ask them. Alfred, six years ago, none of this would have mattered. Now it is everything to me! Isn't it remarkable how completely a man's life can change?"

The two shook hands, then Alfred was on his way. He had a trip to plan and much to do before he and his family were to leave.

To hear a speech given by someone with an extraordinary reputation, a strange woman with a strange name.

Sojourner Truth.

~❧ 50 ❧~

Normally the Littlepage carriage horses were high-spirited but controllable, in part because the entire family spent time with them, touching each animal, brushing it, talking to it. As a result the animals were completely at ease with human beings they recognized and felt less threatened by those who were strangers.

But their behavior after just a couple of days on the road became increasingly uncustomary, even bizarre.

"What in the world is wrong with these horses?" Alfred grumbled at the two animals. "I mean, we hardly need to be racing along, but, even so, they have been acting as though this is the worst chore they have ever had to perform, taking each step like the ground beneath them has been grabbing at their hooves and trying to hold on, and they are able to pull free only through extending the greatest effort."

He had some real empathy with animals, and so did Charity—and to a considerably greater degree.

"I sense the same thing," she agreed, leaning forward, her ears cocked, listening for any sounds that might explain the horses' behavior.

"They could be coming down with some ailment," her father speculated. "I wonder, after all, if we should forego our plans and consider turning back."

He steered the horses over to the side of the road and stopped for a few minutes. Charity got out of the carriage and walked to the horses, examining their eyes, teeth, feet, and legs.

"Nothing that I can see, Daddy," she said.

"Snakes?" he said. "I wonder if they could be detecting some snakes in the vicinity. Hop aboard now, Charity!"

She quickly climbed back into the carriage.

"That could be it," she said.

Alfred guided the animals onto the road again, confident that the reason for their nervousness had been discovered and would disappear.

Except for that momentary concern about the horses, the Littlepages encountered no mishaps whatsoever on the way to Cincinnati. They spent their time talking, singing, enjoying the sights offered by country that was often beautiful, untouched by the ravages of later industrialization that would replace open land and forests with smoke-belching factories, a transformation of states throughout the North.

The three of them passed a number of farms larger than any Charity had ever before seen, with just one moderate-sized home set squarely in the middle and only crops for miles in every direction. But they also saw small villages of a few houses, isolated places where life was slow-paced and calming. And they skirted some urban areas comprised of hundreds of structures, quite different from what would come later in the course of another century.

They stopped just after sundown each night, staying in rented rooms for part of the journey, the rest of the time dropping in on accommodating relatives and friends, some of whom they had managed to alert in advance, but even with the others, the hospitality of the people of that era was inherent and unfailing.

An invigorating few days, the first of its kind for Charity . . .

Until then, she had stayed within a couple hundred miles of her plantation home, having no desire to go elsewhere since all her needs were being cared for.

"I have friends here," she once told her parents. "I have you. This is all the world that I care about."

Many other southern girls felt the same way, their lives so comfortable, so self-contained, that it took a great deal for them to want to change their environment, however briefly. So families tended to stay in one place for a hundred years or more.

But, now, the chance to see Sojourner Truth was another story.

At first, Charity had been willing to come to the subject of this controversial individual with an open mind, but that inclination passed quickly in the face of unrelentingly negative articles in the local newspaper and additional ones she had gathered together from North Carolina, Georgia, Tennessee, and elsewhere.

She understood the question of bias, whether Yankee or southern, but even taking that into account, she found enough that was convincing about Sojourner Truth to make her uneasy.

But Charity was alerted by more than just those sources. She also had had the privilege of being around visiting political and social figures, men who were among the most prominent power centers of that day and who spent time with her well-connected father, making her privy to conversations that were denied the general public.

More than one of these guests painted a dreary, uncompromising picture of the black woman as a dangerous and often irrational figure yet someone around whom a myth-like reputation had been attaching itself, perpetuated by the unending praises published in any number of Yankee newspapers.

"She is being manipulated by the abolitionists for political reasons, that woman," commented a senior aide to Jefferson Davis, "and yet we are supposed to believe that she thinks she is serving purely humanitarian objectives."

He grunted in open disgust.

"She exudes specious nobility of a sort, I suppose, but Jefferson Davis and I consider her not unlike that Hoodoo Jack character you mentioned, with a more genteel facade. You might call her a viper in sheep's clothing."

Even so, the aide could not help admitting that Sojourner Truth had the knack of seeming reasonable and convincing.

"People are being duped by this black woman," the man exclaimed.

"It's her fault anyway, that God-awful woman. Why, it seems to the clear-headed that Sojourner Truth wants nothing less than our destruction!"

He sighed and slumped back in the chair.

"The problem is that she speaks much truth but cleverly colors it, if you will pardon the choice of words, with lies and distortions that make all of us seem as evil as the few she includes in her illustrations."

Charity overheard those comments and others, and finally, after learning that she was going to be part of an audience listening to Sojourner Truth in person, she tried to find out whatever she could about the woman, going beyond the vague impressions she had had until then, which were enough to make her want to go on the trip.

Six feet tall and very strong-looking, Sojourner Truth seemed to have the ability to wring the hearts of those who heard her speak, but as one report stated, she could "also wreathe our faces with smiles and even convulse us with laughter over stories of slave life."

She had been set free nearly twenty years earlier. Ironically, her freedom was gained not from the horrors of southern slavery but rather from a Yankee version of it, and during the time that had passed since then, she seemed to be devoting herself entirely to the spreading of abolitionist doctrine in any community whose citizens would sit down and listen.

Charity decided to talk with her father about his reasons for wanting to expend so much time and effort going to where he could actually hear the woman lash out at the only way of life the Littlepages had ever known.

His reply made her more proud of him than ever.

"I am aware of what you have heard," he acknowledged. "Of course, it gives me some reason to pause. I cannot allow myself to be deaf to such talk."

Charity knew her father well enough to realize that that was not all he had to say on the subject, and all she had to do was wait for him to tell her more.

"I simply want to find out all the truth I can," Alfred Littlepage said predictably. "I want to make up my mind on my own, without the distorted views of others confusing matters. The columnists and those other individuals so ready with so-called insights could be hitting a bull's-eye or perhaps missing it altogether."

Charity hugged him and whispered into his ear, "How I hope that someday the Lord will show me the sort of husband who can be half the father to our children that you have been to me."

After she had left his study, which smelled of mahogany panels recently nailed over what had been plain white walls, Alfred Littlepage sat back in an impressive walnut chair brought over from England by his great-grandfather, a treasured heirloom that was a hundred years older than himself. He sighed as he thought, *May your children be to you even a glimmer of what you have meant to us.*

Just then, Elizabeth opened the door and looked in.

"Charity seems especially content now," she said happily. "She was almost singing as she passed by me a moment ago."

"Nor is she the only one," Alfred replied, motioning Elizabeth over to him so that she could sit on his lap, which she did without hesitating, and soon both fell asleep like that, ignoring the rather Spartan discomfort of that ancient chair as they were comforted by one another's warmth.

In the meantime, though, Charity's own mood was changing quickly, which meant that she was acting not at all the way she normally was given to conducting herself.

During the two days before the carefully planned trip had commenced, she uncovered a much greater amount of information about Sojourner Truth, and she did not like any of what she was reading, because a discomforting percentage of it seemed to suggest an air of mystery about the woman, a degree of orchestrated behavior, or so it seemed, that surely a plain old former slave gal with a poverty-stricken heritage could not have been responsible for developing strictly on her own.

Isabella Baumfree was the woman's given name.

The change had to come as a heavy-handed attempt to gain support, Charity told herself. *She implies that anyone who is white and from the South is not capable of truth. And she waves her ancestry like a flag. In her eyes,* I wonder, *what does that make Little Isaiah and the others who seem content where they are?*

It was a question Charity planned to ask Sojourner Truth if allowed to do so from the audience.

And look at how much time passed after you were given your freedom by a simple change in New York's slavery laws, she thought. *If you were concerned about your people, why did it take so long for you to speak up?*

More than a decade . . . this was the lengthy period that had passed between the year when Sojourner Truth was freed from bondage to slaveholders in New York State and when she started campaigning on the side of the abolitionists.

"All of a sudden, you burst forth from some kind of secret cocoon," Charity said out loud, though she was alone in her bedroom. "Who got into that spirit of yours and seized control of you then? Who pumped the wrong ideas into you during that time, corrupting whatever might be good and decent about you?"

The more she read, the more she became convinced that, far from being someone worthy of admiration, Sojourner Truth instead was becoming ever more sinister, a shadowy figure who could conceivably be a secret ally of someone like Hoodoo Jack, or at least she did not seem like someone who could have been pleased by the news of his death.

One newspaper feature in particular convincingly accused the woman of the most rank of hypocrisies, preaching as she did about securing the overdue freedom of her people and yet living well on money that was being slipped to her by questionable Yankee white men, those whom she should have verbally castrated with the same regularity that she did anyone who happened to live south of the Mason-Dixon line.

"She has ready answers for everything," Charity continued musing, enjoying the role of amateur detective. "But how could she know so much if no one is helping her, and if she is being coached, who is controlling her?"

Apparently, it seemed, Sojourner Truth felt that a man's or a woman's place of residence was enough to earn him or her condemnation, no questions asked.

"She fiercely decries slavery in her many public speeches throughout the North and the West of America," the columnist had written, "and, yet, all the while she is in fact secretly chained to clandestine payments delivered to her in plain paper envelopes under the cover of darkness.

"Sojourner Truth—the very use of that name implicit as it is in her case with a particularly vulgar mockery of the meaning of truth—has been witnessed in the act of selling her pitch-black soul for filthy gain.

"Ivory eyes darting from side to side, she takes the bills and stuffs them into a pocket of her dress and furtively goes on her way, propagating the most destructive notions. And she gains affluence at the same time she works tirelessly to send an entire region of the United States into a devastating economic tailspin."

At first Charity had been skeptical about such interpretations, having dismissed the bulk of the earlier articles as automatically biased against any prominent black person and, therefore, containing conclusions that were suspect. But the growing number of newspaper editorials and other published material proved so consistent that she could not ignore them.

But what if these journalists have the facts? she thought. *What if they are not just southerners first and journalists last?*

She and her parents were due to leave the next morning; and part of the day was gone already. Nevertheless, she had decided to go into town and was hurrying outside when she saw Little Isaiah tending to the rosebushes.

Could he know anything about Sojourner Truth? she wondered to herself. *He doesn't much leave the plantation except to go on errands. And yet could he have picked up anything?*

She approached Little Isaiah, who seemed appreciative of the opportunity to take a break since he had been laboring with the plants—those roses and others across the plantation—through most of the day.

"Sojourner Truth?" he repeated, wiping his forehead with a plain white cloth. "Yes, Miss Charity, I knows some little bit about her."

Charity was not prepared for that sort of response.

"How could that be?" she asked.

"I knowed some relatives of hers who come down from up in Ulster, New York, where she was born."

"What was she like then?"

Charity studied his face, trying to analyze the expression on it, and found nothing negative.

"No one special . . . just another slave strugglin' to survive up north 'til slavery was outlawed there."

"And after she was freed?"

"That was a long time ago, in 1828, I's thinkin'. From what I heerd, she gone and disappeared for ages."

"Until the 1840s," Charity spoke up. "Why is that, I ask myself? Do you have any idea at all, Little Isaiah?"

Little Isaiah sniffed one especially large blossom, his serene manner in striking contrast to Charity's agitated one, making her feel guilty about raising the subject at all rather than waiting and seeing for herself.

"Gettin' closer to God, I hear," he said with the air of someone who was being forced to discuss a matter that meant very little in the scheme of things.

"Getting closer to—!"

Since that particular revelation went contrary to her now more cynical outlook, it made her hesitate.

"How can you be sure?" Charity asked, her tone as uncertain as she was feeling at that very moment.

"Can't be," he replied with no pretension. "But I done heerd it more than once from a bunch of folk. They ain't got no ax to grind, these ones don't; so I'm supposin' they's speakin' only da truth as they's seein' it."

Little Isaiah had been on his knees, carefully pruning one of the stems, but now he glanced up at her.

"You is lookin' for the truth," he said, "and that don't surprise me none, Miss Charity, bein' the way your daddy raised you. But—"

He was struggling for the words.

"I don't have what you need. Wish I did, honey, but I don't."

He looked away but continued speaking.

"Sorry to let you down," he told her, his voice cracking.

Charity knelt beside him and took both of his hands in her own.

"Bless you, dear friend," she remarked. "It might be the Lord Himself is trying to get through to me about something. You did your best. Everything is fine; believe that, will you, Little Isaiah?"

"Miss Charity?" he asked.

"Yes, Little Isaiah?"

"It might be that you can get what you is lookin' for only from that woman herself. It's no good maybe listenin' to heresy and all that kind of thing. It might be . . . that you shouldn't depend upon anybody else to direct you toward the truth."

Little Isaiah winced after speaking those words, and Charity knew why, so she said, "I could never be offended by anything you might want to say to me. You are very, very dear to me, my truest friend."

"I would give my life for you, Miss Charity," he told her.

"And I'd give mine for yours," she assured him.

Smiling more broadly, he broke off one of the stems about eight inches below the bright yellow bloom and handed it to her.

"God created something wonderful when He done this," Little Isaiah remarked. "And He went and did it again with you, Miss Charity."

She thanked him for the rose then stood and walked back toward the plantation house, unable to stop wondering what the Lord would be teaching her over the coming days.

~ 51 ~

AFTER SEVERAL DAYS on the road, the Littlepages arrived in Cincinnati and checked into the city's finest hotel. The next evening they were at the civic building some thirty-five minutes before Sojourner Truth was scheduled to speak and waited outside along with dozens of other individuals, all of whom were evidently wealthy.

The William Holmes McGuffey Hall.

A smallish building just one story tall with a plain whitewashed colonial front, it held barely over a hundred people, which included most of those standing outside in the chilly evening temperature, waiting until someone opened the front door.

"A brilliant man, this McGuffey," Alfred observed with some admiration. "During the past two decades or so, his books have sold more copies than any other except the Bible. It would be wonderful if he were an unannounced guest tonight. I would be honored to meet him."

"Each of his *McGuffey Readers* contains a strong witness for Christ," Elizabeth observed. "Great reading!"

Alfred nodded, smiling at his wife's alertness.

"I hope precious schoolchildren never lose the right and the privilege of having those books provided for them," he told her. "They will if men like that one have any more influence."

"Which one?" Elizabeth asked.

He pointed to a tall, thin fellow standing some eight feet away; he was dressed in a black suit and wore a black stovepipe hat.

"I know a great deal about that one," Alfred acknowledged, not feeling very optimistic about him.

"Who is he?" Elizabeth asked.

"He was elected to the Illinois legislature several years ago, then he became a member of Congress. Before that he studied enough law on his own to become a lawyer. Lately he's been trying for the U.S. Senate."

"What is the problem with him, father?" asked Charity.

"As I see it, this fellow is trying to have his political career both ways by claiming he is not an abolitionist but, on the other hand, that he opposes the extension of slavery to any of the territories."

Coincidentally, the man turned in their direction. As he did he noticed the three Littlepages, his attention centering on Alfred in seeming recognition.

"Father, look!" Charity spoke.

But Alfred had already noticed and grunted as, with three steps, this long-legged stranger was in front of them and starting to introduce himself.

"Sir, my name is Lincoln, Abraham Lincoln," he said pleasantly, though with some awkwardness. "Are you Alfred Littlepage?"

Charity's father nodded.

"And this must be Elizabeth and Charity?" Lincoln added, smiling at them with some degree of personal charm.

"What can I do for you?" Alfred asked impatiently, only marginally successful in hiding his suspicions about the man.

"I admire your stand on slavery."

Alfred was puzzled, not aware that his opinions had gone much beyond the community in which he lived.

"Somehow you have heard of me," he responded. "I cannot imagine how that is possible, sir. Well, I happen to know something about you also, Mr. Lincoln, namely, that you are a Yankee politician. And, thus, I have to take any pronouncements from you with a grain of salt."

"But what I said is true. I have great respect for what you have been reported to say on certain occasions."

"What is the basis for this so-called 'admiration,' may I ask?" Alfred replied, not convinced.

"Not here," Lincoln said cryptically. "There will be a better place for us. Perhaps later tonight or tomorrow morning."

"Why should I bother?" Alfred inquired.

"Because if people like you and I do not bother, we may not have anything left of this nation but the ashes of paradise."

"That is an interesting description, Mr. Lincoln. I know how you mean it, of course. But I was under the impression that Yankees such as yourself considered the South to be anything but paradise."

"I was speaking of the union as a whole, sir, one nation under God. The South is a part of that, at least for now."

"Am I to understand that you are paying some heed to the sentiments of the secessionists?"

"I must pay heed, as you say, to any group that threatens the stability of one nation under God," Lincoln asserted.

Alfred's tone of voice was laced with sarcasm.

"Then why side with those who are misguided abolitionists?" he pointed out, enjoying the seeming contradiction. "They are the ones stirring things up, I must tell you. Because the abolitionists have ranted for so long, we now have the secessionists to contend with—cause and effect, Mr. Lincoln."

"And your people, Mr. Littlepage? What about those editorials in southern newspapers urging conduct that can only bring disaster? I see no hint of compromise in anything I have read over the past months."

"That which is being published these days is only in response to the outpourings of your people, Mr. Lincoln. We, the citizens of the South, still value the sovereignty of individual states."

"You want freedom for yourselves, but you deny it to—"

The doors of the building were being opened up.

"Tomorrow, Mr. Littlepage?" Lincoln asked.

"I think not," Alfred replied. "Stephen Douglas's view of your skills is hardly mine. You seem more like a whiner, Mr. Lincoln, simply another cheap politician straddling fences on a number of issues, particularly that of slavery, while keeping your most personal opinions to yourself.

"You strike me as hardly someone who could debate before any reasonably astute crowd without making a bloody fool of himself, as the English would put it."

Lincoln obviously took offense at that. He turned sharply and walked on inside, never looking back.

"Were you not too extreme?" Elizabeth whispered. "After all, he started out by complimenting you."

"His kind do that like a spider enticing some hapless prey into a net. I want nothing to do with him tonight, tomorrow morning, or any other time, for that matter."

~ 52 ~

O NCE INSIDE, THE three of them took seats near the center of the auditorium.

At one time a youth fellowship hall, it had been donated to the community by the Methodist church, which was on the property next door. The
ceiling was not curved as in some similar structures but flat, the rafters
showing, huge beams from one side to the others. The seats were old pews
that the church's board of deacons had turned over to the community hall
when new ones arrived for the sanctuary. An elevated platform, much like
a mini-stage, had been erected at the front.

Sojourner Truth was introduced by the short, plump mayor of Cincinnati,
and she was in immediate striking contrast to his substantial width and his
pale, albino-like skin color. A full six feet in height, she stood so straight it
seemed she must have been trained in the army.

"I talked to a man earlier tonight who says that women need to be helped
by gentlemen into carriages and lifted over ditches and to have the best
seats everywhere they go," she said. "But nobody has ever helped me into
carriages or over mud puddles or given me the best place anywhere. And
aren't I a woman?"

Abruptly she reached her right arm over to her left, and pushed the
sleeve of her long gray dress up to her shoulder.

"Look at me!" she admonished her listeners. "Look at my arm! I have
plowed and planted, and gathered into barns, and no man could do better.
Yet aren't I a woman? I could work as much and eat as much as any of you
menfolk—when I could get the work, that is—and bear the lash as well. And
aren't I a woman?"

Her voice had both risen in volume and deepened in tone.

"I have borne thirteen children and seen most all of them sold off into
slavery, and when I cried out with a mother's grief, none but Jesus heard.
And aren't I a woman?"

She walked away from the podium and pointed her finger here and there
at the audience.

"Have any of you mothers sitting so primly tonight had your baby torn from sucking your nipple, with fresh, warm milk spilling down over that little one?" she roared at them, then pointed back at herself. "I have!"

She held out her hands.

"These were empty that day!" she told them. "They had grabbed my infant son, broken his neck, and tossed him into some ditch, leaving him there as food to be picked at by birds and wild, roaming dogs.

"Why? You ask that question with your eyes. And the answer is one that none of you will ever have to face: Because my next owner did not want to have me distracted from my work by the duties of motherhood! And yet aren't I a woman?"

For another half-hour, Sojourner Truth continued ripping at their consciences with such precision that only gasps were heard from those seated in that little auditorium. No one moved or coughed or turned away.

Finally she invited people from the audience to respond with whatever they wanted to ask or say.

Alfred could see the trend that was developing, men and women standing, sometimes nervously since they were not accustomed to being the focus of such attention as everyone else turned and studied them. One by one they congratulated Sojourner Truth for her courage and her determination toward the goal of abolishing slavery and emancipating her people.

The first few were like that, but then others took off in another direction.

"We will fight with you all the way!" a man who seemed to be in his mid-thirties spoke up. "I hear that plans are under way now."

"Plans for what, sir?" Sojourner Truth asked.

He winked at her and sat down again.

The bald, older man next to him stood.

"None of us will be deterred," he remarked cryptically, "even if it means shedding our own blood."

Murmuring rippled through the audience, some of the listeners uncomfortable with that last remark.

Surely you will speak up now, Alfred thought, *and disavow any such extremism.*

He waited for Sojourner Truth to do that, to separate herself from the pursuit of violence, even war, to achieve freedom for black people.

But she did not.

Even as others from the audience stood and voiced support for whatever measures were necessary, she offered nothing contrary and seemed to consent to it all by her very silence.

But then Alfred spoke up.

"Do you not see what is happening here?" he asked.

"And what is that?" Sojourner Truth shot back.

"You are helping to incite many of these people," he told her. "By saying little or nothing, you are agreeing with them when they talk of taking up arms and carrying the struggle to Atlanta, Charleston, Natchez, and elsewhere throughout the South."

"What is the alternative, sir?" she asked.

"Do it peacefully."

"While black men and women continue under the yoke?"

"It will take a few more years and much patience, yes, but that would avoid adding their blood to the rest."

"It has not happened yet, after centuries of time."

"So what if it takes another hundred years? How much time is a man's life worth? Or the lives of a hundred thousand men? That which is torn asunder by the ravages of war will take longer to heal. Look at the wounds that would be inflicted! Why not avoid these wounds altogether, sparing generations to come this foul heritage?"

Sojourner Truth stepped down from the platform.

"How many loved ones have you lost to the whip, to hunger, to disease? How many are buried you know not where? You can go to your mama's grave! And your papa's! I cannot do that, sir. And I never shall!"

She swung around and stepped back toward the platform.

"You are not free," Alfred called out. "You are a prisoner of hatred. You wallow in it. You cling to hatred as your sole reason for living. You do not so much want to emancipate your people as to get revenge against an entire region. You are oh so eager to sound the battle cry but only because you yourself are not in danger."

Sojourner Truth was enraged. She faced Alfred again.

"When have you ever known anything but security?" she asked. "You are waited on by my people. You eat from your plenty while they exist from the scraps off your table. They shiver in the winter while you enjoy the warmth from logs they cut and coal that they transport to your front door. You dress in finery imported from Europe while your slaves have only—"

Charity got to her feet, unable to remain silent any longer.

"They have respect for us!" she said.

"Like good little doggies! Do whatever your massa saith. Is that what you mean? Otherwise you won't get your bowl of slop come evenin' time. That's not respect, Missie; that's plain stark fear, fear of hunger."

"They have respect because we have earned it from them, earned it with mercy."

"Oh, when you whip them with a cat-o'-nine-tails, you give them only seven lashes or maybe just five instead of ten or a dozen. Is that the mercy you're talking about, Missie?"

"Mercy is caring. Mercy is loving. Mercy is pity."

Sojourner Truth was silent.

"Where mercy, love, and pity dwell, there God is, too," Charity added. "We have cried with them. We have laughed. We have rejoiced side by side. They eat their meals at a table next to ours in the main dining hall. We now worship together in the same pews in the same church before a man of God whose life was changed when our blessed Violet died in his arms!"

Charity's cheeks were wet. And so were her father's.

"We were not responsible for bringing your people to this land," she said. "But now that they are here, we must do what is best."

"Cast off their shackles!" Sojourner Truth shouted. "Is that not the greatest of merciful acts? Give them their freedom without precept or condition. Just say go! Open the door and stand aside and let them pass. Is that not a gift of love like few others, Missie, if truly you feel this love toward them that you claim?"

Charity bowed her head briefly, and when she raised it, there was almost a glow about her.

"You are a mother who has lost her children, seen them torn from her," she said. "Our coloreds are our children. We do not want them sent out into the kind of world that will destroy them as yours have been destroyed. We want to give them a life without needless pain, as much as pain can be avoided, a life in which they do not have to beg food from passers-by, throwing themselves at the mercy of strangers."

She leaned forward, her intensity startling even her father.

"They can have freedom anytime they want it. My father here has the papers ready with only their names to be completed. But the coloreds we know, love, and respect are aware of what they will face once they leave us. They're not ready, Sojourner Truth. Give them time. Do not thrust it upon them from the ashes of the only life most of them have known as adults."

Charity smiled as she lowered her voice.

"Is it freedom if they go out into the sort of world that will shackle them instead with poverty, poverty that knows no kindness, that offers no mercy, that brings them only shame as their children cry for food that is not there? Are the free blacks of a shantytown really free? If that be freedom, then long live slavery as my family and I practice it!"

Sojourner Truth may have been readying a profound renunciation, but none came from her. Instead she walked down the center aisle and stood before Charity and Alfred, who were two seats away from her.

"If only I could have been a slave of yours . . . ," she said. Then she bowed slightly before the two of them and walked from the hall, leaving an astonished audience in her wake.

~≈ 53 ≈~

THE LITTLEPAGES SPENT another couple of days in Cincinnati, seeing the sights and shopping in the markets. Then they began the ride back toward home. The journey was somber, with Alfred, Elizabeth, and Charity replaying in their minds their encounter with Sojourner Truth. They talked about little else until near dusk when they had to find a place to stay. Sickness in the family of the cousin they had planned to stay with forced them to look elsewhere for lodging.

"I believe there is a bed-and-breakfast farm a mile or so up the road," Alfred said. "We could try that."

"But what if it is full?" Elizabeth asked. "We can hardly stay outdoors."

"But is that so impossible?" he posed.

"You aren't serious!" she replied.

"We used to do that when we were first married. Several of us couples would go camping down near the coast," Alfred reminded her. "We seemed to think it was fun then."

He could tell that Elizabeth remained unconvinced.

"Have we become so sophisticated, so captive to our upper-class way of life," he asked, "that simpler pleasures are beyond our grasp or our desire?"

He was trying to make her feel embarrassed, and he succeeded.

"It was delightful, in those days, to isolate ourselves," she reminisced. "I love our slaves, I surely do, as I love many of our relatives and friends, but getting away from everybody can be wonderful."

"Are you game for this, Charity?" he asked, as always considering her feelings.

The idea was appealing, and she nodded in approval.

"Why not just forget that bed-and-breakfast place I mentioned," Alfred remarked, "and look instead for a camping spot? I wanted to prepare for this possibility, so I put a pile of blankets and some pillows in the back compartment."

Doing something that was a departure from the predictability of their normal way of life enlivened their spirits, and the three of them started singing a ballad they had heard their slaves often perform.

They saw nothing for the next several miles and went back to talking about Sojourner Truth while paying attention to the countryside.

"She is being used by both sides," commented Charity.

"I know," said Alfred in agreement. "That is very sad. There she is, placing herself in the hands of the Lord, and human beings are trying to get in the way."

"I listened to some of them, Daddy. I took their hatred and believed what they said to be fact. Yet you have taught me all this time to use my mind, to be discerning. How could I have been so wrong, especially with something as important as this?"

"Because some truth stands at the center of what is being published and spoken about that poor woman, Charity. If she succeeds, the upheaval throughout the South will be monumental, no doubt about that. They are scared, though none will admit that. They hide behind their venom. It is a moat of sorts around some medieval castle. These people hope to fight off the gathering forces, forces they cannot even see as yet but can only sense and, in doing so, keep things from changing."

Alfred was not being entirely unsympathetic.

"After all, this is life as they have known it, as you and I have also. To rip it from them is almost the same as death. They give up something quite precious if they lose the battle. That is no less true for them as for this family."

He held onto the reins with one hand and pulled Charity close to him with the other. Elizabeth, in the backseat, reached out and patted her on the back.

"In my own life, the battle has already been fought," Alfred continued. "Though Little Isaiah, Willis, and the others have chosen not to accept my offers of freedom, they are free as far as I am concerned. If they walk off tomorrow, it will be something I had anticipated long ago, something I have never felt the slightest need to resist. It is just that I fear for these good people, fear for what happens when that free world beyond our plantation deals them blows that slavery never has."

"But how would you run your business?" Charity asked, not as selfishly as the question might imply.

"I would pay out more money and hire free blacks or men of our own race and color. That would never bankrupt me. This family could lose eighty percent of its holdings and still be considered wealthy by any standard."

Alfred's voice grew husky as he remarked, "I would miss them if they chose to leave, but in that I suspect I would be very much like a father giving each child the freedom to live a separate life on his or her own."

Charity leaned against her father, feeling the most intense love imaginable. She had adored him as long as she could remember, and as she grew older, to that love was added an equal admiration as she learned all that this uncommon man stood for and what this meant in terms of decency and morality.

"Charity, I—" he gasped.

An instant later, Alfred Littlepage slumped against her, something wet touching her, and then she heard her mother screaming.

A knife . . . Charity saw the knife protruding from between her father's shoulder blades.

It had been thrown from an assassin's hiding place in the surrounding countryside, perhaps a clump of brush or from behind some tall grass or one of the thick trees set back only a short distance from the road.

Alfred, still holding the reins, started to fall to the left, off the carriage, but Charity was able to grab him and hold on temporarily.

"I am halting the horses . . . ," he said hoarsely.

They stopped a moment later.

Alfred could no longer hold onto the reins, his hands without strength. He looked at Charity and whispered, "Good-bye, dearest child." He rolled his eyes toward the backseat. "Good-bye, my love."

"Daddy!"

Charity could no longer hold him, though Elizabeth also was trying to help. He pulled away from her and tumbled over the edge.

Elizabeth, screaming, stood up and started to jump off the carriage.

A rifle shot rang out in the quiet of that time of near dusk. It caught her just below the chin. As Elizabeth fell she grabbed her neck and glanced at her daughter, trying to say something, but her vocal chords had been shredded, and only a terrible choking noise came from between her lips.

Briefly, Charity froze, totally disoriented, accustomed to a quiet life, a life that was largely planned, a life where predictability was a virtue; and now all of that had been torn from her, and she was left in the midst of darkness and chaos with an enemy she could not immediately see or hear.

Then came the voices, their evil nature apparent, voices filled with glee at what had been "accomplished."

"Get the girl" one grumbled. "We'll keep her around for a while . . . just awhile."

Charity knew she should be running, though it was impossible to tell in which direction since she could not place where the voices were coming from.

Groaning . . .

Her mother was silent, dead. But her father was groaning.

Charity jumped off the carriage and knelt beside him, hysteria building up in her.

"Go . . . ," he said.

"I can't leave you here like this," she cried.

"Oh, Charity, blessed Charity! You have a full life . . . ahead of you . . . a life that the Lord is going to greatly use . . . you cannot sacrifice it here, now, for us or anyone else. Give Him a chance to do what He wishes!"

"I must stay!" she insisted.

"You must go!" Alfred demanded, the final bit of strength in him pouring into his voice, steady, clear, not willing to countenance disobedience.

He reached out, one finger touching her tears and trying hard to hold onto life so that he could speak just a little longer before he was taken from that place forever.

"Dear Jesus, be with this blessed one," he prayed aloud and then slumped back, his eyes still open; she knew that he was gone.

Daddy, Daddy! her mind cried. *I cannot live without you and Mama. I—*

She leaned over, kissed him on the forehead, gently touched his hands and then closed the lids over his eyes that seemed still to be staring at her. Then she stood.

A rifle was in the carriage, on the floor.

She reached into the back and picked it up, holding it firmly in her hands.

"Come on now!" she shouted defiantly. "I am ready! Show yourselves! Or can you only kill like cowards, from the darkness, with no courage to face me?"

She glanced at the bodies of her parents, sprawled like dolls tossed aside and forgotten, then spoke again, "I have nothing to live for now. Kill me!"

She dropped the rifle, emotions submerging her common sense.

"Please kill me!" Charity screamed while opening her arms wide and inviting them to shoot again.

And they tried to oblige her as two bullets hit Charity, one in the shoulder, another in her thigh. She fell, hitting the ground hard, breaking a rib.

She saw two shapes in the darkness coming toward her, swaggering as they did, so confident that their ghastly mission was going to be achieved and they could soon sit back and gloat over it as they drank their liquor and puffed on their cigars.

Charity's vision blurred for a moment then cleared.

Tall men, with cruel, ugly faces.

"Why?" she demanded as both of them approached, sneers visible on their faces. "Why have you done this? I don't know you. My parents—"

Ever since she was old enough to cope with the more brutal images, Charity had been informed of the cruelties that proliferated in the outside world, and also, the environment on the Littlepage plantation did have its inevitable hothouse aspects.

"We do the same to all nigger lovers like your kind," one of them interrupted, nothing but brutality in his voice. "Those other folk in that building are going to feel our wrath.

"Somebody will stop this!" Charity insisted, trying to keep from showing the pain that was racing along every nerve through her body.

"But it sure enough isn't going to be you!" the second one growled, raising his rifle and aiming it directly at her head, hesitating as he chuckled to himself and then closing a finger tightly around the trigger. "Too bad you won't be around to read about it in the newspaper. Now that is a real shame."

Sneering, he glanced at the other man for a moment and then turned his attention back to Charity like a snake ready to strike at a hapless prey and swallow it whole.

Another shot. Followed by a second.

Closing her eyes, Charity was ready for the sort of pain she had never before known, the pain of death coming from a bullet that, in an instant, would be ripping its way through her brain.

Lord, there is nothing! she exclaimed. *Am I dead and waiting for the gates of heaven to open for me?*

Instead she felt only a heavy body smelling of sweat and whiskey falling on top of her, making her gasp from the impact of its weight, hot, sweet liquid pouring over her face. Then she heard another body hit the ground not far away.

She opened her eyes, saw the one who had been intent on killing her. His rough-skinned, partially bearded face was touching her own, an expression of pain and rage mixed together in an unholy combination.

Charity screamed as she tried to push him off her, but he was very heavy, and she did not have the strength.

Finally, the man was being pulled to one side. Someone bent down over her, speaking comforting words that she could not quite understand, but the tone of his voice convinced her that he meant no harm.

Whoever he was picked her up with infinite gentleness, but seconds later, she lost consciousness in the stranger's arms, surrendering to a greater darkness than that of the passing dusk and the coming night.

❦ 54 ❧

THE BED WAS an unfamiliar one and not at all comfortable to Charity because of its strangeness after sleeping most of the nights of her life in one bed in one room in one house.

Confused and scared, she could feel herself turning again and again on her back, her side, her back, her side, over and over again while remaining largely unconscious.

Mama! Papa! she called out desperately, but there was no answer, only the sound of a rifle's shot and the *whoosh* of a large knife as it sliced through the clear air. *I have been kidnapped and am unable to tell where I have been taken.*

Memories of childhood passed by, floating like jigsaw puzzle pieces, tumbling, turning, one after the other, making her laugh then cry or turn away in childish embarrassment, or she would reach out to her mother, her father as though by touching them, by grabbing hold, she could pull both back into her life.

She saw them look sadly in her direction, shake their heads, and whisper, "We can never return, beloved. But you will not be left alone, Charity. Have faith that, in all of your life, you will never be alone."

"But without you, I am alone!" she protested, but already Elizabeth and Alfred Littlepage were fading from view.

Eventually she emerged from the darkness, opening her eyes to find herself confronted by strangers.

"My mother . . . my father . . . ," she muttered, her mouth dry.

"We are already taking care of them," the middle-aged plump-faced woman sitting on the edge of the bed told her. "Please rest, my dear."

"But I want to go to them," Charity protested. "I need to . . . to see what has to be done, what I must—"

"You do not have the strength. Your parents had identification with them, so we were able to send their bodies back home right away."

"Right away? What do you mean? Why didn't you wait for me?"

The woman smiled thinly.

"Dear, you have been unconscious for three days. We just couldn't wait any longer to do what had to be done."

"They're already being buried? Is that what you're telling me?"

"I suspect so."

"But how can you do that without me?"

"The way you failed to respond to anything, we thought we might have to send you back the same way."

Charity had raised herself up to her elbows.

"It came so suddenly," she told the woman. "We were talking, and then that awful sound . . . and, in a few seconds, it seemed, they both were dead."

"We continue to look for the men, Charity."

"You know my name!"

"We sent a telegraph message on to Columbia. Someone there got in touch with a man named Samuel Fulkerson, I believe. He sent back a message to us, saying that he would leave immediately to come here, along with your family's pastor. And they would bring some of the local militia along with them for protection.

"We in turn have arranged for some of our own men to join you and the rest of your group for the trip home. You were attacked because you came all this distance to listen to a celebrated black woman, so we feel some obligation to you. The issue of slavery brings out the worst in people, I am afraid."

Despite the unique nature of a personal guard consisting of Yankee and southern men, none of that carried any weight as far as Charity was concerned for the moment. Far more important to her was another matter.

"But who's in charge of the funeral?" she demanded.

"One of your slaves."

"He was allowed to do that?"

"We were told that, under the circumstances, your father probably would not have had it any other way."

Charity fell back against the bed and started crying again.

"Does that bother you so much, to have a slave handling the arrangements?" the woman asked.

Charity shook her head.

"Then why are you crying?"

"They loved each other so much. I am glad that Little Isaiah is able to . . . to—"

The woman, seeing that this pleased Charity, added, "Apparently there were no objections from anyone in your home community. I must say that that sounds like a rare turn of events coming from anywhere in the South."

Charity felt a surge of anger at the woman's supercilious attitude.

"Yankees don't know nearly as much about how we live and what we think as they always try to pretend, hoping that honest people won't realize how ignorant they actually are!" Charity retorted, adrenaline sending a measure of strength throughout her body. "What I have been reading in the so-called best of the Yankee newspaper stories these days is more outlandish and concocted to please certain political interests than to present any kind of truth."

"It is my view that any means of overturning the institution of slavery is allowable under the circumstances," the woman replied coldly.

"Wait a minute, Gloria!" someone else in the room protested. "You are not speaking with any rationality."

"I did not ask for your opinion." she told him.

"Nor did I ask for that sort of mindlessness from you!" the other voice responded crisply. "If your influence over others is at the abysmal level of what you just expressed, then I fear for the future! You become the problem, not the solution, my dear."

Charity's attention wandered from that one woman to the two other individuals who were waiting in what she saw now to be a beautifully decorated, expensively furnished room with pale gold-orange walls and French Provincial chairs with red insets, plus a dressing bureau and a nightstand beside the large four-poster bed.

A man six feet four inches tall, with strong-looking frame and homely face showing darkish skin stretched over protruding cheekbones and the beginnings of a beard was standing at the foot of the bed, his expression haggard.

Embarrassed by the bitter clash with the woman, he leaned forward slightly.

"My name is Lincoln, Ma'am, Abraham Lincoln," he introduced himself. "This is Gloria Joinville. Rest well, my dear young woman. You are really quite safe from now on. We will not let anyone harm you."

He indicated the woman with a nod of his head.

"My friend is as wealthy today as I was poor not so many years ago," Lincoln remarked. "But she uses money largely to benefit people, not hurt them, despite what her brutal words may lead you to believe."

"I wish I were not safe at all," Charity blurted. "I wish I were with them!"

He bent down and with almost feminine gentleness, which was startling in a man of his size and chiseled features, cupped her cheek in his hand.

"You will go on," he spoke. "Do not give up. Your loved ones surely would want you to be happy."

"How can I be happy without them?"

He smiled as he replied, "Only faith can sustain you now. For by faith you have given the blessed Holy Ghost, Who is but God's sublime Comforter, entrance to your soul, and there He abides now and always. Listen to Him, for He will be your voice of reason."

She smiled and thanked the man, then noticed the other individual sitting on a chair in the opposite corner of the room.

Sojourner Truth.

"I don't want her here!" Charity said hoarsely.

"She has been here since you were brought in," the woman told her. "She held your hand for many hours."

"My parents are dead because of her!"

"Your parents are dead because some men, filled with the most consuming hatred, let their emotions take over their will, their decency. They became so blinded by—"

"No speeches. You sound like a politician . . . leave me alone!"

The woman nodded sadly, and she as well as the man named Abraham Lincoln started to leave that finely appointed and furnished room through a nearby doorway.

Have they saved me? she asked herself. *Or have they just made me some kind of prisoner being held I know not where?*

Charity could be sure of just one thing.

I have to get home, to be with my own kind. They reek of false self-righteousness, these Yankees. Daddy was right.

For an instant, Charity spotted Sojourner Truth glancing at her sympathetically, then she followed Lincoln and Gloria Joinville out of the room.

"I wish I had never heard your name!" she shouted at the tall figure. "I wish I had never seen that darkie hide of yours."

Three days unconscious . . .

If that information were accurate and if Fulkerson and Marmaduke had left immediately, they would soon be arriving within another day or two to take her back.

"But what will I return to, Lord?" she spoke. "Mama and Daddy both are . . . are . . . dead! What is left for me?"

Simply recognizing that tragic fact covered Charity with chills that touched every nerve.

"How can I go on without them?" she went on. "They have been the center of my world. I am not strong enough simply to stand at their graves, shed some tears, and then go on with my life as though they were visitors who happened to stop by for a while but couldn't stay and finally left without a proper good-bye."

Back home, she would wake up each morning to the odor of a fine breakfast being freshly prepared. She would arise after kneeling in prayer and asking God's guidance for the day, wash and dress, and hurry down-stairs and burst into the dining room.

Gone . . .

She dreaded facing that first morning back in the plantation house, see-ing the two empty chairs at the large table in the center.

No matter how well she might intellectualize the tragedy of her parents' deaths and somehow shove it to the back of her mind and steel herself, as soon as she stepped into that room and did not see her parents there, she would surely collapse—but perhaps not before glimpsing the sad faces of those slaves who now had only her to care for as time passed.

"Pass the butter, please, Mama. This bread is wonderful, but it's just a bit dry this time. Needs some butter."

"Wonderful bacon this morning, Mama. It has a wonderful flavor and isn't as greasy as the other day."

"How was that trip of yours to Nashville a few days ago, Papa? I hear a fine new folk singer's been performing there to big crowds since word has got-ten around. I heard about him before you left. Peggy Sue told me he was wonderful. I hope you were able to catch his act. Next time, if he's still there, I would really like to go with you. Is it all right if I tag along?"

"Did you get to the harbor area yesterday, Papa? I heard that that remark-able new vessel from England had finally come in and berthed, a truly beau-tiful ship. Did you manage to see what it was like, Papa? She was freshly painted before leaving Southampton, as sleek and seaworthy as they come."

"Mama, do you think we could go into Columbia right after lunch tomor-row? I thought I would make a new dress for myself with the material that I could buy.

"I know you don't like to have me go to that sort of trouble when you could have one done up by a dressmaker in the city, but honestly, it's something I would really enjoy creating. You see, I have a certain color in mind. Would you take me with you, Mama?"

"Papa, the main carriage has to have a little work done to it, especially the backseat, which may need to be repadded and restitched. Hester's been thinking about working on it this weekend, but it could take longer than that. Is it all right with you, I mean, if this carries over to Monday? Or do you need him for something else?"

"Just as I was opening my eyes, I heard you singing this morning, Mama. What a lovely sound to wake up to!"

No more.

Simple snippets of the most casual conversation, as mundane as daily breakfast-table chatter can get.

But treasured now as though they were from the mouth of Solomon.

～ 55 ～

A CCORDING TO THE latest telegram, Fulkerson and Marmaduke were supposed to arrive just after one o'clock that afternoon.

Charity had been hoping it would be earlier.

Losing her parents in the way that she had was a monstrous tragedy that was only being aggravated by unfamiliar surroundings and the company of strangers, none of whom she believed could be trusted.

Charity felt every minute of the time that passed, most of which she spent either crying alone in that ornately appointed room or just sitting on the edge of the comfortable bed where she had lain unconscious for several days since the night of the murders.

Sitting and remembering and wanting to die herself . . .

"How can I go on?" she asked out loud but with no one around to hear her. "They were the center of my life."

A center that no longer existed.

Gloria Joinville finally convinced her to eat a truly hefty breakfast, though she consumed it without actually tasting very much of what she mechanically put in her mouth: a large country-fried steak topped with fresh sausage gravy, eggs, bacon, and toast followed by a cup of fresh-brewed coffee.

The militia is coming along to protect me, she told herself, *but how much do I want to be kept from harm right now? Wouldn't it be better, Lord, if an assassin's bullet or knife cut short this life of mine so that I am no longer separated from those I love so much?*

Becoming restless, Charity ventured outside, past a two-story, well-kept, colonial-style building that served as quarters for Gloria Joinville's staff of servants.

Servants . . . she thought cynically. *Even someone so vehemently against slavery has managed to keep black people waiting on her under a different name.*

A garden.

She had seen a hint of color that made her want to investigate the source. What she found made her gasp.

"Oh, Mama, if you could see this . . . ," she whispered. "It gives a hint of heaven; that it surely does."

Roses.

A vast number of the fragrant blossoms confronted her, the most that Charity had ever seen together in one location.

Spectacular rose vines hung heavy with blooms and dominated white-painted latticework trellises. Along the far wall stood seven-foot-high rose trees so thick with blossoms they provided shade against the hot noonday sun. And the fullest, widest, healthiest bushes Charity had ever seen dominated the eastern end of the garden.

A narrow dirt path wound through the garden, and she walked along it, not quite believing the accumulated beauty she was seeing.

"Was there such a collection of scents when you entered the gates of heaven?" she spoke out loud.

Just ahead was a plain wooden bench resting on a bare section of dirt; it was set in a small bower with a wall of multihued roses surrounding it.

Charity sat down on the bench and inhaled deeply. One particular section of roses fascinated her, and she reached out and touched a blossom gently.

Scarlet.

Her mother had raised roses of a similar color but without the special richness of the ones before her now.

"At night . . . ," a now familiar husky voice intruded suddenly, "it is especially nice where you are, with moonlight sneaking in through tiny gaps between all those petals and stems."

Charity opened her eyes and saw Gloria Joinville standing in front of her.

"I come here," the woman observed, "seeking to find some small fragment of peace. And it does come, like something that is will of the wisp, unannounced, unheard, surrounding me with its blissful solitude.

"The only trouble is that such moments are just that, moments, and they never last because, sooner or later, I have to leave that spot in this garden and return to another sort of world altogether. The illusion of heaven dissipates quickly enough."

She reached out and touched one of the petals.

"My hobby," Gloria remarked, stroking it as she would a lover's shoulder in the middle of the night.

"It was the same for my mother," replied Charity. "She enjoyed having more children than she could count. That was what each rose was to her, another offspring she could nurture until it had matured."

"You are an only child, I gather."

"The only child, I imagine, to have roses as siblings."

Gloria chuckled politely.

"It will take a long time for you to recover," she said. "Days and weeks will not do it. Months perhaps, but only as the start of a real recovery. That may be years hence. There are no quick exits, my young friend."

Charity sensed that the woman was not just humoring her.

"You have been through something like this yourself?" she asked.

Gloria nodded with a weariness that showed she herself still felt the aftermath of personal tragedy.

"Many years ago . . . my parents were killed because they made the mistake of befriending a runaway slave. There was no trial. The slave's owner had them shot on the spot, my mother, my father, and the runaway.

"I witnessed everything that happened. They tried to kill me as well, even though I was only six years old at the time, but I managed to escape. And I kept on running, running, running.

"Not long after that, I was adopted by a fine, middle-aged, quite wealthy couple who had never had any children by natural birth. Eventually, just out of my teenage years, I married into a wealthy family near here and was widowed this past December—three days after Christmas, when my husband died of a heart attack. It seems that his legacy was that I have been left with all the respectability that money buys."

"So what does all this have to do with niggers?"

For Charity, the use of that description was natural since both her parents repeated it often over the years and without intended insult, as she just had done, but nevertheless, Gloria grimaced when it was spoken.

"I saw what bigotry could cause," she went on, explaining her unmistakable reaction. "And I know what pathetic conditions black people face everyday."

"Were your foster parents slave-owners?" Charity asked.

"No . . . they hired free blacks, paid them a decent wage."

"So they were servants, not slaves."

"And you are about to ask me what the difference is?"

Charity shook her hand.

"No. I want you to know that on our plantation, the coloreds have always been free to leave, but to this day, every last one of them has refused any such offers simply because my parents treated them all so well."

Gloria cocked her head slightly.

"Out of genuine concern or fear that they might revolt and slaughter you in the middle of the night?" she asked. "Slaves are rising up against their oppressors, you know. This is hardly anything new.

"It has to be said that they would never have started succumbing to the behavior of rampaging beasts if they were not being constantly looked upon as brute animals, period. After so long, they have become the stereotype!"

"But my parents never experienced anything like that, nor did any of the earlier generations in our family. What explanation can there be except that they never treated our slaves as less than human?"

"Not every slave-owner feels the same way."

"Not every slave-owner is a monster either."

"It is the institution itself that corrupts the one at the same time it makes bestial the other. Why not abolish slavery altogether? Remove the occasion to sin as, I gather, the Bible would call it."

"And, I suppose, leave those who are black at the mercy of Yankee opportunists interested in getting their hands on that cheap labor suddenly thrown out into the marketplace? Praise God that there are many within the federal government who are not afraid of facing up to certain special interests supporting the abolitionist movement and that its so-called humanitarian concerns are not to be taken very seriously."

Gloria stepped back to scrutinize the unexpectedly capable and tough-minded young woman in front of her.

"You mention God . . . ," she said.

"You mention the Bible," retorted Charity.

Gloria's eyes narrowed.

"I must say that you sound far too intelligent to try," she said, "and wrap Scripture as a suit of armor around the pro-slavery cause."

"But the Bible has virtually nothing to say against slavery."

"Which hardly means that it goes so far as to support the ownership of one human being by another."

"If the Bible is silent on the subject then, obviously, God has no particular admonitions for or against it. The only slavery denounced is that of slavery to sin. But there are many passages that speak to the issue of being a good slave, an obedient slave, of being a slave not to Satan but to Almighty God, of obeying those in authority over us."

"So you are saying it is all right for Christians to have slaves?"

Gloria seemed genuinely appalled at that notion and expected Charity to deny it with vigor. But, instead, Charity nodded emphatically.

"If those slaves—" she started to say.

Gloria interrupted, "Then I think you and I should not be talking any longer."

Charity was not going to let her get away as easily as that.

"I have noticed, from my father's relationships with certain northern businessmen, that when they have run out of arguments to support their abolitionist views, they just up and leave, period, rather than dig any deeper within themselves—while it is those whose way of life is being demeaned who have the courage to stand their ground!"

"You are remarkable, Charity Littlepage. But my heart is grieved by the fact that a good Christian such as yourself has not chosen the right side."

"I choose the side that has worked very well for many decades. If anything, I think the Lord has blessed us because of the kind of life we have given to our slaves."

"A prosperous life, of course, but one that has been secured on the bruised and bloody backs of helpless black people."

Turning her back with a bit of theatrical flair, Gloria Joinville started to walk away.

"I feel sorry for you," Charity told her straightforwardly. "You support a political philosophy that is founded in deceit."

Gloria spun around, her cheeks not much less scarlet than the petals on the rosebush both had been admiring.

"How can you say that?" she demanded angrily. "What do I have to gain from this? What do any of us gain except being true to our convictions?"

Charity had been well versed by her father, and, later, by Fulkerson and Marmaduke, in terms of a response to that sort of question.

"I mentioned it a moment ago, but you ignored me: a labor pool which many in positions of influence up north covet as they look down their so-called socially concerned noses at my people!" Charity, raising her voice, spoke. "Your abolitionist friends are beckoned by better profits, not better lives for slaves."

She expected Gloria to lash out at her verbally or otherwise.

But the woman said nothing at first.

"Have I struck too close to home?" Charity probed, sensing that she had done just that. "Why are you now so subdued?"

"Because it was never supposed to be that way," Gloria surprisingly acknowledged. "At first, only the noble-minded were in charge, dedicated to freedom and justice for every American, regardless of color. But later it was different. New leaders moved in. They wrenched control from those of us who had only the right motives."

"So you know, then, that I am speaking the truth?"

"And I also know that it is too late. They control everything. And the public stupidly believes them. They would reject anyone like me nowadays if I were to speak up and try to reverse this deterioration."

Her lips curled into a sneer.

"I live with that reality until I think I can stand it no longer. The sound and the taste and the feel of it sicken me. You and I are going to be swept along very much against our will. We can only stand back and—"

"And pray?" Charity suggested.

"Not pray, no! It would be better to hatch new plans somehow, plans to kick out the leaders who have betrayed us, do whatever it takes to accomplish that, even if this were to mean rising up against them."

"Leading to possible retaliation against your own people, I gather? The shedding of blood doesn't matter to you, does it? You reject prayer, but you are willing to embrace riots or, I suppose, outright murder if that is what you find necessary!"

"Where there is no God, there can be no prayer. I would never encourage something in which I did not believe."

"And so you are an atheist?"

"In a world of the most loathsome of institutions, I cannot accept the existence of a God who would allow any of these evils to exist."

A third voice intruded, "Surely you cannot believe that, Gloria."

Stepping into the garden, her form outlined by moonlight, was the now familiar tall, painfully thin, black-skinned figure.

Sojourner Truth.

"God gave us this world," she continued, "and the absolute freedom to make of it what we desire. It is not the Almighty who is at fault with all this madness around us but the corrupt inner selves that we call souls."

Gloria's response was not to speak at all but to stare at her with an expression that could only be called condescending.

"We will discuss this later," she finally said.

Sojourn Truth shook her head.

"But discussing this later is what has delayed any improvement in my people's plight for all these many years," she replied. "We are told in Scripture to resist the devil, not the truth. But good people seem to feel that waiting on the Lord is more important. So they wait and wait and wait and perhaps say, 'We will discuss this later.' But for countless numbers of my kind, later never comes."

"Why are you acting like this?" Gloria asked defensively.

Sojourner Truth pointed to Charity, who was still sitting.

"This young woman's mother and father have just been assassinated! You seem to have let that fade to some foggy corner of your mind. She has lost her entire family, Gloria. That gives her the right to say anything she wants right now without having your mocking rebukes flung in her face."

Sojourner Truth did not relish what she would say next.

"I, too, have been concerned that you and I are being used and for some time now," she continued. The tragedy is that we have left, sheep-like, in the hands of a multitude of others all of that which we should never have let slip through our fingers.

"The mission you and I pledged to accomplish is being drowned out by voices repeating similar words. Yes, I can hardly deny that, but not for the same reasons. I think, sometimes the very opposite—"

"Do not say it!" Gloria interrupted, anticipating where the woman was heading.

"But I shall, dear friend, because I must. With freedom there has to come absolute truth. The two are inseparable, or else we become enslaved to a kind of falsehood that we find so convenient because it justifies what we do. Exchanging one master for another is not the goal to which I have dedicated my life."

"Then join with me, and we will pull the trigger together!" Gloria urged.

"I came to Cincinnati to speak because that is what I do, you know. I go my way, trying to be as honest as I can, speaking to common people and statesmen alike. Some listen and reject what I say.

"Others listen and accept the precepts that I offer to them. The rest do not really listen at all and turn their backs on me, so inflamed by hatred of my skin color that their reason becomes casualty to their bigotry."

"So why is it that you seem to be turning away from—?"

Sojourner Truth sighed as she replied, "No one can subdue the devil by himself or herself; no one can get him to flee if they adopt tactics that make them look, sound, and act as he does. He delights in having imitators just as the Lord delights in seeing us become more and more Christlike.

"When others look to you as a model for their actions, they will either do what you do but more violently, with less purity of motive actually, or they will simply despise you, turn away from the cause you espouse, and do nothing. Either way, evil triumphs, Gloria. I pray that you will see the truth of this before it is too late."

Gloria glanced from the black woman to Charity.

"I am going back into the house now," she said. "One of my servants will tell you when your people have arrived."

She left that garden of roses and did not look back.

"You speak extraordinarily well," Charity said after a brief silence. "This must be a source of great pride."

"Not like a typical nigger?"

"Different, very different," Charity replied without hesitating or acting embarrassed, which she was not. "You worked hard to sound as you do."

"I must tell you that I have been eminently well educated by white men whose only purpose in life is knowledge," Sojourner Truth elaborated. "I was so happy at the time this was starting, so content with the miracles that were being bestowed upon me, including vast numbers of books that otherwise I would have no hope of ever seeing, let alone holding and actually studying at my own pace, plus great piles of reports from Europe and elsewhere.

"Yet, as I think back now, I can only conclude that those benefactors of mine thought of me as some kind of experiment. Instead of a monkey this time, they were fortunate enough to use a skinny black woman.

"I am sure that what they were hoping for was that, with education, my mind would somehow become white though my skin would remain as pitch-black as ever. By replacing my ignorance, they seemed to be saying, 'We are making you more like us, and less like other common blacks.'"

Sojourner Truth stood completely erect, her body tensing as vignettes from years before became seemingly as fresh as when they happened.

"My benefactors have done that, I suppose," she admitted. "I seem unable to prevent myself from recoiling a bit when I hear my black brothers and sisters talk. I look at their dirty rags and smell the odors from their quarters and want to get away as quickly as possible because that is no longer me. I feel that their life is far, far away from me, as though my poor people deserve my disdain for conditions they cannot control. Today I have new clothes whenever I need them and the most pleasant places to stay and much food to eat."

She touched her stomach and her hips.

"I seem unable to gain any weight from all that I am consuming. You know, when I talk of poverty and beatings and hunger and the rest, it somehow seems that I have culled all this from someone else's experience. My hardships have faded, with no real new ones to replace them. To be honest, they appear less and less to have been mine the longer I enjoy more and more of the fruits of the white man's world."

She cleared her throat, frowning as she did.

"Are you all right?" Charity asked.

"Cottonmouth has always been with me, even when I was a child. I seem unable to talk very long at all before the roof of my mouth and my throat are so terribly dry."

"Shouldn't we go inside, then, and get some water?"

"That is kind of you."

They started toward the house.

"I think if war can be delayed," Sojourner Truth remarked, "then people like you will have a chance."

"But I thought that people like me were the problem, not the solution."

"I know something about your family."

Charity stopped as they reached the back porch, which was surrounded on two sides by hydrangea bushes that were more than twenty feet high and nearly as wide.

"How could that be?" she asked.

"Your father seemed interested in finding out what was behind the more rational abolitionist theories."

Charity snorted scornfully.

"I just can't believe that!" she replied. "You surely don't expect me to accept that as the gospel truth?"

Sojourner Truth held up her hand.

"Let me finish, young lady," she said. "He decided that abolitionism would rupture this nation in its quest for goals that could be achieved otherwise."

"That I can believe."

"I think he may have been right."

"But, still, you make your speeches in front of eager audiences, feeding them poison again and again."

"I feed them truth. If these United States must go down in flames, then that is unavoidable if truth be served."

"If a man is about to commit suicide, do you tell him his business has failed, his wife has taken on a lover and is leaving him, and his only child has been shot to death? There is a time for truth and a way of telling it. Otherwise you run the risk of strewing the fields of this country with mounds of corpses and soaking the ground with their shed blood."

"Was that something of your father's that you memorized?" Sojourner Truth asked, sarcasm lacing her voice but along with it a grudging touch of admiration that undoubtedly she hoped would not be noticed.

"It is his, yes, and mine and my mother's as well," Charity shot back. "We lived together, we learned together, and we talked and thought alike. Where is the shame in that, as you seem to be suggesting?"

"The shame lies in not having a mind of your own, which you have just admitted to be the case."

"As you have a mind of your own?" Charity scoffed. "Are you not the worst offender? You have been bought and paid for by those whose views seem destined to plunge the country into turmoil. Are you not the more dangerous of the two of us?"

Charity was becoming ever angrier.

"My parents raised me emphasizing my mind and my spirit. But I was deprived of nothing else! And my father persistently set an example of decency toward his slaves by clothing them properly, by feeding them well, by having them eat in the same room at the same time as we did. He hugged our people, and they hugged him. He sat and talked with them by the hour. He thought of them as children, to be protected. And for this he was often shunned by the other plantationers."

Sojourner Truth responded in a raised voice, showing a temper of her own.

"Can you not understand, as bright as you are, how insulting it is to me and the rest of my people to be thought of as a child?"

"But you are not like the rest. You have admitted feeling different. You have admitted, in so many words, that a barrier exists now and you are concerned with having lost sight of your roots. But that is because you are the exception.

"Others of your race do seem like children and very slow ones at that! I never grew up to hate coloreds the way you hate most white people, even though you are now living your life according to their every dictate.

"Please tell me: Who is more the slave? My family's coloreds who have everything provided for them and are free to leave whenever they wish, or you who may be so bound to your benefactors that you will never get out from under them?"

Abruptly, Sojourner Truth seemed to grow weak, and she staggered. Charity reached out to keep her from falling.

That narrow, bony form, tall and straight, became steadier after a moment, but she was still shaken.

"You should go inside and sit down," Charity urged her.

"Sit down on a piece of furniture in a mansion owned by someone who would be just as happy if war accomplished that which peace approaches with such reticence? Yes, I suppose I really should do that, Charity Elizabeth Littlepage. But shouldn't I break free of this suffocating luxury and experience again more of the poverty I once knew? Shouldn't I shed these fine clothes and dress in the rags of my youth?

"I long to do that, because right now I live while black people die daily, whether they are free or slave. I am eating while they are starving. My old bones are warmed in the winter and cooled in the summer just like life is for wealthy white folk.

"I am taken from place to place, and interested people sit before me in rapt attention, hanging on every word of mine as though Jesus Christ Himself suddenly turned black and female!"

She had difficulty swallowing, but this new bout with dizziness passed quickly, and she was in no danger of falling.

"May I tell you what terrifies me the most?" she asked, a certain desperation in her voice that she had blocked out until then.

Charity said that she could.

"That I have joined one enemy while turning my back on another."

"So you think I may be right after all!" Charity said. "About the organized abolitionists?"

Sojourner Truth nodded sadly, with great reluctance.

"But I have no alternative," she replied. "If I leave now, they are certain to say that I have deserted the cause. And, of course, they have many more ways to spread such pernicious falsehoods than I do. The only outcome, then, is that I would be treated like a leper, claiming neither white nor black as my friends."

Sojourner Truth seemed not so much a crusader then but a woman who was bone-weary and hoping for rest that she had no real expectation would ever come.

"If I declared to the leaders that I am not about to tolerate any more of their hypocrisy, their use of the freedom of my people as a subterfuge to hide their real political purpose, if I told them that they had lost me at last, they would quickly make sure that I would never be accepted again by those who continue in their support of the underground railroad or any of the other means being employed to help my people.

"So many of the other prominent blacks who are heavily involved— including Harriet Tubman, Josiah Henson, Mary Ann Shadd, William Still, Frederick Douglass, Jermain Loguen, the others—they all would think me at best terribly weak-hearted, a coward, and, at worst, a traitor."

"Unless you could get to these people and convince them that the movement has become wrongheaded," Charity said. "Use the gift of communication that God gave you. Your education could become a weapon.

"Tell them what you sense is happening, alert them to the fact that the leaders of the movement, the white leaders, will settle for nothing less than outright war, a military takeover of the South."

Sojourner Truth glanced away.

"What is it?" Charity asked. "Please tell me."

"It would not work."

"But why not?"

"Because most of them have become resigned to the inevitability of war. While the leaders want war as a means to an end, the others abhor the possibility but seem resigned to feeling that that may be what it takes. Either way, the onslaught of war—the North against the South—achieves what both factions covet."

"Does it?" Charity persisted. "Must the South be devastated in order for freedom to come? Isn't there another danger?"

"I know what you are going to say . . ."

"So your outlook is hardly different from mine and what was guiding my father all of his adult life!"

"Yes!" Sojourner Truth said as though the word itself were poison. "My people won't go from the pit of hell to the very gates of heaven overnight simply because the right side wins any war!

"They will continue to be used with utter ruthlessness for many years afterward, not by southerners at all but by certain Yankee interests, while being constantly reminded of what the North sacrificed in order to abolish the slavery that bound them so grievously.

"Grown men and women will be treated as though they are like tiny babies cast out of their mothers' wombs prematurely. Some will die from this treatment, unable to endure. The rest will survive after a fashion, but only a few will survive well! And some of them will not be able to deal with a sense of guilt."

Her entire body was shaking, and Charity began to feel ashamed that she had provoked this reaction.

"May the Holy Ghost soon lift this burden from me by some miracle I cannot conceive of just now or take me to His home of glory where I shall experience blessed peace at last!" Sojourner Truth spoke again, only slightly calmed. "My insides are sore. My head aches. My soul grieves. And my strength ebbs.

"I used to look forward to each morning as a new and vital opportunity for living yet more of what God chose, in His grace, to bestow. I no longer do that, my dear. I see the days ahead stretching on and on wearily before me. I see them only as part of a temporary and meaningless reprieve from darkness descending."

"And what is it that you will be thinking?" Charity remarked. "It may be only this . . . that their security was built on—"

Sojourner Truth held up a trembling hand.

"Do not say it! For I shall do so now! Yes, my people will be confronted with the same awful truth that has been flung in the face of every southern slave-owner since abolition reared up and spat it out."

She closed her eyes while she added, "Whatever security has come their way, whatever opportunity, whatever success, whatever happiness will have been built on a reeking pile of black corpses strewn in their wake by the very white people claiming to be their benefactors. I assume you were going to say something like that, my dear."

Charity could only nod, for Sojourner Truth had guessed correctly.

"I shudder at the future," the black woman continued morosely. "Once my people understand, once they no longer are seeing through a glass darkly, they will surely rise up against this unholy betrayal and, just as surely, blood will run like a hundred raging rivers in the streets of this nation.

"No longer will they be able to trust anyone but themselves! A God-given opportunity to establish harmony and love between whites and blacks will have been sucked through the maw of white exploitation."

"White *abolitionist* exploitation," Charity corrected her.

"As opposed to Dixie's subjugation?" Sojourner Truth countered.

"The way my father favored would take longer, but there would be only vintage champagne in the streets, not blood. Tell me why that is wrong. Go ahead, tell me!"

"I cannot, because it *is* not."

"But how can you go on, then, knowing—?"

Both heard Gloria Joinville greet someone at the front door.

"Your people have come to get you," Sojourner Truth said.

"And yours bid them enter," Charity replied. "Which is to endure?"

The black woman took the white woman's hand in her own.

"I don't want you and I ever to become like the rest will be, dancing with joy when one of us is cut down."

"Nor do I wish that," Charity agreed.

The two of them hugged, not in any perfunctory manner, but with great, genuine warmth.

Then Charity left Sojourner Truth in that garden of sublime roses, glancing back for a moment at the tall, black figure heading for that secluded arbor, with its surrounding roses, briefly stopping to inhale sweet scents carried by feathery breezes before she sat on a lone wooden bench and buried her face in her hands.

∽ 56 ∾

F ULKERSON AND MARMADUKE were waiting outside on the front steps of Gloria Joinville's large, Colonial-styled home, little difference between it and a southern plantation except that the amount of land on which it rested was considerably less.

Behind them, in a single line back along the tree-shrouded pathway that led to the house were a dozen of South Carolina's best state militia volunteers, some of whom happened to have been tough veterans of the Mexican War.

"My dearest Charity . . . ," Marmaduke said. "Everyone in the community showed up for your parents' services."

She rested her head against the minister's chest as her tears began to soak his plain white shirt.

"So many of them despised my father," she muttered. "Why would they want to attend his funeral?"

"Even the ones who had been most vehement would not have sanctioned something like this happening."

She pulled away from Marmaduke.

"But, then, who could have been behind what happened?" she asked, looking up at a man taller than she by nearly a foot. "If those you mention were not responsible for the deaths of my parents, who was?"

"The local authorities are pursuing an answer, Charity. After all, it has been only a few days."

Charity nodded.

"I know, I know, please forgive me . . . ," she muttered.

At that point, Fulkerson spoke up, addressing Gloria Joinville.

"Where are the local men promised to us?" he inquired of her.

The woman's manner bordered on gloating.

"I persuaded them to withdraw their offer."

Charity spun around.

"What was the reason?" she demanded furiously.

"Any such maneuver would be considered tacit approval of an institution that, in time, must be abolished."

"This girl and her parents came here to listen to a leading advocate of abolition," Marmaduke, stepping forward, said with a raised voice. "And you feel that you owe the family's only survivor nothing?"

"Apparently Sojourner Truth was not very convincing," Gloria snapped. "And as for you, Reverend Marmaduke—I've heard of you, oh, yes, we all have! If a list is made up of who owes whom what, you would have nothing left after your obligations are applied to every black man, woman, and child whose slavery has been justified by the foul words dispensed from your pulpit!"

Marmaduke knew that holding in his fiery temper would serve him well, and, doing his best, he inhaled a couple of times before responding.

"Sometimes a pulpit is not made of polished wood, madam," he said calmly. "Sometimes it is paper and ink and distributed from the back of a horse. Sometimes that which emanates from a pulpit, be it wood or newsprint, is devoid of real divinity and infected instead with words and ideas and idle musings strictly from the sinful heart of man."

Marmaduke narrowed his eyelids and leaned toward Gloria Joinville, who pulled back a bit.

"Sometimes, however, what is preached is worse than the latter, far worse indeed, for it is spun from none other than the cankered mouth of the avowed enemy of God and man, entrapping and deluding hapless multitudes, among whom you can be counted!"

He raised a single finger and pointed it at her.

"I know all about you," he said. "You are filled with hate."

"And you are not, I suppose," she snapped, glowering.

"I was but no longer am. My heart has been shorn of deception."

Gloria burst out laughing.

"A man of God, so-called, I might add, who preaches the continued buying and selling of other human beings."

"A woman, I shall add, who writes newspaper columns pleading for emancipation in all its supposed glory, whatever the cost in innocent lives, free man or slave. 'Get those terrible chains off the slaves of the South,' you exhort your readers, 'even if they have to be removed link by link from their dead bodies!'"

"I never said that, John Covington Marmaduke."

"You did not in so many words, of course, but, I ask now, can you deny that you feel as I have said? If you are able to stand before everyone here as well as Almighty God above and declare that there is no truth whatever in this, I shall believe your every word, Mrs. Joinville, and then it will be I who must plead guilty to our Creator for my harsh judgment of another. Just tell us, madam, and that will be the end of it."

"I did not intend to stand here with your kind and kowtow to—" Gloria started to reply but her voice broke.

"Go ahead," Marmaduke demanded, a vivid flash of his famous rage surfacing after all as he sensed her moment of weakness. "But remember that God judges the liar as equally as He does the robber, the adulterer, the murderer, the harlot. Above all, I remind you, our heavenly Father judges the thoughts and intentions of the human heart!"

Gloria glanced from the minister to Fulkerson to Charity and at the men behind them, their attention fixed on whatever she said or did.

"So be it!" she said, the contempt she felt nearly palpable. "If blood, white or black that it is, is to be shed until it is an ocean deep, then that is what must happen. If no black people are left, then that, too, is acceptable."

"Can your abolitionist cohorts be pleased that you stand willing to see matters go that far?" Fulkerson spoke this time. "What about all that cheap labor they have been coveting for so long? What about the devastation to farms and other businesses that the North will need so badly after any war has come to an end?

"Answer me this: Is there anyone—southerner or Yankee, white or black, free or slave—who has any reason to suppose that you will not someday routinely betray them all for the sake of a cause that, if pursued as you surely must envision it, will benefit no one and can only destroy thousands?"

Gloria spat in his face, turned, and started to go back into the house, gasping as she saw the figure standing in the doorway, blocking it.

Sojourner Truth.

Gloria tried to push past her, but the black woman placed both hands on her shoulders.

"Acceptable?" Sojourner Truth repeated, tasting the bitterness of those words. "That was what you said a moment ago, Gloria. Not a great and bitter tragedy that will sadden the very hosts of heaven as it unfolds but something that is *acceptable?* Men, women, and children piled at your feet, their lives torn from them by war, and this is acceptable to you?"

The black woman fought the urge to double the fingers of one hand into a fist and land it on Gloria Joinville's jaw.

"I leave your home now, and to it I shall never return because of that which lives within," Sojourner Truth declared. "May God forgive you, Gloria."

She hesitated then said, "But what about your nights once war starts? What about those accusing voices shouting at you from the darkness? The faces of a hundred thousand dead? Are you prepared for that? Or have you no conscience left?"

"We want the same things!" responded Gloria, her eyes filling with tears as she touched both cheeks, which were becoming bright red. "We need to be united, can you not see that? How can you be so blind?"

Sojourner Truth took her hands away and dropped them at her sides.

"I would rather say to my black brothers, my black sisters, 'You are free. You need answer to no one but Jesus.' I have never wanted to take their crumpled bodies in my arms and weep that only death could set them free."

Gloria's face twisted into an exaggerated sneer.

"You are a weakling," she said. "Your people will surely cast you out once they realize what you have become."

"And yours will not, I suppose, once they are done with you? Or discover that you are more dangerous than a hundred John Covington Marmadukes?"

Gloria grabbed hold of the door, but Sojourner Truth wrenched it from her and shouted, "It would be better, by far, that every last black person in this land remain slaves to men like Alfred Littlepage than become pawns in your bloody hands."

"Jacob, come here immediately!" Gloria yelled.

Her white-haired, rather weary-looking butler came quickly from another room and stood beside her.

"Don't dally!" she demanded hoarsely. "Close it!"

Jacob grabbed the door and tried to wrest it out of Sojourner Truth's grip, but she was younger than he, and he could not.

"Do not strain, dear man," Sojourner Truth whispered. "For the moment, you and I do what the lady wants."

She let go slowly, not wanting him to be injured, but still, the door was flung back, nearly knocking elderly Jacob off his feet.

"Close it!" Gloria demanded of him again. "Now!"

Jacob's gaze met Sojourner Truth's for only an instant, but that was long enough for her to see the hint of tears in his eyes as he finally slammed the door shut.

ᘓ 57 ᘖ

A BRAHAM LINCOLN . . . Though his reputation was growing even during the latter part of that last decade prior to the War Between the States, no mystique had yet become attached to him, history later layering on to the man that which he simply did not possess, including a magnetic personality.

Barely a mile down the dirt road from Gloria Joinville's home, the tall figure, almost gaunt, was standing next to his carriage, which was stopped in the middle of a crossroads just outside the city limits. He was flanked by a dozen armed men waiting on horseback.

No buildings obscured them from view since, in those days, that section of land featured only open farmland, with a handful of modest houses visible but not close by. And traffic was limited to occasional carriages and horses.

Fulkerson and Marmaduke were in the carriage with Charity, six South Carolinians ahead of it and six behind.

Fulkerson had the reins and stopped a few feet away.

"Mr. Lincoln." Marmaduke stood in the carriage as the spokesman for the group after getting the nod from the other man. "I demand to know what is the meaning of this."

He grunted theatrically, his eyes bulging.

"You are blocking the road, Mr. Lincoln. We must be on our way immediately. Too much time has been lost, precious time. This child could not even attend the funeral of her dear parents, taken from her before her eyes. Are you now intent even on further delaying her return to the peace and quiet of home?"

Charity winced at the use of the word "child" but did not register any protest under the circumstances.

Abraham Lincoln stepped forward, his expression grim.

"It is precisely because of what Charity Littlepage has undergone that we are here," he spoke firmly.

"I see your Yankee militiamen. I see their weapons. According to Gloria Joinville, we were not to have our numbers expanded after all, even if this sent a signal to this child's previous attackers, even if this guaranteed the present safety of Miss Littlepage."

Marmaduke smiled slyly.

"There is no purpose for this show of force, if this Gloria Joinville of yours is to be believed. Or do you have some ulterior motive that is so common among you Yankees?"

Before Lincoln could respond, the minister straightened up to his full height and girth.

"I have heard about you, Abraham Lincoln. I know your kind, and I do not like you. I hear that you can prove to be a worthy debate opponent. Stephen Douglas has said that you are the one opponent whom he fears the most."

He let a smirk cross his broad face.

"But I can scarcely imagine why. You seem to me strictly an uncouth backwoods type with a modicum of knowledge and a great deal more ignorance. I see only ill for this nation coming from the shenanigans of your kind."

Lincoln sighed as he walked up to Marmaduke and said, "I am what I am because that is the way the good Lord made me. And I shall be whatever I become because it is into His care that I place my entire being."

Marmaduke was not quite prepared for that; now it was his turn to be quiet.

"We all have people in our respective camps who are the future Judases waiting to betray us, even under the guise of a noble concern for the underprivileged, but I happen not to be one of them," Lincoln went on. "Yet I must confess to being everything that you say or hint, Reverend Marmaduke, for truly am I weak and without polish, and Mr. Douglas and others are far more learned.

"You yourself possess a far greater presence than this bony image of mine. But with the little that I have, sir, I shall pledge before God and man to do the most that I can."

He paused, seemingly examining every inch of the minister's face.

"I wish not one slave freed if it means a single drop of blood is spilled," Lincoln said. "But there are forces in the North as well as the South who may snatch from people like you and me a peaceful end to this dispute and turn it into a nightmare scarring the conscience of this nation for generations to come."

He pointed to the dozen members of the local militia behind him.

"Gloria Joinville will no longer have any association with me," he explained, "and that is entirely because of these twelve men. She continued to persuade them not to come, but when I explained your situation, they volunteered to join your escort back home."

Lincoln then startled everyone by smiling.

"But I am delighted to present these dozen volunteers to you now, and a thirteenth added to their number . . . that uncouth backwoods type you spoke of named Abraham Lincoln."

He reached out his right hand.

"We shall go on this journey with you," he declared, "and may those who lurk in the woods be damned."

Abraham Lincoln, an up-and-coming political figure, was willing to risk his life to add emphasis to what was happening, men from the North and from the South getting together on a common mission.

"I am sure that the benefits to your career will be incalculable," Marmaduke snorted in the dying throes of contempt.

"That may be true," Lincoln rejoined, "but it could become instead part of my eulogy, for I shall be just as accessible to sniper fire as anyone else here. You have to agree, I am sure, that a dead politician is hardly left with any ambitions."

Marmaduke nodded knowingly and extended his own hand, though with reluctance that was hardly subtle.

Lincoln shook it heartily.

"I would like to sit before your pulpit one day," he added, "and hear for myself what others have praised so passionately."

"I think it may be, Mr. Lincoln, that the two of us will come out of this matter with quite different ideas about one another," Marmaduke generously conceded, though it did grieve him that this had proven to be unavoidable, "even while our deeply held convictions about slavery remain irrevocably opposed."

Then, without prelude, Lincoln made a statement that produced gasps from both the minister and Fulkerson.

"Do not be so sure, Reverend Marmaduke, that you and I are as far apart on that subject as you have been assuming."

Marmaduke blinked several times upon hearing that but decided not to pursue it further for the moment.

"I assume then," Lincoln added, "that you can reasonably conclude you may not know as much about me as you presupposed."

"You can certainly assume that if you wish," Marmaduke said, just before he bowed slightly then sat down back down.

The next several minutes were spent detailing the route they would take.

"There is no reason to suppose we will be attacked," Lincoln told everyone, "but it is such a possibility, so we must remain vigilant throughout the journey."

One of Lincoln's men spoke up.

"Mr. Lincoln? May I speak, sir?"

"Of course, lad. What is your name?"

"Billy . . . er . . . William Ethan Mendenhall, sir," the young man promptly responded. "I just wanted to say that while no one really knows who did this to the Littlepages, if it happens to be that my people are responsible, then I declare my shame of them. I cast them out, sir, as the Bible tells us we are to cast out Satan and his demons."

At that, the other eleven members of the northern militia, far younger in average age than any of their Southern counterparts, raised their voices in a common shout of support for what their comrade had said.

Charity was touched by this display and also impressed by the broad-shouldered, dark-haired, dimple-chinned Billy Mendenhall, who seemed only a few years older than she was.

She stood up in her carriage and thanked them all, unaware that the young soldier could scarcely stop looking at her.

❧ 58 ❧

THE TWENTY-FOUR YANKEE and southern militia members were well-armed, with each one having a rifle and at least one pistol, the latter predominantly of Colt manufacture, primarily second- and third-model Dragoons, very sturdy weapons that had given Samuel Colt a monopoly until Edwin Wesson and others came on the scene to challenge him.

An ample stock of ammunition was carried in saddlebags on the back of each horse and by Lincoln in his carriage as well as by Marmaduke and Fulkerson in their own. They all assumed they were prepared for anything that might happen.

But on their second night of the journey, less than two days away from Charity's home, they were brought face to face with a starkly different reality . . .

Charity's energies, which had been flagging at the start due to her healing wounds, had seemed to be reviving well.

And, curiously, she was finding herself drawn to the rather cold-sounding Abraham Lincoln.

"Some consider you a dangerous man," she told him.

"Do I seem such to you, ma'am?" he asked.

The group of more than two dozen men and just one young woman had stopped beside a small clear-water lake where they replenished their water supply and were preparing to bed down for the night.

For whatever reason, Lincoln was keeping to himself, apparently making notes in what Charity correctly assumed was a diary.

"I have thought about possibly keeping a diary, myself," she said pleasantly as she sat down beside him.

He looked up, not seeming perturbed at all, and asked, "And what has been stopping you, young lady?"

"I write letters instead, many letters, to friends elsewhere, relatives."

"Any politicians?"

"Oh, yes. Jefferson Davis is one. And though he is not a politician, I have a regular correspondence going with Robert E. Lee."

"Ah, yes, what a brilliant man!" Lincoln exclaimed, his admiration not false. "But then I am not surprised. His father was a true hero in the American Revolution, as you may know."

"I do know that," she replied. "He is being torn, sir, torn between the abolitionists and those who would cling to slavery even if it means secession. His agony is becoming more and more acute as the months pass."

"Remarkable!" Lincoln said, closing the diary and staring at Charity.

"Are you referring to me?"

"Indeed I am. It is remarkable that you talk so much like a diplomat or a statesman rather than a . . ."

"A woman, sir?"

Lincoln seemed flustered before answering, "Your forthrightness demands my equally honest answer. You are correct. Most of your sex whom I know are not as forceful nor as well spoken as you."

"Then what about Gloria Joinville, may I ask, sir?"

"That woman has twenty years on you," he reminded her. "Besides, I think it would not bother Gloria at all if, one day, she awoke to discover that, somehow, she had become a man overnight!"

Lincoln's previous stiffness of manner left Charity unprepared for that sort of remark.

And now look at him! she exclaimed to herself.

Along with making it, he burst out laughing, and she joined him, the two of them laughing so loudly that others turned and looked in amazement.

"My parents have just been murdered," Charity said after she had stopped the laughter, "and here I am—"

"Enjoying yourself?" Lincoln interrupted.

"Yes . . . I was going to say that," she agreed.

"I think the grieving need such moments, Charity Littlepage. We can become so wrapped up in sorrow that the bodies God gave us suffer severely, sometimes fatally so. It does not honor the dead if the living act as though life itself has lost all meaning."

. . . the bodies God gave us.

That was the second time she had heard Lincoln mention God.

"Are you a Christian?" she asked.

"That I am, my dear, and have been much of my life. However, I am not one of those Christians who have become so complacent in their faith that I can manage to ward off sometimes disturbing questions."

"What disturbing questions, sir?"

He waved his bony hand with its long fingers through the air.

"There is such pain in this world," he said. "I frequently look at it and wonder why. Someday, if this nation is plunged into war, brother against brother, a war between the states of a once strong union, I will kneel before the Father in heaven and ask from the very center of my soul, 'Why have You allowed this to happen?'

"There may be answers forthcoming about these and other questions; there may not. But we go on, do we not? We accept by faith that which we cannot answer by any known means or sources."

Abruptly Lincoln stiffened so noticeably Charity thought he might be having some sort of seizure.

She started to speak, but he interrupted, saying simply, with striking calm, "Charity, my dear, be very calm now; we are being surrounded this very minute. Reverend Marmaduke and that Fulkerson chap have to be alerted, and then the militia. I shall take care of my people. Will you do so with yours, please?"

Charity nodded nervously.

"Be as natural as you can manage," Lincoln cautioned.

"Yes, sir," she told him.

"Whoever it is mustn't suspect that we already know of their presence. For that would force them to confront us sooner than they doubtless had planned."

"How could you have noticed?" she asked, not trying to hide her admiration.

"I grew up in the woods of Kentucky and Indiana. You learn early in your young life what the mere rustling of dead leaves signifies or the minute parting of some tree branches. Your eye must be quick and your response immediate."

They smiled at each other, then each went in a different direction, an attempted nonchalance to their step.

Charity was feeling better, physically, than she had any reason to expect after two gunshot wounds. Since both bullets had passed through with minimal damage and not lodged in either her shoulder or her thigh, she was expected to make a full recovery.

Nevertheless, the trauma of what had happened, both to her body and her mind, was severe enough to make her recovery border on the miraculous, something even Gloria Joinville had remarked upon.

As she approached Reverend Marmaduke and Samuel Fulkerson, she caught out of the corner of her eye a slight movement among the trees. Gulping, she tapped Fulkerson on the arm.

"Yes, Charity?" he asked pleasantly as he halted a conversation with Marmaduke.

She told him what Lincoln had spotted.

"I see," he replied, imposing a sudden calm upon himself that meant resisting the temptation to survey the trees for himself. "I wonder which side they are on. Are they after Abraham Lincoln or us? Interesting!"

"John . . . ," Marmaduke said, "I think perhaps you and Charity should continue this conversation while I amble on over to the militia and tell them to be ready for a fight as we gather everything together and get ready to leave this spot. We must act as though we did not intend to stop here for the night, dissatisfied with it for some reason."

"Why not just stay here and defend ourselves?" Fulkerson asked reasonably.

"Because they could come at us from any direction, Samuel."

"On the road, they would have only the west from which to hit us."

"East of us there are only those open farmlands for quite some distance. We could spot them easily."

"Their charge could come at any time," Fulkerson warned him. "Tell our men that."

The minister nodded and said, "I am very glad, Samuel, that you and I have weapons as well and that my blessed parents were not Quakers."

Charity and Fulkerson did their best to appear to be engaged in only a casual bit of dialogue.

Lord, teach me to be a good actress, she prayed to herself. *The intruders mustn't suspect anything! And give this man the same ability!*

"I wonder if they have any connection with the men who murdered . . . ," she said softly as she felt her self-control slipping but desperately tried to hide her emotions, ". . . my parents."

"It is impossible to say," Fulkerson remarked. "Perhaps we will *never* know."

In the background were the sounds of horses being readied.

"I saw something among the trees," Fulkerson observed. "It was so close."

He trembled despite himself.

"Our enemy is there, like jungle predators, and yet we have no idea why. Animals kill only for food. But this—"

It was Charity's turn to shiver.

❧ 59 ❧

A FEW MINUTES LATER, Charity, Marmaduke, and Fulkerson were back in the carriage, the South Carolina militia in front and in back of them, while Abraham Lincoln and his volunteer militia rode ahead.

After only a mile or so, the first shot was fired, dropping one of the southern soldiers as he was hit in the chest and died within seconds.

The dirt road they were on headed south.

On the western side there was a continuation of the forest that had commenced a few miles back, with only rolling farms prior to that, the trees here providing the most logical cover for any potential attackers.

On the eastern side were small farms, the ground level but covered with periodic clumps of trees between one property and the one adjacent to it.

No alternate route would have been better for them.

And this one was the most direct.

Any other would have added many miles of similar terrain providing additional opportunities for ambush.

And that was where the first shot came from, there among the trees.

"Flip over both carriages!" someone shouted urgently. "They're the only shelter we're going to have!"

By then there was more rifle fire.

Two of the northerners went down, one dead, the other caught in the leg but still able to hold and fire a rifle or a pistol.

"They aren't going to put *me* out of commission!" he bellowed. "The Mexicans didn't do it, and those devils now, whoever they are, are amateurs in comparison."

Lincoln himself grabbed the rifle from the dead man's hand, wrenched it loose, and aimed the weapon, firing into the trees.

A scream.

The wounded attacker stumbled into sight, his otherwise white, long-sleeved shirt dripping with blood.

He fell headfirst just as he reached the road, not more than a foot from the carriage that had been turned over on its side.

"I hunted deer throughout my boyhood," Lincoln muttered. "You learn to aim straight and fire fast."

For a moment, human targets seemed to have been forgotten by the attackers, who concentrated on the horses, methodically and with savage speed shooting the animals down until none were left standing.

The militia members were powerless to stop this and could do nothing but blindly return fire into the woods, twice being successful, judging from the cries of pain they heard, but not knowing how many more men were gathered on that side.

"We have twenty-six men here!" Fulkerson, now next to Charity, shouted to Marmaduke, who was beside him. "That means the enemy surely must have a force of equal or greater number on their side. We could be facing nearly three dozen heavily armed intruders whose positions are largely unknown to us."

"The farmhouse . . . directly behind us!" Marmaduke suggested. "We could get some help from there. Use any carriage they might have for additional cover instead of crowding everybody behind these two!"

Lincoln was only a foot or two away and overheard what the minister was saying.

"You are right, Pastor Marmaduke," he acknowledged.

"Thank you, Mr. Lincoln."

The two men nodded at one another and smiled, then Lincoln turned and quickly told the men in his militia what would be expected of them.

"Wait a minute!" Fulkerson interrupted. "Our men are willing to go. Why not one of them?"

It was a bit of pride that motivated him to say this, for he was rankled by the possibility that a *Yankee* soldier would be picked to do something as important as finding help and shelter.

"And this is *southern* land," he pointed out.

"Am I to assume, therefore, that our attackers are of a southern origin?" Lincoln proposed cleverly.

Fulkerson hesitated, considering the likelihood of any circumstance like that actually being the case.

"Yankees infiltrating the area?" he speculated out loud. "Is that what you hint at?"

"I cannot ignore that turn of events. Can you, my good man?" Lincoln spoke.

"Of course not. All this treachery sounds like something—"

He was going to say, "that only Yankees could devise," but thought better of it and simply muttered, "Go ahead, Mr. Lincoln. Send whomever you want."

Occurring to Samuel Fulkerson just then was the possibility of something going very wrong on that side of the road as well, whatever sort of "wrong" that might turn out to be. And the prospect of sending some young Yankee volunteer to his death was far less disheartening than any sacrifice of southern flesh and blood!

Lincoln nodded deferentially and turned back to the men.

"Who will volunteer?" he shouted.

"I will, sir!"

Standing as straight as he dared, Billy Mendenhall saluted Lincoln while stealing a glance at Charity, who was just a few feet away.

"Go then, Billy," Abraham Lincoln told him. "And may God protect you, son."

"Yes sir!" Mendenhall responded, then turned, and, crouching down, started running toward the farmhouse.

Charity found herself praying about the young man's safe return and for more than just the obvious reason.

~❧ 60 ❧~

BILLY MENDENHALL SAW light coming from one of the rear rooms of the farmhouse. It had not been visible from the road. Bending down, he approached the left side of the window in that easterly part of the dwelling and glanced inside.

Weapons.

Piles of them on top of three rectangular tables and scattered over the floor.

He gasped as he surveyed the rifles, swords, dynamite, and clubs.

Of course! he exclaimed to himself. *They must have realized that this open land represented a possible escape route, so they've taken over—*

Footsteps. And voices.

"We'll keep 'em pinned down, wear 'em out, then attack from this side," one coarse voice was saying.

Billy heard movement on the second floor of the farmhouse.

"They'll be crushed between us!" another added, pointing upstairs.

"Lincoln's the one I want to plug!" a third told the others.

Laughter followed from those inside, coarse, evil laughter that anticipated the pleasure of a perverse act.

It was obvious to Billy that he could never get any carriage past the house with the the men stirring inside. As soon as they heard noise, they would be on him.

He saw a large, square, woodshed to his right. Dropping to his stomach, he crawled toward it. The door was not fastened, and he opened it slightly.

Gallon jugs with cork stoppers.

Billy opened the door wide enough to allow him to crawl inside, and he uncorked one of the jugs, smelling immediately what was inside.

Oil . . . he counted two dozen containers of it.

In Billy's mind he could picture the contents being used against his comrades in Lincoln's militia as well as the southerners.

Screaming . . .

He could see them screaming as their bodies were covered with flame, eventually nothing left but blackened husks.

And Charity Littlepage . . .

Though Billy had not been introduced to her, he felt attracted to this young woman as soon as they made eye contact, and the thought of anything happening to that beautiful face, crowned so strikingly by long red hair . . .

He gulped several times, trying to decide what to do.

If he tried to get back to the others who were being pinned down by firepower from the woods, he might be spotted by the men gathered in the farmhouse. But he obviously could not just remain where he was, useless to everyone else.

The oil!

If he lugged two gallons at a time to the back of the house, he could probably accumulate half a dozen or more without pushing the odds of being discovered any more than would have been the case already. He could empty the oil against the wood structure on at least three sides, two gallons on each one.

And add straw from the barn!

He would need some straw to pile against the house and ensure the wooden structure ignited.

Fortunately Billy already had several safety matches on him—which were patented only a few years before by a Swede named Lundstrom—since he had been a cigarette smoker for most of his adult life, rolling each one himself and sometimes supplying these to a few of his fellow soldiers, all of them agreeing that they owed a debt to the Cubans who had "invented" the little cigars just after the turn of the century.

Back and forth he scurried from the little shed to the house, making three trips, and then again to the nearby barn where he grabbed two handfuls of straw in addition to what he was able to tuck under his arms and under his shirt.

No one had detected him at that point. He had managed to be quiet, praying each moment that he would not trip and hurt himself, praying that none of the men on either of the floors would be looking outside until he had gotten together everything he needed.

Leaning against the house briefly to catch his breath, Billy started placing the straw around the base on each side, grateful that recent rains had not gotten to it and that it proved as dry as he had been hoping. Once these positions were set, he doused each pile with oil and slopped some of the fluid on the wood frame.

Now it was time for the matches.

Billy wanted to have each spot ready before he ignited any of them since, otherwise, at the first indication of fire, the men were bound to react quickly, and he would have little time to set up the other locations or make it back to the road.

Young, strong, a top-notch runner in various meets not too long ago at his school, he had been blessed with sturdy legs that could carry him over considerable distances that seemed likely to defeat most other competitors.

But that night it was not distance that mattered as much as speed.

And Billy Mendenhall was the fastest young athlete anyone had ever seen.

~❧61❧~

L OOK AT THAT!" Samuel Fulkerson exclaimed abruptly, his rich baritone carrying to anyone who was nearby.

Everybody turned in the direction of the farmhouse across the road, temporarily not returning the fire of the shadowy men who had ambushed them from the woods.

Flames spurting from it, and already the smell of smoke reached them.

"It must be Mendenhall's doing!" one of the older members of the Yankee militia shouted disbelievingly. "But why in the world is he trying to burn down a building like that when it might have provided some shelter for us?"

"That's why," somebody else interrupted.

They all spotted Billy Mendenhall racing across the field, away from the house and toward them.

"Look!" the same soldier shouted. "Behind him!"

"That young man is being chased by—!" Marmaduke started to say.

Nearly a dozen men were after Billy, cursing him, ignoring the fact that they themselves were now open targets.

Several more were crouched down, aiming their rifles toward the militia.

Lincoln quickly ordered his best marksmen to turn their attention from the attackers in the woods to those who were after Billy. To Fulkerson he added, "Sir, I suggest your own forces concentrate on the trees. They may think us so distracted by what is happening across the way that they can charge!"

"Give me a gun!" Charity demanded. "I want to help. My father always—"

"No!" Fulkerson interrupted. "That means you will be drawn into the action. We could never allow that."

"But I *am* in the action!" she protested. "Do you know who their target is?"

"Lincoln, I feel certain."

"How can you be sure?"

"I cannot, of course, but—"

It was Charity's turn to interrupt.

"They could be after *me,* you know."

Fulkerson looked at them as though she were experiencing a nervous breakdown.

"That is unthinkable!" he retorted.

"But it was unthinkable what they did to my parents. I am a reminder that they failed. They must get me now or be humiliated."

Marmaduke had overheard this.

"This young lady may be right, Samuel," he said. "Give her a rifle. She will surely need to defend herself."

Fulkerson had two of the third model Colt Dragoons strapped to him, and he handed one over to Charity as he started to tell her how to use it, but she stopped him by saying, "My father taught me."

"You *are* amazing!" he exclaimed.

The men in the farmhouse were coming closer to Billy, raising their rifles.

Lincoln decided to open fire, though knowing there was a strong possibility of hitting Billy Mendenhall.

Charity protested as she ran up to him when she saw several of the Yankees start to aim in that direction.

"He'll be killed!" she screamed.

"He is but one man, however brave," Lincoln told her. "How many of the rest of us will die if we do nothing?"

Just then the attackers in the woods opened fire, but this time they were using another kind of weapon.

A cannon.

It blasted a large, jagged hole through the center of where the two carriages had been jammed side by side, throwing Yankee and southern soldiers in several directions and knocking Charity and Lincoln to the ground.

Billy Mendenhall stopped for a second or two, saw what had happened, then turned and started firing back at the men who were behind him. He managed to shoot down two of them before their return fire caught him in his right leg as well as his side and through his left hand. He fell, dropping his pistol. One of the attackers was very close and seemed to be snarling as he approached the young man's body.

"No!" Charity shouted desperately as she stood, raised her Colt, and squinting, took dead aim, leaning upon what she recalled from those lessons her father had begun to teach her not long after she became a teenager, convinced that, as the family's safe little world eventually deteriorated—and he was convinced this would prove inevitable—she would need to defend herself sooner or later, perhaps again and again.

She never pulled the trigger.

The man who had reached Billy and was about to shoot him through the head suddenly grabbed his own temple, staggered, and—

Charity spun around, trying to find the one who had fired so accurately.

It must have been one of the Yankees, she told herself. *Who could have—?*

"Look at that!" an unfamiliar voice shouted. "What in the—?"

One by one, the men from the farmhouse were being picked off, and not by the Yankee or South Carolina militia, for they had momentarily stopped firing in surprise and amazement.

Lincoln abruptly lost his trademark level-headedness.

"Who is shooting?" he demanded frantically of no one yet everyone. "And where is it coming from? *What is going on here?"*

The men across the road, caught in the open, were being shot down without being able to defend themselves; frantically they turned and started running back toward the burning farmhouse.

But the fire had spread throughout its two floors, and they found no shelter there.

Instead they continued on past it, in the opposite direction from the road, across the field to whatever they could find beyond it.

Yet none escaped. All were brought down, most apparently killed by bullets through the head or in the area of the heart.

"Turn around! Look!"

It was Samuel Fulkerson shouting.

The attackers inside the woods were being *driven out* of their cover, not a retreat so much as a lemming-like plunge over a cliff directly ahead, in this case, into the rifle-and-pistol fire of those they had ambushed less than half an hour before.

The two militia forces lost none of this abrupt opportunity to mow them down. Not a single attacker was left standing.

Silence.

Except for the moaning sounds coming from wounded men on both sides, nothing else could be heard.

And then a shape emerged from the surrounding trees, two rifles held high above his head. Behind him were the barely discernible figures of more than twenty other men.

"Across the road!" Marmaduke shouted.

More figures moving through the moonlight, looking faintly like ghosts rising up from some hidden graveyard. The militia soldiers held their weapons at ready.

If it had not been for so many of the ambushers lying on the ground dead, dying, or seriously wounded, there might have been some cause for them to suspect a demonically brilliant ploy.

Even so, none of the militiamen, particularly the veterans among them, had any intention of allowing even the remotest possibility of being tricked into carelessness.

Apparently having anticipated this, the strangers voluntarily disarmed themselves, dropping their weapons on the ground, and then they walked slowly forward, from the area of the farmhouse as well as the woods.

That first one to show himself stepped around the edge of the left carriage and walked up to Charity.

"I regret that I did not learn of what was going on sooner, Missie," he spoke sadly, his voice breaking. "Aye, I am more sorry than you'll ever know!"

They embraced one another, these two, a broad-shouldered, heavily scarred man of medium-height and a violent history who appeared tough enough to take on a grizzly bear or a mountain lion now hugging a seemingly fragile-looking young woman and both of them starting to sob while the survivors of the battle just won stood by, nursing their own emotions.

Finally, Charity took the man by the arm, and they approached Abraham Lincoln.

"Sir, I want to introduce you to a dear friend of my father's, Max Cutshaw," she spoke through the tears that were still streaking down her cheeks.

"Honored to meet you," Lincoln said, extending his hand quickly. "We owe you our very lives."

Cutshaw obviously had something to say, but, strangely, he hesitated while Lincoln waited patiently.

"Three of my men are headed back to where you came from," Cutshaw told him. "They have in their custody someone who spilled the beans on this ambush."

"What are you saying, Mr. Cutshaw?" Lincoln asked.

"The woman who planned this atrocity . . . she will be in prison by the time you have returned."

Lincoln's throat was constricting as he instantly suspected her identity.

"Do you mean—?" he began.

"Yes, sir, I do. Gloria Joinville."

Charity tightened her grip on his arm.

"Max?" she asked.

"Yes, Missie?"

"Was Gloria Joinville also responsible for . . . for what happened to my parents?" Charity asked, the words as bitter as her feelings.

"Her people were," Cutshaw answered. "She bowed out of that one because she wanted an even bigger plum when she stirred herself to authorize anything like an attack."

. . . an even bigger plum.

Charity thought of what had been her father's approach, a gradual one, an approach based upon love, not violence.

"And Sojourner Truth?"

"As far as I can tell, that woman was *not* involved in any way," Cutshaw responded, blushing when he noticed Lincoln's raised eyebrows. "In fact, I'm kind of thinking that she's going to be devastated by the truth and just might be forced to look a whole lot differently at those abolitionist ties of hers."

Lincoln found this outcome hard to accept.

"It just seems unlike Gloria," he muttered. "She can be mean, yes, but to sanction, to plan *murder?*"

Cutshaw shrugged as he added, "I can't say, sir. All's I know is what I've been told. When you get back, you'll have to find out what's true and what isn't."

"Forgive me, Mr. Cutshaw!" Lincoln spoke again. "Here I am debating something with the man who saved my life, whether or not Gloria Joinville wanted to take it from me."

Charity's mind drifted to an image of Sojourner Truth, knowing when the black woman found out what had happened and the probable involvement of one of her benefactors, she could not help but be thunderstruck.

All of this now, with no war declared! she thought. *But it's as though another kind of war is going on! The shots are already being fired!*

Charity could never have anticipated speaking up about the woman, but that was exactly what she did.

"Think of how Sojourner Truth is feeling now," she interjected. "She must seem like someone without a friend . . . or a country about now."

"I know . . . ," Lincoln muttered. "I shall have to go to her as soon as I return. This must make the foundation of so much of her life suddenly very unsteady."

The black woman was not the only individual Charity had on her mind as she glanced at the carriages which were being righted and Billy Mendenhall taken to the far one. His head turned in her direction, and he seemed to recognize her then his eyes shut.

"Could I ride with that one?" she asked of Marmaduke and Fulkerson as she pointed to the young militiaman.

"And why would you want to be with a Yankee like him?" Marmaduke asked with feigned gravity.

"He's a Yankee who almost died because of us, that's why!" she exclaimed, her temper momentarily flaring. This was one of those times when it would serve her well, though at other times that was hardly the case.

Marmaduke folded his arms and seemed to be examining her before he replied.

"Go ahead, Charity," the minister said, giving in to her just as Alfred Littlepage so often had done. "You should not be issued orders from us in any event . . . now or ever."

"If that does occur," she told him with great warmth, "you will not find me an uncontrollable rebel. I know that you want only my welfare."

"That *is* what your father wanted, dear, and I count as precious those years he and I had as friends. He would have given his life for—"

Marmaduke realized what he was saying and stopped, uncharacteristically burying his face in his hands. After a moment or two, Charity gently pulled his hands away and used a small handkerchief to wipe his face dry. Then she kissed him on the right cheek.

"Bless you, dear man," she whispered. "I love you."

"Love from hate . . . ," Marmaduke said. "What transforming power the Holy Ghost applies to each of us!"

"But we never *hated* you."

"I appreciate that," he said, "but I came to hate myself, yea, what I once was, after that dear black lady died in my arms."

He returned her kiss, and then Charity rushed over to the other carriage.

"Where are you taking him?" she asked Lincoln.

"As it turns out," he replied, "the best doctor is probably the one near where you live."

"And we'll be there in less than two days," she said. "It seems so short a time for us but not for him!"

"We have to be prepared to remove the bullets much earlier, if need be. But that is not a prospect that anyone enjoys, what with the conditions here on the road."

"Can I be in the carriage with him?"

"Why would you—?" Lincoln started to ask, then he narrowed his eyes knowingly before adding, "Go ahead. I see no reason why you shouldn't."

"Is he conscious?"

"I believe so, for now, but he will not remain so indefinitely. There will be, I imagine, periods when he seems as though he is in a coma. Finally, if we do not handle everything as should be done, he will never come out of the last one."

Trembling, Charity reached out her hand, and Lincoln shook it.

"We should dread any turn of history that ultimately makes us enemies," he said, genuinely sorrowful over that possibility.

"That will not happen," she assured him. "The Lord brought us together for a reason that He knows, and that is enough for me."

Lincoln's eyes narrowed but not in skepticism or scorn.

"If I perhaps could be blessed someday with a daughter who is but a mere imitation of you, Charity Elizabeth Littlepage," he said, with no exaggeration intended.

Charity thanked Lincoln and walked toward the carriage a few feet to her left, the odor of fire-consumed wood and attendant smoke so thick now that she was starting to have some difficulty breathing while the sounds of dying or wounded men moaning in agony formed a fading backdrop as they lost consciousness or life itself. When she reached the carriage, an older Yankee militia member approached her.

"May I help you, miss?" he asked. "I know that Billy was talking about you. It will help him if you're by his side. He's not someone to see a pretty girl and act this way about her. He has them gathered around him all the time back home."

"Thank you kindly," she said, smiling.

"My prayers are with you," he whispered. "And I ain't the only one."

Once in the carriage, she saw that Billy Mendenhall was raising his hand unsteadily toward her. She caught it before it dropped back by his side and held it between both of hers as he slipped again into unconsciousness even as a smile curled up the edges of his mouth.

～❦62❧～

AT LEAST ONE problem had to be dealt with in the aftermath of the initial attack and Max Cutshaw's counterattack before they would be able to continue their journey.

The dead . . .

As inglorious as it seemed, a common grave had to be dug for the prompt disposal of those who had been part of the gang of attackers.

Those from the South Carolina militia would be transported back to their homes near the Littlepage plantation. Two volunteers from Lincoln's militia would return the bodies of their fallen comrades back home.

Fortunately, inside the barn, which was located some distance from the farmhouse and unaffected by the fire, two wagons were discovered.

The ambushers who were struck down but not yet dead caused the most controversy. A decision was voted upon by Lincoln, Marmaduke, and Fulkerson that pleased no one but represented the exigencies of what was essentially a battlefield.

And that decision was made from among three possibilities:

One, leave them near the road, with some gauze bandages and water until help could be sent, whenever that would be.

Two, bring the men along and deposit them before the same doctor who would be treating the southern militiamen.

Three, execute them on the spot and throw their bodies into the same mass grave as those already dead.

Marmaduke and Fulkerson voted for execution.

Lincoln held out for leaving them behind and summoning help. No one chose the second option. And so he gave in after talking to both groups of militia.

Once again, Max Cutshaw interceded.

"It should be us to do this grisly work," he pointed out. "We have much more than the blood of these devils on our hands, you know. We shall do it, if you will let us, and no one else need have any of it on their consciences."

Lincoln nodded sadly, adding, "For whom is conscience going to be the greater accuser, those who gave the orders this day or those who carry them out?"

Max Cutshaw and his men did their job well.

One by one the wounded ambushers were shot.

Some pleaded for mercy, but nothing of the sort was given.

"It is done," Cutshaw announced, wiping his hands of some splattered blood.

He insisted upon accompanying the group back to South Carolina.

"We will remain out of sight always," he told Lincoln, Marmaduke, and Fulkerson. "This is not open to discussion, mates!"

The three men acquiesced, recognizing the good sense of what he was saying.

"Fine, then!" Cutshaw remarked. "We are on our way!"

Lincoln was anguished about the outcome even after Marmaduke correctly reminded him that any court would probably have sentenced them to execution either by firing squad or hanging anyway.

"Can you not imagine, Abraham Lincoln, what this does to me as a minister of the gospel of Jesus Christ?" Marmaduke asked.

"Can you not imagine how I feel as a man of conscience?" Lincoln replied.

"Then God will judge us both in the life that is to come. But for the moment, we must live this present existence of flesh and blood and bone, sir."

Lincoln spoke little during the remainder of the journey.

The remainder of the journey back to the Littlepage plantation took longer than expected, in large measure because one of the wheels from the carriage holding Marmaduke and Fulkerson came loose and tumbled off, throwing them onto the ground and shaking up both men considerably, their resiliency shredded by the ambush.

Charity stayed with Billy Mendenhall, wiping his forehead, lifting his head slightly and pressing a cup to his mouth so that he could sip some water, holding his hand, and, at one point, softly singing a verse from one of Violet's old hymns to him.

Lord, I think Daddy must have looked a little like this when he was Billy's age, she prayed to herself as she looked down over the young man's features. *Daddy always seemed so brave; he always looked at life without fear and—*

She was trying to help a Yankee survive his wounds but was never given the opportunity to do the same with her father.

To the astonishment of everyone, Billy Mendenhall's conscious periods were frequent. He had lost much blood but seemed to have an extraordinary reservoir of strength.

"You remind me of my father," she told him while they were waiting for the repair to be completed to the carriage behind them.

"How is that, miss?" he was able to ask, his eyes wide open.

"Brave and determined."

"Was he involved in battle? Did he fight the Mexicans?"

"No. But fighting a war isn't the only part of life where valor can be shown."

"I didn't mean anything by that, miss."

"I know you didn't. It is just that where my parents are concerned, I am a little—"

"Touchy?" he interrupted, smiling.

"Yes . . . touchy."

"You should know, miss, that—"

"Charity. Call me Charity."

"Fine, Charity. And I'm Billy."

Billy started coughing, and some blood spilled over his lips.

"I think I will die . . . ," he muttered weakly.

"That's in the Lord's hands," she admonished him.

"But why is the Lord letting all this happen in the first place?"

Charity had no instant answer for that.

"Why is Almighty God letting black people suffer so horribly as traders kidnap them and transport them across the Atlantic, with so many dying during the trip?" she mused. "I can't say. I can only put my trust in His sovereign judgment."

"Are you against slavery, Charity?"

"No! Just against the slaves' mistreatment by traders and owners who have no conscience. My father never once beat or whipped any of his slaves. All our people loved him."

"How could they love the one who has been keeping them like prisoners?" Billy proposed skeptically.

Charity started to give a well-worn reply when she noticed that Billy's head had turned to one side, and his breathing was becoming erratic.

"I need help!" she screamed frantically.

No one paid immediate attention to her, for they were busy putting the wheel back on the carriage behind her.

Charity pressed her lips against Billy's, blowing oxygen into him again and again until she herself was gasping and had to calm herself, then she was back at it once more.

Fulkerson apparently had heard Charity after all and came running over to her.

"He's going fast!" she said.

"Slide back . . . ," he told her. "I have stronger lungs."

So he took over the job of trying to resuscitate Billy Mendenhall. More seconds passed. A minute, then another.

This tableau caught the attention of Marmaduke, who was the largest of the men there, Lincoln and he roughly the same height but the minister much broader across the chest, with thicker arms and legs.

"Time for a man of God!" he thundered as he reached the carriage and jumped up into it.

Fulkerson scampered over the opposite edge to allow him room.

"I breathe life back into you this very moment, son," Marmaduke declared, "not through any power of my own but through that of the divine Holy Ghost Himself!"

Immediately, he forced air through Billy's mouth and into his lungs once, twice, a third time, so powerfully in fact that those who had gathered around were beginning to be concerned about the strain on the minister's own body.

Lincoln stood straighter than usual, tilting his head upward, his eyes surveying the darkening sky.

"Yea, though I walk through the valley of the shadow of death . . . ," Lincoln started to say, his clear, strong voice needing no amplification.

Man after man, Yankee and southerner alike, joined in with him. For a moment, Fulkerson hesitated, then added his own voice.

". . . for Thou art with me," he said.

He fell to his knees, ignoring the pain of several pebbles that were biting into his skin. As though by this he had signaled the others, everyone else did likewise.

"Thy rod and Thy staff . . . ," those two dozen voices spoke in unison.

Marmaduke continued forcing air into Billy Mendenhall.

Lord, Lord, don't let these evil people claim him as a tribute to their unholy cause, Charity prayed. *Lord, bring him back to us!*

Marmaduke finally felt the exertion to an extent that a wave of dizziness started to overwhelm him.

"Hold me, child," he whispered. "I am about to pass out. Give me some of your strength so that I can—"

As she crawled over to him and put her arms around his waist, he turned to her and said, "I think we may well lose this fine, brave young soul."

"Let me take over," Charity said.

"You are not strong enough."

"And you are too—"

Gasps from men who were used to holding in their emotions shuddered through the group behind them.

Finger tips, reaching up.

Charity felt them lightly touch her right elbow and then stop.

"Pastor, he—!" she gasped.

She and Marmaduke looked down at Billy Mendenhall.

His large blue eyes were open, and he was smiling.

"Praise the holy name of Jesus!" he muttered weakly. "Thank You, Lord!"

And with that arose the sounds of tough, scarred men weeping, some barely audible, others more like wrenching sobs.

≈ 63 ≈

WORD OF THEIR progress was being passed along the route as they crossed over into South Carolina, though none of the members of that caravan were aware of this at first.

For good reason.

They all were too intent on getting back to familiar surroundings for them to pay any real attention to the countryside, particularly since Max Cutshaw's men were always on the fringes, hovering like guardian angels whose physical appearance belied their noble purpose.

But the militiamen as well as Charity and Lincoln were being observed by fascinated farmers and their slaves for most of the way since the route went through rural countryside. Curtains were being pulled aside everywhere, in plantation houses as well as slave quarters wherever these dwellings were located with a view of the road.

The slaves especially were eager to catch a glimpse of the tall, skinny politician who was becoming known as a man of contradictory viewpoints, the one who told many listeners that the best way of taking care of the slave problem was to ship them all back to Africa where they belonged.

That should have been discouraging to all slaves since, on its face, it was an excruciatingly cruel remark, one that seemed to place Lincoln much less in the camp of the abolitionists than was generally believed.

Yet, for some blacks, it was ironically what they wanted to hear, for they would rather be living where life was both free and sustainable, though always at a primitive level, instead of simply being free to roam the unfriendly streets of a foreign land where they had so little rapport with its culture.

Many children were lining up along the remaining segment of the route, waving with great excitement. Dozens of elderly men and women sat in their assorted rocking chairs, waiting for the anticipated group of more than two dozen to come into sight. Even the sick from every age category were being taken outside, some of whom would die within a matter of weeks and have no chance to see any more heroes.

Banners were waved. Greetings were shouted. People dropped to their knees, thanking God for His protective mercies.

Not since the War of 1812 had there been anything comparative, an outpouring to raise the spirits of the militia members, Charity, Marmaduke, Fulkerson, even Lincoln.

"They *believe* so much in valor!" he exclaimed at one point.

"And they also believe so much in *our* cause," Marmaduke responded. "Does *your* cause grab your insides like an iron hand that will not let go?"

Lincoln did not answer then or later, and the minister allowed himself a quick little knowing smile.

But not every observer of the caravan's passage was wide-eyed and sympathetic, ready to cheer the brave survivors of an attack engineered by shadowy Yankees bent on bringing about war with the South. Some were in fact secretly involved *with* those Yankees—if not spies, as such, then so nearly that that the difference was inconsequential. They looked on the survival of the two militias as a flat-out defeat for their cause. Having *both* destroyed would have been ideal, since the Yankees could be told that the southerners were so patently vicious that even the prospect of wiping out a dozen or more of their own kind did not stop their destructive animalistic instincts. And the reverse would have been disseminated to the southerners, with a similar explanation certain to infuriate them as well.

The possibility that a renegade band of blacks was somehow behind it seemed another option for a time. However, since that would have painted an image of ex-slaves contrary to what abolitionists had been engaged in carefully constructing, a viewpoint akin to that of the noble savage nonsense that would come in latter years but regarding American Indian tribes instead of blacks, it proved a notion that never got beyond the casual musings stage.

From farmhouse to plantation to business establishment the messages flowed, telling of the ambush and the survival of most of the defenders. People talked, people rejoiced, people planned a homecoming far grander than anything the area had seen before, save for the return of those who had fought in the War of 1812 and later in the Mexican War.

"I had serious disagreements with Alfred Littlepage," remarked Stapleton Telford Culp two days before the caravan arrived, "but I chose to spend all that time debating with him because I *respected* the man. I would have risked my own life to help defend Alfred or his family if any of them needed me."

He closed his eyes, trying to keep himself from weeping.

"And now Charity is the only one left!" he exclaimed.

Culp pitched in with the arrangements, financing everything himself and making sure that every state government official of any note would be waiting in front of the plantation house for the carriage containing Charity to pull up in front.

But no Yankees were invited.

"It was their kind that caused this great tragedy!" he bellowed when someone suggested that political considerations dictated that the president at least be notified. "Any Yankee who attends will do so as he steps over my still warm corpse! Or perhaps it should be better that I only *appear* dead so that when James Buchanan and others of his ilk are bending over me, I can suddenly jump to my feet and scare them to death!"

None of this would have mattered if Alfred Littlepage had not been blessed or cursed with the ability of making friends on both sides of the Mason-Dixon line. So, it was that welcoming Charity back home should have featured a guest list from across the political spectrum of the times.

. . . a guest list from across the political spectrum of the times.

"Would anyone have expected Christ to invite Judas to dine with Him after the resurrection?" he opined angrily, dismissing a reply to the effect that forgiveness was what the death, burial, and resurrection were all about.

Culp pondered that for but a moment or two before adding, "Yes, but none of us is capable of that kind of perfect behavior."

Marmaduke and Fulkerson had taken it upon themselves before beginning the journey to appoint Culp to be in charge of the various arrangements in the interests of expediency, since by the time they were to return, they would have been gone nearly a week for the round trip and had left no other specific instructions.

The man did well, for while Jefferson Davis could not be in attendance for certain compelling reasons, Robert E. Lee told Culp that he was honored at receiving an invitation and would cancel every competing engagement in order to join them all.

Julia Pegram was someone else who would prove to be helpful.

Culp handled the broad picture while she took care of the social niceties that were so important in the South of that day. She also wanted to be among the first to welcome Samuel Fulkerson, in whom she had developed a rather warm interest.

"I always knew that beneath that rascally facade was the pulsating heart of a hero!" she exclaimed, and all of those in her company made special note of the passion with which she uttered that sudden remark.

~ 64 ~

B ILLY MENDENHALL HAD stopped bleeding temporarily, though he was still very weak while the bullets remained in his body.

That might have seemed cause for hope, but Lincoln felt persuaded by an opposite concern, and he called to Charity after the caravan had stopped to give the horses a rest.

"Miss Littlepage . . . ," he began. "There is something you should know about this brave lad."

"You seem worried," she observed.

"I *am* worried," Lincoln admitted. "And that is why I wanted to speak with you."

"But I am not a relative, of course."

"I realize that, but as you obviously realize, you have caught this young man's eye."

Charity avoided Lincoln's gaze as he mentioned this, hoping the man did not see her cheeks redden.

"I think it could well be that, before we ever reach the doctor, we might have to operate after all," Lincoln remarked after a few seconds.

"Why do you say that?" she asked.

"This young man could be experiencing internal bleeding in the absence of anything that we might be able to see."

Charity could feel beads of perspiration starting to form down her back as she considered that possibility.

"But he appears strong enough," she pointed out. "He can talk well from time to time. He seems to be aware of what is going on."

"But consider the moments when he is not lucid at all," Lincoln reminded her. "You should not focus on any but those. They are the key to what is going on inside him."

They both were standing outside the carriage, the hues of dawn outlining their figures against the fleeing night.

Lincoln reached out and took Charity's hand in his own.

"I have seen what is beginning to transpire between the two of you," he acknowledged. "And that *is* remarkable, this apparent attraction. I hope the good Lord is at the center of it, because it should not be happening at all, you from the South, young Billy a Yankee . . . but happening it *is,* Charity. I am not blind to matters of the heart, though I seem often the coldest of men to those who spend only a little time with me."

He sucked in his breath for a moment and then told her, "I urge you not to get your hopes up about his survival. You respond to him because you have lost your parents so brutally and he is there to fill the emptiness, for however long. But know this, please: Human beings as well as animals often bounce back for a time just before they die."

Lincoln had spoken to her with such unabashed directness that Charity visibly winced at his words.

"Please forgive me," he went on. "I am seldom patient with under-statement."

"You are right, though," Charity agreed. "I *have* noticed what you say in animals. Cats and dogs can be very sick, then suddenly seem to get so much better, and yet they end up dying in a matter of days."

She remembered one special instance.

"One of our cats was born without one of her back legs. She was the most ill-tempered of all, probably hurting in ways none of us could know. But, one day, she seemed to change, becoming affectionate overnight. Two weeks later, she was dead."

Lincoln nodded in recognition of that truth.

"Animals, especially those that are dearly loved by their human family, seem to have a unique sensitivity that we know little or nothing about," Lincoln acknowledged. "We may never know the depth and the breadth of this."

He was frowning as he added, "I cannot accept any notion that waiting even another hour will be helpful. If Billy Mendenhall can be operated on here, now, I think we just might have a chance to save him."

Charity stated the obvious.

"But who would do the operation? There are no doctors among us. That was the main reason for taking him to the doctor near our home."

Lincoln told her, "I have done such operations in the past, in the woods when hunters have accidentally shot a companion and I happened to be nearby and there were no facilities nearby. If the bullets are not too close to any vital organs—"

Charity's opinion of the man was changing further.

"Some might call that reckless, sir," she said, "but I think of it instead as showing courage on your part."

Lincoln's cheeks became ruddy.

"I would say that any agreement by that young man to let me do an oper-ation is an act of far greater courage!"

"Is there nothing that can be given to him to . . . to ease the pain?" she stuttered, not looking forward to the prospect of watching that handsome face contorted any longer or more severely than necessary.

"I think there may be a little whiskey available, but that is all."

Lincoln was climbing back into the carriage as Marmaduke and Fulkerson approached to see if there was anything they could do to help.

"He is, after all, a Yankee," Lincoln reminded them when they had asked what they could do. "Should you not take that into consideration before you offer assistance, gentlemen?"

"He may be a Yankee, yes," Marmaduke somberly replied, "but any man willing to give his life for all of us here, southerner and Yankee alike, becomes my brother regardless of what his heritage is!"

"Well said," Lincoln told him. "As for what you can do, I think hearty prayer is the best choice at present."

Billy came back to consciousness a moment later, and Lincoln explained to him what had to be done.

"I have some whiskey to help with the pain," he concluded. "Are you ready to let me do this, young man?"

"Do I have a choice, sir?"

"You could wait until we get to the doctor, but that will not be until midday at best. I would not want to say that you would be alive by then."

Billy shook his head.

"Go ahead and get the scoundrels' metal out of me."

"Is there anything else, Mr. Mendenhall? Everyone here will be praying for you. I can promise that much."

"There is one thing."

"Tell me."

Billy Mendenhall turned a bit and saw Charity, who was standing on her toes and looking over the edge of the carriage.

"Are you . . . going to . . . stay?" he asked weakly. "It's going to be . . . an awful sight . . . and I have . . . no right to—"

Charity blushed as she replied, "I was going to speak to you about that very matter, Mr. Mendenhall, if you hadn't brought it up."

The young man smiled just a bit.

"It will be bearable then . . . since I'll be able to look up into that beautiful angel's face of yours . . . and imagine a little of heaven without having to go there yet. How could any pain endure for long in light of that?"

Lincoln turned away, more trapped by his public image than he was willing to admit, an image of stoicism that people seemed to expect of him.

I have a desire to stand in the midst of a quite large crowd someday, a crowd comprised of newspaper editors and congressmen and others of influence and power, he thought, *and simply weep or laugh boisterously or do something that would startle them all.*

He glanced at Billy Mendenhall.

But not for the time being, he told himself. *Another burden is on me now. This brave boy's survival rests in my grasp.*

He tilted his head upward, praying, *Father in Heaven, may it be Your doing, may it be Your skill!*

Lincoln had not lost a habit from childhood, that of carrying a hunting knife around with him, left over from his days in the woods of Illinois, and he reached for it immediately. But after looking at the blade, he decided it was too big, a cruel-looking weapon that was unusable for a job as delicate as the one he was taking upon himself.

"Can anyone help me, please?" he pleaded, holding it out before him. "I have only this. It is meant to butcher and only that."

One of the older men in the South Carolina militia approached the carriage and spoke haltingly.

"I . . . have . . . something," he said. "My pappy gave it to me a long time ago. I guess I carry it around for good luck, though I know I shouldn't do that, being a Christian and all."

The man, not much less grizzled-looking than Max Cutshaw, reached into an inside pocket of the gray jacket he was wearing and retrieved a thin-bladed, pearl-handled knife that was precisely what Lincoln hoped someone would have.

"Will you sterilize it for me?" he asked.

Nodding, the other man rushed off to do just that and returned a few minutes later.

"Now those prayers!" Lincoln shouted.

A few seconds later, he was cutting into Billy Mendenhall.

❧ 65 ❧

WHATEVER MIGHT HAPPEN between them during the time just ahead, Charity knew that she would never forget that early-morning bonding with Billy Mendenhall as he tried to avoid screaming out while Abraham Lincoln performed surgery to remove three bullets from his body.

"It's . . . the other men," he muttered. "They must think me brave . . . I must not scream, you know . . . like a coward . . . or a weakling."

"They think you are *very* brave," Charity assured him as his fingers tightened around her hand. "But I doubt that they are the only ones."

People found out about Billy just as they had about the caravan itself. And the way they reacted could not be called less than extraordinary. Men and women came with handfuls of fresh bandages, bottles filled with antiseptic powders, even liquids that were no more than snake-oil concoctions but were offered in the sincere hope that something might help a young man none of them knew directly but whose valor had been whispered from person to person along the route of travel and who was instantly better known in that region than Abraham Lincoln himself. Others brought large family Bibles and sat by the roadside, reading Scripture and offering prayer.

While the operation was proceeding, some families had heated up large crocks of soup and were feeding the militiamen, who could do nothing but stand guard. Even Max Cutshaw and his men broke cover for a short while, lured by the converging aromas.

Everyone stopped once, then again as they heard Billy scream out in pain.

At first, it seemed he would not do so at all, but one of the bullets had penetrated deep into his right side, and Lincoln had to dig through to get it out. At that point, not even Billy could restrain himself.

Since Lincoln was not a skilled surgeon, it was remarkable that the operation went as well as it did. To close the incisions he used ordinary sewing thread brought to him by one of the women from a nearby farmhouse.

"The Lord told me that you had none," she said as she handed it to him.

"God bless you," Lincoln told her, genuinely touched.

"That He does, sir, that He does!"

The caravan started up again but at a much slower pace than it had maintained before Billy's surgery. Billy had to rest as comfortably as possible, and they could not go at the same quick speed that had characterized the earlier part of the journey. This seemed an unfair burden on the other wounded men who awaited the doctor's expert attention, but, in fact, none were as seriously hurt as Billy had been, and a vote had been taken among them, all agreeing to go at the pace that benefited him.

"Remarkable!" Marmaduke ventured. "Yankees and boys of the South pulling together for someone most of them hardly know."

"I agree," Fulkerson told him.

"It makes you wonder if there can be some hope for this Union after all." Marmaduke became silent.

"Why so quiet now?" Fulkerson asked him.

"You just spoke of some hope for the Union."

"I would *like* to think that war can be held off or stopped altogether."

"I never knew you to engage in wishful thinking, Samuel."

"I am just caught up in this moment, John. It is a wonderful moment, to be sure, if you disregard what's actually causing it—Billy's ordeal. I wish it could last even when all the physical wounds have healed."

Marmaduke, sitting in the front seat of the carriage, forced his shoulders back and sat ramrod straight.

"Human nature will not allow paradise to continue for much longer, I am afraid. Look at what happened to Eden."

"But this time it will be different," Fulkerson reminded him.

"Eden collapsed from within, Samuel. Our paradise is resisting pressures from without."

"It is less and less the genteel world you and I once knew. There is growing talk of secession if the North—"

Marmaduke handed the reins over to Fulkerson.

"Are you feeling poorly?" Fulkerson asked.

"I just need to concentrate."

"Concentrate on what?"

"Over there," Marmaduke said, pointing to the farmland on their left.

"What do you see?"

"A man with a rifle. He's—"

He shouted with that deep voice, and heads snapped in the direction of the lone gunman.

A shot rang out.

Abraham Lincoln had been sitting up on the front seat of the carriage in which Billy Mendenhall was resting, with Charity at his side.

The shooter got off only that one shot before one of Max Cutshaw's men dropped him. The attacker's bullet grazed the top of Lincoln's ear.

"I cannot help but think that some group is determined to get that man," Marmaduke observed.

"Do you think they're from here or up north?" Fulkerson asked.

"It may be people who owe no particular allegiance to either side."

Fulkerson was startled by that.

"I find such a notion more chilling than one involving a group of villainous Yankees."

"Some men are determined to plunge this nation into fields of blood, and then when war is over, they will step in, scoop up choice morsels, and multiply their wealth."

"Our land will be ready for them in the aftermath of war," Marmaduke continued. "They will simply walk in and buy up tens of thousands of acres at scandalous prices."

"But if Lincoln is someone inclined to help their cause, though I suspect him unaware of the implications of his conduct, then why would any of those Jews seek his death?"

"For the same reason we were attacked!" exclaimed Marmaduke as though realizing what he considered the truth at the same time he was expounding to the other man.

"To make it seem that the South is responsible and, thus, to fan hatred like a plague throughout the North."

"In chess, I suppose, it would be tantamount to sacrificing a bishop or a rook either to get the queen or to checkmate the king."

Fulkerson glanced from side to side as he realized the profound reality behind what Marmaduke had said.

"Not all the serpents have been routed from Eden," he spoke.

"They are many, my dear Samuel, and they are expert at disguises. Day in and day in, we may be shaking the hand of one without ever knowing it until too late."

"And we can do nothing but wait for the explosion."

"It would seem so," that spellbinding baritone intoned. "It would seem so."

"Lincoln did not allow that very slight wound on his ear to cause further delay but used some of the unused bandages," Charity told the Plantation Letters Society, sighing at the memory, *"and he bound it up himself as the caravan continued on the final stage of that journey."*

~≈ 66 ≈~

No one in the caravan could have been prepared for what they encountered as soon as they pulled up in front of the doctor's office just outside Columbia.

Not a few score people, waving flags and banners, but hundreds. The militiamen, Marmaduke, Fulkerson, Max Cutshaw and his men, Lincoln, and Charity were all astonished.

The *large* crowd confronted them, fanning out across the grass in front of the doctor's home and office.

Men and women of all ages. Children in their mothers' arms—and a fair number of dogs as well, waiting for their masters from the South Carolina militia to return home. As well as a band playing enthusiastically.

But this was only the part of the crowd comprised of local residents. People from all over the state had joined them. And standing beside Stapleton Telford Culp was a man who had just turned fifty but whose hair was already white with streaks of gray.

Robert Edward Lee.

He had just ended his tenure as superintendent of West Point and had not as yet led the U.S. Marines in the capture of John Brown at Harper's Ferry.

Lee was not a tall man, but even those bigger than he felt a certain power coming from the man. This was not in any occultic sense but simply the force of his quiet strength, a personality that seemed a combination of professor and minister and veteran soldier. He had served with distinction in the Mexican War.

He appeared to be much older than his actual age, for there was a weariness and a wisdom about him that would have made him rather ideal to play Moses in a stage play if he had so chosen.

A man interested in the arts, Lee was friendly with members of the family of actor Junius Brutus Booth, and this was not his only relationship with Yankees. The elder Booth was the foremost Shakespearean actor of his day and had two sons who also scored great successes with the bard's plays. Any association between Lee and the Booths required concessions from each party, since Lee was not entirely trustful of Anglo-American "artistic types" and only John Wilkes Booth was sympathetic to the South's growing political plight.

Dressed in full military garb, Robert Edward Lee was the most commanding figure waiting on the steps to greet the members of the returned caravan.

The first hand he shook was that of Charity Elizabeth Littlepage.

"How remarkable you are!" he exclaimed as he took her hand between both of his hand and patted it gently.

"I have survived only because the Lord was with me," she replied nervously—admitting to the soldier that she felt as she did.

"May I ask why?" Lee asked with kind directness.

"Because of what my father told me about you, sir."

"It is I who should be the nervous one, after what good Alfred told me so often about you, my dear."

Charity had not known about the depth of the relationship between Lee and her father.

"We will discuss everything this evening," he said, winking at her, knowing that she would be eager to hear more.

"This evening?" Charity said, nonplused.

"I understand that your slaves have prepared something special for your return, and I have been invited."

Lee seemed genuinely pleased, though he was a man to whom invitations for dinner from presidents and other powerful men had become commonplace.

"I would have been surprised that you were not," Charity replied graciously.

He pressed his hand gently on her shoulder and then went on to see the next awaiting individual.

Abraham Lincoln.

From the vantage of a few decades hence, that meeting would have seemed quite extraordinary, as unchronicled as it was. But in truth it was, at the time, not exceptional at all.

"Hello, Abraham," Lee spoke first. "How unusual, I must say, these circumstances governing this moment."

Several inches taller than the other man, Lincoln felt, as most others did that day, humbled in the presence of someone who had lived far more eventfully than he himself had.

"It seems, from what I hear," Lincoln spoke in a low voice, "that you are as unhappy with a certain institution as I am."

"But I, for one, think more highly of black people than you do, sir," Lee

responded forcefully because he was speaking from the deepest of convictions. "You are, after all, the very man who has mused not so privately with
your cronies of a similar bent that the best course of action for these poor
folk is that every last one of them be forcibly loaded onto boats and
returned to the dark continent as quickly and as efficiently as possible."

Lee grunted his displeasure.

"Very clever, Mr. Lincoln, very clever truly, from a political standpoint,
anyway. But the moral implications for blacks and the economic considerations for the South, well, that is a story for another day."

"Perhaps we can deal with this in another location someday," Lincoln
told him.

"Oh, that *shall* be the case," added Lee a bit gleefully. "You need have
no question about it, Mr. Lincoln."

"I think, perhaps, after dinner this evening," Lincoln went on.

Lee's face paled a bit, for he had never liked Abraham Lincoln and was
not pleased with the possibility of facing him across *anyone's* dinner table.

Lips drawn tight against his teeth, he nodded and glanced toward the two
men standing a few feet behind Lincoln.

Marmaduke and Fulkerson.

"It has been so long," Lee said to the minister, sounding sincere.

"My loss entirely," Marmaduke replied as they shook hands.

"And Samuel, how are you?" Lee addressed Fulkerson.

"Older, but, I fear, only a little wiser since we last met."

Stapleton Telford Culp, who had been on the steps of the porch with Lee
and the others, came up to them.

"I understand that Billy Mendenhall was operated on very successfully on
the way," he commented cheerfully. "This brave young man became quite
alert a moment ago as he was being carried inside and told us some few
details."

Marmaduke and Fulkerson nodded.

"It was as you say," Marmaduke confirmed. "I have to say that Mendenhall
helped everyone, regardless of whether they were southerner or Yankee."

"This Lincoln may be quite a man after all!" exclaimed Culp as he patted
Lee mischievously on the back. "Isn't that right, commander?"

Robert Edward Lee chose not to reply.

～❧ 67 ❧～

After the band had stopped playing and the crowd had dispersed and a group of slaves supplied by their masters was cleaning up what was left behind—banners, confetti, food donated by various local organizations—Charity remained at the doctor's office.

Although she had offered to open her family's plantation home to the wounded militiamen, they had all declined her offer, recognizing the additional burden they would place on her as she struggled to cope with the loss of her parents. Instead, the doctor urged them to stay in his home, which adjoined his office.

Charity settled into a rickety chair beside Billy Mendenhall's bed, talking to him whenever she felt he could understand her, helping him to drink water when he was thirsty, wiping his forehead with a cool, wet cloth as a new bout of fever gripped him, covering his well-muscled body with perspiration. It was, fortunately, a fever that, while it initially hit hard and caused the doctor some concern, did not last long, and once it had broken, Charity was able to doze off without being awakened by Billy's fitful little cries of pain, cries that he tried valiantly to stifle but could not.

"That young man would not be recovering so well if you were not here," the doctor told Charity.

"Anyone who cared at all could have helped him, and he would have done the same," she retorted, scoffing at this.

"Is it because he is Yankee," the doctor asked, "that you refuse to acknowledge your role in his recovery?"

At first she was going to rail against the impudence of the stranger. But this reaction lasted all of three seconds.

"I think you may be right," she told him.

"Well, then, Miss Littlepage, consider, however contradictory this may seem, that your actions thus far have more than attested to the feelings that you apparently have for him," the doctor replied. "Is there anything left that can be hidden, miss?"

. . . the feelings that you apparently have for him.

In fact, she was so embroiled in these feelings that she had remained ignorant of how obvious she was being to people around her.

The first time I really notice anyone, and he happens to be a Yankee! Charity exclaimed to herself. *I must be crazy!*

And yet, noticing Billy Mendenhall was not all that astonishing, whatever the region of the country he claimed as his own.

The boys I was first introduced to always seemed just that . . . boys. Unappealing, callow, and, in most cases, insecure.

She chuckled a bit.

"Did I say something amusing, Miss Littlepage?" the doctor asked rather irritably.

She gave him a look of such warmth that it made him blush.

"No, sir, you did not," Charity replied. "Whatever I was thinking just now had nothing to do with you."

Often, Charity did sense insecurity in the boys who were arranged for her to court. For a long while she could not understand why. Finally she felt that there was no choice but to discuss the matter with her mother.

And as usual Elizabeth Littlepage had provided the answer.

It was as they were being driven into Columbia one day by Hester to do some shopping. A mile or two outside the city, Charity decided to ask her mother about the way she looked at boys.

Elizabeth was not surprised.

"You do not have an insecure bone in your body," she said. "You have seemed levelheaded and confident from a very early age. That intimidates most boys, dearest. That they seem so tremulous in your presence only confirms this."

"Do I seem stuck up to them?"

"It isn't that at all, Charity. Let me give you an illustration: If you went on a picnic in some heavily wooded area and a bear appeared, the boy you were with might shout and scream and run as fast as he could.

"Meanwhile you would pick up a rifle and shoot the bear right between the eyes, watch it fall to the ground, then call out to your beau, 'Everything's taken care of. Let's finish eating now.' Yes, that sounds like a bit of an exaggeration, of course, but I imagine it is very much the way these boys think of you."

Charity could not respond at first. She had had no hint of what was wrong in her relationships with the opposite sex.

"You must learn," her mother continued, "that men want to feel that they are in charge. You may be stronger by will and smarter by intellect than most of those you meet, but still, they must never get the impression that you could take over in an instant."

She smiled before adding, "And, above all, you should never act superior to them."

"Does that mean that I should conduct myself in an *inferior* manner?" Charity asked with some sense of logic.

"Then no man would be able to *respect* you," Elizabeth replied. "What I am telling you may seem to be an impossibility, but somehow, I know you will manage as well or better than your mother."

Charity detected a bit of wistfulness in her mother's voice and asked, "Have you ever felt that you were giving up too much of yourself?"

Elizabeth considered that for a moment.

"Sometimes I have," she confessed. "Would it have been better if I had moved out West where tradition seems to play much less of a role in the lives of pioneering women? Could I have felt more complete by sacrificing a high standard of physical comfort and working harder with my hands, helping to build some log cabin somewhere or shooting down heathen Indians who were attacking my home?"

She sucked in her breath, her eyes wetter than should have been the case.

"I think I can tell you honestly that your father has made all the difference to me. He is a man with whom any woman would feel complete. While he is sometimes a victim of a strait-laced society that assumes anything frivolous and spontaneous and perhaps a bit reckless is somehow a sin of one sort or another, I have never been bored with him. And I have been able to trust this tender, sensitive but virile man throughout all these years with no concern that he would ever give me cause to doubt his fidelity."

"But are you *truly* fulfilled, Mother?" Charity asked.

"Some days I . . ."

Elizabeth stopped herself.

"Mama, what were you going to say?" probed Charity.

"There are times when your father is away and I know in my heart that he has no ordinary flesh-and-blood mistress and that he has been a man of fidelity throughout our marriage. But there is another kind of mistress side by side with him, one he cannot shake because the need has been born into the man you and I both love."

Charity sat in the carriage, waiting for the rest of her mother's revelation.

"This well-bred life of ours . . . ," Elizabeth whispered. "It has been passed with great care down from generation to generation of Littlepages and always with one simple requirement unerringly *bound* to it: that it be *maintained*, that the next generation be given a standard of living and social position as a natural legacy, something to expect."

She shrugged her shoulders wearily.

"So there your father is, maintaining the family's interests whether these interests include, at any given moment, business interests in Raleigh, Baton Rouge, or wherever else they might be. And I am home, managing the household."

She chuckled ironically.

"I have known times when I felt closer to our slaves than to your father," she added. "But as soon as he is back home and we are in one another's arms, the aching in my heart ends—until the next time and the one after that."

Now, for the first time, Charity was deeply involved in having to deal with real feelings for a young man.

How could I not like him? she thought. *He's blond-haired, blue-eyed, handsome, with a smile that makes me wobbly inside—but he's a Yankee.*

Something serious, this problem was, one that could affect Charity, she knew, for the rest of her privileged life. And yet, though needed urgently, her mother was no longer available to sit with her and give her advice.

"I want to be with him whatever the consequences," she said, not realizing that she was speaking outloud.

The doctor noted this with a scowl.

"If that is your desire," he said, "then you will have to live with what happens to you within the community."

Charity did not hesitate to answer.

"If the community is not interested in my welfare after all that has happened," she told him, "should I really be concerned with what they think? Is the community more eager to impose needless restrictions on my behavior than to see that I have someone who *might* be able to fill the void left by my parents?"

The doctor did not strike back with a sharp-edged retort.

"Stay true to your heart . . . ," he whispered, looking faintly conspiratorial. "As long as you have the Holy Ghost within you, I think you will be fine."

He kissed Charity on the cheek and left her standing in the middle of the room.

～❦ 68 ❧～

T HAT FIRST NIGHT back in familiar territory proved to be largely a con-
flicted one for Charity Littlepage.

And she felt embarrassed that this was the case, for surviving all that she
had over the past week should have lifted her spirits and made her deeply
grateful, especially since she had convinced herself that as soon as she
returned to the cocoon that had been wrapped around her for all but the last
few wrenching days of her life, everything would be better, that she could
adjust, however slow the process.

But Charity came to realize that "cocoon" had ceased being the right
description, because the architects of it were no longer inside to enjoy the
benefits with her. And without them, she would never feel the same kind of
stability again.

And then there was Billy Mendenhall.

He was begging her to stay with him.

He did not want to face the prospect of being among strangers.

"I need you here," he said, his voice raspy.

"But something special is being planned at home," she told him. "How
can I not be there, Billy?"

He had raised himself up slightly and now fell back against the bed.

"You're right," Billy relented, smiling weakly but, as far as Charity was
concerned, no less effectively. "You and I have known each other only these
few days, and I can't expect to get away with acting like some old bull
charging around through everything that your life has had set up for you
until now."

He looked rather less sure of himself when he suddenly added, "I'll be
all right, Charity. I really will."

She bent over the bed, which was not much more than a basic cot by the
standards of a later day.

"And what are your intentions?" he asked slyly.

"I have only one thing in mind," she told him just as slyly.

Without saying anything else, she kissed him, not on the cheek this time
but on the lips, and for more than a few seconds.

"I think I feel better already," he said as she was pulling back and standing up straight once again.

Charity blushed and started to leave the room.

"Charity . . . ?" Billy called after her.

She stopped without turning.

"It would be easy to love you," he added.

She left without turning around.

"I mean it," she heard Billy say as she began to walk with some uncertainty down the long hallway to the front door, for a moment seeing in her imagination a mosaic image of all the other boys in her life before that day, each fading instantly until only one young man took their place.

As soon as Charity was outside she stopped short, blinking several times. The carriage!

Little Isaiah was waiting in what looked like the identical carriage in which her parents had ridden when they were shot.

She hesitated, her face momentarily paling.

"It ain't the same one, Miss Charity," Little Isaiah told her, sensing by her expression and the way she stood what she had been thinking. "You left that one behind in Illinois."

He patted the side of the one next to him.

"This is new," he beamed. "Bright, shiny new."

Little Isaiah smiled broadly as she inspected the exterior.

"It's a gift from someone," he said.

"Who would that be, Little Isaiah?" Charity asked with more than idle curiosity, now seeing that this particular carriage was similar to the other but not the same in a number of respects: the shape in the front, the gilt edging, a slight difference in the color of the seats, and other, smaller details. "Was it Reverend Marmaduke or Mr. Fulkerson . . . or, wait a minute, yes, it must have been Julia Pegram! That would seem just like her to do this."

Little Isaiah shook his head.

"None of them," he replied slowly.

"Then who else? Let me know, please," she persisted.

"Sojourner Truth," he told her. "She sent a telegram telling me to pick it up in Columbia yesterday, and she paid the bill in full."

Charity had to lean against the carriage.

"How could that woman afford this?" she spoke, knowing that Sojourner Truth had never experienced material plenty. "How could she?"

Little Isaiah gave her the message that had been left with him: "She said that, since evil people had used *her* message as an excuse to—"

He hesitated, looking uncertain.

"Go ahead, friend," she told him, "finish what you were going to say. You needn't ever keep anything from me."

Little Isaiah tried to smile but was not able to do so and showed that he was still nervous, despite her assurance.

"—to murder your blessed mother and father, you would probably never want to see the old carriage again, 'cause of its memories of what had happened. So she said it was real fittin' that *their* money be used to buy this new one."

He helped Charity climb up into it.

"Smells new," she said.

Little Isaiah simply nodded.

"Smells—" she repeated.

And then she fell into his arms.

"Help me!" she cried, weakness gripping her without warning. "Help me get through what I must."

"The Lawd says in the Bible that He's never gonna leave nor forsake any of us who are His children. And He done let me know just last night, He sure did, that that is what He wants me to be to you, Miss Charity, someone who will always be there, if I still linger in this here world when you's needin' me."

Less than half an hour passed before the carriage pulled up in front of the Littlepage plantation house.

Hester had been leaning against one of the columns on the front porch while he waited with apparent anxiety.

"Miss Charity!" he exclaimed, relieved and beaming as he helped her out of the carriage. "This place has been awful lonesome since—"

He stopped himself and started crying.

"It's been so bad here," he told her. "I keep seein' the massa walkin' the grounds. One night, I thinks I hears his voice, even though I think I'm sleepin' and I wave and hurry to the door and look out but he's nowhere 'round, and I go back to my bed, shiverin' and cryin' like this, wonderin' what we's gonna do now that . . . that—"

Abruptly he seemed to have forced the tears to stop, shutting them off by a sheer act of will that enabled him to get control of himself.

"There I go, weepin' and wailin' 'bout myself," he went on, embarrassed, "and here you are, facin' what you did and hurtin' much more than I's doin'."

Charity touched his cheek.

"We all have lost two special people, Hester," she said, battling to keep tears of her own from starting. "Your pain is the same as mine. They're gone. They'll never, never be back, and nothing can change that. We have to get used to it, Hester. We—"

Charity could not win that battle and surrendered to a new wave of sorrow. She and Hester embraced and sobbed together for several minutes.

~❦ 69 ❧~

L ITTLE ISAIAH HAD organized quite an evening, though Stapleton Telford Culp seemed bent on taking the greater share of the credit. In truth, Julia Pegram had helped far more, since many of the state officials had wives who were successful in persuading their husbands to attend once Julia had worked her "spell" on them.

Every seat at the long table in the dining room was occupied, with Charity at one end. To her right sat Robert E. Lee, and on her left were Marmaduke and Fulkerson with Culp at the right of Lee, the other guests at the remaining places, nearly twenty people in all.

It seemed that the only difficulty to arise, thankfully, was earlier in the evening, long before any of the guests arrived.

A confrontation between Culp and Marmaduke over a piece of furniture . . . the table at which the slaves generally sat, half the length of the main one but identical otherwise.

Culp wanted to use it.

"We can get ten more people into the room," he said. "I thought I would have to exclude some very important folks, a number of men with whom Alfred had done business. But now that is not going to be necessary. They would have been very angry to find out that a bunch of darkies had taken their place."

Marmaduke straightened himself to his full, imposing height.

"My good man, you are using those very slaves to make the coming evening a wonderful homecoming affair for the only surviving member of the Littlepage family," he said, his nostrils stopping just short of flaring.

"I use slaves for *many* assorted duties," Culp shot back confidently. "As Alfred could have told you, I am significantly more sympathetic to their plight than most of the other men in this community have shown themselves to be. I have never been less than that the whole of my life."

He thought that he had bested the dynamic preacher, and his expression was a triumphant one.

"You are, after all, only a recent convert to what I have believed all along, John, that they should not be treated like animals."

"But not quite like human beings? Is that it?"

"Well, I mean, not equal, you know. Smell them especially after they have spent a long day picking cotton. Talk to them. You can see that for yourself. I agree that they are human, but substandard, John. You surely comprehend every bit as well as I do."

Marmaduke leaned forward.

"Substandard because of what they are *naturally* or because that is what we have *made* of them?" he replied, amazed that he was being successful in controlling a temper he knew could be volcanic.

"Listen, John," Culp said, lowering his own voice. "It is the same with that . . . that Cutshaw character and his ruffians. They are nearly as uncouth as those slaves. I certainly shouldn't have invited *them* here either, is that not so?"

Both men were standing in the dining room, after the arrival of the caravan but a few hours before Charity was picked up by Little Isaiah.

"Wait a minute!" Marmaduke exclaimed, finally exploding. "Max Cutshaw isn't going to be here either?"

"Of course not!" Culp yelled back at him. "How could some slaves and those waterfront rats be in the same room as Robert E. Lee. *Are you daft, John?"*

Marmaduke felt as though striking the other man in the jaw to squelch his insufferable ravings would have been considered by Jehovah Himself an act of righteous anger, but still he managed to stop that particular impulse. Instead he dropped his blood pressure several notches, clenched his fists, and spoke in a manner that was as condescending as he could muster.

"I am not daft," the minister replied deliberately, "but I am something else, Mr. Culp, sir, and that is a Christian who finds your very presence a stifling and unbearable stench, not in my nostrils because they are accustomed to such as your kind, and I am not a pure and perfect man at best, but—"

It was Culp who abruptly raised a fist and Marmaduke who grabbed that arm at the wrist.

"As I was *saying*," he continued, his voice so cold that it seemed capable of making his breath visible in front of him, "before a just and holy Creator, the meanness of what you have done or not done, as the case may be, the lack of charity and gratitude—"

"Gratitude?" Culp interrupted. *"Gratitude?"*

"To men who risked their own lives to save Charity's and the others."

"I was not aware of that," Culp lied.

"And the soldiers, what about them?"

"There is no room."

"Granted, yes, I believe that. But to ignore them altogether? You invite Lincoln, but you neglect his soldiers and, I presume, our very own Southern boys."

"Most are incapacitated and could not attend even if they were invited."

"Most are not incapacitated. The ones who still *live* are reduced to sleeping in the barns of wealthy landowners throughout this community, as you call it. How *Christian* of us all! They can shed their blood and give up their lives, oh, that is very fine, to be sure, and we let them do it, but we tell them, by our actions, that there is no room at the inn for their kind, and they must sleep in stables along with common farm animals."

His face was creased by a cynical grin.

"Where have you heard that sort of story before now, Mr. Culp, sir?"

~❧ 70 ❧~

B Y THE TIME the guests started to arrive, Stapleton Telford Culp had worked a kind of miracle by convincing certain important businessmen and state government officials that it would be an act of noble sacrifice if they did not attend the dinner.

"There is just so much demand," he said apologetically to each one. "Charity has so many friends of her own that she never thought she would ever see again, and we must consider her feelings more than ours. Would you not agree?"

In every case, the individual, men who were accustomed to anything but self-sacrifice, nodded yes or grunted assent. When it concerned Charity Elizabeth Littlepage, they could marshal their better instincts.

"This has nothing to do with how much respect and, yes, affection for you there was in that family," Culp added, managing to break his tightly wound composure and shed some tears in what could only be called a top-notch performance. "A new generation is in charge now, as you well know. And Charity undoubtedly will soon be forming her own ties with you, recognizing the good sense of continuing in her father's footsteps."

He smiled benevolently at each man.

"You can be sure that she is an exceptionally intelligent young woman who is very much aware of how essential you are going to be to her future," he said reassuringly. "But for the moment it is important that this young lady surround herself with people she knows, hopefully without offending anyone else."

And they all believed him. Then someone came up with another idea.

"Why not let us come later?" a businessman from Greenville suggested. "That would allow us to avoid taking up space in the Littlepage dining room where the seating capacity is, as you have said, rather limited.

"We could present to Charity certain gifts, chat, offer our sympathies, and leave. I have been in that house before. It is big enough to accommodate us for a short while. What about that, Telford?

"I would like to impress upon the dear girl that we will be there for her should she ever need us to help with any business details. This offer comes from the purest of motives, I assure you."

"That is a wonderful idea!" Culp exclaimed. "Thank you so much for helping out in this time of great tragedy."

And so it was done. After all such details had been taken care of, Culp confronted Marmaduke on the front porch of the plantation house.

"You must feel that I have no heart at all," he said, "no sense of justice or decency or anything of the sort."

"That possibility did—" the minister started to say.

"Just as you are a different man from what you once were, John," Culp interrupted, "allow me similar room for change."

Marmaduke's own manner softened.

"Earlier you walked away quite angry," he observed. "I honestly thought you would never come back. What happened, Telford? Will you tell me?"

Culp was silent so long that Marmaduke was beginning to take that for a negative response to his question.

Finally the other man spoke.

"On the way out to my carriage," Culp recalled, "I glanced to one side and noticed Alfred's slaves. Oh, I had seen them before then, of course, but this time it was quite different, John.

"Not that I could, even now, ever think of them as other than what they are, substandard human beings, no, I suspect that that will never change, for I would be lying to myself if I tried to represent otherwise. And yet—"

Culp hesitated briefly, his eyes closed, as he remembered the details of what he had seen just hours earlier.

"They seemed so possessed . . . ," he muttered.

"Possessed?" asked Marmaduke. "I have to ask what in the world, Telford, you could mean by *that?*"

"Love, John, possessed by love. Every last one of them was working very hard, getting everything ready for this evening."

"Why would that affect you so much, given how you feel about them?" Marmaduke, playing dumb, probed the other man.

Culp looked out over the rolling front lawn of the Littlepage plantation.

"I am waiting, Telford," the minister reminded him in a pseudo-imperious tone, "and I do not have all day."

"Even now that Alfred and Elizabeth are dead and buried, their slaves continue to feel the same way apparently."

"What did you expect?"

"That they act as so many slaves do. After the master is taken by death, they start talking among themselves, no longer afraid of expressing their true emotions, which are usually rift with bitterness, at least until the next master comes on the scene."

Culp's back was to Marmaduke.

"What I detected was love for Charity's parents comparable to the love that you and I are supposed to have for Christ."

The minister, instincts honed after many years of counseling people, detected a forlorn quality to the way Culp spoke those last few words.

"*Supposed* to have, Telford?" he asked. "I have that very love these days. Why not speak for yourself without trying to do so for me, my good man?"

Culp swung around.

"I could not endure what they showed to me," he said, raising his voice. "I wanted to beat it out of them! I could not bear to see that sort of love, love that was so deep, John, love almost holy in its pure and unconditional state."

His face contorted, driven by emotions that were still turbulent.

"Love so deep that it made you cringe—is that it, my dear Telford?" Marmaduke prompted him gently.

"Yes, yes, *yes!*" Culp replied. "But I asked myself, how could any man, even inferior ones such as they were, feel that way about another human being?"

His eyes were wide, bloodshot.

"There I was, with all the generations of breeding that are supposedly mine, and there *they* were, plucked from a jungle in Africa! There I was, with enough money that I could buy the whole lot of them and a hundred times that and still be comfortable financially for the rest of my life, and there they were—"

Marmaduke moved in with an observation that he prayed would help.

"Poor in possessions, poor in education, poor in every other way," he said, "yet so rich in spirit that you suddenly felt like the pauper and had to walk with shame past them?"

"How could you know this?" Culp asked, stunned, not quite believing that Marmaduke was as astute as that.

"It was not unlike how I felt before my outlook was wrenched out of the deception in which it had been submerged for so long," Marmaduke told him. "You and I went through a similar crisis, I suspect, and so did Samuel, from what I hear."

"Fulkerson? *He* came to such a point as well?"

"That he did."

Culp's cheeks were streaked with tiny streams of tears.

"Managing to resist that unholy urge to lash out at those slaves and give them pain instead of the love they showed for Alfred and Elizabeth, I somehow made my way to the front gate before one of them called out to me, 'Massa Culp, sir, are you comin' back soon? Ain't too long 'til all them guests start to arrive, and you was goin' to be at the door greetin' 'em.'

"I could not believe that he had remembered my name, let alone ever knew it. I stopped walking and turned toward him. 'Have we met before?' I asked. This slave replied, 'I's rememberin' you from your visits here, and what Massa Alfred said about you.'

"'What . . . did he say?' I asked. And this was what that slave told me: 'Massa Alfred told me that you are a kind, good man, and that if anything happened to him, he could trust you with everything he had until Miss Charity was on her feet.'"

. . . if anything happened to him.

"I asked him if he remembered when Alfred had made that remark," Culp went on, trying not to be skeptical, "and he told me that it was just a few days before the family left on that trip to hear Sojourner Truth."

"A premonition, is that it, Telford?" inquired Marmaduke, generally not trusting such things at all but also knowing that God could never be limited in what He could accomplish within the heart and soul of anyone.

Culp shrugged his shoulders.

"Who can know?" he remarked. "While I was talking with that one, the others gathered around, anxious to help, to do anything they could."

"How could you stand it, Telford?" Marmaduke quipped cynically. "Did the smell nearly overcome you?"

Culp shot him a glance that made the minister regret that remark.

"I *am* sorry, Telford," replied Marmaduke humbly. "It was only a few moments ago that your attitude seemed so different."

"It was different only a few moments ago, and do not misunderstand my feelings, because these are special circumstances. Generally, I continue to be convinced that niggers should be *thanking* us for taking them out of the trees and bushes and bringing them here."

Culp was obviously straining to believe what he himself was saying.

"After all, John, these people no longer have to hunt down their food each day like the savages they once were and many continue to be, and kill whatever beasts they have spotted then carve open the remains in order to feed themselves and their families, which they seem to expand on a ratio with rabbits in heat."

Marmaduke restrained himself, deciding not to engage in any sort of debate at that late hour, at least until after the evening's festivities had passed, so he let the other man go on without interruption.

"But I think some are different, a handful here and there perhaps, different in that they do *seem* to be somewhat more human and somewhat less like loathsome creatures of the wild," Culp observed. "Whatever the case—and in deference to Alfred Littlepage—they should get their places at the dinner tonight."

His voice cracked for a moment before he was able to add, "It might be, John, that these particular coloreds deserve this more than you and I do."

Marmaduke nodded at that.

"You are probably right, Telford," he replied with some undisguised admiration, "you are probably very right."

71

CHARITY NEEDED SOME time to wash and change clothes. Everything she had packed for the trip had been lost. But she had more than enough replacements at home, a large assortment of clothes for all possible occasions, bought during shopping expeditions to Columbia or Natchez or other cities and, every so often, French and Italian designs brought by her father from Europe.

"You don't have to rush," Little Isaiah told her.

"When will everybody start to arrive?" she asked as she stood at the bottom of the staircase leading to the second floor.

"In 'bout an hour or so."

"That is the time I need. How did you guess so correctly?"

"Didn't need to guess at all, Miss Charity."

"But how could you have planned things that way?"

"'Cause that's how long you always take gettin' ready."

"You know so much about me," she said.

"I've been with you all your life, Miss Charity. Bound to know by now."

She smiled sadly as she told him, "I think I've taken you for granted more than I ever realized before this very moment."

"No, Miss Charity!" Little Isaiah exclaimed. "No, you ain't never done that. You have been kind and loving since you was knee-high to a grasshopper."

That expression amused her, and she chuckled.

"There's more color to your cheeks now," he remarked. "You look a whole lot better, Miss Charity."

She turned to go upstairs but looked straight in front of her and seemed reluctant to take the first step.

"Go . . . ," Little Isaiah told her sympathetically. "The Holy Ghost is inside you, and there are angels all around."

"Am I so obvious?" she asked.

"Yes, Missy, you is," he replied with a gentle smile.

Slowly, her legs barely able to move, Charity ascended a staircase that she had used countless times since she was able to walk as a very young child.

It seems so long, she told herself, *as though new steps have been added. Who would have done such a thing?*

She had almost decided that she would not make it to the second floor, would have to sit in the middle of the staircase and break down and sob from weakness or fear or mourning or a combination of the three.

"Miss Charity, are you——?" Little Isaiah began, concerned that she was faltering and might hurt herself on the stairs.

"Yes, friend," she told him, though her voice was faint.

Finally Charity reached the landing, which, like the rest of the house's flooring, was not covered by any carpeting except an occasional throw rug that had been imported from Europe, the natural wood polished regularly to a sheen that made it seem glass-like, kept in that condition by one or more of the slaves.

She held on to the banister to steady herself.

Her bedroom was to the left; to the right was her parents' huge master suite. In between were two guest rooms.

She walked to the suite, placing her hand hesitantly on the specially carved knob inlaid with a mother of pearl center.

"I should not do this," Charity said out loud and raised that hand for a moment then put it down again, wrapping her thin, pale fingers slowly around the edges. "But I must; oh, Lord, I must! *Help me!*"

She had spoken louder than intended, and Hester, who had just entered the house and was walking toward the warming kitchen, stopped and, alarmed, called up to her, "Are you all right, Miss Charity?"

"So sad . . ." She spoke just barely loud enough for him to hear.

"Do you want someone with you?" Hester said. "The reverend will be here soon. I could send him upstairs."

"Thank you, Hester, I need to get through this by myself or I will never get through it at all. I hope you understand."

"I do," he replied with such feeling in just two words that Charity walked to the railing and looked down at him.

"Tell everyone I may be a little late," she asked. "But there's a good reason. Will you tell them that?"

"Yes, Miss Charity, I will. When you're in there, tell Massa Alfred and the missus that I ain't never gonna stop loving them."

Hester did not want her to see him crying, so he hurried on to the kitchen.

Was it because of your tears or mine? she thought.

Charity approached the bedroom door again, turned the knob, walked inside, and felt weak instantly, familiar odors hitting her nostrils: her mother's perfume, a particular kind of evergreen, homemade soap that her father favored, a pair of leather boots to one side of the bureau dresser, these and other smells mixing together into a kind of common fragrance. She had to stumble to a nearby chair that was made of thick buffalo hide slung between an oak frame, a gift from an Indian tribe with which her father had become friendly a decade earlier, one of several items scattered throughout the house that showed the affection he inspired from other races: a Ming tea set, an inlaid ivory-and-ebony chess set from a French businessman.

Steadying herself, she sank back, the touch of the hide soothing against her bare arms.

You were always here when I came in, she recalled. *I don't think, all these years, that I've ever been in this room alone.*

Yet "alone" was no longer an adequate word. She felt abandoned instead, not blaming anyone but the men who murdered the two most precious people in her life.

"They had no right!" she said, trying to avoid embarrassing herself by keeping her voice unheard beyond the confines of that room but feeling the need to speak out to the walls and the ceiling and the floor as though they were witnesses to her pain.

She tried to stand but was not quite ready.

"Little Isaiah says that he will be by my side," she went on, "and I know that the Holy Ghost is here with me now. But I can't touch Him. I can't wrap my arms around Him and whisper into His ear that I love Him, that I love Him so much."

She reached one hand out before her.

"Mother, do you linger a bit in this world before you go on to glory?" she asked of the empty air, a space with nothing in it where once Elizabeth Littlepage smiled radiantly.

She extended the other hand.

"Father, are you here also? Are you trying to say good-bye? But I can't hear you, I can't see you and mother standing—"

Charity shook her head at that notion, dismissing it quickly, since she was familiar with Scripture from Sunday school lessons and Bible-study times either at home or with some other children at another plantation house, and knew well enough any such prospect was based upon pure falsehood alone.

A faint sound.

She strained to hear what it was.

Branches rubbing against one of the windows, the sigh of the weeping willow next to the house as its leaves were stirred by a breeze that came and went, and that sound for which it was named disappeared, with only a tomb-like silence left in its melancholy wake.

Charity remembered that period in her life when, if frightened or restless, she would climb out of her own bed and hurry down the hallway, which always seemed a mile long at such times, and knock on the door to *that* bedroom, *that* treasured haven of safety, and a voice she loved would say with great warmth, "Come in, Angel."

"And now . . ." She spoke out loud again, forcing the words, "Now you walk with ten thousand angels at your side."

Knowing this was a balm of sorts that somehow eased her loss—eased it but did not go far enough to eradicate it altogether.

Charity managed to stand and walk to the two large wardrobes placed side by side that held the clothes her parents wore, her father's relatively few suits as well as his shirts and her mother's many dresses.

She pictured moments when her parents had worn those clothes . . . at a dinner party or during some political function or for a special lawn party or to church on Sunday.

Some women of that community were determined to be the best-dressed members of the congregation so they would be noticed by others who did not make the grade that day. But Elizabeth Littlepage belonged to another group altogether, those who simply enjoyed "dressing up" but with no intention of doing this to posture for reasons of pride.

"Surely, if our dear Lord had not meant for us to look our best in fine clothes," she would say more than once, "all of us would still be running around naked, just like Adam and Eve did before the Fall."

Remembering her mother's words, Charity started crying again, though not hysterically this time because in that comment was a glimpse of her mother's sense of humor.

I think I miss that almost as much as your love, she thought. *When life became monotonous or far too serious, you would say something funny, and all of us would laugh, especially Savilla and Violet and the other slaves.*

But humor was seldom a part of her father's personality, though he was a loving man, a man who would sacrifice anything for his loved ones.

He always had so much to think about, apart from just his business obligations, Charity recalled, *including what he would learn as he traveled, like those predictions of doom for the Union, which came not from people merely gossiping self-importantly in city parks or as they stood at street corners, chattering away, but from men of stature, men of influence, men of power who looked ahead and saw nothing but fearful events, events in which they might well play some not insubstantial part.*

When she was younger and less able to understand, he had kept such matters to himself, knowing that children could be frightened easily.

"Everything I had depended upon you!" she screamed. "I nurtured the pretense that I was independent, but that was all a facade. *My world was your world, and I knew nothing else!*"

Her gaze darted about the large bedroom, with its twelve-foot-high ceiling.

"You left me behind . . . ," she said, her voice becoming hoarse. "It would have been better if I had gone on with you."

A voice startled her.

"No, young lady, that would have been terribly, terribly wrong," said Julia Pegram.

Charity saw her standing in the doorway.

"But how can you say that?" she demanded, touching her chest. "You are not *inside* me now. You cannot know what I feel."

"How dare you suggest that you are the only woman to have lost someone she loved! When Ambrose died—"

"But he was a—" Charity started to say but caught herself.

"A monster? Was that it? Well, you are right. Ambrose was a monster to every black man, woman, and child he ever met. Nor did very many people in the white community have anything nice to say about him.

"With me, though, there were moments when he was a different sort of man. In his own curious way, he was devoted to me. Knowing that, I allowed myself to ignore the other Ambrose, the cruel side of him, the evil things he did when he gained control over another human being."

"And the man ended up controlling *you*, Julia!" retorted Charity. "How can you not feel so free now?"

"I continue to feel as I did right after he died. And that isn't free, as you so handily assume. I still walk about that house and pretend that I hear his voice. I still call out to him and shiver in my very soul when he does not answer."

She walked up to Charity, who was leaning against one of the bedposts.

"Death has touched both of us," she said. "It has robbed you and me of those around whom our lives were fashioned, for better or for worse. But if I give in to my sorrow that would be a tragedy, because Ambrose Pegram was not worth it. If you give in to yours, you will be throwing away the only legacy from Alfred and Elizabeth that really amounts to anything. Wealth can come and go. This house can stand or fall someday. And they knew that. They cared *only* about you, Charity. They wanted only your happiness. What you make of yourself is what you should be giving back to them, a bouquet of exquisite flowers placed at their grave, its lovely fragrance filling the air, not a straggly thicket of sharp-tipped thorns with your blood on it."

"But I want to see them again!" Charity cried. "I want to feel their arms around me. I want to know that they—"

Julia grabbed the young woman's shoulders and shook her.

"*Listen to me!*" she demanded. "I *abhor* the thought of seeing my Ambrose again now that I can admit to myself what he was. It is good that he is gone. The world has less of a stench each morning I arise from the bed I shared with him."

Julia's expression, which had been stern, softened.

"You have so much *more!*" she said pleadingly. "Your memories have brought you sorrow. Oh, yes, I know that, but, Charity, think of how fortunate you are that you can still look back with such love.

"I do not have that blessing. I feel only shame. I see only the loss of so many years, years that involved my husband building a life for himself and me and our children based upon the terrible things he did, the barbaric things, our wealth growing on the bloody backs and hungry stomachs and ravaged—"

Her face was turning pale, her left hand trembling pitiably.

Charity started to say something, the woman's pain hitting her hard as well, but Julia waved her into silence.

"There was not a single attractive young black woman among our slaves over the years who ever escaped Ambrose's erotic impulses," she went on. "Can you imagine what it was like to know that he was lying whenever he had an excuse for going out certain nights? I told myself that I would have to endure it because of the children. I felt so incapable of running our lives, theirs and mine, by myself.

"That is one of the problems with this society, you know. I love the South. We have so much more here that is life-affirming than the Yankees ever will. They are cold, and they are crass, and I do not see it ever being any different with them. They have been poisoned, Charity, their spirits degraded.

"But here in Dixie, what I detest is that we, as women, live in a man's world. Women are ornaments to be trotted out in public at one function or another. Men run the businesses, the homes, the churches, the government, all of it.

"Their names have been on the ownership papers for every slave who has ever been bought since coloreds were first imported a century or more ago. They have to die before we get any control at all."

"But I have never felt any of that," Charity protested. "I honestly haven't, Julia."

"Only because you had the parents you did, who ran their lives counter to more than one social dictate, sticking with the righteousness held by their consciences instead. And that is what you *have* inherited . . . the enlightened way they looked at the world around them."

"But they still kept slaves," Charity reminded her. "Wasn't that wrong of them? Did their 'enlightenment,' as you call it, stop at the slave quarters behind this house?"

"A hundred years ago, the way they treated your darkies would have been unthinkable," Julia went on. "A hundred years from now, who can say?"

She smiled weakly, a little color returning to her cheeks.

"You must not bury their legacy sooner than the good Lord intended, Charity. You must keep it alive, girl, make it vibrate with *life!* And, please, I beg you, pass it along to your children and hope that they will do the same with *their* own."

Julia stepped back, hands on her hips.

"In a very short while, some extraordinary guests will be gathered together under one roof, this roof, *your* roof. You will come down, will you not?"

"I could not refuse you," admitted Charity.

"Remember that," Julia told her jokingly. "I could be a very good substitute mother to you, dear."

She stepped aside, and Charity started to walk past her into the hallway but stopped for a moment to hug her friend.

"Can we walk together down there, when I am ready?" she asked uncertainly. "I may be a little wobbly yet."

"We'll go arm in arm," replied Julia Pegram confidently. "I would not have it any other way."

As Julia waited, Charity chose a simple outfit, not one of the elaborate dresses complete with a hooped skirt, convinced that even such a dinner, for the reasons behind it in the first place, should not be *usurped* as an occasion to show off the beauty of her wardrobe. The dress she wore was hand-woven silk, mother-of-pearl white, long enough to reach to an inch below her ankles but with no train sweeping the floor behind her. The collar was made of fine lace imported from France; around her waist she wore a narrow, black-satin ribbon.

She greeted everyone with a charming manner that was not at all forced since she was now back among the kind of people she had seen come and go for most of her life. She allowed the men their ritual of kissing the back of her hand while the women put their arms around her and whispered words of sympathy and help.

Some of you, she thought, *despised the way my father treated our coloreds. Where were you when they were still alive and could have been cheered by your support?*

But she kept such words from her lips, however tempted she was to utter them out loud.

Robert E. Lee sat to her right, Abraham Lincoln to her left.

"I wonder if I should change my name," she said, trying to be cheerful after they all had sat down at the dinner table.

"And what would you be called then?" Stapleton Telford Culp, who was next to Lee, leaned forward and asked.

"Under the circumstances, I think that Mason-Dixon would be appropriate!" she exclaimed mischievously.

Even Culp laughed, and not just politely.

A concession made to the times was that the slaves be seated last. Initially, Marmaduke resisted even this small matter when Culp presented it to him.

EVENTUALLY, THOUGH, MARMADUKE gave in, grumbling, and do did Fulkerson.

Only Little Isaiah and Hester remained in the kitchen until the main course was served, and then they, too, sat down at the second table.

Culp's wife, Sue Beth, a thin, pale woman with a rather sour demeanor, was obviously uncomfortable dining in the same room with the slaves, but Julia Pegram felt very much at ease, and the men did not seem to have any trouble.

Since even such a large dining room had practical space problems, given the number of guests ultimately invited, seating the members of the two military groups who were able to attend could have been a problem except for the half-dozen who volunteered to sit with the slaves, all of them Southern men from the South Carolina militia.

It happened to be the soldiers from Lincoln's militia who seemed reluctant, however subtly they betrayed their feelings, a fact that, after dinner, Lee did not fail to comment on as he and Lincoln stood by themselves in the massive parlor that had often doubled as a ballroom for well-attended dances.

"Those who are supposed to hate black people are the first to volunteer to sit with the slaves," Lee said in a low voice, "while others who could be sent to battle on the pretext of overthrowing such a horrible institution as slavery somehow hold back, not quite able to stomach the simple act of breaking bread with the very people who someday may be the object of their valor."

"I have never claimed that all bigots are southerners," Lincoln responded.

"So, then, Yankees do not universally love their black brothers; is that it?"

"They do not."

"And is it not true that Sojourner Truth, whom you know well, received her freedom many years ago from Yankee slave-owners in New York State?"

Lincoln was becoming very uncomfortable and did not answer.

"Well, sir," Lee spoke gravely but with an undercurrent of glee, "perhaps any invasion at the outset of a future war should come from the South instead of the North. If your abolitionists can hint that the owning of another human being is a wrong that must be absolved and their views are praised so universally by the Yankees, why should the South not feel *compelled* to rub the North's nose in its hypocrisy?"

Lincoln did not respond with outrage.

"I wish I could rebut what you say," he went on.

"Yet you cannot?"

"I cannot, as you say. There are nights when I am unable to sleep because I dream of cannons and rifles and sharp bayonets and the screaming wounded as their blood is staining the rich soil of this land."

No one else was in the parlor with them just then. The rest were outside, enjoying the crisp, clean night air and the sight of a sky clearer than any had seen in a long time.

Lincoln puffed out his cheeks then sucked them in again.

"Have you dreamed accordingly, Robert?" he asked.

"I have. I see myself standing in the midst of the worst of battlefields with the greatest number of dead and dying, the most awful carnage, and I am screaming, 'Was it worth *this?*' We would have given all blacks the kind of life they should have if you had just left us alone and trusted the decent and honorable among my people to act henceforth as we have always lived.'"

. . . the kind of life they should have.

Those words rang alarm bells in Lincoln's mind.

"But who determines what that life is going to be like?" he posed.

Another voice interrupted theirs.

"I think Robert E. Lee has already answered that, Mr. Lincoln."

Charity.

She was standing in the doorway, looking slightly uncomfortable for having eavesdropped so blatantly, but she also had to confess to being caught up in what for her was a singularly important matter.

"How so, Miss Charity?" Lincoln asked politely.

"Men and women who are like my father and my mother," Charity went on, "and, yes, like me, sir."

Lincoln thought he saw an opening.

"Will you now voluntarily offer to release your slaves and grant them unfettered freedom?" he ventured.

"I will, sir. But none will take me up on that which they rejected more than once from my father."

Lincoln saw that he had misjudged the situation and sought, as most politicians did, to make the best of it.

"Good!" he proclaimed. "That speaks well of you, of course, and I would not have expected otherwise, frankly, from the daughter of such a man as Alfred Littlepage."

Lincoln paused for emphasis. When he spoke again, he did so slowly.

"But how many others could I expect from the South to hold the very same view? Can you answer me that?"

Charity was ready for him.

"More than you might imagine, Mr. Lincoln. Yet all this talk of armed conflict hardly strengthens *their* hand, sir, for it instead aids the purposes of those men who hold much more extreme views, pushing the two groups together, to their mutual dismay."

"How can that be?" asked Lincoln with skepticism.

Charity glanced toward Lee, who simply winked at her.

"If war comes, the rest of us will have to join with them. Were my father still alive, he would have done the same thing because—"

Her voice broke at that, but she forced herself to go on.

"He would have to say that he abhors the slavery-at-all-costs doctrine that *they* follow, but, in his mind, the greater evil would be to surrender to an invasion fostered by commanders dominated by those political forces that had little interest in the rights of black people but instead acted according to just one overriding passion."

"And what passion is that?" Lincoln asked.

"To see a South that is emasculated, sir, made subservient to their every whim, as they trample on the sovereign rights of every state in Dixie."

It was then that Lee interpolated himself.

"I, who detest slavery, would fight to the death alongside those demanding its continuance," he said, "and I would do so for principle's sake . . . for the protection of our families, our homes, our land, our independence."

Lee's anger, not normal for him in a "social" environment, was apparent.

"We did not throw off the shackles of monarchy less than a century ago only to have those shackles reimposed by homegrown despots, those who may not be so unwise as to claim the title of king but, rather, bear that of senator, representative, or president."

"But no one man can stop any of this," Lincoln told them. "Whatever my warm feelings regarding much of what you have said, I hold only influence in my own local area; that is all."

"Is that all?" Lee pressed. "Be honest with yourself as well as with this young lady and me. Refute certain rumors, and I shall believe you."

"Rumors?" Lincoln repeated, trying ineptly to play dumb.

"That you might run for the highest office in this country. Can you deny this?"

Lincoln looked from Lee to Charity.

"I cannot," he replied. "But even I could not be what you obviously hope, a latent champion of your cause. For what we have been discussing is an irreversible tide sweeping over us. We cannot stop history."

"But history is written by those who are its participants," Lee countered vigorously. "If Napoleon had not lost at Waterloo, if Alexander were less or more than he was, if Constantine—"

Sputtering a bit, Lee reigned in his emotions and then added, "We need time to do peacefully what the abolitionists want to accomplish by cannon, rifle fire, and bayonet."

Lincoln knew what point the other man was making.

"I understand," he replied. "But the moment, I am afraid, has passed. Your ideas are sensible and praiseworthy, and they represent a moderate approach that tests the patience of Americans but does not shed their blood. Yet they are doomed, sir, as doomed as anything noble and fine has ever been in this sin-cursed world."

"How might that be?" Lee probed.

"Some change regarding slavery is manifestly overdue. Delays in correcting its evils have given the other side the advantage it needs, and the wisdom not to let the opportunity slip through its fingers. What if Napoleon had won at Waterloo but lost elsewhere, how much difference would that have made?"

"But slavery's evils have been overstated."

"Are such words coming from a man who has publicly and with great conviction stated his opposition to slavery?"

"And here stands before me someone who defends an economic system that bestows upon black people another kind of slavery, but slavery just the same!"

"That is a very old argument. I would have thought you could have concocted another one. I tire of hearing—"

"But a truth that is as fresh and vital as a morning sunrise, Mr. Lincoln," Lee interrupted, which was hardly customary for him, "sending its beauty and its warmth throughout the land. And you must remember this, sir: God's inspired Word, the Holy Bible, is crammed *full* of old truths that have not changed even slightly for eighteen very long centuries. Only God can replace them, not some political committee or dark, shadowy group of mere conspiring men, and to be thoroughly honest, I *have* never sensed His willingness to do so."

It would have been reasonable of Charity Elizabeth Littlepage and Robert Edward Lee to expect that Abraham Lincoln would find their company intolerable and decide to leave, though giving a nod to civility by coolly excusing himself.

Instead he paused and then spoke, "As you may have surmised, while I abhor slavery, I am not an abolitionist as such. I doubt that some abolitionists would be what they are if they understood, fully, the position of the hard-liners.

"And while I find the treatment of black people in all regions of the nation often abominable, I worry every night over whether they are capable of assuming *any* of the responsibilities that freedom would bring, or whether they ever will be. I wonder if they are not in fact inferior, though by acknowledging that possibility, yea, likelihood, I am not sanctioning the abuse they face routinely, for they are still human."

Lee appreciated the other man's unexpected candor.

"Are you aware that 'the treatment of black people' is actually far worse in the North than here in the South?" Lee said. "Are you aware of the crimes perpetrated against these poor folk by employers who warn them of the loss of their freedom if they do not work their fingers into bloody stumps for trifling wages?"

Apparently Lincoln had not known anything of that, or at least he feigned ignorance rather expertly.

"What are your sources?" he asked.

"Southern journalists of high repute covering the news in northern cities . . . and please do not insult my intelligence by expecting me to believe that these reports are trumped up in any way to make the North seem like a hotbed of hypocrisy. Integrity is not in short supply among *my* countrymen, Mr. Lincoln."

Lincoln winced at the truth of that.

"Nor so with mine," he said with a weariness that seemed like some black cloak he had abruptly pulled around himself. "You are fortunate to have considerably fewer competing voices in your political environment. As for me, I must face the moderate abolitionists, the radical abolitionists, and the country club abolitionists, which means navigating along those who favor a political solution and the others who will accept only a violent, armed one, and I have not even mentioned the conservatives who want nothing at all to happen, preferring the present situation as the lesser of the evils spread out before us."

Lee saw that Lincoln was a man grappling as honestly as he knew how with an issue made complex by too many philosophies.

"You cannot be called a hypocrite," he said. "I will say that much for you."

"And I must make the same statement about you, my good man," Lincoln replied. "Of course, I never did think that of the illustrious Robert Edward Lee, for I have been admiring you for a long time now."

Lee was caught off guard.

"For how long has that been?" he asked.

"Since you served with such distinction in the Mexican War and since your years as superintendent at West Point," Lincoln told him.

"Do you know about my . . . father?"

Lee's manner had softened, especially as memories of Light Horse Harry Lee rose to the surface of his mind.

"Oh, I know about this man, this valorous human being," Lincoln responded. "He was someone I would have been honored to know."

"He is my model, Mr. Lincoln. I look to him as an example for everything I am or will ever be as a man of the military."

"And you do so rightly, Mr. Lee."

Charity discreetly left the two of them and stepped out into the hallway. All of the other guests had left. The slaves were cleaning up.

"I am retiring for the evening," she called to Little Isaiah. "Will you please see our two guests out as they leave?"

"I'll do that; I surely will. I hope you sleeps well, Miss Charity," he replied warmly. "I hope angels carry you off to sleep this night."

"I am sure they will."

He started to return to his duties.

"Little Isaiah?" she asked.

He faced her again.

"Yes, Miss Charity?"

"May those angels be with you as well, dear friend," she told him.

He nodded as he said, "I's 'pecting they will."

Charity went back inside and started up the stairs, smiling as she heard Abraham Lincoln and Robert E. Lee continue to talk in earnest. Later that night, a bit restless even though she was finally back in a familiar bed, she arose to get a drink of water, not expecting to hear their voices at that hour. But she was wrong, for their conversation still met her ears, voices with no longer any seeming rancor in them.

If it could only last, she thought, sighing with a weariness born of what Alfred and Elizabeth Littlepage had taught her about life.

Even so, swathed in the will-o'-the-wisp idealism of that moment, Charity returned to bed and was able to sleep more peacefully the rest of that night, dreaming of a young man in a sick bed who was calling her name.

72

C HARITY DECIDED THE next morning as she walked up the steps to the hospital that Billy Mendenhall really was quite handsome, with striking blond hair and eyes so blue that they seemed almost like reflections of the Atlantic Ocean on an especially clear day.

I think I could look at nothing but your eyes, she thought, *and forget the rest of you, but then that would mean missing your smile, your perfectly formed nose, an aristocratic sort of nose, come to think of it. If not for that Yankee accent of yours, you could pass for a southern boy.*

She blushed as she thought of his dimple.

It's a deep one, she reminded herself, *and your jaw is so strong-looking.*

Chuckling to herself, Charity decided that he actually had what could be considered only one physical imperfection.

Your ears are just a bit too big, she recalled, *but that doesn't matter at all. The rest of you is just right.*

Actually, she had seen quite a bit of the rest of Billy Mendenhall during the course of holding him in the wagon and while watching as much of the operation performed by Abraham Lincoln as she could manage without turning away.

His shirt had to be taken off, and she was able to see that he had an athlete's upper body, a well-formed chest with just the slightest amount of hair, a muscle-rippled stomach, tapered hips, broad shoulders, and muscular arms.

So warm and firm, she remembered. *I wish—*

She blushed again as she reached the front door of the doctor's office, opened it, and went inside, hoping that no one noticed the redness of her cheeks. But Billy was not in his room, and she was momentarily concerned, seeking out the doctor's wife to find out if anything was wrong.

"For land's sake, no!" the older woman exclaimed. "He's in right fine condition this morning."

She started to walk away.

"Where is he?" Charity asked.

"Outside," the woman replied, acting very distracted. "Please, no more questions. One of the young men from our own militia is not doing well, and I . . . I—"

Charity could sense anger in her tone.

"I am sorry to have troubled you," she apologized.

Rather than let it go at that, the woman added, "He's about the age of your Billy Mendenhall. He needs much more attention."

Charity stepped aside and let her pass.

So that's it! she told herself. *If Billy were southern, it would be a different story. Since he isn't, I should never be allowing myself to fall in love with him.*

She caught her breath. That was the first time she admitted something to herself that apparently seemed rather obvious to the people around her.

. . . allowing myself to fall in love with him.

That was happening, and she could not deny it. But then she knew it was hardly a surprising outcome. Billy's bravery combined with his good looks and his flirtatious manner that seemed more charming than presumptuous were certainly not ingredients that would kill any interest in him.

How could I help myself, Lord? she prayed, recalling again the long parade of arranged outings with young men she had had since her parents started allowing her to court the elite of South Carolinian society. *What am I to think when I dream of him at night and he is holding me in his arms?*

In the doorway she saw Billy Mendenhall out on the lawn. He was on crutches, and he was talking to several of the southern soldiers, all of them smiling and shaking hands and embracing as much as their condition allowed in each case.

They nearly died together, these young men, Charity told herself. *There are no barriers now as far as they are concerned. But for people who didn't go through any of that, it's the same as ever, hatred on both sides of the Mason-Dixon.*

"Come on over!" Billy called as he glanced in her direction and smiled from ear-to-ear.

Charity walked though she felt like running.

"See you later," Billy told the other men.

Charity recognized one of the soldiers, a dark-haired, handsome young man sitting away from his comrades. His leg had had to be amputated.

"Johnny Poague!" she exclaimed. "I didn't know—"

The young man's leg had been amputated at a point in medical history when the techniques for doing so had evolved little from as far back as medieval Europe.

"I wasn't with the militia sent to bring you home," he said. "The governor called us to the western part of the state."

"What for?" Charity asked.

"Some rioting darkies. They created a fuss. Most of them had to be shot. None of us died, but a few were wounded. Some, like me, will never be the same."

He started weeping as he pressed his hands against his face.

"Don't look at me, Charity. There's enough shame already. I can't stand much more."

She bent down in front of him.

"What can I do to help?" she asked honestly.

Billy Mendenhall had been standing nearby, but now he stepped back, respecting Charity's privacy and showing no hint of jealousy.

"You never did want me," Johnny told her. "Now nobody else will."

She grabbed his hand.

"It won't be that way," she reassured him. "Not everyone—"

"Charity, Charity . . . ," he interrupted her, his voice at a whisper. "Our time is past. Your new friend is waiting for you. Go to him."

Tears were coming to her eyes.

"I feel so bad, Johnny."

"Don't waste those tears on me. You're going to cry often, you know, because of Billy being a Yankee. That won't go down well with the folks around here."

"And you?"

"If I haven't slit my throat out of self-pity by the time you up and marry him, I want to be at your wedding."

"Don't talk like that," she begged him.

"You don't want me to attend?"

"I mean what you said about . . . about—"

"Killing myself?"

"It's wrong, Johnny. And anyway, folks will stand by you."

"And give me work?"

"Yes!"

"Out of pity? Is that what I am to expect from the good people of this community? That's not something I could tolerate, Charity."

She wiped her eyes with a handkerchief and offered it to him, but he waved it aside.

"At first it might be like that," Charity acknowledged, opposed as she was to lying to anybody about anything, regardless of what the circumstances might be. "But you will earn everything you're paid. That's so much better than things are up North, of course, where the human heart is replaced by a dollar sign."

"I can't ask you to be holding my hand all the time," Johnny told her. "A man's got to stand on his own two feet."

Another voice entered the conversation.

Billy Mendenhall's, as he walked back to where he had been standing minutes before.

"My brother lost both legs during the Mexican War," he said, "I know what he has had to endure. I would be glad to stand with Charity and help you. I think you can get through this. It won't be easy, but it will happen."

"But you're a Yankee. Why bother with a son of Dixie?"

"Your family and mine have been on the same side for a long time—during the Revolution and in the War of 1812 and against the Mexicans. We're all Americans. We've all lost relatives and friends, Yankees and Dixie boys dying together. Why shouldn't I want to do something for you?"

"Speak the truth," Johnny said. "Isn't it really because Charity's involved?"

Billy hesitated, glancing at her then back to the other young man.

"You're right," he replied. "But now it's your turn to speak the truth: Wouldn't you be volunteering to do exactly what I have suggested if the situation were reversed and I were the one in your position right now? Would it be so wrong to want to do something for you and Charity?"

Johnny blinked his eyes several times, definitely wanting to avoid crying anymore under the present circumstances, but he failed.

"I would be honored . . . ," he started to say, then had to clear his throat before he could finish. "I would be honored to let you pitch in . . . along with Charity."

Billy bent down and hugged Johnny.

"That's good," he whispered, "that's so good."

As Charity watched, she could not have agreed more.

~73~

Charity spent most of the next few days dividing her time between the plantation and the doctor's home, for time with Billy by himself, as well as with Billy and Johnny Poague.

Vultures closing in.

That was what certain businessmen seemed to be, those who had come to "honor" her father now trying to maneuver themselves into favorable positions with his wet-behind-the-ears successor, and not all of them trying to do so with any subtlety.

One of the more extreme types was represented by an individual named Linton Halsted Barksdale, someone she remembered spottily from his visits to the house when she was five or six years old and perhaps later. Alfred Littlepage seemed grim in his presence each time, and she had noted that this was not the way he acted with other men, sharing some moments of humor with them, recalling memories that touched each of them.

You never seemed comfortable around this one, she told herself. *Was it his appearance or something much deeper, darker?*

Linton Halsted Barksdale was the fattest human being Charity had ever seen, his substantial weight not distributed evenly but by far the bulk of it resting in the region of his stomach, which protruded to such an extent, and shaped as it was, round like a fair-sized cannonball, that anyone seeing him for the first time could only stare and wonder, perversely, if somehow he was about to give birth to a herd of piglets.

His face did nothing to dispel that impression.

It seemed merely a smaller but no less round version of his grotesque stomach, with eyes so tiny that one wondered whether he could have normal vision or was like a horse with blinders restricting his sight. By contrast, his ears were large, thin, shaped just a bit like an elephant's.

When Barksdale engaged in conversation, though, any perception of his appearance partially gave way to a profoundly different reaction about a mind that seemed, under the circumstances, anachronistically brilliant.

And that voice . . . deep and rich . . . the voice of an operatic baritone trapped inside a loathsome pile of flesh!

She was in her father's study, going over documents dealing with his estate, when she was told that Barksdale wanted to see her about some "family business."

She nearly gagged at the thought of having to be in his presence.

"He is so awful!" she exclaimed, remembering that when she was a child, she had run, screaming, from him the first time she saw him at the front door.

"You's right, Miss Charity," Little Isaiah replied, "but might be better to have him as a friend than an enemy."

. . . as a friend than an enemy.

"I cannot understand how my father could even associate with a man like that, if *man* he must be called," she said.

"Massa Alfred never let color or—"

She looked at Little Isaiah, her cheeks blushing.

"—or anything else on the outside stop him from accepting another human being," she added, nodding.

"You speak the way he did, Miss Charity."

For a moment she wondered to herself if she was going too far in her adverse reaction to Barksdale.

"But the inside, as far as I can tell, is no better than what we can see," she protested. "This Barksdale is truly a dishonest and—and—"

Little Isaiah spoke in a whisper, hoping she would not be offended nor consider him to be interfering.

"Find out for yourself. You have an advantage over him."

He was smiling wisely.

"What is that?" Charity asked.

"You know what he is like, but he don't know nothin' about *you*, Miss Charity."

She had to admit that Little Isaiah was right.

"He probably thinks that I am quite empty-headed, like many of the girls around here, flighty as they are, and certainly no match for someone like him."

"That's his undoin' . . . it sho is."

"He comes here expecting a lamb."

"And finds a tiger, Miss Charity!"

She kissed Little Isaiah on the cheek.

"Bless you," she said for about the thousandth time since she had been old enough to talk and express herself with clarity.

She thought Little Isaiah might have blushed, as was often the case when she spoke as she did then, but there was no way to be sure.

Money . . .

Linton Halsted Barksdale had come not to express his sympathies, although he made a pretense of doing just that, but rather because Alfred Littlepage owed him money, though he did manage to seem surprisingly respectful.

Charity asked him to join her in the sitting room.

"Would you like something to drink?" she asked, noticing that he was sweating as they walked down the hallway. "It must be quite hot outside."

"Thank you," he replied. "Just a good old mint julep would be fine."

She called to Hester, who was hovering nearby.

Not long after they were seated, he had reentered the room, two glasses in hand, each with three small precious cubes of ice.

"You have no female slaves now, do you?" Barksdale asked.

"I do not. My father was in the process of locating one or two when he died. Savilla and Violet are going to be difficult to replace since they were so special."

Her discipline made that reply seem easy, but it was so hard for Charity to speak those words acknowledging once again that her father was gone.

"I could have helped your father," Barksdale interjected. "It seems that I have any number of good females on my plantation all the time."

Trying to appear nonchalant, he began to rummage among the contents of the leather case, much like a saddlebag, that he had placed on his lap.

"Is it proper for a white woman to be alone with all these niggers?" he asked without glancing up, feigning nonchalance.

"I have been alone with them often over the years," Charity replied.

"But with one or both of your parents nearby, I assume."

"I appreciate your concern."

"I am thinking only of the danger to your reputation, Miss Charity."

"My reputation?"

"People do talk."

"About what?"

"In this case, well, it had best be left unsaid."

"Then why did you raise it in the first place?"

"Only to alert you."

Charity smiled as insincerely as she could manage, which was hardly difficult, sitting as she was across from Linton Halsted Barksdale.

"You are only interested in my welfare, then?" Charity asked, knowing that any such motive was the least likely with such a man.

"I liked Alfred and your mother . . . fine, fine people. I know they invested a great deal of effort in your upbringing."

"Invested, sir? You make me sound like one of my father's business ventures."

Barksdale waved his pudgy hand through the air.

"That was not my intention. It is just that you can hardly be too careful, what with people's dirty minds and all that."

Charity's impatience and suspicions were growing.

"Can we hurry this along?" she asked.

Barksdale cleared his throat and continued, "I have taken over the investment firm that handled many of your father's acquisitions."

"And when did you do this, Mr. Barksdale?" asked Charity.

"Perhaps a week ago," he replied, keeping his face emotionless.

"Very good timing."

"How do you mean that?"

"That you became the new owner so soon after my father's murder."

"Do you find this strange?"

"How quickly do you normally make decisions as to where you spend your money?"

"I usually require much more time . . . ," he started to say.

"But not in this case, I gather?"

He sat, unmoving, silent.

"What enabled you to change this time, to make up your mind in just a day or two?" Charity pressed.

"I saw that no one with experience would be at the helm," Barksdale said, "and I wanted to be able to help by—"

"Why would you not simply have knocked on the door, as you did a few minutes ago, and offered to extend this 'help' directly?"

Barksdale seemed much like a cow chewing her cud as he hesitated, his jaw moving but remaining shut.

"Please speak honestly," Charity told him.

"Because I did not think that you knew enough to make an even remotely intelligent decision," he finally replied.

"And by buying that investment firm, which has a contract with my father, you could make those decisions for me. Is that about it, Mr. Barksdale?"

He was obviously uncomfortable but no less determined.

"There *is* a clause that, in the event of Alfred Littlepage's death, your mother would take over, but should the two of them become deceased before you reached the age of twenty-five, regarding the matters involving the firm, the board of directors would assume control."

"But that must have been because my father had great confidence in the men serving on the board. How many of these men remain?"

"None. I dismissed them all. There is now no such board at all. I make whatever decisions are necessary."

"How much control does that give you, Mr. Barksdale?"

"I believe about fifteen or sixteen percent of your father's assets are liquid, and not subject to my . . . expertise."

"And you hold sway over the eighty-five percent that are in land holdings and other such investments?"

"That is quite correct."

His lips seemed to be formed in a permanent sneer, as much from his outlook on life as from the pipe that poked out from a pocket in his jacket.

Looking like some South Borneo warthog ready to charge, Barksdale smiled without warmth, a cold, reflexive movement.

My father was right, she thought. *You are a sinister man who should never be trusted.*

"I can do a great deal to help, Miss Littlepage," he told her.

"And, also, if you were so inclined, to hurt," Charity added pointedly, her view of Barksdale clearheaded.

"It is possible that I might . . . if, as you say, I were so inclined," he agreed.

"What do you want me to do now," she asked, "other than to avoid bedding down with one of the slaves?"

"Your sarcasm is apparent and not appreciated."

"You are free to be as indignant over my sarcasm as I am over the insinuations that generated it in the first place."

Clearly exasperated, Barksdale fell back against the chair in which he had been sitting, and it creaked under the strain.

"I am trying very much to like you as much as I did your parents," he whined.

"And I am trying not to *dislike* you to the extent that they did," Charity responded.

"I came here to help, Charity Elizabeth Littlepage, and yet you treat me as you have been doing. How can you justify that? I have some power, as you know. Is your conduct wise or, I might suggest, rather foolhardy?"

"Whatever label you care to use, I can say this: You can be stopped," she remarked, gritting her teeth as her heart began to pound faster from the escalating tension between the two of them, their surface calmness about as firm as custard.

"I suppose I can be, but the cost might prove substantially higher than you would ever calculate."

"You are not talking about just the financial cost, are you?"

"As you say . . . ," he replied while getting to his feet, though the effort he expended in doing this seemed almost comically exaggerated.

According Barksdale a civility that she neither felt nor he deserved, Charity escorted the man to the front door. As he was walking outside, he stopped and said over his shoulder, "Pause for a moment, Miss Charity, and consider the welfare of that young soldier, why don't you? I surely hope his medical treatment is adequate. But someone in his condition, I mean, however unfortunately, can deteriorate without warning, you know . . . or explanation."

It was as though she had not heard him for a few seconds, his words not grasped because the images they engendered were so unexpected and awful.

. . . someone in his condition . . . can deteriorate without warning . . . or explanation.

Barksdale was nearly at the front gate when she ran after him and stepped in front of him, blocking his way.

"You foul—!" Charity started to say, but she was so emotional that any other words momentarily lodged in her throat.

"I have to be on my way," he told her "I would appreciate it if you would step aside."

"You just threatened someone who nearly lost his life helping to defend my life and the lives of others, some of them *from right here in the South!*"

"I know all about that," he said. "But this Mendenhall is, after all, a Yankee. His death now would be of no consequence to anyone, except to someone who well might be doing more for him than dabbing his feverish brow with a cool, wet cloth!"

A smirk on that contemptible face drove Charity over the edge, and she slapped him across one bloated cheek. Still a bit weak due to her wounds, she thought that she had hit Barksdale with little actual force, but she was wrong.

Barksdale stumbled sideways.

"No one does that to me!" he screamed.

"I just did," she said. "Get off this property now!"

The noise had reached the slaves' quarters. Little Isaiah and Hester and the others were rushing from around the eastern side of the plantation house.

"Miss Charity!" Little Isaiah yelled, trying to quickly survey the situation. "Is you all right?"

Barksdale sniffed the air with contempt.

"Why am I not surprised?" he growled, "A bunch of stinking darkies running to your rescue? Now you can hurry on to the bed of that Yankee lover of yours!"

Hearing that, Little Isaiah let out a roar of rage and barreled toward him.

Eyes widening, Barksdale turned and ran.

Out of breath by the time he reached his awaiting carriage, he had to be helped into it by the two slaves who had been sitting in the front seat.

Barely able to talk, he barked something to the driver about taking off immediately.

Under other circumstances, Charity and the slaves would have burst out laughing, given his bizarre appearance.

"How could he talk to you like that, Miss Charity?" Little Isaiah asked. "What kind of man speaks to a lady as he did?"

"Someone who has no respect for himself cannot respect other people," she said, her face red, her body covered with perspiration.

"Sorry you had to come home to this!" apologized Hester. "It ain't right after all you's been through."

"This is a world in which there is very little that is right anymore," she remarked sadly, "and it's going to get worse."

74

THE ABRASIVENESS AND seething menace embodied so grotesquely in the bloated form of Linton Halsted Barksdale was an unsettling continuation of a pattern that made sleep that night difficult for Charity. Those other businessmen were nowhere near as repulsive as "Pigface Barksdale," their manner much more polished. But the end result was the same: taking advantage of a young woman in a way that none would have dared while Alfred Littlepage was yet alive.

Barksdale in particular was the sort of man her father would have dealt with decisively, either by having him thrown in jail or taking him to court, the latter allowing Alfred Littlepage a forum in which he probably would have served as the lawyer for his side and done so with such effectiveness that any counsel of Barksdale's would have found a coherent defense futile.

"I think I should have studied law when I was much younger," Alfred had mused coincidentally the year before his death. "What would you say about that?"

Charity had been sitting at the dinner table that evening while her mother was out in the cooking kitchen, fussing with some special dessert she had gotten into her mind to prepare, leaving the two of them momentarily by themselves.

"You have the money, the connections," she reminded him. "You could do anything you want. Why not pursue it?"

He seemed to be seriously evaluating the possibility.

"Perhaps I could be your partner," she said, the idea of more than passing interest to her.

"Splendid!" Alfred told her. "We would need a license, but that should not be particularly complicated to obtain."

He chuckled robustly as he added, "After all, that gangly fellow up in Illinois, Abraham Lincoln, is a lawyer."

"And you make *him* out to be a hillbilly," she said, not because she thought he would want to hear this, but it was something she considered true.

"Well, Charity, that is hardly an accomplishment of any special merit since he is a hillbilly to begin with!"

"His only clients are poor people, I hear."

"Oh, no, I think Lincoln has a bigger practice than just some poor white trash and perhaps a colored or two. But I see no intellectual depth to the man. He seems to have some folksy witticism or another for every occasion but nothing more than that. Shallowness is never a virtue."

They talked until dessert was served, and, then, afterward, until midnight.

"Lawyers have to be actors," Alfred said at one point. "They have to be angry in front of a judge or a jury or both. They have to be amusing. There are times when they must feign an almost childlike innocence if that is what it takes to win over men and women who have the power to determine the outcome of a certain case."

Charity asked her father to investigate the opportunities for starting a law firm.

"You really are interested, aren't you?" he asked.

"I am," she told him. "I know, as a woman, I would be talked about behind my back, and you are certain to be accused of nepotism."

"That is very true, Charity," he agreed, admiring her lucid view of the situation, "but neither of us has ever been particularly restricted by the weight of community bias."

And so it went one evening with her father, a dream taking shape that both found tantalizing without either aware that it would never be anything else . . .

THE NEXT MORNING, Charity had Hester saddle up one of the horses.

"You going to the graves?" he asked.

Puzzled, she looked at him and asked, "How did you know?"

"You couldn't go 'fore now, what with looking after Billy Mendenhall and the dinner last night and all, and I's guessing' that you ain't gonna wait no longer, not you, Miss Charity."

"If I don't cry now, it has nothing to do with my feelings for you," she told him. "I doubt that there are very many tears left inside me these days."

"They'll come," Hester assured her. "When you stand 'fore those graves and see them names on the cold stones, you'll cry, Miss Charity, you'll cry."

She held his hand for a moment and, after letting go, climbed up on the back of the horse that he had prepared for her.

"Somebody can go with you," Hester said. "You's not havin' to do this alone less'n you need to, Miss Charity."

She shook her head.

"I have learned that, with a crowd of people around me, I can still feel . . . I can—" she started to say.

"Let me git another horse and follow 'long behind you," Hester persisted. "I won't intrude. You's not gonna see me at all, but if you need me, I'll be there."

"Yes . . . ," she relented. "Yes, I think that would be a good idea after all."

"Go 'head. It won't take me long."

She gently nudged the side of her horse with her foot. It started as it had been trained at a slow gait, moved into a trot, and then settled into a pleasant canter, the wind stirring its long, silky mane and cooling its muscular body.

Charity's hair was blown outward in much the same way. She could have worn a bonnet but decided that feeling the wind touching her scalp and weaving its way through the red strands of her hair that had been such a source of joy and pride to her parents was worth the risk of being labeled disheveled by anyone who happened to notice her.

At the pace maintained by the mare, Charity should have been able to reach the cemetery in about fifteen minutes. But that was not to be. Someone in a carriage pulled out in front of her, blocking the road, someone she did not recognize.

She pulled back on the reins and stopped.

"Charity Littlepage?" the man asked, standing up.

For the second time in a few weeks, Charity felt dangerously vulnerable and hoped that Hester was not far behind her.

"What do you want, stranger?" she asked, remaining seated, both hands clutched around the reins and one another.

"Not your harm," he replied.

She looked him over, saw the broad shoulders, the long unkempt hair, and the thick lips, lips that seemed out of place in someone who was not black.

A scar cut through his left eyebrow. And his smallish nose was pushed back until it was nearly flat, like a bulldog's.

One of Max Cutshaw's men!

Charity thought this might be the case, and she was about to ask him when he spoke again.

"I risk harm for myself by coming here," he muttered. "You have no reason to be scared of me. Be scared of others but not of me."

. . . *be scared of others.*

"The men responsible for wounding me and murdering my parents?" Charity asked. "Is that who you mean?"

The man nodded.

"They're only hired guns like me," he told her. "I've killed before; that's the way I make my living, but I can't do it no more."

"Why have you changed?"

"It's hard to explain, miss."

"I'm willing to listen."

"I've worked for some fine people."

"How could anyone who pays for the murder of another human being ever be considered a fine person?"

"They're smart-looking, handsome, dress real fine, have manners, come from high-society families. I'm dirt next to them. They have the money to spend, and it might as well go my way. I feel as though they're pigs, and I'm rolling in the mud along with them."

Charity stopped breathing for a few seconds.

"Why did you use the word *pigs?*" she asked.

"Some folks make me feel like that. They make me feel dirty even as I'm spending the money they pay me."

"Any folks in particular that you could tell me about, Mr. . . . . Mr.—?"

"Just call me Kane. That's all you need to know."

"Tell me about some of the people who hire you."

"You mean the ones who did the job on your parents, don't you?"

"Yes."

Kane bit his lower lip.

"You seem nervous," Charity told him. "You implied you were putting yourself in danger for coming here."

"I am."

"How did you know where I was heading?"

"I've been watching, at a distance, for some while now."

"And so when you saw me heading in this direction, you guessed I would be going on directly to where my parents are buried."

"Where Barksdale's orders put them," Kane said, announcing the most shocking revelation in a manner that was deceptively casual.

Charity blinked several times, somehow not really surprised but, still, stunned that even someone who looked and acted like that repulsive individual could have gone after her parents' estate in such a manner.

"Did something go wrong?" she asked desperately. "Was there an accident that made everything turn out worse than he intended?"

"I can see why people call you a good Christian," replied Kane. "You try not to see evil. You try to tell yourself that some good can be found in the most foul individual."

He sneered as he added, "Well, you are partially right; this creature is 'most foul.' But you are very wrong when you think he might be capable of the slightest good. He's not, Miss Charity, nor has he ever been, as far as I can tell."

"I have to tell the sheriff," she said.

"Go to the graves first," Kane urged. "Don't let Barksdale or anyone else rob you of this moment."

"Why?" she muttered. "Why did he do this? What could have made him—?"

"I know the answers. I'll tell you on the way home."

Charity nodded, too tired to argue.

"I'll stay nearby . . . ," he said. "Barksdale would want you dead now more than ever if he knew that I had told you everything."

And so ne followed behind her, Charity not happy to have him at her back, despite the convincing little speech he had given.

~75~

Not adjacent to the community's church, which was unusual, the cemetery rested in a spot that, appropriately, was termed Two Knolls since it was between a pair of small, rounded hillocks and adjoined the boundaries of four separate plantations. It extended gracefully over a parcel of land maintained and used by the entire community, excluding any slaves, who had their own burial places provided by black churches in that region, cemeteries that were ill-kept in comparison to Two Knolls, which was a model of proper care, with lawns that were cut to a reasonable height, rose-bushes at intervals throughout, and in the center, an elegant mimosa tree.

Father, father, that was one of your contributions, Charity thought. *You had seen it during one of your trips abroad many years ago and wanted to see if seeds from one in China could be brought to the United States so a mimosa could grow on American soil.*

Alfred Littlepage proved that this could be done. The tree grew even as the number of plots at Two Knolls increased. Twenty years before, there were only a handful of graves, but that figure eventually tripled. And the mimosa became the beautiful centerpiece that Charity could see from the front gate.

She pushed on the gate, which was about as high as her waist, and walked inside, recalling a special time with her mother when the subject was death.

"You have to know certain things; you have to be aware," Elizabeth Littlepage had said the day Charity had become thirteen years old. "One of these is that death is a part of life. You have to face both. Someday, your father and I will be gone. Someday you will have to know what to do in order to take care of our bodies but also how to face life without us."

She had not wanted to listen, had turned away, covering her ears. But Elizabeth had persisted, gently drawing Charity's hands away.

"You must listen, dearest," her mother said. "You cannot pretend this will never happen. You have to face—"

"Would you be able to survive *without me?*" Charity asked.

Elizabeth stepped back, her own emotions strong then.

"We would not want to survive," she admitted. "We would draw this house around us and become very determined never to venture from it again, whatever the consequences. We would let everything that this family has built up over the years collapse, because without you at the center, sweet angel, the rest of it is meaningless. Finally, your father and I would stand side by side out under the stars one night and look up at the heavens and *demand*—forgive me, dear Lord—but demand that He take us from this world that had become so cold, so lonely and . . . and . . ."

Charity reacted to her mother's response with equal passion.

"Mother, that would be very wrong!" she interrupted, only recently a teenager but, as usual, mature beyond what her age might indicate. "Is that all I would leave behind? My legacy? The two of you just waiting for death to take you? How can you say that? How—?"

There was the slightest smile on her mother's face, not a cruel one or a smile that mocked the pain on Charity's, but that "said" in its own language and in its own way, *Now you know, my child; now you know.*

SQUEAKING . . .

Was there a cemetery where the gate did not squeak?

Charity walked inside.

Her feet seemed leaden, as though each weighed a hundred pounds; moving them required special effort on her part.

"This will make it final," she said out loud. "I'll see your—"

Just ahead. Two thick slabs of granite side by side.

She bent down in front of them.

"A hundred years from now," Charity continued speaking, "I will be gone, too, and someone will have placed a stone on my grave long before. We live, we die, and what do we leave behind? So very little, I'm afraid. Cold grave markers for strangers to see, with most walking right on past, caring not the slightest that you both were loved, that, every so often, I will think of you and I will come back here and my tears . . . my plentiful tears—"

She fell forward.

"The last time my arms were around you, your blood covered me," she said, sobbing. "Now there is only all this dirt. I can't reach out . . . I . . . I can't—"

Her face was buried in the bare dirt.

"Others buried you because I was too weak to attend. I could not plan the funeral, I could not pick the flowers, I was not at the mortician's to make sure the right coffins were being used."

Charity did not notice the footsteps behind her, heavy boots crunching ordinary soil, steps that were rapid, determined. She felt a strong hand grab her, pull her up, felt cold, hard metal against the back of her skull, heard labored breathing.

Kane.

"I was going to leave," he spoke. "I was going to turn back, grab a few personal belongings where I've been holed up, and leave!"

He held her more tightly.

"But you talked about going to the sheriff," he reminded her. "How could I allow that to happen? The sheriff would arrest Barksdale, but to make the charges stick, he would have to locate me. I would have to run, and I would have to keep on running. If I was caught, I would have to stand trial. Anyone who rats on Barksdale can count on an early death!"

"But he would be sent to prison after you finished, surely! If a lynching party didn't get him first," Charity tried to reason with him. "What would you have to worry about? You would be free of him."

"You do not know what this Barksdale can do if he's determined," Kane insisted. "Before the sheriff ever laid hold of him, he would hire other assassins to finish the job, and he would take care of every last one of those darkies of yours. They're too much a reminder to the community, the way you all treated them! Even if he went to prison, he would end up owning the soul of the warden, and he would be able to get away with anything."

Kane cocked the pistol and declared, "There are no witnesses."

"One of our coloreds has been following us," she told him.

"Old story . . . ," Kane replied, snorting. "It doesn't work this time. I don't believe a word of what you've said, Miss Charity. And I ain't going to let you—"

"You'd best be startin' to believe her," Hester interrupted.

Charity could sense Kane stiffening.

"If I pull this here trigger," he growled, "her brains is going to be blown into a hundred pieces. No way you can stop me, nigger."

Kane was wrong.

Hester had grabbed hold of his hair with one hand and pressed a knife in the other against his neck an eighth of an inch below Kane's Adam's apple. Now he yanked the man backward, knocking him off his feet. The pistol was fired once, but the shot went wild, and hit nothing. That knife grazed Kane's flesh but only enough to cause a little blood to show. He started screaming, acting as though he was about to bleed to death.

"You's gonna be all right," Hester assured him, "and that's a real shame."

Charity got to her feet, wobbled a bit, then stood over him.

"I am willing to let you go," she said.

Kane's eyes widened.

"I just tried to kill you!" he exclaimed. "What're you talking about, girl?"

"There's an if," she went on. "You've got to be willing to face up to Barksdale, tell everyone what he's like, that he was behind my parents' deaths."

Kane's eyes were bulging.

"That pig's not the only one. A woman, too. There's a woman involved, not here, but up in Ohio somewhere."

"Gloria Joinville? Is that her name?"

Kane was surprised that Charity knew who she was.

"Yes! That dame's the one. They're in cahoots."

"But she's an abolitionist, and Barksdale is one of us, if you can stand the stink. They shouldn't have *anything* in common."

"Here's how it goes . . . ," Kane told her. "Once slavery is abolished, Barksdale will supply her with all the emancipated darkies she wants, and she'll in turn pass them on to the money guys who are backing her. Barksdale's going to collect a real big percentage of what could amount to a steady flow of millions of dollars."

Charity was glad to tell him that Gloria Joinville was in custody.

"I wonder what Barksdale will do now," she added.

"I think he will leave this area and set up shop elsewhere. There is no future here for him."

Charity felt better then but could not help wondering if she would ever come up against Barksdale at some other point in her life.

❧ 76 ❧

I WAS THINKING OF you throughout the night," Billy Mendenhall told Charity as she sat by the bed, dabbing a cool cloth on his forehead.

He saw her cheeks redden and would not let this pass without comment.

"I see that you were doing the same about me," he added.

"Yes . . . I was," she admitted. "There was little else on my mind."

"There was *nothing* else on mine."

"Your fever is nearly gone, Billy. In a few days, according to the doctor, you and the others can be taken back home."

"They will be days that will pass all too quickly, Charity."

She wished he had not said that. What Barksdale had insinuated must have occurred to others within the community. What would happen if they were seen repeatedly in one another's company? Not everyone would be as crude as the pigfaced one had been, but beneath any facade of gentility, the same old social conventions would dictate their reactions, and none of these would be very pleasant.

"I don't know how much time we can spend together," she said reluctantly.

"You are seeing someone else?"

"The estate. I am in charge, you know. There are so many details."

"But many people to help, it seems."

"Yes . . ."

She was removing the washcloth when he reached up and took her free hand in his own.

"You are kind," he told her, his voice sounding husky, "and sweet, Charity, and brave."

"You must know many girls who are all that and more."

"No!" he protested, shaking his head, his movement causing some pain. "I do not know *any* like that. The ones I have dated are empty-headed, Charity, all smiles and chuckles and nothing more. Most of them are concerned with their appearance, their clothes, some social register of events—tea parties and that sort of thing—rather than what is going on inside them or anyone else for that matter. That isn't the kind of woman I find appealing."

How those details matched Charity's own view of the young men she had courted!

He pressed his lips against that hand.

"None could have done what you have," Billy told her. "They would faint, I am sure, or turn away and never come back. My blood has touched this lovely hand, and your tears have covered mine. How could I not now love you with all my mind, body, and soul?"

She pulled back, not prepared for the suddenness of that declaration, hoping that their relationship would progress more slowly.

"In a few days I will be gone," Billy reminded Charity as though he had access to her thoughts as well as her heart. "We don't have much time. You'll have to decide whether you want to go with me or not."

. . . whether you want to go with me or not.

Billy Mendenhall seemed blatantly to be forcing a decision, and Charity was afraid she already knew what it would be.

SHE STAYED IN the plantation house for the next couple of days, except for a trip back to the cemetery, standing at the graves of her parents and wishing she could have been buried with them.

When she returned home, she sat in the master bedroom in a chair beside the bed where they had slept together for so many years.

And she thought of Billy.

She might have decided to go away with him, might have decided to spend the rest of her life with a handsome Yankee, if it had not been for Julia Pegram, at least that was what she had convinced herself of while conveniently ignoring the unsettling thoughts she had been facing before her friend ever spoke up.

"I know about matters of the heart," Julia told her that night after Charity had left the doctor's home, concerned about Billy's obvious overture. "I stayed with a man I grew to hate because it was the proper thing to do. Do you not believe that I, too, met other men over the years of my imprisonment, those who could have laid a claim to my heart if I had let the situation get out of hand?"

. . . over the years of my imprisonment.

Her voice lowered, for an instant, as she spoke those words, showing how deeply they had reached into what she was as a woman, perhaps to the very center of her soul.

"But why?" Charity asked. "You could have divorced him."

Julia smiled ironically.

"Divorce?" she repeated. "Yes, I suppose I could have done that—and thrown away my part in this society. Divorce has no friends in Dixie, you know. We are supposed to be married until death parts us."

"But divorce is not unknown," Charity reminded her.

"No, it is not, but it seems to be reserved for politicians and others of their ilk. My husband was never poor, but he also never had much real influence. The scandal of a divorce would have stuck to him like tar and feathers to a crook being run out of town."

She was starting to shake.

"Julia, are you all right?" asked Charity.

"I am, my dear, I am. Just remembering, remembering the only way my husband could have tried to avoid the scent of divorce of suffocating him."

"How? What could he have done?"

"It is what he could have and what he would have done."

"Tell me, Julia."

"Destroyed me."

"You? You were the blameless one."

"That would not have mattered to Ambrose."

"But you once said that he really did need you."

"I was his whore, Charity. He never paid me money, of course, and a marriage certificate gave an aura of respectability to our relationship, but there the differences ended."

"So he would have ruined your reputation."

"He actually threatened me with that if I ever dared to leave him. He said he would pay off some false witnesses and . . . and he even had my lover already picked out."

"Someone who would have lied about infidelity?"

"That and worse, Charity, for this individual was ready to accuse me of perverse sexual demands as his reason for ultimately abandoning me."

"Perverse—?"

"Yes," Julia interrupted. "The details should be left unspoken between us."

The two women became silent for several minutes.

Charity was the one to speak first.

"Billy seems more and more desirable by comparison," she said finally.

"That was not the point I wanted to make," Julia shot back. "I wanted to show you that each of us is trapped by some circumstance in life, whether we know it or not. Neither you nor I are completely free to do what we wish."

"But I am not married. I have no commitments that would—"

"Wrong, Charity, very wrong. Your whole life is a commitment, a commitment to Dixie, a commitment to which your parents devoted their lives."

"So I cannot have Billy? I must turn my back on him?"

"You must not have Billy Mendenhall or any other Yankee. If there is a war within the next few years, as many believe, what kind of life would you have?"

Julia paused, letting the implications have their full impact.

"A southern woman married to a Yankee soldier? Where would you live? What would you tell your children? In the North, you would be scorned. And you could not come back here. If you did, it would have to be without your husband."

Julia's expression was one of infinite sorrow.

"You must not ever see him again. If you do, you will give in to your passions, and they will control you."

Charity could not argue because her friend's position was unassailable.

"How can I let him go?" she asked, crying. "How can I pretend that . . . that . . . ?"

She fell into the other woman's arms.

"Tradition can be our greatest prison," Julia said, "a prison from which there is only rarely an escape. And this will not be one of those times."

"He wants an answer," Charity told her. "I am supposed to tell him tomorrow morning. Two days later, he will be released to go home."

"You will give him that answer by not going."

"How can I have the strength to stay away?"

"How can you have the strength to stand before Billy Mendenhall and tell him that the relationship is doomed?"

CHARITY DECIDED NOT to go to the doctor's home, at least not close enough that Billy Mendenhall could see her. She did ride a stallion to a point where she could see the old gray-toned building, and the front lawn.

Billy was there, waiting.

It was already an hour past the time when she was supposed to have met him. He stood and paced then sat and stood again, then paced again.

"My love . . . ," Charity whispered.

During the night, as she had thought about what to do, going through a steady grind of sleeplessness that gave her no rest but only increased her anxiety over that which was to come, she admitted to herself that if her parents were alive she might have gone with Billy, and she sensed, in the end, that they would have supported her decision.

But they were gone.

And by marrying Billy Mendenhall or any other Yankee she would have had to wrench herself loose from an imperfect cocoon of sorts, yet a cocoon just the same, and it was this that she needed in order to survive their deaths, so recent as they were, still as fresh in her mind as their blood on her body had been, the reassurance provided by familiar surroundings and familiar people and, most importantly, familiar traditions.

"Good-bye, dear Billy," she whispered.

It was with some irony that, as Charity was burying her head in her hands and starting to sob, so it was that Billy Mendenhall had begun to do the same, for in that single moment, both of them were consumed with a vision of what could have been but now would be denied them both, the ashes of its promise imagined at their feet but no less real to them in time than the coming ashes of Dixie.

Part 4

❧ ❧

We have to do with the past
only as we can make it useful
to the present and the future.
Frederick Douglass

I was well *aware of the reputation that had surrounded New Orleans for many years, but I also knew that any number of folks had moved from elsewhere in the South to Louisiana, discarding 'safer' environs,"* Charity told the Society members.

She remembered so well, even those many years later, what a well-placed businessman had told her weeks before she moved.

"It's a growth state," he had said. "Like the western frontier area, it is often undisciplined, but you can make a great deal of money there if you invest wisely."

Charity possessed all of the money she would ever need for buying anything she wanted. Alfred Littlepage had left an estate that made his daughter one of the richest women in the history of the United States, but a relatively unknown one since she never sought publicity. If she had become a more familiar face, she would never have been able to accomplish what was to be required of her in the years ahead.

The greatest impediment to moving to Louisiana seemed, in Charity's mind, the fact that Roman Catholicism dominated it at virtually every level, for she was a strong Baptist and could imagine that regular clashes would ensue between her and Catholics in the neighborhood of her new property. But she also had been told of a genuine Protestant community throughout the state, one that had managed to survive despite periodic persecution.

Nor did the fact that Hoodoo Jack had been based in New Orleans deter Charity, for she figured that she could withstand anything after all that had occurred in recent years.

"Lord, You have pulled me through so much," she prayed the night before setting off on the trip. *I need Thee now as much as I ever have."*

Recalling that move, Charity told the Plantation Letters Society, "And so the slaves and I left South Carolina and began a journey to what they would decide later was an outpost of hell itself . . ."

A Society member gasped as Charity spoke and then became as hushed as the others

77

THE OLD WOMEN, *Violet and Savilla, could never have made it, even before their health had started to fail,* Charity realized.

This thought caused Charity to reflect upon the Lord's timing.

"You do know what is ahead," she whispered the day before she and Little Isaiah and the others arrived at the new plantation a few miles northwest of New Orleans. "I wish sometimes You gave us more warning, but, then, how would I have reacted if I had had a hint about what happened to my mother, my father? I could not have endured that, Lord, and would have done everything I could to thwart Your plans."

She was in one of the covered wagons that contained as many of her possessions as she cared to take along with her. The poor of that region of South Carolina were given the rest: piles of clothes, linens, shoes, and a great deal more. Much of the stored food was turned over to poverty-stricken families, both white and black.

"There was nothing back there for me anymore," she continued, "not even Billy."

She thought of Billy Mendenhall often, several times a day in fact, thought of what it would have been like for them to be husband and wife, to be the mother of his fine children, to watch them—

But she was realistic enough to know that continuing to let any of this dominate her was unhealthy.

"I am a Littlepage," she declared. "And I shall act like one."

Finally, she started to fall asleep, deliberately pushing images of Billy Mendenhall out of her mind.

Thank You, Lord, she prayed.

Just as it seemed that she would surrender to the night, she heard a sound, someone sobbing.

Little Isaiah.

He had chosen to sleep outside the wagon used by the slaves.

"I don't know why," he admitted. "I jus' feelin' the need to sleep out here under the stars, if it be all right with you, Miss Charity."

And so he got a pillow and some blankets and lay down in front of her wagon.

That was why she could hear him so clearly.

Sobbing . . .

Charity came fully awake and scrambled out of the wagon to find Little Isaiah in an almost fetal position on the ground.

"What is it, friend?" she asked as she sat down beside him.

"This is an evil place," he told her. "Meanin' no disrespect, Miss Charity, I's wonderin' if it's where the Lord really does want us."

"I know about the occultic influence in New Orleans," Charity acknowledged, "but we will be living miles from its center, particularly the Bourbon Street section, and right now we aren't even there and won't be until midday tomorrow."

Little Isaiah was straightening himself into a normal sitting position.

"I's seen 'em," he muttered.

"Seen? Who?"

Charity felt suddenly colder than even the nighttime chill could have explained.

"*Massa Alfred!*" Little Isaiah blurted out.

Charity had not expected anything quite like that.

"You saw my—" she said.

He nodded.

"Standin' right in front of your wagon," he went on. "His face was so pale, Miss Charity, and yet his lips, they's so red, bright red. He turned, stretched out his arms, smiled at me, and motioned for me to stand up so he could put 'em 'round me, so that—"

Little Isaiah was quivering.

"I closed my eyes and prayed to the Lawd Jesus for protection. When I looked again, Massa Alfred, he was . . . he was gone!"

Charity knew that, in some respects, she was dealing with an adult in body who nevertheless had the mind and the emotions of a child. As such, she had to give him a response that was appropriate and not just some predigested pabulum that could be called street-corner Christianity.

"You should have no doubt that I love and respect you," she started to say, "and I would tell you only the truth."

Little Isaiah was nodding, his eyes open wide.

"And I am doing that now, telling you the truth, when I say that you did *not* see my father," Charity declared.

"But, Missie, I—" Little Isaiah spoke up.

She shook her head but not in any irritated or superior manner.

"You saw a demon posing as my father," she told him. "It was a counterfeit. My father is in heaven now with my mother. And that is where they will stay, Little Isaiah."

The big black man started to shake his head then saw Charity's skeptical expression and stopped.

"The massa seemed so real," he said. "He's standin' there and wantin' to hug me like he used to do."

"But then if he was as real as you thought, why did you pray for protection?"

"I was scared, Miss Charity. I mean, the massa bein' dead and then suddenly lookin' right at me."

She bent down beside him.

"Let me hug you instead," she said.

"I's needin' that now," he admitted, "I surely am."

By then the other slaves were awake and hovering around.

Charity glanced up and half-smiled at them.

"We have to be careful," she told him. "The enemy of our souls is after us. I don't know why just yet, but he is, and we will have to stick together more closely than ever before."

Hester spoke.

"We ain't got no one else but you, Miss Charity," he said.

At first she was touched by that, but as she climbed back into the wagon and the slaves went to theirs, she became aware of the implications of what Hester had said.

. . . We ain't got no one but you.

Grown human beings reduced to the position of having no other place and no one else to go to for the rest of their lives!

She was awake for another hour, perhaps a bit longer, thinking about those simple but moving words.

Hester was the youngest, and all the others were at least fifty years old.

Half a century, Lord, Charity prayed. *And my parents and I are the only other people they have been close to most of their lives.*

A feeling of sorrow, sudden and dark, washed away all other emotions temporarily.

What have we done to them, Lord? she continued. *What have we done to them?*

A few second later, she thought of the only righteous answer: Give them a home and love. That's what we did.

Every slave was loved. Every slave was as much part of the Littlepage family as possible. Every slave felt the loss of Alfred and Elizabeth Littlepage nearly as much as did Charity herself.

They have never been mistreated, Lord, she went on praying. *They have*

*always been fed properly and clothed adequately and treated well in every
other respect. And we have done this while facing the scorn of friends and
neighbors.*

It was not a crisis of conscience that had taken hold of her but something
else about what Hester had said.

Regret. That was it more than anything. Regret, not that the Littlepages
had had slaves, for the family's history would show how benevolent they
had been as owners, but regret that those men and women had chosen to
remain what they were.

"Father gave them the offer of freedom again and again," she whispered
out loud to the chill night air. "They were not interested."

But, she realized, as Little Isaiah or one of the others would invariably
say, they would never want to go from the kind of security that they had on
the plantation to the deprivation endured by friends and relatives who lived
north of the Mason-Dixon line.

And yet—

The image of men twice or three times her age having no other place to
go was still a sad one, inexpressibly so as, finally, after wiping away a single
tear, she gave herself to the sleep that was finally beckoning.

What will become of them if something happens to me? she thought.

The night offered Charity nothing in response except the welcome relief
of a few more hours of rest.

78

CHARITY FOUND THAT the people on the plantations around her own were primarily Protestant, not Catholic, a factor that was providential since Charity had made no specific inquiries about her neighbors before buying the property. More than one family had outspoken things to say about the Catholic influence throughout the state.

"Is it a coincidence that there is so much darkness here around New Orleans?" remarked Felicia Lyons, trying to appear matter-of-fact to her new neighbor. "I mean, nowhere else in the entire nation is there this massive amount of evil."

Charity felt like saying she had found as much evil in Protestant areas, thinking of the nightmare she had undergone so recently, with an image of Gloria Joinville as terrifying as anything demonic she might witness.

Instead she decided not to stir up any debate. Perhaps later she could engage Felicia in what could be a spirited but not unfriendly discussion.

"I have known about it for a while," Charity admitted a bit evasively.

"Then why in the world did you ever move down here, of all places?" the other woman asked rather logically.

"Because I thought that that sort of thing was concentrated mostly in the city of New Orleans, centered along Bourbon Street, and had nothing to do with the rest of the state. For example: We have certain areas in Columbia, South Carolina, where many common prostitutes are very active, but, elsewhere, you see, their influence isn't felt at all. You wouldn't say that the whole state is a grossly sinful region just because of what was going on in that one locality."

Felicia nodded, agreeing with the reasonableness of that.

"Besides, what with all that had happened, I wanted to get far, far away from what was familiar," Charity went on to say and then explained as concisely as she could what had befallen her over the past two years.

The two women were sitting in a gazebo in the middle of Charity's backyard. Each had been served mint-flavored iced tea. The day was an especially humid one, even by Louisiana standards, and the air seemed almost liquid in its intensity.

Tiny Felicia was shorter than Charity by a full eight inches, and though she was only a few years older, she seemed much more than that, not in manner but in appearance, with lines around her eyes, frown marks that seemed incongruous in someone of her age, and pale, narrow lips that, on occasion, twitched nervously.

"I don't mean to sound anti-Catholic," she added, "but it is hard to avoid this when you see what is happening around here."

Charity had had some Catholic friends in South Carolina, and her parents had never exhibited any prejudices toward them or others who lived in that region.

"I have some doctrinal differences with them, of course," Alfred Littlepage had commented, "but if Jesus Christ is at the center of their lives as their Savior and Lord, little of that really matters."

At first, Charity was ignorant of such things, but as she matured, she developed an interest in theology, and then she and her Catholic friends engaged in some lively but respectful debates on the subject.

"Protestants tend to forget that the Christian church was largely Catholic for the first fifteen hundred years of its existence," one friend or the other would tell her.

And Charity would have to agree, but then she would deal with such subjects as purgatory and the supposed sinlessness of Mary and others.

But it was all civil and actually fun, to a certain extent, a challenge that she enjoyed since the spirit was one of friendly disagreement.

Only recently, miles outside New Orleans, had she been exposed to a much sharper and considerably more dark divergence between the Protestant and Catholic communities in that area.

"Is it really so bad?" Charity asked, not meaning to sound as though she were calling Felicia a liar but still skeptical that anything could be as bad as she was picturing.

Felicia did not seem to resent any of this not-so-subtle questioning of her judgment by a rank newcomer but acted as though Charity's reaction was understandable and no different from her own when she had moved to that area.

"I think one man knows more than any of us," she replied. "He could convince anyone, I am sure."

"Who is it?"

Felicia smiled and blushed a bit.

"A doctor, a rather handsome one, too."

"Why is he such an expert?"

"He has been battling the demonic influence around here from the beginning of his practice. All of those men, women, and children who are having the worst difficulties seem to go to him for help."

Charity was puzzled.

"But he's a doctor," she said. "Wouldn't a priest or a minister be a better choice under these circumstances?"

"You might suspect that, perhaps, but this doctor is very different, Charity."

"In what way?"

Felicia looked at her with an urgency that seemed unnerving and said, "There is a spiritual dimension to him that many priests do not have, I am afraid."

Charity was uncomfortable as she got a mental image of some fanatic going around with garlic collars, his clothes festooned with crucifixes, his pockets holding several bottles of so-called holy water.

"How did he get started with all this?" she asked skeptically.

Felicia's tone softened, and she spoke almost in a hush.

"His wife was killed by a weird man named Hoodoo Jack."

Charity nearly fell off her chair.

"Hoodoo Jack—?" she repeated, barely able to speak the name.

"A strange one, I know."

"Tall, thin, with bulging eyes, a black man possessed of a hatred of anyone who was white and free?"

Felicia's eyelids shot open.

"How could you know that?" she asked slowly. "How could you possibly know? What's going on here?"

Charity sighed and then told the other woman what had happened back home.

Felicia listened, her mouth dropping open at one point. After Charity was finished, she sat up in her chair for a moment without speaking.

"Dead . . . ," Felicia repeated. "That creature is actually dead. I wonder if the doctor knows. If he doesn't, he will be pleased to learn it."

"The body is, yes, but the entity that inhabited it for so long has gone elsewhere, I imagine," Charity spoke.

She noticed suddenly that the other woman's eyes were bloodshot.

Felicia hugged herself as she said, "Is there to be no rest, no escape?"

"This doctor . . . what's his name?"

The other woman replied while blushing at the same time.

"Payne Preston."

Charity decided not to comment about Felicia's suddenly pink-toned cheeks.

"Did he ever remarry?" she asked instead.

"No. I don't know if he ever will."

Charity surprised even herself with the next question.

"How difficult would it be to meet him?"

Felicia's eyebrows shot up.

"Not very. Why, have you some ailment?"

Charity told her new friend what Little Isaiah had seen that night as they were traveling to their new home.

"Such encounters are commonplace," Felicia commented. "It is a strange place that you have moved to."

Charity needn't have been told that. Already her misgivings were rearing up like physical beasts in front of her.

. . . It is a strange place.

Felicia was speaking both from personal experience and from what other women had shared with her over the years.

"Strange deaths occur with astonishing frequency. And the authorities rarely do anything to solve the mysteries."

"Is the church behind all this?" Charity asked, though not cynically since she had little anti-Catholic bias.

"I used to think so, but lately the cardinals or whatever they are seem to be as disgusted as the rest of us."

"How is it that this Preston fellow has managed to survive so long?" Charity asked, immediately intrigued.

Felicia's reply was direct.

"His soul," she said.

Charity had been taught about the human soul since she was old enough to understand its complexity. But she could not be sure what her neighbor meant.

"His soul?" she asked. "What are you saying, Felicia?"

"It is completely possessed," the other woman replied, no emotion whatsoever showing on her face.

Charity had been sipping some tea as Felicia said that. The remark startled her enough to make her drop the glass on the soft grass.

"Possessed?" she repeated, nearly choking.

Felicia was smiling.

"Completely," she said.

"Oh my . . ."

A grin crept up the edges of Felicia's mouth.

"By the Holy Ghost, Charity. I have never seen a man so given over to the reality of God in his life. He has even begun to make some of the more influential parish priests respond to his entreaties for help."

Payne Preston.

Charity repeated the name to herself.

"He's handsome, you say?" she asked, trying not to appear entirely captivated and yet failing complete nonchalance.

Felicia seemed uncomfortable.

"Payne Preston is the most gorgeous man ever born," she replied, "if I may exaggerate just a bit."

Felicia seemed uncomfortable admitting that to another woman; she shifted around a bit on her chair.

Charity tried to make her feel less awkward.

"I bet you say that about all the men, Felicia."

"Not about my husband I don't."

They both had a good chuckle, and then, aware of other commitments, Felicia excused herself to return to her own home, leaving behind in Charity's mind an image of a man that was not easy to dismiss.

Dr. Payne Preston.

Charity stayed outside for another hour, enjoying the breezes that gently stroked her cheeks and the sweet scents carried past her nose.

"I wonder if I will be meeting you soon, Dr. Preston . . . ," she muttered to the air around her a few minutes later, only to look up and find that Hester was walking toward her.

"Did you want anything, Miss Charity?" he asked.

"I want a great deal," she said, tackling the abrupt onset of melancholy. "I want to be held in my father's arms again. I want to sit with my mother and listen to her tell beautiful stories about Jesus."

. . . beautiful stories about Jesus.

Elizabeth Littlepage had done that often, making the earthly existence of the Savior seem real and vibrant to a young mind.

Oh, Mama . . . Charity sighed, *dear, dear Mama.*

She turned away from Hester, though she had no reason to be ashamed of her tears since he and the others had seen the Littlepages shed them any number of times over the years for any number of reasons.

"But I cannot have any of that," she said, "not in this life."

She wiped her eyes.

"Did *you* want anything, Hester?" she asked, ashamed of what must have seemed like weakness to him.

The black man nodded.

"A visitor," he told her, acting a bit nervous, which was not like him since he and the other slaves usually felt completely at ease with Charity.

"Visitor?" she repeated. "I have another visitor?"

"Yes."

"Who could it be?"

"A man."

"A man?"

"He's askin' to see you. Seems real anxious."

"He wants to see me now? Without an appointment? He happened to be in the neighborhood and just decided to stop by?"

"Think it's more than that, Miss Charity."

She was becoming more interested by the minute.

"Tell me about him, Hester," she asked.

"He's a doctor, Miss Charity," Hester told her.

A doctor? Just after what Felicia had said! How many doctors are there around here? Probably someone quite old and fat!

Her pulse quickened at the same time her mind readily dismissed what seemed to be a coincidence.

"Does he presume to think I'm ill when he has never examined me?" she asked, trying to be jovial but seeming foolish instead.

Hester replied the only way he could.

"He won't tell me, Miss Charity."

Charity wrinkled up her nose.

"Did you ask the nature of his business here?"

"I did, Miss Charity."

"And what was his response?"

"That it was a matter he could discuss only with you."

The presumptuous nature of the man was beginning to irritate Charity more than just casually.

"Tell him I am unavailable," she said, asserting herself and preparing to immediately discard the matter.

Hester hesitated.

"Well?" she asked.

"He might insist," he told her.

"This is *my* house on *my* property," she replied, glaring, "and he is here to see *me*. I am the one to determine what happens next."

"I will tell him," Hester said solemnly, turning to go back into the house.

As Charity straightened the multicolored dress she was wearing, she asked, "By the way, what is this brash doctor's name?"

Hester spoke it clearly.

"Dr. Payne Preston, Miss Charity," he told her.

She gasped, astonished at what had to be God's timing.

"Payne Preston . . . ," she whispered, repeating it not for the first time, a name that she had decided reeked of *machismo,* as the Italians would say, a *machismo* that Billy Mendenhall exuded from the first moment she saw him, but in a more youthful manner, whereas this newcomer had to be older and more world-weary.

"I see," Charity said, hoping the impact of hearing the name was not readily apparent. "Well, he—"

And, then, curiously, her mind went blank for an instant.

"Are you all right?" Hester asked.

"I am . . . ," she said but was hardly convincing.

Clearing her throat, Charity added, "Tell this rather pushy New Orleans doctor that I *will* see him."

Hester nodded and said, "He may ask how long you will be. I think he seems impatient, Miss Charity."

She feigned indignation.

"It will take as long as it takes," she said assertively. "Tell Dr. Payne Preston nothing more than that."

Hester had turned again and was starting to walk toward the back entrance but slowly this time, not convinced she had finished.

"Hester?" Charity asked.

He sighed, half-smiling.

"Yes . . . ," he said.

"Is he a Yankee . . . like Billy?"

The black man turned and was grinning.

"No, Miss Charity, he appears to be a southerner through and through."

She sighed with relief.

"Thank God!" she said. "You can go now."

He waited a few seconds.

"You really can!" she exclaimed, laughing at his little joke. "Bless you, dear friend. I am a bit unsettled now. Don't hold this against me."

This time Hester made it inside.

❦ 79 ❧

L OOKING ABOUT THIRTY years old, Payne Preston was six feet three inches tall, with the broadest shoulders Charity had seen on any man, including some of the brawny slaves she had glimpsed over the years. His arms and chest pushed against his clothes, making them look a little tight on him, but the bulk wasn't from flab that padded his frame. He was just the opposite, in fact, a man of muscle and strength and conditioning. His hair dangled down over his forehead, pitch-black strands with something of a sheen to them.

And his skin . . .

He had an untroubled complexion and skin that was as dark as that of some of the slaves her father had had over the years.

She saw Payne Preston's eyes next, so blue that they could have been drops from the sea itself, and even when he was disturbed, as he was then, she noticed a twinkle about them.

Not to be ignored was his chin, which jutted out and narrowed considerably, and she could trace back from it a strong-looking jaw line.

Charity saw that he needed a shave, but in a man so strong-looking, this hardly detracted from his image.

"Why is it that you are so bent on speaking to me this day?" she asked with a mixture of hospitality and caution in her voice.

"Because I think you are in danger," he repeated without any buildup.

"You *do* hem and hew, don't you?" she replied.

Charity could not resist an outburst of strong laughter. But when she saw that his expression remained serious, she stopped while telling herself that this man would never be the life of any party.

"I have been here only a few weeks," she told him. "I have made no enemies. How could I be in danger? And an even bigger question: How could *you* know about it even if I were, Dr. Preston?"

Preston started to pace on the Italian marble floor of the foyer.

"This is a gateway to the occult . . . ," he went on, his voice trembling.

"My property?"

She snorted as she looked at him.

"That's ridiculous. We are Christians here."

"And I also am a Christian."

"Then start acting like one and stop this nonsense. You come across as rather scared, Dr. Preston."

He winced at that.

"I have a healthy respect for the enemy," he said in a monotone. "While our Lord will be victorious in the long run, we do have to be on guard until then."

He seemed to sense that he was failing to command Charity's attention if not her respect, and his manner changed then, a certain charm settling on that handsome, tanned face with its pronounced cheekbones and its firm jaw.

"Is there anything at all that I could tell you that would make you less skeptical?" he asked.

"About you or the devil?" Charity replied, suppressing a snicker. "I have no doubt about him. It is you who makes me wonder, sir."

Charity was becoming impatient.

"Is there anything else?" she asked. "It is getting late. I am tired. And I really wish you would leave."

"Would you think differently if I told you about Hoodoo Jack?"

"Hoodoo—" she started to say but choked.

"Yes, I know, he's dead," Preston told her. "But he left behind a family."

Memories of Hoodoo Jack had never faded for Charity. Every so often she would dream of him.

"He was married, that evil man?" she asked.

Charity wondered how any sane woman could allow herself to get within ten feet of such a madman.

"Married in an occultic ceremony that was held at midnight in the middle of State Cemetery," Preston went on, "right after they had cut the throat of a newborn infant and wiped its blood across their foreheads."

Charity blanched and turned away as he added, "She knows everything about you. And she is intent on revenge."

"But why has no one else taken any of this seriously?" she asked.

"They do when a curse is directed against them. Right now there seems a kind of harmony."

"Harmony? How could that be, Dr. Preston?"

"A pragmatic approach to life, Miss Littlepage. Louisiana has always lived by it. When merchant seamen from all over the world began arriving years ago, whores took care of them in door-to-door bordellos."

"And the city officials did nothing?"

"The influx of visitors meant money for the city treasury."

"But surely the church must have taken a stand."

"Not a forceful one. Attendance was invariably up, especially those coming to confess their sins."

"But what about the supernatural stuff? Surely the local priests would stand firm against that."

"Some have done that. But you must realize how strong the evil's hold is on New Orleans; it encompasses virtually everyone."

"Why have you remained immune?" Charity asked the handsome intruder.

He took a pocket-sized New Testament out of an inside pocket of the long, black coat he was wearing.

"Because I love the Lord," he said, holding it out before him, "and the Holy Ghost gives me strength."

"Are there so few others like you?"

"There may be many like me, but they fear for their lives. I am hoping that, one by one, they will step forward."

He smiled sweetly.

"It is getting late," Preston said. "I should be going."

"I would be pleased if you stayed for dinner, Dr. Preston," Charity found herself saying, immediately regretting her impetuosity.

"I would like to do that, Miss Littlepage, but there is supposed to be a storm tonight. I live closer in to the city. And I want to avoid being caught in it. The rains here can be devastatingly torrential."

"We have hurricanes in the Carolinas, too," she told him. "The poor suffer terribly because of the destruction to homes that are badly built, many of them no better than flimsy shacks."

"Your coloreds probably fared better."

"They did. When my parents were alive, if it got too bad, we would bring them into the plantation house."

"You did? I hear that sort of thing all too seldom, I am afraid."

"My parents and I always treated our slaves like adopted children."

Charity wanted to make sure he did not forget about her dinner invitation.

"Later this week?" she asked.

"For dinner?"

She nodded.

"As it happens, I am free tomorrow night," he said.

"That is fine with me."

"May I bring something, Miss Littlepage? I am quite well-known for the quality of my butter pecan pie."

She was hardly about to tell him that she could not imagine anyone making it as well as her mother had.

"Sounds wonderful," Charity said instead. "Do bring it."

An awkward moment of silence followed between the two of them.

"Dr. Preston?" Charity asked, finally breaking it.

"Yes, Miss Littlepage?"

"You may call me Charity, if you like."

The handsome young doctor smiled then, outwardly showing his relief, and she knew that, regrettably, she blushed when he did, but it was not something she could control no matter how much she wished she could have.

"And I am Payne," he told her. "Call me that, Miss . . . Charity, I mean."

She threw up her hands in mock confusion.

"What am I to do over the next twenty-four hours to protect myself?" Charity asked, sighing.

"Pray," he remarked. "Our weapons are really very simple, but ageless and effective."

"No garlic, holy water, that sort of thing?"

"That is the stuff of cheap novels."

"Just pray, that's all?"

"And fill your mind with God's Word."

They shook hands then, and he left.

Charity was glad that her palms did not start to sweat until the door had closed behind him.

AROUND MIDNIGHT, CHARITY was beginning to wonder if she would be alive by the next evening.

A storm.

Probably the worst she had ever experienced.

It was a storm of wind and rain that threatened to lift the roof off the sturdy old mansion she had bought through the advice of a former business associate who had visited her father several times a year.

A few weeks before she left South Carolina, Lucas Imboden had paid a visit, and she told him what she was considering.

"I travel throughout the South," he commented. "I would be happy to investigate for you."

"And please charge whatever fee you feel is warranted," she told him.

"I will ask for nothing except a simple 'Thank you,'" he went on.

"But that seems most unfair," Charity protested. "My father would have insisted, and so will I."

"Young Miss Littlepage," the little man said as he twirled his handlebar moustache, "your father was the most honest man I ever knew. He could have cheated me any number of times, but he never did. I owe him something. I owe him for the peace of mind he gave me whenever we had dealings. I saved a fortune on legal fees."

"My father could not have acted any other way."

"Nor can I."

He smiled and reached out a hand to shake hers.

"As you say," she told him.

"Would you do me a favor?" he asked.

"Anything, Mr. Imboden."

"Would you have one of your coloreds take me to Alfred's grave? I could not make it here for the funeral. And, belatedly, I was hoping to spend a little time there. I would go myself, but since I do not live in this area, I am not certain where it is."

"Willis will take you," she said.

"Willis? Yes, a good choice. I met him more than once when I was here with your father. He seems very nice. We can have a good talk, the two of us."

"Will you wait here?" Charity asked. "I'll fetch him."

She had left the foyer and was headed toward the back of the plantation house.

"Miss Charity?" he called after her.

"Yes?" she said as she turned around.

"I loved your father," Lucas Imboden spoke, his voice unsteady. "I am a widower. I have had no one for many years. I think I would have died in your father's place if I could have."

Charity thanked him and continued on her way, thinking, after a few seconds, that she caught the sound of this kind gentleman sobbing, but then she was too far away to hear anything more, and he was quickly gone.

Lucas Imboden had held nothing back about the occultic heritage of Louisiana, but Charity was confident that being a Christian was all the protection she needed. He had neglected, however, to tell her how miserable the weather was, and how dangerous it could be.

That night spelled it out for her.

❧ 80 ❧

WITHIN AN HOUR, *the sudden tropical winds had begun to strike ever harder, first merely rattling the shutters and rustling nearby tree branches then howling as though in warning of much worse to come, and, before long, making the sturdy frame of the plantation house itself shake like some mammoth beast fighting an intruder, and surviving, yes, but still a bit wobbly in any event.*

But the slave quarters were not similarly unscathed. .

Charity had intended to upgrade the smallish building considerably, to put it on a par with what her father had provided the slaves back in South Carolina, but she had only just arrived and had not as yet made the arrangements with any carpenters and others in that region.

Demolished . . .

The slave quarters were demolished by the punishing winds, portions of the roof lifted right off and tossed in the direction of the plantation house, with large tree limbs hitting both the front windows and shattering them instantly.

Only Willis and Hester got out in time. Little Isaiah and Simuel perished, crushed under the fallen structure.

Charity and the remaining two slaves rushed upstairs in the plantation house, the three of them huddling together in the master bedroom.

Though all were Christian, the slaves still had the residue of their African heritage with its superstition-based approach to weather, both good and bad.

"This is the devil's own storm!" Hester exclaimed. "I's lived long 'nough now to know the difference 'tween an ordinary storm and a storm from hell. It's taken those we loved and destroyed them!"

"Only their bodies," old Willis reminded him. "Their souls have gone on to be with the good Lord."

The large house was shaking, timber groaning against the punishment of gusts that must have approached a hundred miles an hour or greater.

Hester turned toward Charity.

"Is you sorry you done moved?" he asked a bit timidly. "Meanin' no offense, Miss Charity."

Charity had never allowed herself to fall into the habit of lying to any of the slaves, and she did not start then.

"I am very sorry, and I can't say that I can perceive the Lord's purpose in it," she admitted.

Howling . . .

"Hear that?" Willis whispered. "Sounds like banshees."

Shrieking . . . sounds like dying creatures headed for the brink of hell itself.

Despite herself, Charity was being reminded of that night of confrontation with Hoodoo Jack. No storm had blown in, but the sense of darkness and the chill that had gripped her then were identical.

"We need to start praying," she told them. "We need to get on our knees, join hands, and do that right now."

She realized that she could be accused of what later would become known as battlefield Christianity since she had been so busy with the tasks involved in moving that she had let her devotions take a backseat.

Charity realized that she was giving in to the superstitious notion that such a storm had anything at all to do with demonic forces, but it was now so strong, so terrifying, that she could not help herself.

The slaves muttered agreement, and, in seconds, they and Charity had joined together and were, in unison, asking the Lord's protection.

Suddenly, a noise.

Different.

Not connected with the storm, it seemed, but from another source, loud, insistent, desperate.

It seemed to be coming from the front of the plantation house.

Banging . . .

A banging sound.

A—

The front door!

Someone was trying to get in.

She stopped praying and stood.

"Miss Charity, shouldn't you be stayin' right here?" Willis, the oldest of the slaves, asked tremulously.

"It might be someone needing help," she said, "someone caught by the storm. I must find out."

Her gaze drifted for a moment to one of the windows in the bedroom and beyond it to the back of that property.

And she screamed.

Bodies.

Half a dozen bodies.

Spewed up from—

"What is it, Miss Charity?" Willis asked as he stood and stepped up beside her.

By the lightning flashes they could see that three had pale white faces.

The others had no faces at all, nothing but bare skulls, vagrant flashes of lightning touching them through the downpour.

"Blessed Jesus!" Willis exclaimed.

Charity staggered back, unable to look any longer.

Willis seemed transfixed, his body shaking but unable to break whatever "spell" had settled over him.

Until Hester pulled him away from the window.

"Did you see—?" Willis started to say.

The sight of those lifeless bodies, ravaged by the process of decay, would stay with him probably until the day he died.

"I did," the other slave told him. "We all caught a glimpse."

"Dead bodies . . . where done they come from?"

"You sayin' the devil's behind this?"

Willis looked forlornly at him.

"I can't accuse the Lord," he said, "so it's gotta be the devil."

Glass shattering!

Down on the first floor.

The banging sound had stopped, followed by that new sound—

Charity opened the bedroom door and stepped cautiously out into the hallway. She had no candles nor any other source of illumination.

Slowly.

She walked slowly, the darkness more unsettling for her than at any time since she was a child.

The staircase.

She approached it one step at a time.

And peered over the railing.

Whatever had been left of one of the large front windows was now totally shattered. Partially covered by shards of glass was a body in the middle of the foyer.

And next to it was an expanding puddle of blood.

~≈81≈~

PAYNE PRESTON, half-conscious, badly cut with injuries that only a proper medical examination could determine.

Willis and Hester started to lift that substantial body of his so they could take him upstairs.

A groaning sound from him stopped them.

"Wait!" Charity spoke up. "He might be injured even worse than he seems on the outside. There is no way of telling. If any ribs are broken, he could—"

Preston's head turned toward her.

"Listen," he muttered. "Here . . . is how . . . to do it . . . I . . . I think my ribs are intact . . . Listen carefully."

He was about to say something else, but a wave of nausea overwhelmed him, and he blacked out.

Charity had remembered something that a nurse friend had told her a number of years before.

Thank You, Lord, she thought. *I never knew the purpose of that chat until now.*

"Internal injuries," she told the slaves. "Do as he told you. And walk very, very slowly, please."

She bent down next to him and gingerly probed his neck, his chest, his stomach to see if he reacted.

Nothing.

His eyes were still closed, but he had begun to mumble.

"The storm . . . a bridge . . . gone!" Charity could hear him say. "I . had to come . . . back . . . here."

"We have to get you upstairs without any more delay."

Preston nodded painfully and reached out, closing his fingers lightly around her slim wrist.

"So sorry . . . ," he whispered, "so sorry to place this burden on you."

The two slaves carefully lifted Preston step by step up the spiral staircase, which was like so many others in plantation homes of that period.

Both men had reached the middle of the first flight of stairs when, an instant later, the continuing wind seemed to intensify.

And, without warning, the wind ripped the front door off its hinges and sent it slamming against the opposite end of the foyer, glancing off the staircase and causing it to shake.

Startled, Willis and Hester nearly dropped Payne Preston but somehow managed to hold on to him until they reached the second-floor landing.

"The smaller bedroom!" Charity yelled. "And we need to get bandages as soon as possible."

Carrying a lamp, she rushed ahead of them and swung the door open. There was only one small window in the far wall, and it was still intact.

Willis and Hester rested Preston on the bed.

Charity already had grabbed some fresh blankets and sheets from a linen closet in the hallway and brought them with her.

"Hester . . . please . . . help me undress him!" she told them as she struggled to get his heavy coat off. "We need to find where his cuts are and bind them up as best we can."

The bleeding seemed to have slowed down, but Charity knew enough to avoid taking any chances.

He had a gash just below his neck, another on the back of his head. A large chunk of glass had ripped through his trousers and into his thigh.

"I can take care of that, Miss Charity," Hester told her.

She nodded, turning away, embarrassed, for she had never seen even her parents naked, and being in such a situation with a stranger, especially one as handsome as Payne Preston, made her blush. She felt very sheltered just then despite the experiences of the past few years.

Preston had regained some semblance of consciousness and was trying to talk, his eyelids opening and closing in rapid succession as he strained with the effort.

"I can't understand you," Charity said as she leaned closer to his mouth, his lips brushing against her cheek.

Preston tried again and managed to speak more clearly this time.

"Alcohol . . . ," he said in a whisper. "Clean the cuts only with alcohol."

"But that will hurt awfully bad," Charity reminded him.

"So will dying."

Intuitively, Hester tapped Charity on the shoulder. She looked at him, smiled sweetly, and nodded. He knew where all the medicinal items were kept and dashed out of the room.

"And thread," Preston muttered.

"Thread?"

"Yes . . . for the cuts that need it."

"To sew them together?"

"Yes . . ."

"But I've never sewn—"

"I might die if you don't."

He coughed several times, and the flow of blood quickened, staining Charity's plain white nightgown.

So pale, Lord, she thought, *he's beginning to look—*

And she turned her head away for a moment, hoping that Preston did not glimpse her distress, for that tanned face of his was quickly beginning to lose its color as he grew weaker and weaker.

Charity resented being thrust into a life-or-death situation with a stranger.

Why should I have the responsibility for you? she thought. *I don't know you. I'm not sure I even like you.*

Charity choked on that last part, for she realized that she was kidding herself, since she had to admit that she was drawn to the man, if only on a physical level, and to think of him dying in her arms because she did not do everything she could to help him live was not an image she could accept.

"Willis," she said, "will you get the needles and thread?"

He nodded as he started to get to his feet, his old joints protesting.

"And boil them, Miss Charity?" the old man asked, reminding her of what had to be done.

That would mean going downstairs and into the kitchen, past all the shattered glass and the unrestrained ferocity of the storm.

"It's too dangerous," she said. "You must not take that chance."

"Then the doctor-man could get infected and die, Missy," he said, hoping she would not feel he was trying to argue with her.

Charity sighed, knowing he spoke truthfully, and there was no other choice.

"Be very careful, dear friend," Charity told him. "I've known you all my life. Take Hester with you just in case."

"I's too old and slow to be anythin' but real cautious," he said, smiling a bit. "'Sides, you might need Hester here, to lift the doctor-man. I ain't gonna be fit for that, Miss Charity, no more than I would be sprouting wings and flying to heaven right now. But I'll do what you wants me to, as I always has."

She touched his cheeks gently.

"Just be careful," she said. "I love you so much."

"And I's gonna be lovin' you, Miss Charity, until the day the Lord decides to call me home. When that happens, I'll be perched right at the gates for you, waitin' until it's your time to leave this world and join your mama and your daddy. I's gonna be standing' right next to 'em."

Willis was crying as he spoke, years of affection now coexisting with the loss that he felt over the deaths of two of the three kindest white people he would ever know.

"So sorry . . . ," he said, "so sorry to be blubberin' like I's doin'."

"Bend toward me, please," she asked of him.

And Willis obeyed as always.

"I's truly ashamed . . . ," he muttered.

"Shush," she told him.

Charity kissed the black man on the forehead.

"Bless you . . . ," she said simply.

And then Charity could only wait for him to return as blood dripped from Payne Preston's badly cut body onto the bare wood floor, little streams of it trickling between the tongue-and-groove joints.

~82~

WILLIS FOUND THE thread and packet of needles, then headed for the staircase, which trembled beneath his feet as he hurried down to the first floor. He paused at the bottom, hearing the fearsome wind and seeing the shadowy shapes playing across the water-drenched, glass-littered foyer.

For a moment he forgot where the warming kitchen was as age-old superstitions reared up in his mind, fear of darkness and sounds and—

"Lord, please be with me as I walks through the valley of the shadow . . ." he whispered as he took one tentative step then another and—

The warming kitchen was just ahead.

Whispering . . .

Voices.

"Who's there?" he asked out loud. "Who—?"

Then he shrugged, thinking it was the wind playing tricks on him, and walked faster as he reached the kitchen.

HE HAD JUST REACHED the door when the voices became clearer, seemingly more insistent.

Die . . . old man . . . die.

"What the—?" Willis said then clamped his mouth shut, sensing that he should pay no heed to whoever or whatever was responsible.

Die . . . now . . . nigger . . . and roast in hell.

That was a mistake.

He stood up straight, turned, and faced the darkness around him.

"I ain't gonna go to hell!" he declared. "I got the Holy Ghost inside me. I's going straight to the Lord, not the devil!"

But those voices, insinuating, almost hypnotic, would not give up.

White man's lie . . . . Jesus doesn't take black souls, only Satan does . . . You're lost, darkie . . . lost forever.

Perspiration covered Willis's body, and because of the rain that had buffeted him in the foyer he was now soaked, every inch of him, and feeling chilled.

"Leave me 'lone!" he cried out. "I's gotta—"

Rush to save whitie . . . rush at the command of that vicious woman upstairs . . . don't do it . . . let them both die this night.

"But the others, they—" he tried to say.

The voices were much stronger now, louder, even meaner.

They sold their souls to a white master . . . you can reclaim your own now.

Another mistake.

Willis was knowledgeable enough in spiritual matters to recognize the siren call that was being sent.

"And serve da devil?" he shot back. "Be enslaved to him for eternity?"

Willis hurriedly opened the firebox of the warming stove and stoked the coals still glowing there from supper. Next he fumbled for the spigot on the hot-water reservoir, filling a kettle with the steaming water and dropping in the thread and needles. He set the kettle on one of the burners and stood, trembling in the near-darkness, as he waited for the water to return to a boil.

As he waited, his heart pounding, the voices swirled around him.

You are a fool . . . old . . . lost . . . useless . . . you will die before you reach the staircase . . . You will die in the grip of the worst pain of your senseless life . . . You needn't let that happen . . . Give up your loyalties to your white oppressors and start over by—

Hearing the kettle hiss with steam, Willis hurriedly jerked it off the stop and stepped quickly toward the kitchen door, noticing that rainwater was now covering the floor and rising.

Willis . . . Willis . . . You're going to die . . .

Now angry and always stubborn, Willis shook himself rather violently as he cried out, "I's claimin' the power and the protection of Christ Jesus through His shed blood. You can't harm me or those I love."

Love, you say? All they have ever done is use you. You have been valuable to them all these years. They have no love for you. And you must have none toward them.

Suddenly, Willis felt very weak and nearly dropped the kettle; but he managed to reach the door, open it, and enter the hallway outside, the water now up to his ankles.

He could see, illuminated in the lightning flashes, that the foyer seemed to have become a small lake, with the level of water rising rapidly. He would have to wade through it in order to get to the staircase.

Odors.

Rancid odors.

Like those that could have emanated from an ancient, fetid swamp but somehow worse than any he had ever come across before.

So strong.

Their source must be quite near.

He tried to breathe as little as possible.

Abruptly his legs were pushing *against* something.

Willis glanced down—and screamed.

A body. A decaying body, bare bones showing.

"Lord, Lord, help me!" he cried out loud.

Other bodies. Half a dozen.

Most had little or no flesh or organs left, twisted skeletons looking even more eerie as the silver-tinged flashes of lightning touched them.

Willis had had a pain in his chest for the past minute or two, and it was not going away but was becoming worse as he made his way through the floating bodies to the staircase and onto the first step.

No more voices purred temptation into his ears.

Now there was laughter instead.

Loud laughter.

Laughter that was so coarse and cruel and harsh that it seemed, in itself, obscene and unholy.

"I's goin' to make it to the room," he called out to the darkness, "and I *will* give Miss Charity this kettle, and she will save that man's life and—"

Despite the duration of the storm, the wind was no weaker now; if anything, it seemed stronger.

A violent gust swept through the open front door and the empty window frames and struck Willis hard across the back, and he could easily have been knocked down. But he was holding on to the banister with one hand and the heavy kettle that acted to balance him, and so he was able to get to the landing and into the hallway and then stumbled toward the bedroom door.

His legs seemed to weaken all at once though he fought, fought hard to keep them from buckling under him.

No use, no use at all.

It was as though they had a suddenly independent streak, ignoring his orders by rebelling and acting on their own.

And so he fell.

Fell hard.

Hitting the bare hardwood floor with enough impact to break one or more bones and wrench tendons and muscles to such a degree as to nearly immobilize him.

Oh, Lord, he thought, *it hurts! How bad it hurts. I can't 'member such pain before.*

Willis tried so hard not to fall, tried desperately to keep going, knowing how much Charity needed him, tried out of the love he felt for her not to fail a child who had become a woman before his eyes, but he could not continue, his old, aching body giving in to the toll that exertion had exacted.

No strength left.

His heart seemed to be pounding in his ears, and a wave of nausea overtook him.

"I's comin', Miss Charity," he yelled hoarsely. "I ain't gonna let you down, not this friend of yours!"

By sheer will, Willis inched himself down the hallway, pulling and pushing the kettle beside him and using his other hand to gain one inch, then two, three, four, five inches, a painful inch at a time, until he knew he could no longer do even that.

The door to the bedroom was a little over a foot away.

"Miss Charity!" he called, hoping that his weak voice somehow could be heard above the continuing noise of the raging storm outside.

Footsteps.

He caught his breath.

Could she have heard me already, Lord? he wondered. *Could she know that I am here and that I won't—*

He gulped, not so much out of fear over death but rather disappointment, for he had been hoping for some time to leave the increasing weariness of his body and take on the new one that Scripture had promised, yet to live without helping Charity one more time was a blow as bad as anything physical just then.

Will I be white, Lord? he asked silently. *Oh, how I have wanted to be white so that no one would hate me anymore.*

The bedroom door was swung open, and Willis could hear Charity gasp.

"The kettle," he said weakly. "Make . . . no mind 'bout me . . . Take the kettle . . . I boiled the thread and needles in it for the doctor-man . . . My years is up, Miss Charity . . . That man's got . . . a whole lifetime 'head of him."

Hester was right behind her. She picked up the kettle and asked the other slave to start treating Payne Preston while she sat down next to Willis and cradled his head in her lap.

"What happened down there?" she asked.

He was trembling.

"Hell . . . Miss Charity," he told her. "It was . . . somethin' like what hell must be . . . 'cordin' to . . . my way . . . of . . . thinkin'."

"And that odor? That ghastly odor?" Charity spoke as she tried to ignore it but was unable.

"It . . . will . . . get . . . worse . . . Missy."

Willis wanted to prepare her, to lessen the shock, but there was no longer any time for that.

"But what's causing the awful smell, Willis?"

He could not speak.

"Willis?" he asked. "Won't you tell me?"

His eyes were open, but he was not blinking.

As her tears started, she reached down and gently closed the lids then sat there for a moment, rocking back and forth as she hummed a simple tune that Savilla had taught her long before.

Finally she rested his head on the floor and stood, her legs wobbly. She walked hesitantly to the railing and looked down at the scene below.

More bodies, their rotting stench assailing her.

She staggered back and into the bedroom.

Hester had retrieved the needles and thread from the steaming water and was now standing over Payne Preston's body, waiting for her to begin the suturing. He sensed what had happened.

"Is Willis dead, Miss Charity?" he asked.

She nodded, not able to speak.

"I's threaded the needle; it's ready for you," Hester said simply.

"You didn't come out to see," Charity managed to say. "Why didn't you come out to see?"

"I couldn't," he told her honestly. "I couldn't. I loved him too much to stand there while he was dyin'. I think—"

"Yes . . ."

"I think I might have done somethin' to myself afterward, like dyin', too, maybe. I wouldn't never do that to you, Miss Charity, but then I don't think I could have controlled myself, just watchin' him like that, just watchin' him pass away as though he never was, as though all those years he lived meant nothin', Miss Charity, nothin' at all."

Forcing back some tears of his own, Hester went on, "But then I asked myself, what would Massa Alfred have thought of me to run off and leave you like that. I couldn't spit on his memory, Miss Charity, and I couldn't desert you, so I decided to go on, to let the good Lord take over, and—"

Payne Preston, who had been unconscious, started moaning.

"Shouldn't we be takin' care of the doctor-man?" Hester suddenly asked, abruptly changing the subject. "We gotta think of him now."

≈83≈

As Charity was finishing the task of sewing up Payne Preston's wounds, she noticed that his face had remained untouched except for some dirty smudges. The scars, and there would be many, some rather extreme given her lack of experience in such matters, were all from the middle of his chest downward.

You can still woo any damsel who catches your eye, she told herself. *You—*

He had been in and out of unconsciousness.

Coincidentally, just as she was in the midst of that thought, he opened his eyes again and seemed more coherent this time.

And he winked at her.

Charity pretended that this had no effect on her, but she was deceiving herself, and for about the tenth time, she blushed as her hands worked on ·his flesh, sewing the skin back into place as cleanly as she could manage.

Before tonight, she thought, *I could only imagine what a man—*

She cut herself off.

Preston was beginning to regain full consciousness.

"How bad was it?" he asked weakly, slurring his words slightly.

"You're alive," Charity told him. "I would say it is not bad at all."

He felt pain over much of his body.

"Many cuts?"

"Many, yes."

"All over?"

"None on your face. Only elsewhere."

She was biting her lower lip, anticipating where the conversation seemed to be heading.

"Elsewhere?" he repeated.

"Yes . . . your chest, your thighs."

"My back as well? It hurts there."

"Yes, your back was cut."

He tried to move but stopped immediately.

"Will I be able to sit down in a chair anytime soon?"

"No problem there. You had no cuts at all on your—"

Preston became a bit mischievous.

"You had to go over every inch of me, didn't you?"

Charity nodded.

"I am sorry to have put you through all that. It must have been rather awkward for a well-bred young lady such as yourself."

"I did what had to be done, Dr. Preston."

He inhaled.

"That odor . . . ," he said, wrinkling his face.

"Downstairs."

"Bodies?"

Charity had just finished tending to the last cut and was winding the thread back onto the spool and opening the little wooden box where she kept her sewing supplies.

"How did you know?" she asked, her head jerking up.

"You aren't the only one to face something like that."

The thought that others would face a similar night of horror jolted Charity, and she had to force herself to speak.

"I'm not?" she spoke. "It's happened before?"

Preston's face showed his own feelings of distaste.

"Any number of times . . . during a major storm such as this," he said, grimacing at the grisly recollections. "I have a very small patch of land halfway between here and New Orleans. I have had to clear bodies from my property five times in six years."

"But where do they come from?"

"Any cemetery in the vicinity. This is all basically filled-in swampland. The water pushes the contents up through the surface and carries along with it innumerable coffins and whatever else. Often the coffins are so rotted through by the moisture that's here for so much of the year, even when no storm is in progress, that the wood crumbles, and the bodies are simply washed away."

"How horrible!" Charity gasped.

Preston nodded in agreement.

"And yet little can be done," he added forlornly. "It's one of the many hazards of life here."

He smiled again.

"People used to think it had something to do with the occult."

"I can see why!"

"Even though it doesn't, the Satanists still have a field day. They go ahead and grab as many of the corpses as they can handle."

Charity was beginning to feel sick.

. . . one of the many hazards here.

"What are some of the other 'hazards' I need to know about?" she asked.

"Gators . . . ," he stated simply. "And snakes, particularly water moccasins, among the most deadly snakes anywhere in the world. And any number of insects, some of which are armed with poisons of their own."

"But the gators and the snakes . . . they're way off in the swamps, right?"

"They're in the swamps, yes, but, you must remember, no location is what you would call 'way off,' Charity. Everything here could turn back into a hodgepodge of swamps across practically the entire southern section of the state if not kept up properly year after year with fresh soil brought down from the northern parishes.

"The greatest danger always comes from the Mississippi side where the river seems prone to threaten a crisis whenever there is heavy rainfall. Conditions like those tonight are ripe for catastrophe."

Overflowing . . .

Charity's mind filled with images of houses being swept away or buried under water or mounds of mud. And homeless people, many of them used to the comforts bought by great wealth, suddenly with no more protection than the displaced poor.

"I would think that the Mississippi's overflowing tonight is going to be unavoidable and will raise the water table all over this part of Louisiana. We will be living with the impact of this storm for weeks. Some families will take longer than that to recover."

He grinned and added, "But there is one good outcome in such cases, a remarkable display of the reconciling power of the Holy Ghost."

"Catholics and Protestants forgetting their differences and working together for their common survival," guessed Charity.

"That *is* it," Preston remarked. "I'm impressed . . . Charity."

Though earlier both of them had agreed that using first names would not constitute a breach of southern etiquette, he had found it awkward to call her that.

"Finally!" she exclaimed. "Well, Dr. Preston, it seems that you and I—"

Her face reddened as she realized what she was saying.

"Payne, I mean!"

He reached out and brushed a lock of hair back from her forehead.

"The most beautiful shade of red I have ever seen," he said in a slightly husky voice.

"It is so unkempt right now," she told it. "I must say that when it has been shampooed and brushed, it looks quite—"

Again, some blushing.

"I was going to be terribly immodest," she admitted, "because I have been told, too often I suppose, that I have the best-looking hair of any woman in the South."

"But stating only the truth, I am sure, Charity," he said, an admiring expression on his face. "In fact, I agree with anyone who has ever told you that."

Charity did not say anything more for several minutes, and Preston respected her need for silence.

"So many I loved are gone . . . ," she muttered, overcome with melancholy as the storm continued relentlessly. "My mother, my father, Savilla, now Little Isaiah and Simuel and Willis and—and—"

She seemed not so much a grown woman in her early twenties but a child faced with a frightening world.

Hester touched her on the shoulder.

"I won't never leave you," he said. "We can get some new slaves anytime and start all over again, Miss Charity."

When she turned and looked at him, her eyes were red-rimmed and bloodshot, with dark circles beneath.

"I am so tired of saying good-bye," she said.

She leaned her head on Hester's shoulder.

Payne Preston looked at the two of them, as though unaccustomed to witnessing that kind of bond between white owner and black slave.

"I would like to help any way I can," he spoke up. "I don't think any of us have any clue why the Lord brought us together like this, but He truly has done that, and I trust Him to show us the reasons."

Charity held out her right hand, and he reached up and closed his fingers around it briefly then fell back, still too weak to move himself very much.

Just then, they heard what seemed like the groaning sound of a large, tired, wounded beast ready to collapse.

"This house is old," Hester said. "It might be ready to—"

He and Charity glanced at one another, and he said nothing further.

≈ 84 ≈

TOWARD MORNING . . . The storm's seemingly maniacal rage appeared to have dissipated markedly. Some gusts still kicked up, but they were becoming less and less powerful, and just before sunrise, they stopped altogether.

"We should consider going outside now," Preston commented, "and surveying the damage."

Charity and Hester had arranged pillows on the floor, and they both had managed to get a couple hours of sleep somehow, giving the young doctor the real bed all to himself, though due to the size of it, they could have shared it with him and not been crowded. But Charity had decided against this, in part because he needed to be kept as comfortable as could be managed under the circumstances, and, also, the notion of being in bed with two men, regardless of what had happened that night, was not something that could be reconciled with her rigid southern sense of propriety.

Preston had seen them starting to awaken, and that was when he spoke.

"Are you strong enough?" Charity asked.

"I feel remarkably well!" he declared and added rather mischievously, "I suspect someone must have been praying for me."

Hester stood and seemed unsteady.

"Are you all right?" Charity asked.

"Just thinkin' . . . ," he replied.

"About Willis?"

Willis was just about old enough to be Hester's grandfather, and the two had become close over the years of their slavery.

"Yes, Miss Charity."

"We will take care of him later on," she said. "Nothing can be done now until the water subsides."

. . . until the water subsides.

"It will; I knows that," Hester agreed. "Until . . ."

"The next time," Charity finished that thought for her friend. "It may not happen again for years, a storm as bad as this one, but there will *always* be a next time, won't there, Payne?"

"Would you—?" the big black man started to ask.

"Would I what?"

"I shouldn't say anything, Miss Charity. "It isn't my place."

"You can finish if I ask, and I am asking, Hester."

"Would you think of movin' back now?"

"To South Carolina? After so short a time?"

"It ain't gettin' no better if you live here just a few weeks or many years, Miss Charity. We is jus' one step from hell."

Preston nodded and remarked, "It's inevitable that today will be like tomorrow, and tomorrow will be the same ten years from now unless something is done, but the parish leaders appear unconcerned. They seem to be saying, 'It doesn't matter. The rich use cemeteries on higher ground. They're not much affected. Why be concerned with what the poor have to face?'"

"Their consciences have become as hardened as that?" asked Charity. "What about the Bible's admonitions to feed the poor? Is it possible that they have turned away completely from that sort of mission?"

"Oh, there is an effort to seem beneficent, at least with something that looks good to the public, but finally, anything that requires real sacrifice is neglected while the parish leaders wallow in their relative prosperity!

"Is it any wonder that we are being cursed with such an onrush of severe occultic activity at present, as well as accelerating government corruption from the local to the county and, ultimately, all the way up to the state level? I wonder, as well, how much Washington, D.C., is being affected. How many there can be trusted to act in a Christian manner for the betterment of a Christian nation?

"I think Louisiana will never be anything but a haven for dishonest people of all types. After all, New Orleans was nothing more than a promenade of brothels when it came into being. And it continues to offer wall-to-wall whores even today."

He anticipated Charity's next question by adding, "But such conditions also point to where the need for redemption and regeneration is the most urgent, wouldn't you agree, Charity Littlepage?"

She had to acknowledge that he was right.

"I cannot contest anything you have said, Payne, but then you are a doctor instead of a minister."

"A *Christian* doctor," he emphasized. "Are only ministers and deacons to be concerned with the salvation of the lost?"

He sighed with more than a touch of exasperation.

"There are churches everywhere," he said, "but most are half-full. I've attended several services in different ones and have yet to find a sermon being delivered that would challenge anyone spiritually."

WILLIS'S BODY REMAINED right where it had fallen.

Hester stood beside his old friend for a moment, sobbing fitfully.

"Forgive me, Miss Charity," he said. "I just ain't able to help myself."

"Why don't you take him into the bedroom and put him on my bed?" Charity suggested. "Wouldn't that be more fitting?"

He glanced at her, his eyes widening.

"You don't have to do that, Miss Charity," he said. "I know it's just his body there. His soul's in heaven."

"Yes, but I am thinking of respect," she said. "That body was all that we have known for so long; it was all that we saw. You can do what you want, Hester, but I am willing to turn over my bed if you decide to do this. And as soon as we can, we'll need to tend to the bodies of Little Isaiah and Simuel, too."

He nodded, thanking her, then bent down and gently lifted Willis's body in his arms and carried it down the hall.

Payne Preston and Charity waited a couple of minutes, with the doctor leaning against the wall for support.

Finally, concerned but not impatient, Charity walked to the bedroom doorway and glanced inside.

Willis's body was on the floor, lying on a pile of pillows, with a comforter draping over it.

"Not the bed?" Charity asked.

"That bed is yours, Miss Charity," Hester told her. "No one 'cept the man who da Lord sends as your husband should rest on it. Willis would be pleased just for this much of your kindness."

He said good-bye, for the moment, to that body that had been so familiar for decades and rejoined Charity and Payne Preston.

⤙ 85 ⤚

THE ODORS WERE worse, but that was not what stunned them as they surveyed what had become of the foyer.

Hurricane-force winds had shattered not only the windows but their frames as well, and ripped away part of the front of the plantation house so that there was only an irregular, gaping series of large and small holes.

At least the water level had receded substantially since the height of the storm. Now the half-dozen disinterred corpses could be seen more distinctly in the morning light, their grotesque images like fragments of a scene out of Dante's epic vision of hell, phantasmagoric figures made all the more unsettling because they were once animated living human beings of no special distinction but were now transformed into the stuff of eerie drama and foreboding.

Even Payne Preston found the sight an overpowering one.

"Dear God!" he muttered prayerfully, breaking out, momentarily, from behind the super-masculine image that he perhaps unconsciously underlined by the way he talked, walked, and generally conducted himself.

Charity turned away, gasping for air, knowing that the bodies of her parents would appear similarly if they were seen now in their present state.

She fell against Preston, who was none too steady himself, but he instinctively leaned back on the railing for support as he rested his hands on her shoulders.

"Inhale slowly through your mouth," he told her, "then exhale slowly. Initially, the smell will make you want to gag, but you mustn't let it. Do this several times. Do it *now*, Charity, or I shall have to carry you downstairs, which would be rather like the blind leading the blind, I am afraid, given the way you and I both feel."

She had been close to blacking out and welcomed the strength of his hands, which felt surprisingly soft on her partially bare shoulders.

Once, twice, again, again, as he had told her, she inhaled, then exhaled, then—

It worked.

Her surroundings stopped spinning, and she felt steadiness return.

"We must not waste any more time!" Preston declared. "We cannot stay here. There is no telling what structural damage has been done to the house."

"You heard that noise during the night?" Charity asked, surprised.

"I did. It was really awful. I think it came, in part, from what happened to the front of the house, as we see it now. But I suspect, also, that we were being warned about the stability of the rest of the structure."

Charity had never been suckered into anything before then, nor had her father, and the possibility that the purchase of this property had been a sham made her angry.

"Right now, there isn't much wind and only a little rain," Preston went on, "but if the storm intensifies again, as so often happens in this semitropical region, it could collapse on us, and we'd be dead for sure."

The tone of his voice deepened.

"The three of us must get outside, see what everything looks like there, and hope that some portion of the road is passable. I want to get to my own house as soon as possible. There might be nothing left of it."

"You seem so much stronger," Charity said with open admiration. "How quickly you recover."

"I am a doctor," he remarked casually. "Didn't you know that we're better at recovery than anybody else?"

And then Preston laughed.

"And you are better at bouncing back than most other women," he told her. "Believe me, that isn't any joke. So many southern belles seem to wallow in self-pity when misfortune interrupts their well-ordered lives."

He reached out and cupped his hand around Charity's cheek, kissed her on the forehead, then pulled back quickly.

"Let's go!" he said as he led the way down the staircase.

When the three of them were halfway down, Preston stopped and faced Charity and Hester.

"One other thing," he said.

He seemed especially nervous.

"What is it?" Charity asked.

"Something to watch out for."

She felt chills then.

"Tell us, Payne," she insisted.

"You have a fair-sized open swamp near you," he said portentously. "Are you aware of that?"

"I wasn't."

Charity was yet again forced to think of herself as a stupid lamb that had been led to slaughter by some opportunistic men, men who must surely have gotten together sometime after the transaction and gloated.

"This particular one has always been known as a breeding ground," Preston told her, "for some elusive reason considerably more so than others, even the much bigger ones. From there, through various water routes—"

Charity gulped as she interrupted, "Breeding ground? For what?"

"Water moccasins, one of the most dangerous snakes known in the United States. Not more than four feet long and belonging to the pit viper family, they're also known as cottonmouths because when they are startled or angered, each one raises its head and opens its mouth where the interior is the color of freshly picked cotton.

"These deadly creatures—more silent than rattlers and more deadly as well—can hide away in total darkness and still catch prey because special organs, called pits, help them sense the heat from any living, warm-blooded creature."

Perhaps, Charity would think later, she assumed there was some virtue or safety in trying to be dumb, for why else would she come up with the question that next passed her lips?

"So what does that have to do with—?" she started to say, until the reality of what he was insinuating got through to her.

Preston nodded knowingly as he saw her expression.

"Now you understand!" he exclaimed.

And that she did.

"Here?" she asked. "Could they have been carried right into this house?"

"More easily than corpses can be floated up from their graves and swept right into your foyer—"

Nausea.

Charity felt it grip her.

And something else.

A sense of evil.

Hoodoo Jack's wife! she exclaimed to herself. *Could she—?*

Charity shook her head rapidly, trying to clear her mind of images that were dark and unsettling.

"What's wrong?" Preston asked.

She told him.

"I can see why that might occur to you," he acknowledged, "especially after what I told you about her. But, remember, Charity, God is in control. If we give in to our fears, we hand Satan a victory that should never be his."

At first she resented being preached to by a stranger but immediately had to recognize that he was telling the truth.

She forced herself to deal with the *natural* threat facing them without letting suspicions about the occult confuse her.

"Snakes down there?" she repeated. "And gators, too?"

"The snakes, yes, I would wager, but not the gators, unless it's the very young ones. The adults are simply too heavy. Besides, the immature gators are no serious threat. They tend to be far more skittish."

"How can we know?" Charity asked. "How can we just walk into that mess, not knowing whether—"

"It's difficult," Preston interrupted. "Let me be your eyes. I've gone out to rescue people lost in the swamps. I have an eye for the snakes."

Hester offered to help as well.

"I's seen them a few times, yes I has. That was a long while ago, but you's never gonna forget them, you's can't because they look so black and slimy and—"

He was shivering.

"And quick," Preston added. "They could move from one end of the foyer to another in seconds, striking before any of us could stop them."

"Then how can we get out?" Charity asked reasonably.

"Yea, though I walk through the valley of the shadow of death . . . ," he reminded her pointedly.

"I know we can't stay, with the house in the shape it may be in," she replied, "but the thought of setting foot in that water, among those bodies and wondering if—"

He put his arms around her because she was noticeably shaking.

"I have been thinking just as you are," he remarked. "Remember that I have no one left either."

Charity had let that truth slip away until he reminded her of it.

He has no family, she thought, *and I have none either. Surely, Lord, that is why you brought us together.*

"Let's go," Preston said.

They walked the remaining few steps until they reached the first floor.

"I's goin' first," Hester insisted.

"I can't let you do that, dear man," Charity protested, but he was not listening to her and stepped forward, the water reaching to his ankles whereas earlier it would have gone up nearly to his knees.

"I's gonna make it," he said, looking over his shoulder at them, a smile crossing his coal-black face.

Then he stopped abruptly.

"What is it?" Preston asked.

"My ankle," Hester spoke, his voice tense.

The doctor's own tone changed.

"What about your ankle?" Preston asked slowly, with an edge of dread apparent.

"I felt somethin'."

He wore no socks but had shoes on over otherwise bare feet.

"Slippery . . . ," he said. "It felt—"

Hester hesitated, his body seemingly frozen in that spot.

"Could have been debris," Preston pointed out.

"Could've been, yessir . . . ," Hester said, trying to reassure himself, and yet his body was soaked with perspiration.

"Go ahead then," Preston advised. "Ignore it."

The black man nodded as he continued wading through the water.

Floating directly in front of him was a corpse.

But this body was not one of those that had been unceremoniously regurgitated from a nearby grave and carried from it by flood waters after being long-dead and now in the midst of the repellent rotting process.

Dead only hours before.

"Sweet Jesus!" Hester prayed, pressing his hands together and closing his eyes to try and control the shock.

"Push it aside!" Preston called out to him, his view partially blocked by the black man's large form.

The slave swirled around and faced Charity.

"It's Little Isaiah, Ma'am," he cried in desperation. "Poor Little Isaiah! I can't let him just float around like a piece of wood or some other kind of junk. He ain't no junk, Miss Charity; he's my friend."

"But where can we put him?" she reasoned. "If this house collapses, he'll be part of the wreckage anyway, just like Willis upstairs. We can't take him with us because we just don't know what it's going to be like outside."

Preston glanced at her, admiring her clarity.

"But I gotta do something," Hester added. "Willis is resting on a soft, fine bed. How can I let Little Isaiah stay where he is and maybe be washed right away again, endin' up who knows where?"

He looked so helpless that Charity told him that he could go ahead and take Little Isaiah's body upstairs. Preston offered to help, but Hester knew that this would be too arduous and said he would do it by himself.

They stepped aside as he carried his old friend up the stairs.

After Hester had struggled up the stairs with Little Isaiah's body and disappeared into the bedroom, Preston leaned over and whispered to Charity, "I think we are going to have a problem."

"More than we have already?" Charity asked.

"Water moccasins."

"You saw one?"

"I saw a whole displaced bed of them."

Charity's mouth dropped open.

"As many as a dozen at the far end of the foyer. But I could be wrong. It might be less, but it could also be more."

"What can we do?"

"It will be a grisly business."

"What do you have in mind?"

"They seem to be lurking near where all but one of the bodies have accumulated. I see that loner just to our right, not far from the bottom step."

"But what about it, Payne? I thought you said they would attack only something their heat pits detected."

"True," the doctor told her. "But we have to wrap that one body in one of your blankets and set it ablaze. They will flock to it with such speed that you'll almost want to watch the spectacle, attracted as they are by the heat."

"You said it was going to be grisly."

"Very. I caught a glimpse of the corpse's condition. Hester and I will have to have strong stomachs."

Charity's hand was shaking.

"I'm going back to South Carolina after this is over," she warned. "I could endure their autocratic ways and their enslavement to tradition better than this. At least they are, at heart, decent Christian people."

"I don't blame you. I feel as you do. Around here, finding real Christians is a time-consuming and frustrating task."

She was surprised by the sudden turnaround in his attitude.

"You would leave here, after what you told me yesterday?" she asked.

"Fighting the practitioners of voodoo and Santeria practitioners is one thing, Charity. But when you add to this the raging storms and the corruption of the city and other governments and whatever is wrong with this hellhole, you finally have to admit to yourself that this is one of those places on the planet where you just take off your shoes and get rid of its dust and move on."

He was no longer so self-assured.

"Just yesterday, I was telling you about my Christian duty," he reminded her, "about sticking it out. The truth is that I wasn't anywhere near as determined as I sounded. Life in this swampland of a state is rotten. And it seems to breed moral and ethical rottenness at every level of life and work.

"I don't think that will change. I am convinced that, fifty to a hundred years from now, Louisiana will remain a symbol of degeneracy and corruption. This is where Satanism entered America. This is the nation's Achilles heel . . . always has been, always will be, despite its pretensions toward culture and all the rest."

He seemed almost a pitiable figure then.

"I was raised in what was really not more than a village near Baton Rouge. I think it is only by the grace of God that I avoided being sucked into the malignant undercurrent of this nightmare place. My parents were dedicated Christians—that certainly was a major reason for my avoiding the pitfalls.

"But never having been contaminated by any of the destructive spiritual cancers typical of New Orleans and all its tributaries throughout the state, well, this has definitely made me a prime target.

"The forces rampaging across Louisiana, as they attempt desperately to hold on to all that they have gained over the past hundred years, find me to be a problem, a reminder that they are not all-powerful after all, that people can withstand them and therefore defeat them and their master."

"Why don't you go back to South Carolina with me?" Charity suggested, speaking before she had thought the question through.

"Is there a demand for doctors in that region?"

"Definitely. The doctor is constantly overwhelmed."

A moment later, Hester rejoined them, understandably depressed.

"I's sorry to take so long," he said.

"Never mind that," Charity told him.

Preston grabbed his shoulders and looked straight into his eyes.

"My dear man," the handsome young doctor spoke, "there is something you should know."

❧ 86 ❧

T HE CORPSE NEAREST the staircase happened to be one of the least decayed among those that had been swept into the foyer. But that did not mean it was being left untouched by the ravages of death. Payne Preston and Hester had to work very hard to ignore all the grisly details as they wrapped a blanket around the body then set it ablaze and sent it floating in the direction of what must surely have been a haphazard nest of water moccasins.

What if the snakes reacted to the movement or sensed the heat from Preston's and Hester's bodies? Charity wondered fearfully.

Preston had anticipated that.

"Before we do anything," he said, "we have to completely soak ourselves in water. It will temporarily lower our body temperature, but we must act very fast afterward, for the effect will be short-lived."

Neither liked the prospect of wallowing around in water that carried the debris of corpses and no one knew what else. But Preston's idea made sense, and so they did it as quickly and as calmly as they could.

The odors continued unabated.

By the time the two of them were completely soaked, they both smelled of ancient graveyards.

As Hester finally stood, he nearly let out a scream but clamped his hand over his mouth to help stifle it as he looked at Payne Preston's ruffled white shirt, now black with dirt, with wiggly maggots clinging to it.

The black man pointed at him.

Preston had not detected the maggots at first, but Hester's reaction made him look, and he staggered as he noticed the slimy creatures.

Dozens of them! And something else, bigger and smoother.

Each was blindly but instinctively trying to tunnel into his living flesh.

"Leeches!" Hester warned him. "There are leeches among them."

Instead of picking them off one at a time, he unbuttoned his shirt and flung it from him, most of the slug-like creatures going with it.

Except one.

A large, obviously ravenous leech.

Its head had partially disappeared below the level of Preston's skin.

Preston was grabbing the tail and started to pull it off.

"No!" Hester shouted. "The other end, the head, press your fingers against it tight and pry it loose real slow by lifting it up and away from you."

The pain was severe, but there had not been, as yet, any substantial blood loss. Preston threw the leech back into the water, then, still wincing, he moved in measured fashion, hoping not to attract the attention of the gathered water moccasins and cause them to attack from across the semi-circular foyer, which was large enough to have been considered a ballroom in any other house.

In the meantime, Charity had gone back up to the bedroom and gotten the blanket. She blanched as she saw the corpse resting across the bottom step.

"Will you be all right?" Preston asked with great concern.

"I cannot see where I have been left with much choice," Charity replied grimly. "Can you, Payne?"

The two men closed what was left of the corpse's hands around the ends of the blanket, leaving as much of the soft material on top of it and away from the water.

"Match . . . ," Preston said, sounding like a veteran surgeon who was on the verge of performing an operation.

Charity had gotten several, and she handed him one while avoiding any glimpse of the foul-smelling remains.

After looking at the blanket a final time, Hester and Preston pushed the rotting body toward the center of the foyer.

The blanket ignited without delay as one more push sent the corpse toward the group of snakes.

While the two men scurried back to the staircase, the creatures reacted to the sudden burst of heat and became frenzied as they scrambled toward it.

"It's working!" Preston proclaimed, watching for a second or two as nearly a dozen water moccasins tore into what was left of a body that once had contained the living soul of a human being created in the image of God. "But hurry! Now! They will lose interest quickly when they discover only cold meat under all those flames."

Charity stepped down into the water and headed for the gaping hole where the front door and all the windows around it had been.

Fresh air from outside touched her face, and she felt better after she had passed cautiously through the jagged opening.

Preston motioned for Hester to go next.

"Me?" the gentle giant of a man asked uncertainly

"Yes! No delays, please."

"I's nobody of any 'portance," the slave said. "I can't do what you's askin'. The world needs doctors. Nobody needs more of my kind. If I make it, fine. If I don't, what's the loss, Massa?"

But Preston would hear nothing more in protest.

"Charity obviously loves you," he observed, "and that's plenty good enough for me as a reason."

While Preston was reaching for the black man to push him toward the shattered entrance, Hester's face contorted with pain, and he staggered backward, one of the water moccasins clinging to the back of his right leg. As he was falling, another of the snakes latched onto his neck, his cries of pain suddenly cut off.

In seconds, Hester's upper body was covered with what looked like the displaced and repugnant contents of that nearby vipers' nest, their dark, slimy bodies pulsating as they seemed bent, in their reptilian brutality, on killing him quickly and then feasting on his still warm flesh.

❧ 87 ❧

CHARITY LITTLEPAGE SEEMED *even more ancient and frail-looking than she had minutes earlier, a very old woman reliving one of the most devastating periods of her life.*

"It was almost impossible for me to accept the deaths, within the span of twenty-four hours, of all those slaves whom my family and I had loved most of our lives," Charity paused before the Society members, tears soaking her cheeks, her voice unsteady. "One day, they were all around me, and we were happy, enjoying our new home, and then—"

Charity had to stop, words giving way in the face of images that she had not recalled for many, many years.

And those members, of an age similar to hers, were being affected as she was.

Even Loreta.

She was so deeply moved that she had to leave the room. She returned some ten minutes later, having regained her composure only to lose it again as Charity told them of the aftermath of that monumental storm and how her life was being changed in such a way that she felt utterly powerless to do anything but let the will of God take its course.

"I think, though, without Payne Preston, I might not have survived," she acknowledged.

And that was when several Plantation Letters Society members glanced at one another and smiled through their tears . . .

Rescue came soon—but too late for Hester.

Eventually all the bodies were found and were buried in what was called State Cemetery less than a mile from the heart of New Orleans.

Tragically, just days later, Charity was told by Payne Preston that their graves were dug up and their remains used at precisely midnight in a voodoo ceremony while young children were forced to watch as part of a process of inculcation.

"Was Hoodoo Jack's wife responsible?" she asked.

Preston shook his head.

"No," he told her.

"How can you be sure?"

The fact that anyone hated her as much as that woman apparently did was hard for Charity to face.

"I can be very sure, Charity," Preston told her, smiling slightly. "The wife of Hoodoo Jack as well as their children died in the storm. Their bodies were found just this morning, an entire family wiped out in an evening."

Charity was spending the first of two days in a shelter set up by the archbishop of the diocese of New Orleans and run by a group of priests. Preston stayed with her since there was nothing left of his home.

That first night, something happened that neither Charity nor he could have guessed was possible.

A priest named Father Piton approached their row in the large assembly hall of the Roman Catholic Cathedral near the garden district of New Orleans.

"Payne . . . ," he said, looking rather sheepish.

"Hello," Preston replied, his voice a monotone.

"I have to tell you about what this storm has done to us," the little man, bald and thin, told him.

"It will cost you much money to repair your buildings, I suppose."

"It's not that. We have had losses from storms before now."

"But none as severe as this. I can only imagine how much depletion your treasury will suffer. Perhaps it won't be so bloated at last."

The priest winced at that.

And Charity stood just behind Payne Preston, increasingly amazed at the doctor's manner.

"What I am about to tell you," Father Piton continued, "has nothing to do with money . . . It has nothing to do with anything material or physical at all."

Preston saw an uncustomary urgency in the man's expression and decided not to interrupt.

"The archbishop and I, but not us alone, Payne, we have seen God's hand in this. As badly as we all have suffered, do you know where the devastation was at its worst?"

Receiving no answer, the priest added, "Our parish homes, Payne; we have suffered the greatest loss. On a street that included official church property, for example, but also the property of laymen, including those who are non-Catholic, we were wiped out, but the others survived intact.

"I have never seen the likes of this before. The flood waters should have wiped away almost *everything* in their path. The extraordinarily high winds should have done away with whatever might have been left.

"But, again and again, it was the clergy that proved the hardest hit and the common, everyday families who were able to salvage a great deal and quickly begin the process of reshaping their lives."

Father Piton was wringing his hands.

"We did not know what to do," he said. "So much in which we have believed has made us go astray. It is awful, Payne. We feel like rudderless ships."

Surprisingly, Preston was sympathetic.

"It is not necessarily your beliefs that are at fault," he said, "but, rather, whether you truly lived by them or not, and how much you misused them in order to dominate your congregations."

"But you are the one who invariably opposed us at nearly every turn," Father Piton reminded him. "Why would you want to do anything to help us now?"

"If you thought I would turn my back on you, why have you mentioned any of this in the first place?" Preston countered.

"I hoped, I suppose, that you would not prove to be as hypocritical as the rest of us seem to have been."

"You were right, Piton. I shall not walk away from this, though I was hoping to make other plans."

"Leaving this area, Payne?" the priest asked suspiciously. "Is that what you are suggesting?"

"I have never *wanted* to—"

"—but the church seemed less interested in antagonizing the Satanists than in expanding its membership rolls and having donations increase as a result. Is that about what you were going to say?"

"It is exactly where I was headed. I see material pursuits taking the place of spiritual ones."

Father Piton looked at him and then held out his hand.

"We have come to that very conclusion," he said. "We regret the time that has been lost and the souls along with it."

Preston brushed away the hand and hugged him instead.

"I get so little sleep at night," Piton muttered. "I am afraid even to close my eyes."

"You have had demonic encounters?"

"Not demonic, Payne. I would call them encounters of conscience. I see, when I do sleep, the haunting faces of countless numbers of people writhing in the flames of hell. And I wonder, over and over, how many of them are there because I was pursuing new members rather than ministering to their deep-seated needs."

~ 88 ~

I WAS TEMPTED TO *stay there near New Orleans,"* Charity recalled for the other old women who could not take their eyes off her as she paced back and forth in front of them. "I did not want to admit this to myself at first. How could I, in view of the losses I had experienced on a personal level, with no one from my old life alive to reassure and comfort me? But I also realized that I was developing some very warm feelings toward Payne Preston, despite the fact that we had known each other for less than a week.

. . . some very warm feelings toward Payne Preston.

One of the members gasped slightly, but the others ignored her, and for this she was glad since she embarrassed easily.

"We had met only days before, and yet the conditions were intense and the struggle for our lives demanded whatever courage and cleverness and determination we could muster. I saw what kind of man he was."

She smiled at the memory.

"I was falling in love with him," she said. "Yet it looked as though we would part within days, and there would be little opportunity for us ever to see one another again. He had his calling in New Orleans, and I was being called, I assumed, away from that foul place."

Falling in love . . .

None of the members had known the love of a man for many, many years. Nor had Charity either, for that matter.

However, this now frail-seeming figure spoke with such renewed vitality that she set herself in even greater difference compared with the rest of them, particularly as they commiserated about their past tragedies, allowing a cold, lonely invocation of age to overtake them. In contrast, Charity Littlepage was celebrating the beginnings of passion, passion that newly enlivened her as she continued her pacing with emboldened steps.

"I decided that if I left I would miss what I had never truly known, having Payne's arms around me, and feeling his warmth against my body," Charity continued, "and wondering what it would have been like to—"

A woman of her age blushed at the implications of that more youthful time when she was confronted by the stirrings of sexual nature.

"It was one part of my life in which I had never known any satisfaction," she assured the members. *"But envisioning all of that changing with Payne Preston was a rather beguiling fantasy, and yet one without any hope, it appeared, of ever becoming reality."*

None of the other women seemed even to be breathing just then.

"I decided to leave him behind with his ministry and return to—" Charity started to say, then choked up.

Her eyes were moist at that recollection, and she fell briefly into silence, but then, looking out over the taut and aged faces in front of her, she smiled slightly, cleared her throat, and continued. And none who heard that which followed were disappointed that she did.

CHARITY CONTINUED TO live in the New Orleans area for a few weeks after the storm had dissipated, but, in the meantime, she was able to send a series of telegrams back to Columbia, South Carolina. Replies from Reverend Marmaduke and Samuel Fulkerson were helpful, assuring her that the old property had not been sold as yet. While the Louisiana plantation was damaged sufficiently to cut its value to a substantial degree, perhaps by half or more, it had been purchased with funds from her parents' estate, and she still had the worth of the original family home if she needed any money, but that was unlikely since Littlepage investments in various companies, plus other land holdings, could be disposed of as necessary to yield immediate cash. She would come to depend heavily upon Fulkerson for advice, the irony of that not lost on her.

Charity stayed in the home of the archbishop of the New Orleans diocese and could see that he was a man of conscience, however latent that still, small voice had been, a man who had been irritated rather than convicted by Payne Preston's hard-line stance over the past several years. But, as it turned out, Archbishop Vatier Watteau was slowly being brought under the transforming power of the Holy Ghost, though, once again, it took the widespread ravages of that storm to drag him to the point where he fell to his knees in front of the young doctor and first, prayerfully, asked for the cleansing provided by his Creator and then also begged Preston for forgiveness.

"You could turn away from me now," the bone-thin Watteau admitted, "and that would be understandable. I am the one who has been behind the lack of cooperation you have gotten. At first I said to myself that you were just a doctor. What could you know about spiritual matters? But your wisdom and your maturity in the area of faith became obvious if only through your persistence."

The man groaned.

"How many victories has the Prince of Darkness gotten over the years?" Watteau speculated.

"But were my youth and my profession the only causes of this resistance of yours?" Preston asked. "No, they were not the only ones."

"What were the others?"

"Just one, Payne, just one."

Preston waited for the rest of what the archbishop was struggling to say.

"I was frightened," he finally blurted out, "truly frightened."

"You, frightened of me? But how could that be?"

Watteau winced as he heard that word repeated back to him from the lips of a man to whom he had been an antagonist for so long.

"Well, perhaps *nervous* is a better word," he said.

Still, Preston was dubious.

"But why would you feel that way?" he asked.

"I was worried that, compared to you, the parishioners would see me for what I was, a fraud, someone using his clerical position to satisfy a need for *controlling* people and dressing in fine gowns and eating imported foods while remaining oblivious to the poverty around me, the hunger, the spiritual decay.

"None of that was true of the Satanic forces raging through this whole area, though. They saw what was happening and *expanded* their influence. For example, many of the whores of New Orleans are not hapless women 'merely' trying to feed themselves and, in some cases, their little bastards, but they are coven-born witches, aggressively attempting to enslave men in body as well as soul. And, as stupid as it sounds, the city government nevertheless approved the appointment of an openly militant witch-whore to sit on the local committee of civil administrators.

"Occult shops now offer for sale shrunken heads, magic potions, and other voodoo-oriented items right on Bourbon Street, along with the brothels and saloons and whatever else that is part of the most decadent atmosphere of any city in the nation, worse than San Francisco, if you can imagine that. Bribes have been flowing freely. I myself have had a share of those."

Preston had suspected as much.

"Father Piton was telling us about the extent of the storm damage to church property," he remarked.

"A much higher percentage than the common folk suffered," Watteau confessed reluctantly. "But I can assure you, my dear Payne, that the message God sent has been received and will be heeded as the weeks and months pass; what a pity that it took a catastrophe to move the hearts of men such as myself."

The archbishop looked at Preston then at Charity.

"My residence sustained only modest damage, ironically," he acknowledged. "I would be honored if you would stay here, in separate quarters, of course."

"Why are you doing that?" Preston inquired, unable to fight back a flare-up of cynicism.

"It is not to get on your good side," Watteau retorted, "though I can understand your hesitancy. Allow me an opportunity, please, to do the kind of penance that my faith demands of me."

The doctor nodded and extended his hand without delay. Which the archbishop accepted in his own.

AND SO CHARITY Littlepage and Payne Preston moved into one of the most palatial residences in all of New Orleans, but the doctor was gone much of the time, helping the Catholic priests and ministers from a number of denominations comfort and relocate families affected by the storm.

Preston did not spend much time inside but cooperated with the priests by bringing together other Christian doctors as well as various Protestant clergymen to help in the task of ministering to the poor and the displaced, many of the latter from upper-middle-class families who were not accustomed to sleeping in the same large room with families from a variety of races and cultures.

There was one afternoon, however, when Preston took time off and invited Charity for a walk.

Down Bourbon Street.

"They sell themselves mostly at night," Preston said, describing the prostitutes who in the evenings hung over the balconies and posed on street corners. "They rest during the day. Sometimes they service six to eight men in one evening."

Charity gasped.

"I am not surprised that that shocks you," Preston remarked. "I had the same reaction at first."

"Night after night . . . ," she whispered.

"It destroys their bodies, their emotions, their souls."

"Haven't you been able to help them?"

"A few. But there are so many. At night, they line up on Bourbon Street or hang out of windows and cajole passersby, men and women alike."

"They have women as their customers, too?"

"I have to say yes. It is perversion on top of perversion, if you'll pardon my choice of terms."

"Why haven't you been more successful in reaching out to them?"

"They are addicted to what they do. It is all most of them have ever known. Some have told me, 'Give up this life? Why should I? I used to do it for free with my father or my brother. At least now I am earning a living.'"

Charity stopped walking.

"Are any possessed?"

"I believe so. And I have found that I am not an effective exorcist."

"But the priests? How about them? Are they not supposed to be well-trained in what to do?"

"Too scared," he said.

"They're scared?"

"Oh, they are, Charity. They have lived for so long without challenge or adversity that they have become very soft. The results of the storm will change all that, as we already have seen, but a truly great transformation will take time."

"And time is not on their side, is it, Payne?"

"No, Charity, it is not. Every so often, one of the whores is found after having slashed her wrists or had her throat cut by a sadistic customer, or she's drowned herself in the Mississippi. Time will not treat any of them kindly."

"What happens when they become old and tough-looking and no longer attractive to any man?"

"They drink themselves to death usually," Preston said, sighing sadly, "or they are used in voodoo rites at midnight in State Cemetery."

Preston shed much of the sense of *machismo* he had been projecting, and looked more helpless than anything else.

"It is why I am torn between staying and leaving, changing my mind one way or the other sometimes by the hour," he admitted. "If I stay, I don't feel that I will be any more effective two years from now than I have been over the past two. If I don't stay, I will bloody myself emotionally over that one whore or two or three or whatever the number that I might have reached for Jesus Christ at the same time I could have taken care of her battered and spent body."

He touched Charity's shoulder.

"It has been depressing, Charity, more than you may ever know," Preston said. "You have been a bit of sunshine for me this day."

She saw the expression on his face and avoided his eyes as they headed back toward the archbishop's residence.

❧ 89 ❧

CHARITY GENERALLY HAD little to do on her own time and was largely left alone to wander the hallways of the archbishop's large home, left alone to think and pray and to anticipate her return to South Carolina while having no clue as to how she would cope with those very conditions that had forced her to leave in the first place only a few months earlier.

One day Archbishop Watteau caught her sitting in a chair in one of the hallways, her head on her hands. She had not been sobbing, but, rather, she felt tired and overwhelmed and more than a little uncertain.

"May I intrude?" he asked.

She looked up and smiled.

"You would not be intruding at all," she said politely.

"Everything that has happened must be very perplexing to you," the archbishop remarked.

She had to admit that he was right.

"I came here to escape conditions that I thought were intolerable," she confessed, sighing at the recollection.

"Only to encounter conditions that have turned out even worse, though in a quite different way?"

"You are very astute. I have lost everything that was once precious . . . my parents, our slaves. And I am surrounded by strangers."

She threw up her hands.

"I have never had to experience anything like this before now," she told the archbishop. "The only real upset I had to survive was the death of a favorite pet."

Watteau sat down in a chair next to the one she was occupying.

"Would you be willing to tell me what is on your heart?" Watteau asked.

"But I have never confessed to a priest before," Charity quipped. "I am, after all, a Baptist."

"And I am, above all, a Christian."

So the two of them sat and talked, Charity telling Watteau why she was feeling as she did about wanting to leave and not give New Orleans another chance.

"I do not blame you," the archbishop reacted. "Life here is not what you are accustomed to."

"But another part of me hates to see how weak I am by wanting to leave rather than stay and fight."

"Have you had any occultic encounters before now?"

"Just one."

Charity described what had happened in the case of Hoodoo Jack.

After she had finished, Watteau bowed his head and engaged in a quick but fervent prayer and then straightened up, some tears trickling down his cheeks.

"I am the one who has been weak, not you, Charity Littlepage," he muttered. "I ask this, young woman: Who is the greater coward, one who admits her weakness and her lack of preparation, not to mention experience, and leaves—or one who has been here much of his adult life, and has all the necessary techniques and training as well as spiritual and physical weapons at his disposal but is too scared to force a confrontation with the powers of darkness throughout this city and this region?"

He turned away from her.

"I have admitted that to no one else, not even God," Watteau said. "But you need to know that leaving here is no act of shame, because you cannot be taught overnight how to stand up against evil."

"Back home, I had Reverend Marmaduke to intercede," Charity remarked.

"You know that man?"

"He was my family's pastor for the longest while."

Watteau was impressed, far more so than Charity could have expected, since she was unaware of the minister's standing beyond the borders of South Carolina.

"We could use a Marmaduke here," Watteau commented. "We could use ten John Covington Marmadukes."

"Payne Preston will be a help, I am sure."

The archbishop faced her again.

"He plans to go back with you," he told her.

"He plans to—" she repeated; then more words would not immediately come.

"I was supposed to keep this to myself, but I cannot, under the circumstances. You need to know. I will miss him, but the truth is that now there is a new spirit among us, a willingness to give up material things if necessary, since so much has been taken from us, and to concentrate on spiritual victories instead."

"But he knows so much. He has such a conviction about his work here."

Watteau nodded as he said, "I understand that, of course, but this is one time where following his heart may be the same as doing God's Will."

"But I can't let Payne do this. I would never be at peace again."

"Even if it may be what God wants?"

"How could that be? Combating the devil here is not God's will, but having Payne enslaved to his infatuation with me is? I doubt that God would ever want that to be so."

"Ah, now, you are doing what we Roman Catholics have been accused of over the centuries."

Charity bristled at that notion and had no idea what he was talking about.

"You talk in riddles," she said irritably.

"But have you done any less?" the archbishop persisted.

"Done what? I don't know what you're saying."

"Putting words in the mouth of the Almighty, young woman. Our authority to do this has been maligned for hundreds of years. And so should yours be. To be very honest, you have no idea what God wants in this matter."

Charity stubbornly rejected what Watteau was telling her.

"I still refuse to believe that he is meant to leave behind everything that is here," she added, "those men, women, and children whose bodies he has cared for and whose souls he has tried to reach."

"There is one flaw in your outlook, if I may say so," Watteau persisted.

"And what is that?"

"Any man who is merely *infatuated* with a woman would be foolish, yes, but not one who is in love with that woman."

She was becoming more and more disbelieving and irritated.

"In love with me?"

The archbishop smiled sweetly as he replied, "Passionately, desperately so."

"But Payne has never said anything, never shown me any hint, except for what he might do for any Christian who found herself in need of someone to help her."

The archbishop smiled again but with no hint of disapproval.

"Can you be so sure?" he asked gently. "Have you been alert to all the signs, young woman?"

"I believe I have. And I am surely not as naive or stupid as you are inferring just now. Payne Preston has shown me nothing more than kindness, for which I am deeply grateful, but that is where it ends."

"Because you have never *allowed* him to do more," Watteau offered.

Charity was very close to accusing the well-intentioned archbishop of meddling, and this made her instinctively want to turn her back on him and ask, with the right touch of indignation, that he leave her alone, to tell him that she was not ready to feel affection toward anyone because, as soon as she did, she would become obsessed with the fear of losing that individual tragically, as had happened with her parents and with the slaves and, in a sense, with Billy Mendenhall as well.

I can never permit myself to love again, she thought. *Lord, is the archbishop so blind that he cannot see this?*

But she could not lie to herself or Watteau or God.

. . . because you have never allowed him to do more.

Charity's shoulders slumped, for she was annoyed that a stranger had seen through her so easily and, in doing so, had been more accurate and to the point than someone back home who might have known her all her life.

She started nervously twisting her earlobe.

"I have turned away from him so many times in so few days," she said, sighing, "trying to pretend that I had no feelings at all for this man."

. . . no feelings for this man.

Now all pretense seemed as meaningless as the move to Louisiana in the first place, for that pretense served the same purpose: enabling her to run away from the truth, but not for very long.

You tried to show me how you felt, she recalled with regret, *whether it was the stirrings of love or a kind of gratitude posing as love. You tried, but I would not listen. I could not listen. I did not want to listen.*

After she had sewed up his wounds and while he was momentarily conscious, Preston had reached out to hold her hand, but she had moved it away from him. And then he had blacked out. But that was not the only time he had attempted to express himself.

How could he expect otherwise? Charity thought then and later, as she revisited that moment. *Or was he only trying to take advantage of my vulnerability?*

And when she did not have even the last of her slaves, Payne Preston was right there, by her side, wanting to do what he could to console her, but she had refused him again.

. . . I tried to pretend that I had no feelings of my own for this man.

She was snapped out of her reverie by the archbishop's voice.

"And have you been successful?" Watteau asked knowingly.

"Successful?" Charity repeated, finding it awkward to shake those recent images from her mind.

Watteau was determined to be patient with her.

"Have you been successful at having no feelings for this man?" he probed. "Or have you perhaps been playacting your indifference?"

"I thought so, until now," she replied rather coldly.

Watteau's less-than-subtle look of disapproval cut through her more than a thousand words of rebuke would have.

"How could he possibly care? I mean, I've been so callous toward him."

"He cares because he sees your pain, Charity, and he wants to ease it."

She stood as she declared, "He will never succeed in doing that. No one can. I will have no peace until I die."

Watteau got to his feet with some effort, years of battling bone-and-joint problems not helped by the humidity of New Orleans.

For a moment he seemed to stagger, and Charity reached out to steady him.

"You have wrapped around yourself a cloak of sorrow," he said after thanking her. "Each new loss has added another layer. It will eventually suffocate you. Someday, when you want someone at your side, that will no longer be possible because you will have chased everybody away."

Charity felt a chill then.

"Then that is the way it will have to be, archbishop," she said, determined not to change. "I shall probably die alone then."

"Is that the legacy your parents would have wanted?"

She could not face that question then. Perhaps she never could.

"Thank you for your kindness in letting me stay here," she said. "My train will leave tomorrow, and I shall be out of your hair by noon at the latest."

As she left him and headed back down the hallway toward her room, Archbishop Vatier Watteau had come close to deciding to engage in a practice that he had learned from the Baptists over the past forty-eight hours, something that would have seemed too "Protestant" and homespun before the storm brought havoc in its wake, havoc that would change many lives permanently.

"We must gather together, a group of us who are believers, Catholics and others, and pray for you," he whispered. "We must ask the dear Lord Jesus Christ to melt that well-guarded heart of yours."

And he knew that God probably would have to do even more than that.

～ 90 ～

A N HOUR LATER . . . One of the priests had offered to take Charity back to the plantation house so she could gather together any belongings that were left, including jewelry in a concealed compartment in a bureau dresser that she had bought just a day after arriving in the area.

During the carriage ride from the heart of New Orleans, she saw that people were trying to rebuild their lives as they worked on homes that had been badly damaged. Some had sustained little apparent damage, but, still, the owners were refastening doors that had been wrenched partially or entirely off their hinges, repainting, rehanging shutters, replacing window panes, and doing whatever else was necessary.

It was the black people who succeeded in catching and holding her attention more than any others. They seemed completely at a loss as to how to do anything but walk aimlessly along the roadside, looking frightened or confused or both.

No one is doing a thing to help them, Charity thought. *Their misery has been forgotten while rich and middle-class white folks are given nearly all the attention. Homeless animals are treated better than that in South Carolina. What a horrible place, this Louisiana!*

Little black children walking around and around in circles, others sitting by the road, sobbing.

"Can't something be done," she asked the priest.

"There are only so many funds to go around," he replied. "We have to take care of our own first."

"You're a priest," Charity rebuked him. "Are you not concerned about their souls, whatever the color of their skin?"

"Miss, can we be sure that black people have souls in the first place?" he asked without changing expression.

She fell into silence, feeling too helpless to say or do anything else.

It is right for me to leave here, Charity decided to herself. *I wish Payne Preston the very best, but from what I have seen, I think he will fail, and I don't want to be around when he decides that has happened.*

She did not say anything further until the carriage pulled up in front of her plantation house.

SEEING THE DESTROYED house, smelling the horrible odor of decay, it all came rushing back to Charity's memory—the loss of Simuel and Little Isaiah when their quarters were decimated, the floating, eyeless bodies, poor old Willis, dying on the floor in her arms, Hester, killed by the writhing mass of snakes . . . Suddenly the sorrow and misery she had endured overwhelmed her, and she nearly collapsed.

"Are you all right?" the priest asked rather coldly, it seemed.

"I . . . I . . . It's just so hard to think of all that happened here. I had thought I'd begin a new life here, and instead I opened a whole new chapter of horrible memories and loss," she said, not looking at him. "I'll . . . I'll be all right. Just let me catch my breath. I won't be long. I certainly won't be tarrying here!"

She picked her way across the debris-strewn lawn and climbed the two rickety steps up to the porch. At the doorway, she had one more mental glimpse of the awful, horrific scene that once had filled this foyer. She drew in a breath and quickly proceeded across the entryway. At the bottom of the stairs, she took a step back, but as she did that, she could feel herself starting to tumble . . . but only until a pair of very strong arms caught her and turned her around.

Startled, she found herself looking up into Payne Preston's face seconds before blacking out, just as she heard his voice say, "Don't worry, Charity. You are not alone. I will take care of everything—and you."

When Charity regained consciousness, she found herself back in Archbishop Vatier Watteau's residence.

Payne Preston was sitting in a chair beside the bed.

"As soon as I found out where you were heading, I kept hoping that I could get to you before you actually reached the plantation house," he told her. "I didn't think you were ready for that, not just yet, and especially not without someone beside you who . . . cared about you."

"I . . . I care about you, too, Preston, I do," she said earnestly, looking into his eyes and finding warmth and kindness there.

"I appreciate all that you've done for me. If I haven't made that perfectly clear, I want to do it right now."

"I wanted to do it, Charity. I care about you . . . and . . . I want to be with you—here or in South Carolina," he said clasping both of her hands in his.

"But . . . I'm afraid your calling, your duty, may be here. I want to be with you, too, but I can't stay here. I just can't, not after all that's happened. And yet, I wonder if God is showing us all these problems to tell us you should stay here and finish your work," she said, her voice trembling.

"Yes, Charity, at first I had the idea that that was what I should do, but I feel differently now."

"Why? Aren't you deserting a cause the Lord has given you?"

"Archbishop Watteau can carry on well enough. The past few days have made him a changed man."

"I won't let you make that kind of mistake, Payne. How could I face my conscience if I did?"

"How could I come to grips with mine if I missed an entirely new mission that the Lord had in store for me?"

She looked at that strong face, with the pronounced cheekbones, those bright blue eyes, his wide, sensuous lips, and she wanted to pull the young doctor down to her and give him the most passionate kiss she could manage.

Lord, how can I know what to do? Charity thought. *My heart wants me to embrace this man, yet my spirit seems to be telling me that he must not give up what You have had him doing for nearly two years now.*

And so she told him to leave. And with an effort, she pulled on a mask . . . and a powerful resolve to do what she felt was right, even if it went against what her heart wanted.

"I don't want to see you again, Payne," Charity said, hoping she could keep from crying. "Never again!"

Preston tried to ignore what she was saying.

"You are tired," he replied, "and you are sad. You can't mean what you are saying; you can't!"

She sat up, trying to glower convincingly at him.

"I do," Charity added ruefully. "A couple of weeks ago, I didn't know you existed. And now you are here talking to me like this. What gives you the right? You haven't earned my feelings yet, and you never will."

"But, Charity," he protested.

"How could you expect me to care," she continued, "I mean, really care, for someone I have spent so little time with? You ask too much, Payne."

Charity had to get Payne Preston to leave soon because she could no longer hide her true feelings.

"I do want you to get out of here," she demanded. "It would not be seemly for a minister to refuse me that."

Broad shoulders slumping, Preston nodded sadly.

Then, without warning, he reached out, grabbed her right hand and kissed it on the back.

"I shall never become used to saying good-bye," he muttered. "It is too hard for me. So I won't do it now."

Preston stood, bowed slightly to her, and left the bedroom, not turning to look back, but staring straight ahead.

When Charity was sure he was gone, she allowed the tears to flow.

~ 91 ~

THE TRAIN HAD been scheduled to arrive in New Orleans about noon, but it came in nearly twenty minutes early.

Charity was already at the station a full hour before, primarily because she wanted to make sure she did not run into Payne Preston again.

The same priest who had been with her at the plantation house was given the job of making sure she had no difficulty leaving, obviously ordered to do so by a decidedly vigilant archbishop.

"I feel a bond with you," Watteau had said as he saw her to the front door of his Garden District residence.

Charity was surprised, and not a little dubious, that the man had changed so dramatically from the image painted of him by Payne Preston.

"It is comforting to hear you say that," she remarked.

Watteau was grinning.

"But you cannot imagine why, isn't that so?" he said.

"Something like that."

He lowered his voice until it sounded almost conspiratorial.

"May I suggest an answer?" Watteau ventured.

She had no objection.

"You face a terrible task, Charity Littlepage. As do I. Somehow you must get your life back together again. And I am in the midst of doing the same. So much of your world has been dealt a terrible blow by nature. And so much of my own has had to endure the same thing."

He cleared his throat, looking thinner and more pale than usual.

"I have no idea what is ahead," he admitted. "Nor can you feel any more secure about your future, I imagine."

. . . You must get your life back together again.

Three times that had happened to Charity.

The first was after both her parents were murdered. The second was when she realized that she had fallen in love with Billy Mendenhall but could never have him. And now, the Louisiana plantation as well as her emotions had been ravaged by one of the fiercest storms in state history.

"You have eliminated the possibility of any further contact with Payne Preston, have you not?" Watteau inquired.

Charity decided she had nothing to lose by being totally candid.

"I have," she said.

Watteau licked his lips as though having to prepare himself for what he was about to tell her.

"Charity?" he began.

"Yes, Archbishop Watteau?"

"Payne Preston?"

"What about him?"

"He may have fallen in love with you; do you realize that?"

She was afraid he might be saying that, and she had a ready answer.

"I can't accept that possibility. You have no idea how unlovable I have tried to be. No man could get past that. He's deluding himself."

Watteau was curious but did not seem surprised.

"Why do you say that?" he asked.

Charity was frowning.

"You mean, why have I rebuffed him?"

"Yes . . ."

"Because I could love him so deeply, so completely, that if I ever lost him, I couldn't survive it. There has been too much loss in my life. I do not plan ever again to let go of my emotions to that extent."

Watteau was sympathetic.

"Then, surely you must stay," he urged a final time. "Deal with your fears. Treat them as though they are demons hobbling your spiritual growth, Charity. Confront them through the protection of God's Word and the covering of His Son's shed blood, and they shall flee from you."

"Thank you for trying," she said, "but it is too late. I will never change."

Now, SITTING IN the train station, Charity was brought back from that moment with the archbishop as the priest's voice interrupted her thoughts.

"I'm sorry about all that's happened to you, and I'm sorry if I have not seemed as understanding and sympathetic as I should have been back at your home," he acknowledged without looking at her. "Will you forgive me, Miss Littlepage?"

So quiet and withdrawn had he been as he drove her to the plantation house to retrieve her jewelry that she had nearly forgotten he'd even been with her.

"Yes, of course," she told him absent-mindedly.

. . . back at your home.

That plantation house was never her home.

Charity had not occupied it long enough to make it one. Everything about her stay in Louisiana would become only an unfortunate misstep, a series of bad memories arising from a misguided decision on her part.

The priest had been sitting with her on a bench, waiting as she was for the boarding call to be given. Now he stood and told her, "I must be leaving now, Miss Littlepage."

Now it was Charity's turn to feel guilty about her manner.

"I am afraid I've been a bit distracted," she told him, "Will you forgive me if I haven't seemed responsive to you? I accept your apology, even if it wasn't needed."

"Good-bye, Miss Littlepage," the priest said, shaking her hand and then hurrying away, looking back at her with a smile as he climbed into the carriage and headed the two horses back toward the archbishop's home.

CHARITY HAD A Bible with her and read portions of it again and again during the return to South Carolina. And she hummed a couple of ancient hymns that Savilla had taught her years before.

But not everyone on the train wanted to overhear the church songs.

A middle-aged woman, dressed in fur apparel, approached her and asked, "That's a darkie tune, is it not?"

Charity nodded cheerfully.

"Only whites are allowed on this train," the woman responded.

"And I am white."

"Then act like one!"

"The music deals with spiritual redemption."

"Then why are coloreds singing it?" the woman scoffed indignantly. "They have no souls. What is redemption to them?"

"How do you know that they have no souls?"

"The Bible says so."

"It does not, madam! Here's my copy. Find it for me."

The woman was flustered then.

"I certainly do not have to prove my Bible knowledge to you or any other stranger!" she declared.

"Then prove it to God," Charity retorted as she started to thrust her copy toward the woman.

"I think not," the other said, and walked away.

Charity put the Bible on her lap and closed her eyes.

Lord, it is everywhere, she prayed, *this meanness. I enjoyed a home where it was never present, and now I see the world beyond those familiar walls.*

She looked out the window beside her.

I can learn to forget Billy, she went on, *though that will take a long time, if I can live again among people who treat coloreds as human beings and not as mindless work animals. It isn't perfect back home, but it will never be as bad as what I have just left*

She dozed off for a bit, the sound of an old black woman's voice in song still vivid in her memory.

Two days later, the train was just a few hours away from the Columbia, South Carolina, station.

For Charity, it seemed impossible that she would be returning at all, but especially without any of the Littlepage slaves. She would have taken the train on her way to Louisiana, but blacks were not allowed on it except in one of the cattle cars, and she was not going to subject any of them to that humiliation.

Gone . . .

She repeated that cold, sad word.

They were with me throughout my childhood, Charity thought. *Now I return to my childhood home and they're dead . . . all of them, dead.*

In time, she knew, there would be friends trying valiantly to take the place of the loved ones in her life, people such as Julia Pegram and John Fulkerson as well as Reverend Marmaduke and undoubtedly others whom she previously had given little or no opportunity to really get to know her, separating herself as her tragedy consumed her.

And yet no one else would be able to help, at least for a while. She had heard that mourning ran a course lasting from one to three years, but that was usually the case for a single loss, a parent or a dear friend, but not both parents and not so many dear friends.

Little Isaiah and Willis and Hester and . . .

They were like the brothers and the sisters, aunts and uncles she never had, the color of their skin mattering not at all to her.

Charity had been so accustomed to *seeing* her mother and her father every day of every week of every month of every year of her existence, talking with them, laughing, breaking bread with them.

And the slaves as well

Hearing them sing their spirituals at night. Listening to their hearty laughter. Seeing the love in their eyes as she or her parents approached with a question or a request or whatever the case might be.

"How do I do this, Lord?" she prayed out loud. "How do I go on? How do I pretend to myself and others that I actually want to go on?"

And then she thought of Payne Preston.

Am I doing what You want, Lord? she prayed. *Is Payne doing what You want?*

Hanging out the fleece.

It was a notion that her mother often depended upon, citing a biblical character who wanted to discern the will of God in his life before he embarked upon a certain course of action, so he hung out a cloak of lamb's wool on a tree branch, and said, "God, if I am to do what You seem to have put before me, then let the fleece be bone-dry in the morning. If not, let it be as it usually would be, wet with dew."

She felt some mighty urging to try hanging out the fleece, to offer up to God a condition that seemed impossible, and if He met it, then she could be certain that the outcome was what He wanted.

If Payne is waiting for me in Columbia, she prayed, *Lord, I will be at peace. I will know that, should he propose marriage, I am to accept and become his wife and begin a new future, a new family, a whole new life.*

Charity felt weak.

"I can never be whole without Momma and Daddy," she said, realizing that she had spoken out loud and hoping that no one heard her.

. . . I can never be whole.

She honestly felt that way, and wondered if it was a truth to which she would be chained for whatever years God had left to give her.

Charity felt a hand on her shoulder.

The woman who had objected to the hymns she hummed earlier.

"I see that you are going through some distress," she observed, "and I wanted to tell you how much I regret speaking so harshly."

She smiled with not inconsiderable warmth.

"May I sit beside you?" she asked. "Perhaps we could share some moments that might help us both."

"Are you hurting as well, Ma'am?" Charity asked.

"So deeply that I wonder if my poor heart can stand it much longer. You see, our slaves revolted three months ago, slaughtered my husband, our two children, and nearly me. I can scarce bear the fact that I yet live while my family is six feet under. Now you can understand why I have no love for blacks. We treated them well. But some unholy urge took control of them, and now I am alone in this world."

"Like me," Charity told her.

The woman's eyes widened, and her cheeks did not remain dry for very long.

"Bless you, my dear," she said.

"May the good Lord bless us both," Charity reminded her.

And so the two of them spent the next few hours talking and reading God's Word, and trying to make sense of what had happened to their lives.

Columbia was the next stop.

"I am so nervous," Charity confessed.

Emily Plummer, who had hardly seemed a candidate for Charity's friendship at the beginning, had in a very short while become very close to her.

"Think of this," she said. "You have people to return to, my dear."

"But you have friends, don't you?" asked Charity.

"I do not. They tolerated me. My husband was the center of their atten-tion. That was something I had to live with all the years of our marriage."

"But why would that be the case, Emily?"

"Look at me!" the other woman said as she stood and turned around once, then again. "I am overweight. I am not pretty. I have no pleasing per-sonality. There is nothing left for me, Charity, nothing."

"But surely there is someone left for you."

"No one. I am paying the price for so many years during which I ignored everyone except my family."

"How can I be any different?" Charity asked logically and with some apprehension as she considered the coming weeks, months, and years.

"You and I are different," Emily reminded her. "I do not easily draw people to me. But you are the opposite. You beckon them, and they come. I smile, and they seem to run in the opposite direction."

Charity privately questioned any purpose God might have in bringing about this unexpected contact with a middle-aged woman who was doing nothing to elevate her emotions that had been battered so badly.

Oh, Lord, surely this could not be to cheer me up, she prayed to herself. *Emily is in a bad way. How could that be—?*

Charity swallowed hard several times.

And in my present state of mind, how could I inspire anyone? Are You showing me this woman to make me comprehend where I could be heading if I do not change?

The conductor went down the center aisle, telling everyone that the train would be pulling into the Columbia station in a few minutes.

"If you have no place to go," Charity told her, "why don't you get off with me?"

"I could not impose upon you," Emily remarked.

"It is not an imposition. I would be pleased and honored."

But Emily would not accept.

"I am not ready," she commented. "I could not face a single black per-son without wanting to kill him."

"We could keep you isolated until you felt better," Charity persisted. "And anyway, all my coloreds are dead; it will be some time before I can replace them."

Emily looked at her and asked tellingly, "Will you ever feel better?"

"Right now that seems inconceivable, I must admit."

"And you may have a man in your life now."

"Payne Preston? I think it's unlikely that this will be what—"

The other woman interrupted her.

"But there is that possibility, Charity. For me, I have nothing of the sort to anticipate. I shall be wandering from place to place until the day I die."

The Columbia station was now visible.

"Please reconsider," Charity begged her. But Emily Plummer would have none of that. She set her jaws tightly together and retreated from any further discussion.

Charity stood, taking with her a single small piece of luggage, and walked slowly to the exit.

Waiting for her outside were Julia Pegram and John Covington Marmaduke and, it seemed, half of Columbia, crowding the station to its full capacity and then some.

She looked back at the train and saw Emily through the window, dabbing at a flow of tears that had started.

Lord, help her to find someone, Charity prayed. *Help her to shed the loneliness.*

"Forgive us, Charity," Marmaduke's booming baritone shifted her mind away from Emily Plummer. "We acted very badly, and our consciences have given us no rest ever since you left."

He smiled broadly.

"If you want to have Billy Mendenhall return," he added, "we could learn to somehow overlook his Yankee blood, or at least not let it bother us. What is more important is your happiness and the kind of legacy for your parents that we allow to survive."

"But could he ignore what we are?" Charity replied. "I've had time to think about all of this. The only difference between everyone here and me was that I wanted Billy to love and to hold, I think, for the rest of my life. Otherwise, we are the same, you know, products of a society we dearly love."

She sighed with the impact of a truth that she would have preferred to pretend did not exist, but there was no time for pretense.

"Billy probably could never have adjusted," she went on. "He might have ended up hating me as he would have hated the rest of you. We are of Dixie heritage, you and I, proud of it, too, and that can never change."

Most of the people who had been waiting for her started to cheer until Marmaduke gave them one of his sternest expressions, and they stopped instantly.

"You must be very tired," he said, taking hold of her hand. "We should take you home now."

As Charity left the station, she looked for Payne Preston, but he was not there waiting for her as she had imagined, not waiting around some corner, ready to step out in front of her suddenly as she had dreamed. She tried to praise God for this answer to prayer—not the one she wanted but an answer just the same. Yes, she tried, but she failed, and for that she would seek His forgiveness just before falling asleep once again in the bed she had left only a month before.

~⊰ 93 ⊱~

CHARITY SLEPT THROUGH that night and most of the following day. She did this in part because she dreaded getting up and walking through the emptiness of the only house in which she had ever really lived. But she was also physically drained by the wrenching events of the past two weeks.

And there was something else.

Depression.

Losing her parents, losing the slaves she loved, were the primary tragedies that undermined her resiliency. Not finding Payne Preston waiting for her at the Columbia train station should not have mattered a great deal in comparison. But it turned out to be the proverbial final straw, and the finality of that lost future crushed her ability even to open her eyes in the morning.

By late afternoon, though, she knew she could not allow her familiar old bed to become some kind of premature coffin.

Even if Charity had decided not to get up at that time, Julia Pegram would have forced her to do so.

"I was just going to drag you from bed single-handedly," Julia told her as she entered the bedroom. She had insisted on staying in the Littlepage plantation house the first few nights Charity was back, and she had brought along with her two of her house slaves to help with the cooking and housework.

Charity was sitting in a high-back plain wooden chair her mother had used whenever childhood illnesses had struck and it was necessary to stay by the little girl's bedside to give her medicine or simply to comfort her whenever she awoke in pain.

But it was not the only chair placed near the bed.

A second one was on the opposite side in a similar position, the chair that Savilla or Violet would occupy, one or the other singing or humming softly to help send a child off to a more peaceful sleep.

Charity told Julia about that empty chair.

"It will always haunt me," she admitted. "My thoughts will frequently go back to those years when two black women and my mother cared so much for me and would nurse me back to better health, and make me feel less miserable while I was sick."

"Then put it elsewhere," Julia offered. "That old chair doesn't have to be where it is if seeing it causes you some anguish."

"Even if it were destroyed," Charity told her, "that would solve little. Every inch of this house provokes memories. That was one of the reasons I left, to get away from anything that reminded me of—"

"Love? Is that what you are saying? Anything that reminded you of being loved? We are, I think, entering a period in Dixie when hatred will rise and love will fall, and we shall be *glad* to have our memories of what once was."

Julia stood with her hands on her hips.

"But why did you come back then?" she said as though demanding an answer and not willing to settle for less than that.

"Because what I headed into was worse than what I left."

"That doesn't surprise me, Charity. You were so blinded by anger and mourning that, I suppose, Alaska would have seemed a more hospitable place in comparison. What you failed to see was that you carried your memories and their pain with you, and suddenly you found yourself in the midst of strangers. At least here you have friends to whom you can turn, even if what they tell you is not what you want to hear."

"But I wanted Billy so badly."

"He was your first love, the first man to stir you sexually. Of course you would feel the way you did about him. Isn't that what passion is all about?"

Charity winced at her friend's candor.

Julia smiled as she added, "You will surely feel that way about someone else."

"I do, dear friend; at least I think so."

"I assume you mean Payne Preston?"

"You could tell from the way I was going on about him on the way here from the train station?"

"It was like you were talking about Billy, only more so."

"More so, Julia? I can't be sure I feel that way at all."

"Here's why I am certain: You couldn't have had Billy, I know that, but there is nothing standing in the way of a lifelong relationship with Payne Preston. Even now you're hoping that he will appear in that doorway, for you know that if he comes he will never leave without having you firmly in his arms."

"But he isn't coming, Julia. He has his work in New Orleans, and if that is where the Lord wants him, I have no right to confuse him."

Julia abruptly changed the subject.

"There is a welcome-home dinner tonight in your honor," she announced formally. "I think you should attend."

Charity protested, but Julia would not stand for it.

"Samuel and Reverend Marmaduke have gone to some considerable trouble putting everything together," she stressed. "And your friends are eager to show you how glad we are that you've come back to us. Please don't disappoint us."

"But don't my wishes mean anything?" Charity asked irritably, wondering if she had taken a step backward in her life.

"Not if it means you mourning your life away, my dear. Would your mother and father have wanted that for you?"

"Of course not."

"Then plan on being ready by seven this evening."

"Where is it being held?"

"Right here, Charity. We thought it would be good to have this house filled with life once again."

"Only to wake up tomorrow morning to find it as empty as before?"

Julia smiled and left.

Charity spent the rest of the day alternately angry and touched, angry that she had not been consulted, touched that people were trying so hard to fill the void that was haunting her.

Charity had not taken all of her clothes with her when she left for Louisiana but had left instructions that the remainder be sold and the money be used to purchase food and clothing for poor black families in the area.

"When I learned that you were returning," Julia Pegram told her, "I sent some of my own garments to a seamstress in Columbia and had them altered for what I hope were your correct measurements.

"You are bustier than I am, with slimmer hips, and I hoped I could make the right guesses. Then someone found one of your old dresses and brought it to me. I measured it, and you know what? I was less than half an inch off!"

Julia was very pleased to be able to say that.

"Forgive me for bragging," she said cheerfully, "but I was, well, just so pleased with myself."

The women enjoyed that moment before Julia glanced out the window in Charity's bedroom and saw carriages already starting to pull up out front.

"Some guests are arriving early," she said. "Please hurry. There are several choices. But I think I know which one you will like the most."

"But the cooking, the serving," Charity asked, "who is doing that?"

"It's all being taken care of. Now is your time of rest. You will be working hard soon enough as you get your life together again."

"Julia?"

"Bless you. So much trouble from everyone!"

"If the whole bunch of us had acted differently just a few weeks ago you might never have left."

"I could never have married Billy."

"Not unless hearts could have been changed. But people just had no time to let that happen, you know. And that is my regret, Charity, and it is also the regret of others.

"We love our traditions, but they are often like bars of a prison for each of us. We might as well be locked up and the key thrown away."

"Who will be next? Which dashing young fellow will I meet only to have him taken away from me? Dare I try ever again?"

Julia shrugged her shoulders and shut the bedroom door behind her.

A moment later, Charity began to cry, grateful that her friend and others were trying so hard to help but feeling unworthy.

How can I ever endure tonight? she thought. *I feel so weak, dear Lord. I need strength. I need the strength that only You can give me.*

She waited for a familiar sense of dread to descend upon her, but this time it was not to be so.

ᨒ94ᨒ

A FTER CHARITY OPENED the bedroom door, she paused, listening. Voices. People talking, laughing.

That was the way it had been before she and her parents had made that trip to see Sojourner Truth. Whether from slaves or businessmen or dinner guests or one of her mother's social gatherings, voices were seldom not heard. The Littlepage plantation house was almost never a place of silence.

Until Charity had returned, alone, from Louisiana.

Empty. And suffocating.

And this impression was aided by the fact that everything else seemed, in a physical sense, normal!

None of the furniture, most of it from a previous Littlepage generation, had been moved. The curtains still hung from where they had been for years. Cooking and other utensils remained in the kitchen. Only the people had been removed, as though sucked out by some invisible tornado that left everything else untouched. Only the contents of the closets had been emptied.

Now there were voices, some she could recognize even from a distance. *They send me away in anger*, she thought, *now they want to welcome me back.*

Charity fought a sudden desire to leave the plantation house, unseen, and disappear again, not allowing any of the guests to assuage their guilt by saying a long and well-rehearsed list of nice things to her now, though every last one of them had deserted her when she truly needed them.

"Where were you?" she asked out loud.

Charity had walked to the edge of the staircase, hesitating before setting foot on the first step.

"Not where you needed us," a familiar voice called up to her.

She looked down and saw Samuel Fulkerson standing on the bottom step.

"I loved him," she replied. "I should have gone with Billy."

"Forsaking *everything?*"

"But I was left with nothing. If I had gone with Billy—"

"The slaves would have wanted to be with you. And yet that kind of life for blacks isn't tolerated in Yankee country; I do not have to tell you that."

She paused, not knowing what to say.

"What would have happened to them?" Fulkerson continued. "They would have been cut loose, you know. Your Billy most certainly would have demanded that. None could have survived up there."

Charity tried to interrupt him, but he would not let her.

"Yankee companies eat up and spit out countless numbers of black people day in and day out, but none of this is ever covered by newspapers because those companies are expert at concealing truth that conflicts with Yankee self-interests. You would have condemned them to a horrible existence, Charity, most horrible!"

"But I could have hired all of them as free blacks to work for me. They would have been employed then."

"Billy would never have permitted it."

"How do you know?"

"Because I discussed it with him, Charity. I discussed it with Billy Mendenhall while he was still here at the doctor's home."

She was feeling unsteady and grabbed the banister for support.

"I knew where you were heading, at least what was in your heart, and I tried so hard to help."

"But what did Billy say when you told him of the plight of black people in Philadelphia and New York City and Boston—?"

Fulkerson had walked up the steps and was standing next to her.

"Billy Mendenhall could not believe the truth. He was accepting all of the ridiculous Yankee propaganda, Charity. Billy thought I was just trying to confuse him, and he ordered me to leave."

"So we might have split up over this?"

"I think so. And you would have headed back down here to Dixie, to face a moment such as this one, and a welcoming party given by people who really do care about you because, Charity, you are one of us. While we have our faults, we are decent people trying to do the right thing for you, for our own families, for our slaves."

He reached out and took her hand.

"The guests are waiting rather patiently," he said. "Won't you join us now, my dear Charity?"

She nodded and walked down the stairs with Fulkerson at her side. The ballroom was through the doorway to their left. As Charity entered, she steeled herself and for good reason, as it turned out.

Thirty or more people stood before her, many of whom she recognized as one-time business associates of her father's. Others were friends from other plantations in that part of South Carolina. But a few were former Littlepage enemies, the very individuals who would talk about Alfred Littlepage behind his back.

"Some folks here want to say something to you," Samuel Fulkerson told her, following a script he had worked out with great care.

Julia approached Charity and stayed on her other side.

And then, one by one, men and women came up to Charity and spoke briefly, either professing their love for her parents or offering heartfelt regret over some nasty business regarding her father.

It wasn't like this even after my parents died, Charity thought and shared her thought with Julia.

"There is more guilt now," her friend replied. "It has had more time to accumulate, my dear."

Charity had been left with no one. And, as Samuel Fulkerson had hinted, a large percentage of the people gathered in front of her in that familiar ballroom felt responsible at least for part of her loss. If they had acted differently, as individuals and as a community, she might not have been compelled to leave, and if she had not left, the slaves would not have perished as they did. Southern mores, while burdened with some seemingly innate hypocrisy, had real strengths as well, forcing a degree of decency and conscience that seemed to be largely missing or else retarded north of the Mason-Dixon line.

Finally that part of her reentry into the local society was over, to Charity's relief, and it seemed that they all would settle down at the banquet table in the dining hall across the foyer; but one other "ceremony" had been planned, and for Charity, it would prove far more unexpected.

Five blacks.

Two women and three men.

They walked slowly through the crowd of wealthy white folk and stood before Charity.

"We's your new slaves, Miss Charity," one of them, a tall but thin man, told her.

She could not speak but nodded at him.

They introduced themselves, and then Marmaduke hugged each one, turning to Charity afterward.

"It took some doing," he said, "but we traced them pretty good."

"Traced them?" Charity managed to ask.

The preacher smiled broadly.

"Each is related to one of the coloreds you lost," he told her, "though I could not find any women linked with Savilla and Violet, I am sorry to say."

Again they stepped forward.

"I am Savilla's grandson," the tall, thin one named Parker said.

"I am Willis's nephew," five-foot-tall Willie identified himself.

"I am Hester's sister," a young, attractive woman named Fannie remarked.

Charity put her hands on the other woman's shoulders.

"Hester spoke of you again and again," she said. "But I thought you could not be found or that you were dead."

"I tried to git letters out, you know, to mah brother, but the massa I had never let me post any of 'em."

Charity was trembling with emotion as she spoke.

"You *knew* where he was?"

"I sho did, Miss Charity. Ya see, I was in North Carolina all this time, and Hester never knew it. So close we was, and yet he died not knowin'."

"But how did you find out about him?"

"I read somethin' in an old newspaper about your daddy," Fannie explained. "It mentioned some of his slaves. My brother was one of 'em."

Charity hugged her as she asked, "How did you get here?"

"Massa Fulkerson bought me and sent two of his slaves to pick me up. I got here this mornin'."

Then Charity was introduced to the remaining two blacks.

"I's Sylvia," the robust, heavyset woman told her cheerfully. "Tougher than a mule, I's told."

"And my name's Joe," said a six-foot tall, military-erect man in his early sixties, his hair a brilliant white, his manner curiously shy.

"And who are you related to?" Charity asked, taking to him right away.

"I am Hester's father," he told her, his voice with a slight lilt to it.

Blinking her eyes several times in rapid succession, Charity looked at him for a moment without speaking.

"Do you know where my son is buried?" he asked.

"I do . . . but . . . ," Charity stuttered, not wanting to tell him what had happened to the bodies in Louisiana.

"How did he die, Miss Charity?"

Fulkerson stepped in at that point, knowing that the details were grisly.

"Any answers can come later, boy," he said to a man who was at least a decade older than himself. "This is a time for reunion, for celebration."

The slaves obediently stepped back.

"Help Mrs. Pegram's coloreds in the kitchen," Fulkerson told them rather sternly, some of his old autocratic nature resurfacing.

He turned to Charity.

"I understand that dinner will be ready in just a few minutes. Why don't we all go to the dining hall now?"

Charity impetuously kissed him on the cheek.

"A Littlepage kissing a Fulkerson?" he responded jestingly. "Have we coloreds entered an age of miracles?"

~95~

SOME GUESTS HAD not arrived. As Charity was being seated at the banquet table, she noticed several empty chairs, including the one at her left.

Samuel Fulkerson was apologetic.

"I wanted everything to be flawless," he said, fretting, as he and Julia Pegram settled into seats at her right.

"But that isn't to be."

Within the next few minutes, however, the stragglers did enter the dining hall and offered reasons for their tardiness. Fulkerson was gracious though undoubtedly seething under that facade.

Finally, only one seat remained empty . . . the one next to Charity.

"Tell the coloreds that they may come in now," Fulkerson announced.

One of his own slaves left the hall and returned with Joe, Willie, Sylvia, and the others. The new slaves were told to take their places at the smaller table next to the one where the thirty-odd guests were seated.

Charity gasped audibly.

And Fulkerson picked up on this right away.

"This is your house," he told her. "As little as possible should be changed, wouldn't you agree?"

She reached out and touched his hand gently while noticing that the man's eyes were very nearly as moist as her own.

Charity sensed a curious mood among the guests as well as with Julia Pegram and Samuel Fulkerson. No food had been served more than five minutes after the slaves were seated. Everyone seemed to be making idle conversation as though to fill time.

Fulkerson was scowling. But then that mood changed seconds after the front door was opened, then shut.

Footsteps.

Now there was no conversation at all, a hush silencing everyone as a few more seconds passed.

Charity felt a hand lightly touch her bare shoulder.

She froze, unable to move.

"How could I not come?" a voice reached her ears.

"Dear God . . . ," she whispered prayerfully.

"Yes, Charity, I think God had *everything* to do with it."

She did not need to turn as Payne Preston sat down in that remaining seat, nor could she have done so, every muscle in her body seemingly unable to obey any command from her brain to move, to show any kind of emotion for those first few moments, that moment too unexpected, its suddenness freezing her where she sat.

He had something in his hand.

A small box.

"This is for you," he told her.

Finally, Charity regained the use at least of her arms, though she still was numb and dazed as she reached out for the box, opened it, and saw the sparkling diamond ring inside.

Pushing his chair to one side, Preston gallantly got down on one knee, and looked at her directly as he said, "I have only one question now, dear Charity."

With her free hand, she touched him on the lips.

"Please, don't—" she tried to say, afraid to hear what she knew he would ask, but even more afraid of her answer.

He kissed those fingers and then pulled her hand aside.

"But I must, Charity, I must," he said. "It is the desire of my heart."

She tried to block out the words that she could repeat to herself before he ever spoke them.

"Would you marry me, Charity Littlepage?" Payne Preston proposed. "I want us to spend the rest of our lives together."

Abruptly, beads of perspiration appeared on her forehead and trickled down the back of her neck.

"But we scarcely know each other," she protested.

"Just enough to realize there is a bond between us that cannot be ignored."

"Yes, but—" She saw out of the corner of her eye virtually everyone else at that table putting their fingers to their own lips, and she could not help but burst out laughing and crying at the same time, because most of them had seemed so stern, so boring to her before then.

"Getting married may be a mistake," he acknowledged, "but staying apart may be the greater mistake."

"Your work . . . the Lord . . ." She tried to continue resisting.

"Can we be so sure that my work is not now here, with you by my side? Neither of us can know without a second's doubt what God has in mind; I realize that, Charity. We can only go ahead in faith, believing. Can He expect any more of us than that?"

Charity nodded as the laughter ended but the tears continued.

They stood together. She wanted to hold him, but she was not quite ready for that.

Marmaduke approached the two of them.

"I have never felt more peace," he said. "I have never felt that a union would be more blessed by the hand of God than this one. I would be honored to perform the ceremony anytime, anywhere."

"Charity . . . ," Payne Preston said, "will you become my wife, so that we can hold one another, cherish one another for as long as our hearts are beating and we are able to breathe the air of Dixie?"

The tears had slowed for Charity but had not stopped altogether.

She looked at Marmaduke and at the other guests, then back to Preston.

"I was raised with love," she said, "yet I was prepared to live without it, sad and alone perhaps for the rest of my life. But I know that would not be living at all."

She cleared her throat and wiped her eyes.

"I *will* become your wife, Payne Preston, and you *will* become my husband, and I *shall* love you with all my heart."

The guests began applauding as Charity and Payne finally kissed one another, having no idea what was ahead of them but quite willing to put their trust in Almighty God for time and for eternity.

CHARITY BECAME *Mrs. Preston Payne exactly one month later. The marriage ceremony was the social event of the year for the entire state. The crowd was so large that no church building could contain the number of those demanding attendance. So a civic auditorium in Columbia was used instead. Even it provided barely enough room.*

The Reverend John Covington Marmaduke officiated with a grand flourish. He also provided a one-hundred-voice all-black chorus and acted as conductor for the orchestra that accompanied them.

The reception was held in three different restaurants, Charity and Payne having to go from one to the other. All costs were assumed by Julia Pegram and Samuel Fulkerson.

Finally, tired but extraordinarily happy, the bride and groom went on their honeymoon, but Charity asked to stop en route at the little cemetery where generations of Littlepages, including her parents, had been buried.

"I would have liked to have known your parents," Payne remarked.

"They would have adored you, my love," Charity assured him.

And then they left, returning a bit more than two weeks later, unaware of how much their love would be tested during the years ahead . . . yes, the love and the devotion to one another that was at the very core of their lives together.

Epilogue

SARAH, SEVENTYISH, SHORT, thin, and gray-haired, looked around at the other members of the Plantation Letters Society after Charity had finished reading from the pile of letters and sharing the stories that had held the attention of everyone present for so long. All the ladies were staring at Charity with an expectant hopefulness.

"I am afraid there are no more," Charity said. "It has been a wonderful experience for me to go back over them. I never would have imagined that so many had survived."

The members appreciated that. It was largely because of their efforts and the people around the nation who were helping them that a whole class of historical records had survived so well. Before the Plantation Letters Society was founded, letters were a ridiculed source of information. What the Society started would live long after it had disbanded several decades later.

"Can you recall any others?" Loreta asked, always anxious to add to their storehouse, which had grown for so many years that the sources of supply seemed to dry up.

"Perhaps so," Charity replied. "I may have some that were returned to me over the years because of someone dying or moving with no forwarding address. You plan to continue all this, then? Am I understanding you correctly?"

Loreta spoke for the rest.

"To us, it is a reason for living . . . ," she replied.

"That is what I was afraid you would say," Charity told her.

"What do you mean?"

Charity smiled graciously.

"I have been greatly touched by these letters," she commented simply, tapping the pile, her manner clearly suggesting the deepest of emotions, her upper lip quivering, a slight blush to her cheeks, an unsteady voice at times.

Instantly the others sat up straight in their high-back chairs, reacting in an almost comically exaggerated manner—except for Sarah, who had always been the most dour of all, a woman who had waved good-bye to her four sons as they went off to war at one point or another and never saw any of them return to her again.

"But ladies, I think you grieve our blessed Lord," Charity said with vocal clarity.

The remark took the Society members completely by surprise. But there was no uproar, just shock that kept them momentarily silent.

But then Charity had thought about and prayed over those words long before saying them. She wanted to believe that her time with the other women could be of some value apart from reading her own letters.

"I think that by dwelling on your sadness you grieve the Lord," she repeated. "And I hope, no, I pray that the contents of these letters are used by the Holy Spirit to minister to you as they have done to me. At least that is what I have asked of Him for many days and nights prior to coming here," she went on, speaking so softly that it was difficult for the others to hear, though they all were seated closely together in the small room. "They have surely ministered to me."

"Tell us more!" Abigail, a regal-looking woman nearly seventy years old, spoke up, expectancy giving a more vibrant tone than usual to her thin voice.

"I have lost loved ones in more than one war, you know," Sarah started to say, explaining her reasons for extended sorrow, though she need not have reminded the other women, every detail of everyone's personal drama having been memorized long before.

"That was not what I had in mind; I wanted Charity to—" Abigail spoke with some impatience then immediately silenced herself, realizing from the stern expressions being shot her way by the other Society members that she should let Sarah go on to what the poor woman desperately wanted to tell them.

Sarah cleared her throat and then reminded them about her two older sons, just barely out of their teens, who had been blown apart by cannon fire during the Civil War, nothing left of them to bury, and the two younger sons who had died in Cuba during the Spanish-American War.

She sighed, remembering again the pain of hearing they had died. Then she lifted up, in both hands, the three-inch-thick pile of Charity's letters that she had brought to share with the group—and with Charity.

"I found these in a lovely old building located on a little back street in the oldest part of Columbia, one of the few that survived the monstrous fires that were set in that city, though this one had been damaged significantly," Sarah continued. "It once had served as a doctor's office. And these letters were primarily written by the doctor's wife, a remarkable woman named . . . Charity."

Sarah beamed a feeble smile toward Charity.

"I know you so well now, Charity," Sarah said. "I have read your letters and have seen your diary, and I even have a few letters that your mother and father wrote."

The women turned to smile tenderly at Charity, too. Someone murmured about the beauty of the name, assuming it had been taken directly from the Bible.

Charity . . .

"Yes, it is a very lovely name, and you are a lovely and intelligent woman," Sarah agreed, nodding toward Charity as she retrieved a tiny, frill-edged, silk handkerchief from a small pocket in her pink-brocade dress, dabbing it slowly across both eyes. "These letters—and the details you have added—have told us a wonderful story, the most remarkable one we have stumbled upon after so long a search by each of us, my dear sisters.

"I thought we all might be encouraged if we knew Charity's story, a story that might put our own personal tragedies in perspective, dear friends. This dear soul went through what we have and much, much more. The results are not what any of us would have expected or have endured ourselves."

Then the members all leaned back in their seats again, unified by the very real anguish that they had experienced but which had been made so much worse by their hanging on to their grief far longer than was necessary because of their stubbornness or weakness or a combination of the two.

Charity was right. Every last one of them had allowed their battered emotions to drag matters on and on far longer than could be deemed healthy, revisiting their losses repeatedly, in forlorn little moments of dwelling on the past of another century.

Now they saw how their years of grief had eaten away at all of them, grief that they still clung to as a perverse reason to survive, the airing of their sorrow year after year after year.

The members were waiting, wondering who would break the silence—perhaps even help them break free from the sorrow that had held them so long.

Finally it was Abigail who spoke. "Let it finally be so, dearest friends. Let this valley of the shadow, this ancient veil of tears, be left behind at last, for each and every soul here, and may sunlight shine on our faces once again!"

Abigail drew in a deep breath, feeling the weight of the years of searching weighing heavily upon her.

"Our grief has been with us all for so long that it has seemed we would never be without it, but I pray that a change will start this day as a result of what we all are hearing."

"Go on, Abigail," Sarah said. "We will continue to listen."

SARAH WAS RIGHT. The story of a young woman named Charity Elizabeth Littlepage Payne—and her remarkable endurance and fortitude in the face of overwhelming sorrow—had inspired them to deal with their own grief—and then to set it aside. One by one, they began to speak of something that had rarely been mentioned in their previous gatherings: the future. They were setting aside their grief, and, instead of sharing their sorrow, they began to share their hopes, their dreams, for themselves and the generations to come. Their conversation about themselves—and about how Charity had touched their lives—would keep them talking together throughout the rest of the afternoon, and not even the coming of dusk would dim their fascination with someone who seemed destined to change their lives for time and eternity.